YO-DCO-619

THE TIME OF THE DRAGONS

TRANSLATED FROM THE GERMAN

BY RICHARD AND CLARA WINSTON

ALICE EKERT-ROTHOLZ

The Time

of the

Dragons

New York · THE VIKING PRESS · *1958*

Wo Tränen verboten sind
Copyright 1956 by Hoffmann und Campe Verlag, Hamburg

The Time of the Dragons
Copyright © 1958 by Alice Ekert-Rotholz

Published in 1958 by The Viking Press, Inc.
625 Madison Avenue, New York 22, N. Y.

Published in Canada by
The Macmillan Company of Canada Limited

PRINTED IN THE U.S.A.

For
Genevieve, Haruko, and Noboyuki

CONTENTS

A FEW OF THE PRINCIPAL CHARACTERS

KNUT WERGELAND, Norwegian consul at Shanghai and later Bangkok, connoisseur of the arts, father of three daughters, by French, Chinese, and Norwegian mothers respectively.

ASTRID, Knut's eldest daughter, a silvery blonde, whose search for love leads her through many troubles.

MAILIN, his second daughter, cheerfully adaptable but ever charmingly Chinese.

VIVICA, his third daughter, willful, bewitching, who almost finds life too much for her.

HELENE WERGELAND, Knut's sister, the repository of the family's common sense, who saves the day in many crises.

AKIRO MATSUBARA, also known as Major Kimura, a high-born Japanese, upholding all the traditions of his station. He enters the story early, rises to brief authority when Japan seizes power in Southeast Asia, survives the war, and is still on the scene ten years after.

PIERRE DE MAURY, whose French charm creates some disturbance in the lives of two of the sisters—and also among the Japanese, who suspect him of being "Foxface," the wily chief of a spy ring.

MR. HSIN, a powerful Chinese aristocrat, rich in worldly goods, whose pride loses him his most cherished possession, a daughter.

VERA LESKAYA, White Russian assistant in a beauty parlor, whose avocation is to spy, impartially, for the Japanese as well as the Chinese.

HANNA, a Jewish refugee from Hitler's Germany who finds fresh tragedy and then happiness in Shanghai.

DR. YAMATO, consecrated to the ideals that spring from his devotion to Japan and the Catholic faith, who lives and dies like a hero of his nation and his church.

YURIKO, Matsubara's girl assistant—as a spy and in other ways—and deeply in love with him.

TIMOTHY WILLIAMS, M. D., a major with the United States forces in the Far East, an excellent specimen of New England manhood. He appears opportunely when Vivica needs a rescuer, but that's not the end of their story.

THE SCENE: Shanghai; Norway; Bangkok; Japan.

THE TIME: 1925 to 1955.

PROLOGUE

The Flower Bridge of Shanghai

Man withers like the cherry blossoms of Kyoto;
the Imperial Chrysanthemum is not subject to
the vicissitudes of Time.

—Ashihei Hino, *Flowers and Soldiers*

1: *Consul Wergeland's Reception*

Consul Wergeland's reception in Shanghai began with a connubial disagreement. Such quarrels between the consul and his French wife occurred before every party. The scene had been brought to such perfection by years of repetition that it unfolded like the latest performance of a successful play, without the slightest slip. The drama was well rehearsed. No prompter was needed, since the couple knew their lines as well as they knew the city of Shanghai. The script called for Madame to talk and the consul to listen.

The scene began some two hours before the reception, with Yvonne Wergeland's calling through several doors to inquire where the consul was, what he was doing at the moment, and when he was going to condescend to dress. Instead of answering his anxious wife in a friendly manner, the consul—likewise calling through several doors—asked whether he could not be alone for five minutes in his own house without drawing up an official report on himself.

This was the cue which brought Madame to the stage in a trice. She entered her husband's room—cool, elegant, and inwardly furious —and studied him with a pair of lively, realistic eyes. Those eyes were too close together and betrayed a faculty for jealousy. Yvonne's jealousy arose less from overwhelming affection for the consul than it did from a characteristic French love of property. A prudent wife guarded her husband as carefully as her securities and family jewels.

The consul was still lying on his Japanese mat, attired in a kimono, looking outrageously comfortable and lost in unidentifiable thoughts. At the beginning of each scene he regarded his wife with amazement, as if seeing her for the first time. How was it possible for a statue to contain so much explosive material? Yvonne in her evening dress of night-blue brocade, with her hair rolled into a Greek chignon, and her set, white face, actually did look like a statue. Only her flashing eyes and her somewhat too fleshy earlobes, which turned a feverish pink in the course of the scene, showed the vitality of this statue's inner life. Madame was a Fury in apparent repose.

The more aroused she was, the more measuredly Yvonne spoke. The consul's eyes infuriated her most of all—those ironically amazed light blue eyes which led their own incomprehensible life, and which showed her that Knut Wergeland's thoughts were far away. He slipped out of her verbal snares with an absent smile, and let her arguments drop to the ground like empty oyster shells.

Dr. Wergeland had met Yvonne toward the end of the First World War, when she was staying in Switzerland with her sick mother. She had piqued his curiosity the very first evening, in the hotel dining room. Norway had no girls like her. In spite of her youth Mademoiselle Clermont was unusually polished in manner, extremely chic, and proud in her bearing. She seemed made to dominate a consular corps. For a few weeks Knut had observed Yvonne with speculative curiosity, and then had precipitately proposed to her. The Clermont family of Paris found him a highly acceptable suitor—part heir to a well-known Norwegian shipping line, brilliant in appearance, and a man of high social position. Yvonne had been reared for just such a marriage. It would have been considered ideal if Dr. Wergeland had also been French, but after all you could not have everything in this world.

Professionally the marriage had been a scintillating success. A charming, decorative couple with many-sided interests and a private income were highly esteemed in the consular service. Privately life had been one long disappointment, sheer bankruptcy resulting from contradictory temperaments. Neither good will nor greater love could have bridged this gulf. Yvonne was by nature sociable. The consul, on the contrary, secretly regarded the inevitable social obligations of his profession as an oppressive burden. He was a hermit who with the passing years found the superficial social activities of embassy circles more and more repellent. He preferred a quiet hour with his art collections to any other entertainment. At bottom he had little use for a wife. Even a woman who had suited him better than Yvonne would have been condemned to solitude. As soon as Knut Wergeland had exchanged the anticipated pleasures of the mind for the definite fulfillment of the body, a woman no longer interested him. She ceased to stir his imagination; she became an earthbound creature with all sorts of foibles, demands, and weaknesses.

The Clermont family had been unable to guess that the consul was such a romantic. Most Frenchmen, by the time they made marriages and established families, had long since been cured of this disease. They were realists; even their dreams were distinctly more logical than the dreams of Nordic eccentrics. A Frenchman usually knows by instinct and experience, long before marriage, that on closer acquaintance women are neither mysterious nor sublime. It would simply be against reason to expect such qualities of a competent and thrifty wife.

So it was that the consul's feelings toward Yvonne oscillated between irritation and respect. He was by no means blind to her good points. She was amusing and yet steady, and also a woman who took care of her appearance. On and off he felt sincerely sorry that Yvonne had happened to marry him. She should have married a professor at the Sorbonne, who would undoubtedly have been enchanted by her wit, her cooking, and her chic. In the Far East a Frenchwoman could not enter the household kitchen without receiving the shock of her life; and when a cook was spied upon in his own domain he lost so much "face" that he could be prevailed to stay on only by a raise in wages. *Mon Dieu*—what a stench in the kitchen, what filth, and what a cynical waste of food! It was enough to make any sensible woman go out of her mind. Fortunately Yvonne's mind was so sound that it could stand a few strains.

The consul usually listened to her tales of woe with no more than one ear. In Shanghai no husband listened to anything his own wife said. He preferred to go to the races or to *thés dansants,* or to chase after Chinese women and art dealers. With such persons Consul Wergeland always showed his best side. He could be silent with the Chinese women and talk with the art dealers. When purchasing a porcelain vase, the consul came to life; if the object was a lacquered box, he became virtually eloquent; and in negotiating over a wall painting of a few bamboo shoots and a duck in a pond, he was the match of the most loquacious Frenchman. The consul was truly a connoisseur; he had the needful interest in significant detail.

Whenever the consul did listen to his wife during one of their scenes, he invariably thought of his sister Helene. The contrast between the two women was too amusing for words. Helene Wergeland was the only member of the female sex who had never disappointed the consul. That gangling spinster who occupied their old family home in Trondheim, together with her protégées from the factory and waterfront districts of the city, was spiritually akin to him. To be sure, she lacked the polish he had acquired from living abroad. When her patience gave way, laconic Miss Wergeland flung her frank opinions into people's faces. But Helene's cross generosity, her taciturnity, and even her hearty rudeness restored to the consul, during his rare holidays at home, that tranquillity his whole nature imperatively demanded. As a matter of fact, Miss Wergeland had expressly warned her younger brother against marrying Yvonne Clermont, and not only because she was reluctant to surrender her favorite brother to another woman. She knew his likes and dislikes, his Norwegian bent for dreaminess, and his unfitness for marriage. Miss Wergeland too had little talent for marriage, and she had consequently remained single. When could she have found the time for marriage anyway? Mornings she worked with her brother Olaf in the Wergeland Shipyard's office, and the rest of the day was devoted to her charges in Trondheim and the vicinity. But above all, Miss Wergeland suspected that husbands occasionally gave advice which they liked to see taken. Helene was a highly independent person; she was the one to give advice. She had never had any use for Yvonne, nor Yvonne for her.

Yvonne too thought of Helene during her scene with the consul. Was she to endure this boorish, tyrannical female again, since the consul wanted to spend his leave back at home before he started at his new post in Bangkok? No, never again! She would take her daughter Astrid—the consul's child also, but during such scenes Yvonne always referred to her solely as "my daughter"—and leave the ship in Marseille. Knut could then pick her up—after he had spent *his* months skiing or hunting whales!—at the Clermont home in Paris when it was time for their return to the Far East. Miss Wergeland and her ways were an indispensable component of every scene. What did that woman think she was? Her advice on Astrid's education was altogether superfluous. Yvonne was raising her daughter as she thought right. . . . There followed a lecture on French educational methods that would have done credit to any professor of psychology. But the consul remained unimpressed. He had heard this lecture at regular intervals ever since Astrid's birth. Meanwhile Astrid had reached the age of seven.

Two days before Consul Wergeland's farewell reception in Shanghai, an airmail letter from his sister had arrived at his house in Shanghai's International Settlement. Astrid, Miss Wergeland wrote with her customary graciousness, looked in her last photograph like a skinny herring and had too precocious an expression. The child would have to spend at least a year with her in Trondheim, eat porridge with cream and fresh cod in butter sauce, swim in the fjord at all temperatures, and go skiing with her aunt until she was hard as nails. From everything Knut wrote, Shanghai must be a horrible city, for all that those Chinese poetically called it the "City above the Sea." Poetry didn't make clean streets. Helene personally had already seen enough in the photographs. She could tell that the shops and goods were never dusted. Astrid would learn a thing or two in Trondheim. The poor child had never seen a clean city. Here even the lively *torvet*, the marketplace, was sanitary and orderly.

Consul Wergeland had laughed aloud as he read this letter, but there was a good measure of loving forbearance in his laughter, and of his old pleasure in his sister's view of life, in which love of nature and a fantastic sense of order mingled harmoniously. At any rate, Miss Wergeland seemed to take it for granted that Astrid would certainly come to Trondheim, for she wrote that the child would stay in the blue room. She intended to put Knut and Yvonne in the yellow room, which at the moment was occupied by her distant cousin, the Widow from Aalesund. This lady, who seemed to have no other name, had recently taken the post of Miss Wergeland's housekeeper, and helped her in caring for her protégées. The "Mother Carey's chicks," as Helene called these homeless girls, occupied the rest of the rooms in the east wing of Villa Wergeland.

Yvonne was outraged. When her torrent of speech subsided, the consul straightened out his tall frame and said, "Now that is enough. Of course Astrid is going to Trondheim with us." When Yvonne retorted hotly, he declared that he wished his daughter to make the acquaintance of her father's relatives, of Villa Wergeland, of the shipyard and the skiing terrain around Tröndelag. How long Astrid would remain in Trondheim could not be decided in advance here in Shanghai. In any case, he wanted to hear not another word about Helene. She was a remarkable person.

After this flight of eloquence the consul relapsed into his accustomed silence. Ordinarily he was the soul of patience, but he could not hear his good old Helene maligned. He could see her before him, with her prematurely gray hair, her keen, steely blue eyes, her emphatic nose, and her exasperated smile when her chicks brought her their touching gifts. There was a sizable number of unmarried mothers in Trondheim and the vicinity who but for Miss Wergeland would have jumped into the fjord or committed some other such folly. Those chicken-headed girls did not dare return to their homes after their misadventures. They were put up in the east wing of the big old country house and fed with creamed porridge, hygiene, and Miss Wergeland's advice until—with the newborn infants in their arms, a few crowns in their purses, and layettes in their shabby suitcases—they dared to venture back into ordinary life. Quite often Helene, with the aid of the Widow from Aalesund, succeeded in locating the fellow who had got Ingrid or Marie into trouble. The Widow from Aalesund was a regular old gossip, capable of tracing down every stray herring. If the man was not a sailor from some foreign freighter, she invariably found out who had taken advantage of a bright, mild night to increase the population of Norway. In such cases Miss Wergeland took the Nordland Railroad to some distant point, or drove into a waterfront alley in Trondheim, and descended personally upon the shirker. For the belated wedding at Villa Wergeland, cod with melted butter or partridge in cream sauce was served, according to season, and for dessert the Widow of Aalesund's famous cream puffs. Then the young couple was permitted to depart with a kitchen set, brand-new skis for the entire family, and an extra portion of advice. Later the shirkers and the Mother Carey's chicks visited Miss Wergeland on all possible occasions. They clung to this benevolent and imposing lady and were scolded for clinging. What was all this talk, what all these gifts? Sverre and Marie were getting along so nicely by God's help and their own hard work, weren't they? Miss Wergeland would claim no part in it. But secretly she was delighted to see Marie's round, red-cheeked face as pretty and happy as ever, and the shirker apparently wholly wrapped up in his tiny image. . . . The consul thought involuntarily of such visions, which he had witnessed even as a boy at Villa Wergeland, when his wife spoke of his sister without a spark of understanding. Helene was still the finest person in the world, even if she was not always the pleasantest company.

The scene frequently took place in the Japanese tea room which Consul Wergeland had brought with him from his stay in Tokyo. It was an almost empty room with delicately painted sliding doors. Its contents were only a few low lacquered tables, the usual floor mats, the tea utensils, the *hibachi*, or basin of charcoal, and boxes and chests containing the master's treasures.

In the traditional raised niche hung a choice scroll, in front of which was kept a porcelain vase of flowers. The vase, the flowers, and the scroll formed a landscape of their own—a gentle, subtle illusion which gratified the aesthetic sense and purified the mind. The light in the tea room was also muted by bamboo curtains over the windows, like clouds over the sun. The quarrels with Yvonne in this room shattered its peace and left in Knut Wergeland a lingering weariness and discontent which could only be alleviated by redoubled silence in the "Place of the Imagination," as the Japanese call their tea huts. In this room Northern dreaminess often entered into a temporary union with Japanese philosophy and art of living. . . . At present the consul was trying to collect himself before his guests arrived.

Knut Wergeland had entered the consular service because, like many Norwegians, he had in his blood the longing for foreign worlds. Yet by nature he was, like his sister Helene, a solitary who preferred to eat his herring without spectators. Now the irony of fate imposed upon him extensive social obligations year in and year out. For hours at a time he had to smile affably, follow the diplomatic rule of reflecting twice before saying virtually nothing, and chat animatedly with guests from all parts of the world. Without Yvonne he would scarcely have managed it. She was thoroughly at home in international salons. The consul expressed his gratitude by gifts which Yvonne called "our professional jewels." She possessed valuable family heirlooms of her own and wore the professional jewels only on official occasions. Her parties were highly esteemed. Even Fu, the Chinese cook, reluctantly admitted that Madame knew a great deal about cuisine. He listened to Yvonne's suggestions apparently half asleep, but was in reality alert as a lynx. Like so many Chinese, Fu pricked up his ears whenever he could learn something gratis. Fu, too, had that respect for Yvonne which every just person had to accord her.

But Yvonne was not content with respect. She had expected something different from marriage—had, in fact, expected the thing which her Uncle Antoine in Saigon had once called the "miracle of intimacy." That was a force that transformed human beings and released them from their ordinary state of fruitless narcissism. They became softer toward the lonely crowd outside them, and harder toward themselves. With Yvonne, as with every other disappointed woman, the reverse had happened during the eleven years of her marriage. She was too intelligent not to notice that self-pity was making her more and more unlovable. Her regular penances in the chapels and cathedrals of the Far East had helped little. When she knelt before the altar or in the confessional, bitterness rose up out of the depths of her soul and robbed her prayers and appeals of their radiance. But all the disappointments and memories of a loveless marriage that had been stored up within her over the years poured out in glittering cascades of words during the scene she invariably had with her husband before every reception in their home.

On December 7, 1925, two hours before "the wolves came"—that was the consul's secret term for the arrival of his guests—the scene took place before a new scroll in the tea room.

The scroll was a parting gift of the Japanese consul-general in Shanghai. Yesterday his nephew had unexpectedly arrived from Tokyo and had naturally been invited to the Wergelands'. The result was that Akiro Matsubara, second-oldest son of a Tokyo industrial baron, had in all modesty thrown the carefully planned order of precedence at table into confusion. Where was one to place a young man who had never before been out of Japan? He was too young to merit a place of honor at the table. On the other hand his family, who belonged to the *zaibatsu*, the nobles who controlled Japanese industry, was too important to permit his being thrown together with the young fry from Europe. He was certainly too much of a horror to occupy a place beside brilliant Yvonne, and finally he was too

Japanese to be seated alongside candid Americans or maliciously smiling Chinese. Shanghai was at this moment a hot pavement. The Chinese hated and sneered at the Japanese "island dwarfs," who were trembling with hidden lust for conquest and making themselves at home everywhere. Young Matsubara might, of course, be placed beside Miss Borghild Lillesand. She too was a newcomer in Shanghai, and just as shy as a Japanese. Or rather, Miss Lillesand was absent-minded, not shy. And even the youngest and shyest Japanese expected in all humility the most devoted attention on the part of their interlocutors. Otherwise they suspected that the sons of Nippon were not being paid the respect they had a right to demand as members of the most modern, industrial, and industrious nation in the Far East. . . .

The devil take Baron Akiro Matsubara, the consul thought nervously. Although in private the Japanese were wonderful friends and hosts, they formed an island all their own on social occasions. Even among friendly Europeans they were never really relaxed. Sitting in a corner, they listened surreptitiously and tensely to the discussions of businessmen of the West and East whose tongues had been loosened by a good deal of liqueur or whisky. They themselves said as little as possible. But weeks, years, or decades later they acted—without warning—on the basis of the information they had so assiduously gathered. Even tourists like young Baron Matsubara amassed information. Japanese were listeners with a purpose and enjoyed it.

While Consul Wergeland was meditating on the order at table, Yvonne was saying that Baron Matsubara could very well sit beside Miss Lillesand. Her husband, however, saw fit at this point to tell her that Miss Lillesand was already *his* partner at table. And here the scene really began.

"*C'est impossible!*" Madame exclaimed. "Do you really mean to lead in that goose? Is it sheer chance or a law of nature that you always pick the youngest and silliest woman in the company?"

Since the consul did not reply, Yvonne assured him that all Shanghai was already making fun of his arrangements. The consul threw a veiled look at his wife. "Miss Lillesand amuses me," he said at last. "I see nothing odd about that."

Madame thought it extremely odd. She had observed Miss Lillesand at the races, and also at the home of friends of Captain

Lillesand, who had dragged his sister Borghild all the way to Shanghai to show her a really different corner of the world. Borghild dressed with a remarkable lack of feeling for fashion. She had not a trace of conversation and *savoir vivre*. She was dull as some melancholy northern kingfisher. In a word, Mademoiselle Lillesand, the concert violinist from Oslo, was exactly as amusing as a rainy day in Norway.

"I am certainly not prejudiced," Yvonne remarked, "but at Mademoiselle Lillesand I draw the line, my dear. You know, I have heard some very curious things about her. She *had* to leave Oslo very shortly after her first concert. I mean to find out why; the American vice-consul's wife unfortunately never listens closely enough when anyone is telling something interesting. Mademoiselle Lillesand would not be the least bit averse to compromising you. Her career seems to be ruined already. I imagine she would like to ruin your career now, but she has failed to take *me* into account. Do you think I've worked for it day and night for nothing?"

The consul regarded his efficient wife with his light, ironically wondering eyes. "Kindly leave concern for my reputation to me, my dear Yvonne," he replied with provoking gentleness. "Borghild will sit beside me; she can hardly speak French or English. Baron Matsubara will be well placed alongside the British vice-consul's wife; she knows the Japanese and is a good listener. Miss Lillesand knows nothing about the Far East."

"She knows nothing about anything but her violin. What in the world do you see in this colorless, depressed little creature?"

Yvonne had a gift for stripping every female in her vicinity of her charms with two or three pointed adjectives. Borghild Lillesand was in fact colorless and small and gave the impression of being somehow crushed beneath some burden.

The consul lit a cigarette and regarded the new scroll-painting in the *tokonoma*, the alcove of his tea room. A pupil of the great Miyamoto Musashi had painted it in the style of the seventeenth century. A tiny bird sat in a silver mist on a long, thin branch that seemed on the point of breaking. Underneath, the artist had written: "Songbird on a Dead Twig." The bird seemed utterly isolated from the rest of the world. Its situation and its attitude, moreover, suggested a typical Japanese virtue: the heroic and, to the Westerner's feeling, senseless determination to break into ecstatic song in the face of a death that might have been avoided by the exercise of a little caution.

"I asked you something!" Yvonne glowered at her husband with her dark eyes, which were somewhat too close together. Knut had slipped away from her, as he so often did. Her hand flew to her heart. Once again she had felt that painful stab.

The consul continued to study the scroll. That was Borghild Lillesand for you: a songbird on a dead branch. That she went on singing was, in a profound and romantic sense, amusing. If the consul had attempted to explain this to his wife, she would not have understood, for she was utterly devoid of romanticism. She observed, analyzed, and drew her conclusions. "Miss Lillesand is not well," the consul murmured.

"I am not well either, but I contrive not to look rumpled. Why does the girl go to parties? She doesn't have to go out. Why doesn't she take herself to bed with an electric pad and a couple of aspirin?"

"It isn't that sort of illness." The consul looked at his watch. Barely an hour before the wolves would be coming. "You smoke too much, Yvonne," he murmured. "It's a good thing we are going to Norway for our leave. I take it we're agreed on that?"

"Whatever led you to think that? I am taking my daughter to the boarding school in Lausanne. We have already discussed the fact that you are to pick me up later in Paris."

"*You* have discussed it, my dear. Astrid is coming with me to Trondheim. If you don't want to bother about her, I'll take the amah along. She will be coming with us to Bangkok later on anyway."

The old quarrel over the child was in full swing. The scene had reached its climax. Madame was determined to enter Astrid in the boarding school where she herself had learned deportment, logic, and *haute cuisine*. In Lausanne the child would forget her Chinese and fragmentary Norwegian and become a little Frenchwoman. Later Astrid would marry a prosperous, proper Frenchman. She must have a better life than her mother's.

After earnest persuasion, Yvonne at last yielded and agreed to spend a month with "her daughter" at Miss Wergeland's. The consul sighed with relief. "But your sister isn't going to get Astrid in her talons," Yvonne concluded the scene. She was content. The consul had at last risen from his mat. It was high time. Back in their hotels and houses the wolves must already be changing clothes for the party. Yvonne would have liked to say something to Knut about Astrid's future husband, but he refused to go into that. "Must we discuss that too?" he asked with nervous irritability. "We have a bit of time to spare before Astrid marries the fellow."

He suddenly laughed. The thought of his pale seven-year-old daughter's future husband amused him. Yvonne arranged marriages in her mind with all the realistic details. The house the couple would occupy, the young man's income, solid education, and distinguished family played an ever lively part in her picture of the future.

Yvonne's ears flushed. Knut was making fun of her again. And yet it was absolutely essential to consider Astrid's future before it was too late. How quickly a girl grew up! And how rapidly she could become an old maid like Miss Helene Wergeland!

Yvonne lingered for one moment more at the door of the tea room. Her ruby necklace and the earrings she had inherited from her great-grandmother lent her a peculiar charm, austere and darkly burning. Her countrymen characterized her as an "ugly beauty." In any case, she was a lady—a *grande dame*, in fact, such as one seldom encountered in the motley society of Shanghai. Her full red lips turned downward with more than a trace of bitterness.

"Yvonne," the consul murmured, patting her gleaming dark hair, "why are we always squabbling? We ought to try— Hm." He gave an embarrassed cough. "Everything will be better in Trondheim," he added hastily. "Shanghai is dreadful. Sometimes, on Nanking Road, I have the feeling that this city is bent on swallowing me alive."

"Don't talk nonsense. Shanghai is amusing. We are very happy here."

"That's fine, then. May I dress now?"

"I have been waiting for an hour for you to start. What is going to be any better in Trondheim? You're hiding something from me. But I have good eyes and ears, my dear. I know your secrets!"

The consul thought he had not heard aright. *What* did Yvonne know? There she stood, with her rigid smile, in her night-blue brocade dress, stretching her cormorant's neck inside the ruby necklace as though she were striving to catch fish for her empty, dreamless soul! Dr. Wergeland pulled himself together. His nervousness before the beginning of evening receptions was assuming morbid forms. Had Yvonne really discovered Borghild Lillesand's shameful secret? Had someone gossiped? Or was Yvonne referring to something else, something that had not happened on Bubbling Well Road and Avenue Foch, but in the opium mists of the Chinese City? Nonsense! Yvonne only wanted to provoke him and catch him in her verbal traps. She could not possibly know anything. The consul wiped the perspiration from his brow. He felt suddenly chilled, in spite of the glowing basin of charcoal. Shanghai had a cold winter. Old men and Chinese children lay down quietly by the edge of the road and waited to freeze to death, while the foreigners in this greatest port of the Far East continued to dance on a volcano. Less than a year ago Sun Yat-sen, the father of the Chinese Revolution, had died in Peking of cancer of the liver. The country was rent by disturbances. Would General Chiang Kai-shek be able to complete the work of unification without China's becoming a Russian province where foreigners would no longer be able to trade? Everything was uncertain—except for the growing Russian influence and the ubiquitous social misery. The consul sighed. Here not even Helene could have helped. There were too many homeless persons and too few fires in this vast, Westernized city through which Russian and Japanese spies roamed.

Without another word the consul went to his dressing room, where the boy was already waiting. The bath was ready. It was high time to dress. The wolves were drawing closer.

Half an hour later Consul and Madame Wergeland received their guests in the vestibule of their house in the International Settlement. This was their last official party in Shanghai. They did not intend to depart until March, but in a few weeks they would be auctioning off all dispensable household objects. Their Shanghai life would be packed away in trunks, and the family would move to the Cathay Hotel until their departure. When they arrived in Norway the Hardanger Valley would certainly be already green and flowering. Shanghai would vanish; it was no city one longed to return to as one did to old Peking with its solemn, sleepy palaces and temples, or Kyoto with its glory of cherry blossoms.

They would not miss their Shanghai acquaintances either, the consul thought as he stood at the side of his elegant wife, greeting the wolves with a radiant smile. As in the Japanese *kabuki* drama, the actors reached the stage from the left by a narrow corridor, and had to step upon the main stage by crossing a *hanamichi,* a bridge of flowers. In the Japanese drama new actors were constantly walking across the bridge of flowers, and others unexpectedly vanished from this second stage through a trapdoor. In Shanghai there were many bridges of flowers, and each possessed a trapdoor. The consul's guests, too, were actors; but he did not precisely know their function in the play. He could only guess at the thoughts concealed behind their flowery speeches. Perhaps for that reason there was an electric charge in the atmosphere: anticipation of those equivocal conversations that were a specialty of Shanghai.

When, a good hour later, they sat down to dine at the oval table, the consul knew that his party was going to be a success. His guests knew one another well enough not to become too familiar, and not well enough to be indifferent about the way the conversation went. Yvonne was discussing with a member of the Banque Industrielle de Chine the pink, blue, and cubistic periods of Picasso. Monsieur Vallin knew quite as much about modern painting as about finance and French interests in China. It was so easy to be a good hostess, Yvonne thought. She had leafed through her notebook under the heading "hobbies" and found in the Vs that she must talk about modern painters with Monsieur Vallin, and, moreover, only about those who set the tone in Paris. . . . On her left sat Mr. John Edwards, chief manager of an important British building firm. His hobby was horse-racing. He was the man who had the best tips and the worst results on all the tracks between Shanghai and Hong Kong. Sporting events bored Yvonne to death. But a little bell of memory rang inside her head: track. To be sure, she had seen and judged Borghild Lillesand for the first time at the track. She glanced as if it were accidentally at the head of the table, where the girl sat, and raised her eyebrows. How in the world could any woman, even if she knew nothing about clothes, wear a red dress with her silvery-blond hair and her pallid face, without a touch of make-up? What did Knut see in this drab little creature? Did he pity the girl? He never felt any pity for his wife. . . .

"Will you play for us afterward?" Consul Wergeland was at the moment asking his partner at table.

"If you like," Borghild murmured obediently as a child, and absently brushed her wispy blond hair from her forehead.

Her way of wearing her hair irritated Yvonne beyond anything. She had already inquired of her husband whether blond women really thought they could do without visits to the hairdresser. Did they imagine it good taste to sit down at a formal table looking as if they had just got out of bed? "You can ask her," the consul had suggested. But Yvonne was already resolved not to exchange a word with this disorderly, drooping little violinist.

Borghild Lillesand sat staring into space. Was she thinking of her shameful secret? She looked as if she were listening, half in a trance and half with deep attention, to some music, to a song of the Far North, a sweet and melancholy melody. Borghild's lower lip twisted downward in helpless grief. She started as her other neighbor, the chairman of the Chinese Chamber of Commerce, turned to her with a polite question about how she liked Shanghai.

"Oh—very interesting," she murmured in poorly enunciated schoolgirl English.

"Have you seen the bird market yet?" the influential Chinese asked, regarding this queer girl with secret sympathy. That she was not talkative pleased him. She might have been the daughter of a Chinese in that respect. At this thought, Mr. Hsin Kao-tze's slanting, deep-set eyes clouded. Since his daughter had run away from him because she was unwilling to marry the man her father had chosen for her, Mr. Hsin had stricken the word "daughter" from his vocabulary. In any case a daughter was not worth wasting any thought on. Her brain was too insignificant to grasp the Confucian doctrine of veneration of parents.

Borghild did not reply to Mr. Hsin's question about the bird market. The consul frowned. Yvonne was probably right—as always. The girl was impossible, even though, in a fleeting hour, the miracle of intimacy had blossomed between him and Borghild. They understood each other without words—which was the way it should be. "Miss Lillesand is dreaming," he apologized smilingly to his Chinese guest, "a bad habit of our Far North."

"A very praiseworthy habit," Mr. Hsin replied in flawless English. "Unfortunately we forget how to dream in present-day Shanghai. It has become a city with a mechanical heart. Our great teacher Chuang-tzu maintains that he who has a mechanical heart in his breast loses his innocence and becomes fickle. That is Shanghai—a fickle city. To my mind, innocence remains only in the bird market."

Mr. Hsin Kao-tze (his given name meant "High Purpose") inclined his long, narrow head over his plate. He himself resembled a bird. In Shanghai he was called "the Crane"; he had the crane's long, skinny neck. When he was not smiling, his face expressed distaste and skepticism. His full lips, which contrasted oddly with the rest of his melancholic, ascetic face, betrayed a fondness for sensual pleasure. His small, glittering eyes had a mildly crafty expression. Those eyes pierced through all the "fool projects" of his enemies. Mr. Hsin had many enemies in Shanghai, but even more friends, especially in the consulates and the foreign trading companies. For them he was a barometer that faithfully showed the political weather. He lived behind Bubbling Well Road in an old-fashioned Chinese house with thick walls and many small pavilions. Consul Wergeland had visited there frequently; among the bird cages and Chinese vases he could recover from the wolves. Mr. Hsin had fits of indolence. At such times he switched off his telephone and forged plans. Although his daughter had left him and there was no longer any son to make sacrifices to the ancestors in the house of Hsin, there were still his songbirds, the exciting game of high finance, and his own plans for China's future. Among other interests, Mr. Hsin controlled the *Shun Pao,* the oldest Chinese daily newspaper, read every day by "at least 150,000 families." Anyone who controlled a newspaper in Shanghai held one corner of power. Mr. Hsin rarely went to his newspaper offices on Hankow Road. He held many conferences, however, in the old-fashioned house back of Bubbling Well Road. There he reminded the editors not to print everything they knew. Only the things one knew and did not say gave one that portion of power which the Chinese adherents of Soviet Russia and the Japanese island dwarfs in Shanghai so bitterly coveted.

Mr. Hsin glanced with that crafty, mild alertness of his at the Japanese consul-general, whom he knew well, and then at young Baron Akiro Matsubara, whom he had never seen before in Shanghai.

The young man was at most twenty, the age Mr. Hsin's son and heir would have been. Tin Po—"Protection of Heaven"—had been involved, along with other students and Shanghai workers, in the May 1925 uprising against capitalists and foreign imperialists, and had been killed in the streets by a bullet intended for a more important person. That had taken place on May 30, five years after the flight of Mr. Hsin's daughter. She had covered her tracks completely, was gone from his world as thoroughly as Protection of Heaven. Mr. Hsin had become only a little more withered, a little slyer, since the death of his son. Now he had only his birds and the great porcelain vases preserved from times when children obeyed their fathers blindly. Mr. Hsin's concubines did not count; they could not follow him on his lonely ways. Nor were they meant to. They were cicadas who sang with shrill voices in the night, and were afterward silent.

What was this young Japanese doing in Shanghai? Was he one of those tourists with good German cameras who supposedly took snapshots of romantic corners of the Chinese City and were so unexpectedly encountered at the waterfront, surreptitiously photographing or sketching installations and fortifications? Mr. Hsin stretched his crane's neck. . . .

Young Baron Matsubara was feeling dreadfully uncomfortable and therefore smiled as if he were sitting under flowering cherry trees, enjoying a picnic with good friends. What irritated him most was a Dutch still life. The painting hung directly in front of his nose, in the center of the wall of the long dining room. Since he stared through his glasses (which he wore only to conceal his shyness) fixedly at the lobster, the fruits, and—horror of horrors!—the few flowers which were assembled with bland incongruity on the canvas, the wife of the British vice-consul asked, "Isn't the painting marvelous? There really is nothing to surpass a Dutch still life. They are so calming, don't you think?"

"I am entirely of your opinion, Madame," Baron Matsubara replied in careful mission-school English. He felt boundless pity for the ignorant female. How was it possible? A person with only a spark of culture would never permit a painting of foods in a dining room. One's digestion and all one's pleasure in the mulled wine were churned up if one had to look at painted edibles while dining. The smile on Baron Matsubara's sensitive, finely chiseled features, which bespoke his *samurai* family, was distorted by effort. In the torment that the sight of the still life produced, he even forgot temporarily the unspeakable affront that America had committed against his nation. Over a year ago, on May 26, 1924, Congress had passed the law limiting Japanese immigration into the United States. Thus the Japanese, who after all were descendants of the sun goddess, had been placed on the same level as Koreans, Chinese, and other "undesirable aliens." Before dinner Akiro had discovered an American among the consul's guests—he had recognized him at once by his casual bearing and unmistakable accent—and had twitched inwardly even as he gave a courteous low bow at his introduction to Mr. Horace Bailey of Clifford Motors, Inc. Matsubara had so intensely admired these foreigners and had learned so much from them at the mission school. And these Americans had sent millions of dollars to help alleviate the mass suffering caused by the last great earthquake in 1923. Akiro could not resolve these contradictions. Like many students in Tokyo, he still admired the foreigners. One had to abash them by wisdom and generosity. Probably that was the way to their hearts.

At last the meal came to an end, and Akiro fled with the other guests to the music room. There the Dutch lobster could not pursue him. The young baron loved European music beyond all else. German music, in particular, sometimes moved him to tears. It was disgraceful for a proud Japanese to weep so easily. Akiro had therefore begun ascetic exercises on the advice of his uncle, who was a follower of Zen Buddhism; these exercises, he expected, would train him in hardness and firm bearing. Life was a difficult task, full of duties and rules; only music and the chatter of geishas gave Akiro a degree of relaxation. The powerful figure of his father cast a shadow upon all his actions and feelings. The father had to be respected—that too was one of the duties of a well-reared Japanese.

His train of thought was interrupted by a violin solo played by a young foreigner with colorless eyes and fearfully unkempt hair. Akiro had never heard such beautiful playing or seen so plain a girl. He closed his narrow dark eyes and surrendered to the music, outwardly unmoved and inwardly quivering. . . .

Borghild was playing Grieg. She stood in solitude among these strangers and gave to them a magical sound-picture of the world.

In this incomparable moment she had power over those who were more powerful than she. In the act of giving, she seemed to grow. Her delicate face was tinged a lovely pink that wonderfully animated her. She was no longer crushed and absent-looking; in the magical transformation of the world she herself was transformed. Her pale hair glistened like spun gold, and in her dreamy eyes, ordinarily addled by grief and fear of life, there shone creative concentration. The audience, released from the prison of convention into realms of their own feelings, bowed their heads so that no one could see the way the masks over their faces crumbled.

Consul Wergeland alone had not bowed his head. He sat bolt upright, staring at this terribly young thing. In this frail, shy creature in the cheap red dress, in those limpid eyes and the tones of the violin, the reticent spirit of the Northland found expression. Borghild was now playing those soaring and charming melodies which he had heard as a boy. The consul was the most enchanted of all the listeners, for this music sang of gay beginnings in fjord country in spring, and of buried life in foreign quarters of the globe. She is a nymph, he thought confusedly. One of these days she will carry me down into the water, if I do not watch out. I dare not pity her. The helpless are full of cunning dodges. . . . His face and his glinting eyes hardened. Yvonne was right—as usual.

At that moment Borghild Lillesand lowered her bow, surrendering her power. Consul Wergeland rose and in the name of all the guests thanked the young lady in the ill-fitting dress for an enjoyable half-hour.

Late as it was, Astrid had not yet slept. She was always overexcited when her parents gave a party. She was also offended because she had to stay with Yumei, her amah, up in the nursery, while downstairs people were eating, dancing, and playing music. She was very tall for her seven years, and so pale and thin that Miss Wergeland had been justified in calling her a "skinny herring." Astrid wanted to cry because she had been excluded from the party on the floor below, but then Yumei would have laughed at her with her deep, rough laugh. It always struck the young Chinese nurse as utterly ludicrous when the little foreign girl cried. A girl child cried because it had no rice, or had to work too long at the spinning-mill, or had been beaten by its father for not being a son. Yumei had once been such a little girl; that was why at seven she had known and cheerfully endured so much more than did little Missie in the big heated house with the many ricebowls.

Yumei had pity for Astrid in only one respect: she thought her as ugly as the nine-headed bird which is used to frighten children. Little Missie had no color at all, neither in her face nor in her hair. It did no good to twist red hair-ribbons into her braids; the plaits still dangled down like bleached hemp around her doughy little face. Yumei had her own ideas about beauty. Coal-black, glistening hair, apple-red cheeks, and a fat, round body—that was the way a pretty child should look. That was the way Yumei herself had looked in spite of the work in the spinning-mills of Shanghai. Years ago her family had set out from a famine-stricken village one day, traveled down the great river with all their belongings, and descended upon a second-second cousin in Shanghai's Chinese City. Three days later they were all working in the spinning-mill. But Yumei had grown up in the village and during the first years of her life had benefited by fresh air, unpolished rice, and a fruit now and then. Now she was fifteen years old and watching over little Missie instead of laboring for many hours in the factory. Her elder sister worked eleven and a half hours every day in a cotton mill for starvation wages. As a ten-year-old Yumei had also accompanied her mother to the mill every day and "helped" for eleven hours as an apprentice, in return for two bowls of rice and a little dried fish. On the way to work the family had eaten one or two dried wheatcakes for breakfast; at the factory they had the privilege of washing down the dry food with hot water. Only evenings did they all eat hot rice, vegetables, and even meat together in the kitchen, and drink wonderful hot tea along with it. Yumei had always considered everything fine and had never cried. Little Missie tried her patience, but at the same time she was terribly sorry for her. Astrid's tired blue eyes looked out so jealously from her little white bean-flour face, looked out with such a hunger for love that Yumei would take the tall, thin child on her lap again and again, embrace her heartily, and whisper that "Missie Astlid" was Yumei's dearest little sister, even if she was a foreign devil's child.

Then Astrid was content and forgot her misery. She would so have liked to be a Chinese girl with shining black eyes and a big jolly family. Yumei sometimes secretly took her into the Chinese City—on the moon festival, or, last time, for New Year's. Youngest Brother had had a nasty fever at the time, but he insisted on sharing his stuffed dumpling with the little foreign girl, and so the two of them had taken alternate bites of the dumpling, amid the laughter of the entire family. *Maman* would undoubtedly have exploded with outrage if she had known where Yumei took her daughter on their "walks." Yumei had threatened Astrid that the evil storm spirit of Wuliain Mountain would seize her by the hair and throw her through the air if she ever told *Maman* a word about the dumpling. Yumei was superstitious and took the typical Chinese delight in horror tales. She often frightened the sensitive child far more than she suspected. But still, Yumei was all Astrid had in the world: sister, playmate, storyteller, and an oven pouring out a consoling, unvarying warmth. *Maman* had little time for Astrid, for all that she was so concerned about the child's future. The future seemed so important to Yvonne that she somewhat forgot the present life of this pale child, so hungry for love, who would have liked to be gay and in on everything. Papa too had little time for her. Either he was having conferences or was at his club, or in the Japanese room, which Astrid was not allowed to enter. "Papa is thinking," she had once explained to Yumei, and had been very proud. She herself never knew what to think about; she had not an ounce of imagination. Yumei had to tell her stories constantly, to which Astrid listened greedily. Although she was mortally frightened by Yumei's vixens and dragon-gods, to hear a voice cheerfully rattling away bloodthirsty Chinese fairy tales was better than just sitting around with nothing to do.

Astrid had seldom been quite so excited as she was over tonight's party. She had heard somewhere that a violinist from Oslo was going to play; and suddenly—after anxiously waiting for Yumei and some delicacies from the table—Astrid heard the first notes of the violin. She climbed out of bed, posted herself in her thin Chinese sleeping-gown on the landing of the stairs, and listened. She was quivering with cold and agitation but did not know it.

And then something happened that could not be grasped. It happened quietly, and yet it was far more terrible than Yumei's black-faced dragon with the red hair and mouth that was a bowl of blood.

Astrid suddenly heard a scream that came from *Maman*'s bedroom. A girl in a red dress with blond hair that hung wanly over her forehead stood before the dressing table, uttering a penetrating scream, while Papa took an article of jewelry from her limp hand. But the most frightening thing was *Maman,* who stood stiffly in the doorway. Astrid could not understand precisely what she was saying, because *Maman* was whispering on account of the guests, and she slipped hurriedly into the bathroom. From there she peeped shakily through the curtain. Papa placed his arm around the strange woman and said, "You are sick, Borghild. Of course you are not a thief. I'll explain it all to my wife."

But *Maman* laughed as shrilly as a heroine in the Chinese theater, which Astrid sometimes secretly attended with Yumei when they were supposed to be walking in the park. And *Maman* went up to the stranger and raised her hand as if she intended to slap her. But *Maman* was much too well bred to do that. She only said, "Give me your handbag; I want to see whether you have also stolen silver spoons!"

Papa held his hand over the stranger's mouth to muffle her screams, because after all there were guests downstairs. And *Maman* did not take the stranger's bag after all, but only said to Papa, her eyes flashing, that he should take his arm from that tramp's shoulder. "Tramp," *Maman* said. Astrid understood the words quite well—*"Cette vagabonde."* On *Maman*'s instructions, Astrid was learning twenty French words a day. And then Yumei came rushing in and asked, loudly and without embarrassment, where little Missie was; and Astrid felt terribly frightened and ran into Yumei's arms and hid her head against the warm breast.

Maman said to Yumei, "You are dismissed at once." She spoke Chinese, and Astrid understood every word. But Papa waved his hand, and Yumei went contentedly back to the nursery with little Missie. After putting Astrid back to bed, Yumei told her another thoroughly shivery story about mountain spirits and joyously stuffed herself on sweets from the kitchen, because Astrid was trembling so hard that she could not even eat chocolate cream. She screamed twice during the night. Yumei took the child into her arms, wrapped her in her own wadded jacket which she always wore in the "bitter month," the twelfth month of the lunar year, and sang in her rough, cheerful

voice an aria which the two had heard together in the Chinese theater. At last Astrid fell asleep again, smiling faintly; Yumei had assured her that "Miss Astlid" was her dearest little sister. Astrid knew
perfectly well that Yumei was not telling the truth; she undoubtedly
loved Youngest Brother far more, because he was, after all, a man
child. But Astrid did not care. At seven she was already fond of a
loving little lie. And Yumei must like her somewhat, anyway, since
Astrid did so many favors for her.

The child sighed in her sleep. It was like the delicate, wailing tone
that welled up from the throats of the little Chinese birds Mr. Hsin
had collected in his house behind Bubbling Well Road.

Fifteen-year-old Amah Yumei lay down on the sleeping mat at the
foot of Astrid's bed. Why had Madame been so angry? Unfortunately
they had been speaking the foreign language. Madame had already
dismissed Yumei several times, but Master had always nodded reassuringly. And what the master decided was done in this world.

Yvonne had left the bedroom as suddenly as she had entered it.
She would have to warn Captain Lillesand at once, and without attracting attention, so that he could take his sister to their hotel. With
all her energy she chased a tormenting vision from her consciousness: Knut with his arm protectively about that tramp. Yvonne had
observed his face at that moment; his light eyes had not regarded
Borghild with that ironic curiosity which was their usual expression
when he looked at Yvonne and at most other human beings. Rather
there had been a kind of reluctant tenderness in them. Knut could
not seriously see anything in this depraved magpie who stole glittering things! Certainly he was a dreamer, but he was a man of honor.
His conceptions of order were not so fantastic as Miss Wergeland's
visions of the world as it should be, but the consul also hated chaos.

She stopped in front of the door to the smoking room and struggled for breath like a drowning woman. Then she drew herself up
and approached Captain Lillesand with a gracious smile. Borghild's
brother reluctantly moved away from the brisk talk of the men. Silently he ascended the stairs at Yvonne's side. Yvonne too—quite contrary to her habit—said not a word. After all, the Oslo captain was
her guest.

In the bedroom deep silence had succeeded Yvonne's disappearance. The consul did not look at Borghild. She sat hunched in a chair, moaning. "Now, Borghild, do be calm," he murmured. He was still feeling that curious tender repugnance. Suddenly Borghild sprang up and came close to him. She did not even reach to his chin. Her hair hung loose, lifeless, like gold threads falling to her shoulders. They were touching, childish shoulders, too weak for the burden they had to bear.

"I would have brought the bracelet back tomorrow," she whispered. "I can't stop myself. I'm—I'm sorry."

Her lower lip drooped like a child's. She seemed more crushed and without attractiveness than ever. With that same tender repugnance the consul brushed her hair back from her forehead. "It's quite all right," he said absently. If only the captain would hurry, he thought. Why is she standing in front of me? What does she want now? I cannot help her.

But while he was thinking these thoughts, his repugnance deepening, Borghild had thrown her thin arms around his neck, standing on tiptoe to do so. It was ridiculous, shocking, and a breach of all propriety. She laid her tousled head against his chest and whispered, "I need someone who will be kind to me when—when . . . it . . . comes over . . . me." She looked up at him, her lower lip quivering. An impossible little person. *Une vagabonde.*

"Stop this silliness, Borghild," the consul said hoarsely, and gently but firmly freed himself from her helpless arms. Not a moment too soon! Yvonne and Captain Lillesand entered the room.

"Please come to the smoking room," Yvonne said to him. "People are wondering where you are."

She did not so much as glance at the tramp as she politely bade the captain good-by. A delightful party indeed! But there would be no scandals in Yvonne's house. She would see to that—with or without the consul's aid.

In the smoking room businessmen from all quarters of the globe sat recovering from the strain of conversations with their ladies at table. Shortly before departure they would return to the ladies in the salon, but at the moment they had their peace, their whisky, and their fun. Thank God the violin-playing was over for the evening, Mr. Horace Bailey thought. He was not musical, and proud of it. He was in fine humor, as he always was as soon as the ladies vanished. He had sat down beside Mr. Hsin and was radiating benevolence and business acumen in all directions. Mr. Bailey was making a study tour of various cities of the Far East. He wanted to learn personally by what means and to what extent the sale of Clifford automobiles could be increased still further. The Japanese wanted to conquer Asia commercially. That was a bit nervy of them, Mr. Bailey thought, casually studying young Baron Matsubara. Fortunately that modest young man sat in the farthest corner of the smoking room; thus Mr. Bailey could discuss the business and political situation in peace with "the Crane." He was enthusiastic about Mr. Hsin—a true friend of the West.

In actuality Mr. Hsin wished the foreigners who exercised economic dominion in Shanghai a pleasant old age in their own honorable countries. He too had plans, just as did the Japanese. But they concerned less the greatness of China than its unity, as well as the abolition of foreign administration and the foreign big businessmen and banks. Thanks to his people's long memory, Mr. Hsin had not forgotten that in the International Settlement in Shanghai a large placard had announced one morning: *Chinese and dogs are not allowed in the park.* But Mr. Hsin still needed his foreign business friends. Was General Chiang Kai-shek the right man for China? Any man would suit old Mr. Hsin who expelled the foreign police who had shot down his son in May. But he had more patience than the Japanese dwarfs. He sat still and waited. For the present one must sit still and gaze at the clouds. There was a time to go fishing and a time to dry nets.

"I am buying raw materials," Mr. Hsin announced after a pause, and he stretched his neck as if the Japanese were at this moment on the point of falling upon his investment. "That is the safest investment if the Japanese should swallow up Shanghai some day."

Mr. Bailey gave a booming laugh. "You are a pessimist, my friend."

"We must always be prepared for the worst and hope for the best," the Chinese replied quietly.

At this moment Monsieur Vallin and young Baron Matsubara sat down near them. The conversation stopped so abruptly that the clever Frenchman felt compelled to leap into the breach so that the game could continue.

"What do you intend to study in Paris?" he asked the young Japanese, who was to "learn about Europe" in Paris for several years.

"Art and literature; these are my deep interests."

This grave reply produced a fit of laughter on the part of Mr. Bailey, who unfortunately drank too much whenever his wife was not watching him. "Art and literature!" he exclaimed genially between gasps and slapped the young Japanese baron on the shoulder with his big red hand. "Who do you think you're fooling? Do you want *me* to tell you what you intend to study in Europe, my dear young man? The same subjects as all your countrymen: strategy, tactics, chemistry, and cheap ways to build railroads and blow up locomotives. Art and literature—hahaha!"

Young Baron Matsubara was so stunned that he did not even shake the big red hand from his shoulder. It lay upon his Western evening jacket like a Dutch lobster. A mist had formed over his eyes, through which he could only dimly discern the men from the West and the Chinese Crane. He had been insulted, and Nippon had been made ridiculous in the eyes of the world. There could be no forgiveness for this crime, neither now nor in the future. Baron Akiro was a son of the *samurai* on his mother's side; one of his forefathers had received the Imperial Order of the Chrysanthemum. And here he stood, at the beginning of his life abroad, shamed, mocked, and accused of warlike designs. And yet Japan had had an open door for the Western Powers since 1854, and only three years ago a World Peace Exhibition had been held in Tokyo. Along with other aristocratic students in Tokyo, Akiro had plunged into the stream of liberalism. What he proposed to study in Paris in addition to art and literature was no concern of this oversized shopkeeper from the American Middle West.

Naturally, Akiro did not show by the slightest change of expression that he was mortally insulted. He smiled stiffly, by a superhuman effort. "It will be hard for us to do full justice to Western humor," he murmured, making a deep, humble bow. "We know we have much to learn."

An awkward pause followed. Mr. Bailey looked around in dismay. He cleared his throat. "Don't take it amiss, young man," he said good-naturedly. "My wife always says, 'Horace,' my wife always says, 'if you would only stop your silly jokes. Talk is mostly hot air, remember that!'"

He boomed out liberating laughter, in which Baron Matsubara apparently joined. At least the high, hysterically shrill sounds that he produced at the cost of all his strength were supposed to represent an approving chuckle. Moreover, he no longer kept his eyes lowered, but stared from the side directly at this well-disposed American with his huge lobster hands and his sound but indiscreet common sense. At that moment of deadly disgrace Akiro, who had intended with the best will in the world to learn technology and poetry from the West, developed the Japanese X-ray eye. That penetrating, disillusioned keenness was born of hatred. It was a hatred preserved by a phenomenal memory and by the Japanese principle of education, which held vengeance to be a noble masculine duty. Revenge of an insult was one aspect of *giri*, the duty that every Japanese owes to his family, the state, and the Tenno, the Son of Heaven. As young Baron Matsubara, on his first night abroad, stared at the tactless American, he felt for the first time the fullness of his powers of concentration. Here too was something basically and typically Japanese, an odd peculiarity of that inscrutable nation: that a cruel shock did not make a Japanese cynical or indifferent toward his enemies. It intensified his vitality.

Suddenly Consul Wergeland's reception was over. The gentlemen had flirted for a while with the ladies, paid compliments to Yvonne, and expressed admiration for the little Norwegian's violin playing. What a pity the young *artiste* had been so exhausted that her brother had had to take her back to the hotel! But that was the Shanghai air for you; it sometimes acted upon a visitor like an electric shock.

Akiro Matsubara of Itoh bowed very low and stiffly to Consul and Madame Wergeland, and in careful English expressed his delight and his gratitude for the honor of being present at the reception.

"I hope that you have been entertained, Baron," the consul said, giving Akiro a jocund and somewhat conspiratorial look. "Unfortunately I was unable to offer you festivities in the Japanese style. That would have been more to the taste of the two of us."

The young Japanese made a second, still lower bow. "I could not have spent my time better, Consul Wergeland," he murmured. "I am greatly indebted to you."

2: Japanese Interlude

Young Baron Matsubara did not take a cab back to his hotel in Hongkew, where—contrary to the official tale that he had just arrived in Shanghai—he had been living under another name for several months. In this district to the north and east of Soochow Creek, whose cloudy waters separated the rest of the International Settlement from the Chinese world of factories and traders, the student from Tokyo, acting on instructions from government circles, was engaged in studies that had no connection with the fine arts. Since he would enter government service after spending several years in Europe, the twenty-year-old was already beginning to gather information, sound out tempers, and establish contacts. He had already taken a number of first-rate photographs of Shanghai's waterfront district, of North Station, and of large industrial plants. In addition he had dispatched to Tokyo a proposal concerning the silk industry. If Shanghai was occupied by the Japanese for its own good within the next fifteen years, and a new order was established there, the silk industry ought to be concentrated in Hongkew, he suggested. Sending cocoons into the foreign settlements in Shanghai ought to be strictly controlled at first and later banned entirely. Several Japanese firms should supervise the export of the raw silk from Hongkew. For years Shanghai had in any case been the center of the raw-silk-export trade, which was now shared between Japanese and Chinese firms. Fortunately Baron Akiro had today made the acquaintance of Mr. Hsin, who resembled a crane—the very man his report had suggested approaching. Before his departure he could find occasion to propose to him the creation of a Sino-Japanese silk-processing industry in Hongkew. In spite of his insufferable humiliation, he had not missed a word of the conversation between the Crane and the American, and had been deeply gratified to observe that Mr. Hsin told his business friend from the United States only half-truths about the economic situation in Shanghai. It was not essential for foreigners to know about the rice and transportation conditions north of the creek and east of the Whangpoo River. Mr. Hsin's behavior had been a revelation to young Baron Matsubara. Intelligent Chinese seemed to hate the foreigners almost as heartily as they did the Japanese in Shanghai. Perhaps the Chinese would realize in the course of time that the busy, determined sons of Nippon were not only their true friends, who wished to lend them a paternal helping hand, but Asiatics as well. . . .

For the rest, Akiro would answer tomorrow Tokyo's inquiry about Clifford Motors, whose representative was the gentleman with the lobster hands. Their products were poor, their sale in Shanghai very small; Tokyo would be well advised not to be deceived by this new firm! That was Baron Matsubara's rejoinder to Mr. Bailey's harmless little joke. Akiro smiled contentedly. He called a cab to take him to the Japanese restaurant near Kiangse Road. That street was also the location of Norinaga's art and antique shop. Norinaga and his eldest son, who sold Japanese and Chinese *objets d'art* of bronze, lacquer, tortoise-shell, and ivory, were not only agents of a large Tokyo firm but voluntary associates of the Japanese Secret Service. Even with the best of intentions, a person was highly exposed in this filthy and corrupt city! From Mr. Norinaga Junior, Akiro Matsubara had received the address of a first-class Japanese restaurant near Kiangse Road, a few steps south of Nanking Road. He had already taken the precaution of ordering a late supper there, and he was now going for it. Madame Wergeland's Franco-Chinese cuisine had been, as was only to be expected, thoroughly vile.

Just as Akiro was about to enter a cab, his dark eyes widened in alarm. A small blond foreigner with straggling hair and an absent expression was running straight into an automobile. That is, she would have run straight into it if Akiro had not pulled her back. He sprang to her aid so quickly that his glasses fell into the filth of the gutter, where they instantly became the center of a scramble by beggars and children. Mr. Tse, member in good standing of the Shanghai guild of beggars, who slept by day and by night patrolled his route as a "blind beggar" in the International Settlement, won the battle.

While his glasses were still on, Akiro had recognized the young lady whose honorable violin playing at Consul Wergeland's reception had penetrated so deeply into his soul. What was the girl with the wan eyes doing in the street at night? That was contrary to reason and etiquette. She was no "girl of the dark," no prostitute. Baron Matsubara was confronted with a riddle. Was the yellow-haired girl running planlessly through the streets of this city of vice for amusement? She did not look exactly happy. Had she wished to put an end to her life because of some unknown sorrow? All these speculations shot through Akiro's head as he held the trembling Borghild firmly by the arm and fumbled for his spare pair of glasses, which had cunningly hidden themselves somewhere among the many pockets of his Western suit.

"What are you doing here at this hour, Mademoiselle?" he asked at last shyly, in faultless French. "Are you ill? Were you seeking a doctor?"

Borghild looked distractedly at the young Japanese and replied truthfully that she was doing nothing at all on Bubbling Well Road. Then she suddenly opened her eyes wide, startling Akiro, and demanded, "Who are you?"

Akiro swallowed the insult smilingly. Mademoiselle had seen him only an hour ago at the consul's! After her playing he had paid her a solemn compliment, a poetical Japanese compliment expressing respect and understanding. He had murmured that Mademoiselle's honorable playing had aroused in his unworthy spirit that unhoped-for happiness which Japanese felt when they snatched from the foam of the waves a carnation-conch—a *nadeshiko-gai*. The carnation-conch was a great rarity, the dream of every seeker of seashells. His speech had been fairly long, but gratitude for such music should not be expressed curtly. To do so would have been dreadful discourtesy.

It had afforded Akiro great pleasure that the violinist had listened to his tribute in numbed admiration. In reality Borghild had not been listening at all, but only waiting for Consul Wergeland to pull himself together and make her some acknowledgment. But he had not answered her gaze. And that disappointment had thrown her off balance. She had gone to Yvonne's bedroom because she had sud-

denly realized that Consul Wergeland did not wish any more intimate relation with her. In the bedroom a bracelet, one of Yvonne's
professional jewels, had been lying on the dressing table, and Astrid's
Amah Yumei had vanished silently in her felt slippers. But Amah
Number Two, who was excessively devoted to Yvonne, had taken
the precaution to spy on the stranger through a crack in the curtain,
and had instantly gone for Consul Wergeland when Borghild hastily
tucked the bracelet into her brocade bag and then stood staring
numbly into the mirror instead of running away as any sensible Chinese thief would have done. The amah had wisely informed the
consul instead of subjecting Madame, with her weak heart, to excitement. But Yvonne's eagle eye had observed her amah, and she had
gone to the bedroom after her. And now Borghild had attempted to
throw herself in front of a car because she could not bear having
been so shamed before Consul Wergeland. To be sure, her brother
had told him about her unfortunate tendency, and also that she was
in the habit of secretly returning the stolen ornaments after a short
time. But she was mortally ashamed, even though he had been
forewarned.

Young Baron Matsubara, whose hungry and sensitive stomach was
contracting more and more painfully with each passing minute,
asked Borghild whether he should take her back to her hotel. He
had to repeat his question, for the foreign girl only opened her eyes
wide again, and began to cry. What extraordinary bad manners! So
abashed was Akiro for his suddenly acquired companion (who was
also twenty years old, but an infant in experience and breeding in
comparison to him) that he hastily told the driver to take them to
the White Chrysanthemum Restaurant on Kiangse Road. Subconsciously he hoped that the quiet and purity of a Japanese dining
place would help this foreigner who had so utterly lost self-control.
With what decorum Japanese suicides proceeded! Certainly the
public was rigorously excluded from the solemn performance.

At all costs Baron Akiro wanted to spare himself and the foreigner
any further lingering in the street. An ever larger throng of children
and beggars had formed around them, all demanding tea-money and
appreciation for their watching and, so to speak, collaborating in the
drama. It was astonishing how many children and adolescents
drifted about the streets of Shanghai at night. It was obvious that

Shanghai could not govern itself properly. It was also obvious that the foreign woman could not be left to her own devices in her present state. Akiro was far from enraptured that the gods had chosen him to guard the footsteps of this undisciplined young person, whose honorable violin had fortunately remained in the Cathay Hotel. Baron Matsubara would have mourned over a smashed violin as he did over the fish which he found so toothsome but which he nevertheless sincerely pitied for having to end their lives in a lacquer bowl. Life was complicated for a sensitive Japanese who, in addition to his responsibilities toward the emperor, his family, his honored teachers, his chosen profession, his noble ancestors, and his own honor, would also have liked to enjoy a little fun and aesthetic pleasure. Young Baron Matsubara had by no means lied when he expressed enthusiasm for the arts of the Occident. But in Japan one regulated pleasure and enthusiasm quite as carefully and strictly as one did the great burden of duties and the mourning ceremonies for people, fish, and violins.

The White Chrysanthemum, where curious foreigners and homesick Japanese found well-prepared food, attentive service, and the bliss of quiet and cleanliness, was outwardly an inconspicuous place. But after you removed your shoes in the vestibule and entered the private room Akiro had reserved for himself, which was separated from the restaurant proper by sliding doors, you found yourself transported to a segment of Japan. There was also a dining room for Western patrons, furnished ostentatiously and in dubious taste. There it was possible to obtain, along with Japanese specialties, dishes that the Japanese cook considered to be European.

Baron Akiro Matsubara, who had lifted his incognito for the first time tonight, was shown to the best private room in the house. Borghild went along, quite stunned; she was no longer weeping but was again utterly absent. She had wanted to protest when she was asked to remove her shoes, since she had a hole in her left stocking. But after all, a hole in the stocking suited a tramp, which was what Madame Wergeland had called her. As a child Borghild had traveled from city to city with her mother and her mother's admirable maid, for her mother was a concert pianist with engagements all over Europe. Her parents were separated; her father had wanted a wife

in the house and warm food on the table. He had kept their son and
left the small daughter to Sigrid, who had little time and less patience for Borghild. At night, playing in hotel rooms, Borghild had
often decked herself out in Mama's jewelry, which brought the
brightness of stars into the dreariness of strange rooms. When Sigrid
Lillesand's career ended—an automobile accident had left her with
a paralyzed hand—she had crept back to Oslo with her twelve-year-
old daughter, to a life without triumphs, without music, and without
the starry glitter of the jewels which had been such solace to Borghild. Mama had sold the jewels in order to pay doctors' bills. From
then on Borghild had had only her violin and the thirst for the lost
sparkle which made throat, arms, and fingers come to life. It was
cold and gloomy in the Oslo apartment. Borghild sat at table between stony parents. Councilor Lillesand had no talent for forgiveness, for all that he wished not to bear a grudge toward his wife for
her "willful abandonment," as the courts had called it. Sigrid had
taken all the blame upon herself, which was only just. Borghild had
been too small to wonder about the "uncles" who gave her sweets
and who spoke a different language in every city. Mama was unfortunately a fine artist and a tramp by nature. But she had had an
admirable maid who darned the holes in her stockings.

Akiro Matsubara endeavored to ignore Borghild's torn stocking
and to present an imperturbable demeanor before the waitress while
he savored bouillon with sea cucumbers, raw fish, and tempura
picked out of the lacquered bowls with his chopsticks. In the alcove
hung a colored print showing a scene on the revolving stage of the
kabuki players. Under the stage several men were turning a large
crank, and the *kabuki* players in their splendid garments acted on
the stage above until they had to give way to other actors and other
destinies. No doubt about it, the seventeenth-century Japanese
drama had made use of the revolving stage long before Europe. Perhaps that was why Japanese players in life also turned more agilely,
noiselessly, and thoroughly at each new turn of the drama.

A bit of sea cucumber had stuck in Borghild's throat, and she had
been forced to remove it with her fingers, but in contrast to most
foreigners she ate the artfully prepared foods with curiosity and appetite and handled her ivory chopsticks with unusual skill.

"Have you often eaten Japanese fashion, Mademoiselle?" he asked at last. "You are remarkably skillful with chopsticks, if I may be permitted this remark with no offense."

"I watched the way you did it," Borghild replied with childish simplicity. "It all tastes wonderful. You are very kind to me, Monsieur."

Young Baron Matsubara swallowed the wrong way out of sheer happiness. This foreigner had a hole in her stocking and was fearfully ugly, but she had praised Akiro and Japanese cuisine in all sincerity. In his heart the hatred for Westerners collapsed as suddenly as it had arisen. (Only a single honorable flame of dislike for Americans remained; sometime or other a noble Japanese would have to avenge that insult. He must not allow himself to forget it, because it had been directed against Nippon.) Nevertheless, not for nothing had he admired Shakespeare while still in Tokyo, worshiped Beethoven, and learned to appreciate the paintings of the French impressionists. The West still sometimes conferred an unexpected joy upon the sons of the sun goddess, a pleasure as great, radiant, and rare as *nadeshiko-gai,* the carnation-conch which had to be snatched so dangerously from the waves. For intercourse with foreigners remained a risky matter. This very year Tokyo had passed the law for the suppression of "dangerous thoughts." The chance of harboring dangerous thoughts naturally increased a thousandfold when one associated with Westerners. Akiro was fully aware of that; but by her praise Borghild had created for him a blossoming landscape of the soul.

"The meal is worthless, but the insignificant cook endeavored to serve you, Mademoiselle," he replied politely, quivering with pride.

Late that night, long after Borghild in the Cathay Hotel had sunk into deep, restful sleep, aided by hot rice wine, Akiro sat in his hotel, reading the letter from his honorable uncle at the Ministry of Education in Tokyo. Uncle wrote that Akiro's father, Baron Jiro, had hurt his hand and was therefore prevented from writing. It was his duty, therefore, to transmit an important communication to his nephew. Akiro was to go to Korea first, postponing his trip to Paris. There would be time for him to become acquainted with Europe by and by. A Japanese who had dedicated body and soul to the Tenno must first become thoroughly acquainted with Asia.

Something incomprehensible and utterly scandalous had happened in Korea. A high Japanese official, closely related to Akiro's mother, had been assassinated while attending a Friendship Meeting with Koreans, which he himself had arranged. This was all the more incomprehensible, Honorable Uncle wrote, since Nippon had annexed wretched Chosen for its own good as long ago as 1910, and ever since had been civilizing the country. No effort had been spared in the course of these fifteen years to win at least the propertied and conservative Koreans over to support of the Japanese regime. Nothing much, after all, could be expected from the rice-farmers. When underground resistance among the educated classes began growing, vigorous methods to combat it had been adopted. General Sanuki, Akiro's mother's cousin, had for the past three years been arranging many successful Friendship Meetings between Koreans and their paternal protectors from Nippon. And the ingrates had now treacherously murdered him. To think of all the Japanese had done for Chosen! Precisely what they intended to do everywhere as soon as they occupied certain other countries for the good of those same countries. To be sure, Nippon needed Formosa's salt, rice, and opium, and also needed Korea as a base for further expansion and domination in Asia; but look at what had happened to these areas under Japanese rule. Railroad lines, ports, highways, technical and military installations had sprung up. Industrial expansion and a higher standard of living were gifts which the ungrateful people of Chosen obviously did not sufficiently appreciate.

Akiro put down the long sheets of rice paper and closed his eyes. Everywhere Nippon was encountering resistance from the little Asian brethren. And yet it was so benevolently showing the less capable, less industrious, and less ambitious peoples the Way of the Gods, exercising sternness only where absolutely necessary. Akiro suddenly felt very tired; he had no desire to go to Korea and ferret out Nippon's enemies there. But he must become acquainted with "the world"; that was his duty.

Once more he took up the rice-paper sheets and read the rest of the honorable missive. Uncle had conferred with Akiro's honored father on his son's further activities in Shanghai, and that High Person did not wish his son to establish any connection with Mr. Hsin in regard to Sino-Japanese factories. It was at least seven years too early for any such measures. Moreover, the High Person asked quite brusquely whether his son had become megalomaniac. A tiny insect like Akiro did not make proposals to a powerful Chinese. Had he not yet understood that he must gather experience while remaining as invisible as the *minomushi*-insect with its curious hood that hid it from the sight of even its own kind. Staying unseen was the most important art a future member of the Kempetai, the Japanese military secret police, had to practice. Worthless young son must promptly assume a better camouflage. Moreover, the High Person desired that Akiro in Korea and later in Paris and London keep strictly away from "dangerous thoughts" and direct his interests less to the art and literature of the West and more to military science. He must never forget that the Kempetai, which in the next twenty to thirty years would be confronted with vital tasks in a Japanese-directed Southeast Asia, was a branch of the military, not a branch of a blossoming cherry tree or any other lyrical object. The time would come when Akiro would—like all the best among his fellow countrymen—be personally responsible with his *samurai* blood for the safety of Nippon. He must therefore realize early during his apprentice years that Nippon was surrounded by all the world's spies, and that no Chinese and no man of the West could be trusted across the street—certainly not when they made flowery speeches, which were only intended to cover up their sinister intentions. Above all the High Person wished that Akiro, during the next five years of his apprenticeship, should have dealings with foreign women only for purposes of information and not with any amorous activities in view. The yellow-haired, long-nosed ladies of the Far West were all active in the secret services of their countries and aimed only to batten on the blood of the sons of Nippon and lead them astray from the kind of thinking approved by the state.

Akiro did not read the letter to the very end; he skipped the many formal, circumstantial greetings. He could hear Borghild's voice and see the honest expression in her eyes. And yet what she had said which had pleased him so much—these had been precisely flowery speeches. Akiro, as Greatly Honored Uncle had rightly judged, was a stupid little insect with a stupid little insect mind. With a sigh, young Baron Matsubara stretched out on his sleeping mat.

Ten days later Akiro paid a call on Consul and Madame Wergeland to thank them for the party. Following the custom of his country, he brought them a gift which was gracefully and carefully wrapped in flowered silk. In Japan pearls were not packed in rice straw. Baron Matsubara wished to present Madame with a precious kimono such as high-born Japanese ladies wore for the *O Cha-no-yu,* the Sublime Tea Ceremony. Actually the gift was intended to give pleasure to the consul. Akiro thought the consul wonderfully friendly and sincere, whatever his honored uncle in the Ministry of Education might say. Consul Wergeland and Akiro had met by chance the week before on Bubbling Well Road, and had harmoniously and with great pleasure partaken of sukiyaki together in the White Chrysanthemum. Akiro had prepared this deliciously fragrant dish with his own hands, over a small brazier of charcoal, for this alien and yet kindred foreigner friend. They had drunk a good deal of saké; and the consul had settled down on his mat with almost as much ease and grace as a Japanese. Afterward, he had taken the young Japanese home with him. In the tea room they had chatted quietly and delightfully about Japanese woodcuts and the art of *haikku* poetry. Consul Wergeland's wife could don her kimono when she came to the "Japanese room," Akiro thought, for he was already aware of the fact that foreigners spent a certain portion of their time with their wives, and that a foreigner's wife did not drink her tea *after* her husband but with him. These ladies seemed to have no particular respect for their masters.

Two days after the strange supper with Borghild, Akiro had also gone to the Cathay Hotel to leave a bolt of *habutai,* a white, taffeta-like silk, there for the young violinist. But the yellow-haired girl had departed, leaving no address. When Akiro asked whether Mademoiselle would be returning to Shanghai, the clerk shrugged impatiently. Akiro had left with the silk, feeling a stab of disappointment. Borghild had promised to send word to the Japanese consulate when she would have another tempura dinner with him. Akiro had looked forward to this occasion. And now she had left without a line. When she smiled, she had really not been ugly. Akiro would have taken pleasure in seeing her dressed in the white Japanese silk; he had been more horrified by Borghild's cheap red dress than Madame Wergeland—less on account of the color than because of the quality of the silk. The foreign violinist had no sense of patriotism if she showed herself in such materials abroad. It did not occur to the young Japanese that such considerations never entered the minds of most Europeans.

When Akiro arrived at the Wergelands', the villa looked utterly lifeless. There were no lights anywhere, although it was already twilight. Sublime Virtue, the Number One Boy, laid Akiro's gift carelessly on a table in the hall and mumbled that no one could be received. For one heartrending moment Akiro suspected that the consul was not receiving *him*. He stood shyly in the big vestibule, and the boy did not ask him to sit down. Sublime Virtue would not put himself out for one of the island dwarfs. Finally Akiro asked the obvious question, which was the last to occur to his complicated mind. He asked whether he could wait, since he wished to deliver the gift to Madame personally. "No good," Sublime Virtue replied. "Waiting velly bad. Madame in hospital. Heart velly bad—bump, bump, thump. Master with Madame. Velly bad."

Akiro asked the boy to take the kimono to the hospital, since he himself was leaving for Soochow shortly. He would not be back in Shanghai for quite a while. "Velly good," Sublime Virtue said; it remained obscure whether he meant that he would obey the order, or that he regarded Akiro's absence from Shanghai, or the pagodas of Soochow, as very good. He accepted Akiro's tea-money with a medium-low bow. Finally Akiro pulled himself together and started to leave, after impressing on the boy his addresses in Soochow and in Shanghai. After the shock of hearing of Madame's illness, he found it difficult to plunge into action again. How very, very unfortunate this was—and that it should happen only a few days before the foreigners' festival of lights and exchanging presents.

Akiro was looking forward to Soochow after commercial Shanghai. In Soochow there prevailed that Chinese spirit of wisdom and temperance, of resignation and nirvana, which had so tremendously influenced Nippon in past centuries. In Soochow, Buddhism was still a living force.

He felt abandoned and forlorn when he at last left Consul Wergeland's villa behind him. His second uncle, the Japanese consulgeneral in Shanghai, had more important things to do than to waste time on a stupid young nephew. Akiro was living at his home now and found him rather terrifying in his alternations of melancholy gravity and wild gaiety. In the gaiety phase his honorable eyes sparkled like the eyes of actors behind the slits of the No masks. The consul-general was in his mid-forties and hostile to foreigners. At home in Shanghai he wore only the kimono, unless he happened to be receiving a Western guest in the "foreigners' room," which was furnished in Victorian style. The parlor could not be surpassed for superfluity of frightful bric-a-brac. Only an enemy of the West could have accumulated so many horrors. Yet the consul-general seriously believed that the foreigners admired "their" room. After receiving a longnose in the overstuffed plush cave, Akiro's honored uncle would every time be seized by such savage amusement that he could tame it only by a few calligraphic exercises in his own choicely decorated rooms.

Young Baron Matsubara stood forlornly at the intersection of Avenue Foch and a side street where there was a consoling flower-shop window. He had driven here in order to have a flower arrangement sent to Madame Wergeland's hospital room. Naturally the boy, like all Chinese, must have exaggerated enormously; an illness had to be dangerous, in the minds of the Chinese, or it would not be worth mentioning. These Chinese! Akiro thought. But the flowers for Madame now gave him a pleasant subject for reflection. They must rise out of a bed of moss in a shallow rectangular bowl—silent, poetical "friends in suffering." Only lilies, of course; they were the sign of respect. The lotus was for meditation, which Madame did not understand anyway; and imperial chrysanthemums would have been an unforgivable *faux pas*. They were flowers which encouraged the sons of Nippon to struggle. As soon as Madame's health improved, young Baron Matsubara would invite the consul to Soochow for a week end; the consul was his best friend, and friends made life abroad bearable. Akiro could swallow Borghild's forgetfulness, since he secretly had a friend in Consul Wergeland.

His enthusiasm for the civil but indifferent Norwegian sprang from fanaticism, loyalty, and bottomless private loneliness. Young Asians, inexperienced in the ways and emotions of the West, so frequently glorified their few foreign "friends." There was a tragic naïveté about it; they would have been ready to lay down their lives for these friends, and in any case gave them far too expensive gifts, which produced a shaking of the head and embarrassed thanks. The kimono from Imperial Kyoto, for example, was an object so valuable that Yvonne and the consul would never have dreamed of expecting it. Yvonne had scarcely exchanged three words with the young baron from Tokyo. In a moment of nervousness the consul had wished he would go to the devil for having upset the arrangements at his dinner; later he had treated him with natural friendliness at a chance meeting. In so doing, he had been acting only out of the smooth and well-meaning courtesy of the experienced Western diplomat who knew the customs and feelings of Asians. But he had not given Akiro another thought, for he had to treat countless persons of the most varied races and nations with naturalness and friendliness—the whole art lay in the naturalness of his conduct. Had he received it, the precious kimono for Yvonne would only have embarrassed the consul.

But Knut Wergeland never set eyes on the kimono from Imperial Kyoto. Sublime Virtue spirited it away with intent to sell it. When the consul returned home an hour after Akiro's visit, Sublime Virtue sent the cook to make an apology for him: Great-Grand-Aunt Lung was mortally ill and was mustering her relations around her bed in a village on the Yangtze River. Sublime Virtue would never have ventured such a dodge under normal circumstances, but Master was constantly busy nowadays. He had to prepare for the auction, which was to take place as soon as Madame recovered. The boy would have to look for a new job in any case, since the master was going to Bangkok. And so he hid out with the precious kimono in the Chinese City. After Master's departure he would cautiously offer it, through an uncle who knew the great-uncle of an art dealer, to the firm of Norinaga on Kiangse Road. That was all very simple and happened frequently in Shanghai.

Consul Wergeland paid no attention to the story the cook told him about Sublime Virtue's absence. He had other worries than his boy's great-grand-aunt. Yvonne was seriously ill. Her difficulty with breathing had grown worse. She had certainly smoked too much, wrought herself up over imaginary wrongs, and received and paid far too many visits. Everything would improve as soon as they were in Trondheim. Before they left, however, he wanted to confess something to her that weighed heavily on his conscience and that only his sister Helene knew about. But now he could not talk with Yvonne about it. The doctor had strictly forbidden all agitation.

In Soochow young Baron Matsubara received no letter of thanks from the consul for the kimono. On his return to Shanghai he found at the consulate only a card, dated the day of his call, in which the consul thanked him for himself and in Madame's name for the flowers. Consul Wergeland had already left Shanghai.

Akiro decided that his gift of friendship had been ignored or despised. The recipient had not thought it worth a word of thanks. Never in his life had young Baron Matsubara been so deeply hurt. Mr. Bailey was only a chance acquaintance of an hour; there was no danger that Akiro would ever encounter him again, since he would consistently avoid him with that consistency that only Asians understand. Borghild had been the lightest of disappointments; as a woman, she was too far beneath a man's notice to offend him seriously. But the consul was not only a man of the world; he was also Akiro's only European friend. And now he had done something unforgivable. By not expressing his thanks in all due form for something he had never received, he awoke in Akiro's proud and sensitive heart that dangerous and inextinguishable mistrust which has constantly prevented any genuine understanding between West and East in our century.

Thus Consul Wergeland, in whom the future officer of the Japanese Secret Service had fervently believed in spite of all warnings from Tokyo, became the last European whom Akiro trusted—because of a rascally boy whose theft was never exposed.

While Consul Wergeland was still planning where he would take his wife for her convalescence, and wondering when he would be able to reveal his secret to her, Yvonne lay on her deathbed.

3: The Jade Bell

On January 6, the Feast of Epiphany, a sharp wind sighed through Shanghai. A great many things happened in this restless city. Young Baron Matsubara set off for Soochow. Mr. Bailey submitted to a lecture by his wife on his intake of alcohol. The Chinese Crane, in his old-fashioned house back of Bubbling Well Road, drifted among his bird-cages and pensively examined their small jade ornaments, as well as the curtains which assured the birds a degree of private life. All the while he thought about his vanished daughter. It was ridiculous for him to waste valuable thoughts on a worthless female person, but so he did. His daughter had trilled more beautifully in her high, clear voice than his best Mongolian songbird, whom he was having instructed by a singing master.

Then Mr. Hsin drove in his Buick to the Willow Tree Teahouse in the Chinese City. His youngest concubine sat in the front with the chauffeur, a bird-cage on her knees. This particular bird was very stupid about singing. Mr. Hsin, who had grown so rich because he avoided unnecessary expenditures, had decided to save on expensive singing lessons for this stupid bird. He ordered his concubine to secure a free place for the bird in its carved cage in the bird pavilion of the famous old teahouse, beside a "lark of the hundred spirits." There the fool could learn to sing free of charge. Next week Mr. Hsin intended to send it as a small convalescent present to Madame Wergeland, who was still in the hospital.

Much and little happened on this day. Toward evening Father Pierre de Lavalette of the Society of Jesus in Shanghai stood at the deathbed of Yvonne Wergeland and strengthened her in her last hour with the Sacrament of the Church. In the corridor of the hospital stood Consul Wergeland, clutching Astrid's cold little hand. Yumei and Amah Number Two crouched in the corridor, weeping with discreet noiselessness. Both amahs had twice a week brought incense and offerings to a temple in the Chinese City, putting the extra expenditures down to "household purchases." They had done their best and did not understand why Madame nevertheless had to commence her journey into the spirit world.

In the sickroom the only light was shed by the candle burning on the night table with its French lace doily. With failing breath Yvonne had confessed her sins and received Extreme Unction from the hand of her spiritual adviser and friend. In the light of the candle Consul Wergeland, Astrid, the two French nuns, and the amahs were now kneeling around her bed while the priest murmured the prayers for the dying. Yvonne was already washed clean of earthly frailty and rested in the mystery of divine forgiveness. And while Père de Lavalette and the two nuns said an intercessory prayer, as pious souls the world over do when a friend is dying, and while Consul Wergeland was struggling to retain his composure and Astrid covered her cold little face with her cold hands as she knelt at *Maman's* bed, the peace of death spread over the features of that restless soul.

Father de Lavalette gently closed Yvonne's eyes and commended to the Lord the soul of His servant Yvonne Thérèse, that she, dead to the world, might live in Him. Then he turned his attention to the widower and the trembling child; at the moment of death the living were the ones who always needed his help.

So Yvonne Thérèse Wergeland died on the Feast of Epiphany, a good and peaceful death after a life full of effort in the wrong departments. She left in her husband a feeling of indescribable emptiness and futile regret, such as all husbands feel who have withheld from their wives the miracle of intimacy. To her daughter Astrid, Yvonne Wergeland left the dark glow of her jealousy and her rubies, her faultless taste, and the collected writings of St. Theresa of Avila.

When Consul Wergeland returned to his solitary home, life seemed to him for a moment to stand utterly still. He paced back and forth in Yvonne's bedroom. It was as though he were looking for his wife in this room for the first time in many years—a vain search. A grief he had never before experienced assailed him as he sat forlornly on Yvonne's bed and mechanically smoothed out her pillow. A short while before, he had thrown himself down on her bed—and Yvonne hated this slovenly habit. Heavily he stood up and smoothed out the wrinkles he had made in the damask bedcover. This was the most loving and the most senseless act in all his career as a husband.

In this empty house—and in the empty house in Bangkok into which he would move in a few months' time—no one would ever again ask Knut Wergeland where he had been, what he was doing, and when he was going to change his clothes.

The consul sat down on a low French hassock and cupped his hands over his burning eyes. It was too late for questions and answers. A broken vase might be skillfully mended, but a lonely man remained a lonely man. He had only duties now. He must live his professional life and rear his daughter without a mother's aid. At this thought Knut Wergeland realized that he had never been able to tell Yvonne his secret.

A week after the funeral the consul drove into the Chinese City. There, in one of the gloomy, narrow stone houses, lived the honorable pawnbroker and art dealer Mr. Pao. He did not read news of the foreign devils' family affairs, and had therefore sent his boy Hei Lien —Black Face—even after Yvonne's death to report that he had a rare jade ornament which would be just the thing for Madame. Since he had been supplying the consul with art objects for many years, and respected the consul as a connoisseur, it would have meant a great loss of face for Mr. Pao if the consul had ignored the invitation.

Mr. Pao's pawnshop was situated in the heart of the old Chinese City, which concealed within its narrow streets and gloomy houses so many memories, treasures, indefinable smells, and so much dirt. Here was the true center of the art trade, not in the glamorous, brightly lit district of Nantao to which hotel porters directed sentimental foreigners who sought "the true China" in Westernized Shanghai with its banks and splendid shops. In Mr. Pao's dim rooms you could find, alongside all kinds of trash and imitations, the genuine article: old porcelain, hand-embroidered tapestries, bronzes and jade that withstood all files—hard, "cloudless" jade, as precious as the best pieces to be found on the jade street in Canton.

Mr. Pao served the consul green tea in ethereally thin cups, and in the course of its drinking learned of the foreign devil's great loss. He ceremoniously expressed his condolences, interjecting—by way of consolation—that a wife mourned for her husband three years, a husband for his wife only one hundred days. Then he sent Hei Lien to the front room to wait on customers, and turned to business. From a carved chest he took an object wrapped in brocade. "This is *chen-yu*"—genuine jade—he prefaced, "and by no means *Ts'ui-yu*" —the cheaper jadite, such as his son-in-law in Nantao sold.

"A man brings a son-in-law into the house to have him become a common peddler." Mr. Pao chuckled. Then he became serious. He let the wrappings slip aside, and murmured, "A jade bell! *Chen-yu!* It will bring a hundred advantages to the buyer, sir."

The consul stared speechlessly at the two translucent jade disks, which rang finely at every movement of the hand. This was an antique Cantonese ornament, and he knew it better than he did Yvonne's rubies and his own soul. He forgot his manners and proper ceremonial, snatched the jade bell from the dealer's hands, and held the thin, magically shimmering disks against the light so that he could decipher the engraved inscription. It read: *Ch'ing-chao* (Limpid Light), *Li Hsia* (beginning of summer), *Shanghai.* The inscription meant that a girl by the name of Limpid Light had been born in Shanghai at the beginning of summer—around the sixth of May.

"Where did you obtain this gem?" he asked hoarsely.

"A Russian woman brought it to sell. She came on commission for a Chinese woman. A very rare piece of jade, sir. Carved by a master."

"I know."

The old Chinese looked at the tall foreign devil in astonishment. What did he know? The foreigners' thoughts were like uncombed hemp. And the art of the jade-carver was, to most of them, a sealed book. The foreigners had crude hands. They felled a tree to catch a blackbird.

At this moment the assistant, Black Face, thrust his head through the curtain and reported the visit of Mr. Hsin of Bubbling Well Road. He wanted to look at jade. Black Face, whom his parents had given this repugnant name in order not to arouse the envy of the gods over such a splendid specimen of boy, whispered the name of the caller reverently. Mr. Hsin was a great man. To offer him genuine jade was not throwing good wares at a rat.

Consul Wergeland made a decision. His glacier-blue eyes, which were surrounded by dark rings of exhaustion, gazed keenly at the dealer. He offered a price. Mr. Pao demanded twice the sum, since Mr. Hsin was waiting in the adjoining room. His presence was a form of credit on which it was unnecessary to pay interest. Mr. Pao knew men, and he could see by the foreign devil's quivering nostrils that he meant to buy the jade bell at any price. But Mr. Pao was a Chinese gentleman of the old school; when they had agreed on a compromise and the consul had written out an enormous check, Mr. Pao took a delicate Chinese bronze mirror from an ebony chest. It was circular and bore on the center of the back a pierced stud for the silken string. The mirror too bore an inscription: *Always preserve your high rank!* Around the raised part in the center of this antique work of art writhed animals and Taoist divinities. To those who knew the worth of such things, it was a tiny treasure; work in such perfection was no longer conceived in the twentieth century, let alone fabricated.

"A wretched parting gift, sir!" Mr. Pao whispered in his hoarse opium voice. The consul thanked him in good Chinese, with great solemnity. Emotional effusions were not in order. Mr. Pao smiled because he knew that beautiful objects and good human beings were rare articles in this world.

On his way out Knut Wergeland greeted the old Crane, who was not yet so old, but who looked as if his life were behind him. The consul's measured bow was answered with equal measuredness. If Mr. Hsin had seen the jade bell the consul had in his coat pocket, he would have taken a collector's interest in it and glanced at the inscription. A jade bell was a talisman and, following Chinese custom, bore an inscription on the second disk. This one read: *Haste is error.*

Mr. Hsin had had this inscription engraved upon the jade bell when his only daughter, Limpid Light, was born. The ancient motto, which for thousands of years had served as a warning and guide to the Chinese, had proved its truth once more. Ch'ing-chao had left her father's house in haste because she did not wish to marry the man destined for her. And this haste had proved to be an error for both father and daughter.

But Consul Wergeland entered his automobile silently, the jade bell in his pocket. Thus Mr. Hsin did not find out that the foreigner knew his daughter, though not under the name of Limpid Light, but as Lily Lee, singsong girl in Shanghai. Hsin Ch'ing-chao had ceased to exist after she left the house of her father back of Bubbling Well Road in mistaken haste, in the bitter month, toward the end of the moon-year. Consul Wergeland had met her under the name of Lily Lee in a night-club in the French Concession when Yvonne had gone to Saigon for six months. Mr. Hsin did not visit night-clubs frequented by foreigners, where White Russians sat at the cashiers' desks.

So it happened that two men who knew the same girl and the same piece of jewelry came within a hair's breadth of a conversation which would have clarified and changed many things. But life consists of missed chances. The consul was too reserved to show his Chinese friend the jade bell, and Mr. Hsin was too Chinese to conduct a private conversation in the presence of a dealer. Mr. Hsin thought he would have time enough to chat with the consul over mulled wine. But in this he was mistaken. Two weeks after the silent encounter with Mr. Hsin, Consul Wergeland left Shanghai.

For the present, however, he drove, with the jade bell in his coat pocket, to a shabby boarding house back of Avenue Joffre.

The house in which the singsong girl Lily Lee occupied a room gave the impression of being tired and hungry for money. It looked as if the tenants were always in arrears with the rent, which was in fact the case. On the ground floor two White Russian women ran a beauty shop which had scarcely its like for shabbiness and disorder. Next to this a French milliner exhibited hats which had been fashionable in Paris shortly after 1918. On the second floor lived a Franco-Chinese bookkeeper who spent his nights at the gaming table in the Chat Noir and his days wondering whom else in Shanghai he could borrow money from. In the room opposite lived the singing girl Lily Lee with her small daughter Mailin. Lily Lee had been in great demand for a few years, but now there were younger stars in the Shanghai amusement world. Shanghai consumed youth and beauty like a tiger. Lily Lee was the only person in this house who, in spite of everything, had been able to pay her rent. She frequently gambled, out of boredom or despair, with Monsieur Latour in the Chat Noir next door, and paid her debts whenever she made a haul. That happened now and then, for she played cautiously; she had learned seven years ago that haste is the mother of error, and had suffered the consequences. Since then Lily Lee had also learned that haste is the grandmother of gambling debts. For years she had hidden in Chapei from her father, and had been living for only a year in this boarding house, whose owner never showed his face; his "checker" was sent to collect the back rent. In the adjoining room lived Vera Leskaya of the beauty shop below, whose face was of so sinister a cast as to frighten her clients.

It was this sinister young lady who received Consul Wergeland as he climbed the worn stairs of the boarding house. He was determined to find out why Lily had parted with her talisman.

"Where is Mademoiselle Lee?" he asked the Russian woman in French. "I should like to see her."

They stood in the dim corridor; a naked bulb, feeble from age, let light trickle down upon the visitor and the Russian, who was wrapped in an old military cloak. In this house no shades were bought for electric lights; the light was not in need of any filtering.

"Lily Lee is not here," Vera Leskaya said.

"Is she at the pharmacy? That Chinese 'nightingale lotion' is worthless. I have brought her better medicine." Evidently the consul knew the Russian woman and the house and was aware of Mademoiselle Lee's trouble with her hoarseness.

Vera Leskaya looked nervously around the corridor; footsteps were approaching from below. She hastily opened a door. "Please wait in my room, Monsieur," she murmured hurriedly. "I—I must speak to someone downstairs—a pupil whom I instruct in French conversation. Please wait! I—I have something important to tell you."

She gave the consul a feline look, with the hint of a smile, and pattered downstairs in her embroidered Chinese slippers. She was still quite young, but faintly depraved and with the bloom of youth already faded.

The visitor who was waiting for Vera Leskaya looked impatiently up at her. His deep-set Chinese eyes flamed. He had with him neither text nor notebook. At her beckoning he followed her into a small room separated by a partition from the beauty shop and from the office of Madame Ninette, the owner of the shop. This lady, a corpulent middle-aged person, was upstairs drinking vodka with another tenant, a former Russian general. Vera Leskaya was alone with her "pupil."

"He is no longer in Hongkew," she whispered.

"Did he leave anything behind?"

"Only his French exercise books—in my opinion."

"What do you mean by 'in your opinion'?" the Chinese asked; he worked for the newspaper *Shun Pao* and was obliged to report privately to Mr. Hsin on Japanese newly arrived in Shanghai. "Who is this young student? He was probably living under a false name in Hongkew. We are not satisfied with your services, Mademoiselle. We want to check the correspondence of Japanese living in Shanghai. We went to know all about the butterflies who flutter over here from Tokyo. What about it?"

Silently the Russian took several sheets of paper from the pocket of her military cloak. "You need not go through this performance, Mr. Ho," she said firmly. "You are satisfied and only want to force the price down. I have obtained what you wanted. The young man left this letter locked in his wardrobe when he drove to a flower shop in the Concession. I was in his hotel and spent silence-money. Here is the bill. The young Japanese is in reality—" She paused, lowered her eyes, and asked, "How much?"

The visitor named a sum that seemed to please her. She was also paid for the copy of the letter. The letter had been written by Akiro Matsubara's uncle in the Ministry of Education in Tokyo. The Chinese visitor skimmed through it.

"If Mr. Akiro intends to enter the Secret Service, he still has a great deal to learn," he remarked scornfully. "How can he let such letters simply lie around? Where, by the way, did you learn Japanese, Mademoiselle?"

"From my Japanese pupils in Shanghai," Vera Leskaya replied with half-closed eyes as she pocketed the check without a word of thanks.

"Would you like to work for—or, as the case may be, against—the Kuomintang people sometime?" the visitor asked. "We should like to know which ones among them are completely pro-Russian. Chinese and international financial circles in Shanghai have no use for Communists."

"But Chiang Kai-shek was trained in Moscow, after all," the White Russian demurred with an expression of innocence.

"That is just the reason." The visitor grinned. "Sooner or later he will have to have a reckoning with the Communist elements. Well, would you keep your ears open?"

"No."

"Why not? Our Russian liaison agent is sick. You could very well take his place. Big expense account. Night-clubs. All expenses paid. You have cosmetics right here in your beauty shop. What is your objection?"

"I don't like Chinese," Vera Leskaya replied impudently.

"Take care."

"Never fear, I can take care of myself."

"Does Madame Ninette know anything about your—sideline?"

"She hasn't the faintest idea. When shall I insert another ad for French lessons?"

"In a hundred years, Mademoiselle! You are dismissed from our information service."

Vera Leskaya turned very pale. Fear ran like ice water down her spine. These Chinese—these beasts! "Why?" she asked, stunned. "I've just delivered first-class work to you."

"The usefulness of an employee is measured by her humility," Mr. Ho replied and took his leave with a polite bow.

The Russian woman felt weak in her knees. It was not good to forget politeness even for a second in the Far East. Then she shrugged. After all, she could vary things by working against the Chinese and for the Japanese. There were innumerable possibilities in Shanghai. Everyone betrayed everyone else. And everyone turned in another direction in the course of time—as on a revolving stage. One of these days the Japanese might be masters of the scene in Shanghai and the surrounding territory. Vera Leskaya had nothing to lose. In this city there was always a job for a go-between.

As she climbed the stairs to Consul Wergeland, a cigarette between her thin lips, she considered when and how she could offer her services to the Japanese in such a manner that the men of the *Shun Pao* would not find out and secretly and politely twist her neck. Little spies died daily in Shanghai, but new little spies daily replaced them. One had to live. Shanghai gave away nothing to White

Russians. People without a country had to accept any kind of work in China.

In the meanwhile the consul had been pacing restlessly back and forth in the Russian woman's dim room. On the wall hung two photographs. One showed Vera Leskaya, who must now be about twenty-five, as a young girl, arrayed in probably her first evening dress. In the picture she looked like a special, luxurious edition of herself. Her hair, which now hung in limp and wayward locks—surely a depressing sight to the clients of her beauty parlor—was carefully curled and piled high. The evening dress exposed one shoulder, which gleamed out of the silk, round and young and innocent. In her eyes was an expression of anticipation and melancholic reverie; that was how well-bred young Russian girls had looked before the Revolution. The prominent Slavic cheekbones lent her face a piquant attractiveness. Vera Leskaya must have hung up this photograph of the springtime of her life out of typical Russian liking for self-torment. Alongside it was the portrait of a young Russian man with sleepy eyes, a round face, and a lazy, sensual mouth. It bore the inscription: *For Vera, in eternal love. Boris.* Boris was wearing a highly decorative uniform, something like those favored by the princes and generals who worked as doormen in the night-clubs of the Settlement and the French Concession. "Eternal love"—how easily those words glided from the lips and pens of people in prewar days! The corners of the consul's mouth drew down in disapproval. It never lasted. The love of flawed creatures remained flawed love. One ended by being sorry for the woman—as he had been for Yvonne and Lily Lee, the former Limpid Light. He was sorry for little Borghild too—but at least she had her violin. After every fall she renewed herself by the magic of music. Eternal love—a delightful and stupid illusion. The consul too had succumbed to that illusion at times. But he could not run off, like other men. He was bound to the women whom he had once thought, under the spell of that illusion, he loved eternally.

He had heard Lily Lee singing in a night-club that time Yvonne was away. (In those days she did sing as sweetly as the best of her stern father's songbirds.) She had attracted his attention because of her refined grace and her expensive brocade dresses. The girl was terribly young, but she must have rich friends to wear such clothes in a rather ordinary night-club. That was his first error. Lily Lee still wore the dresses she had owned at home. It was only a year since she had run away. She was full of *joie de vivre* but unspoiled; a Chinese girl of an old aristocratic family—cultivated, honorable, hard as jade and at the same time soft as silk.

When the consul pitied her in later years, that was again an error on his part. Lily Lee was much stronger than he himself, or Borghild, or even poor Yvonne with her arrogance and her consuming jealousy. Lily Lee knew what she wanted. By instinct, however, she also knew what men wanted of a Chinese singing girl—gentleness, style, poetry. Singsong girls were no prostitutes. They existed for the entertainment of men, but no patron had any right to them which they did not voluntarily grant him. Lily Lee fell in love with Knut Wergeland. She did not know that he was married. When he told her, it was too late; a child was already on the way. There were no scenes, no tears, no attempt to force the foreigner to break away from his wife and small daughter by blandishment or blackmail. When her hopes collapsed, Lily Lee ceased to be the gentle little songbird who recited carefully prepared poetic speeches. She suddenly became Hsin Ch'ing-chao again, Limpid Light of the Hsin family. Like her father, she began to calculate and to forge stubborn plans. The consul pledged himself to pay a monthly sum for the child—not too much and not too little—and to remember the son or daughter in his will. That meant that Knut Wergeland would some day have to explain to his wife how the child of a Chinese woman had found its way into his will. Yvonne's death had relieved this situation. He would no longer have to reveal his secret.

Lily Lee had furthermore set down in writing that the consul, in case she should prematurely die, or in case of some other unforeseen situation that rendered her incapable of caring for the child, would himself adopt the child. After bitter disputes the consul had also agreed to this astonishing demand. After all, the question would never actually come up. Chinese always wanted to provide for a thousand years in the future. Lily Lee had considered everything and knew, once again by instinct, how yielding men with guilty consciences were. Her father could not have arranged matters more forethoughtfully. The consul had learned at this time, to his amazement, that Lily Lee had no family left. Her kin were all dead, she maintained. That was strange, probably pure obstinacy. This was the consul's only correct assumption in his relationship to her. Lily Lee possessed the obstinacy of so many Chinese; she would not veer from a resolution once taken. As part of this obstinacy, she would never again allow the consul so much as to kiss her fingertips, and she never again accepted a gift or money from him for herself—only things for the child, for the son whom she would some day bring to its grandfather. When her condition forbade her singing, she earned money at the gaming table, gave younger Chinese larks lessons in singing and deportment, teaching them, in return for good Shanghai dollars, the conventional but poetic phrases and songs that had enchanted Knut Wergeland. Naturally the consul, like so many foreigners, might have somehow escaped all these obligations. He need not have gone to the lawyer with Lily. He could have given only a sham consent. But the consul also came from an honorable family. He was a respectable romantic. Moreover, his position was such that he could not afford public scandal. And so, before the birth of Lily Lee's son, he had arranged everything as decently as possible.

Then the child turned out to be a girl. Limpid Light buried her secret hope of one day propitiating her harsh father by presenting him with a grandson. A granddaughter is nothing but a disappointment to a Chinese. She called the little girl Mailin, "the Lovely Lily" —in other words, "Purity." And when the infant, delicate and enchanting to look at, lay healthy and contented at its young mother's breast, everything changed once more. The consul conceived a deep fondness for this child of love, this little creature of good Norwegian and Chinese stock, who looked quite like a small aristocratic Chinese woman, but had the long body and the thin, bold nose of the Wergelands. He felt much closer to Mailin than to Astrid; she was a tiny, precious songbird on a dead twig. When he sat in his Japanese tea room he thought of this darling child with tenderness and concern. He would have preferred to acknowledge Mailin legally as his daughter and take her into the house. Astrid was lonely; she would certainly be pleased by a playmate—so the consul assumed, since he knew nothing at all about his older daughter. But Lily Lee would never part with her little one. For all her practical sense, she was a true Chinese mother. And she raised her child like a true Chinese mother—decently and healthily in an impossible environment.

Mailin was now four years old. Around her neck there always hung the jade bell which Lily Lee, so she told the consul, had once received from an "admirer" in gratitude for her singing. The two thin jade disks on their silken string were a small legacy for the fatherless child.

Helene Wergeland had repeatedly urged her brother to make a clean breast of it to Yvonne. She did not like the idea that Knut too must be classed among the shirkers, and she expressed this view in no uncertain terms.

Vera Leskaya had entered the room noiselessly in her Chinese slippers. She was still feeling the shock of Mr. Ho's dismissal. Seeing her visitor absorbed in the photograph of Boris, she remarked, "My former fiancé. He worked for three years on the Chinese Eastern Railway."

"Is he dead?" the consul asked, only to say something.

"He is engaged to the daughter of the railway director. They offer him roast duck, innocence, and pure-silk coverlets. What can I offer him? Only eternal love! How abysmally stupid we women are. Footmats for men. Stupid, tearful footmats."

Vera Leskaya was not actually talking to the consul but to Boris, the shirker in the fancy uniform.

"Where is Mademoiselle Lee?" the consul asked impatiently.

"Gone! Address unknown, Monsieur."

"When did she leave?"

"Four days ago. Was she not right to? What good was it to stay here?"

The consul stood like a man who has just received a blow on the head and then been asked whether he did not deserve it. For years he had pondered how to take Mailin into his home without imperiling Yvonne's health and his career. He had been naïve enough to believe that one could flee the consequences of a thoughtless action without seriously injuring anyone. And now that the situation had changed fundamentally because of Yvonne's sudden death, Lily Lee had taken revenge upon him. So she had not forgiven him after all;

she had disappeared without a word. A Chinese farewell! She had
snatched his sweet four-year-old Mailin from him. Lily Lee knew
how to strike him to the heart, silently and secretly—following the
best Chinese prescriptions for vengeance.

"Would you like a glass of vodka, Monsieur?" Vera Leskaya asked,
closely scrutinizing the pale, tall man with the dark rings under his
piercing blue eyes. The consul pulled himself together. This was no
time to make mistakes. Naturally this Russian woman knew precisely
where Lily and Mailin were. He took the jade bell from his coat
pocket.

"Did you sell this to Mr. Pao?" he asked dryly. "Does Mademoiselle Lee know about it? Were you commissioned to do it?"

"Of course. The money has been deposited for the child at the
Hong Kong and Shanghai Bank—in the name of Mailin Lee. The
child will need something to live on. I cannot support her."

"Where is she?"

"Upstairs, with Madame Ninette and her friend. The general en-
joys playing with Mailin. Shall I fetch her?"

The consul was now completely bewildered. He understood only
that Mailin was here.

Vera Leskaya took from her desk two sealed letters and put on
her glasses in order to read the addresses. With the glasses she
looked like a respectable Russian schoolmistress who had just got
out of bed, her hair down, and was correcting pupils' notebooks in
slippers and bathrobe.

"This one is for you, Monsieur," she murmured and went off to
fetch Consul Wergeland's younger daughter.

In the letter Lily Lee informed the worthy father of her daughter
Mailin, in courteous phrases, that she had met in the Chat Noir a
wealthy businessman from Singapore whose benevolent approval
had been aroused by her insignificant person. Since she was at the
end of her strength, she had decided to place Mailin's education and
future in her father's hands, in accordance with the agreements made
before the child's birth. She herself, now that she was an old woman
of twenty-seven, preferred the life of a respected spouse. However,
she would forfeit all chance of marriage into an honorable Chinese
family if she attempted to take into the marriage an illegitimate
daughter by a foreigner. Mailin's honorable father would cer-

tainly understand that, since he had not wanted to introduce Mailin into his own honorable family, for all that she was of the best Chinese stock. But the situation had probably changed with the death of his chief wife. Otherwise Lily Lee would have had to abandon her own plans for an honored old age in distant Singapore. The consul and she herself—the letter concluded—had unfortunately never been of one mind and one body. Only when two partners were of one mind could they transform clay into gold.

A postscript informed Mailin's honorable father that the daughter, when she reached the age of fourteen, was to go to the Chinese lawyer and notary Chang. There she would be given a letter from her mother enlightening her as to her mother's family. Circumstances had compelled Mailin's unworthy mother to conceal her origins from Mailin's honored father. Since her miserable lung would probably not last until her daughter was grown up, she had chosen this way to inform her. It was possible that Mailin might later wish to live as a Chinese, and a Chinese without family was like a tree without roots, which any gust of wind could blow over. There followed the address of the notary in Shanghai's Chinese City.

The consul put down the letter. Within ten days, without his own intervention, the lives of all of them had changed. Life was merciless. Helene had rightly shaken her head at her brother's penchant for regarding life as a grand picnic. It was no picnic. An unfathomable providence directed every man's fate, for all that he might imagine he was meant for pleasure, amusement, comfortable distraction, or sheer joy. And no one loved anyone else adequately. Lily Lee had deserved more love and respect than Knut Wergeland had accorded her. But he had met her as a singsong girl and not grasped her innate dignity and soundness. He did not even have a picture of Mailin's mother, only the jade bell with the inscription: *Haste is error*.

This time Lily Lee had not acted in haste. She had carried out a carefully preconceived plan at precisely the right moment. The silent heroism of a Chinese mother would not allow her to ruin her daughter's chances in life. She herself, of course, did not marry and go to Singapore; only a European would believe that a respectable Chinese businessman would bring to his honorable mother a daughter-in-law who was a tubercular singing teacher from Shanghai. A week after the consul's departure Lily Lee returned to the cheap lodging house. There she died three years later from the disintegration of her "miserable lung," without tears and without regrets, in unrelieved solitude. With farsighted Chinese sense of family, she had smoothed the way for her daughter Mailin to return eventually to the home of her forefathers, and in the meanwhile she had assured her a full ricebowl.

Consul Wergeland sat in his car with his daughter Mailin, taking her home. Attired in wadded pantaloons and fur-lined jacket, Mailin slept in his arms. Beside her stood her little bird-cage with her pet, Gold Oriole, whom she loved dearly and tended daily. Around her neck hung the ancient ornament that the grandfather she did not know had given to her mother at birth. At every movement of the sleeping child the jade bell rang with a soft, ghostly purity. . . .

Astrid stood in her Chinese dressing gown at the bed of her new sister and regarded her unmovingly out of pale blue eyes that were a little too close together and betrayed a talent for jealousy. Mailin had now been in the house for three days. She never cried, and bowed solemnly in Chinese fashion when Elder Sister handed her a toy which she did not know how to use. Hitherto she had had only Gold Oriole and the old Russian general for playmates. She had been told that her mother was away and that for the time being she would live with tall old Father, Elder Sister, and Amah Yumei. Mailin had nodded gravely and again solemnly bowed when she received this information. Good manners and love for birds and family were innate in her. She smiled in innocent politeness at glowering Astrid.

For three days Astrid swallowed her tears, for Amah paid far too much attention to the new sister. Fear that Yumei would now love this suddenly arrived child more than herself was like a great lump in Astrid's throat, so that she could scarcely eat and swallow. When Astrid asked Yumei whether she loved her "most of all," her young nurse had replied that she must also love Younger Sister and the bird Gold Oriole now, since they all belonged to one family.

Astrid stared at the sleeping child. Papa certainly loved Mailin more than he did her. He had never taken her on his lap. In spite of her wadded Chinese dressing gown, Astrid shivered. She put her

long, thin hand into the bird-cage and took out Gold Oriole. As if
he guessed his fate, he fluttered in her cold hand precisely in the
tempo of her wounded little heart. Teeth chattering, she crept to
the window to open it and let the tiny singing enemy disappear so
that Amah would return to Astrid at least a part of the love which
now went to Gold Oriole. Would losing her bird at last make Mailin
cry? Papa had said that Astrid should imitate her little sister and
stop her eternal whimpering. The recommendation had sounded
much harsher than the consul had intended. He himself was not in
the best state of mind after the events of the past several weeks.
Astrid did not have the gift for winning love effortlessly; this made
it all the worse that she always wanted to be loved more than others.
Her persistent questions on this score even tried Yumei's almost lim-
itless patience. "Do you love me just as much, Yumei? More than
Younger Sister? More than anybody else in the world?" At last Yumei
had given her a very gentle slap on the mouth which yammered
so much silly talk. Then she had brought feed to Gold Oriole and
tenderly chattered with him, and had taken Mailin and danced
around his cage. Yumei herself was still almost a child, after all. The
lump in Astrid's throat had grown so large that it had forced her to
throw up and ruin Mailin's first Western dress. Yumei had scolded,
and Gold Oriole had sung mocking songs at Astrid. That was why
Gold Oriole must go out into the cold winter night now. He would
never again make fun of Astrid.

When at last she managed to get the window open and wanted
to let Gold Oriole fly away, he lay cold and immobile in her icy
hand. She had pressed too hard. Astrid began uttering loud, sharp
screams, and she was standing at the window with the dead bird in
her hand when the consul came bounding up the stairs. Yumei—like
many Chinese servants, no matter how devoted—was blind and deaf
as long as she was eating her rice.

Papa was very kind and very alarmed. He took Astrid in his arms
and carried her to her bed.

"I didn't mean to, Papa, I really didn't!" she said between sobs.

"I know," the consul murmured, and he patted his unattractive little daughter's soft, too soft blond hair. He covered the bird with a
handkerchief and later gave it to the gardener to bury. Then he sat

down, sighing, at his desk to finish up his correspondence. Among his private letters was an unopened one from Hong Kong. It had been written three days after the reception and mailed, in a rather crushed condition, from on board the *Kingfisher*, Captain Lillesand's passenger-freighter, which at the time had been in port in Hong Kong.

On Board the Kingfisher
December 1925

Dear Consul Wergeland,

Since I have decided to return with my brother to Norway, instead of continuing to drift around the Far East, I want to bid you good-by. I am sending this letter to your office, since it is intended for you alone. In our family, letters to my mother were opened by Papa, and I don't know whether that may not be the custom in all families.

I do not want to apologize to you and Madame for the incident, since there is no excuse that will not sound silly and untruthful. I certainly would have returned the bracelet; I only wanted to look at it for a night. Cheap, sham jewelry, such as is suitable for a tramp, only depresses me. Since we will never see one another again, I should like to confide something to you. Although you are so much older than I—my brother told me you are already thirty-six—I am terribly in love with you. You cannot imagine how awfully trouble-some this feeling is. My agent has sent me an offer for concerts in Paris, and I cannot practice because I am always thinking of you. Utterly idiotic. If you had given me a single kiss, I would certainly be calm and contented now. That was very unkind of you, not to. It certainly would not have made much difference to you. I would not have been taking anything from your wife. Although I am a tramp, I have strict principles. They come from Papa. He is in the Civil Service, but I think he is entirely without desire for— Oh, what nonsense I am writing. My head aches. It's your fault. I hope I forget you as quickly as I forget everything else.

Many thanks for your understanding. I have firmly resolved not to endanger my career. Perhaps some rich old gentleman will give me genuine jewelry if I do my hair better, don't wear my shoes down at the heels, and become as well conducted and boring as Papa. What do you think?

If you see Baron Matsubara in Shanghai, please tell him that I am most grateful to him. He unfortunately saved my life after your party. But on the other hand, I'm very glad about that, because I want to play the fiddle.

Baron Matsubara thought I would have a great success in Tokyo. Perhaps I shall go there after my engagements in Paris next fall. He has an uncle in some ministry who might be able to arrange some concerts for me, he thought. Unlike you, Baron Matsubara is very kind. Unfortunately, he interests me no more than my violin case. I will never marry because I know that I shall never meet a man whom I could be as crazy about as you. Please excuse me for writing that. I don't know whether it's proper. Unfortunately, I had no education aside from my violin lessons. My teacher was always deploring that. But in the years when other girls learn manners and so on, I was living in hotels and out of suitcases. That must be it. I would be very happy if you and Madame were to forgive me. I am terribly ashamed and will try never to do it again. It would be nice if you could like me just a little, even though you don't want to kiss me.

I should have said good-by to the Japanese, but I forgot all about it. I hope he is not angry. I shall write him from Norway. I've tied a knot in my only nice handkerchief, to remember.

Au revoir! Oh, nonsense. I meant to write: Adieu!

Borghild

Consul Wergeland thoughtfully tore the letter into small bits and dropped them into the wastepaper basket. For a moment he saw Borghild vividly; then he shrugged. He had other worries. At dawn he drove to the birdsellers' street and bought a new Gold Oriole. He brought it to Astrid as she lay in bed, and told her she had only dreamed about the death of the bird. Astrid did not believe him, but she smiled at him with touching gratitude for the kindly lie.

Consul Wergeland did not reply to Borghild directly or through his friend Lillesand. In spite of her mature talent, she seemed to him an ill-bred adolescent. Mailin had more dignity, the consul reflected, and his thoughts returned to his daughters. Since the incident of the bird, Astrid had been following him around like a puppy. It made him nervous, but he controlled the feeling.

On the morning of their departure it was raining in the city of civilized discontent. There was not the usual swarm of friends and servants at the port, for the consul had kept the day a secret. Yumei chattered away in joyful excitement with Astrid and Mailin; she would be returning to the Far East in a few months, after all, and she had promised her numerous brothers and sisters gifts from Norway. Astrid said not a word, but kept count to see whether Amah spoke to her exactly as much as to Younger Sister. Mailin held the cage with Gold Oriole's double in her left hand; her right hand she had placed trustfully in Astrid's. After a while Astrid succeeded in shaking off the tiny hand without anyone's noticing. Mailin, under her new woolen dress, wore the jade bell with the inscription: *Haste is error.*

On board it occurred to the consul that he had not yet informed Helene that Yumei was with them. He promptly wrote a long airmail letter, explaining to her that after poor Yvonne's death the amah had been the only person who could manage Astrid. When the possibility of separation from Yumei had been mentioned, Astrid had made such a fuss that the consul had seen no choice but to take Yumei along. In any case, four-year-old Mailin also needed a nurse who spoke Chinese. He was very worried about Astrid, he said; she dutifully went on learning her twenty French words a day, but was unaccountably indifferent to her sweet little half-sister.

In conclusion, the consul wrote that a year thence Astrid would be sent to a convent school in French Switzerland. That had been her mother's plan. Although the Wergelands' religious views differed, he was determined to respect Yvonne's wishes in regard to Astrid. Mailin was no problem at all; she was as merry and peaceable as a bird, and one could not help loving her.

The consul wiped the cold sweat from his brow. Since Christmas his world in Shanghai had collapsed, he wrote, and he was now bringing all he had saved from the ruins to Helene at Villa Wergeland. She must try to make Astrid and Mailin as much as possible into good Norwegian children who knew where they belonged. And he hoped she would not be too upset by the Chinese amah and the bird, Gold Oriole.

The consul folded the letter. At least he had now prepared Helene in regard to Astrid's character and the Chinese invasion of Trondheim. He knew that Miss Wergeland detested three things: shirkers, scenes, and surprises.

4: Family Reunion in Norway

"Poor Knut," said the Widow from Aalesund, drying a tear. "I know what it means to lose suddenly the person you have loved most in all the world."

Miss Wergeland regarded her poor relation with pinched lips. The Widow from Aalesund had a round, self-complacent face, an eternally red nose, a small mouth with pouting upper lip, and pretty blue eyes that wept easily and gave her permanently reddened lids.

"Don't talk nonsense, Laura," Miss Wergeland said sharply. "You know you twice ran away from your husband."

Miss Wergeland never showed the slightest consideration to anyone when the truth was at stake. She had taken in the widow, fed her, and wounded her by adhering to the unvarnished truth. Laura Holgersen jumped at her words. "That was only at the beginning," she murmured. "Later on I grew accustomed to him. Sverre was the best husband in the world."

Whereupon the Widow from Aalesund wiped away another tear and gave a sneeze. Helene was an unpleasant person; she threw the truth into your face like a wet dishrag. But Laura was dependent on her. Her husband had left her without a penny, and Laura was greatly attached to eating, drinking, and gossiping. She was extremely good-natured and extremely sentimental. At night she polished up her marital recollections until she had converted her unfeeling husband into a paragon of every virtue. Then she slept soundly and placidly, while Helene lay sleepless, thinking about Knut's last letter from the Far East. Here was a fine mess! A Chinese child in the family! To be sure, Helene had always urged Knut to tell the truth to Yvonne, and to remember the child in his will, but she had not meant the child to live with the Wergelands. Helene had little fondness for foreigners, and none for Chinese and heathens.

"Are the guest rooms clean?" Miss Wergeland asked her house-keeper next day. "Everything in its place? The children will sleep in the blue room with their Chinese nurse, I take it."

"I thought they were to have the yellow room."

"Do me the favor and don't think!" Miss Wergeland said. "Leave that to me in the future."

Laura Holgersen sighed. She gave her energetic cousin a mournful look. Helene was right, after all: ever since Sverre's death her memory had gone to pot and she always thought the wrong thoughts. She was altogether intimidated in Villa Wergeland. Everything here was so strange and on such a large scale—those unwed mothers and the infants in the east wing, Helene's depressing oil paintings, and Helene herself. When Helene contracted her bushy eyebrows and rose briskly from her chair, mild Laura trembled as she had before her teacher when she was a child in Bergen. At the same time Helene was so good and helpful. But she was formidable; there was no getting around that.

The widow looked at Miss Wergeland in mute penitence. Somehow Helene could not endure that look and that twitching upper lip. Faced with helplessness, she always laid down her arms. She rose and patted Laura lightly on the shoulder. "I'm a little short sometimes," she said with a forced smile. "You must not take it personally."

"Why, Helene, you're always so good to me!" The Widow from Aalesund was horrified that Miss Wergeland, whom she simultaneously feared and admired, should have virtually apologized to her. "Whatever would I have done without you?" she murmured.

"I have no idea," Miss Wergeland said. "I suppose you would have done something. A woman who can make such cream puffs would never go a-begging."

"Do you really think so, Helene? Or are you just saying that?"

"Why should I just say that?"

"To make me feel better."

"Stuff and nonsense! I don't have to make you feel better. You whimper your troubles away," Miss Wergeland said penetratingly. At bottom she envied the Widow from Aalesund. The dream house of her memories had pink curtains and artificial sunlight. Miss Wergeland saw things as they were. She could not dilute her memories with cheap tears until they lost their stinging taste. Moreover, she despised her cousin's cream puffs, but she had kept this feeling to herself from the first. One did not pluck a helpless chicken's last feathers.

Never in her life would Miss Wergeland forget that arrival of her favorite brother and his daughters. It was already evening. The ship had been two hours late, and now a strange procession from the Far East came walking toward Helene Wergeland. In the van was Knut, who, as always, towered by a head over all the other passengers and nevertheless looked stooped. Behind him came a sturdy-looking young Chinese girl in a satin jacket and padded pantaloons, with a flower in her glistening black hair. At her side minced the thinnest, palest child Miss Wergeland had ever had to feed back to health. In her arms the young Chinese was carrying a small, sleeping something with a checked traveling cap, from under which peeped a fringe of soft black hair. On her back hung a bird-cage covered by a square of gold brocade—a fragment of Oriental beauty. For a moment the little group paused, stood motionless in the bright northern night—messengers from a strange, colorful, and incomprehensible world. Even the jolly, ever-chattering Yumei had been stunned into silence. She stood wide-eyed with the little Missies and Gold Oriole in the austere silvery light of the Far North, and stared at the Nid River, which washed romantically and usefully around the ancient fortress of bishops and kings. No coolies laughed or sang here; an uncanny and unnatural orderliness reigned in this port. For the first time in her life Yumei was frightened, and at the same moment she resolved, with Chinese obstinacy, not to be frightened.

Meanwhile Knut Wergeland had been looking for the figure of a woman who would be towering over all the others. There she stood, Helene, a still, familiar, and stern figure out of a life the consul had left behind him. Helene, the cathedral, the mystic-heroic air of the Old City, and the uncompromising cleanliness of the streets—all this was home and youth with its dreams, hopes, and fleeting griefs. . . .

The consul shook himself and strode like a sleepwalker toward his sister. His eyes probed the expression on her face. "Here we are," he murmured, gesturing toward the little group, which had followed shyly and obediently at his heels.

"Welcome home, Knut," Miss Wergeland said. "So here you are!" She ignored Yumei's low bow and drew Astrid close to her.

"*Bon soir, ma tante,*" Astrid said formally, evading her aunt's steely blue eyes.

"Well, well," Miss Wergeland exclaimed so loudly that two sailors turned around and looked grinningly at her, "what's this *parlez-vous?* Can't she say *god aften?*"

The consul told his older daughter to greet her aunt in Norwegian. For a moment Astrid stood like a stick; she was afraid of this tall, loud-voiced woman with the sharp eyes. Then she ran to Yumei, hid her face in the satin jacket, and began sobbing. Miss Wergeland gazed in consternation at her brother and at the skinny, sobbing child. A fine beginning this was! But she would find ways to manage Astrid. Never fear!

Yumei threw a faintly triumphant look at the big old Missie, who already had many gray hairs. Little Missie knew who was her comforter.

Astrid's sobbing, which became more violent with each passing minute, awakened Mailin. The black gems which were her eyes blinked about; then she wriggled out of Yumei's arms, prattling away and tugging at the brocade drape which concealed Gold Oriole. Yumei nodded crossly, but at last she did as Younger Sister wished and handed her the small cage. Mailin, now fully awake, went up to the tall woman, bowed solemnly as her amah had, and held out the cage to a speechless Helene Wergeland.

"Gold Oriole will sing pretty songs for big old Mistress," Yumei whispered in Chinese. Mailin looked imploringly at her father. She wanted him to explain to the aunt that Mailin liked her and therefore wanted to give her her dearest possession. The consul stooped, trying to understand her stammering words. Mailin had thought about this moment during the whole long voyage, ever since Papa had explained to her that they were going to see the tall old aunt.

"Mailin likes you," the consul said, and he coughed. "So she wants to give you her Gold Oriole."

Miss Wergeland lifted the little girl and pressed her mutely to her heart. Her eyes had suddenly acquired a soft gleam; it was a light that came from the depths of her soul and restored her youth. This was how she had sometimes looked at Knut when he unexpectedly made her happy, absurdly, excessively happy, with a gift for which she had as little use as she did for Gold Oriole. Helene peered closely at the strange, pretty child. Mailin was smiling, half asleep again. She was not in the least afraid of this imperious Miss Wergeland who gave so much and so seldom received. Trustfully Mailin laid her black-haired head against Helene's shoulder. "Mailin tired," she murmured.

The checked traveling cap had fallen from her head. Miss Wergeland brushed the silken black hair back from the round forehead. The child looked up at her and smiled with innocent charm into those stern, steely blue eyes. And that look decided her relationship to this aunt who was by nature so alien to her. In that mute encounter of two pairs of eyes and two worlds, a subtle and indissoluble bond was formed between Helene Wergeland and Hsin Mailin, the Pure Lily of the Hsin family. Out of Western dubiousness and Oriental childish innocence, affection was born, a laconic and passionate fidelity. In that decisive moment Helene Wergeland transferred the love which Mailin's father so often seemed to have no need for to this daughter who was and would remain Chinese.

"A sweet little thing," Miss Wergeland said to her brother.

Astrid had stopped crying, since there was no hope of making a scene. She went slowly up to her aunt and mumbled, *"God aften!"* But no one paid any attention.

That was unfortunate, for Astrid very rarely made any effort to please, although she longed for nothing else more intensely. Only a single person, who had remained modestly in the background, noticed her action. Laura Holgersen went up to Astrid, smiling amiably, and greeted her. But Astrid only looked haughtily at this stranger and murmured, *"Je ne comprends pas."*

Laura stepped back; she had felt the unfriendliness even without understanding the words. Instinctively Astrid renounced pity and the second best when she could not have the best. At seven she sensed who were significant persons, as Helene Wergeland and her brother Knut always were without effort. Laura Holgersen was born to be a subsidiary figure on the stage of life, and with such Astrid Thérèse Wergeland would have nothing to do. She wanted all or nothing. Laura Holgersen thought her horribly unsympathetic, but she said to herself that a child of only seven, who in addition was dead tired, should not be taken seriously. In this the Widow of Aalesund was mistaken, as usual.

Knut Wergeland stood before a large oil painting in the main salon of Villa Wergeland and regarded the first forefather recorded in the family's history. A modern painter had done the portrait of old Olaf Wergeland from a faded engraving. A giant with steely blue eyes and broad shoulders looked down on the consul. Old Olaf had been a farmer in Tröndelag, a short-spoken, rough, intelligent, and far-sighted man. From his own woods and small sawmill he had provided wood for shipbuilding, and toward the end of the eighteenth century had risen into Norway's democratic moneyed class. His sons and grandsons had then built ships of their own. Thus the Wergeland Shipyards in Trondheim had been formed. His grandsons had stepped higher; they had been educated at the technical academy. Knut's father had married the daughter of a shipowner. A thrifty woman who loved life, she had handed on to Knut his glittering eyes and his bent toward reverie and beautiful objects. With her daughter Helene she had never got along. Helene was like old Olaf. The consul smiled at this thought. Family tradition had it that their ancestor had also thrown the truth like a wet dishrag into everyone's face, but was the first to help wherever help was needed.

This evening the fiftieth birthday of Knut's brother, the present Olaf Wergeland and head of the shipyard, was being celebrated. Knut was not fond of him. Olaf Wergeland was a fiercely honest man without a spark of imagination. His sister Helene tartly called him "the Eyewitness" because he recognized the reality and validity only of things he had seen with his own eyes. The Far East did not interest him because he had never seen it. It was only a place to which ships could be sent, a sphere for trade.

Olaf Wergeland greeted his brother Knut frostily and surveyed the children with a cold gaze. A bachelor himself, he had no use for children. Astrid stared at him out of her pale blue eyes. Mailin hid from him behind Miss Wergeland's skirt. The tall, thin man with gold-rimmed glasses and drooping mouth frightened her.

Olaf thought it entirely in order that his brother should now be becoming acquainted with the seriousness of life. He sat stiffly in his chair and looked on, frowning, as Helene tried to enliven things for the children. An itinerant circus was nothing compared to Knut's family. Moreover, children did not belong in the company of adults. Perhaps it was customary in the gypsy world of the Far East, but not in Trondheim. Olaf Wergeland sat up still more stiffly.

"I suppose you will be taking the Chinese child back to the Orient with you?" he asked his brother, chewing each word between his big yellow teeth. "She would create an unpleasant stir here. I cannot afford that in Trondheim."

The consul looked at his elder brother with that same surprise he had sometimes displayed toward Yvonne back in Shanghai. How was it possible for anyone to be so narrow-minded and altogether heartless? The savage hatred he had felt as a boy, after the death of his parents, for this Eyewitness who forbade or spoiled all his amusements rose up in him again. He looked around. Helene, Laura, and the children had gone into the orangery. That was just as well; it gave him an opportunity too good to be missed. In a quiet voice Consul Wergeland proceeded to tell his brother a few things. He forgot the diplomatic language of his profession, and the ties of blood. Olaf had insulted Mailin. Sweet as she was in every way, this child with her gold-tinted skin and almond eyes would create an unpleasant sensation in the marketplace, would she? That was what Olaf had meant, wasn't it? Then Knut wanted to tell him that . . .

The consul was still standing in the middle of the room with the handwoven rugs and the oil painting of Grandfather Wergeland, continuing to tell him, long after the Eyewitness had left the house.

Knut looked around as if he were awakening from a nightmare. He was swaying slightly when he went into the orangery to see Helene. "We must talk alone," he explained to the Widow from Aalesund, who was regarding him with devouring curiosity.

Cousin Knut looked as if he wanted to wring someone's neck. Laura reluctantly took the children to the east wing, where Yumei was already waiting. Yumei was by now completely at home in Villa Wergeland. Thanks to the extraordinary adaptability of most Chinese, she enjoyed her rice even in such foreign surroundings.

"Where is Olaf?" Miss Wergeland asked. "We are ready to eat."

"I've thrown him out."

"Are you out of your mind?"

"On the contrary, my dear Helene." The consul fixed his eyes upon his dear Helene. "I have discovered that my daughters and I have no business here. We are leaving."

Miss Wergeland sat alone in the big hall, lips tightly compressed. Two weeks had passed since the abortive birthday party. A pleasant surprise that had been! Knut knew perfectly well how she abhorred surprises. He had actually left the next morning to visit the Clermonts in Paris. Naturally the children and Yumei had remained behind in Villa Wergeland. He had not succeeded in taking the children—or rather Mailin—away from his sister. It would have been easier to take a kit from a tigress. He had promised Helene to return in two months. Then, for the rest of his home leave, he intended to sail farther north.

Miss Wergeland had won a partial victory, but she felt cross and grief-stricken. For so many years now she had been waiting for Knut. At any rate, she would go to Bangkok with Mailin in six months, to run her brother's household—after first taking Astrid to the boarding school in Lausanne. Laura Holgersen would stay to close up Villa Wergeland. Since she would never be able to manage Miss Wergeland's protégées, she would have to bake her cream puffs elsewhere. Naturally Helene had provided for Laura, as she did for all hapless chicks.

For Helene Wergeland life had begun again after a chain of disappointments, since from now on she would be living with her favorite brother. And she had Mailin. She would learn to endure Astrid. The child annoyed her—there was no denying that. She was an envious little thing who kept a sharp eye out to see that Miss Wergeland did not show a preference for the younger sister. Astrid went her own way, Miss Wergeland thought disapprovingly. It did not occur to her that she too went her own way—though she was certainly not of an envious disposition.

At this moment Astrid came into the sitting room. She had entered so softly that Miss Wergeland involuntarily started. Had she attracted the child by her antagonistic thoughts? Astrid now spoke such a mixture of French, Norwegian, and Chinese that Miss Wergeland had decided to converse with her niece in French for the present. It was really scandalous that Knut had taught a seven-year-old girl only scraps of her mother tongue.

"What do you want?" Helene asked in her harsh French.

Astrid held out her schoolbook. "My twenty words," she said, looking up at her aunt. "While *Maman* was living, I learned twenty French words every day. It used to make her glad. Are you glad too, Aunt Helene?"

"Of course," Miss Wergeland said hastily. She did not like to lie, but the child had such a curiously hungry way of looking at one. . . . Hm. . . .

In the middle of the lesson Astrid stopped and once again gazed unwinkingly at her aunt.

"What is there to stare at?" Helene asked, not in the friendliest tone. The child really could make one nervous.

Astrid started, but she felt that she had to say it. Then Aunt Helene would love her more than Mailin. "It's a secret," she murmured and began to tremble.

"Well, out with it," Miss Wergeland said, not very encouragingly. Astrid always had some secret to reveal; so Helene had already discovered, to her distaste, in the past two weeks. "Why are you trembling?" She made an effort to be kindly. "Don't you feel well? Would you like hot lemonade? What is the matter, child? Out with your secret!"

"Would you really like to know, Aunt Helene?"

"Of course."

Astrid stared into space. "Mailin is not the same as we are," she whispered quickly.

"How do you mean that?"

"I mean—she is Chinese! In Shanghai we were not allowed to play with such children. They're—something—not as good as us. I know all about it, Aunt Helene," Astrid went on, the words coming out in a rush. "No Concession child invited Chinese children to play. They weren't allowed to eat with us either."

"Well!" Miss Wergeland suddenly rose to her full, terrifying height. "Is there anything else you'd like to tell me?"

Astrid's too-soft hair had become damp. She felt that Aunt Helene was frightfully angry, though she was reining her anger in. Astrid was wise for her seven years. She suddenly had the feeling that she was about to plunge from a phantom mountain into one of those seething abysses that Yumei always told her about before she went to sleep. The secret that was to win Aunt Helene's love had only made her compress her lips more harshly. Astrid could feel that her aunt was closing her heart toward her.

"You listen to me," Aunt Helene said sternly. "There are no as-good and not-as-good children. There are only good children and bad children. Do you understand me?"

"No," Astrid said obstinately. She stood her ground before her aunt as though her feet were rooted to the mat.

Miss Wergeland considered. How should she answer this monstrous declaration of the child's? She did not understand Astrid. Here the child clung to Yumei, who was also Chinese. What was this all about? Miss Wergeland had never been in Shanghai. She could not possibly know what the foreign "sugar dolls" talked about with one another.

"You're fond of Yumei, aren't you?" she asked at last in her perplexity.

"Of course," Astrid murmured, and tossed her head back haughtily exactly as Yvonne had done. "But Yumei is not my sister, she's my servant. Almost all Chinese are our servants in Shanghai, and so are their children."

Miss Wergeland shook Astrid vigorously and administered her a ringing slap in the face. "That's all!" she cried at the livid child. "I'll lock you up in your room if you ever say anything like that again."

Abruptly she released the child, who stood staring open-mouthed at her. What had she done? She had mistreated a child who wanted to be loved by her, and who had picked up misguided notions in the Orient—she, Helene Wergeland, the protector of children and helpless grown-ups.

"Come," she said hoarsely. "Let us go to see Aunt Laura. I think she has just baked some cream puffs."

"*Merci beaucoup,*" Astrid said with a great effort. She was alarmingly pale but no longer trembling. Rather, she seemed stunned. Astrid had never been slapped. She had told Aunt Helene nothing but the truth. In Shanghai the children of Chinese servants helped to serve the foreigners. And European parents did not invite the children of their Chinese friends to their houses. Astrid was not bad; Aunt Helene was bad.

"I want to go to Papa," she cried, sobbing. "You're bad to me."

Helene took the child on her lap and said with unwonted gentleness, "That is nonsense. I'm very fond of you, Astrid. Tomorrow we will go on a nice outing together."

"Thank you, I must study my twenty words tomorrow." Astrid swallowed her tears. Something had happened that neither she nor her aunt understood. An alarm bell had roused Astrid from childish yearnings. After the slap she could not breathe properly, and her stomach ached, but that was not the worst of it. For now she no longer wanted Aunt Helene to love her more than she loved Mailin. Aunt Helene had slapped her for confiding a secret to her. Therefore she must not tell Aunt Helene anything—and no one else either, certainly not Yumei or Mailin. Papa had gone away. She would steal away at night and go looking for Papa.

Had not Yumei, in her loyalty and love for little Missie, pursued the bewildered Astrid when she attempted to creep out the door in her nightgown, the child might very well have fallen into the water or been run over by an automobile in the delirium that developed two hours later.

Yumei carried the sick child to Miss Wergeland. There was no need for her to say anything; Helene saw for herself. The doctor, summoned in haste, feared a very grave illness, but it did not turn out quite so badly. Day and night Helene sat by the child's bed, listening to her delirious fantasies in Chinese and her French dictionary words, and the ever-recurrent God aften and Jeg forstar ikke, "I do not understand." Jeg forstar ikke—that was what Astrid had cried out in her fright at being slapped.

During those days Helene came to know and appreciate young Yumei. The raw-boned, worried Norwegian woman and the jolly little Chinese girl understood each other without words. To Yumei, Fröken Wergeland became an astonishing new mistress whom she was ready to serve for all eternity. At the time Miss Wergeland knew nothing of this precious gift of loyalty that was cast into her lap during those long days and nights after Knut's departure.

By the time Knut Wergeland arrived in Trondheim again to begin his trip to the north, Astrid was almost fully recovered. All three stood on the terrace—Astrid, Helene, and Mailin—and waved to him as he approached. Yumei knelt in front of Miss Wergeland, waving a garland of flowers.

Astrid seemed to have forgotten everything. She was treated with anxious caution by her aunt. But something had changed: Astrid never asked whether she was loved most of all. And she listened to Yumei's fairy tales with only half an ear. She could not say why these stories no longer fascinated her. Perhaps her child's soul was beginning to suspect that reality is far more frightful than the most frightening of Chinese tales.

5: *The Maid in the Swan's Dress*

Knut Wergeland spent several weeks in the Lofoten Islands, fishing, breathing the good air, and thinking things over. This was the first time in years that he had been entirely alone; and he rested thoroughly and fruitfully after the upheavals of recent months. Mild summer air, bright nights, and swarms of seabirds, which accompanied him from island to island, inspired him with a kind of rapture —that sober rapture, lifting one above the world of tinned fish and lumber, which the pantheistic soul needs now and again. For days the consul scarcely spoke a word. But this was not the silence of defiance with which he had been wont to treat Yvonne; it was the silence of inner contentment. The lack of superfluous bustle, the primeval stillness of the mountains and the water, did wonders for him. The colorful jackets and shawls worn by the girls, the big milk jugs in the cafés of the small towns, the dances and songs of the valley dwellers, became for him—a cosmopolitan come home—the symbol of that indomitable Norwegian spirit which flourishes on hard work among beetling cliffs, rocky coasts, great forests, and the thin soil of oft-tilled fields.

Then he rode back—past fjords, sheer mountain walls, velvety meadows, and sandy coastal strips, past villages shimmering in light and smelling tangily of cod. In the fishing port of Stamsund the consul wrote a letter to his brother. He had recovered his balance now and must apologize for his outbreak. He had been suffering from "Shanghai nerves," he said—a term he did not define. How could he explain to Olaf Wergeland the breakdown of the emotional life and of propriety produced by such a city? There were no words for the horrible sensation of thrashing about in the net of an irrational civilization, that gasping in an alien atmosphere fatal to one's moral being—thrashing and gasping like a cod in the net of a Lofoten fisherman. Back in his native land, Knut had found himself again. The pure air, the wide landscape of mountains and fjords, the certainty of undisturbed solitude which a homeland in the Far North can give to its sons even in the age of cocktail parties and travel bureaus— these had cleansed his mind and senses more profoundly than the stolen hours in the Japanese tea room in Shanghai. With his eyes on the wooden racks for drying fish, the consul requested his brother to forgive him for the scene at Villa Wergeland. He never received a reply to this letter. Olaf Wergeland was incapable of forgetting or forgiving; he lacked the imagination. He had stricken his brother from his files.

Knut did not return to Trondheim directly but took a voyage to the island of Hitra, where in his youth he had hunted deer with Olaf. It was truly a puzzle why he sailed to this remote wooded island where everything must inevitably remind him of his brother: the pale twilights, the sleepy little coastal harbor where ships took on loads of kelp, the scattered wooden houses, and the discouraged moorland between Trondheim and Kristiansund. In the yellow sunset the post office of Hestevik looked like a week-end bungalow for trolls.

Knut had gone to the island of Hitra with the idea of completing the round of visits to places that loomed so large in his memories. But perhaps he had really gone because destiny was awaiting him there. And his destiny made use of the basest power of seduction in the universe: music. Under the wan moon of the trolls' island the notes of a violin sounded from a wooden house in a tangle of heather and reached the consul's ear as he stood looking at the house. He might have fled; in that case he would have saved his sister

Helene further surprises and assured himself peace and contentment. But Knut Wergeland instinctively pressed forward into danger zones when his ear was bewitched. Perhaps he felt that life is
too short and monotonous to be lived without music.

It was around ten o'clock at night when he entered a large
room hung with brave-colored old tapestries. In the wall-cupboard
gleamed silver cups and pitchers, the traditional Norwegian coffee
service. They were the work of Henrik Moeller of Trondheim—the
consul recognized the plain, noble styling. Pewter utensils and fine
ceramicware filled other shelves in a house that outwardly could be
distinguished only by its size from the cottages of the woodsmen.
This was some Norwegian family's week-end cottage, like so many
in the vicinity of Trondheim and Kristiansund.

A girl in a white dress lowered her bow, stepped forward to meet
the visitor in the moonlight, and whispered a magic welcome. Borghild Lillesand said, "You came because I was waiting for you."

Borghild had changed, but the consul could not at once decide
why she seemed more vital and attractive. He regarded her silently
with that speculative curiosity he invariably felt before plunging into
an adventure. Uncertainty had slid from Borghild's shoulders like a
mousy gray cloak, revealing a different girl, a creature glowing quietly from within, utterly free of neurotic traits. She must have a man,
the consul thought innocently. He did not know that she had *him*.
This change had taken place in Borghild after her brother informed
her of Yvonne's death. Her eyes had lost their absent, despondent
look; even her hair was better groomed. One of her stockings, it was
true, had a hole in its heel again, but she was not sitting shoeless
on a Japanese mat with young Baron Matsubara. She stood lithe and
slim in her white dress. Her sensitive lips quivered very faintly as
the consul said, "Well, well, what are you doing here?"

Borghild gave an eminently sane reply. She was staying here with
friends who happened to have gone to Kristiansund for the week
end. In the fall she intended to give her first concert in Paris. She
had already been here for a month and intended to leave tomorrow.
Actually she had decided on this departure after she saw the consul.
His ship, he had explained, was going to Kristiansund. He wanted
to visit some friends before returning to his sister's in Trondheim.

What a coincidence! That was the very ship Borghild was planning to take. But would there still be room on the ship?

The consul saw through the trick and thought it as touchingly young as Borghild herself. Of course there was room; the consul would sleep on deck and Borghild could have his cabin. He had drawn her head to his shoulder and was asking her about the Paris concert and about her teacher, who prophesied a great future for her. Then she sprang away from him and went to get her violin. Was it only the desire to please, or a great love, that electrified her? In any case, she had emerged from her vacuum. Her simplicity and honesty had remained. There was nothing insipid about Borghild.

They walked across the moor under the pale moon and looked at craggy cliffs and the dark sea. Borghild had tied a lace scarf, a heritage from her mother's concert days, over her hair. And her imagination produced for her the delusion of a fulfillment she had longed for since Shanghai. The consul was walking at her side, had put his arm around her. The future was a path strewn with roses. Borghild's imagination was as compelling as that of a child who despises realities because she does not know them. And these innocent assumptions of hers, combined with the elevating effect of her music, momentarily put to flight the justified doubts of a mature man and made Knut believe that love was the greatest force in the world.

"Why are you looking at me that way?" Borghild asked. They were looking down from the peak of a rock upon the sleeping strip of beach, where three girls and a solitary horse stood about, waiting for someone.

"You remind me of the Maid in the Swan's Dress," Knut said in playful tenderness. That maid in white had married a human man and so lost her feathers and the power of flight. Years later she came across her swan's dress again and was seized by longing for far places. Singing, she flew away from her human husband.

Borghild too had heard this fairy tale from her mother's maid, who used to tell her stories in cheerless hotel rooms. "I would never fly away from you," she whispered and stood on tiptoe in order to look into the eyes of the man she had waited for all these months.

Knut Wergeland evaded her gaze. He should not be trifling with her. She was—like every artist—an innocent child in a world of reckoners and careerists without illusions. "I hope we have committed no more follies since Shanghai?" he asked, tipping up her soft chin in a paternal gesture.

Borghild shook her head with the spontaneity and candor of a child. She was no longer ashamed before the man she loved; indeed, she had been ashamed only before Yvonne. That Knut Wergeland knew of her sickness only lent a deeper attraction to her relationship with him. It was a miracle of intimacy, even though in a negative sense.

She looked up at him, enchanted and enchanting. She was so small, so frail, and had even left the recourse of the helpless behind in the cottage. The consul sat down on the trunk of a tree and took her on his lap. Already he had ceased to believe that she was a child of chaos. He picked up the lace scarf, which had fallen to the ground, and wrapped it around her. "It is getting chilly," he murmured. "I must return to the ship."

"No," Borghild begged. "Don't—go away! Please don't go away!" Her eyes filled with big tears. She wanted to wipe them away but had no handkerchief.

He wiped away her tears with his handkerchief, as he was accustomed to do for Astrid. As a father he was irresistible. Borghild evidently thought so, for she threw her arms around his neck and buried her face in his shoulder. "I've waited so long," she whispered.

He kissed her tenderly, and still half in play. What was she but a lovelorn little girl who had not yet found a boy who suited her? He came very close to saying, as he had done in Shanghai, "Stop this silliness, Borghild!" He stood up and raised her to her feet.

"Did you receive the letter I wrote you?"

Knut Wergeland considered. He should have said no, but the affectionate repugnance he had felt in Shanghai had now become affection. Borghild was no longer weeping. She looked fixedly into his eyes and said calmly, "Then you know how I feel."

"That is sheer nonsense. You have no idea what love is." Absently he caressed her. *He* knew that no amount of initial happiness outweighed the throes of eventual boredom. Suddenly he took Borghild into his arms. "Silly little girl," he said. "I am much too old for you!"

In his thoughts he added that he had two daughters. But it was already too late. Borghild's desires were stronger than his reason and experience, because clearly defined desires have an extraordinary power. Borghild was young, fearfully and wonderfully young. The consul sensed in her a fanatical capacity for devotion such as Yvonne had never possessed. It was a wordless, innocent surrender which he found as touching as her little ruse about the ship, and as exciting as the midnight sun in all its streaming radiance. He carried Borghild into the cottage, which waited with lighted windows in the midst of this wild landscape, into the big room lined with silver utensils. As he bent over her she threw her arms around his neck and kissed him with desperate inexperience, a chaste tramp, disorderly and intoxicating. Trembling, she started undoing the buttons of her white dress; this was her notion of how to express surrender. He did not tell her to stop the silliness, but took her hands, kissed her pensively on brow and eyes, and covered her with a white blanket.

"You'd best go to sleep, darling," he said, evading her fixed gaze. Then he returned to his ship. He was not undertaking the seduction of virgins; no member of the Wergeland family could be that romantic. And that incautious.

Next morning Borghild appeared with lowered eyes, in a faded summer dress, on board his ship. Her hair hung in wisps; over her left arm she carried a battered raincoat and in her right hand her violin case. Her swan's dress lay crushed in the shabby suitcase which the consul had carried to his cabin. Borghild was not a lady who spruced herself anew after every fling.

The consul's canvas tent already stood on deck. If the weather turned bad, the first mate had promised to lend him his cabin.

"Well?" The consul smiled at Borghild out of his glittering eyes. She blushed like a schoolgirl and sat down, pale and confused, in the darkest corner of the dining room.

"Please forget everything," she murmured at last. "I am an idiot. I simply don't know how to behave. Promise me that you'll—that you'll forget—last night."

"I have not the slightest intention of doing so," Consul Wergeland replied. "I could not forget it even if I wanted to."

"Is that really true?" Borghild asked, reviving.

"Of course," Consul Wergeland replied with the utmost gravity. "I suffer from good memory—an occupational disease. Come now, what is there to cry about?"

At last the children had gone to sleep. They had taken their dolls, Romsdal and Trondelag, who were dressed in the picturesque costumes of Nordland, to bed with them. Yumei too had a costume doll, dressed in the red and gold jacket of Telemark; in China these were the colors of gladness. Yumei had never before had a doll; she promptly wrapped it in a dustcloth and stowed it away in her suitcase. The doll was far too precious to touch. Later, in Shanghai, she would show it at the New Year celebration.

Astrid had asked Aunt Helene whether she could wear a costume like that, with all the embroidery, and was rewarded with a cordial look. In fact Astrid had not been motivated by any patriotic feelings; with her innate sense for beauty, she had been greatly impressed by the Nordland costume. Moreover, she knew instinctively that the white blouse and the green bodice with the bright flowered trimming would become her. She had Yvonne's marvelous taste.

Now the consul and Helene were sitting by themselves in the parlor. Out of sheer nervousness Knut was drinking his fourth cup of tea. He had a surprise in store for his sister. Helene was uncommonly loquacious. She informed Knut in her precise, energetic manner of her plans for Villa Wergeland. She wished to make the huge private house into a home for mothers, to be administered by the city. Trondheim was a city that already owed many of its social institutions to the generosity of its citizens. Miss Wergeland was quite pleased with her arrangements. She would live with Mailin and Knut in Bangkok henceforth. She regarded her brother with secret maternal pride. She had been a grown girl of seventeen, and Knut only twelve, when they lost their parents. Time had scarcely altered the basic relationship.

"Yumei is first-rate material," Helene concluded. "When we get to Bangkok, I intend to teach her order, punctuality, and cleanliness." She seriously imagined that these Norwegian virtues could be transplanted to Southeast Asia.

"Helene," Knut Wergeland said and fell into contemplation of the Japanese scroll he had brought for his sister. It was the "Songbird on a Dead Branch." Miss Wergeland had not cared for the picture, but she had made the best of it since it was a gift from Knut. She herself painted what she saw. Her oils were very neat. After all, she painted only for her own amusement.

"What's the matter, my boy? Has the cat got your tongue?" Miss Wergeland, who was not the most patient person in the world, eyed her brother sharply, her forefinger tapping the table—a habit that had always irritated Knut. He studied his sister as he considered how to deliver his surprise in the most merciful way. But all considerations went up in smoke at the sight of that familiar energetic face with the steel-blue eyes and the firmly compressed lips. Helene had always been a lifeboat to him, and now—

He ventured to dive headlong into the sea of uneasiness. "My plans have changed, Helene," he said quietly. "For the present you need not give up the villa."

"Do you want to stay here? Now that would be sensible! I could do a splendid job with the children. Besides—what is the sense of all this gypsy wandering around Asia? Olaf is not getting any younger."

"You've misunderstood me, Helene. I am going to Bangkok, of course, but—I intend to remarry after the year of mourning is up."

Miss Wergeland sprang to her feet. Hadn't Knut had enough of one mistaken marriage? She was tempted to ask him whether he was raving mad, but Knut was a sensitive person. He was the only person on earth before whom she would watch her tongue. And so she listened with compressed lips to what Knut had to say. A fledgling of no more than twenty, a chit who scraped away at a violin and knew nothing about household management! Miss Wergeland's assumptions were, in fact, amazingly correct. Borghild would eat dry bread rather than cook for herself. She and her mother had always left cleaning up to the maid. When the maid was not around, no cleaning was done. In this respect, Borghild would be a good mistress for a tropical household.

"Lillesand," Helene muttered. "Is she related to Sigrid Kronstad-Lillesand?"

"That was her mother. She gave concerts all over Europe."

"And caused scandals all over Europe. A disorderly family." That was a death sentence.

"Borghild is different," the consul said quickly. "She is—" He paused. It was impossible to express how pure Borghild was.

He is already defending her. I must hold my tongue, Miss Wergeland thought bitterly. She felt Knut slipping away from her from minute to minute, felt that he had already transferred his loyalty from her to this unknown girl. He no longer needed her. That was new and unendurable. Instinctively she realized that Knut was plunging into a marriage for love. He was no longer struggling between reason and temptation. Once again he saw life as a picnic.

Miss Wergeland went to the bay window and looked out on the darkening fjord and mountains. In the past Knut had discussed every decision with her, but this time he had stepped roughshod over her own plans and hopes. How frail were human ties! And how heedlessly people in love inflicted pain upon others. Helene compressed her lips to a thin line. In the shadow of renunciation she gazed after the fleeting clouds.

"She needs me, Helene."

Helene turned brusquely. "Does she?" she said and dropped into brooding silence. Don't I need you? she thought. What was the use of all the talk? She would have to forget all her own plans. At least she still had Astrid and Mailin and her protégées in the east wing. How many people had as much as a dog or a cat? Miss Wergeland smiled bitterly, yawned loudly and openly, and called out, "Time for bed! Good night!"

The consul jumped up and placed both hands on his sister's shoulders. They stood facing each other like two wrestlers—both tall, but she was of granite, he of a softer, more sensitive material.

"Be good to her, Helene," he pleaded. Then he relaxed the pressure of his hands and began shyly to pat his sister's broad, strong shoulders.

"Stop this silliness," Miss Wergeland said hoarsely. "I'll give her Mother's pearls for a wedding present. When is she coming?"

"Whenever you like. She's waiting at the hotel."

Miss Wergeland leaned out of the window and shouted in a stentorian voice for the chauffeur. "I'll drive over alone," she said to her brother. "What's the matter with you, silly boy? Save your kisses for your fiancée."

Contrary to all expectations, Helene Wergeland liked Borghild. Somehow her heart went out to the girl who approached like a terrified schoolgirl and was unable to speak a word. This girl was really no siren who had cunningly ensnared Knut. But Helene had gloomy forebodings that Knut would make the poor child utterly miserable.

Borghild seemed to be completely without wiles. Helene did not consider that her violin was a dangerous instrument of seduction—for Helene was not musical.

Years later Miss Wergeland recalled a little scene with Astrid. The child came to her in the middle of the night to reveal another of her secrets. *Maman* had called the lady with the violin case *une vagabonde*. But Astrid no longer remembered exactly why. From this disclosure Helene learned that Knut had already met Borghild in Shanghai. "I think she stole something from *Maman*," Astrid whispered, already half asleep again.

"You're dreaming, child! Come, I'll carry you to bed."

"Piggy-back, Aunt Helene?"

"Yes, piggy-back," Helene said, lost in thought.

6: A Bundle of Letters

BORGHILD WERGELAND TO HELENE WERGELAND (TRONDHEIM)

Bangkok, July 1926

Dearest Helene,

Do not be angry with me for not having written for so long. It is so frightfully hot here, and my head aches most of the time. You would not like it here at all. The foreigners are so debonair and pleasure-seeking and behave toward the Asians with arrogant modesty. I am expressing myself stupidly, but perhaps you know what I mean. Yumei is my only consolation. She is absolutely unchanged, whether she is in Shanghai, Trondheim, or Bangkok: always good-humored and hard-working and dear and loyal. I do not know what I would do here without her. She massages me when I am exhausted, cooks for me when I can't bear the eternal "rice and curry," and comforts me in every way.

Dearest Helene, do not be angry if I whimper my troubles to you, even though you cannot stand whimpering females, as you once said in Trondheim. When I think of you and Mailin and Villa Wergeland, I should like to run away from here and come to you at once. With you I felt sheltered for the first time in my life. Perhaps because you care for so many helpless chicks. Here the people all pretend to be so terribly happy and interested in everything, and they have sharp lines in their faces and do not listen at all when one tells them something or plays for them. Knut's Siamese friends smile charmingly, but I feel that they are somewhere else entirely in their thoughts—in the glittering halls of their temples or in their rest pavilions, or somewhere else. Baron Matsubara in Shanghai was quite different from them. I think I told you that he was the one who happened to save my life. He was rather boring and terribly solemn; but he listened closely to whatever was said to him, and he loved Beethoven and Grieg. He was *sympathetic*. Quite the opposite of Knut, who isn't at all sympathetic. But you know that better than I. After all, you've known him much longer.

You ask how I have adjusted to my duties in the consular corps. Not at all! They nauseate me. Excuse my throwing the truth into your face like a wet rag, but I've learned that from you. Knut is naturally a diplomat and raises his eyebrows when a button is loose on my evening wrap, and my hair flies around. Of course he says he doesn't care, but he hates it. With me he really doesn't have to lie in bed in his dinner jacket. (That was a phrase Mama had for men who continued to put on airs when they were all alone together. Mama sometimes had awfully funny expressions.)

As far as Knut is concerned, I have been completely disappointed in one respect. I used to think in Shanghai (isn't it odd that he never told you how long we'd known one another?)—what was I saying? Oh yes, in Shanghai I thought that Knut was utterly miserable with his wife. But that cannot have been the case. He is constantly telling me about Yvonne's virtues, her intelligence, her elegance, and her way of dealing with the servants, and then he is angry if I cry over these reproofs or shut myself up with my violin and let only Yumei in to see me. I shall not be able to stand it much longer. He was so sweet and tender at home. There must be two personalities in him. Sometimes he's himself, and then other times he's a diplomatic monster whom I'm afraid of as a child is afraid. I adore him nevertheless —that is the trouble! I wish I could be proud and unapproachable and a statue like Yvonne, but I cannot be that way. I become more and more uncertain, the more often Knut tells me that my slatternliness and my *faux pas* do not matter to him. If he would only once praise or encourage me! But no—he smiles like an icicle and says, "Silly little girl," and hates me. I'm certain of it, Helene, he doesn't love me any more. He only makes a pretense of it and is dreadfully bored. Most of the time he sits in that absurd Japanese room which he brought here from Shanghai, or goes off to see art-dealers. He seldom comes in to listen when I play my fiddle. So often I play his favorite pieces and wait, and then the bow falls from my hand and I have to throw up, and Yumei massages me or makes me laugh. Or I look at the pearls you gave me for the wedding, and put them on, and some of the glow of them passes into me. I never before had any genuine jewelry. You're so good, dearest Helene. Excuse my saying that to you again and again. I know you can't stand being thanked.

The pearls remind me: Knut was absolutely terrifying recently. We were invited to visit a Siamese princess, and after tea Her Highness showed us an old necklace with enormous gems in a fabulous gold setting. Lost in thought, I held the piece in my hand, taking pleasure in the glitter of it. Suddenly Knut came up to me, glared at me like a tiger of the jungle, and literally wrenched the necklace from my hands, whispering, "Give me the necklace instantly," as though I intended to steal it! And he smiled for the princess and the two Americans, but his face was all twisted. My eyes filled with tears. At home Knut was fearfully angry; he did not say a word and slept in the Japanese room. Instead of remaining in my room, proud as a statue, I went to him at eleven o'clock that night to apologize; for I suppose I was a little off balance at the princess's, while I was holding the necklace in my hands, and did not even know that I was still staring at the gems. Or something like that. I wanted to tell him during the night that I was expecting a baby. It's due in November. But Knut did not even open his door, although I told him it was something important and that he must not stay angry with me. Do you think that kind of him? Here in Bangkok there are a great many young girls, and with them he is as tender and charming as he was with me in Shanghai and on Hitra. But I am already twenty-one years old and a married woman, and I know enough about life to know that husbands exert their charm only for other women.

You must not think I care that Astrid never writes to us. She is a puffed-up brat anyhow, and I did not like her in Trondheim. But I think Knut is very upset at her silence. She has written him only one letter from her school in Lausanne, and he tore that to pieces at once, before I could read it. Isn't it ridiculous for Astrid to be angry that her father has married again? Perhaps she has something special against *me!* Though I cannot imagine why; she met me for the first time in Trondheim. It's all so strange. Knut refuses to tell me what she wrote in her letter. He always has secrets, and that torments me. Please do not write Knut about any of this nonsense, but I have to pour out my heart to you or I would simply burst with grief. Knut is right; I'm a bull in the international china-shop, and I'm bored when I have to primp and say, "How do you do?" when I don't care a bit how the puppets we meet everywhere are feeling.

Perhaps Knut is too old for me after all. Papa always said that a man should be at most five to seven years older than his wife. He himself was fifteen years older than poor Mama, who could never adjust and could only look charming (unlike me) and who led a "disorderly life," as Papa called it, and was a real artist. Sometimes I envy her because she's dead and at peace.

Couldn't you come to visit us? Knut is much nicer when you are around. When we talk about you, we completely agree. That is the only thing in the world we completely agree about.

Excuse the disorderly appearance of this letter. All the spots are from ink, perspiration, and tears; everything flows together. I hope you are not too disgusted.

Come to visit soon with sweet little Mailin. And give my regards to the Widow from Aalesund and your chicks and the funny shirkers and everybody who visits you and robs you of your time—as does your loving

Borghild

CONSUL WERGELAND TO HELENE WERGELAND (TRONDHEIM)

Bangkok, October 1926

Dear Helene,

Thank you for your long letter. I sent Borghild to Chiengmai in the mountains two months ago, with Yumei to look after her. It is cool there, and there is a first-rate American hospital where she will have the baby. She is very tired and unfortunately oversensitive, but I hope that the baby will bring her happiness and she will come to her senses somewhat. Please do not give me advice on how to treat my wife! I am treating her correctly; there is no need for you to worry. Naturally I did not know that she had so little adaptability. I suppose Yvonne had spoiled me. I must attend to everything my-

self when we have guests. If it were not for Yumei, we would have
no servants left. Borghild does not know how to handle them at all;
she is always getting angry or dismissing them. It is a real cross.

I am very worried about Astrid. It is scandalous that she does not
answer my letters at all. I have written to Father Laudin, who is the
children's spiritual director. He replied immediately, asking me to
have patience. I certainly have plenty of that; without patience I
would get nowhere at all with either Astrid or Borghild.

Kiss my little darling Mailin for me. I am happy that she is such a
joy to all of you. I too could use some of this joy. I miss you, old girl.

Love,

Knut

TELEGRAM FROM BANGKOK TO HELENE WERGELAND (TRONDHEIM),
NOVEMBER 1926

Your niece Vivica just arrived Chiengmai Hospital. Mother and
baby doing fine. Very happy. *Borghild. Knut.*

HELENE WERGELAND TO BORGHILD WERGELAND (BANGKOK)

Trondheim, December 1, 1928

Dear Borghild,

From your last letters I was happy to learn that Vivica is doing
well under Yumei's care, and that you have recovered from your
fever. Thank you for the photographs of yourself and the baby. You
look a little peaked, but I suppose that is from the fever. The baby
seems quite pretty. But take care that she doesn't grow up vain
among all the foreigners there. If Vivica takes after her little mother,
she'll know how to talk straight from the shoulder. Let's hope for
that.

Don't brood so much, my dear child; keep yourself occupied. And
don't keep writing me how hot it is in Siam. I know that by now.
But otherwise you must go on writing me about everything, as you
have done right along. Things will work out between you and Knut.
It would be better for you to show him your teeth occasionally. Too
much love and sweetness is not good for men.

It is very wrong of you to have given up your violin. Although I myself am not fond of music, I know what it means to you, my girl. Besides, you're good at it. Incidentally, I rather like your "Norwegian Peasant Dances."

Happily there is nothing new to report on ourselves. Mailin is receiving private lessons from a shirker who has since married his girl and has turned out quite decently. Mailin learns slowly but thoroughly. She still speaks a mixture of Chinese, Norwegian, and a little pidgin English she learned from Yumei. Give Yumei my regards. It is nice that she intends to marry your cook. Ask her what she would like me to give her for the wedding. Something practical, of course. Good that she will stay with all of you in Bangkok for the present. Vivica must be thoroughly accustomed to her by now. But it is pure nonsense that you could not stand it without Yumei, my child. One can stand anything, let me tell you that. Life is not always fun, but with a sense of order and good will it can be got through. Only we must not pity ourselves. At the moment I cannot visit you; at Christmas the house is always jammed with girls who first commit their follies and then come and cry on my shoulder. The snow here is up to the eaves. Our Mailin has become quite skillful at skiing. Everyone is fond of her. I don't intend to send her to you two in a hurry, though; a school-age child must not be sent from country to country as if by parcel post. It needs peace and an ordered life above all. And Mailin has that here with me. But that is my only reason, you silly girl! Don't imagine that I am unwilling to entrust Mailin to you. You know perfectly well what I think of you. I certainly do not intend to repeat it in every letter.

A good Christmas to all of you!

Helene

BARON AKIRO MATSUBARA TO VERA LESKAYA (SHANGHAI)

Paris, December 1928

Chère Mademoiselle,

Permit me to send you and your honored friends my most humble good wishes and greetings for your festival of lights. Holidays, after all, are throughout the world highly welcome opportunities for persons to remember their honorable friends and patrons with profound respect. As an unworthy testimony of my gratitude for your excellent instruction in French and in the ways of the West, I am taking the liberty of sending you an old Japanese fairy tale, a French edition of which I found here in Paris and have had bound in brocade for you. The "Tale of the Bamboo Cutter" is more than one thousand years old. Matsubara Akiro modestly hopes that his wretched gift will find approval in the honorable eyes of his esteemed teacher. May her stupid but diligent pupil also mention that the *Taketori Monogatari,* as the fairy tale is called in his language, has been praised by our great woman poet Murasaki Shikibu as the "father of all tales." In this poet's novels, which the world does not yet sufficiently appreciate, we observe as early as the eleventh century the glorious rise of a Japanese national literature and a concomitant liberation of a political and cultural nature from morally and politically decaying China. May my highly honored teacher forgive this digression, whose sole purpose is to prepare the teacher's mind for a Japanese fairy tale.

Paris is a pleasant place in which to learn; luckily I have met several friends from Tokyo here. That is very consoling in a foreign land.

Respectfully and in all humility yours,
Matsubara Akiro

P.S. In Shanghai, Matsubara Akiro called himself by another name; but he is so unimportant an insect that the worthy teacher would in any case have forgotten his worthless appearance.

M.A.

MADEMOISELLE M. DE BERNIÈRES (HEADMISTRESS OF A BOARDING SCHOOL IN LAUSANNE) TO HELENE WERGELAND (TRONDHEIM)

Lausanne, 1929
Chère Mademoiselle,

It gave me great pleasure to have the honor of meeting you and Astrid Thérèse's little half-sister in Lausanne. Father Laudin and our teachers are sincerely happy that Astrid, who has so many personality problems, has a maternal protector in you. Unfortunately the dear child's father is so far away and cannot keep properly in touch with her.

To our regret, little has changed in the past six months. Astrid continues to incline to haughtiness, excessive ambition, and cherishing of secrets. In all my long experience I have never before encountered so pronounced a character in an eleven-year-old girl; more-over, the dark and the light sides of her character are mingled to a degree I frankly call distressing. The arrogance Astrid displays can-not deceive an experienced teacher, or a spiritual director such as Père Laudin, as to the child's overwhelming unhappiness. Our prayers, and the Father's energetic intervention, have at last induced Astrid Thérèse to take a rational attitude toward her father and her young stepmother. Since, with your express agreement, I ad-vised Professor Clermont in Saigon that it would be best not to send her to him, Astrid has become even more withdrawn. My own sister is in the mission service in Indo-China. From her letters I know that neither the climate nor the conditions of life in Saigon could be help-ful to the development of this problem child of ours. Astrid ought to finish her education in Lausanne, as was planned. Then, to be sure, it will be up to her father to decide her future—and we are convinced, *chère Mademoiselle,* that you will advise Consul Wer-geland sagely.

May I take this opportunity to tell you that Astrid is passionately attached to you, although she shows her feelings so little. She has bitterly repented her unseemly and un-Christian behavior toward her sweet little half-sister. And she has done so not only in confes-sional but in deed. I am sending you under separate cover a batiste dress which one of our ladies cut out and which Astrid sewed with her own hand and embroidered with her own design. She has placed a card inscribed "For my sister Mailin" in the package.

To our regret, your niece still has not made any friends among our dear good girls. I am sorry to say that this is due solely to her own character. She cannot tolerate a relationship of friendship; she al-ways wishes to dominate. Recently there was a painful relationship between Astrid and a fellow pupil from Paris, which ended with lit-tle Marie-Béatrice's parents taking her home. Astrid terrorized the child so badly that Béatrice began having nightmares and could be calmed only with sedatives. Astrid bows only to authority and shows herself in a good light only when it seems worth while. Her sharp intelligence, her industry and energy will prove no blessing to her unless she becomes humbler. Fortunately she attends Holy Mass with sincere attentiveness and reverence. We hope, therefore, that divine grace and Astrid's own efforts will bring about a change.

It grieves me to inform you that the child has developed certain traits which needlessly complicate her relations with people. She is what schoolchildren call a "tattletale"; she tells us, her teachers, "secrets" about other pupils which are intended to lower our opinion of the girls. This greatly troubles us, all the more so because her motives are not apparent. She is first in her class and has no need to win credit at the expense of the others. It is our principle here not to be sparing of praise where praise encourages. With Astrid Thérèse, however, we must be extremely cautious in praising, since in this regard she is insatiable. No child under our roof is more in need of Christian instruction and good example than your niece.

If Astrid is to spend summer vacation in Trondheim, Père Laudin and I would be grateful if you were to give the child duties in connection with those unfortunate girls whom you have so generously been caring for in your own home and guiding back into life.

Rest assured, *chère Mademoiselle,* that our House, in prayer before the altar, commends you and your family to the special favor of Our Lord.

> *Cordially yours,*
> *Monique de Bernières*

CONSUL WERGELAND TO HELENE WERGELAND (TRONDHEIM)

> *Dalat (Indo-China), January 1930*

Dear Helene,

At the end of the month Captain Lillesand will be in Bangkok and will take Borghild back to Marseille. From there he will take her to a sanitarium near Paris. Her condition has become unbearable. Only through the kindness of a Swiss friend in Bangkok, in whose home Borghild stole a ring, has a scandal been averted. It would have cost me my career. The day after the theft I took Borghild here, to Dalat in the mountains. Yumei has remained in Bangkok with Vivica; the child must not see her mother in her present broken state. Vivica is uncommonly perceptive.

Borghild is no longer fighting against my arrangements. We will live separately henceforth. In my position I can scarcely afford a divorce, but naturally I cannot expose Vivica to the influence of so unstable a mother. Astrid, with her outrageous memory, never forgot a scene in Shanghai, and alluded to it in her first letter from Lausanne. Since she cannot be shut up in Lausanne for life, but will be coming to me some day, Borghild must go. It is impossible to bring the two of them together. I regret to say that Borghild must

bear the consequences of her actions. So must we all. She is a creature of chaos, and her art is a product of the abyss. I recognized this
too late. I must ask you in the future to spare me reproaches on
account of my conduct toward Borghild. You have not had to live
with her in a society of foreigners whose favorite sport is gossip and
backbiting. You have not had to live with her at all! I am not cruel,
as you think, but at forty and with my gall-bladder trouble, which
must also be charged to Borghild's account, I am no longer young
enough to respond to an adolescent love which lacks all stability,
dignity, and rationality.

Borghild is going to a sanitarium for nervous illnesses. I stress this
because otherwise you are sure to write me that I have "put her
away." She will enjoy freedom of movement to a certain degree, and
will be under discreet observation. During this period the doctors
will decide whether it will later be necessary to assign her to an
asylum. I hope not, and want to ask you to make the sanitarium
palatable to her. At least Borghild still listens to you, though to no
one else. At the moment she is sitting on the veranda and weeping
heartbreakingly. I am not inhuman, as you sweetly maintain. But
Borghild has carried things too far. I do not want ever to see her
again. If she recovers, she can resume her musical career. I hope she
will. Then she will also be able to lead a tramp's life, according to
her tastes.

Try to understand my decision and don't withdraw from me what
is left of your sisterly affection. I should be sorry if you were to take
a one-sided attitude toward this regrettable affair. You are the only
one I have left.

Always your
Knut

TELEGRAM FROM HELENE WERGELAND (TRONDHEIM) TO CONSUL
WERGELAND (DALAT)

Will pick Borghild up in Marseille and tend her back to health at
home. Objections useless. Am beside myself. *Helene.*

TELEGRAM FROM CONSUL WERGELAND (DALAT) TO HELENE WERGELAND
(TRONDHEIM)

Borghild killed in fall. In despair. *Knut.*

PROFESSOR ANTOINE CLERMONT (MEDICAL SUPERVISOR OF THE DISTRICT
OF SAIGON-CHOLON) TO HELENE WERGELAND (TRONDHEIM)

Saigon, January 1930

Ma chère Mademoiselle,

At the moment your brother Knut is in no condition to inform you
about the tragedy at Dalat. He is in bed with a severe case of inflammation of the gall bladder, at my private clinic in Saigon. Infec-
tion of the biliary duct was a constant danger since his bout of
typhoid in 1922. The continual agitation Knut has had since his second marriage unfortunately contributed to his susceptibility. I hope
that the inflammation will subside within a few days. Afterward a
furlough in Europe, a water-cure in Sculs-Tarasp, and a quiet life
with his family should put our friend back on his feet again. The
tragic death of his young wife, Mademoiselle, is a horrible business;
the life of those two in the Far East was a horror without end. My
ties with Knut were not limited to the memory of our dear Yvonne,
and I have been seeing him regularly in Bangkok. The couple,
along with Vivica, a dazzlingly beautiful child, were frequently at
my home in Saigon, and so I have been a witness to this marital
tragedy. Permit me to express my sincere condolences for the death
of this unfortunate young woman. A true artist, but a chaotic spirit,
who needed a great deal of love, has left this world before her time.
The Lord in His infinite mercy will forgive Madame Borghild her
act of desperation.

Since we, the living, must concern ourselves with the living, I beg
you, my dear Miss Wergeland, not to condemn your brother too
harshly. As any objective observer will tell you, he doubtless wished
to clarify in his own way an untenable private and professional situation. The prospect of losing simultaneously her husband and her
daughter made the young woman so distraught that in an unsuper-
vised moment she threw herself from the hotel balcony. She died in
Knut's arms.

At this time Knut needs your sisterly aid. We must remember his condition: troubled by gall-bladder attacks and by asthma, and temporarily in a state of emotional rigor. In these circumstances he certainly proceeded too harshly toward the young woman, whose shameful secret was scarcely a secret any longer. But, *ma chère Mademoiselle,* who are we to cast the first stone at Knut? I beg you to write to him at once. He asks about mail from you every two hours. Life is difficult for persons whose vitals are torn with reproaches that a little more love and understanding might have averted some terrible happening. I say expressly "might have." Providence goes its own ways. For that young woman had an intense inner longing for peace, the kind of peace that only the grave can give. Knut, moreover, was at his wits' end, and his health was rapidly declining. A disillusioned romantic is the harshest husband in the world. We Frenchmen love a woman with or because of her weaknesses; these weaknesses bring us closer together, until the miracle of intimacy arises—a very substantial miracle, Mademoiselle, and the wellspring of marital happiness.

During these past days I have pondered a great deal about Knut, who has always won women's hearts so effortlessly. In my niece Yvonne and in little Borghild he sought the typical dream of the romantic: the virginal wife, who is a creature of fable. Romanticism is a serious disease, Mademoiselle, and much harder to cure than a broken leg or an inflamed biliary duct. It has always been my humble opinion that the Church in its wisdom has fostered the veneration of Mary so that we unreasonable and unjust men should not seek on earth what exists only in Heaven. Your brother, Mademoiselle, was forever irrationally looking for a rose without thorns. But that blooms only in the mystic garden around the corner from Golgotha.

As a result of these sad events, I have decided to take my one-year European leave now, in order to accompany Knut to Marseille. He ought not to travel alone. I hope that I shall meet you, my grandniece Astrid, and charming little Mailin in Marseille. Details by cable as soon as our poor friend is capable of travel. Do not be alarmed by his appearance, *chère Mademoiselle!* For all that he is only forty, at the moment he looks like a broken man, spiritually and physically. His next post will be in Singapore, if he returns to the East within a year, as he intends. He hopes that you and his daughters will live there with him for a while. Establish for Knut the only kind of family life he seems to be made for. It means leaving your native land—but that must be.

With sincerest sympathy I am
Your friend and kinsman
Antoine Clermont

Miss Wergeland sat numb for a moment. Five years had passed since Knut and Borghild had left Trondheim, a radiant, loving pair. Once again she took up this letter from the strange world of the Far East, and in the twilight she painfully deciphered it word by word, like an old peasant woman. The Widow from Aalesund found her thus.

Laura Holgersen switched on the electic light and in her blind zeal knocked over a chair. "Am I intruding, Helene? Why are you sitting in the dark?"

Miss Wergeland sat immobile at the window. Laura stared open-mouthed at her, with a rather codlike expression. "Why, you're crying," she exclaimed compassionately and tactlessly. She stood stunned. No one had ever seen Miss Wergeland weeping.

"Let me be, Laura." Something alarmingly gentle in that vigorous voice checked Laura's prattle. She cast a troubled glance at the tall, motionless figure by the window and stole out of the room. Who could have written to Helene from Saigon? Well, she would find out somehow.

At last Helene Wergeland rose heavily from her armchair and stepped out onto the terrace where she had awaited her brother five years before after his vacation in the north. She saw Borghild before her eyes—terribly young, shy, helpless, infatuated, so innocent and so fundamentally honest that in spite of her draggling skirt hem Helene had taken her to her heart at once. And then the nocturnal scene with Astrid—Yvonne had called Borghild *une vagabonde.* And the wise and friendly letter of this unknown French doctor. Her heart contracted. Her boy Knut a broken man! And life went on—quickly, numbingly slowly, merrily and frightfully. There was never a moment of rest. One stood on a stage that turned continually, and one had to turn with it, willy-nilly. Anyone who jumped off was a shirker.

Miss Wergeland looked up at the clouds. They were drifting restlessly over the mountains and the fjord, coagulating into dark clots and suddenly scattering so far apart that a spot of light appeared on the horizon.

"Laura," Miss Wergeland called, picking up the chair that had been knocked over, "bring carpenter's glue and a paintbrush. You broke one of the chair legs."

"Oh, how terrible, Helene!"

"There are things more terrible," Miss Wergeland replied, and she began mending the chair leg. After a while she stood up. She was so pale that Laura asked whether she was ill and received the reply that Helene could not afford to be ill. Finally she informed Laura of what had happened. As she spoke, her face was utterly expressionless; Akiro Matsubara would have appreciated her bearing.

Late that evening Miss Wergeland asked her faithful companion whether she would like to go to the Far East with her and Mailin. Villa Wergeland would become a maternity home after all. Knut would never live in Norway again—he had said that often enough in his letters. And he needed his family more urgently than ever before.

Laura Holgersen stared at her cousin. She had been intensely unhappy five years ago when Miss Wergeland was planning to go to Bangkok. "B-but Helene," she stammered, "you know I get on your nerves. Do you really want me along?" Tears ran down her honest, foolish face.

"Don't ask such silly questions," Miss Wergeland said. "If I didn't want you along, I would not have asked you."

"How can I thank you?"

"What for? For the prospect of dirt, heat, and vexations? Come now, Laura, it is I who must thank you." Miss Wergeland stood up. "Put the chair back in its place," she said sternly. "The room looks a mess. Do you think you are already in the Far East?"

BOOK ONE

Songbirds on Dead Branches

THE FAR EASTERN REVOLVING STAGE, 1930—1941

The years Miss Wergeland spent with her family in Southeast Asia, until the outbreak of the Second World War in that part of the world, were years of internal revolution for the peoples of the Far East. The moral and political reorientation of these nations, which lacked a solid middle class, had begun after 1928, and developed as slowly as does everything in the Far East. The Europeans scarcely noticed the awakening of the Asians; their business flourished and the dancing girls smiled. Had they read fewer economic reports and more of the Chinese philosophers, they might have come across the admonition that "high position is accompanied by severe torments, since the person in high places thinks too much of himself and too little of the crowd at his feet." So, at least, the wise Lao Tzu (Lao-tse) maintained, that one-time archivist who learned such bitter lessons at the court of the Chou kings that he ever afterward avoided persons in high places and took up mysticism.

The businessmen, colonial officials, and plantation owners from the West in fact gave not a thought to the crowd at their feet. For almost two hundred years they had been the "white gods" and were treated accordingly in the Far East. This state of affairs, with which Miss Wergeland became acquainted only shortly before it ended, lasted precisely until December 7, 1941.

At seven thirty-five o'clock in the morning of that day Japanese bombers blazoned with the Rising Sun appeared above the rose-colored Royal Hawaiian Hotel, flew over the placid beach at Waikiki, and dropped their bombs upon the American fleet anchored in Pearl Harbor. That was the end of almost two hundred years of evolution; it was also the result of intensive preparation by Japan ever since the First World War.

The white gods in the Far East had been, during the last decade of their rule, the selfsame middle-class gods who had begun modestly in the fifteenth century with the spice trade and had risen in our times, with tin mines and rubber monopolies, to the summits of world commerce. From Singapore to Batavia they exuded a pleasant fragrance of whisky, Yardley's lavender soap, and success. In the year 1938, after all, some 54 per cent of the world's tin came from Southeast Asia, and more than 90 per cent of its rubber from Malaya and Indonesia. The coolies were willing and cheap. The dances and songs of the natives did not especially interest the middle-class gods. The Chinese bored them, and, in the years before Pearl Harbor, Chinese smuggling of rubber could not trouble them since they were scarcely aware of it. A Chinese smuggler is slightly more difficult to find than a needle in a haystack.

During the years from 1930 to 1941 the Far East was visited with increasing frequency by Western journalists, who found the shockingly low native standard of living picturesque and sent home glowing accounts of entrancing festivals in Singapore, Bangkok, and Saigon. The private palaces of their hosts, the magical gardens, and the number of white-clad "boys" so bedazzled the Western observers that they overlooked a crucial fact: how many of the indubitably excellent businessmen were intellectually limited and emotionally immature.

In addition to the correspondents and photographers, between 1930 and 1941 more and more women came from Europe and America to the Far East, to try their hands at being white goddesses. They were addressed, according to region, as "Missie," "Memsahib," "Mem," or "Madame." Lifted from the small towns and suburbs of their own continent, these ladies—who at home had scrubbed their own kitchen floors and shamefacedly turned collars on winter coats for the second time—became the very pinnacle of society. In British Singapore, Colombo, and Rangoon, in the little Paris of Saigon, in elegant, dreamy Dutch Batavia, and in cosmopolitan Bangkok and Shanghai, they lived like people of great wealth. Far, far below them was a class of whites whose existence they were to some extent unaware of: missionaries of all the Western churches and emigrants from all the Western dictatorships. The myth of white supremacy, combined with an excess of alcohol and servants, had turned the heads of the missies and mems. Not even the tropical heat suggested to them that they might be dancing on a volcano. The social life of the white gods in some ways resembled the ferment of amusement into which the French aristocrats had plunged before the Revolution of 1789. The differences were ones of climate and manners. Certainly the missies and mems before 1941 contributed their own small part to the ultimate awakening of Asia.

They could not help doing so many things wrong, for they had risen too swiftly from painstaking domestic souls to great ladies. In a similar way Baron Akiro Matsubara was transformed during those years far too quickly from a worthless aesthete to an esteemed member of the Kempetai, the Japanese military intelligence, whose sole interest henceforth was the Rising Sun. Surrounded by envious rivals, weaklings and spies in Korea, Manchuria, Paris, and London, Lieutenant Matsubara had sought strength and consolation in the state religion of Nippon. Shinto—that was the golden Imperial Chrysanthemum, which was not subject to the mutability of time. Since the Meiji Restoration of 1867, Shinto had gained steadily in intensity and in the decade before Pearl Harbor had acquired so brilliant a radiance that some rays of the sanctity of Nippon and of the imperial family fell upon Lieutenant Matsubara and all other young Japanese. One might live in concealment like a hooded *minomushi*-insect; still the radiance remained. But the price for it had to be paid. In order to counter the "debilitating influence of Western thinking," state Shintoism demanded strict obedience, fanatical adherence to Japanese customs, and contempt for death where the welfare of Nippon was at stake. The leading statesmen and generals of the new Japan sprang—like Lieutenant Matsubara's family on his mother's side—from the ancient knights of Japan, the *samurai*. They made use of the more or less liberal Japanese financial aristocracy because industrial barons like Akiro's father represented a salutary counterpoise to socialistic and communistic revolutionary movements, and because they could finance Nippon's holy campaigns of conquest in Southeast Asia.

Many of the Japanese agents who appeared all over Southeast Asia as modest tourists with Imperial Chrysanthemums in their buttonholes also belonged to the leading families of Nippon. They had the noiseless way of moving, the springlike inner tension, and the fantastic presence of mind of Japanese acrobats. Privately they were art-lovers; as such they were able after 1941—like Lieutenant Matsubara—to add effortlessly to their collections of Japanese and Chinese art some rare pieces of Annamite, Malayan, Javanese, and Siamese miniature work. Since they belonged to the *zaibatsu,* the few great families in whom power and wealth were concentrated, they always had plenty of money for pursuing their hobbies.

The army which was to effect the conquest of Southeast Asia consisted, by contrast, of thousands of peasants' sons—an army of the people, in which the best soldiers could rise into the officer corps. Distressed tenant farmers in particular believed fervently in the propaganda which promised that in the army their families could rise to share in the glory of holy Nippon. Supported by these willing masses, the greatest police state of the Far East thought itself safe in beginning a war of conquest. Between 1930 and 1941 the tourists had gathered sufficient information on the white gods and the Chinese so that Pearl Harbor proved a brilliant initial success. They were convinced that it would inevitably be followed by further triumphs.

On July 7, 1937, Japan launched at Marco Polo Bridge in Peiping —formerly Peking—a grand dress rehearsal. It was tactfully referred to by the reporters and historians of various nations as the "conflict" between Japan and China. If, as the Oxford Dictionary maintains, a conflict means a "test of strength," this clash was no conflict. The comparative strengths of unified Japan and of a China torn between Chiang Kai-shek and Mao Tse-tung were too uneven. Moreover, a feudalistic Japan of military castes, intoxicated by the lust for conquest, was clashing with a China of bankers and political orators. But on that day of the visible outbreak of war between China and Japan, a Chinese united front against the Japanese aggressors began to grow, with Chiang Kai-shek as national leader. The Chinese dragon was tougher than Nippon had imagined.

The Chinese in Shanghai drew all sorts of conclusions from the clash in Peiping. Mr. Hsin, the grandfather whom Mailin Wergeland did not yet know, looked even more withered, more melancholy, and more sly than usual on the day after the clash at Marco Polo Bridge. He left behind his birds in the old-fashioned garden back of Bubbling Well Road and for once attended a conference in the rooms of others. Along with other leading bankers, industrialists, and newspaper men, he decided upon something that the Japanese consul-general in Shanghai later called an illegal militarization of the city. It was an emergency measure of self-help against Japanese aggression. Long before the "conflict," the far-sighted Crane had proposed to the British Foreign Office, through its representative in Shanghai, the creation of an internationally protected neutral zone around the city—a bastion to shelter bankers, songbirds, white gods and goddesses, and the many sensible Japanese businessmen of the city of Shanghai, who regarded bombs and tourists with profound distrust. For we must not assume that during this decade the Japanese were all heroes and tourists armed with cameras and notebooks. There were then, as there are still, large numbers of humble, hard-working shopkeepers and their clerks, who had nothing to say, lived and loved undramatically, and occasionally died under the hail of bombs that fell upon whole families of Japanese who did not want to conquer or occupy anything. Of such a family, for example, was the "tourist from Urakami" who until 1941 helped to prepare Southeast Asia for the joy of Japanese occupation. He did so against the will of his honorable family, who wanted to earn and consume their rice in peace.

Unfortunately the British Foreign Office did not respond to the proposals made by Mr. Hsin and his liaison men in Shanghai and London. Although Shanghai was, by virtue of its industrial and commercial activity, a vital base for America and Europe, the British thought defensive measures against the Japanese inflammatory or premature.

During the years before the clash at Marco Polo Bridge, whenever Mr. Hsin met the friendly English gentlemen at the Shanghai race track, he asked himself when the white gods would be harvesting the fruits of their China policy. During that decade Mr. Hsin was in the habit of telling his songbirds—since he had neither son nor daughter to listen to him—that foresight is a deep pond which never dries out. He did not even know of the existence of his granddaughter Mailin. Nor did he remember that in 1925 he had eaten a protracted dinner in the Shanghai home of her father and listened to the horrible music produced by an unkempt girl. Of Consul Wergeland's reception he recalled only that he had met a young Japanese and secretly rejoiced because Matsubara Akiro had been mortally insulted by the foolish, good-natured remarks of an American businessman.

On July 7, 1937, while Mr. Hsin in Shanghai was pondering the mysteries of suffering, and while the Sino-Japanese war flared into its acute stage at Marco Polo Bridge, Consul Wergeland sat with his favorite daughter, Mailin, in a spacious tropical house in Bangkok, regarding with his tired, glistening eyes a Japanese scroll which until 1930 had hung in Trondheim and during the last six years had adorned the wall of his tea room in Singapore and Bangkok. From the stairwell Miss Wergeland's voice broke into his solitude. With her usual doggedness, Miss Wergeland was trying to put the house in order in preparation for Astrid's arrival in the Far East. She was receiving no support at all, since Yumei was at this time having her third baby. Although Astrid planned to stay with them only three months, and then return to Paris, Miss Wergeland wanted the house to look as clean as the marketplace in Trondheim.

Consul Wergeland smiled forbearingly as he listened to Helene's imperative voice—although ordinarily he could not bear loud voices. Mailin sat at his feet. The jade bell around her neck gave a soft ghostly sound, as it had done in Shanghai in 1925 when he first brought his little songbird home. He had since adopted the curious habit of placing his arm around Mailin's shoulders with great firmness, as if he feared that someone was trying to take her away from him.

Sitting so, on July 7, 1937, he contemplated his Japanese scroll, "Songbird on a Dead Branch," by a pupil of the great Miyamoto Musashi. The little bird, which somehow reminded him of Borghild, sat still upon a long, thin branch that seemed on the verge of breaking at any moment.

Such was the position of the white gods in the Far East midway in the year 1937.

1: Consul Wergeland's Daughters

During the seven years she had spent in the land of smiles, Miss Helene Wergeland had smiled remarkably little. In the first place, she was of the opinion that life was no picnic. In the second place, her keen eyes penetrated so deep behind the shimmering curtains of the Far East that she discovered more reasons to weep than to smile. Hunger, dirt, and fatalistic submission existed so openly and visibly in picturesque marketplaces and charming huts on piles everywhere east of Suez, that Miss Wergeland could only wonder at how little the white gods noticed. And the longer she lived in the Far East, the more hopeless she saw her efforts to transplant order and cleanliness to places where neither was missed. Even Yumei, dear, cooperative Yumei, whom she had trained personally in Trondheim, once back in her own milieu had fallen back into that good-natured slovenliness which Miss Wergeland detested as thoroughly as she did scenes, surprises, and shirkers. As far as housework went, there seemed to be nothing but shirkers in Southeast Asia. With compressed lips Miss Wergeland pondered whether Malays or Siamese deserved the palm for laziness. Even after seven years she still believed that cheerful singing early in the morning is no substitute for careful dusting.

On the day Astrid was to arrive, Helene sat at noon, when all other Europeans rested, in her roofed orchid pavilion, doing her daily stint of painting. At all other times the child, Vivica, never gave her a moment's peace. Miss Wergeland sighed. Astrid had always had an outrageous memory and a hungry look; Vivica, on the other hand, was obsessed with an insatiable curiosity. And not only that; the lovely child with silver-blond hair and greenish eyes displayed an unstable temperament which filled Miss Wergeland with gloomy premonitions. It was not going to be easy to raise Vivica properly. At the thought, Miss Wergeland compressed her lips still more tightly and mixed an angry chrome green on her palette. Vivica had not a trace of Borghild's lovable sincerity. She had inherited only her disorderliness. What bothered Helene most of all was that one had no idea what the child was thinking when she spent hours regarding her father's collection of *objets d'art*. For Helene those scrolls and pieces of porcelain and jade were among the most unpleasant of the surprises the Far East had visited upon her. The previous year his gall-bladder trouble had forced Knut to resign from the consular service. Since then he had gone into partnership with a Dutch friend in the firm of Sun (Bangkok, Singapore, Shanghai). He was one among many Europeans who regarded the Far East as a permanent paradise. He had bought the house on Sathorn Road with the assistance of a Siamese friend.

When her brother informed her of his plans Miss Wergeland had remained silent for a while and at last observed that she did not intend to live in these disorderly countries forever and a day. Knut had said he certainly did not want to keep her in Asia if she did not feel comfortable there. It was agreed that in three years she should take Vivica to Trondheim and send her to school there. At the moment the child was attending St. Joseph's Convent School at the corner of Sathorn Road. Vivica learned quickly and forgot even more quickly. Sometimes, in the midst of lessons or in Helene's painting pavilion, she burst into tears and declared that she was horribly bored. The first time Helene heard this she gave Vivica a slap. A regular tempest followed. Next night the child opened all the shutters in the house, and the two doors to the nursery as well. She never said why. Ever since then Vivica had been sleeping with open doors, under Yumei's supervision. Her father had ordered this—he never refused Vivica anything because she aroused in him guilt feelings which he had not overcome since Borghild's death. However, he kept his chests in the Japanese tea room securely locked. What if Vivica should . . . They must not lead Borghild's daughter into temptation.

When Helene had proposed to him that she take the child to Olaf in Trondheim, Knut had made a scene—he must have learned that from Yvonne. Miss Wergeland had been so astonished that she became speechless. Thereafter she had sat all day long in her pavilion, without painting, and resolved to be gentle and sweet with Knut and Vivica. He was indeed a broken man, although he did not look it in any way. Women still pursued him, but the difference was that now he ran away from them without their remarking it. But he was still all Miss Wergeland possessed in this world.

Helene lowered her palette and regarded her still life with a satisfaction which was the due of a better work of art. Her orchids and bougainvillaeas had little of the exotic beauty of the originals. They looked rather like daisies in warpaint. Unconsciously Helene Wergeland robbed the tropical products of her new environment of all their strange magic and transformed them into symbols of inconspicuousness. She was trying to achieve something similar with Vivica—without any visible result.

Consul Wergeland never commented on his sister's artistic productions—he hated arguments just as much as he had in the past, when Yvonne had insisted on having her discussions with him. In any case, he traveled a great deal. He attended auctions and, amid the sweepings of others' lives, between Singapore and Batavia discovered with a sure instinct the best among really good things and among clever imitations. He had a penetrating eye for true beauty, as did his sister for human worth among sweepings. For that reason she was out of place in the Far East, where everything is exhibited plainly in show windows. Nevertheless, she put up with it, because Mailin would never again return to Norway. Mailin had never said that in so many words, for she offended no one if she could help it—least of all her Aunt Helene, whom she loved and admired with deep-felt reticence.

But Mailin had returned to the Far East like a small fish to its proper element. Here she breathed the air that suited her. Every Chinese was kin to her. Starting with Yumei and her family, she loved every Chinese baby and every beggar in the overcrowded Bangkok market. This love for her own kind was as wordless, profound, and sober as Chinese love is in all of life's situations—a product of nature, elemental, indestructible, and cloudlessly gay. Mailin was the only gay creature in the Wergeland family. Neither Knut nor Helene could conceive of life without her.

Mailin was sixteen years old now. Two years ago she should have gone to a lawyer in Shanghai to receive the letter left for her by her mother, Lily Lee. But Knut Wergeland had burned her mother's last letter and as yet had said nothing to his daughter. He could not bring himself to do so. Not even Helene knew of this sin of omission. From year to year he postponed enlightening her. It would be early enough when Mailin was twenty-one, he told himself. Then she would have reached her majority and could decide for herself whether she wanted to return to her mother's family. In a man's way, Knut Wergeland preferred postponing unpleasant matters. Consequently he was altogether unprepared when the bomb burst.

It burst three hours before Astrid's arrival, on July 7, 1937. Mr. Chang, the lawyer and notary in Shanghai, had, after protracted investigation, learned of Knut Wergeland's present whereabouts and written to Bangkok a flowery letter with highly direct injunctions. In it he asked Miss Mailin Wergeland, daughter of his client, Lily Lee, to visit him shortly in Shanghai, since he had important matters to communicate to her in regard to her mother's will.

Knut Wergeland sat alone in his Japanese room, staring at the letter. At the moment Mailin was decorating Astrid's room with tropical flowers. Helene was still in her pavilion, working now on a painting of a Siamese temple—it looked like a Trondheim frame house with unsuitable ornamentation. So the time had come. There was no point in pondering the riddle of the suffering that hovered in the rain-filled air. The rainy season was always a difficult time for Knut and Helene. The summer monsoons brought melancholy thoughts, fevers, and undesirable letters.

Knut Wergeland found his sister sitting idly before her easel and informed her that in August he was going to a Shanghai auction and would take Mailin with him.

"Why should she go there?" Miss Wergeland asked in a tone of merely moderate opposition, but in too loud a voice. She looked so keenly at her brother that he nervously turned away from her. Then he informed her, with averted face, what reason Mailin had to go to Shanghai. For a long while Miss Wergeland said not a word. Finally she observed that she thought it altogether right for Mailin to make the acquaintance of her mother's relatives and that no pleasure lasted forever, as they all knew perfectly well. She would take Vivica to Trondheim sooner if Mailin— She fell silent again.

"Do you think that Mailin will—leave us?" Knut asked hoarsely.

"Nonsense," Miss Wergeland said amiably. "She belongs to us and knows it. Why are you glaring at me like that? Mailin is so reasonable, after all."

"This has nothing to do with reason, Helene."

"Do you think so?" Miss Wergeland commented sarcastically. "As far as I know, the Chinese base their decisions solely upon reason. At least so you've always told me."

"Mailin is no Chinese."

"Don't fool yourself!" Miss Wergeland heard herself saying, to her own surprise. She had maintained otherwise for all of Mailin's life. And now she had suddenly expressed what she had always known. It must be the shock. She ran her big hand over her moist face.

"I must take a shower," she murmured. "This heat! And Yumei in labor!"

"Helene," the consul said without looking up, "I simply could not bear it if Mailin were to remain in Shanghai."

"The rest of us are still here," Helene said dryly. Nothing in her expression showed that Knut had offended her. He offended everyone who loved him. In these years with him, Helene had asked Yvonne's forgiveness for many harsh thoughts about her—to say nothing of Borghild. Knut was far more careful with his Chinese and Japanese porcelain than with the hearts of those closest to him.

"Yes—*you* are still here," Knut said. And this one word, that carelessly spoken *you*, changed the whole aspect of the world for Helene

Wergeland. She coughed out of sheer happiness and said that Knut ought to take his pills. No scoundrelly Chinese lawyer was worth a gall-bladder attack.

"I wonder whether Astrid will eat fish in sweet-and-sour sauce," she said as she went out. "As a child she was always very choosy about food, though I did my best to wean her away from her finickiness."

"Well, she's nineteen by now and may have good manners," the consul consoled her with an ironic look.

In this case he was to prove a good prophet. Astrid had wonderful manners—such wonderful manners that she almost drove Helene mad.

Astrid stood straight and tall at the railing of the coastal steamer that was taking her from Saigon to Bangkok. She had spent a week in Saigon with her great-uncle, Antoine Clermont, before continuing on to her Norwegian family in Bangkok. The little Paris of Indo-China had happily bridged the contrast between the city on the Seine and Bangkok. Astrid stood looking straight ahead. Between her rather too close, pale blue eyes a little nervous fold twitched. She felt little eagerness at the prospect of seeing her Aunt Helene and her odd half-sisters again. Since leaving school she had become thoroughly accustomed to life with the Clermonts in Paris and was preparing herself to be a fashion designer. In this work the exquisite taste she had inherited from her mother would be a help to her. Her way in life was fully determined in her own mind. Astrid demanded rigid programs of herself and others. She had imagination only in matters of fashion; in all other affairs of life she depended on her sharp intelligence and her self-control. She had become a very independent spirit who brooked contradiction no better than her Aunt Helene.

Quite a dame, thought the young man beside her, regarding with interest Astrid's profile, her haughtily arched eyebrows, expertly painted lips, and chic, extremely slim figure. There was not a girl like her in all Berlin. Ernst August von Zabelsdorf had seen Astrid at the office of the Société des Affreteurs Indo-Chinois, where they were both arranging their passage to Bangkok, and had not let her out of sight since. He intended to visit a friend in Bangkok and then sail on to Shanghai, where he held one of the more important positions in the Deutsch-Asiatische Bank. During the voyage from Saigon to Bangkok he had sat at table in the dining room with Astrid and industriously made conversation; she had participated only with a frosty smile and monosyllabic replies. But Herr von Zabelsdorf was a Berliner. This meant that he could chat pleasantly with a block of ice. His tongue never failed him in any situation, nor his presence of mind and incisive wit. And so he stood beside Astrid at the rail, in the best of humors, and remarked that tropical sunsets were not at all so banal as one might expect. His French was flawless.

Astrid discreetly studied the towering, loquacious man with the face of a thoroughbred horse. In spite of his youth, his hair was thinning slightly. He had lively, sharp eyes which looked out into the world ironically and with extreme acuteness. Between his lips dangled a cigarette, as always. They were rather mocking but sensitive lips. Ernst, Baron von Zabelsdorf, was altogether a far cry from Astrid's picture of "the Germans." She wondered whether he said *"Heil Hitler"* when he met fellow countrymen in the Far East. But what did that matter to her? She had her own worries.

Herr von Zabelsdorf had his own worries too, but at the moment they were in abeyance, in Shanghai.

The glow of the setting sun lent a rosy tint to Astrid's transparently pale face. For a moment she looked like a statue with a soul. But the gentleman from Potsdam had raised his binoculars to his eyes and was sweeping the Bangkok pier. His friend should be there to meet him.

The small coastal steamer wound its way sluggishly through the oily waters among the sampans, canoes, and ocean liners waiting in the rain—rain that brought no cooling breeze but only a kind of damp fire. River sailors in pointed bamboo hats stood like bronze manikins in their narrow sampans. Gigantic trees and bizarre temple roofs thrust into the blood-red sky.

"There are my people," Astrid murmured, lowering her binoculars with a curiously exhausted gesture. In a toneless voice she bade good-by to Herr von Zabelsdorf, who was nonchalantly waving his silk handkerchief to a man on the pier. Then he wished Astrid a pleasant time in Bangkok and earned a last frosty smile.

Five minutes later Herr von Zabelsdorf's long cavalryman's hands

were shaken heartily. "*Grüss Gott,* Bibi," his friend exclaimed in unmistakably Austrian German. "Say, how long is it since we've seen
each other?"

"Don't try to figure it out; it'll give you gray hair."

Baron von Werner glanced at Astrid with a faint smile; holding
her father's arm, she had just nodded slightly at Herr von Zabelsdorf.
The gentleman from Potsdam had been extremely helpful, after all
—though Astrid had not the slightest notion where Potsdam was.

"Who in the world is that?" Konstantin von Werner asked inquisi-
tively. "She's a snappy number."

"That is *La Muette de Portici,*" Herr von Zabelsdorf replied, tossing his cold cigarette into the darkening river. "Every word from her
costs a pound note. I've gone broke on this trip."

"So you are my sister Mailin," Astrid said, staring unabashedly at
Consul Wergeland's favorite daughter.

Helene Wergeland said loudly, "Come, children! Dinner is waiting
at home, and Vivica will go out of her mind if she has to wait any
longer for Astrid."

"Does she go out of her mind so easily?" Astrid inquired.

"I was only joking," Miss Wergeland said irritably. She herself did
not know what it was about Astrid she disliked. The girl was extremely polite—though Helene did not care much for politeness—and
spoke good Norwegian, though with a slight French accent. All these
years Astrid had studied Norwegian faithfully. There was really
nothing Helene could reproach her for. Probably the tall, distinguished girl with cool blue eyes found it just as hard now to win
friends as she had during her childhood. Did she still desire so intensely to be the "best loved" everywhere? It was impossible to tell
from her face. Miss Wergeland turned with a shrug toward Mailin.

Mailin gazed into Astrid's eyes with a tranquil smile and offered
to carry her raincoat and hat. The beautifully fashioned bouquet she
had brought for the occasion Astrid had left on the pier. A person
doesn't have seven hands and eight feet, Mailin thought forbearingly
and dismissed Astrid's unfriendly act forever from her memory. Big
Sister looked exhausted.

She is beautiful, Astrid thought in astonishment, and so sane. This slender, delicate creature with the wise almond eyes, the somewhat too small nose, and the strong, joyously sensuous lips, radiated a smiling serenity that was not without its effect upon Astrid. Mailin's ivory features were slightly and artfully made up. She was full of life, but also full of tranquillity—a person one had to trust. Mailin was a very solid songbird.

"I'm so sorry that I forgot your flowers," Astrid said almost shyly and earned a first friendly glance from Miss Wergeland.

On the big veranda stood a child in a pink dress with tropical flowers in her silvery-blond hair. Vivica had studied herself in front of the mirror for hours in order to achieve the proper effect. Her dress was torn in one place, but she had concealed the rent with a blossom —quite a trick for an eleven-year-old.

The tramp's daughter, Astrid thought; she had instantly sighted the rent under the blossom. Life was not easy for her, with her gift of observation and her outrageous memory. For years she had not thought about the *vagabonde* who had stolen from her the father she worshiped. But Vivica's costume at once revived the recollection.

The child devoured Astrid with her green, mysterious eyes. Vivica had been burningly curious about her big sister and had looked forward to her coming with great eagerness. She was sure she would never be bored again, once her big sister, who had seen so many cities and people, arrived. But Astrid's cool look and her erect, elegant figure in its impeccably tailored suit sobered her. Disappointed, Vivica was unpredictable. Suddenly she burst out into loud laughter.

Miss Wergeland frowned. Vivica ought to outgrow such nonsense. Astrid regarded the pretty, moody child with studied composure. "Why are you laughing, Vivica?" she asked evenly.

"I don't know," the child murmured. Her upper lip, a rosy, boldly arched line, quivered with a kind of delicate vexation. She threw herself passionately into Helene's arms. "Astrid is horrid, but she has a pretty hat," she whispered into Helene's ear, between laughter and tears.

"Come to bed, child!" Helene spoke with amazing gentleness. She carried the *vagabonde*'s daughter into the house like a baby.

Helene turned very pale as she undressed Vivica and found herself staring at a certain piece of jewelry. It was Mailin's jade bell, with the ancient inscription, *Haste is error*. She resolved to do nothing in haste.

"Why did you put on the jade bell, Vivie?" she asked quietly. "And why did you have it under your dress?"

"Mailin gave it to me," the child murmured sleepily with averted gaze. "But it didn't go with my flowers, so I hid it."

Miss Wergeland could feel in her bones that Vivica was lying. This was the first time she had stolen anything.

"Give it back to Mailin. I don't like the jade bell," Vivica said, closing her eyes. The delicate vexation now lay like a shadow over her charming little face.

"Sleep, child." An abyss had opened up. As Helene deposited the jade bell back in Mailin's black lacquer box with its golden Chinese dragon, she reflected that life steadily became more complicated instead of clearer and simpler. The thought of her corner room in Trondheim with its view of the fjord and drifting clouds gave her an almost physical pain. Did not the branches of a tree necessarily wither when the trunk was sawed down? And now, to make matters worse, Astrid with her critical looks and her politeness and her memory would be spending three months in the house. Miss Wergeland scolded herself. She was ashamed to realize that she now disliked her eldest niece more than she had in those distant days when the girl begged for love and appreciation. Astrid had changed a great deal.

Helene returned to the veranda, where her brother was showing his daughters Chinese porcelains. Astrid was holding a bowl in her long, slender hands. It was porcelain of the "Rose Family," from the Ch'ien-Lung period, around 1785. The center of the big round bowl showed in delicate colors the star-myth of the shepherd and the weaver girl. The consul was explaining that the festival of this legendary pair of lovers took place at the beginning of autumn, in the "Month of the Hungry Spirits." He was in the midst of the romantic love story when Miss Wergeland joined the group. Astrid was eagerly studying the colors of the garment which floated like a rainbow around the form of the heavenly weaver. Those colors would be just the thing for a Paris spring ensemble, she was thinking, and made a note in her gold-bordered notebook, a gift from Great-Uncle Antoine.

The love story, which aroused in Mailin a gentle sadness every time she heard it, had not made the slightest impression on Astrid.

"What would the bowl bring at an auction?" she asked her father.

"There's no question of selling it," Knut Wergeland replied, slightly put out. "Incidentally, I am going to a big art auction in Shanghai next month. How would you like to accompany me, my young ladies?" He did not look at Mailin.

"May I speak to you for a moment, Mailin?" Miss Wergeland asked. She was still pale from the shock, but very composed. She must clarify this matter at once and advise Mailin to lock her jewel box if necessary.

"I wanted to go to Shanghai in any case," Astrid remarked. She did not say why, and her father did not ask. In this family every word cost a pound note, after all—as Astrid's traveling companion from Saigon had rightly observed.

At this moment Ernst August von Zabelsdorf sat with his Viennese friend on the veranda of a house separated by only a few other houses from the Wergeland home. If you went up to the second-floor balcony, you could watch the Norwegians eating. Not that Herr von Werner would ever watch anyone at eating or at prayer. A Viennese would never do that.

"I'm expecting company," he said, slapping two mosquitoes at once. "They all want to say hello to you, Bibi!"

"Who is all?" Herr von Zabelsdorf had a penchant for precise information.

"Well, if you must know: my friend Joseph Bopfinger, from Munich; and then Dr. Engel of the Bayer Works. He is bringing a Japanese with him."

"All we need is an Italian to round out the Anti-Comintern Pact."

"The Japanese is shy as they come, Bibi. You'll scare him to death if you talk so fast and laugh in addition."

"I'm awfully shy myself," Herr von Zabelsdorf said, and he stood up to greet Dr. Engel of the Bayer Dye Works at Leverkusen, and the Japanese guest.

"May I introduce Baron Matsubara from Tokyo," Dr. Engel said in accented English. Akiro Matsubara took an unobtrusive look at Herr von Zabelsdorf. Wasn't this one of the prominent men in the

Deutsch-Asiatische Bank at Shanghai? He would find out for certain. Probably an important contact.

"Haven't we met before in Shanghai, Baron?" Herr von Zabelsdorf asked the Japanese. "In some bar or somewhere?"

"I am so terribly sorry, sir. I have been in Shanghai only a few days, as a tourist."

Dr. Joseph Bopfinger, commercial attaché at the German Embassy in Bangkok, came late as always, and as always he was quite out of breath. Dr. Engel greeted him with *"Heil Hitler."* The Bavarian murmured a cross *"Grüss Gott."* He wore dark-tinted glasses; the fierce tropical sun had affected his eyes.

The five men conversed in English—Baron Matsubara regretted immeasurably to say that he did not know German. In outward appearance they presented the greatest possible contrast: the Viennese aristocrat, smooth, frivolous, utterly charming, and caring not a shred for the German policies which would soon make possible for him a comfortable life in fantastic surroundings as a legation councilor; the hulking, worldly-wise Berliner, who had startled his family of army officers by going into banking; the plump, musical commercial attaché from Munich, a visionary with a bent for arithmetic, a Bavarian-baroque personality, who carried with him, in addition to his considerable weight, a heritage of dreams and healthy realism; Dr. Walter Engel, tall, ambitious, and member of the National Socialist party, whose motto was "On to immortality with Bayer-Leverkusen"; and in the midst of them Baron Matsubara in his tropical suit, a respected member of Japanese military intelligence.

What did these Germans want in the Far East? Akiro was asking himself. To reconquer lost territories? Or only to sell chemicals and machines? Lieutenant Matsubara had received from Dr. Engel a number of Bayer products by way of advertisements for Tokyo. He had already had them analyzed; they could easily be imitated and put up in cheap packages with the same labels, in case Japan should conquer Eastern Asia during the next few years and should wish to cut off European imports. In wartime imitations always won out. Lieutenant Matsubara had sent the products to the proper place in Tokyo, with the proper instructions.

Dr. Engel had also inspected chemical factories in Tokyo, and he now suddenly exclaimed in German over the ridiculous crudity of the equipment, the slowness of the workers, and the poor quality of the goods. The Japanese could learn a good deal from the Bayer plant any day they cared to, he commented.

Zabelsdorf threw a look askance at the Japanese guest. "Look here," he whispered to Engel, "take a deep breath and shut your trap. Our friend here—"

"Doesn't understand a word of German," Engel reassured him.

At that moment the Japanese rose from his distant corner and expressed his overwhelming regret that he must now leave his honored friends from Germany. He bowed low and solemnly to all present, keeping his arms pressed against his body. His eyes avoided those of his honored German friends. And at that moment it came to Herr von Zabelsdorf in a flash where he had seen Baron Matsubara in Shanghai—not in any bar, but with Anna Weber, his own Annie, who gave German lessons to Japanese. Hm. Engel sure has put his foot in it, Herr von Zabelsdorf thought. He said not a word about his discovery, but he looked after the departing Japanese and remarked that shy Baron Matsubara was in his opinion a slick article. His comment was received with uproarious laughter. Dr. Engel laughed loudest. He knew the type and he knew Baron Matsubara like the inside of his own pocket, he blustered, and raised his glass.

Herr von Zabelsdorf excused himself; he had been on his feet all day and needed his beauty sleep, he said. His Viennese host showed him to the balcony room with the big mosquito net and the small prints of Old Vienna on the white plaster walls, which were otherwise adorned only by water stains.

"What's the matter, Bibi?" Herr von Werner asked. "A fly fall into your soup?"

"Nothing's the matter." Herr von Zabelsdorf stepped out onto the balcony. "But one of these days you'll blab your heads from your shoulders with these Japanese, my boy."

"What's that?"

"Listen, if you can still get something through your thick head. . . ."

Von Werner was appalled by his friend's revelation. "B-but Baron Matsubara expressly said he did not understand German," he stammered. "I'd better go right down and talk to Dr. Engel—"

A long arm pulled him back by the sleeve. "Take it easy. Tell me this. What the devil do you people learn in your diplomatic kinder-garten?"

The Viennese laughed in lieu of reply. "Can you lend me a hundred ticals?" he asked.

"Out of the question. Money deals spoil a friendship."

"On the contrary, Bibi! I assure you—"

"You still owe me twenty marks from the races in Auteuil. I have witnesses. Well, well!" Zabelsdorf exclaimed, gazing at a veranda where people were still dining at this late hour. "Why, there is—"

"Who?" Baron von Werner asked.

"*La Muette de Portici,*" Herr von Zabelsdorf said. "What a world! From Saigon to Bangkok she hardly said three words, and now she's talking like a phonograph record." He lowered his binoculars.

"Since when have you gone in for watching women from a distance?" his Viennese friend inquired.

"G'night, Maxie," Herr von Zabelsdorf said.

"How's your Shanghai Annie?"

"If you mean Fräulein Anna Weber, she is well."

On the veranda below, Werner's guests sat talking about the mineral resources of Southeast Asia: tin, petroleum, manganese, copper, and tungsten. These were blessed lands, certainly, but others held the sources of wealth: the British in Malaya, the French in Indo-China, and the Dutch in the Dutch East Indies.

"The next ones to control these resources will be the Japs," Dr. Bopfinger prophesied.

"That would be fine. We are allies, after all!"

"You know a great deal about chemistry, my dear Engel, but less about politics than our host." Dr. Bopfinger sat down at the piano to "take a breather," as he phrased it. He had spent four years in Japan and knew the economic situation only too well. Japan needed a war —too many people and too few raw materials, the old story, like Germany since the World War. Japan was producing only forty-three million tons of coal and about seven million tons of steel, and even at that had to import ore from Korea and Manchuria.

"The war began today," Bopfinger said to Dr. Engel.

"Which war?"

"For the present, war between Japan and China—at the Marco Polo Bridge at Peiping."

"We can't afford one yet," Dr. Engel remarked. He closed his eyes and exposed himself to the base seductiveness of the music. It was Beethoven, the favorite composer of Lieutenant Matsubara, who understood German music. He also understood the language of the Germans, but not their thoughts. Until late that night Akiro sat on his hotel balcony, writing a report, to which he added a number of documents headed by a great many names.

Next morning a young Japanese called on Lieutenant Matsubara. He delivered a sealed package which Matsubara was to hand personally to Captain Saito—or, to put it more discreetly, to the "tourist from Urakami," who was at the moment touring Indo-China. Urakami, on the lovely Urakami River, was the highly industrialized suburb of the city of Nagasaki, near the peninsula of Hisen, which juts so surprisingly from the island of Kyushu.

That same day Lieutenant Matsubara set out for Shanghai in order to perfect his knowledge of German under the tutelage of Fräulein Anna Weber.

2: *The Tourist from Urakami*

Two or three weeks after Astrid's arrival Miss Wergeland sat on her private veranda in Sathorn Road, writing a letter to the Widow from Aalesund. To be sure, Laura Holgersen was no longer a widow. Two years ago she had married a Danish forester who worked as an employee of the East Asiatic Company (headquarters in Tokyo) in the teakwood concessions in Northern Siam. Miss Wergeland was not at all pleased that Laura had hied herself off to the jungle, but she was accustomed to having members of her family make surprising marriages and then weep on her shoulder.

That rainy morning Helene had been reading Laura's last letter with furrowed brow. At her feet sat Yumei with the new baby son and her two other children, doing nothing. Miss Wergeland had the mistaken notion that Yumei must recover after her confinement. Smilingly Yumei obeyed this whim, and for the present was embroidering napkins for Missie Laura Nielsen. Laura was living in Pré while her husband spent the greater part of the year in the jungle with elephants and coolies. Wiping the perspiration from her fountain pen, Miss Wergeland wrote:

Dear Laura,

Many thanks for your letter of last month. I cannot understand why you bewail your fate all the time. If you are afraid of elephants, you have to go on living in Pré and continue to bore yourself with the American missionaries and the wives of the Danish foresters. Perhaps it would be nice if Astrid paid you a visit as soon as she returns from Shanghai. In spite of my warnings, Knut has gone to an auction in Shanghai with Astrid and Mailin. I don't trust the Japanese; they might very well drop a few bombs on Shanghai for a change. But Knut and Astrid will never take advice, as you know. Mailin has promised me to look out for both of them. What Astrid wants to do in Shanghai and whom she intends to visit is a deep, dark secret, of course. She has changed a great deal. But you will see that for yourself. Mailin may remain for some time in Shanghai. In that case I shall visit you in Pré with Vivica. Our visit will be no expense to you. You are a dear soul, but stingy. Well, you know yourself best.

If any Japanese tourists visit you again, pretend to have typhoid. That is the best excuse in the rainy season. Since I do not assume that your marriage has made you any less forgetful than you used to be, I should like to remind you to have yourself and all your servants inoculated. How extremely poor your memory is, I see from your last letter. You write of how wonderfully entertaining your first husband was in comparison with Mogens. But I recall from Trondheim your telling me that Sverre used to talk of nothing but herring.

I am well, thanks for asking. I do still have my rheumatism during the rainy season; but then, we do not get any younger.

At the moment I cannot tell you when I shall finally return to Trondheim. In five years at the latest. After all, I am no spring chicken at fifty-two, and the surprises my family constantly has in store for me do not make me any gayer.

Still and all, chin up! Anyone who gets married must take the consequences. Don't say I didn't warn you. To my mind, your

Mogens is quite a decent fellow; one must not ask too much of any one man. Our poor Borghild made that mistake. Since you ask me: I think I am the only one in the family who has not forgotten that dear unfortunate child. So much has changed since Borghild's death, in the world and in our own immediate family. The girls have grown up. Knut has become a solitary eccentric. As far as I am concerned, Knut tells me that I am as patient as a tigress and as gracious as a mole. Still, he seems to be glad I am around, for recently he made a face like a week of monsoon rains when I mentioned the possibility of my returning to Trondheim.

Don't let the jungle get you down! Things are never as bad as they seem.

Warm regards to both of you,
Your old Helene

Just as Laura Nielsen was on the point of opening her cousin's letter, the boy reported a visitor, a Japanese tourist who had run out of gas and been forced to leave his car near Pré. It was late evening, and the tourist from Urakami, to his unspeakable regret, had been unable to find a room at the tavern in Pré. He was so exhausted from his tramp through the rain-soaked jungle, and so badly bitten by insects, that he ventured to ask the foreign lady for shelter for a single night.

Captain Saito remained in Pré for two days. Over the week end he met the master of the house and was invited by Mr. Nielsen to visit the jungle station, where he could observe how teakwood was moved by elephants and could gather all sorts of information on the international lumber trade. His touristic enthusiasm so amused the Danish foresters in their lonely bungalows that they proudly answered his endless succession of naïve questions. Such an eager little schoolmaster from some unknown region in Japan! This was his first visit to another country, and he admired the Danes so warmly that they supplied him with a great deal of Carlsberg beer and still more information. Thus the shy tourist from Urakami, who was so eager to learn, found out that the English, Danes, French, and Chinese had organized the teak business very skillfully since the nineteenth century and built up a large and profitable export trade to Europe. The natives were employed as coolies and elephant drivers. That was all they knew about the lumber business. The governments of the countries involved received large sums from the foreigners for licenses and in taxes. Thus things were organized for the good of everyone, were they not? But no, the Germans had no share in this economic paradise. They had been in on it only at the start, when they sent foresters and engineers into the jungle. The Germans preferred making war to doing business, Mr. Nielsen smilingly remarked.

The tourist from Urakami tried in vain to grasp the humor of this quip and therefore laughed as loudly as he could. In the evening he modestly retired to his wooden guest bungalow to read his mail and develop his photographs. He took pictures of everything with naïve enthusiasm—of the Danish officials, the grinning coolies, the lithe elephant drivers, the methods of work in the jungle, and the poetic, fever-damp monsoon jungle which was so interesting to drive, ride, and walk through. How splendid it would be if the Siamese and Burmese, under Japanese supervision, should experience a new era of prosperity in the teakwood regions. How much more just and Pan-Asiatic that would be! Moreover, such an arrangement would have the advantage that Nippon could obtain preferential prices on the importation of teakwood. Such were Captain Saito's silent reflections as he sat during the sultry August nights in the single-roomed bungalow that Laura Nielsen's husband had hospitably placed at his disposal. Siam was a delightful country and a magical ricebowl, a source of teakwood, and a first-class air base. In wartime a whole army could be fed from Siam.

After Captain Saito had finished dreaming these tourist dreams, he took up the package of letters Lieutenant Matsubara had forwarded to him. Here, in the quiet of the jungle, he had the chance, for the first time on his inspection tour, to study the contents. After a short time he laid aside the report on the situation in Shanghai and turned his attention to the personnel files which Lieutenant Matsubara had prepared in Shanghai and Bangkok. Nippon was constantly on the lookout for foreign agents and "friends" of the Imperial Chrysanthemum, which still blushed too often unseen. Even a police state with a genuine love for flowers and meditation needs friends. And even a Japanese Catholic, who was simultaneously a patriot, could become quite as intoxicated by the glory of the native chrysanthemum as by the fragrance of the mystical rose. For Captain Joseph Kitsutaro Saito was a deeply believing Catholic. He came

from Urakami, after all—that region around Nagasaki in which, since
the seventeenth century, at least half of the three hundred thousand
Japanese Christians have lived. Captain Saito's forefathers—farmers,
teachers, and priests—had experienced persecutions and massacres in
the name of the cross; and the greatest cathedral in the Far East
stood near that peninsula of Hisen which jutted so surprisingly from
the island of Kyushu.

Joseph Kitsutaro Saito had attended the military academy at
Tokyo against the will of the family. There, because of his special
abilities, he had been trained as a tourist of the first rank for the
foreign service of the secret police—a tourist equipped with Kodak,
secret ink, and a rosary.

A medium-sized, stocky island farmer with a round head, exceed-
ingly large ears, three protruding incisors, vigorous, finely shaped
lips, and round, sad eyes that bespoke a divided soul—such was the
appearance of the man who sat in the gloomy jungle of northern
Siam, surrounded by a thousand animal noises, reading reports from
Shanghai and Bangkok. Captain Saito owed his perpetual smile to
those three front teeth, which kept his lips slightly parted. That smile
was another little trick of his, like the secret inks, the amateur photographs of strategically interesting areas of Southeast Asia, and the
gentle art of jujitsu.

Next morning at half past four Captain Saito rose and went for
a stroll in the tropical, rain-sweet woods. He found it difficult
to breathe in Siam and wanted to enjoy the untainted morning cool-
ness of the jungle. At the same time he considered the problem of
modern methods of transporting teakwood. The elephants inspired
him with an inexplicable horror. Moreover, they were expensive and
moody and could suddenly run amok. Captain Saito sought and at
last found a section of narrow-gauge railway which had been installed by the East Asiatic Company east of Pré. He took a lovely
nature photograph that included this. The gigantic teak trees with
their deep green foliage cast tranquil shadows; some still wore their
snowy white crowns of blossoms for adornment. Captain Saito found
this sight even more enchanting when he considered that this was
the veritable teakwood paradise of the world; there were some
three hundred and seventy-five cuttable teak trees per square mile

of forest. In this poetic region Captain Saito sought and found a pretty place to cook rice. Here he decided to have his breakfast, and then bid his host good-by for the present. He found a spot among wild orchids, a tiny tea room filled with stillness and beauty, surrounded by wild mountains and dense, useful forests.

Soon a gay little fire blazed up, and Captain Saito began boiling his rice. Wherever he was, he carried his cooking utensils with him in his suitcase. At the bottom of the suitcase lay a thick bundle of letters—Lieutenant Matsubara's documents. Saito tossed the bundle into the fire. He had already digested the information; he possessed a faultless memory. The personnel files concerned a number of very different persons—some future agents, some whose acquaintance should be cultivated, some whom it was advisable to avoid. Among the latter was a chemist named Dr. Engel of the Bayer chemical company. The others whose origins, occupations of the moment, mentalities, noteworthy physical identifying marks, and possible uses were so carefully listed were: Herr von Zabelsdorf, Deutsch-Asiatische Bank in Shanghai; Fräulein Anna Weber, daughter of a German union leader of Breslau, language teacher, and poor as a church mouse; three Siamese aristocrats whom it would be rewarding to educate at the military academy in Tokyo; Monsieur Pierre de Maury, associate of the École Française d'Extrême-Orient in Hanoi, at the moment visiting Shanghai; and Mademoiselle Vera Leskaya, assistant in a White Russian beauty shop in the foreigners' quarter of Shanghai. Leskaya, formerly an agent for Chinese financial circles, had been serving Nippon on occasional jobs through the Norinaga art-dealers in Shanghai for some years now. Lieutenant Matsubara recommended her warmly. She was intelligent, had a gift for languages, had been basely deserted by her lover, and had a "knowledge of human beings." There followed a detailed outline of where and how Mademoiselle Leskaya could be employed as a star agent, without attracting the attention of the Chinese or Europeans.

Captain Saito was thinking about the practical implementation of this chatty letter when his Danish host, seated high upon an elephant, surprised him in his sylvan tea room. The papers had long since burned to ashes, and the morning rice was cooked. Mr. Mogens Nielsen, whom the former Widow from Aalesund found such a trial and cross, looked like a good-natured hippopotamus.

"Hello, mister," he called out amiably. "I see you're having a regular picnic. That's the kind of tourist I like to see."

Joseph Kitsutaro Saito smiled with the aid of his three incisors, and invited Neilsen-san with low bows and in faulty English to share his insignificant morning meal with him.

He had all the fixings: a tin of crisp kelp, smelling of iodine; pearly rice for the lacquer bowls; and a small pot of tea.

No doubt about it, for the tourist from Urakami life at this time was a picnic.

3: Lieutenant Matsubara's Marionettes

Ever since her arrival in Shanghai, Astrid had had the feeling that she had never been away. When she looked out of her window in the Cathay Hotel at the cosmopolitan crowd; when she sat in Jessfield Park, considering how strange it was that now a small Chinese girl was playing on Yvonne's veranda, and her amah was telling her blood-curdling fairy tales, or rubbing her mouth with paper money (a plea to the god of wealth as well intentioned as it was unhygienic) —everywhere, Astrid had the warm feeling that she was intimately familiar with the air, the people, the stones of this city. After her brief but significant visit to Father de Lavalette something had flowered within Astrid which secretly made her very happy. Naturally she did not say a word about it; she did not have the ability to be intimate with Mailin, although she wished to be and was surprised to find this wish in herself. But still more she wished to be called to the telephone in the hotel. And that happened at last on August third. Contrary to her habit, Astrid had been dawdling about while the consul waited impatiently in the lobby, for the auction was beginning in fifteen minutes. Then the telephone rang upstairs. A boy came and called, "Mademoiselle Clermont-Wergeland wanted on the telephone, please Missie!"

"So you have really come to Shanghai!" a voice said.

"Yes," Astrid said.

"How are you?"

"Very well, thank you."

"Do you still feel like visiting a real Japanese restaurant? Or was that only a Paris whim, Mademoiselle?"

"Not at all," Astrid said.

"Are you alone in Shanghai, Mademoiselle?"

"No, but it doesn't matter. I . . ."

"You did not finish the sentence, Mademoiselle."

"That is so." Receiver in hand, Astrid fell into thought.

"You are very reserved, Mademoiselle. Would you mind explaining a bit? *Eh bien*—I shall wait!"

"*Au revoir, Monsieur,*" Astrid said, still holding the receiver. Her pallor was even more intense than usual. She hated gaiety which she could not and would not share. She was nineteen years old and took men with deadly seriousness. This man she loved. This restiveness, the pounding of her heart, the desire to be alone with him— that must be love!

"Do you have an hour free for a Japanese Montparnasse this evening, Mademoiselle? I should be delighted to show it to you."

"Where is it?"

"I'll come for you in a cab, of course. As I did in Paris."

"No," Astrid said quickly. "That won't do."

"Why not, *ma chère?*"

"Where is the place?" Astrid asked nervously. Her father was approaching the telephone nook. In despair she clutched the receiver in her long, thin hand. *Where* could she find her only friend in all huge Shanghai?

"The White Chrysanthemum Restaurant, back of Kiangse Road, south of Nanking Road. Will eight o'clock suit you, Mademoiselle?"

"Perhaps," Astrid said and hung up.

"With whom were you on the telephone so long?" her father asked.

"With a friend from Paris, Papa. He has invited me to dine in a Japanese restaurant tonight."

"Well, well! Who is he?"

Astrid told her father the name and hastily added that the young man came from an excellent old family.

"Where did you meet him?" Knut Wergeland asked, unimpressed.

"At my cousin's, Amélie Clermont."

Knut Wergeland made a face as if he were suffering from tooth-ache. "Horrible female," he remarked. "Well, come now. The auction won't wait for us."

"Please forgive my holding you up, Papa!"

"You always do whatever you please and then apologize," Knut Wergeland said distractedly. His mind was already at the auction. Ming vases, lacquer bowls, and Japanese woodcuts were being sold —works the very sight of which made a man younger. Astrid, more-over, seemed to have inherited his taste. She came to life whenever she saw Oriental art. Already there was developing between father and daughter an intellectual bond which was very different from Knut's love for Mailin, but which gave him great pleasure. He was secretly proud of his elegant nineteen-year-old daughter. In Paris As-trid had learned to make the best of herself. If only her eyes were not so close together. She had none of Mailin's touching grace. She was an ugly beauty, like her mother—but still more attractive, the consul thought. In profile she was bewitching. He had no objection to her meeting a male acquaintance from Paris. Once she was back in that city she would be meeting innumerable friends, after all, and her father would be unable to interfere. Moreover, Astrid knew very well how to look after herself; that was quite evident.

"Where is this important dinner taking place?" he asked good-naturedly.

"In the White Chrysanthemum, back of Kiangse Road," Astrid said without hesitation, "not far from the hotel." She was quite ready to have her father know where she was, but she did not want him to see her friend. She wanted him for herself alone.

"A nice place, the White Chrysanthemum. At least it was in my time. I used to dine there frequently with Japanese."

Astrid did not answer. Whatever her father had done in Shanghai twelve years ago seemed to her to belong to a shadow-play for elderly gentlemen.

The consul decided to go to the White Chrysanthemum at ten o'clock to pick up Astrid. By then she would probably have covered the essentials of whatever she had to discuss with her friend from Paris. He did not consider that to allow two hours for a talk with

Astrid was to allow very little. He himself intended to dine in the hotel with Mailin and take the opportunity . . . The notary was waiting!

Astrid would never be able to take Mailin's place for him, Knut Wergeland thought as they entered the auction room together. Many eyes followed the tall, handsome Norwegian and the two young girls at his side. Were they his mistresses? many European and American women asked themselves. Astrid would have been stunned if she had known that her father did not seem so ancient to all young women as he did to her.

As through a mist, Astrid saw treasures of art, feverishly excited people of every race and nation—and Mailin, a delicate ivory figurine with a thin nose and deep-set Chinese eyes. At this moment she decided on no account to let her friend catch sight of Mailin's exotic and touching beauty. He had an eye for Asian beauties.

Never! Astrid thought. For a few seconds she stared at Mailin as if her sister were an utter stranger. Then she turned her attention to the prices that were being paid for works of art in war-threatened Shanghai. Her father sat immobile in his chair. He had placed his right arm around Mailin, as though someone were trying to take her away from him. It was very convenient that Astrid was going out for dinner tonight.

Astrid stared into the mirror. Her too soft hair—her eternal grief—looked more lifeless than ever, and damp besides. She couldn't possibly appear like that this evening. She looked at her watch. Her white dress was lovely, and she intended to wear her mother's rubies with it. Lifting the telephone, she asked for a beauty salon. She had two red spots on her left nostril. The humid heat of Shanghai in summer was ruining her transparently pale skin. Then she took a cab to Madame Ninette's, a White Russian beauty shop on Nanking Road.

"First-class," the concierge had murmured; he received a percentage from Vera Leskaya for every client he sent to her. Only white women were employed as assistants by Madame Ninette. One could obtain anything there: facial massage, removal of small skin blemishes, coiffure, manicure, pedicure, information, lovers, and spies of all sorts—although the last three specialities of the salon were not noted on its card, which was lyrically adorned by a Parisian bottle of perfume and Chinese plum blossoms.

Astrid still had three hours to make herself beautiful. Her father was resting at the hotel, and Mailin was writing her diary. Actually she painted in this diary; she had the Chinese habit of writing in pictures. The Japanese passion for expressing thoughts and feelings on paper in words was alien to Mailin.

Lieutenant Matsubara's diaries, on the other hand, contained not a single drawing but endless pages of neat script indited with ant-like industry. The lieutenant employed a typewriter only in emergencies and for official communications. Painting his letters with a very fine brush, Lieutenant Matsubara was at the moment devoting himself to a second Japanese passion: concocting new combinations and moving human beings about like marionettes on invisible strings. In his Shanghai hotel he had a number of particularly fine pieces from his precious inherited collection of ceremonial marionettes. They reminded him of his home in Tokyo and entertained him in a remarkable manner.

One of his living marionettes was at this moment arranging the soft dull-blond hair of a young Norwegian woman dressed with Parisian chic.

"May I try a new coiffure, Mademoiselle?" asked Anna Weber, former student of medicine from Breslau, in naïvely clear schoolgirl French. "I think if we do it up in braids twined around your head, your hair will look fuller than it does in a chignon."

"A wonderful idea!" Astrid exclaimed, electrified. She determined to give the skillful girl a good tip.

"Did you have a beauty salon back home?" Astrid asked.

"No, Mademoiselle," Anna Weber said tersely. "I come from the Riesengebirge, the mountains. It was more or less by chance that we lived in Breslau later on."

Astrid repressed a yawn. But the new coiffure was turning out beautifully; she tried to be friendly. "Is Breslau near Potsdam?" she asked, to show interest. Amélie Clermont always said that people worked much better if you showed a personal interest in them.

Anna Weber almost dropped the hairbrush. For a moment she opened her blue eyes wide. How in the world had this stranger happened to mention Potsdam? Ernst August von Zabelsdorf was the only person from Potsdam in Shanghai and the vicinity. But really, how silly, the girl must have read something about Potsdam in an illustrated magazine. Anna pinned the second braid firmly and explained that Breslau was nowhere near Potsdam.

"Do you happen to know where the White Chrysanthemum Restaurant is?" the client asked. Again Anna started. Was she dreaming? That was where she often met "Ernstel," as she called Herr von Zabelsdorf. Did he intend to meet this young woman with the fine figure and elegant clothes there? Was he cheating on her? Anna looked into the mirror of the pink-draped booth and saw her own face, pale and slightly distorted. And yet it was a face with clever, frank eyes and a mouth that could not conceal its readiness to smile, although it seldom smiled gaily nowadays. When one is twenty-four, the death of feeling is still far away.

She explained the location of the restaurant to her client. Not far from . . . She still could not keep herself from starting back when a tip was handed to her—a silly habit out of the past. Anna was the first member of the Weber family who had ever received a *pourboire*.

"*Merci, Madame,*" she murmured, and curtsied as Madame Ninette insisted her employees do. Astrid left the pink shop with a gracious nod of her head to the girl. That was how all the Clermonts nodded; Astrid had learned the gesture from them.

Anna went to the office and asked for an advance. Landlords would not wait forever for their rent, even in the cheap exiles' quarter of Hongkew. She had already sold all her jewelry—except for the consecrated medal of St. Hedwig of Breslau, which no Chinese dealer wanted anyhow, although the Silesian saint bore a faint similarity to Kuan Ying, the goddess of mercy.

"Have you got what you were supposed to get?" the chief assistant, a cigarette-smoking, sallow-skinned Russian woman, asked. "Our employer needs Mr. Hsin's correspondence with the Deutsch-Asiatische Bank."

"I have had no opportunity, Madame," Anna murmured.

"Then make one. The Japanese don't give high ratings to agents who wait until opportunities fall into their laps."

Anna remained silent. It would be easy to go with Ernst von Zabelsdorf to his apartment and look through his desk while he was mixing drinks. And yet it was too hard. And besides it was a sin.

"'No metal is so hard that fire cannot melt it, and no trouble so bad that money cannot repair it,'" Vera Leskaya quoted from the *Wisdom of the Chinese Alleys*. She had learned this wisdom twelve years ago in a broken-down boarding house, after Boris had left her. It was, as a matter of fact, no longer true. Everything turned about in the world, including Vera Leskaya and Madame Ninette. If this thickheaded young German girl did not want to turn with the rest, she could see where she ended. Morality was something for the rich.

"Then your only choice is the other way. There the demand is greater than the supply. Shanghai is the city of love, after all," Vera Leskaya said, lighting her thirtieth cigarette for the day.

Her gray dress, her sallow complexion, her avaricious, crafty eyes, and her pinched mouth, set in this Japanese-financed pink beauty salon, looked like a study by Goya in one of his bitterest moods. By now Vera Leskaya looked as if she had already died but had not yet received the news in the morning newspaper.

"Do you think you are too good for Nanking Road?" she asked viciously.

"I cannot do that," Anna Weber whispered. "Please give me an advance, Mademoiselle Leskaya."

"If you do not want to use a source of earnings, it is your own funeral," Vera Leskaya said as sternly as a moralistic schoolmistress. "Bring me what I ask, or do what I suggest. Those are the choices. *Au revoir*."

Anna felt that she was shivering in spite of the fiery August heat. Her sturdy young country girl's body in the flowered cotton dress swayed for a moment like a tree in the winds of her Silesian mountains. She was a slow, deliberate person, this Anna Weber who had studied medicine in Breslau. In her second semester her father, who had not changed with the times, had been sent to a concentration camp and, somewhat later, "shot while trying to escape"—a commonplace fate in the Third Reich. Anna's mother had then died. And Anna had remained behind in the empty Breslau apartment with its ghosts. Then, one evening, a neighbor had come to her, a Jewish lawyer to whom no one ever took a case nowadays. Herr Dr. Goldberg had proposed that she emigrate with him and his young wife to Shanghai. His little daughter was no longer with them—he did not say what had happened to her a year ago—and Annele was all alone and never saw a soul since what had happened to her papa and mama.

"What in the world should we do in Shanghai, Herr Doktor?" Anna had asked, quite stunned. With the wisdom of his people, Dr. Goldberg had replied that they would "live" in Shanghai. Living was a great and good thing. At the moment he was learning how to sole shoes from his good old cobbler—who railed so much against the Nazis and their "damfoolishness" that Dr. Goldberg could already see him ending up in a concentration camp.

"B-but," Anna had stammered, "Shanghai is so far away, Herr Doktor. If only it were a little closer to Breslau." And, since Dr. Goldberg had exactly the same opinion, he told her to stop her damfoolishness. Anna had paid one last visit to her parents at the cemetery, and then she had set out for Shanghai to begin anew, in her thorough and deliberate way, the difficult business of living. Within a short time Anna had become the Salon Ninette's best hairdresser, but her friend the Breslau lawyer was no longer soling the shoes of German and Austrian refugees. He was now defending the righteous and the unrighteous in a Silesian heaven, Anna had said as she and Hanna Goldberg and hundreds of exiles conducted the Herr Dr. Goldberg to his last resting place in foreign soil. In one corner stood the Chinese in whose house in Hongkew the Goldbergs had lived; they were dressed in their white mourning garments and stared with helpful sympathy at the dethroned white gods. The foreign devil from Silesia had been a scholar, and so they and their wives and children and concubines paid him the last honors.

Henceforth Anna had to work for two, for the young widow knew nothing but how to dress prettily and run a handsome household. However, Hanna Goldberg was learning how to empty chamber-pots in a Chinese hospital. Her Chinese landlord had introduced her there so that she could earn her rice and not be such a burden to the other young missie. In China one must begin small; one could not start a mill with a single grain of rice, Mr. Wen had murmured consolingly. He was fearfully embarrassed for this impoverished *tai-tai*, this lady; she did not fit into his set, ceremonial picture of the world. For centuries the white gods had been active in trade and finance in

China; they had always possessed the finest houses, the best cooks, and the most lightfooted dancing girls. Their missies had always given orders, and the daughters of Mr. Wen had obeyed and served. And now here was a reduced white goddess whom Mr. Wen was trying to save from starvation. The *tai-tai* was twenty-seven years old and knew less about the struggle for existence than Youngest Grandson, who sold fish in Hongkew and helped his honorable mother drive up the prices, which were in any case climbing steadily higher because of Shanghai's insecure position.

Hanna Goldberg was Anna's great problem child. She was one of those who forever proclaimed that everything had been cleaner and nicer "back home." In the long run nothing came of the Chinese hospital; Hanna could not get along with the nurses or with the patients. Her pretty dark eyes were perpetually red from weeping. She had always heard that the Chinese were so polite. She still had to learn that no one in China is polite to poor people. One evening, when Anna came home from the beauty salon to their little hole near the marketplace in Hongkew, she found Hanna gone. Late at night the widow returned, dressed in her fur coat and her best Breslau evening dress. Anna said nothing when her friend thrust the money at her, but she cried for the first time since the death of her parents. It was Hanna who had to console her. "Don't take it so hard, Annele. I just close my eyes and pretend I'm with Bertel in our summer house in Agnetendorf. . . ." It was fortunate that Bertel had by now been a full year in his Silesian heaven. His lungs had not stood the strains of travel, although his heart had remained staunch and his mind unimpaired. Within a short time he had spoken Chinese like a native. For all that he was so much older, Bertel had been everything to Hanna—a friend, husband, and father.

And now Anna Weber stood before Vera Leskaya and was told to close her eyes and think of something else in order to pay the rent. She was no longer taking care of Hanna Goldberg. Some time ago a rich Chinese had established that lady in elegant quarters near Bubbling Well Road. A white-skinned "pastime woman"—that was something which gave Mr. Chou a great deal of face in Shanghai banking circles in 1937.

Perhaps some more Japanese students will come to me for German lessons, Anna told herself. She did not know that the students were not coming because Lieutenant Matsubara had so ordered.

Anna Weber, after all, was just a silly chit who could not bring herself to steal correspondence from a fellow countryman's desk. So only the other way remained open to her. This evening, she decided, she would meet Ernst in the White Chrysanthemum for the last time —but not tell him anything. It would be a private farewell, for herself alone.

Lieutenant Matsubara, whom Anna knew under the name of "Dr. Tekiho," and whom she had successfully taught German, did not suspect that this marionette was distinguished by Silesian thickheadedness. He needed an intelligent German who would spy on her honored countrymen. But the Anti-Comintern Pact had not promoted mutual confidence. Dr. Tekiho distrusted everyone.

Anna went to the beauty salon's telephone booth and dialed a number. A cheerful man's voice answered in English. "Zabelsdorf speaking!"

"It's me, Ernstel!"

"Are you through work already, Anna?"

"Yes." She did not say that she would never be going back to work at the beauty salon because she was being asked to spy on him. She was still shivering. Herr von Zabelsdorf knew little about her life, no more than that she worked in the Salon Ninette and gave German lessons—a fine, upstanding girl.

"How about a snack at the White Chrysanthemum for friendship's sake?"

"I'd love to. Thank you, Ernstel."

"You have a shaky voice today. What's the matter, kid?"

"Nothing."

"I'll meet you at eight, then. So long until then, and don't take any wooden ticals."

"*Auf Wiedersehen*—till this evening."

Ernst August stood holding the receiver in his hand. What was the matter with the girl? "Hello—Annchen!" he called into the telephone, but Anna had already hung up. He frowned. Something was troubling her. He shook his head and telephoned Baron Matsubara to say that unfortunately he could not dine with the baron this evening. He had caught cold and was running a high fever. After all, he wasn't likely to run into Baron Matsubara this evening, he thought. Anna called him so seldom and so rarely accepted an invitation—a girl among thousands. Herr von Zabelsdorf whistled under his breath. He was a sensible and clear-headed Berliner, but at the moment he had taken a plunge into an abyss. One did not cancel an appointment with an aristocratic Japanese, even if one was on one's deathbed. Rather drive to dinner in the hearse; otherwise there would be hell to pay.

Times change, and restaurants with them. The White Chrysanthemum, which twelve years before had been a genuine Japanese restaurant, had changed as much as Madame Ninette's beauty salon. For exclusive foreigners and Japanese, however, there still existed the old wing where young Baron Matsubara had eaten tempura with Borghild Lillesand. But the Chrysanthemum had expanded considerably. It now had a Western restaurant with such vulgar decor that it was constantly jammed with foreigners. There was also a dance floor with dazzling illumination. Lieutenant Matsubara always walked, blinking, through this modern inferno of light into the old wing with its private rooms and wall niches for scrolls and flowers. He felt well only in a world of finely tempered shadows without electric light and the mass products of industry. It took semidarkness to stimulate the mind and soul. Protected by dark sunglasses, Akiro hurried through the barbaric reception hall and with a sigh of relief entered a private room in the old wing, where a Japanese waitress, kneeling, handed him the kimono and took off his American street shoes.

"Has he come yet?" he asked.

"No, Master."

"Report his arrival to me at once."

"Yes, Master. He ordered Room Seven; a Japanese dinner for two persons."

"This is the man." Lieutenant Matsubara took a photograph from his briefcase. The waitress studied it with silent intentness. "I am going to Tokyo tomorrow. I must speak to him tonight, but it must seem like chance. When you bring the tea, leave the door open. I will pass by at this moment and greet my friend from Paris. Is that clear? Listen closely to what Monsieur and his companion say. Is it a lady?"

"He ordered Dinner Number One for himself and a lady. He spoke in French."

"Bring my dinner now."

"Yes, Master," little Yuriko whispered and scurried off. She was afraid of Lieutenant Matsubara and homesick for the University of Tokyo. But there was no combating love. Love was always mingled with fear; Yuriko had come to accept that. Tomorrow Akiro-san would be leaving again. He had not said that she should wait in his rooms for him tonight. Lieutenant Matsubara was a hard master and a difficult lover for a young student who had wandered somehow into the Secret Service. Yuriko wiped a tear from the corner of her eye, being very careful not to smudge her rouge. As a waitress she was not allowed to wear glasses, although she was nearsighted. Be-spectacled marionettes spoiled the romantic atmosphere for which the foreigners paid in dollars at the White Chrysanthemum.

She had no time for tears. More and more foreigners came to the White Chrysanthemum these days, and all of them talked without restraint in front of the little waitress. Yuriko had spent a year in Paris and a year in New York at government expense, and had learned the foreigners' languages. The headwaiter of the popular res-taurant regularly sent to Lieutenant Matsubara lists of the guests who ordered private rooms. Today he had discovered on the list the name of the Frenchman with whom he had struck up a friendship in Paris. Monsieur de Maury was planning to dine in Room Seven at eight o'clock this evening with a certain Mademoiselle Clermont.

Astrid was happy as she sat with Pierre de Maury in Room Seven on silken cushions with a small lacquered table before her—so happy that she had difficulty in seeming cool and collected. She had cate-gorically rejected the kimono which Yuriko, with a bow, had offered to her. It would have spoiled the effect of her white dress and her rubies.

Pierre had come from Hanoi to Shanghai to talk with Père de Lavalette, consulting scholar of the École Française d'Extrême

Orient and an associate of the weekly *Indo-Chine*, a journal well known to scholars, of which Pierre de Maury was an editor. Pierre had turned from journalism to archaeology. He was of medium height—in fact somewhat shorter than Astrid—and had two faces. In profile he was an ascetic, from the front a witty cosmopolitan. On his travels he always carried three things with him: his coffee-maker, a pharmaceutical kit of alarming proportions, and the writings of Montaigne. Like many Frenchmen, he considered all the cities of the Far East except Saigon and Hanoi absolutely unbearable. As soon as the Congress of Orientologists ended, he planned to return to Hanoi. So warmly did he speak about the excavations in the jungle and about his editorial activities that Astrid listened attentively, although she usually found such subjects wearisome. She could never make Pierre out. If he was really in love, and not merely toying with her with a delicate, feline cruelty, then his way of loving was certainly not hers. But ever since he had entered her cousin Amélie's drawing room in Paris, Astrid had been at his mercy. Fortunately he had not realized that yet; Astrid no longer flung hungry looks at the people she wanted to have for herself. But the hunger was there inside her, gnawing away like a rodent. It hurt her when she smiled. Why didn't Pierre kiss her? He squatted gracefully and contentedly on the cushion and extolled the Japanese food. Astrid had not yet learned that Frenchmen treat dinner and love separately. Since it was humiliating to be longing for a kiss from a young man who reverently fished unpalatable foods out of lacquer bowls, Astrid put on her haughtiest expression.

"Do you find Shanghai unbearable too, Astride?" Monsieur de Maury attached a French *e* to her name, and drew the *i* out so long that it sounded like a cry of yearning. But all this was deceptive, for he promptly turned his attention to the sukiyaki which Yuriko, kneeling before them, was preparing on a tiny charcoal stove. As she cooked the finely cut strips of meat, Yuriko listened in despair. The foreigners seemed to be ignoring politics completely. The pallid young woman was eating virtually nothing. Monsieur, on the other hand, seemed to be interested mainly in the food. He drank hot saké and listened to what the lady had to say about her childhood in Shanghai.

"Why, you're not eating anything, *ma petite!*"

"I'm sorry, Pierre, I really can't stand this Japanese hodgepodge."

Yuriko made a mental note of the foreign woman's insulting hostility to Japan. To think of calling so wonderfully prepared, artistically cooked a meal a "hodgepodge"! A small surge of hatred passed through Yuriko, along with the hope that the longnoses would at last begin revealing their secret plans for the annihilation of Nippon.

After the sukiyaki Pierre de Maury ate something which Astrid thought must be either a fried snake or an eel, and then ordered the traditional rice and tea as the conclusion of the meal.

Yuriko arose, quivering. Tea! The spies were at last going to lay their plans on the lacquer tables, and the young woman would receive her instructions. Meanwhile Yuriko must fetch the tea and leave the door open for Matsubara Akiro. . . . But she had nothing to report to him—an unthinkable disgrace for an agent.

"Why are you so nervous, Astride?" Pierre asked. "Don't you like your Bangkok family? When can I meet your father and your Chinese sister?"

"Papa is not well."

"I saw him at the auction today. He seemed lively enough."

Astrid's pale face flushed. Pierre looked at her with flickering eyes, a smile twitching at the corners of his mouth. Mockery? Pity? The superiority of the person who permits himself to be loved?

"Papa is exhausted after every auction. I really don't know what there is to smile about in that," Astrid said coolly. Pierre regarded her with sudden admiration. This decorative beanpole from Norway was only nineteen, but she had poise. And that was something that Pierre de Maury, like every Frenchman, appreciated. Astride would not let him treat her badly. Women ten and twenty years older than she could well learn from her!

"You're *charmante* this evening, Astride!" His voice had the basely seductive powers of music. "And what a wonderful hairdo you have, *ma chère*. Chic and dreamy!" Astrid was breathless with joy. If only the tea—and that stupid little Japanese whose zealous service upset her—did not come just now.

"I invented the hairdo myself," she lied.

"It gives you a kind of shepherdess look. Adorable!"

Astrid took a deep breath. Then she said something so curious that Pierre de Maury was not to forget it for years. "I don't care whether or not you mean it, Pierre," she whispered. "It sounds so nice. I'm grateful for a pleasant little lie."

Her eyes were filled with Nordic melancholy, and with something that Pierre was unable to decipher. What a strange girl! Suddenly he wanted to kiss those tart, girlish lips. They were trembling faintly, in spite of Astrid's self-control. What had happened to this child that she did not believe she had any beauty or any seductiveness?

"Astride," the young Frenchman whispered, "my enchanting little—"

He dropped the arm he had placed around Astrid's shoulders; in the doorway Yuriko had appeared with the tea and rice. And behind her a distinguished Japanese gentleman passed by the door and exclaimed, "Monsieur de Maury! What a surprise! I thought you were in Hanoi. I am delighted to have the privilege of greeting you in a Japanese atmosphere."

This was the beginning of a ceremonial speech, in the course of which Baron Matsubara spoke of his "ardent desire" to celebrate worthily their meeting again, as well as of butterflies (dreams) of the city on the Seine—all this in the veritable intonations of Paris. Then the Japanese gentleman in the dove-gray suit fell silent and allowed his eyes to linger on the scroll in the niche. Pierre took advantage of this pause to make the introduction. "Baron Matsubara of Tokyo—Mademoiselle Clermont of Paris."

Astrid was always called Clermont among her French relations for convenience' sake. "Wergeland" was a difficult task for the French tongue. Consequently Akiro failed to learn the interesting fact that this cool-eyed young lady was the daughter of the man who years ago had not even expressed his thanks for a precious kimono from imperial Kyoto.

Baron Matsubara was in an irritated mood and therefore smiled as all-lovingly as an advanced Zen Buddhist. On the way to this private room he had detected his Berlin acquaintance in the restaurant with Fräulein Anna Weber. He had instantly turned his back on the man who had disdained his invitation by alleging a cold. That was what they were like, these people who had concluded a pact against the

Communists with divine Japan. His stomach—always a restless tourist's most sensitive organ—had almost turned over when he heard Herr von Zabelsdorf's contented laughter.

Astrid forced a smile to her transparently pale face. The hungry rodent inside her was gnawing close to her heart now. This circumstantially polite Japanese had rent the fabric of her first dream. She would never forgive him for that. Astrid was one of those persons who cannot accept disappointments. No more could she revise basic emotional attitudes. Her spontaneous, irrational dislike for Japanese sprang into being at this moment and was never revised by her intellect. The moment she had longed for day and night was irrevocably gone now. She loved Pierre and wanted, for all her reserve, to devour him whole. She would marry him or no one, she was determined. Pierre's gift for telling colorful stories dispelled the inner emptiness which had tormented her even as a child in Shanghai. His charm, his gentle irony, and his evasions both provoked and enchanted her. He was the first man who had ever impressed her. Perhaps it was only his greater experience, or his feebler attachment, that made him irresistible in her eyes. But in any case she had framed her plans. After three months in the Far East she would finish her education in Paris, correspond with Pierre, then suddenly marry him and steer him back to Paris. To reside in dusty Hanoi with museums and excavations was out of the question for her.

But all the plans for the future which she had been spinning now suddenly became terribly remote. Pierre was chatting animatedly with this "Parisian Japanese," as only a Frenchman can chat after an interrupted idyll. The shepherdess of the idyll no longer appeared to exist.

"Was this your first Japanese meal, Mademoiselle?" Baron Matsubara asked smilingly. "May I ask how you liked our cuisine?"

"I found it delicious, Baron," Astrid replied unwillingly. Akiro bowed with pleasure, and at Pierre's request gracefully dropped down on a cushion, while Yuriko, with lowered eyes, poured the tea into the thin bowls. This was the flour-faced female's eighth lie.

Baron Matsubara threw a brief, sharp look at the foreign girl. His eye, trained in the Secret Service, saw a great deal more than the retina received. He saw the dislike for him, for Japanese cuisine, and for holy Nippon. Then he invited Monsieur de Maury and Mademoiselle Clermont to lunch in his own rooms on the tenth of August. He would be back in Shanghai that day, he said; and on the eleventh of August he planned to fly by military plane to Tokyo again.

In the course of the conversation Akiro Matsubara handed his Parisian friend a small, beautifully illustrated booklet. It was the newest volume of the "Tourist Library" which was being published by the Office for Industrial Tourism in Tokyo: a series of brochures intended to acquaint foreigners with Japanese miniatures, drama, the flower cult, Buddhism, the tea ceremony, and the significance of ceremonial marionettes—in short, with all the cultural properties which Nippon could with justified pride display to foreigners. Akiro Matsubara himself was a collector of ceremonial marionettes and had recently acquired a rare piece, a *gogatsuning-yo* figurine of the Yedo Period, which was always exhibited with spears and irises at the Iris Festival on May 5, in honor of Japanese boys. These warlike marionettes were something after the heart of a Japanese aesthete.

The Tourism Office was not planning a brochure on the organization and methods of the Kempetai.

As Baron Matsubara had foreseen, Monsieur de Maury became wild with enthusiasm as he leafed through the brochure with the wonderful reproductions of Japanese miniatures. Thence it was only a natural conversational jump to the weekly *Indo-Chine*. What more obvious than to invite Baron Matsubara to Hanoi, the center of the colonial spirit at its most elegant? The baron was delighted at the prospect of making the acquaintance of this city. While Pierre was describing to his Japanese friend the Louis Finot Museum in Hanoi, a brilliant plan took shape in Akiro's mind. Nippon would prepare Indo-China for Japanese occupation by cultural exchanges. Baron Matsubara offered to deliver lectures in Hanoi on the various Japanese centers of Buddhist pilgrimages, which he had visited as a boy with his honored father. Then Monsieur de Maury would come to Tokyo at government expense for six months and help foster Franco-Japanese relations by lecturing in his turn at the Japan-France Cultural Institute.

"A brilliant idea, Baron," Monsieur de Maury said. "I shall do my best. In our minds, too, cultural exchange is the most satisfactory way to promote international understanding."

Baron Matsubara smiled happily; the marionettes were beginning to dance. Not a word was wasted on Tonkin's economy—maize, cane sugar, coffee, soya beans, and significant resources of anthracite coal. At the moment Nippon had to import coal from Indo-China at high prices. Culture would change all that.

Stimulated by the tea and the conversation, Baron Matsubara crowned the "happy reunion with Paris" by offering a compliment to the mute young lady who sat like a carved image on her cushion, heroically repressing a yawn. As was only proper, he resorted to lyric poetry and recited in a gentle voice several celebrated short poems, or *haikku*. This art form, developed in the fifteenth century, had ever since had a magically soothing effect upon the Japanese. To Akiro, the soul of poetry was concentrated in this courtly literature with its prescribed number of syllables.

Astrid let the words trickle past her ears. She could not make anything out of them. Miss Wergeland would call the *haikku* "stupid nonsense," Astrid thought suddenly and involuntarily smiled. Unfortunately the Japanese interpreted her smile as high appreciation and now recited: "You—the old pond. A frog hops in. The water whispers." He looked expectantly at Astrid. What would she say to this pearl of seventeenth-century verse?

At that moment Astrid's self-control snapped like a too taut silken thread. Out of the depths of her disappointment, of her frustrated desires, she exclaimed impatiently, "That has no meaning at all, Baron! These observations are not a poem as we understand the word. It sounds to me like a child's game."

"We are too simple for Europeans, Mademoiselle," the baron said regretfully. "We only imply where you express."

He stood up and with complete graciousness expressed his thanks for the tea and the conversation. No sooner had he vanished than a tall gentleman with keen, bright eyes entered the private room.

"Aren't you going to introduce me, Astrid?" Consul Wergeland asked, scrutinizing the Frenchman with the jealous curiosity of a father who wonders why his daughter should go out at all with strange men.

Baron Matsubara had missed by a hair meeting again his first Shanghai friend, who had so deeply disappointed him.

Akiro entered his private rooms in the White Chrysanthemum in a black mood. The hotel part of the restaurant had only a few suites available for prominent Japanese. The rest of the Japanese colony lived north of Soochow Creek in a thickly populated industrial area of dreary business streets. In this district of the International Settlement, and in the adjacent streets north of the creek, lived many Japanese who regarded Nippon's rise to military power with anxious concern. All of them were crowded together here—the respectable merchants with their clean shops and the small manufacturers whose old-fashioned factories had aroused Dr. Engel's scorn, people with happy family lives and charming, round-headed children in bright kimonos. Altogether they were peaceable souls, distinguished by their industry.

One member of this group was Mr. Kinichi Komiya, who was awaiting Lieutenant Matsubara in the hotel's reception room. Poor Mr. Komiya; he could scarcely have chosen a more unfavorable moment to speak with a military man in civilian dress about Japanese commercial interests. For the lieutenant had just had his noblest feelings outraged by a flour-faced foreigner. To call Japanese poetry a "child's game" was a slur that could not be forgiven in a thousand years. It was as if someone had doubted the timeless beauty of the Imperial Chrysanthemum. Moreover, Akiro Matsubara was suffering from stomach cramps, the result of suppressed indignation. In short, circumspect, plump, industrious Mr. Komiya was most unlucky in choosing eleven o'clock this evening for his respectful "friendship conversation."

"How do you dare call on me *here?*" Baron Matsubara shouted without a trace of the famous Japanese politeness.

"An abnormal situation, Baron," Mr. Komiya murmured. Out of fear and respect he drew breath so audibly through his nose that it sounded as if he had a bellows concealed in his tensed abdomen.

"I do not understand you," Baron Matsubara said haughtily, although he knew perfectly well what Mr. Komiya meant. With a thousand delicate apologies, which the bellows forced like hissing steam out of his mouth, Mr. Komiya, owner of a sizable cotton-spinning mill north of the creek, described the abnormal situation of the businessmen. Rumors—always a Chinese specialty throughout the world—had swelled to torrents that were threatening to overwhelm Mr. Komiya's miserable, industrious existence, together with the miserable, industrious existences of thousands of others. He himself had been selected by the group of patriotic Japanese businessmen in Shanghai, in spite of his reluctance—at this point Mr. Komiya drew his breath almost thunderously into his nose—to inquire of so influential a patriot as Baron Matsubara whether Shanghai was going to continue its peaceful existence. For if not, the Japanese would prefer to leave this city with all their kith and kin, notwithstanding that they would have to accept losses as mighty as sacred Mount Fuji. For everyone realized that in that case the Chinese would plunder the factories and the miserable shops which the Japanese had been building up for years. War rumors brought with them commercial ruin and the destruction of familial felicity, concluded Mr. Komiya, sucking air mournfully through his nose.

A long pause ensued. Plump Mr. Komiya tried to hide himself from the fixed gaze of the Secret Service lieutenant. The city pigeons in Shanghai had different views from those of the war buzzards in Nippon. Fear prevented him from even privately formulating the heretical thought that he would sooner have the cherry blossoms in Kyoto wither than have his two little sons struck by bombs.

Lieutenant Matsubara thought fast, sharply, and without any aid from poetry. A panic among his countrymen in Shanghai—this fat city pigeon before him was trembling like jelly—would amount to disaster. Mr. Hsin, whose correspondence with the Deutsch-Asiatische Bank was probably being stolen this evening by the beauty-salon agent (why otherwise had she been dining in the White Chrysanthemum with Herr von Zabelsdorf?)—Mr. Hsin, the Chinese Crane, was already doing enough to generate a mood of panic. The newspaper controlled by him carried ceaseless incitements against the Japanese, "who like cormorants want to swallow the city of Shanghai in their greedy gullets." The bankers advised by Mr. Hsin—both Chinese and foreign devils—were hurriedly buying foreign currencies. Shanghai's insurance companies—this was outrageous beyond words—had already refused to underwrite Japanese ships. Valuables were continually being moved, with Chinese cunning and caution, to safe places. The Kempetai was working at full steam. The exodus of Japanese civilians from Shanghai had been secretly in progress since the middle of July. On the twenty-fourth of July a Japanese sailor had

disappeared. Thanks to his secret investigations, Lieutenant Matsubara had succeeded in discovering the sailor on board a British
steamer in the Yangtze River—the man had simply deserted. What
an error, he apologized, to have imagined that the Chinese were trying to kidnap members of the Japanese fleet! Thereby Lieutenant
Matsubara had contributed significantly to an abatement of the Sino-
Japanese wave of distrust. They were all good friends together again.

And now here stood this limited, money-grubbing buffalo, blub-
bering about the danger of war, panic, and mass flight of the Japanese. *Prematurely!* The evacuation would be ordered, all right, but
not by Mr. Komiya and his like. Moreover, it would be ordered only
in the Yangtze Valley. Japanese factories in Shanghai were vital and
must be retained. In a few days the Third Fleet was to assemble in
Shanghai. On August tenth, the day Monsieur de Maury and the
foreign woman were to lunch with him, four Japanese cruisers and
seven destroyers were expected in Shanghai. If the surprise was to
succeed, the Japanese in Shanghai must keep quiet. Nippon's future
was at stake.

Accordingly Lieutenant Matsubara changed his tactics. He ordered Yuriko to bring tea and sweet cakes to his private rooms—no
one else must be allowed to see Mr. Komiya with his buffalo face
twisted by fear. While Akiro heroically suppressed another stomach
cramp and sipped green tea—he left the cakes to the buffalo—he
gradually reassured his guest, lulled his suspicions with exquisite
tact, and finally as good as pledged that there would be no war in
Shanghai. Mr. Komiya and his friends could rest easy.

"Business as usual," the baron murmured, watching the relieved
buffalo through half-closed eyes. What a pretty mess it would be if
his marionettes should begin to dance independently! With three
deep bows, which were answered by three deep bows from Lieutenant Matsubara, the pacified businessman took his leave. The Japanese north of the creek would sigh with relief, just as the buffalo
now drew relieved breaths through his nose with a faint whistling
noise.

Eleven days later the bombs crashed down north of the creek,
upon the peaceful Japanese businessmen. Lieutenant Matsubara was
at this time in Tokyo, promoting that Franco-Japanese cultural amity

which he had initiated in the White Chrysanthemum. But Southeast
Asia was not to be conquered in a day, either with culture or with
cannon alone. What counted were the puppet-masters who made the
marionettes dance and die at specified times.

After Mr. Komiya had left, Akiro had his humble mistress rub his
back and prepare an almost boiling bath, in which he lingered a
good three-quarters of an hour, luxuriating in the warmth. In spite
of the sultriness of the August night, he had shivered when Mr.
Komiya bowed himself out of the room with such gratitude for the
reassurance—a decent, complacent, average Japanese who had never
harmed a fly and was now innocently and submissively waddling off
to his death. The buffalo had loyally and intelligently reported to
him on the industrial and financial situation; for the past two years
he had been well paid for this side activity. The military could not
get on without the Japanese businessmen in hostile China. Lying in
his bath, Akiro Matsubara closed his eyes in order to efface from his
mind the decent face of the good buffalo. A frightful surge of pity
suddenly shook his sensitive Japanese soul, which had nothing to do
with his cold and calculating mind. That soul hovered in a deadly
vacuum between personal impulses and the mission which Nippon
had imposed upon its best and most able sons. The dissolution of
individuality in the service of Shinto forced him to take the path of
private suffering. But whereas the riddle of suffering had driven his
powerful Shanghai adversary, Mr. Hsin, into the society of songbirds,
it drove young Baron Matsubara into the crystal-clear discipline of
Zen Buddhism, which his uncle in Tokyo had recommended to him.

Akiro stepped from the bath with compressed lips and raging
stomach cramps. In his magnificent dark kimono, with his intrepid,
finely carved features and his athletic body—very big for a Japanese
—he represented the ideal man to little Yuriko, who awaited him in
naked humility on a mat in the adjoining room. Nothing in her immobile face betrayed her hunger for love and her boundless submissiveness—emotions which dominated the modern girl students of
Japan as utterly as they had their mothers and grandmothers. Lying
with downcast eyes, she seemed like a helpless doll that had been
stripped of its ceremonial adornments. But Yuriko was no doll. When
she saw her lover's frowning brow and cold eyes she drew the peach-

colored kimono over her delicate naked figure with a touching gesture.

"Come here," the black-browed young man said. Troubled, she tripped toward him, wrapped in the protection of the kimono.

With a brutal gesture he pulled the silken wrap from her and stood examining her. He knew that his intestinal cramps and his melancholy would vanish with gratification of the sensual desires which were slowly flaming up in him. But that was not the way to become lord and master of the base suffering which had assailed him this evening. Pity and self-pity must not corrupt him. The peace which Yuriko's naked young body promised was a fleeting, animal peace which one desired but nevertheless utterly despised. Directing his fixed, greedy gaze upon Yuriko's tender nakedness, Akiro Matsubara concentrated with all the force of his mind and all the subtle technique of Zen discipline upon the objects of meditation. After that hour of tea with Mr. Komiya, he felt that his physical energy and intellectual harmony would not be furthered by sexual gratification. His dilemma required different medicines. And so he stood, staring at the trembling girl until, sobbing, she clasped her arms around his knees. "I want to go home," Yuriko whispered, humiliated.

Lieutenant Matsubara was so remote from her that he drew away almost gently. "Don't cry, Yuriko," he said serenely. "It has nothing to do with you." Whereupon Yuriko, like a true woman, was even more hurt, and sobbed so noisily that Akiro frowned. But his frown was very slight, for the experience of *muga*—the extirpation of emotion, especially of self-pity, by intellectual concentration and Zen meditation—had already made him free and calm. Since his hands were wet from the so-called "sweat of the *muga*," he dried them carefully on a towel embroidered with the crest of his family. He had just experienced an ecstasy of the mind that made all other pleasures seem shallow. Only those who knew how to conquer themselves could conquer the world for Nippon.

Going to his desk, he took out a letter. It contained instructions for Yuriko's further activities in the Secret Service. "You will leave Shanghai tomorrow."

"Am I flying with you to Tokyo?" Yuriko asked, new hope in her old-fashioned Japanese girl's soul.

"Don't be so foolish," Baron Matsubara said impatiently. "You are accompanying Mademoiselle Vera Leskaya to Bangkok and will help her set up an elegant beauty salon there."

"I know nothing about beauty culture," the marionette whispered, a tiny note of obstinacy in her voice.

"You need not," Lieutenant Matsubara replied amiably. "Your task is to watch over our star agent. I do not have a hundred eyes, but I must know with whom she associates and make sure she is not playing a double game with us. These Russian women are deep," he concluded with strong disapprobation, as if he himself were as shallow and transparent as a pool in morning light in his dealings with people and marionettes.

He telephoned for a cab for Yuriko and brusquely turned his back on her. She was becoming a burden to him with her love. Moreover, for all her charm, she had that regrettable defect of Japanese women, a tendency to bow legs. Tonight this had struck him for the first time, when he had regarded her for a while without desire. For a few seconds he thought of Mademoiselle Clermont; she had a wonderful figure. As Yuriko crept slowly and sadly toward the door, he suddenly called her back. She came, lifting her little face expectantly. At least he wanted to take kindly and ceremonial leave of her. Oh, how infinitely grateful she should be to be noticed at all by such a man!

"Our agent in Bangkok is Mr. Narihira on Silom Road. He keeps a retail shop: toys, household utensils, and stationery. There you will receive further instructions and information. Your replies will be transmitted by Mr. Narihira directly to Tokyo. When you first call at the shop, ask for tea bowls with a chrysanthemum pattern."

Bowing, Yuriko left the room where her dreams of love had collapsed.

Baron Matsubara lay down on his mat with its hard pillow roll to refresh himself with sleep. He was one of the few guests in Shanghai who slept well these days. In a room in the Cathay Hotel, Mailin Wergeland at this hour started up out of an uneasy dream. She had obtained a sleeping tablet from a mute, nervous Astrid after the latter's return from her dinner in the White Chrysanthemum. But the tablet had put her into a kind of delirious sleep that lasted only for minutes at a time.

She switched on her bedside lamp and once more read the letter of an unknown lawyer named Dr. Chang of the Chinese City of Shanghai. He wrote that he had discovered her name in the list of newly arrived guests and that he had important information to give her about her mother, who had died nine years ago in Shanghai, and about her family, who now lived in Shanghai. He had been trying in vain to get in touch with her for several years, and requested her to call at his office at eleven o'clock the following morning.

Mailin lay down again. The night lights of the restless city danced on the ceiling. So she had a family in Shanghai! Poor Papa, she thought suddenly, and her loving heart pounded violently. Mailin knew no technique that could think out of existence love in its thousand forms. Aunt Helene—she too was a powerful shade who came to Mailin's bed at night and with rough tenderness smoothed her braids, the nighttime coiffure of a little Norwegian girl with a Chinese soul. And with Chinese wisdom and resignation Mailin knew that a chapter of her life had come to an end.

On tiptoe she stole into her father's room and stood studying with a deep but restrained love his fine Norwegian face. Some gentle compromise must be found. She settled quietly, in the precious Chinese dressing gown which she had put on over her nightgown, on the mat at her father's feet. The riddle of suffering, which had for the first time touched her serene soul, filled her with anxious premonitions. Dear Papa, she thought, eyes filled with tears, how can I save you from grief? By instinct and intelligence she grasped completely her father's vulnerability.

Sitting silently at his feet, traces of tears on her delicate features —that was how Consul Wergeland found her next morning. "Did you have a bad dream, darling?" he asked, strangely touched, and in his strong arms he carried his songbird back to her bed. "Or did you want to guard my sleep, my sweet dwarf?" He had the strangest pet names for Mailin. Never would he part with her!

"Yes, Papa," Mailin whispered, "I guarded your sleep."

In the distance an airplane roared. Baron Matsubara left the city of a thousand discontents. He had his newly acquired ceremonial dolls in his baggage.

4: Cannon and Kisses in Shanghai

On August 10, four days before the bombing of Shanghai, Mr. Hsin awaited, in his venerable house back of Bubbling Well Road, the first visit from his granddaughter, Mailin Wergeland. Immediately after receiving a letter from the Chinese City he had called upon his lawyer and with immobile features altered his will in Mailin's favor. His philanthropic bequests for the poor of Shanghai remained unchanged, as did his bequest of the house and his property in Shanghai to his nephew, Mr. Chou Tso-ling. Tso-ling was a banker who had recently introduced a German wife into his mother's house. Tso-ling and the German woman would some day live on Bubbling Well Road with Mr. Hsin's birds. Mailin, on the other hand, would inherit an impressive fortune in securities and American dollars, all of it safely in the Chase National Bank in New York. Only a fool left all his wealth in Shanghai in these days. Foresight, Mr. Hsin believed, carried a man as in a secure vessel across the ocean of life.

Mr. Hsin had pondered long and silently upon the ways of destiny and was now ready to receive into his house the unknown daughter of his daughter with dignity and with love. Heart-stricken at first, he had swiftly recovered his equanimity. His anger against the foreigner who had covered his daughter with dishonor, and whose rice he had unknowingly eaten in Shanghai, had already evaporated. In the meanwhile the foreign devil had no doubt, like everyone else, registered his own "losses of happiness and contentment." That much, at least, seemed evident to Mr. Hsin from the long letter that Consul Wergeland had written to him after Mailin's visit to the lawyer.

In the meantime Knut Wergeland sat in the Cathay Hotel, waiting for an invitation from Mailin's grandfather. It had not yet come. The consul was so extremely nervous and so tormented by constant gall-bladder trouble that he resolved to take Mailin to Soochow after her visit in Bubbling Well Road. Astrid had declined his invitation with a frosty smile; Monsieur de Maury would still be in Shanghai. Since the evening at the White Chrysanthemum she seemed to be without vitality, lost in brooding. She suddenly looked ugly, her father observed to his astonishment—colorless, skinny instead of slim, and with lifeless eyes. How could one and the same girl possibly look so different at different times? Mailin was always lovely; her ivory face was a pleasure to see at any time. Her father had no intention of "surrendering" her to the old Chinese; that was his private phrase for it.

Thinking of this horrible possibility, he drank a forbidden whisky without soda as he stood at the hotel window watching Mailin walk away. She wore an almond-green linen dress that enclosed her fragile body right up to the neck—a dress of Chinese cut and taste—and carried a pocketbook of Norwegian needlecraft which did not at all suit the rest of her costume, a gift from her father, which Mailin never parted with. Knut Wergeland decided that he would, with all due regard for ceremony, talk sense to the influential old gentleman. Mailin was still a minor, he would point out. In four years she could decide whom she would prefer to live with henceforth. But she would visit her grandfather in Shanghai regularly—perhaps once a year.

After a sleepless night Knut had calmly spoken of all this to his songbird—but at the same time anxiously watching her out of the corners of his eyes. She had seen the pretended calm, the fear, and the great love in her father's face, and had nodded reassuringly. "Yes, Papa. It will all turn out well. But first I shall go to call on honorable Grandfather."

As it happened, there was no occasion for Knut Wergeland to go to Soochow. Ten minutes after Mailin set out he was struck down by an attack of bilious colic, lost consciousness, and was whisked off by an alarmed Astrid to a private hospital in the French Concession. Astrid was even paler than usual, and not only from fright. This morning Pierre de Maury had telephoned her at the hotel and informed her that Baron Matsubara, to his regret, had been forced to cancel the invitation to lunch because of urgent conferences which would keep him in Tokyo. Pierre had not proposed that they lunch together alone somewhere. French leave, Astrid thought, and compressed her lips in the manner of Helene Wergeland.

Old Mr. Hsin was on the point of donning a heavy dark gray silk reception robe in honor of his granddaughter when the servant brought him a visiting card. He glanced at the card, and signed to his servant, Hsüan-ch'ing, "Jewel of Understanding," to hand back to him his Western suit. The intelligent Jewel was so confused by this unforeseen order that she held out to him his gray trousers and the robe.

"Show the caller into the *Ta Shu Fang*." Mr. Hsin, with completely expressionless face, decided to receive the visitor in the study.

"Where do you wish to have the feast served, sir?" a boy asked, hovering at the door.

"I'll order that later," Mr. Hsin murmured, and he went to meet his visitor. He had not the slightest desire to receive him and therefore smiled with particular benevolence. This was not the first visit Herr von Zabelsdorf of the Deutsch-Asiatische Bank had paid to powerful Mr. Hsin, but it was going to be the last. Only the first and last visits in a home really count; they are as irrevocable as friendship or a summons to pay.

Mr. Hsin had twenty minutes for his visitor. This time was precisely apportioned from the first: ten minutes for the introductory polite conversation on his own health, that of the guest, and the health of the Hsin and Chou families, as well as on Chinese bronzes in the *Huai* style. The pretext for these last remarks would be standing in front of the visitor's nose, on the rosewood table. Five to seven minutes would be due for the foreign devil's business, and the rest of the time would pass in waiting for the visitor to finish his tea, thus giving the signal for the end of the call.

The prelude over, Mr. Hsin listened in silence to the Berlin banker, his deep-set, oblique eyes fixed on Ernst von Zabelsdorf's face. But when he had heard the business, he stretched his long, withered neck. The Deutsch-Asiatische Bank, Mr. Hsin instantly recalled, was a consortium of thirteen German banks. It had been founded in Berlin in 1889. In 1920, after the war, it had with remarkable tenacity and skill once more gained a place in the economic life of the Far East. It had had branches in Shanghai, Tsingtau, Tientsin, Canton, Hankow, Peiping, Yokohama, and Kobe; however, the branch in Yokohama had not reopened after the great earthquake of 1923. In 1932 the Kobe branch had also closed its doors. But in China the bank's business had shown a steady upward development. In the past Mr. Hsin had often recommended Chinese businessmen to the Deutsch-Asiatische Bank. And this was what Herr von Zabelsdorf was now concerned with: the Chinese customers were boycotting the bank. There could no longer be any doubt about it.

Mr. Hsin smiled sympathetically and reminded his caller that he lived a very retired life; he was a foolish old man who occupied himself with his songbirds and bronzes. He rose to show his guest a rare piece, a teapot with dragons and animal masks. Herr von Zabelsdorf wiped the perspiration from his brow. He had understood. This was a refusal, administered as politely and indirectly as possible. Mr. Hsin considered his visitor too intelligent for there to be any need to explain the defection of the Chinese customers. The bank had always participated successfully and graciously in the issues of Chinese loans and had carefully built up a good reputation; but last year Germany had become Japan's ally in the Anti-Comintern Pact. Given this new connection, the bank would have no trouble—Mr. Hsin also said this by his silence—in reopening the branches in Kobe and Yokohama, and could therefore limp along without its business in Shanghai. The editor of one of Mr. Hsin's newspapers, who had ventured to attack the Japanese, had been imprisoned on the insistence of the Japanese consul-general only a few days ago. But everywhere Chinese were wearing anti-Japanese badges in the streets and merrily looting Japanese shops and Chinese shops they suspected of dealing in Japanese goods.

"Do you belong to the party of the National Socialists?" Mr. Hsin asked between two remarks on art, as abruptly as an interrogating detective.

"No," Herr von Zabelsdorf said. "My family is old-fashioned." He hesitated. Then he murmured that here in the Far East he was working for his country. Parties came and went; no doubt that was also the case in China.

Mr. Hsin nodded. This was not the language of a fool; but nevertheless the young man had missed the point. Because Herr von Zabelsdorf was intelligent and had good manners, and because Mr. Hsin had allowed for another five minutes of conversation, he decided not to let him depart in error. Therefore he explained with the aid of Chinese figurative language just how his visitor had erred. A political party was a powerful current, indeed a torrential one; either you swam with it or you went under. But those who swam with the stream inevitably left familiar shores behind them. Consequently there was no choice; it was necessary either to swim or to walk aloof along the shore and watch the swimmers. Never was it possible both to swim and to remain ashore. Mr. Hsin fell silent. His mute visitor could draw for himself the unspoken conclusion that in Shanghai at this time one could not do business simultaneously with the Chinese and the Japanese.

Ernst August von Zabelsdorf finished the tea. Every swallow ran bitterly down his throat, although it was mild and fragrant jasmine tea. Then he rose to his considerable height. He had chosen to swim with the stream. Back home in Potsdam the aging members of his family were watching the swim from the shore. Their familiar shore was dearer to them than Hitler's millennial kingdom, the Thousand Years of National Socialism, which the others were swimming toward.

"It was a great honor and pleasure to me to receive you in my modest home. May I express my sincere wishes for the prosperity of the bank," Mr. Hsin said gently. Bows. Retreat through the vaulted passage to the big door that led out into the street. The Chinese doorkeeper bowed low. He wore the badge of the Anti-Japan Club.

Not until he reached the street did Ernst August von Zabelsdorf realize that Mr. Hsin Kao-tze, one of the most powerful men in Shanghai, had spoken of their friendly relations in the past tense. Ernst August whistled softly under his breath as he beckoned a cab and got in to drive to his flat in the French Concession. He was the first Zabelsdorf who had ever been thrown out of a house—even though it had been done in the most delicate way. Everyone was turning away from him—first Anna, who had suddenly vanished from his life, and now an old friend with whom, not long ago, he had eaten Peking duck and litchi nuts in the Western Flower Room.

Life these days consisted principally of thorns in the flesh.

On the Avenue Foch stood a Chinese soapbox orator, the proprietor of a modest embroidery shop in Yangtzepoo, delivering a fiery speech against the Japanese. Mr. Feng was cautious enough to speak at a good distance from his shop, but his language was not temperate. A goodly crowd stood around him—mothers with babies on their backs, beggars, ricksha coolies, street peddlers, and idle passers-by. One person with an anti-Japan badge shouted agreement with Mr. Feng at the top of his voice; all the others joined in cheering him. Contented, Mr. Feng set out on his way home. Next evening he was found murdered in his shop; his wife and children had been away at a Chinese temple. No one knew who had killed Mr. Feng, but evidently someone with an anti-Japan badge must have been a Japanese spy. . . .

There was really no chance for banks that concluded political alliances with Japan. The monster city on the Whangpoo River was trembling with premonitions of evil. The first Chinese refugees, activated by caution and fear, were streaming out of the Chinese quarters and into the Settlements, where they thought themselves secure. But for the most part life went its course undisturbed.

While Herr von Zabelsdorf was driving back to his flat, and Mr. Feng, contrary to Chinese custom, was making speeches that were direct and to the point, Mailin Wergeland entered the reception hall of the house of Hsin in her almond-green dress. An old man in a ceremonial silk robe stood between the east and the west walls of the flower-decked hall. On his right and left other sages gazed out of clouds of golden silk. These were portraits of the ancestors of the Hsin and Chou families, who waited against yellow silk backgrounds, dressed forever in their precious robes, for greetings and offerings from later generations. Along the walls stood stiff ebony chairs in which the members of the Hsin and Chou families were accustomed to sit when they gathered around the patriarch on feast days and brought him their "miserable and useless"—that is to say, expensive—New Year gifts. In the childless house of Hsin respect, stillness, and a sense of family still reigned.

The old man in the dark gray, gold-embroidered robe was also uncannily still, but his suffering, knowing eyes regarded Mailin with deep attention. Mr. Hsin saw a delicate girl child—more delicate and fragile than purely Chinese daughters. She wore just such an almond-green dress as Limpid Light, the bitterly mourned daughter, had been fond of wearing.

Around her neck Mailin wore the jade bell with the inscription: *Haste is error.* At every step she took it gave forth a gentle, ghostly ring. Something happened to Mailin in this reception hall with the portrait of Confucius on the north wall, something she could not grasp with her reason. She felt that she had been here once before, years or decades or hundreds of years ago. She knew that here the story of her life had begun—her life with her love for Gold Oriole, with her loyalty to the Wergelands, with her obscure longing for another, a Chinese way of living in which wish was already fulfillment and the opinion of the world suddenly became personal insight. She felt her membership in an ancient and enormously vital people, felt it like an electric shock; for a brief second she reeled, and then slowly walked on. As yet the old man in the solemn festival robe had said not a word. Mailin too remained mute as a dreaming bird as she approached with lowered eyes that bent, dignified figure. As in a dream she made the three prescribed bows before honorable Grandfather. Suddenly, with cupped hand, he lifted her bowed head in a gentle but imperious gesture, lifted it lightly and carefully as a bowl of eggshell china, and gazed into her eyes. He saw—with a great rush of happiness—Chinese eyes that reflected the three lofty virtues of woman: steadfastness, gentle love, and that sound common sense which is all the more effective because it remains modest and laconic. These were really Chinese eyes, deep, gleaming, and gaily intelligent.

The lonely old man said quietly and solemnly, "Hsin Mailin, daughter of my daughter Limpid Light, welcome to the home of your forefathers!"

Four days later Astrid left the Cathay Hotel to visit her sick father at the hospital in the French Concession. Mailin was staying there, since her presence calmed the sick man. When he first awoke, Knut Wergeland had asked, "Where is my daughter?" and had poorly concealed his disappointment when Astrid came to his bed. Astrid had noted it and bitterly sent for Mailin, but they were sleeping alternately in the small room meant for the nurse. Now that he was feeling somewhat better, Knut Wergeland had complete control of his emotions once more; but Astrid filed the little scene away in that outrageous memory of hers.

On the morning of August 14 they did not know that Consul Wergeland's bilious colic was going to save the lives of all of them. By evening Nanking Road, the Cathay Hotel, and the Palace Hotel lay in smoking ruins. Two hundred bodies lay about in front of the entrance to the Cathay at the time the consul usually ate lunch with his daughters there. On Shanghai's fateful day he lunched with Mailin in the hospital. On the table before them stood an old Chinese porcelain bowl filled with litchi nuts, sent by Mailin's grandfather. Mr. Hsin had not yet visited because the consul had been too ill hitherto. However, he had announced a brief visit for today, the fourteenth of August, at four o'clock in the afternoon. Mr. Hsin had such definite plans for his granddaughter that for the present, with inscrutable Chinese courtesy, he was leaving her to the sick foreign devil. He knew by now that haste is error.

When Astrid left the Cathay Hotel on August 14, it was a day like any other, and a day like no other. But in the spinning-mills and international banks, in the Chinese bakeries and laundries, in the foreigners' breakfast bars, in the waterfront taverns and the Hongkew and Pootung factories, in the enormous cosmopolitan beehive of Shanghai, people worked as usual and ate their morning rice as usual, laughed, spread fresh rumors, and thought only of the moment.

Astrid had all morning to herself and sauntered slowly down Bubbling Well Road. Her real goal was the White Chrysanthemum Restaurant, where Monsieur de Maury usually had his lunch, as he had mentioned to her. Astrid did not mind contriving a chance meeting if need be. She rarely deceived herself about such things because she had no imagination. Her life, consequently, was a little empty, but her reasoning was all the more accurate.

As she set out on her manhunt in a flawless white suit, with a witty hint of a hat, long gloves, and a white leather bag redolent of Chanel's, heels clicking under long, thoroughbred legs, she was every inch a white goddess of the settlement and the colonial paradise—a somewhat ill-humored goddess, though. This morning she had no premonitions that death lurked around the corner. Had she taken the trouble to visit such impossible districts as Chapei, Hong-

kew, or Pootung, she would have seen sandbags and barricades, behind which workers, factory-owners, prostitutes, opium dealers, and
such decent Japanese water buffaloes as Mr. Komiya, north of the
creek, were seeking protection from rumors and bombs. All these
hard-working, life-loving ants were Asians and therefore understood
the trick of survival. They regarded even the most miserable existence—and Shanghai was rife with a misery that reeked of sweat,
filth, suppurating sores, humiliation, and repulsively sweetish opium
—as worth living and loving. That is one of the Asian secrets
which Westerners with their bathroom civilization and their luxurious dream worlds cannot understand. Astrid, with her lack of imagination, her taste for beauty, and her habituation to regular,
expertly served meals, could not at all comprehend such a thirst for
life and such a joy in life.

In any case, only one thought filled her mind this morning: Pierre
de Maury. Yet she did not know him, understood nothing of his interests in Asia, had no knowledge of his personal background. He
was the first man who had made any impression on her; he had
served up to her charming little lies that filled the emptiness in her
heart. Naturally there were all sorts of reasons for this deviation from
the sensible conduct of life for which Astrid was essentially made.
She was nineteen years old. How should she know that love is based
upon giving, and that marriage consists at least seventy per cent of
sick-nursing and common troubles, and is essentially a pilgrimage toward heights that the average couple never reaches, if only because
it cannot see these heights? Like Fuji, the sacred mountain of the
Japanese, they are wrapped in clouds.

While Astrid sauntered along, bored and wondering how to fill out
the time until lunch, she thought of Madame Ninette's beauty salon
and betook herself to it. The young German who had transformed
her into a shepherdess with Parisian chic was no longer working there,
she was informed. Accordingly she put herself into the hands of a
fat Russian who told her a host of stories about persons she did not
know. Madame Ninette, the fat Scheherezade, was fond of recount-
ing whole novels about people out of her private set of acquaintances.
Astrid was one of the few clients who found these stories interesting,
for all that she looked bored. She would have listened to Madame's

tales for hours, devouring this conversational feed as greedily as in childhood she had devoured Yumei's Chinese horror stories.

"Just imagine, Mademoiselle," Madame Ninette concluded one of her short novels in ebullient French, "poor Sonya was so desperate after this cruel Englishman had simply let her wait in the Chapei opium den that she—please hold still, I'm putting the herb mask on now—that Sonya Petrova went to confession again for the first time in years."

"To what church?" asked Astrid, who always wanted to know things precisely. Since Madame Ninette had made no use of the Church's benefits since her arrival in Shanghai in 1920, she was unable to supply this information. She therefore changed the subject to a White Russian dancing girl who had left her third-class nightclub at three o'clock in the morning to return in a ricksha to her hardworking parents, and had been basely robbed, raped, and subsequently murdered by the ricksha coolie.

"Natasha's horrible death broke my heart," Madame Ninette concluded after a lengthy account of the girl's parents and *their* sad fate, and she waddled good-humoredly to the cash register. Astrid paid the high fee gladly; she had spent the time pleasantly. She decided to come regularly to Madame Ninette's.

At the entrance to the White Chrysanthemum, in the vicinity of Nanking Road, where the first bomb fell later, stood Pierre de Maury, looking for someone. This someone was by no means Astrid Wergeland, but was probably the reason that Astrid had heard nothing from him. His eyes had a restive, almost harried look, and he started in alarm when Astrid came sauntering long-leggedly toward him and exclaimed, as smoothly as Baron Matsubara, "What a surprise!" It really was a surprise—to Pierre, who, however, immediately surrendered to his fate. The person he hoped for had not come. He had already waited, like a fool, for an hour. And he was not fond of waiting like a fool. Shanghai was the most unreliable city in the world—a department store of secrets.

They again took their lunch in the intimate Japanese room where they had chatted so delightfully with Baron Matsubara. Today, after a long interval, there was again hanging in the alcove the scroll showing the revolving stage of the *kabuki* players. In front of it stood a bowl of choice flowers. With his usual loquacity Pierre at once expatiated upon the *kabuki* theater, although he had not yet been given that particular volume of the Tourist Library. The surprising appearances and disappearances of the *kabuki* players on the *hanamichi*, the bridge of flowers, teased his imagination. He himself came and went in a similar way. He always took his leave so swiftly that others scarcely noticed and lingered too long alone on the revolving stage. There was no one to warn Astrid against so difficult a lover. What good could come of it when a *kabuki* actor and prim innocence dined together?

Astrid listened with only one ear, but she regarded Pierre fixedly with her pale blue eyes. What did she care about the Japanese theater? It had been invented by people who at the most unsuitable moments indiscreetly thrust their way into private rooms.

"Why haven't we seen each other for so long, Astride?" the seductively musical voice asked suddenly.

"I've had a great deal to do; my father is in the hospital," Astrid replied. Did Monsieur imagine she was running after him? He had failed to invite her to lunch four days ago. A cold wave passed slowly through her heart. She did not yet know that attractive men in particular are often inclined to torment women. And although Astrid would not allow anyone to treat her badly, she still suffered, like any woman, and probably more than most, from amiable neglect. How long would she be able to go on listening to Pierre without bursting into tears? With a great effort she swallowed and put on her haughtiest expression.

Monsieur de Maury had zestfully fished his share from the lacquer bowls and was now telling her that his favorite writer, Montaigne, had furnished a bedroom on the first floor of his palace in order not to be constantly near his wife, and that his study on the third floor had been his favorite refuge.

Pierre went on to relate that on his last European furlough he had visited this palace in Gascony. On the wall of the study Monsieur Montaigne had placed a Latin inscription expressing the hope that he would be able to spend the declining days of his life in this room "in perfect security and independence," far from domestic disturbances. The inscription, Pierre said, was virtually a sign saying "No entry" in golden letters. Smiling, Pierre sipped his tea.

"That seems to me altogether horrid," Astrid said. "After all, people marry in order to be together all the time."

"Wherever did you pick up this ghastly idea, Astride?" Monsieur de Maury asked in alarm.

Astrid was so outraged that she could not answer. Her naturally pale face had become snow white, an almost tragic mask beneath the playful suggestion that was her Parisian hat. "It is not *my* idea," she said frostily, lighting a cigarette. "I never have ideas. The majority of people hold that opinion, you know."

Monsieur de Maury regarded the charming beanpole out of halfshut eyes. She was simply indescribably young. Only someone so young could have taken him so terribly seriously. He should not have lunched with her. She knew nothing at all about his life. Certainly it would be best for her to marry some boy who wanted to be with her all the time.

"Have you really no imagination at all, Astride?" he asked after a pause, and smiled at the Japanese waitress—an act that Astrid noted with displeasure.

"Fortunately not. Imagination only leads to drawing false conclusions from the facts."

"Do you worship facts, then?"

"Worship is scarcely the right word. I reckon with them."

"Poor child," Pierre murmured. The pity in his voice also contained a faint note of boredom. No doubt about it, this beautiful girl was not for him. In spite of her wonderful figure and her fine profile, she had missed the boat as a woman. She served a fellow facts instead of dreams for lunch. Pierre de Maury needed dreams; that was why he had waited vainly in front of the restaurant for someone else. Naturally he did not want dreams constantly; no Frenchman could do that; but he did want to withdraw to the world of dreams at certain times. He had learned that from the Asians.

Astrid stared into space. "Poor child," Pierre had said. "You need not pity me," she remarked coolly. "There is no reason at all to." Never would she permit a man to humiliate her. The sense of coldness grew so intense that she began to tremble. In her soul, which hungered for devoutness and goodness and in spite of earnest prayer did not attain either, despair welled up—a shadowy emotion that was sinful. And yet she was not alone; she only felt as if she were.

She still had God, Whom she had loved from childhood. She knew this; in Lausanne she had grown up in the consolation of this love. The writings of St. Theresa of Avila, which she had inherited from her mother along with the rubies and her talent for jealousy, were still reckoned among the few books which she devoured again and again with a strange, tragic hunger. But the love which had inspired the Spanish nun demanded nothing and therefore received everything. Astrid suddenly sighed. The sound she produced was so weak and despairing that Pierre de Maury, who knew something about sighs, put his arm gently around her. She quivered, and he pretended he did not notice.

"I must go," Astrid murmured. "Thank you for the lovely lunch."

"Did you really think it lovely, Astride?"

"Of course. *Au revoir.*"

"Why the hurry? I'll take you back to your hotel."

"Thanks, but I must go to the hospital in the French Concession." She could no longer bear to look at him. It hurt too much. She must escape, quickly.

"That is on my way," Pierre said firmly. "Come, Astride. How that little hat becomes you! A real creation! Congratulations."

"It's my own model."

"I thought you had no imagination."

"Only where hats are concerned."

On the way to the door Monsieur de Maury met the person he had awaited in vain. Astrid on his arm, he went past her without a greeting. The time for dreams had been missed for today.

They stepped out of the White Chrysanthemum just three minutes before the first bomb exploded on Nanking Road.

Later Astrid could scarcely recall just how she and Pierre had plunged suddenly into the inferno. The Chinese air force had wanted to carry out its first attack upon the Japanese battleship *Idzumo*. On the way to the quay near the Japanese consulate-general it dropped bombs into the Whangpoo River, opposite the Shanghai Club. Other bombs landed by mistake far beyond the quay and killed many waterfront coolies, as well as several persons with sizable bank accounts—nothing is more democratic than a bomb. So began the dilettante bombing of the Japanese warships, which led to such dreadful consequences when the Japanese retaliated. The streets of the giant city were at this time already jammed by thousands of Chinese refugees who wanted to seek shelter in the settlements, and who met death on Nanking Road. The ants of Chapei and Kiangwan fled with all they owned; with wives, babies, bird-cages, great-grandparents, and bundles of rice, fled with stoic faces and trembling hearts, into the citadels of the foreign devils who had so often shown them the way out of sickness, dirt, and hunger by taking them into their hospitals and kitchens. But now the honorable foreign devils were themselves trapped—and Astrid and Pierre with them.

At one o'clock the bomb fell on Nanking Road. At four o'clock in the afternoon more Chinese bombers flew toward the *Idzumo* and were greeted with violent Japanese fire. Astrid and Pierre had been pressed forward by the crowd, caught up in a sea of yellow and white ghosts with wide-open mouths and limbs that held them fast and threatened to crush Astrid to death. She uttered one sharp cry, then fell, fainting, into Pierre's arms. Not for the rest of her life would she overcome the phobia of an Asian crowd which she acquired this day in Shanghai. When she opened her eyes she lay, in her stunning suit, with rows of corpses on both sides of her, near the Palace Hotel and her own Cathay. As if in a nightmare she saw the upper stories of the Palace sway and then dissolve in sheets of flame. Pierre had tried to take her back to the hotel, but it was already burning. She sat up and looked into his eyes.

"*Chérie,*" he murmured. His light hair was a paste of soot and blood. Beside him a Chinese mother vomited over Astrid's suit. She wanted to draw away but found that she could not move. Then she too had to throw up, right on Pierre's jacket, and was so ashamed of herself that in the midst of death and destruction, groans and screams, she began to weep the tears she had been unwilling to let come in the White Chrysanthemum. "Oh, Pierre!" She sobbed and wept as though her heart would break—for herself, for Pierre's jacket, for her frustrated hopes, and because death had no pity on mothers, children, birds and coolies.

Pierre looked at her. He brushed her pale golden hair back from her forehead. "Can you walk?" he asked, and then he slung her like a flour sack onto his shoulders. He must get her out of here. Somewhere cabs were riding down side streets. Here they would both die either from bombs or from the crowd. The expensive shops were collapsing on all sides. Pierre joined another procession of people who were pressing out of Nanking Road, for he could not swim against the stream.

Astrid had clasped both arms around his neck and dangled between him and a helpful young Chinese who carried her feet. What exactly had happened? Before she sank back again into the night of unconsciousness, she caught a glimpse of a store sign in an unknown side street jammed with people. It read: *Chum Li-seng, Hardware. Successful in all business.* Successful Mr. Chum lay peacefully dead beside his fine sign with its inscription in gold letters. Relaxed, legs outspread, he lay as he might have lain under the plum tree in his home village, which he had left twenty years ago for the city by the sea. Beside him lay his dying son, his wife, and his honored mother. They were gasping their last breaths, and the son still held in his cooling hands a bird-cage with a gold oriole like the one Astrid had once killed in Shanghai. She screamed, and her arms fell slackly down.

"Missie dying, quick, quick!" the young Chinese whispered. He held out his hand. *"Kumsha!"*

Pierre gave him the tip, then kicked aside a solitary hand that lay in his path. It had belonged to a singing girl. It was a bloody scrap of flesh with a diamond ring. The helpful young Chinese stooped, drew the diamond ring from the scrap of flesh, quickly wiped the ring on Astrid's skirt, slipped it on his finger, and hurried on. On Nanking Road the top story of the Palace, which Astrid had seen swaying in her hallucination, was now really collapsing. Fiery-hot walls plunged to the street. One piece struck the young Chinese. He staggered, crying, *"Ai, ai!"* He had not enjoyed the diamond ring for long.

Window panes shivered; automobiles began to burn. Two bombs fell at the intersection of Tibet Road and Edward VII Avenue, annihilating hundreds of refugees—men, women, children, cooking utensils, rice bags, hopes and fears. A twelve-year-old Chinese girl stood with her three brothers, surrounded by death and horror, feeding the smaller children rice from a tiny pot. She was Elder Sister, and it was her duty to take care of the three sons of the Wen family. Thousands of persons around her had been killed and wounded a moment before, but she stood in a burned-out shop and equably continued the business of life. She did not know whether the rest of the family was at the moment alive or dead. Wide-eyed, she watched as two foreign devils in a burning automobile turned to ash; she murmured, "*Ai, ai,*" and went on feeding Youngest Brother. The fish that jumps into the frying pan is done for, but for the present Elder Sister stood in the burned-out luxury shop and was alive. That was all there was to it. It was very simple, and yet to the wounded and moaning Europeans on the avenue it was utterly incomprehensible. "These beasts!" a foreign woman whose car could go no farther muttered to her husband. He shrugged his blood-smeared shoulders. "Chinese!" he said, feeling that he had said everything necessary.

While masses of people were still pouring from the Chinese City and Shanghai's suburbs over the huge bridge into the settlements, toward evening hundreds of bodies were put on display, in hastily knocked-together coffins, in the streets opposite the race track, so that they could be identified. Hundreds were never recognized by their relations, hence could not be buried with the traditional rites, for they had lived in Shanghai as in a no man's land—village people who had been seeking their little fortunes in this great city only for a week; opium smokers known only by their opium dealer, who had also perished; White Russian and German refugees who had been unable to endure any longer the memorial tea parties given by their fellow countrymen and had crept off to hide away far from these companions in misery; children of all races and nations who had lost their parents in the crowds; nurses, doctors, priests, thieves, procurers, and saints. All lay opposite the race track in the reddened, smoke-filled air; they had all lost the last bets in the great race of Shanghai. But many bodies continued to lie for days in the hot August sun in Hongkew and Yangtzepoo; they were partly eaten by starving street dogs and in this horrible condition photographed for the edification of posterity by the best reporter on the *Shanghai Evening Post and Mercury*. In those districts fires went on raging for days. The Chinese Christians crossed themselves because they thought the Last Judgment had begun and they were already in the midst of the purgatory fires. The great department stores, Sincere's and Wing On's, where Astrid had often bought pretty trifles, had also been wrecked by the bombs; on the other hand, the Japanese

hotel-restaurant near Nanking Road had come through compara-
tively unscathed. Close by it a pair of lovers, one Korean and the
other Japanese, were found dead in such close embrace that they
could not be separated. And everywhere in the streets, among the
dead and the wounded, lay the wretched possessions of the fugitives
—all the things the Chinese had considered so valuable that they
attempted to save them from the spirits of fire. A whole cultural
history, from ancestor tablets to blue and white porcelain soup
spoons, lay spread out in the shattered streets and alleys of the vast
city; but no one except a few photographers noticed. Life had become too difficult an affair for anyone to pay heed to such minor
details.

Between a Swiss clock and a broken bottle that had formerly contained a Chinese secret medicine—the label read: *Good for con-
sumption and a hundred other diseases*—lay Astrid's white leather
handbag, filthy and bloodstained. Astrid herself had been injured.
She lay unconscious in a Chinese hospital on North Szechuan Road.
An overworked Chinese nurse was bending over her; a European
nurse renewed the icebag and whispered, "She has come to now.
Please call her sister, Nurse Wei."

Nurse Wei scurried out, and Astrid was left alone with the German nurse in Foo Ming Hospital, for which Mr. Chou Tso-ling in
conjunction with his uncle, Mr. Hsin, had provided the equipment.
Here Chinese mothers could bring their young into the world in
cleanliness and peace—not that all the wives of workmen and coolies
in Shanghai enthusiastically rushed to the hospital. Most of them
preferred the age-old way of bearing children in their own homes
on a dark, ill-smelling street, in the presence of numerous relatives.
They did not hanker for the cleanliness introduced by the foreign
devils. But many came nevertheless, for they received Chinese food
and had Chinese nurses. The hygiene and the instruments brought
from America were inescapable, but they took these drawbacks into
the bargain.

Astrid tried to recall where she had seen this European nurse before. And although she was very dazed, her outrageous memory
functioned through all the shock: this was the girl who had done her
hair so charmingly some time ago. But it had not helped.

Anna Weber whispered to her, "Your sister is here, Mademoiselle."

Then Mailin was kneeling beside Astrid's bed, and Astrid wanted to grip her hands and pull herself up out of the reddish mists that beclouded her mind. But she could not. In the pressure of the crowd, one of her ribs had been broken.

"What is wrong with me?" she groaned feebly. Then she fell again abysmally deep into the mists, and human beings dropped like lumps of rock on her chest.

"Dr. Chou says we must try to prevent secondary shock," Anna Weber whispered to Mailin. "That would put a great strain on her heart."

Mailin looked at Astrid with misted eyes. Elder Sister did not have the vital resistance of even the most delicate Chinese girls. Her forehead was damp with perspiration and her eyes deep-sunk in their sockets.

"A specialist must be brought here at once, or else we must take Mademoiselle to a private hospital in the French Concession," an angry man's voice exclaimed. Pierre de Maury stepped into the dim circle of light around the bed. Astrid had the only bed in a private room in which, at the moment, some thirty persons lay on mats on the floor. The Chinese on the mats, those who were conscious, looked up with insatiable curiosity at the group of foreign devils, who were barely shielded by a tattered bamboo screen.

"These conditions are frightful," Monsieur de Maury said heatedly. "I must speak to the head doctor at once, Nurse."

Anna Weber regarded him as if he were some antediluvian sea monster. She was too young to know that human beings are far stranger than sea snakes. "But Monsieur," she said in her deliberate schoolgirl French, "the doctors have their hands full at the moment. Thousands of wounded people are lying in the streets. The city is in flames from one end to the other."

"I'll dig up a cab somewhere and take Mademoiselle to our hospital," Monsieur de Maury replied obstinately. "*Au revoir!*"

"You have a head wound, Monsieur! Dr. Chou has forbidden you to move at all. Please lie down again. And besides, Mademoiselle Clermont must not be moved at all." Anna spoke sternly, an obstinate German to an equally obstinate Frenchman.

"I'll telephone Dr. Bardot at once. I will not permit some Chinese quack . . ." Monsieur de Maury's voice failed him.

"Dr. Chou is not some Chinese quack, Monsieur! He passed his examinations in the United States with highest honors. He has given first aid. At the moment no more can be done. I assure you, Dr. Chou is a first-rate surgeon. He has reduced the fracture and averted complications as far as possible. Now he must help others. If you like, I'll show you the X ray. Do be reasonable, Monsieur."

Anna's appeal to French rationality accomplished what medical data, assurances of the doctor's competence, and allusion to other patients could not have done. Monsieur de Maury brushed a damp lock of hair back from his fine, stubborn forehead. As he did so he accidentally touched his head wound and felt a stabbing pain. Whatever had he been storming about?

"I am sorry, Nurse," he murmured. "I've just come out of that inferno. You will understand . . ."

"She's looking at us," whispered Anna, who had not for a moment stopped watching Astrid. Anna did not understand at all. The attitude of Western men toward the Asians was altogether alien to her. Most Westerners treated Orientals either too placatingly or too condescendingly, depending on their importance to the West. Most Westerners were alternately embarrassed or contemptuous and never natural.

Mailin had remained silent all this while. She had always been surrounded by so much love that Monsieur de Maury's remarks had offended her. At the same time she felt sorry for him; he had lost his head and, with it, promptly lost all sense of courtesy. That would never happen to a Chinese. In this alone the Chinese were certainly the stronger. Mailin gently drew the foreign nurse out of the room. She sensed that Astrid wanted to see no one but this arrogant and courageous Frenchman.

"How are you now?" Pierre spoke in a low, tender voice.

"I think I'm going to die," Astrid murmured in tones of wonder. "Oh—Pierre! Isn't Père de Lavalette coming?"

"He's surely coming. Just be patient a little, *chérie!*"

Astrid's thoughts became jumbled. She had always had so many good intentions and yet committed so many sins. The bird; . . . "Mailin is not as good as we other children in Shanghai, Aunt Helene"; . . . the tramp's daughter; . . . arrogance, emptiness, desire; . . . prayer without penitence; penitence without prayer.

Pierre. . . . I want him, I must have him. . . . Holy Mary, Mother
of God, pray for us sinners. . . . The old pond; a frog hops in. Is
it Baron Matsubara? The water whispers. *Haikku* are silly nonsense.
. . . Father, forgive us. . . . *Haikku* . . . Holy Mary, Mother . . .

Astrid groaned. Pierre stooped over her. "Forgive me," she whispered, bemused. "Darling, I wanted . . ." He listened. Astrid's voice
was only a breath. He bent toward her so carefully that her head
with its pale gold hair lay against his chest. He was no longer dressed
in bloodstained trousers and silk shirt, but in a pair of black Chinese
satin knickerbockers and a torn white cotton shirt which left bare
half his chest and his muscular arms. After the bombing the Chinese
had hurried to bring mountains of old clothing to "their" hospital.

Through the thin cotton Astrid heard Pierre's heart beating. It
seemed to her that all the music in the world was in this rhythm.
She lay still, for the first time without gnawing desires, against
Pierre's heart. She listened. Pierre's heartbeat seemed to give her
vital strength. It was as though her crushed body were flying on shining clouds toward the moon. For she was so made that love quick-
ened her imagination and gave her hair gloss—love alone.

"I hear your heart. . . ."

"It belongs to you, Astride," he said straightforwardly and with
some astonishment, for he himself had made this discovery just now.

"I should like to live," Astrid whispered in a high, lamenting, birdlike tone that he would never be quite able to forget.

"Tomorrow you will feel better, *chérie*."

"Yes . . . tomorrow," Astrid breathed. She seemed to grow paler
every second. She had lost a great deal of blood from cuts.

At that moment Père de Lavalette entered the room to give Astrid
Extreme Unction as a necessary precaution.

"We must be hopeful," he murmured when he saw Pierre de
Maury's expression. Then he remained alone with Astrid.

When Father de Lavalette stepped out into the corridor again he
met Dr. Chou. The doctor's young face with its high cheekbones was
hollow from exhaustion, and yet the night had just begun. More and
more wounded people were being brought to the hospital in trucks,
in automobiles, and in the arms of their relatives, to be made well
again "for all time."

"She is asleep," murmured the tall, stooped Jesuit who twelve years before had administered the last sacrament to Astrid's mother. "I shall wait out here, Doctor."

"Please lie down for a while, *mon père*," said Dr. Chou, who would have done well to follow this advice himself.

But the priest shook his gray head. "I knew her mother," he whispered. "Will she make it?"

He could not wait for the doctor's reply, for an ancient Chinese bowed before him, at the same time tugging imploringly at his cassock. "Noble Teacher," the old man whispered in a hoarse opium voice, "the son of my son leaving the world. Please, quick, quick, come. Son of my son best Christian man in Shanghai. Every month many dollars for mission. Noble Teacher must show way to paradise, quick, quick. Son of my son not go to eight-stage hell. Is good Christian man with good Christian gambling house."

"I am coming, Grandfather." The priest laid his big, sinewy pianist's hand on the old man's spare shoulder. He had been long enough in China to know what the death of a grandson meant—the break in the chain of generations. Immediately he followed the half-naked old man through the overcrowded corridors to the cellar where the dying owner of the Christian gambling house was waiting for his passport to paradise.

"Ten thousand happy years for you, Noble Teacher," the old coolie murmured, satisfied. For years his grandson had been paying; he had a just claim to all the joys and advantages of the Christian heaven.

Pierre de Maury kept vigil alternately with Mailin. During the night Astrid awoke. Mailin was sleeping in a corner of the room. When Astrid opened her eyes, she looked into Pierre's.

"Astride." For the first time he kissed those inexperienced girlish lips, which in disappointment were wont to become so tightly compressed. And Astrid Wergeland began slowly to live again—against all the doctor's expectations and against the will of the "Hungry Spirits" in the death month of 1937. Perhaps she remained alive because she knew why she wanted to live. That was a good deal in the years between 1914 and 1955, a period of organized, scientifically devised annihilation in which few people were privileged to die private deaths and still fewer to live private lives. Precisely that was given to Astrid at this moment, when she was on the point of taking leave of the world. From Pierre's kiss she gathered strength. A kiss can be everything or nothing; for Astrid it was everything. Henceforth all her joys and her many bitter sorrows were linked with this man who had saved her life and who alternately took it from her and restored it to her again. At this moment she knew Pierre de Maury no better than she had in the White Chrysanthemum, and perhaps that was well. Crows, as old Mr. Hsin was in the habit of saying, are black the whole world over—and men are changeable the whole world over.

Mr. Hsin lay two rooms down from Astrid in "his" hospital. But he lay dying, although he wanted to live, since only a few days ago he had welcomed in the hall of his ancestors Hsin Mailin, daughter of his daughter, spirit of his spirit, and blood of his blood. On the way to the French Concession Mr. Hsin Kao-tze had been hurled by blast from his car, and his tired heart could not recover from the shock. People in flight had trampled over his frail, withered body. His bookkeeper had found him gasping, and had brought him, dying, to his own hospital, not in his big American car, but in a ricksha with one wheel missing. The ricksha coolie and Mr. Hsin's bookkeeper dragged the ricksha all the way to the hospital by their joint efforts. The coolie recognized powerful Mr. Hsin. Who did not know him, his newspapers, his philanthropies, and his wealth, which gave face to all the poor devils in Shanghai? But no one can sew without a needle, no one can row without the Whangpoo River, and no one can live without air. And in spite of his money and his property, Mr. Hsin could not get air. He struggled for breath like a tubercular coolie; he looked no richer; and his agony was the same.

And so, at three o'clock in the morning, Mailin stood by his bed. The Hsin and Chou families—nephews, nieces, in-laws, grandsons of relatives, and a few discreet concubines—thronged together in a corner of the room. But the old man saw only Mailin, who was truly his beloved daughter Limpid Light. At this moment he was going to the New Year celebration with her. Limpid Light wore a red smock and her jade bell, inscribed: *Haste is error.* "*Kung Hsi Fah Tsai,* Happy New Year," she chirped. Suddenly she vanished.

Mailin whispered, "I am here, venerable Grandfather." Why

"Grandfather"? But Mr. Hsin could not answer this question, for the jade bell on Mailin's neck grew before his dimmed eyes until it was a green bird-cage. And within stood Limpid Light, singing as though to outsing his feathered friends. She must never again leave her father even for a moment. And so a fine, withered old man's hand suddenly gripped Mailin's jade bell. Mailin was now wholly Limpid Light in a green dress, and they were together in the bird pavilion in the garden back of Bubbling Well Road.

"Limpid Light," old Mr. Hsin gasped, clinging with his last strength to the jade bell. At this moment it began to ring with a thousand voices. The old man uttered a sigh of contentment.

He was with his daughter in the paradise of songbirds.

Mailin did not know how long she had been kneeling at her grandfather's deathbed. A hand touched her shoulder. She looked up into the face of a young man she did not know. It was a face more full of life than any she had ever seen. "May I help you, Cousin Hsin?" said the well-bred young Chinese with the glowing eyes behind intellectual's glasses. He spoke in flawless English. "I came to Shanghai by chance day before yesterday. What a city! Oh, permit me to introduce myself. I am your cousin, Jimmy Chou, from Singapore."

At that moment a strange procession arrived at Foo Ming Hospital. A Chinese workman and his wife from Yangtzepoo, with three sons clinging to their coattails, were pushing a handcart in which lay a long-legged European who had rescued the youngest son from a burning house. The handcart had been stolen somewhere; crushed fruit still lay in it. On the dreary way to the hospital the European's arms and legs had been dragged through dust and blood. The rescued son, a fat baby, was sleeping peacefully beside the unconscious rescuer.

"We must amputate the arm; it is already gangrenous," Dr. Chou murmured. "He must have lain for hours like that." At this moment Ernst August von Zabelsdorf opened his eyes. He was not surprised to see his Anna; nothing could surprise him now, for his head felt very light.

"Ernst," Anna Weber whispered close to his ear, "you'll be all right, but your arm must be operated on."

"Go ahead," Herr von Zabelsdorf croaked vaguely.

"Your arm must be taken off; do you consent?" Anna asked insistently, while Dr. Chou stood impatiently. First-aid stations had been set up in the streets, and every minute a nurse came for him.

"No!" Ernst said distinctly. "Out of the question. I need the arm for riding. Tell him that, Anna." But then night swept down upon him again, beating monstrous wings, and Dr. Chou operated anyhow so that Ernst could stay alive in this city of sudden death.

Toward morning he awoke, still half stunned and in great pain. He screamed fiercely and was given morphine. Anna looked in on him as often as she could. He lay on a bamboo mat on the first floor, between a dying water boy and a delirious singsong girl from Chapei. "Anna," he murmured and sank back into blackness. Where was she? She must not go away. Why was she hiding from him? Why, there was Anna, looking at him like a young Silesian Madonna who was simultaneously a schoolgirl in a nurse's cap. Where was his right arm? "Anna," he cried, "where is . . ." Dry sobs and rising fever shook him. Anna knelt beside him and laid his head against her breast, where no man's head had ever rested. She was so strong and helpful and pure in the midst of this city of perfumed vice. And she rocked the half-stupefied man in her arms until the terrible dry sounds stopped.

"*Mannla* . . ." she whispered.

It was the sweetest word of love in the Silesian dialect.

Old Mr. Hsin's funeral was one of the last social events in dying Shanghai—in the Shanghai of merchants and bankers of every race and nation; in the Shanghai of free Chinese, respected foreign devils, and patient, contented worker-bees in Chinese textile mills, exchange offices, rice shops, cook shops, night-clubs, docks and warehouses; in the Shanghai of Fuh Tan University, curiosity shops, Christian churches, and quiet Confucian temples; in the Shanghai of luxury hotels, filthy opium dens, and millions of frugal households. Until the outbreak of hostilities the city on the Whangpoo River had, for all its hectic bustle, stood solidly upon its own feet. Now it was already turning like the *kabuki* stage, and would continue to turn until it fell, weary, shattered, and stripped of all its virtues, to the Japanese. Nothing remained in its place; there were new masters, new servants, new vices—and new, terrible poverty for the Chinese worker-bees and the European refugees.

After the bloody Saturday the stillness of death had prevailed for a while. But soon thereafter new aerial and artillery battles began between Chinese and Japanese forces. The Japanese warships anchored farther up the Whangpoo River, at the mouth of Soochow Creek, and an era came to an end. But as yet the inhabitants of Shanghai did not suspect this. Neither foreigners nor Chinese foresaw that the Japanese victory parade had only just begun, that within a few years the Japanese would dominate all Southeast Asia, imparting a tremendous whirligig motion to the Asiatic stage and turning everything topsy-turvy. And although people are supposed to learn from trouble, in this city they learned nothing from their troubles, for they clung to property and prestige until they held nothing but ashes in their hands. Yet all the time, until the fall of Shanghai, life went on, with cannon and kisses, with celebrations of births and deaths. And the celebrations—without which the Chinese would be like every other nation—gave old Shanghai a magical radiance once again, and immortality in the bargain.

And so, a few weeks after Shanghai's bloody Saturday, the city's greatest Chinese financier and benefactor of widows, orphans, and coolies was conducted with traditional solemnity to his family grave. Before the event the Hsin and Chou families had sent out those celebrated obituaries which vividly conjure up for the benefit of the survivors all the deceased man's most sterling qualities. The booklet had a portrait of the financier on the first page. In subsequent pages prominent members of the Chinese Chamber of Commerce and writers for Mr. Hsin's newspaper described his importance to Shanghai's public life. Then followed the solemn lamentations of the Hsin and Chou families, in which they heartrendingly accused themselves of "inattention" toward Mr. Hsin Kao-tze. A compact biography of the great Crane of Shanghai concluded the green leatherbound volume. The chief mourner—who in this case was Mr. Chou Tso-ling, since Mr. Hsin had had no living son—had provided the editor-in-chief of Mr. Hsin's newspaper with a list of the most important dates

and events in the deceased man's life. The names of male relatives
in order of their importance and age were also included, in this way
stressing the high rank of the family. Right at the end stood a name
which engendered a great many rumors and conjectures in both
Shanghai and Singapore: *Mailin Hsin-Wergeland, granddaughter,
daughter of Hsin Ch'ing-chao, Shanghai.* This disturbing notice had
been inserted by the young Mr. Chou who had introduced himself
to Mailin at her grandfather's deathbed as Jimmy. To others he was
known as Mr. James Chou of Singapore, architect and son of the
millionaire apothecary Chou Yu-tsun, who had invented "butterfly
balm" for hoarse singsong girls.

Since the old-fashioned house back of Bubbling Well Road had
suffered only minor damage from the bombs, Mr. Hsin's mortal remains lay on the bier in the reception hall. He wore the prescribed
"wardrobe of last garments" which he himself had assembled with
great care during his lifetime and had preserved for years. There
were some twenty such garments, some of thin, some of stout material, in preparation for different seasons of the year, and all two
sizes too large—that the dead body might be the more easily dressed
in them. The outermost garment was of gleaming silk, embroidered
thickly with gold threads and pearls. A number of gems and pearls
were also placed in the big coffin, for the head of the family must
not set out on his voyage to the hereafter without some material
goods. A giant pearl was placed in the dead man's mouth.

Before the vast procession began moving through war-torn Shanghai—the possibility of a renewal of the Japanese bombardment was
stoically ignored by all concerned—the memorial ceremony took
place. Innumerable guests came and went through the reception hall
on this day, paying their respects to the deceased. Each of the guests
was greeted thunderously by a band and walked to the coffin amid
deafening howls of lamentation from the hired mourners. These
professional mourners were for the most part women, who in the
Chinese view can wail louder and better than men. Two of Mr.
Hsin's oldest servants, Purple Cuckoo and Faithful Goose, wailed in
the chorus voluntarily, without pay. Never again would they serve
such a master! He had found wives for their sons and provided
dowries for their daughters. Both the old women had sat at his feet
in the bird pavilion and borne with him the sorrow of his solitude. In

his will he had been so generous toward them that they would have no cares for the rest of their lives.

Purple Cuckoo and Faithful Goose had made for Mailin a white mourning gown of finest linen. They hovered around the grand-daughter with despotic humility; long ago they had served her mother, Limpid Light. Their tenacious and talkative loyalty extended to all who were in any way connected with Mailin. Nights, they took turns watching over Astrid in the hospital, since there were no private nurses available for the multitudes of sick and wounded. Of their own accord they already regarded the Wergelands as their second family—Chinese loyalty passing through revolutions and graves. After the funeral Faithful Goose remained with the Shanghai Mr. Chou and his German wife, in order to await the birth of the "grandson" who would then be given into her care. Purple Cuckoo returned as Mailin's personal servant to Bangkok, where she promptly began a silent but intense war against Miss Wergeland.

While the professional mourning women uttered their piercing howls every time a new guest made his bows before the coffin, automatically breaking off as soon as the gesture of respect was finished, the Singapore Mr. Chou regarded his new kinswoman with restrained delight. Mailin united Chinese virtue with European charm. Jimmy Chou had studied in England and Paris and was by no means insensitive to the graces of foreign women. Mailin was moved, but displayed the poise of a well-bred Chinese girl.

"May I call on you in Bangkok, Cousin Mailin?" he asked softly. Mailin nodded.

"Then you must meet my fiancée in Singapore," Cousin Chou whispered, looking at her with those incredibly lively eyes of his. A faint shadow passed over Mailin's face, though at the moment she was bowing low before a new member of the family, one of the querulous great-aunts of the Hsin branch. Was she disappointed? She had thought a great deal about Jimmy Chou during these past few days. He observed the shadow upon her delicate features and placed his arm around her shoulders.

"Are you already engaged?" he asked. "Your husband will have a favorable wind for the voyage of life."

"You are very kind, Cousin Chou," Mailin whispered. She did not look at this merry, urbane cousin of hers, for looks are born in the heart. This ancient Chinese wisdom was embedded deep in her. A sense of melancholy filled her; she longed for her home in Bangkok and for Aunt Helene, and decided she would remain with her forever. Why did Jimmy want to visit her? . . . The women howled; another guest was bowing before the coffin. He was some high official; in the breathless silence that followed the wails he painted a red sign on the dead man's wooden soul-tablet, which would be preserved on the family altar for posterity. The sign was a Buddhist "letter of recommendation" for the hereafter.

The indoor ceremonies concluded, it was time once more to display old Mr. Hsin's "face" before the general public. For on that day the Hsin and Chou families, the old-fashioned old people and the highly modern young people, paraded the deceased's social and financial position with princely pomp. Through the shattered streets of Shanghai wound an endless procession of relatives, foreign and native business associates, and spectators so taken with the splendor that they straightway joined the parade. For bombs and fireworks, weddings and funerals, all tragedies and all comedies, have their spectators in China; neither Christian nor Marxist teachers can do anything to change the inborn love of the Chinese for all kinds of spectacles, and their pleasure in pomp and circumstance.

The procession took place on a sultry September day four weeks after Mr. Hsin's death. A military band, consisting partly of police, formed the van. It was followed by a troop of Shanghai officials in uniform. Two huge lanterns bearing the name of Hsin, and two gongs, "smoothed the way" for the procession. Innumerable Europeans had sent expensive wreaths; wealthy Chinese had presented huge silk banners, which were proudly borne by hired coolies. An automobile carried the dead man's portrait, which faithfully recorded his reflective look and his long, thin crane's neck. Buddhist and Taoist monks accompanied the portrait toward paradise. The Hsin and Chou families walked behind the monks. Mailin and Dr. Wergeland followed in a car. The Hsins and Chous were invisible behind the white mourning curtains held protectively around them by many coolies. Then followed the coffin, on Mr. Hsin's big Chrysler. A drapery of richly embroidered silk concealed it from view. The coffin was surrounded by all the things that old Mr. Hsin would need in paradise. There was spirit-money in precious, hand-painted lac-

quer boxes, and a faithful model of his home in colored paper—
American bathroom and Chinese library included. On the summit
of the coffin stood a touching and utterly enchanting replica of the
bird pavilion, for everyone knew that old Mr. Hsin would think he
had entered the realm of spirits by the wrong door if he did not find
all his songbirds there. A wooden dragon adorned the coffin to in-
dicate that a man was being buried—when old Madame Hsin of the
Chou family had died, it had been a stork. And then followed several hundred private automobiles, cabs, rickshas, and humble pedes-
trians from the working-class quarters whom Mr. Hsin had provided
with rice year in and year out. They carried small handmade gifts
which they intended to smuggle into the High Person's grave at the
cemetery. Their wives, children, and grandsons marched along in the
procession, for they felt it as a kind of tribute to themselves that
Mr. Hsin was to be buried in a quiet little cemetery in the heart
of the old Chinese City. The High, Benevolent Person had wished to
be laid to rest in pure Chinese soil, so that he might set out on the
road to paradise together with porters, coolies, petty officials, and
workers. This was the highest honor that had ever been accorded
Shanghai's worker-bees. They stood, silent and reverent, far down
along the narrow side streets, whispering to their sons and grandsons
that virtue was the surest way to paradise.

So all Shanghai bade farewell to a man and to an era. Mr. Hsin
Kao-tze had been a friend and objective critic of the Europeans
and an irreconcilable enemy of the Japanese, a father to the poor,
a solitary listener to the song of birds, a far-sighted schemer and in-
triguer, a fit antagonist for Lieutenant Matsubara. Mailin sobbed on
her father's shoulder; the consul had risen from his sickbed for the
first time since his illness. By the workings of destiny Mailin had
been restored to him. What possible evils could come his way now?
Old Mr. Hsin would probably have told him that destiny is thin as
paper and that a father must not steal his favorite daughter from her
husband by keeping her too long. But Mr. Hsin could no longer
preach reason. Perhaps he had chosen the better part; the business
of life had already become a highly dubious affair. The Europeans
in the Far East were like songbirds on dead branches.

On the morning after old Mr. Hsin's funeral the newspapers nevertheless carried an item to the effect that Ernst August, Baron von

Zabelsdorf, had quietly wed Fräulein Anna Elisabeth Weber of Breslau. The couple would not be going away for a honeymoon for obvious reasons: Japanese bombs were raining down upon China.

Because death was so close, love produced some strange blossoms. For love is by no means always the same, as many people think. Now, however, it displayed more varieties than Japanese chrysanthemums. Sometimes it looked very much like hatred. Or it was fearful, like the love of Lieutenant Matsubara's much-envied wife. And these fears had a good basis and were more baneful than the bombs falling upon the city of Shanghai.

5: *Varieties of Love*

Lady Tatsue Matsubara had married because her father and old Baron Matsubara, both of whom were important figures in the Japanese combines, had so decided. She herself had not been asked, nor had she expected to be. Love played no part in Japanese marriages. If a young husband wished entertainment, he contemplated the moon over Enoshima. One did not marry for entertainment—during lunar eclipses there were the geishas, after all. One married in order to have sons who would obey their fathers as blindly as Akiro had obeyed his bland and cunning father during his early manhood. But a woman who brought only daughters into the world was a wife remiss in her duties, even if, like Lady Tatsue, she came of a great family and had perfect command of the arts of flower arrangement and the tea ceremony. The more disappointed Lieutenant Matsubara was in his wife, the more anxious grew Lady Tatsue. This September, anxiety almost suffocated her, for the doctor had informed her that she would be unable to have any more children. Now she sat with her two charming little daughters, whom their father almost completely ignored, and felt the weight of anxiety and shame crushing her.

On the day of old Mr. Hsin's funeral in Shanghai, Matsubara Akiro had departed from Tokyo for Enoshima, to admire the moon there, without so much as a farewell to his wife. This was the first time in their seven years of marriage that he had so baldly shown his contempt for Lady Tatsue. Hitherto she and Akiro had always contemplated the moon over Enoshima together and been harmoniously bored. That is to say, Akiro had been bored and Tatsue had not dared to speak to him. For although there were already emancipated wives in Tokyo who chattered away unbidden and who wore far too bright and glowing kimonos for their age, Lady Tatsue was not one of them. She obeyed her mother-in-law; followed her honored husband through the streets of Tokyo at a respectful distance, carrying his Western briefcase for him; never spoke unless addressed; and concealed her two small girls, Sadako and Eiko, as best she could from their father's cold glances. Akiro had never responded to the ardent love which had grown in Lady Tatsue soon after their wedding. When the first daughter was born he had frowned; at the birth of the second, shrugged. Now he usually traveled about as a tourist, and when he returned to Tokyo on leave he rarely spent his days and nights in the fine house in the western quarter of the city, not far from the Tenno's palace.

After Lady Tatsue had somewhat recovered from the blow of not being invited to Enoshima, she took a resolve. She was in such despair over the doctor's sentence that for the first time in her life she displayed initiative. She was by no means stupid; she had merely acted all her life in obedience to the authorities in Japanese family life—father, mother-in-law, and husband. Now she was twenty-seven years old, a quiet young woman with an aristocratic, reticent face and a limp—at the age of seven she had broken a leg, and her tender bones had knit poorly, the consequence of careless medical treatment. Akiro had nevertheless married her without objection. It had been clear from the first that he would some day marry into a combine. During the period of her engagement Tatsue had taken refuge in the reflection that she would most of the time be kneeling before her young husband—while he drank his tea, while she served his evening rice, while she took off his shoes. And when they went for walks she would have to follow him at the prescribed distance, and he therefore would not observe her unfortunate limp. She spent a tre-

mendous amount of time artfully doing her hair in order to please
her stern master. Stern he was, for Akiro forbade her even the few
harmless pleasures that an aristocratic Japanese woman was permitted to enjoy in the circles of her female kinswomen. Let Tatsue first
do her duty; once she was the mother of a young Baron Matsubara,
she could enjoy herself all she liked. To be sure, he had never said
this to Lady Tatsue in so many words; but in spite of his pressing
political work he was able to supervise Tatsue sufficiently to cut her
off from all possible pleasures. Each time the bans were laid down
with a polite smile. For Akiro had secretly begun to hate his wife,
not only because she had only daughters but because she obstinately
and mutely pursued him with her shy passion. A useless woman had
no right to passions. Lieutenant Matsubara believed that the student
Yuriko, who had spied privately for him in Shanghai and was now
working in Bangkok, had far more right to bore him with her love.
Yuriko was a first-rate agent and had sent him so much information
from Bangkok that as a reward he had invited her to come at intervals and admire the venerable Lady Moon in Enoshima with him.
He intended to spend two weeks there and then visit Bangkok—as
a tourist, of course. Yuriko was in seventh heaven.

Tatsue had a suspicion that her husband would not be alone in
Enoshima. She secretly went through his correspondence but found
only bills or invitations. Matsubara Akiro was not for nothing a member of the secret police. Only so innocent a loving wife as Lady Tatsue could think that he would leave Yuriko's respectful love letters
in his briefcase or in the desk in the Western Room for his wife to
examine.

Lady Tatsue had taken her two daughters to her mother-in-law
and asked her to take charge of them for the week end; she wanted
to visit some friends at the beach in Katase, she said. From this resort
it was possible to see across the water to Enoshima.

And so she sat alone in the train from Tokyo to Katase, repressing her fear. Her luggage consisted of a beautiful silk shawl in which
lay a well-worn volume of poems and a lock of hair from each of
her daughters. Lady Tatsue never left the house without her poems
and a memento of her two little girls. She loved and pampered them
to compensate for the High Paternal Person's indifference. For this
she got little thanks from her daughters, but she was so accustomed

to having her love despised that she even accepted Sadako's and Eiko's childish contempt. In accord with that inexplicable principle which awards love to those who neither desire, earn, nor even deserve it, Sadako and Eiko adored their youthful father. That they saw him so rarely only increased their affection. They were gay little creatures in bright dresses and kimonos, who in character had inherited some of Grandfather Matsubara's bland slyness. Since they were still very small, the family did not yet relegate them to second place, behind their male cousins. That began only when girls were growing up.

Lady Tatsue looked out at the fleeting landscape. Huge, dusty Tokyo lay behind her, and she was already entering the realm of Japan's thousand islands. At a station she bought from a platform peddler tea, rice, and an *umeboshi*—a large plum preserved with salt and spices. She by far preferred new-fashioned ice cream to *umeboshi*, but a woman who could no longer bear a son had no right to any such indulgences. So she rode on, out of twilight into denser dusk. . . .

Evening had come. It was a wonderful moonlit night. With lowered eyes Tatsue hesitantly left her frugal hotel, where she had taken a hot bath in order to give herself courage. Once more she went over in her mind that last terrible marital scene. In her despair she had lied to Akiro, telling him she was expecting a child again—and received for her pains only a smile from him. Her tricks were too simple for this esteemed member of the Kempetai. The baron had promptly telephoned the doctor and learned the truth. He was in the habit, after all, of assuming that persons who wish to obtain an advantage will embellish the truth. Furious, tormented by stomach cramps, he had appeared in the tea room and so deeply humiliated Lady Tatsue as to drive her to this desperate expedient on this moonlit night. He had struck her. To be sure, it had been only a single blow and he had instantly apologized, but it was done. Lady Tatsue, whom her honored husband privately thought of as a "limping mouse," had a proud Japanese soul. Her soul flew; only her body limped in the dust of this transitory existence.

It was ten o'clock in the evening when Lady Tatsue limped to a lonely spot on the beach at Katase and there sat down in the moonlight to meditate. All around her lovers whispered the enchanting

nonsense Tatsue had never heard from Akiro. Tatsue contemplated
the streaming whitish light, the beach, and the great bridge that led
to the magical island of Enoshima. There, perhaps, Akiro might at
this moment be climbing up to the terrace temple and inhaling with
delight the incomparable sea air. *Akiro!*—husband eternally loved
and eternally lost. With *samurai* courage Lady Tatsue swallowed her
tears. Her honored great-grandfather had been so famous that Tokyo
school children still learned songs about him. No member of such a
family could permit herself to be struck—not even an obedient lame
wife who had failed in her duty.

Certainly she was dreamy, spoiled her daughters, persecuted her
honored husband with boring "love in thought"; but now at last she
knew what she must do. Only thus could she restore her honor and
prove to Akiro that in spite of all her faults she had not been entirely
unworthy of him. She had mailed her letter to him before taking
the train for Katase. For a moment Lady Tatsue placed her fine,
sensitive hand upon her breast, and then upon her unfruitful, unac-
commodating womb. Later she walked forward and sat down so
close to the water that a single step would have brought her to the
bridge which led to Akiro. . . .

Hours must have passed. The beach was deserted now. The honey-
mooning couples had gone to their hotels and were begetting sons.
Lady Tatsue alone sat like a statue in the moonlight, letting her mind
once more run over the course of her marriage. She had been so
proud of her handsome, unapproachable husband. Her heart had almost stopped for happiness at their wedding, when they drained together the traditional cup of saké. She had always been so ignored
—a lame girl. And now she was an old woman of twenty-seven and
had accomplished nothing at all—nothing, except for the one thing
that remained to be done and that would set everything to rights.
Now she would glow in the dark.

She contemplated her gray kimono. Underneath it she wore a garment embroidered with chrysanthemums, the symbol of her glowing, hidden soul. Lady Tatsue looked around once more. Then she
threw the mouse-gray kimono into the sea. For a moment she stood
erect in her chrysanthemum gown. The flowers glowed in the moonlight. She was carefully powdered and rouged. Never would she have
undertaken this step with unadorned "morning face." Around her

long, frail neck—the sign of noble blood—hung a cheap talisman which she had bought before the birth of her first son—who was never to be—and had worn until this day. The *tamuki* was meant especially for boys. She took the talisman, touched it gently to her lips, and threw it into the sea so that future mothers of sons would not trample on it tomorrow. It had cost only thirty sen, but still it had been intended for a *taro-san*—an "important little man," the usual title for an eldest son. She leaned her weight on her ivory cane. Then she walked slowly into the sea and became one with the venerable Lady Moon. Matsubara Akiro would now have the chance to beget many healthy sons with a worthier wife.

Lady Tatsue smiled before the waves received her.

In China the moon god is called Yüeh Lao Yeh. He is an old man who arranges marriages. It is his duty to bind engaged couples to each other with a red thread. This thread is supposed to hold for life, and Yüeh Lao Yeh sees to it that none of the husbands takes flight. "Marriages are made in the moon," the saying is in China. Everyone believed that, from the banker to the river pirate and from the singsong girl to the German wife of Mr. Chou Tso-ling, who after the death of his uncle, old Mr. Hsin, moved into the old-fashioned house back of Bubbling Well Road.

On the moonlit night on which Lady Tatsue Matsubara took flight from life, a son was born in the old-fashioned house in devastated Shanghai. He was a vigorous boy in whose veins flowed the blood of a Chinese banker and a Jewish banker from Breslau. His mother was the helpless young widow of a once famous Breslau lawyer who had taken her and her friend Anna Weber to the city across the seas, there to practice the business of continuing life. So curiously and wisely had Moon God Yüeh Lao Yeh tied the red threads of marriage that Chou Tso-ling had brought Hanna Goldberg into one of the mightiest families in Shanghai. Hanna had simply not been born for the role of pastime woman, and the moment she was married she once more became a Breslau girl from a respectable family.

On this moonlit night Hanna lay, relaxed and happy, in the old-fashioned bed that had belonged to Mailin Wergeland's grandmother, in which Mailin's mother and the short-lived son of the house of Hsin had been born. Several people moved softly and busily in the big moonlit room: the Chou family's doctor, Anna Weber von Zabelsdorf, and Mailin Wergeland. The child had just been born; Anna put him, in an embroidered Chinese infant's gown, into Hanna's arms. "Here is your son, Hanna," Anna whispered. "I'll go for Tso-ling. They are all waiting in the bird pavilion."

Then Anna and Mailin, together with Dr. Chou of Foo Ming Hospital, left the room, and Hanna Chou was alone with her son for the first time. He lay still at her side, and she regarded with amazement the miracle of the tiny hands and the dark, almond-shaped baby eyes. It had been a long road from a pastime woman's apartment to this patrician household so steeped in tradition, and Bertel, who had now been resting for two years in Chinese soil, would certainly be content with the way things had gone. He had wanted Hanna to find a good husband and protector in this foreign city, had told her this with his last breath. And somehow the son who now lay at her breast was in a way Bertel's son too, Hanna thought mistily. During the few minutes she was left alone with her newborn son in the magnificent bed with its heavy brocade curtains the stages of her Shanghai life rushed as in a film past her mind's eye: the wretched room in the Hongkew quarter; Bertel, stooped over a Chinese shoe, coughing his lungs out as he tried to repair it; Bertel, scholar's glasses on his penetrating, kindly eyes, reading Lao-Tzu in the original. Then the last cough, the last kind word, the last veiled look, still protectively loving even in utter helplessness.

"Good-by," he had whispered, and so departed, liberated from a fugitive's existence. Bertel—a great lawyer; a cheerful, practical, paternal husband, who had never fully understood why Hanna, so much younger and finer than himself, had married him.

The funeral in Shanghai . . . the Chinese in white mourning robes . . . the heartache of solitude . . . "I can never stand it in the Chinese hospital, Anna! I can't do it; Bertel pampered me too much." Anna's words of comfort, and Anna's wages . . . dismissal from the hospital. . . . "The white lady is much too good for our miserable hospital. It is unworthy of the white lady." Chinese courtesy in firing a silly female. A *tai-tai* without dollars was worse than a cur without a master.

And then that frightful night in her last Breslau evening dress and the motheaten fur coat. Hanna had never had to fuss over her clothes.

The maid had attended to that for her, or Bertel, who hated to see things spoiled because he knew how hard they had to be worked for. Hanna had closed her eyes tightly and in the arms of a Chinese thought of Bertel. For she was determined to contribute her share of the rent and food money. The only daughter of Councilor Stein could not let Anna support her forever.

One night in a dance hall Mr. Chou Tso-ling, old Mr. Hsin's nephew, had appeared at her table. "Say, there's a good catch. Go after him!" the manageress, a White Russian, had whispered to her. But Hanna had not gone after him. Mr. Chou had danced with her, ordered champagne, chatted. Never had he expected to meet such a woman in the Blue Lotus Emporium. Here was a lady who spoke good English, who was modest, and who had utterly lovely grief-stricken eyes. "Where do you live, Madame?" . . . Hm—a sad address for a white goddess. They rode home in Mr. Chou's brand-new Cadillac. "May I see you again, Madame?" Any time; you have only to pay. I am employed at the Blue Lotus. Bedroom, opium room, mirror room on the second floor . . . Naturally Hanna had not said that; that was not how one replied to such requests in Breslau. "I shall be very glad, sir," she had murmured.

Then Mr. Chou Tso-ling had discussed the case with his two cousins, Dr. Chou of Shanghai and Jimmy Chou of Singapore. And Jimmy, the cosmopolitan young man with the lively eyes which made Cousin Mailin Hsin-Wergeland's heart pound, had advised Tso-ling to set this remarkable lady up in a little place of her own.

Naturally Hanna had not taken anything for nothing from Mr. Chou. Without protest, with eyes firmly shut, she had paid for her apartment. She was alone most of the day. In the afternoons, however, she invited Anna Weber for lunch and cooked all Bertel's favorite dishes. Cooking—that was the way it had really begun. "We can do without the cook-boy, Tso-ling," Hanna had said. "I cook a great deal better." With time she had made a home out of the insipid little whore's apartment—a gracious, pleasant home to which young Mr. Chou repaired with a sigh of relief after the day's business affairs were done. Hanna had found herself again. Though everything in her life was topsy-turvy, she was back in a place for which she was suited. She could not empty chamber-pots with good grace, but she knew how to keep house and she could embroider. That was something she had learned in a feudalistic finishing school, luxury embroidery on precious materials. It had cost her many a bitter tear, but she had learned well. Anna saw some of her things and offered them to clients at Madame Ninette's beauty salon. She sold every one of them.

Then the great moment had come, an evening like any other in Shanghai, and yet for Hanna an evening of rebirth. When Tso-ling arrived for dinner she was not wearing a Chinese mandarin gown or a pair of silk pajamas. She wore a raw-silk dress from Breslau, so simple and unadorned that it must have cost a fortune. Over the coffee came the moment that proved to be the great turning point in her life. She stood up, once again with the ladylike grace that was a part of her upbringing, and handed Mr. Chou an envelope. "Here is the rent, Tso-ling," she said quietly. "I am earning so much from my embroidery that from now on you will be my guest in this apartment. I am very happy to have you here, my dear."

The young banker stared speechlessly at his pastime woman for a moment. His intelligent dark eyes shifted from the dress, which seemed all the more fashionable because it was a little outmoded, to the tablecloth, which Hanna had embroidered, to the room, which she had cleared of all superfluous ornament, to her fine oval face with its mournful eyes.

"Tell me about your family, Hanna," he said at last, very quietly. It was like a decoration unexpectedly pinned on one's breast. Hanna told him about herself for the first time. She spoke of her childhood, her parental household, explained that her father had been a financier, spoke of her marriage to Bertel—and spoke of Bertel again and again. All of Breslau would come to hear a case when he was conducting the defense. . . . She conjured up their big summer house with its view of the lake. And then Shanghai. She spoke softly, as if it were someone else's life she were relating. But it was her life. She was drawing up a balance sheet—like any banker, in Breslau or Shanghai.

"I would be very happy if you would come with me to visit my mother next week," Chou Tso-ling said.

Old Madame Chou's house lay on Great Western Road, at the rim of the great city. At the end of the road, where the Chous' mansion stood, one looked out upon open country—fields, lanes of plane trees, and canals in which the pure lotus blossomed. There Madame Chou had scrutinized her closely and let her have the family's treasured recipe for preserved ginger. That had been the first visit. Afterward old Madame Chou had appeared for tea at Hanna's, accompanied by innumerable servants and grandnieces. She had looked around the flat of the German "embroidery mistress" and examined with a professional eye the napkins Hanna had hemstitched. Then, until the wedding, Hanna had lived in her mother-in-law's house. When Anna Weber lost her job at the beauty salon, old Madame Chou had found her another as assistant nurse in Foo Ming Hospital. So everything had turned out well. . . .

Suddenly Tso-ling was standing in the moonlit bedroom. He stooped solemnly, silently over his wife and his son—a fine, strong grandson for old Madame Chou, who had so warmly taken his Hanna to her heart. By now she would not have preferred a Chinese daughter-in-law to Hanna. Hanna could cook, entertain guests, and bear sons. She had brought the Chou family "a thousand felicitous hours."

"What shall we call him?" Hanna asked, her eyes glowing like dark suns.

"Herbert Chou," Tso-ling said, kissing her.

So it came about that the eldest son of Banker Chou received the given name of a refugee Jewish lawyer from Breslau.

Outside, in the bird pavilion, it was very quiet. They were at the moment all staying with Chou Tso-ling and Hanna in the house back of Bubbling Well Road: Consul Wergeland, Astrid in her sickroom, Mailin, and Jimmy Chou, who would be returning to Singapore on the morrow. With Chinese hospitality Tso-ling had insisted that Mailin's relatives stay with him and Hanna until Astrid recovered. If there were danger of more bombing, they would then all be together, as was proper for a large family.

Astrid slept restlessly. She was recovering very slowly, for Pierre had left again, and she only half lived without him. Moreover, she had the tormenting feeling that her fiancé led a full and colorful life without her—which was in fact the case. She now had a lifetime to find out about the lives and transformations of a single man.

At their parting there had been a slight discordance, the first of many such slight discordances between this unlike couple to whom love meant basically different things. In her concern for the future, Astrid had had Mailin write a letter at her dictation to Amélie Clermont in Paris. She had told Amélie of her engagement and asked her to inquire in Paris whether Pierre might not be able to lecture there on the archaeological finds in Indo-China, or again obtain a good post with some newspaper or magazine. They planned to be married in two years; by then the Clermonts, with their connections all over Paris, would certainly have turned the trick. For all her love, it seemed to Astrid utterly out of the question that she should bury herself in Hanoi among Tonkinese and Chinese. She still wanted to open a millinery salon in Paris. She was a modern girl and hoped she would be a wonderful wife.

Amélie had answered that there were certainly excellent prospects for Pierre there. Everyone in Paris realized the cultural importance of the excavations in Indo-China. But instead of blithely thanking his fiancée for her efforts, the free-tongued Monsieur de Maury had at first remained silent as a Trappist. Finally he had remarked coldly that he did not like fiancées to be concerning themselves about their future husband's careers. Since Astrid unfortunately always wanted to know things precisely, she asked Pierre whether he no longer loved her.

"I love you passionately, my darling arranger of lives," Pierre had replied, but the answer displeased Astrid. She had been forced to postpone the quarrel, since Monsieur de Maury had promptly left for Bangkok. Whom he was going to meet there, why and wherefore he was going there, he had not revealed. Astrid had successfully swallowed her tears and received Pierre's parting kiss with closed eyes. Now she lay motionless in the moonlight and was able to cry at leisure. She so seldom cried that she enjoyed it greatly. Then she prayed, aridly but doggedly. *What* was she doing wrong? How should she arrange matters so as to possess this man completely? No solution came to her. Pierre! This was the only thought she could keep in her head.

Astrid hoped she would soon be well enough to leave. But Shanghai had brought her one great good—friendship. During those days when nothing but bombs, kisses, and death seemed to exist in Shanghai, Astrid, sick, weak, and bewildered by a love full of problems, made a friend for life—Hanna Chou, the German wife of her host. The two young women from such differing physical and emotional worlds had come together without Astrid's lifting a finger. It was a veritable miracle. Perhaps she had aroused Hanna's sympathy and affection because for once in her life she had not planned anything and had not struggled to be the best-beloved. Perhaps, too, Hanna with her experience in suffering, which had made her mature and loving far beyond her years, sensed that Astrid was terribly lonely, and arrogant from fear of disappointments. Gently, in the most light-handed way, she had given Astrid much good advice on how best to treat Pierre de Maury. Astrid had followed none of her advice, and so she persisted in saying the wrong thing to her fiancé at the right moment, and the right thing at the wrong moment.

"Out with it, Annie," Herr von Zabelsdorf said to his newly wed wife on a moonlit veranda in the French Concession. "Why did you skip out on me before the eggs began to drop?"

"There were a number of reasons." Anna hesitated. "I think I was very silly, Ernst."

"Out of the question."

"Yes, I was. A—a Japanese waitress at the White Chrysanthemum came to have German lessons from me. On account of the Anti-Comintern Pact, she said, so many Germans were patronizing the restaurant now."

"What has that to do with us?"

Anna suddenly looked stern. "She said to me—in her artless Japanese way, I mean—that she, that you . . ."

"Out with it, my girl."

"That she often helped you pass the time. You understand . . ."

"I don't understand a word, Anna."

In the moonlight his long, intelligent, horsy face with its sharp eyes looked hard at her. "What kind of dirty trick is this, now?" Herr von Zabelsdorf murmured thoughtfully. "What was her name?"

"Yuriko. I found out by chance at the restaurant. She had paid in advance for the lessons because . . ."

"Why?"

"Because I had no money left, Ernst," Anna said almost desperately. "For a while I had to take care of Hanna too, you know. And so . . ."

"I see you had a lot of faith in me." Ernst August von Zabelsdorf did not smile. "This damned city, and a little thing like you astray in it . . ."

"Yuriko left suddenly—for Bangkok, I think. I still owed her two lessons." Anna still had no suspicion that Lieutenant Matsubara's agent had tried to anger her to the point of stealing Ernst von Zabelsdorf's correspondence with the Chinese banker. Akiro suspected the Germans of supplying the Chinese National Army with arms. Arms for Chiang Kai-shek would be a good business, after all.

"Forget about it, Annie. Come, give your old invalid a kiss. You don't have to worry about me. I'm a damn fool dog, faithful-like."

Only Jimmy Chou of Singapore remained behind in the bird pavilion. Like an old-fashioned Chinese he contemplated the moon, the friend of Taoists and pacifists. From Hanna Chou's wing came the sound of happy voices; a son had been born.

Jimmy intended to leave Shanghai next day. In this old house the life of his forefathers seemed to be going on as if there were no war and the Japanese were not bombing the towns of the Yangtze to smithereens. From far away came the muted beat of a drum. Taoist monks were praying for the hordes sick with cholera on the outskirts of the city.

Mr. James Chou once more read his mail from Singapore. He nodded three times, like an old bazaar god at a Chinese fair. So his father was not opposed to the change of plans. His own mind was already made up.

Mailin appeared in an apple-green dress. "A son has been born, Cousin Chou," she called, not looking at him. "Won't you come to see Hanna?"

"Later, Cousin Mailin. Please join me here in the pavilion. Tomorrow will be too late. I am returning to Singapore."

"*Bon voyage,* Cousin Chou."

"The name is Jimmy, Cousin Hsin."

Pause. Jimmy and Mailin contemplated the moon. The birds slept. The world slept.

"My father has written me, Mailin. He would like you to visit us in Singapore. My elder brother would also like to meet you."

"Thank you for the honor," Mailin said, bowing like a well-bred Chinese girl, "but I intend to stay with my father and my Aunt Helene when we leave here. We should be able to leave in another week. Astrid is going to stay with Hanna and Tso-ling until she is well."

Jimmy Chou looked down from his considerable height upon tiny Mailin. Little bird, he thought, and remained silent for a moment. His ordinarily lively face was somewhat frozen. "Does that mean that you will never visit us, Mailin? Would you mind being European for a change and telling me the candid truth?"

"I want to stay in Bangkok. That is all, Cousin Chou."

"Wouldn't you like to meet my bride?"

"Why do you ask?"

"Mailin, we want to bind you closer to our family. You would make a wonderful wife for my brother."

"I shall never marry, Cousin Chou." Mailin bowed her head because looks are born in the heart.

"But at least you will come to my wedding?"

Mailin did not answer. A woman lost virtue in showing her heart to a man, above all when he disdained it. But suddenly she raised her head and looked full at Cousin Chou. The Wergeland heritage in her soul burst through. "I will *not* come to your wedding. Good night, Cousin Chou." The moon stabbed at her like a dagger.

"But then I cannot be married," Jimmy Chou exclaimed in comic horror. But there was something else in his voice—an earnest question which, after the Chinese fashion, he hid behind a joke.

"What do you mean by that, Cousin Chou?"

One of the birds awoke and began singing drowsily. The tops of the fir trees stood like silver swords in the moonlight. Love was a sword forged by old Yüeh Lao Yeh, the man in the moon. No silken thread could cut so deep.

"Have you ever seen a wedding without a bride?" Cousin Chou inquired, catching Mailin in a net of ardent glances. He lifted her up like a cloud of feathers, and in the light of the matchmaking moon regarded that delicate face with its unfathomable Chinese eyes and the narrow nose of the Wergelands.

"Mailin, bird-girl," he whispered, "don't you understand yet?"

In this way Mr. James Chou informed the granddaughter of old Mr. Hsin that he had broken his engagement in Singapore and intended to bring Mailin into the house of Chou as honored wife and mother of many sons. Jimmy Chou had already spoken with her father. The consul recognized that daughters were gifts with a time limit. Above all, he had realized that Mailin's life would have to be a Chinese life. He had lived too long in the Far East not to see that marriage with a Chou would be the best possible solution for his favorite daughter. He himself would simply spend part of the year in Singapore. Subconsciously he had long ago decided to settle forever in the Far East, in order not to lose Mailin. His loving father's instinct had warned him that Mailin would never again wish to live in Europe.

Late that night, when everyone had congratulated the newly engaged couple and drunk mulled-wine toasts to a thousand years of happiness for them, Mailin asked her fiancé whether he would be disappointed if she presented him with a daughter instead of a son. She did not know what had impelled her to pose this question. She had only been studying that face, livelier than any other she had ever seen, and a minuscule Asian anxiety had risen in her—not the choking anxiety that had driven Baron Matsubara's wife to her death, but a need to search out her future husband's moral countenance.

"A daughter would be all right with me on one condition," Jimmy Chou said with more energy than the occasion required. "She would have to look like you."

He was a member of the new generation that had grown up in Singapore under the English. And he was Chinese. He was not surrounded by thorny hedges of duties like Lieutenant Matsubara—and like most of his own countrymen.

All were asleep; even Astrid had at last ceased to fret. Only Miss Wergeland in Bangkok could not go to sleep. For the fifth time she read a letter from Shanghai with surprising news. Although almost everything else changed, so that an outsider could scarcely recognize the life in Asia that had been before the stage revolved so jerkily, dropping some off the scene and lifting others onto it, Miss Wergeland did not turn and did not change. She still hated surprises, scenes, and shirkers. She loved Mailin, put up with Astrid, and was anxious about the child Vivica.

But her stability was of no avail. The Far Eastern stage was whirling for Baron Matsubara and millions of his countrymen. It was already turning fast on that night in 1937 when the birds began singing in the moonlight in the house of Chou and the dead branches made cracking noises.

Yumei appeared, barefoot, upon Miss Wergeland's veranda in Bangkok. It was two o'clock in the morning. "Youngest Sister is screaming, Mem," she reported, "screaming again like a fox-ghost."

"Silly nonsense," Miss Wergeland said, getting up. "She is only dreaming. . . . What is it, Vivie?" she asked a moment later, shaking the child awake. The lovely little face was twisted with fear.

"The door, Aunt Helene," Vivica whispered, wide-eyed. "Someone closed the door. Was it the moon goddess?"

"Nonsense, the door is wide open. But come!" She carried the trembling child under her own mosquito netting.

What will come of this? she thought. Knut should never have allowed that business of open doors to start. She frowned down at Vivica in perplexity. There were so many things a person had to endure in life. If Vivica could not stand closed doors now, what would happen when, some day, she had to? In Trondheim in winter, or in hotels—or even in a prison? Good Lord, whatever put that last idea into her head? I'm losing my grip, she thought, yawned, and went to sleep.

BOOK TWO

===

Where Tears Are Forbidden . . .

"Tenno heika banzai!—Let us die for the Emperor!"

Political earthquakes have happened so frequently in our time that they really ought to surprise no one any longer. Nevertheless, countless numbers of our contemporaries are always unprepared when the earth suddenly cracks and swallows them up with kith and kin, bank accounts and stamp collections. The Europeans in Singapore, Bangkok, Batavia, and the vicinity were still drinking cocktails and playing golf when the Imperial Japanese Army stood at the gates of their athletic clubs and palatial dwellings. After December 8, 1941, the earth cracked asunder; the white gods of Hong Kong, Singapore, the Dutch East Indies, and the Philippines were led away to Japanese internment camps or to forced labor on the Siam-Burma Railway—those of them who were American, British, or Dutch, that is. In Japanese-occupied East Asia only Scandinavians, Swiss, Vichy French, Germans, Italians, and Russians remained as "free guests." Among these privileged souls were the members of the Wergeland family, who decided not to return to German-occupied Norway. They preferred Japanese-occupied Siam. There Miss Wergeland could still throw the truth like a wet dishrag into every visitor's face —a habit that would have brought serious trouble down upon her in Trondheim during those years. But when the earth in Bangkok also opened to swallow the Wergelands, they were still wholly unprepared. Like most Westerners, they had ignored Japanese preparations for the struggle for world domination with a naïveté that they now bitterly paid for. The lesson Japan administered to the white gods during the period of the Rising Sun shook them roughly out of their sleep of indifference. Willy-nilly, they had to concern themselves with the Japanese now. Too late Americans and Europeans learned that travelers like Captain Saito and Lieutenant Matsubara had been anything but tourists, and that in addition they were inflexible foes of the white face; and that the land of chrysanthemums, geishas, and lovely courtesies was a police state led by a military group intoxicated with power.

The years between Pearl Harbor and the sunset at Hiroshima ought not to be forgotten by the West, and not only because Japan unleashed the greatest racial war of modern times—the Tokyo press and radio referred to it as a holy war against the white race by a thousand million Asians. This brief period which brought death, suffering, and madness to thousands of Europeans and Americans conveyed the lesson that in the future indifference toward the peoples of the Far East might mean the end of the Western World. It is a vital necessity for the West to understand Japanese, Chinese, and Indians. Lieutenant Matsubara and his marionettes were already principal actors upon the Far Eastern revolving stage while we were still regarding them as extras. Any day they can begin again to raise those Shinto chrysanthemums which we see as pretty garden flowers. It is their national sport. And the mania to die for the Tenno still exists. All that can be said now is that the Japanese do not sing so much.

Aside from the death propaganda which from 1941 to 1945 sent those famous Japanese suicide brigades into the battle for the Pacific, there was also economic propaganda for the conquered "little brothers" in Southeast Asia. The Co-Prosperity Sphere was assiduously preached but put into practice in a somewhat one-sided fashion. It was an economic plan on glossy paper, intended to win for Nippon the raw materials she lacked, as well as the gratitude of the Asians in Malaya, the Dutch East Indies, Indo-China, Siam, Burma, and the Philippines who had hitherto been exploited by the West. Under the slogan of "Asia for Asians," the victorious legions of the Tenno, with sacred zeal, seized from the natives of these territories their rice, rubber, coffee, and other vital products. In return the Tokyo radio, the newspapers, and Lieutenant Matsubara of the Kempetai told the little brothers that they were now the masters of New Asia.

The third phenomenon of the period of the Rising Sun was the lightning transformation of the Japanese tourists of prewar days into Japanese victors. The speed with which this change took place was truly incredible. The Chinese, to be sure, maintain that a virtuous victor is as rare as a five-legged water buffalo; but in this case the masks fell from the faces of the polite, admiring tourists with startling rapidity.

Nippon failed in this war above all because the mechanics of success engendered in the fanatical souls of the Japanese two phenomena inimical to success: a static megalomania, which was the direct opposite of the dynamic striving for world dominion; and a mystical trust in victory. Both these attitudes are a creeping moral corruption which attacks equally the Caesars of East and West at the peak of power. Thus Lieutenant Matsubara of the Kempetai already sat in the prison cell of success long before he and millions of his fellows plunged into the depths of defeat. He had meanwhile been advanced in rank and had sniffed about everywhere in occupied Southeast Asia for enemies of the sacred state, as well as for saboteurs among the Chinese and free Europeans. During those years of triumph there were irritating cases of industrial espionage in the Siamese, Indo-Chinese, and Burmese regions. Major Matsubara, also known as Major Kimura, dealt especially with such cases. The traitors, who worked in the dark like the hooded *minomushi*-insect, again and again informed the Allies where the sons of the Rising Sun were setting up factories and establishing munitions depots on lands lush with dreamy tropical flowers. Everywhere the Japanese had confiscated the largest and most retired dwellings of the fallen white gods and were raising orchids and munitions in them. Major Matsubara was so ingenious in tracking down such traitors that he was generally called "the bloodhound" in military-intelligence circles. When he laid hands on one of the Allies' marionettes he took it apart thoroughly, in order to see how much sawdust and how many secrets were concealed inside. Shortly before the apocalyptic end, Major Matsubara had the opportunity to take vengeance on a white goddess in the name of the Kempetai. This revenge aroused in the major private emotions that ill suited a descendant of the *samurai*.

For, aside from longings for a glorious death for the Tenno, private emotions were strictly forbidden to a bloodhound. It was meet for him only to smile at the progressive "destruction of the white race," which one of his countrymen had announced as early as 1938 in the famous book *Nippon Kakushin nosho,* "The Book of the Renewal of Japan." And Major Matsubara smiled frequently while the sun was still rising; he smiled and even laughed, like thousands of his countrymen—a high, shrill, unending laughter which sent icy chills down the spines of victims of the Kempetai. The more shrilly he laughed in those days, the more freely flowed the tears of those who provided such amusement for him.

1: *Finale in Angkor*

In the rainy season of the year 1942 Miss Wergeland sat on her veranda in Bangkok, writing a letter to Hanna Chou, Astrid's friend
in Shanghai. It was late evening, and the mosquitoes were buzzing
around the dim electric light. Miss Wergeland was dressed in white,
and her hair had also turned white. At her feet crouched faithful
Yumei, who had left her husband and children in the cook house in
order to keep Fröken company. Helene was wearing a black band
around the sleeve of her tropical dress. The band was new, as if for
mourning.

Suddenly she laid her pen aside and listened, frowning. Through
the garden with its swaying banana stalks a low song broke into the
nocturnal solitude. Yumei too raised her head.

Three Japanese soldiers were marching through the fearful, quivering, deathly still city. They were singing the "Shinto Hymn of the
Year 1942":

> "Nippon, the sacred land,
> Fights for the peace of the East
> And destruction of the foreign powers.
> Listen, you peoples of the earth!

Once there was Japan and other countries;
Soon there will be nothing but Nippon.
Listen, you peoples of the world!"

"Is the door locked, Yumei?" Miss Wergeland asked.

"Yes, Mem. Khum Yam is watching." Khum Yam was the Indian night watchman.

"They broke into the home of a Dane recently."

"Yumei takes good care, Mem! Now that . . ." Yumei fell silent. Tears filled her eyes.

"Very well, Yumei," Miss Wergeland said, compressing her lips.

The doorkeeper, wakened from his doze by the song of the Japanese soldiers, had crept to the gate and, concealed behind a palmyra palm, had surreptitiously examined the new lock once again. They came in the night sometimes and took away an Indian or a Chinese or the whites. They sang and won battles and marched, and commanded their little brothers in Greater East Asia to follow their biddings.

Khum Yam shook his round head and softly sang himself to sleep. His only son was in the cellars of the Kempetai, where he was being quizzed about other Indians. Khum Yam knew he would never see him again. When anyone in this "allied" city heard the word "information" or "Kempetai," he was seized by cold shivers. On the veranda Mem was still sitting, the black band around her arm. She continued writing.

Khum Yam hummed an ancient Hindu song to fend off the choking anxiety over his son. He rocked his big round head, tapped time with his bamboo staff, and sang:

"There is no sense in weeping
Where tears are forbidden."

He sang very low, in order not to disturb Mem Wergeland.

Helene Wergeland brushed her white hair back from her forehead and read over once again what she had written to Hanna Chou, Astrid's friend in Shanghai. She had met her at Mailin's wedding two years ago and come to think highly of her—a dear, sensible young woman who knew that life is not a joke. . . .

Dear Hanna,

Many thanks for your last letter. I would have replied long ago, had not my brother's sudden death plunged us all into grief. I long ago pleaded with Knut to have an operation, but no one in my family has ever followed my advice. When the severe attack in Singapore came, it was probably already too late to save him. Mailin was at his side when he died. He did not live to see his grandson born. Mailin is very well. Purple Cuckoo, her Grandfather Hsin's old servant, now tyrannizes over her and the baby. I am planning a trip to Singapore to see them, if the uncertain political situation and my family cares permit.

Since, Hanna dear, you ask so sweetly about Astrid, I shall be perfectly frank with you. You are her only friend and know what a problem child she is. Astrid has now been happily engaged to Monsieur de Maury for five years, and still there is no talk of marriage. I was against this engagement from the start, but as I said, no one listens to me. Monsieur de Maury always speaks of the war as the obstacle to marriage. I should like to know what the war has to do with this muddled affair. Astrid could very well help Pierre clean up his dusty pieces in the museum at Hanoi. Believe me, Monsieur de Maury is a shirker. It doesn't take any special keenness to see that. In my long life I have accumulated a good deal of experience with shirkers, I assure you. It's a mystery to me that Astrid, with her intelligence, doesn't see through the business. I grant you, circumstances have complicated the lives of all of us and made Astrid's future a dubious matter also. Since the German troops marched into Paris on Mailin's wedding day, Astrid and Monsieur de Maury could not very well go back there. But he has been leading her around by the nose here, instead of coming out with the truth. I know that you understand my concern, Hanna dear. It is good, at any rate, to know that you are the happy mother of three sons and have a full life in your family. Please give them all my warmest regards. Old Madame Chou is a person after my own heart. Not a trace of nonsense in that woman, and not a speck of dust on her furniture. I still think back with pleasure on my visit to Shanghai shortly before Mailin's wedding. Monsieur de Maury with his *parlez-vous* could well learn from your husband how a man ought to behave. But then, Tso-ling is his mother's son!

I want to be perfectly honest, so that you will understand why I am making this request. Would it be possible for Astrid to visit you for a few weeks after her trip to Angkor? I know that the Japanese are spying outrageously on prominent Chinese these days, so that if your husband does not wish to have a European in his house let me know without beating about the bush. I am well aware of the low state we have fallen to since the Japanese occupation. If I did not know you to be a sensible and sincere friend of my family, I would not make this suggestion.

The relationship between Astrid and Vivica is at the moment so painful that I think it would be better if Astrid were to live for a time in another environment, and under your influence. The antique business that my late brother helped build up years ago is so well managed by the Suns, his Chinese partners, that Astrid could well take it easy for a while. As you probably know, she worked her way into the business while my brother was still living, and continues to buy at auctions with discrimination and good business sense. I am very glad she has found an occupation which keeps her busy and also brings in money, since our account at the Hong Kong and Shanghai Bank has been frozen. The Japanese promptly arrested the English manager and confiscated the deposits of all foreigners. At the moment we are also receiving nothing from Trondheim. No word has come yet from my brother Olaf. I do not even know whether he is alive, or what has become of the shipyards. Astrid has set up an office of her own on Prahurat Road and conducts her business there. That is all I know about it. Perhaps you can find out more.

Vivica, who has developed into a veritable minx, will call Astrid nothing but "the duchess." It is amazing to see how furious Astrid becomes over such childish teasing. I must admit the child is sometimes a real cross. And what is worse, this sixteen-year-old minx is already making eyes at Astrid's fiancé. After a recent visit of Pierre's there was a terrible scene between the sisters—I prefer to spare you the details. In the end Astrid lost all self-control and called Vivica a tramp. The child had foolishly wrapped herself in Siamese brocades and was doing a dance to entertain Pierre until Astrid returned from her office. I assure you it was simple childish fun, and I had to tell Astrid she was wrong. She is in a state of high tension and offensively arrogant toward all around her. I have never seen a person for whom regular attendance at church does so little good as Astrid. Only recently I had a long talk with Mère Seraphine, who has been kind enough to give Vivica music lessons at St. Vincent de Paul's convent school. The child is as musical as her dear, long-dead mother. But Borghild was a model of sincerity and fidelity. Since she died in tragic circumstances—some day I shall tell you about them—I am always concerned about Vivica. Along with great beauty, her mother bequeathed a great many odd and incalculable traits to the girl. Vivica's very beauty deeply worries me. Beauty is almost always a snare.

Astrid, as I mentioned, has gone to Angkor to meet her fiancé. Why the two have chosen a city of ruins for a meeting, I do not know. I suggested that she ask Monsieur de Maury whether they were to wait until she became a ruin before he marries her. Unfortunately, just for this rendezvous in Cambodia, Astrid has made herself a hat which would drive any suitor to the end of the world, it is that fantastic! But since it does no good to give Astrid much advice, I held my peace. What her state of mind will be when she returns to Bangkok is anyone's guess. If the meeting turns out as inconclusively as all the others, Vivica's morbid curiosity and her childish jokes will be simply unbearable for Astrid. I hope there will be some kind of decision in Angkor; as things are, it is a protracted malady. Astrid is twenty-four now. Since she is so bent upon marriage, she should accept Dr. Lafitte of Saigon, who has been courting her for some time. Astrid's great-uncle, Dr. Clermont of Saigon, would be very much in favor of this match. Gaston is his first assistant at the hospital, and although, like all Frenchmen, he has an amazing gift of gab, he is really an extremely substantial man. Perhaps a bit boring; his personal interests—apart from Astrid—are only for Cambodian musical instruments, and he can tell you so much so fast about them that you simply gasp for air. I mention Dr. Lafitte because I would be grateful to you if *you* could find occasion to mention to Astrid what a chance for an orderly and happy marriage without scenes and surprises she is missing. Astrid's affair with Monsieur de Maury reminds me of a Chinese opera—without any apparent end, and exhausting for all concerned.

In conclusion, one more request, Hanna. I should very much like to know *before* Astrid returns from the jungle whether she can visit you. Then there would be something pleasant awaiting her when she comes home. As soon as I have your reply I can also write to Monsignore de Lavalette in Shanghai. Perhaps he can set her to rights and remind her that there are other human beings in the world besides Monsieur de Maury who need our thoughts and our help. Monsignore knew Astrid's mother in Shanghai; we have been corresponding with each other for years. Even though he was so overburdened with his Chinese flock, he went to a great deal of trouble with Astrid that time she was injured in Shanghai in 1937—which unfortunately led to her engagement to Pierre de Maury. My late brother also made efforts to bring Astrid to her senses. He made inquiries and discovered that Pierre, in addition to his work in the museums of Hanoi, has long been occupied with mysterious business. I am sending this letter to you through the Danish consul-general in Bangkok, who is traveling to Shanghai and will also take your reply back. The Japanese poke into every private letter nowadays as if it were bound to contain "information."

Warm regards to you and the whole Chou family. For your little Herbert I am sending an English picture book which Vivica was given as a child. How is your new baby? It is a true pleasure to think of you and your young ones; one sees that life goes on its steady course even in difficult times. Naturally, your husband has a great deal to do with that. Tso-ling is the salt of the earth!

It is good of you to ask about our war orphans. Yumei and I have had her husband, who cooks for us, build a third bamboo pavilion on the estate, where we dispense rice to the Chinese boys and girls whose parents have vanished into the Kempetai prisons, and teach them to make themselves useful. Yumei finds employers for them among the huge Chinese population of Bangkok. After they have been with us for a while, they are orderly and punctual, and we can recommend them without hesitation. As you know, Chinese children are industrious and good-humored by nature. Enough for today!

> *With all my best wishes,*
> *Your affectionate*
> *Helene Wergeland*

On the trip to Angkor, Astrid had as yet had no opportunity to have it out with Pierre. He had invited her to Pnompenh, the capital of Cambodia, in order to show her the Buddhistic Institute, founded by the French in 1930, as well as the School of the Arts in Cambodia, which was famous all over the Orient. Most of the time Astrid looked hungrily at him out of her pale blue eyes and pretended to be interested.

In the five years since their engagement in Shanghai she had scarcely changed outwardly. But the gleam of vitality which the cannon and kisses of the city by the sea had conferred upon her had by now been lost. She was thin instead of slim, and well on her way to becoming skinny. Deep bluish shadows underlined her eyes, which had a tendency to squint. She had become nearsighted but wore glasses only when she did figures or attended movies to watch the way all other girls in the world got married and—at least before the wedding—were loved, kissed, and boundlessly adored in close-ups. Then she compressed her lips as tightly as her Aunt Helene. Nevertheless, Astrid went at least four times a week to the air-conditioned movie theater in Bangkok to see old Hollywood films over and over again. No new ones had come in since the outbreak of the war.

As she walked, mute as a fish, beside her talkative fiancé through the art school in Pnompenh, casting only cool glances at the art works of the Khmer people, she pondered desperately how she could pin Pierre down to a wedding date. He gave her no encouragement and had said nothing about her new hat. With appreciation she stole a look at herself in a mirror. Her tropical suit, her lovely blouse, and the amusing trifle of a hat—a hybrid between an orchid and a bird's nest of golden threads—lent her an inimitable elegance. She liked wearing rather loose jackets nowadays; then she did not look so thin. Her elegance had a special quality. In Paris she had worn the mink coat inherited from her mother as if it were some casual thing she had just thrown on; here in the Far East she wore a trifle of a hat as though it were a golden crown.

Something reminded her of Vivica, and she smiled contemptuously and uneasily. She had not at all forgiven Vivica for trying to steal Pierre—just like the tramp.

"You're off your head, Astrid," Aunt Helene had blurted out during the ensuing scene. "It's time you were married."

It certainly was time! When Astrid returned, dead tired, to the Pnompenh inn, she had accomplished nothing at all. She stood bolt upright in her room and looked at the silver compact Pierre had given her after their tour of the crafts school—a consolation prize for passion. The box was decorated with a relief of Cambodian dancers bending their bodies in sly sensuality, as Vivica had bent with innocent slyness before Pierre, smiling at him all the while—in play, of course. A sixteen-year-old brat with the sluttish instincts of her mother and a vigorous Nordic beauty inherited from her father. A young vixen, like the ones in the horror tales that Yumei used to tell little Astrid in old Shanghai.

From the street sounded the cry of a Chinese cook. It began to

rain monotonously, unwearyingly. Astrid opened her Chinese oiled-
paper umbrella and strode, bolt upright, out of the inn and into a
narrow side street. It was ten o'clock at night. Through open doors
she saw families in sarongs, gaily chattering, nibbling garishly colored sweets, and apparently enjoying each other's company. They
had certainly never attended the art school and were certainly not
as tired and bored as Astrid. There was virtually no furniture in these
huts; Cambodians were not interested in tangible property. They
left that to the Chinese, who in Pnompenh, as everywhere in Southeast Asia, lived in magnificent houses.

Hungry dogs with sulphur-yellow hides padded close to Astrid as
she walked down toward the river, absorbed in her thoughts. Behind
a high wall stood the royal palace, with roofs incurving toward the
sky. These roofs were as nostalgic, as strangely twisted and sensual,
as the bodies of Cambodian dancing girls. In front of the palace a
beggar squatted. Teeth flashed in his dark face. Singing softly, he
held out his beggar's bowl to Astrid.

From her crocodile leather pocketbook she took the silver compact
with the dancing girls and threw it into the beggar's bowl. Then, still
walking bolt upright, she went back to the inn.

In the Grand Hotel of Siemréap, the tourists' suburb of Angkor,
sat two Japanese officers, talking in excited but low voices. Colonel
Saito and Major Matsubara had just returned from Angkor and were
planning to fly to Saigon next morning. They were not in uniform;
not long ago two uniformed Japanese had been shot from ambush
while visiting the temple ruins of Angkor. The two had spent considerable time in Colonel Saito's hotel suite, and were now relaxing
in the lobby of the Grand Hotel. Major Matsubara, who had always
had an eye for culture, was regarding with interest several artistic
photographs of Angkor Thom, the royal city of the Khmer people.
The monumental blue-gray and ruddy stone structures belonged to
times too remote from modern life to reveal their wonders at first
glance. A brilliant, warlike past, when the Khmer kings had won
fame in battle and for munificent festivities, had been lost in Cambodia through the sluggishness and the inadequate sense of honor
of the native populace—had evaporated like mist on the bridge of

Seta. Only the monumental ruins still testified to the heroic spirit of the past. Major Matsubara wished he could give a push to these lazy little brothers. They had not even excavated their honored ruins themselves; a Frenchman had had to do it for them in 1859. The French were causing Nippon a great deal of worry in 1942. In Indo-China there were as many resistance fighters and saboteurs as there were grains of rice in the warehouses. But they could not be simply seized, like the rice. They hid from Major Matsubara in all the nooks and corners of Indo-China. But as far as culture was concerned, the French were just as zealous as the Japanese. Pierre de Maury's cultural visits in Tokyo, and Major Matsubara's visit to Hanoi shortly before the war, had yielded much fruit.

"Is he coming to Siemréap today?" Colonel Saito asked. "I should like to meet him. He is still our most trusted man in a country I do not trust."

At that moment Monsieur de Maury entered the hall of the Grand Hotel, accompanied by Astrid. Major Matsubara looked at his archaeological friend's companion and recognized her at once. As was only proper for a high military-intelligence officer, Akiro enjoyed a phenomenal memory. He had no sooner set eyes on Astrid than he recalled Room Seven in the White Chrysanthemum in Shanghai. There this flour-faced foreign female—Clermont, that was her name, the same as the old French physician in Saigon; he must check the connection—there Mademoiselle Clermont had made a contemptuous remark about a famous Japanese poem. "The old pond. A frog hops in. . . ." She had called *haikku* a children's game. Not in a thousand years would Major Matsubara forget this insult. He had not known that Monsieur de Maury in the meanwhile had married this uncultured woman.

But behold! At this moment she was again introduced to him as Mademoiselle Clermont. Major Matsubara smiled radiantly. Astrid's presence in Siemréap was most welcome. He showed no surprise that she was still unmarried—at twenty-four a girl in Japan was either a mother or a rice widow, and in any case a ruin not worth looking at. Nor did he allude to the fact that a certain Dr. Clermont in Saigon had been mentioned to him as an opponent of Nippon. He wanted first to inquire quietly whether a relationship existed.

Instead of contributing anything to the conversation with the long-noses, Colonel Saito only flashed those three big incisors which gave him so jolly an appearance. He thought about other things while he drank the champagne cocktails. Never had he felt such an intense longing for mulled rice wine! Politely out of sorts, he swallowed the horrible beverage which friend of culture de Maury had ordered. So this was what he looked like, this friend of Japan whom Baron Matsubara had won for Nippon with the aid of temple art and *haikku*. The magazine *Indo-Chine*, which Pierre de Maury was help-ing to edit in Hanoi, published in every issue speeches, proclama-tions, and exhortations by the "Japan marshal" Pétain. No doubt about it, Monsieur de Maury was doing his part. Colonel Saito studied his pale face, with the blond hair, the ascetic profile, and the ironic smile. So this was the man. The colonel bared his front teeth, exposing the easily inflamed gums. He did not even glance at Astrid. Foreign women did not exist for Joseph Kitsutaro Saito from Urakami. For a second he thought of his wife back home, an ex-emplary Catholic wife and mother. Then he resumed his covert examination of the liaison man between Nippon and the intellectuals of Hanoi and Saigon. He had to limit himself to looking, since his French was none too good.

Major Matsubara, with his Parisian intonation and his Japanese slyness, directed the conversation. As always in Cambodia, it turned about the temple art and ruins of Southeast Asia. Suddenly the major gave a giggle, so high and thin that Astrid's brows contracted. "I recently visited the temple of the Cao Dai sect near Saigon," he re-marked. "It reminded me of operetta décor. Do you know the cathe-dral of Tay-Ninh?"

"I was there once years ago." Monsieur de Maury smiled at the memory. "You are right, Baron! As against the tremendous cultural monuments of Asia, this cathedral is like Madame Butterfly com-pared to real Japanese women."

Major Matsubara bowed in delight. "Let us rather speak of the im-mortal sculpture of Angkor," he murmured modestly. "These reliefs with their gods, warriors, and fabulous beasts"—he forbore to men-tion the stone dancing girls—"affect one by means of that same poetic suggestiveness which we Japanese also employ in art. Take our short poems," he concluded. "What is a *haikku*, my friends? Just a few

lines! All the rest is hidden meaning." He ran his delicate hand
dreamily over his hair and recited an eighteenth-century poem:

> "Loudly, as though she sees not
> The bars of her cage,
> The nightingale sings."

Then both gentlemen rose as if at a secret command, the major
having recited the *haikku* again in Japanese. They made their stiff
Japanese bows and wished their honored friends and art-lovers an
enjoyable visit to Cambodia's past. It was the usual abrupt Japanese
farewell in the midst of a lively conversation, and gave the impression of Colonel Saito's and Major Matsubara's having seen or heard
enough.

That was precisely the case.

"Your French associate was nervous," Colonel Saito remarked a
while later. They were sitting in the colonel's drawing room and
counteracting the taste of the cocktails by eating slices of sea-tang
from tins. "Did you notice that de Maury's left eyelid twitched when
you mentioned the cathedral of Tay-Ninh? I always watch the left
eyelid," the colonel added smugly. "A man has no more power over
it than over his Adam's apple."

"We must pursue our investigations, Colonel! Not that I trust him."
Here Major Matsubara laughed. "But it may also have been some
other Frenchman. If we dangle our hook too soon, we may frighten
off the fat carp."

"The matter is pressing, Major! That secret radio station which is
constantly giving the Allies information on our transports must be
silenced. If it is that sect which is the nest of these traitors—" Colonel
Saito showed all his incisors. He had a faculty for looking simultaneously jolly and grim. He rubbed his nose with his big finger, placed
a pair of cheap, steel-rimmed glasses on his strong peasant's nose,
and began reading the latest report from his chief agent in Saigon.
One passage he read over twice. Either he particularly liked or particularly disliked it.

In any case, he gathered from the summary on the Cao Dai sect
that its priests had built up a private army, which they were employing with extreme caution and skill against the Japanese army

of occupation. Troop trains were being constantly attacked, trucks hijacked. Worst of all were the bombings of factories located amidst dense tropical growth. Someone must be spying out their location and then—presumably through this militant sect—betraying it to the Allies. A few weeks ago the Japanese agent in Tay-Ninh had observed a Frenchman visiting the Cao Daiists. The Frenchman had been blond, with a sharp profile. He might be Pierre de Maury. He might also be some other Frenchman.

The sect, the report concluded, had been officially founded in Cochin China in 1926, by spiritists. Their religion contained elements of Catholicism, of Buddhism, and of Taoism. The Cao Daiists' calendar of saints embraced such diverse personalities as the Maid of Orleans, Count de la Rochefoucauld, John the Baptist, and the Chinese Jade Emperor. The sect had a pope, a hierarchy of dignitaries, a legislative body, a medical "corps of charity," and its private army. Captain Saito fished out of a portfolio a small book in French, which he gave to Major Matsubara. It was the *Histoire et philosophie du Cao-Daiism; religion nouvelle et Buddhisme nouveau en Asie,* by a French author named Gobron who had died in 1941.

"Tell me tomorrow whether this heretic speaks of the sect's private army, in addition to its religious nonsense," Colonel Saito said. "When did Monsieur de Maury purport to have visited the cathedral the last time?"

"He said it was several years ago, Colonel."

"For his sake I hope it was." Colonel Saito showed his incisors and the inflamed gums. He was a believing Christian and had no right to give up hope.

"Send the agent Yuriko from Bangkok to Saigon," he concluded. "She knows Monsieur de Maury from Shanghai, doesn't she?"

"She occasionally obtained opium for him, Colonel."

"Did he sleep with her?"

"No, sir. I questioned the agent closely on this point. He only liked to talk to her. Yuriko speaks good French and is clever. De Maury is talkative, like all Frenchmen."

"When he comes to Saigon, have her watch his every step for the first three weeks, before she calls on him. Let her go on selling him dreams."

"I will issue the necessary instructions," Major Matsubara murmured. "Vera Leskaya can take care of Bangkok for us, after all. She recently put us on the trail of three Chinese Chungking agents." Major Matsubara withdrew, respectfully bowing. With regret he replaced a silk-bound volume of Japanese poems in his suitcase and turned to the *History and Philosophy of Cao Daiism.*

There was no time to listen to nightingales singing.

Every trip through jungle country bored Astrid to tears. She was a creature of cities, or, properly speaking, of the city of Paris. Never would she have returned to the Far East if Pierre had not been in Indo-China. Astrid had inherited her father's love for Asian works of art, but the people and the landscape remained a book with seven seals to her. The only strong feeling she had in regard to Asia was panicky fear of crowds. Otherwise she was merely seized by an endless boredom that robbed her of the last vestige of her vitality. She was already in a state of agitated irritability by next day, when in the company of her fiancé she entered the legendary kingdom of the Khmer people, which Frenchmen had dug out of the jungle.

Pierre was transformed. His ironic smile had vanished; his eyes burned with an unfamiliar fire; his ascetic profile looked unapproachable. He was farther away from Astrid than ever before. The museums in Hanoi and Pnompenh had only been the vestibule to hell for her. Pierre lavished on the sculptures of the Bayon temple, and on Angkor Wat, all the love and admiration he had withheld from Astrid since their last meeting in Paris.

In the evening they drove out to Angkor Wat once more, to see the ruins by moonlight. Astrid had set all her hopes on the moon. Although she herself did not have enough imagination to be spurred to original remarks by the moonlight, she knew that such nights automatically put any man into a romantic mood. Even Frenchmen, with their all too alert intelligence and their irony, could, in general, not resist the spell of an Asian moonlit night. The moon was surely the best of allies if one wanted to pin a suitor down to a wedding date.

Astrid's reasoning, in fact, seemed correct. After all, it was almost invariably correct. She walked arm in arm with Pierre up the gigantic temple stairs. So remarkably was the temple situated that an illusion of completeness and perfection emanated even from these ruins. Theirs was a unique clarity, harmony, and solemn magnificence.

Cambodian torchbearers accompanied Astrid and Pierre on their way to the Wat. The rain had ceased; the stream of moonlight and the red glow of torches made the ruins a landscape of stone and fire. In Angkor Wat life and death held a continual whispered dialogue. Intoxicated, Pierre de Maury tramped through the endless galleries and terraces. The moonlight showed huge trees growing among the stones. Two modest Japanese tourists in gray tropical suits passed by. They whispered reverently of a past which in the ninth century had rivaled Nippon's heroic spirit.

The sight of the Japanese stirred feelings of uneasiness and displeasure in Astrid. She scowled slightly and said loudly in French, "Let us go."

In the shadow of a sandstone tower they stood mutely side by side for a moment. Had Astrid startled her lover out of a propitious trance? She had meant well; at the moment something had occurred to her that she had been wanting to tell Pierre since the evening in Siemréap.

"I don't like that Baron Matsubara and the colonel, Pierre. They were looking so hard at you all the time, as though they were taking mental notes on what you said."

"Whatever put that idea into your head, *chérie?* You're seeing ghosts! Tonight we want to see only the ghosts of Cambodia. They're far more attractive."

But Astrid had taken a grip on her subject and would not let it go. "You might pay attention to me," she said in Helene Wergeland's tone. "I know what I am talking about."

"Then you are an exception in the human race, my dear."

"There's no need to make fun of me," Astrid said, deeply offended. "I know I have no ideas, but on the other hand I see things all the more clearly. Those Japanese exchanged glances when you were talking about the Cao Dai sect."

Pierre burst into laughter. "You have a fear-psychosis. Why don't you consult Dr. Lafitte? He is a first-class psychiatrist."

"When was the last time you were in Tay-Ninh, Pierre?"

"Is this an interrogation? There are no girls there, you know."

"When were you in the temple?"

"The last time I visited that operetta temple was several years ago, as I told Baron Matsubara. He is deeply interested in temple architecture. That was why he came to Angkor. Are you content now?"

"Do Frenchmen often go there?"

"So this is an interrogation after all. You're boring me, my child. Why, yes, I remember now; Gaston Lafitte often visits the place."

"Gaston? Why in the world?"

"He is writing a study on the Catholic element in this circus religion of theirs. Then, too, he is friendly with one of the abbots."

"The Cao Daiists are supposed to be working against the Japanese, Pierre. Gaston is in danger. We must warn him."

"From whom have you heard all this nonsense?" Pierre de Maury asked quickly.

"From Madame Ninette, the White Russian proprietress of a beauty parlor. I know her from Shanghai."

"Those White Russians can dream up all kinds of things." Monsieur de Maury gave a very French shrug. Then he drew Astrid to a stone relief that had fructified the whole art of Southeast Asia. Every figure of a dancing girl on a Siamese, Burmese, or Cambodian powder box had been patterned after this *apsaras*, the divine nymph of the Khmer people. On thousands of utensils in the modern Far East— vases, knife blades, boxes, wall hangings—she danced with inimitable suppleness, danced with innocent slyness and ceremonial voluptuousness the unending dance of the gods of Angkor.

Astrid's thoughts digressed: then Gaston was making studies in the temple of the Cao Dai sect. She must warn him; he was so utterly unworldly. But the principal thing was that Pierre had nothing to do with it. She had no desire to be constantly frightened over a man. Men were foolish out of pure carelessness. Although she would never marry Dr. Lafitte, she wanted him to keep out of harm. *Marry!* Now the moment had come.

"Isn't she wonderful?" Pierre whispered, devouring the stone nymph with his eyes. For a moment he closed them—and saw a sixteen-year-old brat cavorting on a lawn in Bangkok. Vivica! A name like champagne. And a girl like champagne. She was childish, did not yet know the power of her beauty, but had an instinct for things that Astride, for all her intelligence, quite lacked. The sixteen-year-old girl, as radiant with victory as the forest nymphs of the Far North, already knew the one means a woman could employ to hold a man through the years. Vivica tried to cheer him. Astride wanted to bind a man by force of will, but she could not and did not want to entertain or amuse him; she was too haughty or too bereft of ideas for that. And Astride showed, in a thousand unconscious ways, how much she needed him. There was her cardinal fault, Pierre thought, eyes still half shut. The man ought to need the woman so badly that he would even marry her—not the other way round.

Astrid's pallid, aristocratic charms evaporated before Vivica's vivid color and playful grace. At least so it seemed to Pierre when he stood before the relief of the dancing girls with his fiancée, regarding them pensively and thinking about Vivica. He must clear the decks now, and he had a natural male disinclination to do so. For this reason he sought still another reason for postponement.

They strolled into the Northern Gallery with its Brahmanic battle scenes and turned, still arm in arm, into the northwestern pavilion, which contained some of the finest sculptures in Angkor. Could he take a look at Astride's powder box with the dancing *apsaras,* Pierre asked, so that he could check the quality of the drawing against the original? He had a strong interest in the art school of Pnompenh, where he had given Astrid the box as a substitute for passion.

"I have lost the box," Astrid said with a manner not in the least regretful.

"I suppose this is one of your rare jokes."

Astrid flinched inwardly at the coldness of his tone but controlled herself perfectly. Her impulse was to tell Pierre that she had given the box to a beggar because she despised dancing girls. But a residue of caution restrained her from so disastrous a statement.

"I am sorry I lost the box, Pierre!" Since Pierre did not condescend to answer, she asked whether he had never lost anything.

"Of course not," Monsieur de Maury brashly asserted. "I learned early to have a regard for my property." This was perfectly true. Pierre came from a family of civil servants with a low income and the habits that went with it.

Frowning, he looked at a statue of the god Vishnu resting on a snake. He would be in precisely the same situation if he married Astrid.

"That is the last present I will ever give you," he said angrily.

The last present? What did he mean by that? Astrid was seized by panic. Did Pierre wish to use this little disagreement to escape from her without a kiss and without setting a wedding date? If he did, he would find he had miscalculated. She changed her tone and tactics, brushed the soft hair back from her forehead, and murmured that she was really very sorry. Her voice quivered, though not from regret over the loss. They were standing in the western bay, in front of a wall showing Sita's trial by fire, the glorious scene from the Indian epic *The Ramayana*. Sita, the loving princess, was ascending the burning pyre to prove her faithfulness to her husband. Naturally she came out of the trial by fire unharmed and justified. The ancient stone tablet was a fragment, but Astrid saw only the fragment of a fragment because unwept tears dimmed her eyes. Pierre had never adopted such a tone toward her. Poor Astrid, who knew so much about art and so little about men, never for a moment realized that this matter had come up very opportunely for her fiancé and was being used by him to bring himself into the right mood for saying something painful. His anger was already half dissipated, but his courage had increased considerably. Men often wait until they are angry when they wish to make unpleasant revelations.

They were still standing in front of the relief when Astrid's world of wishes collapsed.

At first she felt no pain, like someone whose leg has been blown off by a shell. She stood like a stone statue in the moonlit ruins of Angkor and became aware that Pierre de Maury was asking her to forgive him for not wanting to marry her. It was all *his* fault, of course. He had been trying to tell her this for two years without hurting her, he said. They did not suit each other. No, *chérie*, really not. Probably he was unsuited for marriage altogether, like so many Frenchmen. She was a wonderful girl—so clever, so elegant, so efficient; in a word, much too good for Pierre de Maury! She was only twenty-four, had her whole life before her. It would be unfair to tie her to a husband who would constantly be making her unhappy without intending to. That was just the way things were.

"Is it another girl?" Astrid asked. She felt a dullness in her head, and a loss of substance, as if part of her body were gone. Pierre replied with a touch of impatience that there was no question of another girl. Did she really not understand? he asked himself in despair. He was sick of the whole tormenting relationship. He had labored hard all these five years, out of pity, cowardice, and diplomacy. What was the name again of that fellow who had to roll a block of stone up a mountain in the nether world? Sisyphus, that was it. Well, he, Pierre de Maury, was the successor to Sisyphus in Indo-China. Naturally he did not say this to Astrid; he spoke to her very gently and tactfully—a surgeon winding a wreath of roses around his knife.

Astrid stood as motionless as Princess Sita during her trial by fire. Rigidly, without tears, she regarded the fragmentary portrait of Prince Rama, who waited without visible emotion for his wife to throw herself into the flames. That was how things were. This was how they would always be. Women were simple-minded when they loved. In their hunger for love they would risk their lives if there was the slightest chance that such risks would warm a love grown cold. All very well if one died during the trial by fire, Astrid thought, staring at the extraordinarily lifelike stone monkeys which tumbled at Prince Rama's feet and seemed to be pleased as Punch at the loving wife's imminent roasting.

Astrid squinted, pondering hard but vainly on something, as Pierre continued to talk away at her. Aunt Helene was right; he was indeed a marvel of loquacity. The wave of coldness within her reached into the chambers of her heart. Her eyelids slowly swelled from repressed tears. She hoped that she was dreaming. This could not be possible—that this man should have saved her life in Shanghai five years ago, only to take it from her now. She tried to pull herself together. Alone now, humiliated to the depths of her soul, she must go down that gigantic staircase of Angkor Wat, step by step. She raised her head in the haughty pose her mother used to adopt for such moments. But the effort of thrusting her head back gave her such violent pain that she uttered a feeble sound—the dim echo of a terrible scream that would have cracked the stones of Angkor. Instantly Pierre sprang to her side.

"Did you hurt yourself? You're standing much too close to the slope, Astride. Before you know it a stone will fall on your head."

He had not the slightest suspicion that in the past few minutes several monstrous blocks of stone had fallen on her head. Men really are idiotic, Astrid thought. She saw her future stretching before her as a dying man might envision all his past in a moment: a ruined world of listening to the radio and making Parisian hats. Of course she could marry good Dr. Lafitte, who sincerely loved her. But Astrid was not one to be satisfied with second best. She had not the faculty to settle down comfortably in a surrogate world. That was how she had always been. Years ago it had had to be Aunt Helene and not the Widow from Aalesund from whom she wanted praise and love. Now it was Pierre de Maury, Astrid's first and only man. If she could not have Pierre, she would far rather live as a stone statue in her private world of ruins.

"Say something, Astride," Pierre implored her in his most winning voice. In spite of the sultry tropical air, he wiped the cold sweat from his forehead. *Mon Dieu,* what an operation!

What should Astrid say? Nothing ever occurred to her, as Pierre well knew. They walked in silence through halls and ornamental terraces to the great staircase. There Astrid turned to go. "Good-by," she whispered. "I'm sorry I bored you for so many years."

"For heaven's sake, Astride! We cannot part like this."

Astrid looked at him once more: his stern profile, gleaming hair, bright, predatory eyes, mouth, fine hands. . . . His heart she could not see. It had once belonged to her. He had told her so in Shanghai. And she had believed him as foolishly as the most chickenheaded girl in Trondheim believed her shirker. Aunt Helene would scold Astrid now as she did her chicks, and support her, although she was far fonder of Mailin and Vivica. Astrid had no illusions about that.

"Don't look at me that way, Astride! You know how much I think of you. You deserve all the happiness in the world."

Astrid continued to stare at Monsieur de Maury out of her pale blue eyes. Her mother's rubies were the only spot of color on her.

"You'll always find me a good friend," Pierre assured her nervously. Why in the world wasn't Astride making a scene? For all her haughtiness, she was first-class when it came to scene-making.

"A good friend . . ." she murmured at last. "How nice!"

Long pause. The other tourists had scattered. Astrid seemed to be asleep on her feet. She was as pale as the figures of legend upon the stone walls of Angkor.

"Are you ill, Astride? Would you like an aspirin?" As always, Monsieur de Maury carried his personal drugstore along with him on his pleasure trips. "Say that we will remain friends, Astride!"

"There is a marvelous reply to that venerable chestnut," Astrid said. "Unfortunately I can't remember it at the moment."

Without looking back, she strode down the great staircase of Angkor Wat.

As soon as Miss Wergeland saw her niece's face she knew what had happened.

"Don't worry about it," she said hoarsely. "The rotter isn't worth it." Her heart contracted at the sight of Astrid's fine, lifeless face wearing the cracked rouge of pride. Never had Miss Wergeland in all her long practice seen a chick suffering so fiercely from the behavior of a shirker. The mystery of suffering had allowed a grotesque gulf to arise between Astrid's social conduct and her wounded heart.

"Go to sleep, Astrid. You must be exhausted from the trip. I'll bring you some hot buffalo milk with palm sugar."

No reply. Astrid stood in her new traveling suit and her witty trifle of a hat, absolutely immobile in the doorway to the veranda, staring fixedly at her aunt. Miss Wergeland's skin began to crawl. Suddenly she recalled a long-forgotten scene out of Astrid's childhood. The child had stood just so, staring just so rigidly, and whispered that Mailin was not as good as the "white" children. That was how she had sought to win Helene's love, and had been snapped at and slapped for her pains. Everything had changed since that day in Trondheim, but now again Astrid was standing immobile, regarding the powerful protector of her childhood with the same hungry look.

"Why is it that no one can love me?" she asked suddenly. Astrid too must have been thinking of that day in Trondheim.

"Don't talk nonsense. I'm very fond of you." Miss Wergeland could have slapped herself for the lukewarm phrase. It was love Astrid wanted!

"Thank you, Aunt Helene." The humility of her tone cut Helene

Wergeland to the heart. If only Astrid would make a scene! But she only stood still, thanking her aunt for being fond of her.

"There's a letter from Shanghai for you, from Hanna Chou. She'd like you to visit her."

"Did you by any chance ask Hanna to invite me?" Astrid asked acidly. Her mind was beginning to function again.

"Have you begun to imagine things?" Helene replied. "I have other things to do. Our third pavilion is jammed full with bombed-out families."

Astrid breathed a sigh of relief. Her only friend had not yet forgotten her. But at the moment she felt no special longing to visit happily married women. Her rude aunt would be far better company, the way she was feeling now.

"I don't feel in the mood to go to Shanghai right now."

"As you like, but Hanna will be disappointed." Helene could think of nothing but the necessity to remove Astrid from Vivica's presence. It would be frightful if the high-spirited child were to tease Astrid now. That was one scene Helene would prefer not to witness.

"Do you really think Hanna cares one way or the other?"

"Don't look at me like that!" Miss Wergeland exclaimed. "Of course I think so."

"Then I'll go. You're so good to me, Aunt Helene."

Miss Wergeland went to rummage in the refrigerator in the pantry. Then she called, in that ringing voice which always cut Astrid to the nerves, for Yumei, and gave her the milk to warm. Contrary to her custom, Yumei scurried off to the kitchen house without a word. Elder Sister looked like a ghost who had met a tiger.

"Good night," Miss Wergeland said, yawning as heartily as a Japanese rice farmer after a full day's work on a poor field. "Tomorrow everything will look different."

But both of them knew that tomorrow everything would look exactly the same. Under her Parisian hats, Astrid had the Nordic tendency to brood. Innumerable women of all nations married men on the rebound and were even happy with them—because they expected less and were therefore vouchsafed more than they expected. But Astrid was like one of those big birds of whom the Chinese proverb says that they "are not content with small grain."

Perhaps Astrid's refusal to be content started the ball of misfortune rolling. Perhaps it was a careless remark by Dr. Lafitte, who had brought her through a near nervous breakdown in Saigon. But probably disaster descended upon the Wergeland family because Astrid suffered a loss of virtue after that night in Angkor Wat—not of her maidenly virtue, but of virtue in general. Such losses are curious: they are not noticed in daily living; they are not written up in the newspapers or broadcast over the radio. Loss of virtue is a creeping disease, more dangerous than cholera or malaria, and as hidden as a cancerous tumor. Dry despair gnawed at Astrid's soul. That was all the more dangerous because she had been raised in the faith that despair is a sin. She knew the tyranny that sin wields as soon as it is permitted entry into the soul, but she continued to walk her dark path. She had lost faith, love, and hope. She locked away the writings of St. Theresa in a camphorwood chest. For the first time in her life she did not attend Mass.

And so she had nowhere to turn when, three years after the breaking of her engagement, disaster fell upon the Wergeland family. On that day Astrid was sitting, all unsuspecting, in her office in the center of the city of Bangkok, and Helene was putting in her daily stint of painting in the orchid pavilion. Nineteen-year-old Vivica was at Madame Ninette's and Vera Leskaya's beauty salon, where she worked as a receptionist. Astrid had found the job for her, and, after protracted resistance, Helene Wergeland had reluctantly agreed to the arrangement. Young European women could not be choosy in Japanese-occupied Southeast Asia, and Vivica could not very well sit around the house. The imp needed something to do, and she found it very entertaining there, Vivica assured her aunt.

The fourth of April, 1945, began like every other day in Bangkok. But it proved to be unlike any other. The Allied bombers shattered the two power plants on the Menam River, so that the population found itself, between one moment and the next, without electric light, telephone, streetcars, refrigerators, and radios.

On that same day Miss Wergeland received some visits which within two hours cruelly changed her life. And yet those two hours were only the final outcome of a development which had begun in the ruins of Angkor.

2: *The Arrest*

Miss Wergeland had not been feeling very well at breakfast on the fourth of April, 1945. The hot season placed a strain on her heart. She was no longer so young, but quite ignored this fact, to Astrid's annoyance. Astrid, who now wore glasses almost constantly and no longer did her hair shepherdess-fashion to please a man—Astrid now had in her life nothing but the cinema, her manifold business affairs, and her secret thoughts. Orderly Helene Wergeland would have been horrified if she had been able to see the dangerous disorder within Astrid's mind; but Astrid locked that as carefully as her desk, concealed it as she did her valuables, especially her mother's rubies and her collection of Burmese gems. She always sighed with relief when she was able to retire to her first-floor room after a dispute with Aunt Helene. If no occasion presented itself for a dispute or a scene, she sat on the family veranda, preserving the frosty silence of a dethroned duchess.

Miss Wergeland, then, was sitting in her painting pavilion instead of resting in a darkened room. She had eaten her lunch alone, out of old habit having Yumei rather than the cook serve her. But not even Yumei could persuade Helene to lie down after tiffin. She had never rested by day in Trondheim; why should she do so in the tropics?

Mixing a strong purple on her palette, she sailed into the next orchid. This time the exotic flowers on her canvas looked like violets in warpaint. No one but Astrid ever dared to criticize Helene's pictures. Even the consul had withheld comment on them; without blinking an eye, he had been in the habit of hanging Helene's work beside the most glorious products of Asia on the walls of his houses in Peiping, Tokyo, Shanghai, and Bangkok.

Knut! To this day Miss Wergeland had not got over his death. She missed him everywhere, although she had so often had violent quarrels with him over his daughters. That is to say, Helene had scolded and the consul had listened, his thoughts evidently elsewhere—just like Vivica. When that child looked at her aunt out of her mysterious green eyes, and smilingly tossed back her silvery-blond hair, she was beyond influencing. Miss Wergeland sighed. She loved Vivica with the same protective love she had felt for Borghild from the very start; but Vivica would not allow herself to be loved. In this respect she was thoroughly Knut's daughter. She also had the careless charm of his younger years. If she wished to she could twist anyone, man or woman, around her finger. Not even Helene was entirely immune to Vivica's negligent and mysterious charm. And the child cheered her. Evenings in Astrid's company would have killed the strongest man. Helene Wergeland herself, of course, was not exactly sociable, and not easy to live with. Knut had always said she was as patient as a tigress and as sociable as a mole. By now she was sixty and assumed the right to think whatever she liked. Even in her younger years she had been relatively indifferent to the opinions of her fellow human beings; now she did not care at all about them.

Helene laid down her brush and wiped the perspiration from her high forehead. White-haired, in a white dress, she sat stubbornly erect on her Chinese hassock, thinking of Olaf, of Knut, and of the girls. At this noonday hour she was always undisturbed. The servants were sleeping. The bombed-out Chinese families in the fourth pavilion had at last realized that the tall stern missie had a very different idea of "rest" from theirs. Relaxation for a Chinese family consists of incessant, deafening chatter.

But although all was quiet inside Miss Wergeland's domain at this time, irritating waves of noise surged in from the street: the shrill cries of peddlers; the Japanese radio program, turned on full blast in the house next door; the continual screeching of the geese, which are kept to drive snakes and thieves out of gardens; and the marching songs of passing Japanese troops—loud, rough voices clamoring monotone heroics into an atmosphere quivering with heat. Miss Wergeland closed her eyes. She wished she were on Mount Aksla, which rises so proudly and quietly above Aalesund.

Heavily she rose and lay down on her cot after all. It was protected from mosquitoes by wire netting, but her thoughts kept her awake. And yet she knew that all her pondering about Astrid and

Vivica could not make the atmosphere of the house any pleasanter. But this war, too, would some day end. When it did, she was resolved, she would return to Trondheim with Vivica and there look for a husband for the unpredictable child.

Later Helene remembered how her mind had dwelt on the return to Norway as she fell asleep. She dreamed, and breathed heavily. A black curtain dropped around the pavilion, covering the orchids, the garden, and herself. Suddenly the monsoon blew the curtain away, and Helene was sitting on her balcony at Villa Wergeland, happily watching the drifting clouds and recuperating from Asia. She must have been looking at the fjord for months, for Astrid and Vivica had become pleasant, untroublesome shades. Suddenly she saw an eider duck on the shore—or was it Vivica? Blood was flowing from the bird's soft feathers, and it looked up so imploringly that Helene wanted to rush down to take it into her arms. She had always sheltered and helped others; that was her mission in this world. In her dream she groaned because she could not move, and tears streamed down her face. Awake, Helene Wergeland never wept. Perhaps the girl had stolen something—but Vivica had never done so again since, as a child, she had taken Mailin's jade bell. Mailin, at her wedding, had given the bell to Vivica. Perhaps Vivica needed the admonition, *Haste is error*, more than Mailin. . . .

Miss Wergeland started up out of sleep. She had the feeling that someone was watching her. But it was only good Yumei in her black pantaloons and white starched jacket, standing over her and holding out a bowl of ice and a towel.

"Visitors have come," she said gently.

"Visitors?" Helene asked in horror. "And at midday!"

"Russian ladies," Yumei explained. "Russian ladies from where Third Sister works. Want to speak to Missie right away."

"Impertinence," Helene muttered. "They could just as well have written." She hastily rubbed her face with the ice. Yumei had closed the bamboo curtain. Now, kneeling, she held out a fresh white dress to Helene. For years she had been servant, confidante, and guardian of the household. Her neat appearance and her sound common sense gave Helene strength when the nieces proved too much of a problem. Through Yumei she was far more strongly attached to Asia than she knew. Chinese loyalty is powerful and a great consolation.

Helene imagined she knew what Madame Ninette wanted. Vivica had spoken to her of a big party the fat Russian woman wished to give, in spite of the danger of air raids. She could have saved herself the trouble of calling; Miss Wergeland would not attend. But she would take this opportunity to inform the Russian woman that Vivica would be giving up her job in the beauty salon. Astrid must find something for her with French friends in Bangkok. Madame Ninette was constantly sending nineteen-year-old Vivica to Indo-China to buy cosmetics and jewelry—with good reason: the girl was so grown-up, so charming, and had a passport that made border officials kowtow. But these trips were a constant source of anxiety to Helene. The child was far too young, too frivolous, and too beautiful to go gadding about Saigon alone. Alone? What did Helene really know about Vivica's doings, even though she stayed in Saigon with Dr. Clermont, Astrid's great-uncle. Once Vivica had mentioned that Pierre de Maury had been in Saigon, and that they had spent a lovely evening together in a night-club. Astrid had stared speechlessly at her sister through her glasses. Then she had stalked up to her room.

"What's the matter with Astrid?" Vivica had asked, giving Helene one of her cunningly innocent looks. "Pierre threw her over, after all. Does that mean he can never again go dancing with a girl?"

"Be still!" Helene had snapped. She would really have liked to give the imp a spanking. That had happened just three months ago. Vivica's craving for pleasure knew no bounds. Was she a creature of the depths, like her unfortunate mother? Or a spirit of the air? How could one tie down a spirit of the air? Vivica was a grown girl; she listened smilingly to reprimands and went dancing. Molly Sun, a rich young Chinese girl in Bangkok, was constantly inviting her to parties that went on long into the night. Vivica had a hunger for new faces and places, as though life were too short to see everything and to experience all the hidden possibilities for sensation.

While Vivica danced, Helene and Astrid sat grimly at home in Sathorn Road. Helene could not go to sleep until the child was safely back. She scolded herself for having become a mother hen in her old age, but still she could not go to sleep. She would have been even more apprehensive if she had known with whom Vivica danced like a passionate elf at the home of her friend, Molly Sun. Once Astrid had been invited by Miss Sun; she had not accepted and had told Vivica she would not sit down at the same table with Chinese war profiteers. Vivica had not been overmuch impressed by this. More and more she regarded her elder sister, who for all her perfect figure was without a spark of life, with gentle mockery. Poor Astrid! How ridiculous to always look and act like a governess. She ought rather have her limp hair done up decently and not wear her glasses all the time. Not a single man was in love with her. Vivica had a host of suitors whom she graciously led around by the nose—except for Pierre de Maury, of course. He was the last man to be led around by the nose—not even by beautiful little girls. But he could be very amusing. And he did not ask permission when he wanted to kiss a little girl. He kissed her. . . .

Miss Wergeland had made up her mind. First she would give the Russian women notice for Vivica, who was still a minor, after all. And then she would thank them politely for their idiotic invitation. She laid aside her comb and told Yumei to bring lemonade to the Russian ladies. Then she raised herself to her full imposing height and strode militantly, without the trace of a polite smile, into the reception room, which was dim because all the curtains were drawn. The room had last been used at Mailin's wedding.

The reception room contained two comfortable wicker chairs for guests of honor, many stiff ebony chairs with Chinese carving, a large vase of the Ming period, and several paintings on the white plaster walls: two oils by Miss Wergeland, showing wild Norwegian landscapes in ghostly colors, and the precious Japanese scroll, "Songbird on a Dead Branch." Twenty years ago in Shanghai, Yvonne had made scenes in front of this scroll, and young Baron Matsubara had believed in the possibility of friendship with Europeans. Everything had changed since, except for the songbird on the dead branch.

The two Russian women were studying this painting when Miss Wergeland entered the room.

Madame Ninette had settled without a qualm in one of the two armchairs reserved for guests of honor, where at Mailin's wedding old Madame Chou of Shanghai had sat in modest dignity. The years had not dealt too kindly with Madame Ninette. She was now a massive block of fat upon which the pink-rouged cheeks and implausible blond chignon looked absurd. When she had first prettied Astrid in Shanghai for the lunch with Monsieur de Maury—that was now eight years ago—she had been a plump but prepossessing Scheherezade who beguiled Astrid with her spicy tales about unknown persons. Alcohol, greasy Chinese foods, and a disinclination for all movement had greatly changed Madame Ninette. What remained the same were thirst, her Russian sentimentality, and her inclination to tell perfect strangers dramatic biographies of unknowns. Her affable smile, too, was still ready; in spite of all proofs to the contrary, Madame seemed still to consider life a picnic at which the vodka flowed freely. She was now some fifty-eight years old, but had made up her mind to look eighteen. For this reason she wore a pink frilled dress with such a violent flower pattern that Helene Wergeland almost took her for a particularly strange, gigantic orchid.

Madame Ninette was saying something in a loud and excited voice to Vera Leskaya, who, as in Shanghai, functioned in the Bangkok beauty salon as cashier, secretary, and private spy. Vera, who had once spied for the Chinese against the Japanese in Shanghai, had for some years been hunting down Chinese on orders from Nippon. Chungking agents were her favorite game.

The years had dealt just as unkindly with Vera Leskaya. She looked like a crow now, a gaunt figure in her mid-forties, wearing a gray dress. Even her Slavic face with its high cheekbones and small, covetous, mistrustful eyes, was gray rather than white. Her bitter mouth was firmly shut, but her nostrils fluttered like leaves in the monsoon wind. These nostrils alone conferred a little life upon her pasty gray face. Miss Wergeland thought that she had never seen two more unsavory creatures. And Vivica spent much of her day with these women! That had to end right away!

It was curious that the crow did not sit down, but remained standing in a servile posture near Madame Ninette, enduring with stony resignation the torrent of talk. She had been standing beside Madame Ninette for years, ever since the woman had picked her up in the back alleys of Shanghai after her father's death and had clothed her and given her work. Vera belonged to that army of intelligent and refined White Russian women who for decades had been living in painful but indissoluble community with their more successful and more ordinary fellow exiles in the Far East. Madame Ninette had apparently never worried about where the money for the smart beauty shop in Shanghai and now in Bangkok came from; she knew only that Leskaya somehow raised the necessary funds. She considered it only right for Vera to show gratitude for Madame Ninette's not having let her starve as a girl in Shanghai. Accordingly, she made fun of her without restraint and treated her with alternate brutality and affection. The relationship had become established along these lines at the beginning, and outwardly it was still the same. Vera Leskaya, who could have all the money she wanted from the Japanese, evidently had her reasons for staying with the fat Russian. These reasons were as opaque as her mask of servility and colorlessness. At the moment Leskaya was indispensable to Madame Ninette because she spoke Japanese. Many Japanese women came to the beauty salon and paid fantastic prices—since the Japanese printed their own money in occupied territory. Moreover, Vera Leskaya arranged things with the Japanese authorities whenever Madame Ninette wanted to buy perfume and jewelry in Indo-China, or bring anything over the border, such as French champagne, which could not be had in Bangkok but which flowed like water at the parties given by certain circles. A great many things were being smuggled over the border between Siam and Indo-China—luxury goods, people, and information.

Vera Leskaya came regularly to the beauty shop at seven o'clock in the morning, and was the last to leave the place to return to her small hotel in the Chinese quarter. Not even Madame Ninette knew where and with whom the crow spent her solitary evenings. Nor did she care. She never invited Vera to the noisy, costly parties which Vivica liked so well.

Madame Ninette had not yet observed Miss Wergeland's menacing shadow in the doorway. In her fire alarm of a voice she asked whether there was not a single bottle of brandy in this house. Madame Ninette spoke French, in the hope that someone was listening. Miss Wergeland's heavy eyebrows contracted and she graciously informed her uninvited guest that her home was not a bar. At that moment Yumei entered with iced lemonade, which Madame Ninette waved aside with a burst of mocking Russian laughter. She blinked sardonically at Leskaya and observed in Russian, "Hospitable Saint Julian in the flesh!" Her voice rolled like a rumble of thunder. As she spoke, she remembered a story about a remarkable hostess in Shanghai, and related the tale to her secretary in swift Russian while her sharp bright eyes took measure of the tall old Norwegian woman. An unsympathetic person, this Miss Wergeland, she concluded.

"What brings you here?" Helene demanded, coming a step closer. Madame Ninette pulled herself with some difficulty out of the chair for honored guests and approached her frowning hostess with outstretched hands.

"Dearest friend," she murmured, "my soul is athirst for consolation!" Madame Ninette had many dearest friends whom she knew no better than Miss Wergeland. "Did I say brandy?" she went on in her rapid, harsh French. "It might be a glass of gin, or a light, cheap peppermint liqueur. My secretary would certainly be content with that."

Vera Leskaya bowed mutely. Miss Wergeland remained grimly silent. So outraged was she that for a moment she was at a loss for words. Astrid had told her that Madame Ninette was "all right," and Helene had relied upon this information when she allowed Vivica to work at the beauty parlor. Helene resolved to have a word with Astrid this evening. Something was amiss. How could Astrid, usually so discriminating, endorse a creature like this Madame Ninette? Perhaps, in spite of her competence in business, her misfortunes had really disturbed her mind a little. But no; Helene rejected this thought. Astrid had a cool head on her shoulders. The mystery remained; Helene Wergeland simply did not know how grave a loss of virtue Astrid had suffered.

Finally Madame Ninette introduced her secretary. "Vera Leskaya, my right hand. I could not have a prettier one, eh?" She laughed raucously.

Miss Wergeland did not answer: This fat creature was a fool to provoke this other silent, burning female. Vera Leskaya, with her forced smile, looked like a martyr at the moment. But although Helene's sense of justice was aroused so that she pitied her, she also felt distaste and impatience. She had not much use for Russian women anyhow.

"If you came here to ask me to your party," she said brusquely, "I must decline with thanks. I never go to parties."

For a few seconds the great mass of fat let her sharp, pale blue eyes linger in speechless amazement upon the fierce, white-haired figure before her. Then the storm burst.

"Did you hear that, Leskaya?" she screamed hoarsely in Russian. "This old tigress who doesn't even have peppermint liqueur for her best friends is talking of *invitations!* Merciful heaven!" Madame Ninette toppled back into the chair reserved for honored guests. "Brrrandy," she moaned.

Miss Wergeland's small store of patience was exhausted. These women were utterly impossible. She should rather have locked Vivica in her room than permitted her to work in the beauty parlor with such creatures. Astrid would hear something when she returned from the office today!

"Will you kindly leave my house," Helene said coldly, regarding the enormous woman with savage dislike. Lightnings flashed in her steely blue eyes. "And may I take the opportunity to inform you that my niece will no longer be working in your business. That is final. Good day."

She had reached the door in three huge steps when she felt a light pressure on her arm. Whirling around, she stared straight into Vera Leskaya's small eyes. The lifeless face bore an unfathomable expression.

"Madame," the woman in gray said with the ceremonial pathos of a cultivated Russian, "our visit is in no way a social one. My employer has been attempting in her own fashion to prepare you for a—hm—unpleasant surprise, but she is too soft-hearted."

The soft-hearted colossus nodded, flattered, and lit one of Astrid's French cigarettes, which were kept in an Annamite silver box on the teakwood table beside the chair.

"And so *I* unfortunately must tell the tale," Vera Leskaya went on slowly. "For decades it has been my sorrowful lot to be the bearer of ill tidings."

Miss Wergeland stared angrily at the gray-clad secretary. The woman spoke in a singsong chant that was enough to lull one to sleep. Couldn't these Russians ever call a spade a spade? Helene was not interested in this gray creature's sorrowful lot. What an exaggerated way to talk! But—what was this about an unpleasant surprise? Was it anything about Vivica? Miss Wergeland wanted to ask what the devil it was all about, but her voice would not obey her. In spite of the heat she suddenly felt chilled.

"Madame," said the chanting voice, "it grieves me to inform you that—" She hesitated, and then said clearly and forcefully, "Miss Vivica Wergeland was arrested an hour ago by the Japanese secret police."

The furniture in the reception room rocked before Helene Wergeland's eyes. Was she not still dreaming in her orchid pavilion?

The colossus in the chair seemed to think that the situation called for a Russian outburst of emotion. Suddenly a tremendous fit of weeping shook her body. The rouge streamed down her puffy cheeks. "Vivica, my dove, my only friend in this icy world," she whimpered. Icy world indeed—a bold assertion when the temperature was a hundred in the shade.

"Vivica, my dove!" Madame howled. "So young, and a jailbird already! Leskaya, give me a handkerchief." And then she said quite audibly, even as she noisily blew her nose, "Brrandy, or at least a mild pink gin. This house is rridiculous. No drrinks, no music, no amusements. Console me, Leskaya!"

Vera did not stir; she had been accustomed for twenty years to these eruptions on the part of her employer. "Console me!" Madame Ninette shrieked furiously. "Don't stand there like a plaster saint."

But for once the shadowy secretary was not dancing attendance on Madame Ninette. She was ringing for ice water to revive Miss Wergeland, who had fainted. . . .

As Yumei pattered toward the reception room, Vera Leskaya slipped into the big hall and returned with towels and Astrid's cardiac drops. She had a supernatural gift for finding bathrooms and desks in utterly strange houses. Then, with Yumei's aid, she tried to bring Miss Wergeland to.

Meanwhile Madame Ninette was enjoining her in Russian, "Don't go on talking to this frrightful old dame. She'll drag us all into the affair. She reminds me of Lisaveta Kruszova, who always made a point of involving all her acquaintances in her affairs. Let me think, now, Lisaveta was the niece, no, the second cousin of . . ." There followed a lengthy tale about the lady in question. "Vera, listen," Madame continued. "You know that I had no idea that the last batch of Saigon silk was stolen goods, don't you? It was offered to me; I examined it, bought it . . ." Madame Ninette recounted the course of events like the plot of a classical tragedy. "I knew nothing, nothing at all—you remember, don't you?"

"Of course you knew nothing, Nina Ivanovna! How could you possibly have known?"

Madame threw a sharp look at her "right hand." Was there a touch of mockery in that narcotic voice? Nonsense! Leskaya was too stupid for mockery.

"Leskaya," Madame went on, "just what did that Japanese say, the one with the little mustache and the crocodile-leather briefcase—it must have cost him a pretty penny? What did he say to you when he arrested the girl?"

Leskaya murmured long official sentences, as if she were reading from a file. "The Jap asked whom we rented the shop from, and whether he was pleased about the new Pan-Asiatic Co-Prosperity Sphere, and whether he read English books or listened to the Allied radio. He asked how long we have been in Bangkok and for whom we used to work."

"What does that mean, 'for whom'?"

"I thought the question queer too, Nina Ivanovna. Of course I told him we have always worked for ourselves, that we are poor Russians in exile and have to struggle to earn a bare living."

"Verry true and verry good." Madame Ninette applauded with her fat beringed hands as though she were attending a theatrical performance. "But that wasn't all. He chatted with you for fifteen minutes, my dove."

"He asked how long you have lived in China, and whether you prefer the Chinese to the Japanese."

"I hope you told him Nina Ivanovna wouldn't be able to say which she thinks more charrming. What did he ask about the little conspirator, Vivica?"

"I've forgotten, Nina Ivanovna."

"Then rremember. And fast!"

"He only asked how long Mademoiselle had been working for us. And whether she associates with you outside business hours. And then he told me to prepare a list of our clients by tonight."

"Over my dead body! The Jap is rridiculous."

Vera Leskaya disregarded the objection. She would deliver to her employers whatever they wished. The client list was, in fact, the only true detail in her whole account. Narrowing her eyes, she decided to put the fear of God into Madame Ninette—discreetly.

"I remember now; the younger officer wanted to know, right at the end, who bought the silk and cosmetics in Saigon, and how often your buyer has crossed the border to Indo-China in the last three months."

Madame Ninette had turned very pale. "What else?" she asked hoarsely.

"And whether you are interested in politics, and what our European clients, especially the German women, talk about. And whether you think Germany may be able to win the next world war. And whether he could have some skin lotion for his 'consolation lady.'"

"What was the name of the older officer, who stood in the background and did not say a word?"

"Major Kimura, as far as I know."

"He reminded me of someone, Leskaya! You used to have a Japanese student in Shanghai. He looked like him."

"They all look alike, Nina Ivanovna," Vera Leskaya murmured. "Oh, the young officer drove me distracted with his questioning."

"It doesn't take much to do that, Leskaya. Did you tell him that I am not the least bit interested in politics?"

"How could I say that, Nina Ivanovna? You know you listen to Tokyo Radio day and night!"

"You ought to be boiled in coconut oil," Madame replied in a harsh, sober voice. "Do you want to see us all in the Kempetai's cellars, goose? Did you also tell him what the clients talk about, you educated idiot? Women who want to be beautiful must keep their mouths shut, above all. Too much talk makes a woman ugly—you're a good example of that!"

"I'm sorry, Madame, I meant well."

"Since you're such a chatterbox, did you at least tell the Japanese that I hardly know the Werrgelands and wanted to fire that silly girl anyhow?"

"This is the first I have heard of it, Nina Ivanovna! You always called Mademoiselle Vivica your dove. You told her ever so often that she was your only friend in this icy world."

"Take care, Leskaya!"

"I'm terribly sorry if I've said anything wrong. Forgive me, Nina Ivanovna."

"You are a damnable chatterbox, Leskaya," Madame Ninette said with an effort. She must not show this idiot her fright. More and more Europeans were being arrested daily.

"Please forgive me, Nina Ivanovna!"

Madame Ninette threw a long, cold look at her "right hand." "I don't know why I picked such a chatterbox out of the back alleys of Shanghai, at no profit to myself," she said at last. "I wouldn't mind seeing you—"

She fell silent. Miss Wergeland had come to and was looking at her.

Helene Wergeland's ears were ringing, or was it her head? She had never before fainted, and was cross with herself at the paralyzing weakness she still felt. Only by the utmost effort could she recall why these Russian women were in her reception room. Her heart took several uneasy jumps.

"Do you feel better, Madame?" Vera Leskaya asked with concern. From her shabby handbag she took a crystal flask of French brandy, which she poured into the silver cup that served as a cap. It was a precious traveling flask, obviously a relic of Czarist Russia.

"Please drink," she said, observing Miss Wergeland's distaste. "You will need your strength, Madame. I always carry some cognac with me. Madame Ninette is so liable to attacks; as soon as the sirens howl, she collapses."

Madame Ninette looked mollified, snatched the bottle from Vera's hands, and drained it in one draft.

"Vera, my dove," she said with emotion, "your good heart moves me to tears. Let us flee, dearest Leskaya! This house is rrridiculous. No drrinks, no singing, no amusements!

"Best friend," she went on, turning to the speechless Miss Wergeland, who had never before witnessed the effect of really good cognac upon the Russian soul, "my heart weeps for your sake. But have you any objection if my dove Leskaya and I now leave this place?"

"A splendid suggestion." Miss Wergeland rose to her full height. She had recovered, though she was still deathly pale. "I shall call upon the police, in any case," she continued acridly. "Your beauty shop must be closed. It is a public menace."

Before Madame Ninette could throttle her "best friend," Vera Leskaya interposed politely but firmly. "Permit me to give you some good advice, Madame. It is pointless to attempt to place the responsibility upon my employer. We do not know why your niece has been arrested. Would you be so kind as to recollect that Madame Ninette at first did not want to employ your niece? Mademoiselle Vivica's social background is not that of girls who generally work as beauticians. My employer insisted upon having your written permission. The document is in our hands. Needless to say, we would only submit it to the secret police with the greatest regret, indeed, with bleeding hearts. Is that not so, Nina Ivanovna?"

The great mass of fat nodded so vehemently that all her chins shook. "I hired the girl with dark forebodings," she agreed. "With great, dark, fateful forebodings."

"Your niece was in no way suitable for us," Vera Leskaya went on. "But the young lady wanted to work for us to 'collect faces,' as she called it. She referred to the beauty salon as her 'hunting grounds.' A very strange young woman."

"Not in the least strange," Miss Wergeland broke in. She was prepared to defend Vivica against the whole world and her own better judgment. That was how she had behaved with Borghild also. "Vivica is an innocent child who wanted to make herself useful somewhere."

Vera Leskaya listened respectfully to this description of Vivica Wergeland's character.

"An innocent child," Miss Wergeland repeated obstinately.

"Certainly your niece is young and inexperienced," Vera Leskaya put in diplomatically. She looked toward the door as if she were expecting someone. "But I must with all due respect protest energetically against any attempt on your part to drag my employer's good name into this sorry affair."

An uncomfortable silence followed the gray crow's words. It seemed to Helene that the burning sunlight pouring through the cracks in the wooden shutters momentarily darkened. Why should this unsavory but very polite Russian woman defend her rude and spiteful employer so energetically? Miss Wergeland knew nothing about the irrational hate-love which cemented Russians in exile. Yet what Vera Leskaya said sounded like truth, and Helene Wergeland had always had a sensitive ear for the truth. It was pointless, and moreover dangerous, to anger this secretary who so politely proclaimed death sentences. Fixing her honest eyes on Vera Leskaya's unlovely face, Helene said bravely, "I beg your pardon."

The Russian woman bowed stiffly and held out her arm to Madame Ninette. As she steered her employer toward the door, something seemed to occur to her. She turned once more toward Miss Wergeland, who stood motionless in the middle of the room. Helene's strong features were frozen with despair.

Vera felt a stirring of pity, a thing she had scarcely felt in the past twenty years. Almost gently she said, "Permit me a final warning, Madame! If you have any compromising documents in the house, you ought to destroy them before the secret police search through everything."

Helene drew herself up angrily. "This is too much!" she exclaimed harshly. "Do you think we are a gang of conspirators? In my whole life nothing like this—" She broke off and laughed hoarsely, but her heart again skipped a beat. She forced herself to continue. "It may seem strange to you, Mademoiselle, but we live here in an absolutely orderly and uneventful manner. Absolutely *orderly*, do you hear? Our only documents are our passports and our birth certificates." Miss Wergeland gave another short laugh. It sounded like a sick bird trying to sing in a cage.

"Come, Leskaya!" Madame Ninette waited impatiently at the door, humming a melancholy Russian song. But Vera Leskaya was still looking at Miss Wergeland. An expression that might well have been genuine pity had come into her frigid eyes. Hesitantly she opened her bag and produced a sheet of Vivica's letter-paper.

"In your interest I have already looked through Miss Vivica's room," she declared with the blandness of an experienced espionage agent. "I deduced where it was located from remarks Miss Vivica has made. And I found this paper. I said nothing to you before because you seemed to be so agitated, Madame. It is my sorrowful destiny to be the bearer of ill tidings."

Helene stared in silence at Vivica's jade-green letter-paper.

"Before I leave you forever, Madame, I should like to tell you that

I am very fond of Mademoiselle Vivica. Never have I seen so radiantly beautiful and fearless a girl. I know, Madame, that she is young and thoughtless. Please destroy this paper. It might well be regarded as incriminating evidence. In occupied territory the Japanese secret police pounce upon every piece of paper with writing on it."

Miss Wergeland glowered at the green paper, which was covered with enigmatic signs. "Thank you, Mademoiselle," she said at last. "Vivica needs friends now." Her repressed love for the frivolous child threatened to choke her. "But are you not being overnervous? How could my niece—" She broke off, and her eyebrows drew together. It was all silly nonsense, an error. Out of her daze only one thought rose clearly: for the first time she felt glad that Knut was no longer among the living.

Vera Leskaya examined the sheet of paper with a pocket magnifying glass of Japanese manufacture. Then she said in an oddly solemn manner, "I am inconsolable, Madame. This is certainly part of a secret code. I know from my days in Russia what such things look like." Without asking Miss Wergeland's permission, she struck a match, burned the paper over an ash-tray, and crushed the black ash into a fine powder.

Helene did not stir; but she was far too intelligent not to be shaken by the Russian woman's warnings. As soon as they left, she herself would search every nook and corner of Vivica's room. It must all be a mistake. Vivica was only nineteen, an ignorant girl. And she herself, with all her experience, had really not the slightest conception of what a code looked like. These Russians were always either instigating conspiracies or discovering them; without that they could not be happy, Helene thought wearily.

She looked at the clock. What had she meant to do? With all her might Helene tried to dispel the thin mist from her brain. She had wanted to say something important. Now she knew. The thing was to ask Vera Leskaya for help, instead of wasting precious time babbling about sheets of paper. Naturally it went against the grain to ask this unknown and rather unpleasant woman for aid. She had never done that before, but this situation was different. The child must have tobogganed into something, although the affair would certainly be cleared up before long. After all, she knew Vivie. Vivie was not one to sacrifice herself for a political idea.

Madame Ninette had sunk back into the chair of honor and was snoring peaceably after her full flask of cognac.

"Mademoiselle," Helene said in her frosty school French, which had always rasped the nerves of Astrid's mother, "would you be so kind as to accompany me to the Kempetai? You see, I am no longer very sociable—at least so my late brother always maintained—and I might not find the best tone to use with these Japanese. Let us go at once. How in the world could that child have come into possession of a secret code? Why, it's ridiculous."

Miss Wergeland tried to laugh heartily, but all she produced was the choked echo of her anxiety. "Where have they taken the child?" she asked hoarsely. Suddenly the cruel reality of the arrest had dawned on her. Politics, which she had never troubled about, was beginning to destroy her orderly world. For a few seconds she found herself thinking that nothing as bad as this could ever have happened to them in their own country. They had stayed here in order to escape the German occupation; in their ignorance they had thought Japanese occupation less dangerous. Now, like thousands of their fellow Europeans, they were paying the price for their ignorance of the Far East.

"I believe Mademoiselle Vivica is at Saladeng Station at the moment. That used to be the office of a British company. The Kempetai uses it as a detention house for new prisoners. I am sorry, Madame, but I cannot accompany you. Please understand that the arrest of someone connected with our salon has made all of us suspect."

"Surely you take too black a view, Mademoiselle."

"My friends consider me an optimist," Vera Leskaya said gloomily. "However, I would like to ask you particularly not to go to the Kempetai. I too hope that your niece was arrested by mistake. Certainly this code on the letter-paper is evidence against her. But perhaps the young lady was writing a love letter in cipher. At her age girls often waste time on such jests. She really is still very much of a child."

Miss Wergeland nodded dumbly. Vera Leskaya studied one of Helene's Norwegian landscapes, whose wild melancholy appealed to her. Then she observed slowly, with great emphasis, "A great deal can be said against the Japanese as victors, but they have behaved in an altogether gentlemanly manner toward the civilian populace of this city. At the moment, of course, they are nervous. The British are making tremendous progress in Burma; the Russians have taken Silesia; the bombing of Japan is on the increase; and recently the Americans have landed on Luzon. Consider what Luzon means to the Japanese!"

Miss Wergeland had not the faintest idea what Luzon meant to the Japanese, and did not want to know. What had all this to do with Vivie? She fought heroically against her rising impatience as Vera Leskaya continued, "The breath of liberation is in the air, Madame! The liberation of Paris was a symbol for decisions in the Far East. Italy has collapsed. Germany will soon follow. I am fairly certain that—"

"Please keep to the point, Mademoiselle."

Like all Russians, Vera Leskaya did not like keeping to the point. She scowled at Helene. There was no life in her gray eyes, only a kind of passionate attachment to death.

"Naturally many spies in this part of the world are turning their coats," she continued. "The rats are abandoning the Nipponese ship. Pardon, Madame, I am digressing again. Political discussions are a Russian vice."

Helene had begun to wonder why the Russians did not go, if they were not going to help. She was reminded now of what Knut had once said: that Russians could remain from morning till midnight in a stranger's house, once they began talking politics.

"Consider, Madame, that it would only harm your niece if you went to the Kempetai. An arrest is no occasion for a family gathering. If you go, the Japanese will not release your niece but arrest *you*."

"Stuff and nonsense," Miss Wergeland replied. What could she do to make an ally of this Russian? Did the woman want her to beg on her knees? Was she longing for a cheap triumph over secure people? That might be forgivable. Helene was ready to sacrifice her pride; she resolved to do anything to win Vera Leskaya's help. After all, this woman had behaved in a civilized and even a considerate and protective manner. She had burned Vivie's letter-paper with the suspicious markings. She had offered French cognac and warned against taking reckless steps. Had she not even said she was fond of Vivica? Moreover, she looked like a respectable village schoolmarm. To be sure, Helene, who herself hated all excess of emotion, had never before met a person who so utterly lacked human warmth. Vera Leskaya had the ghostly chill of a chapel where no one ever prayed. Nevertheless, Helene tried a last plea. The Wergelands had produced some strange birds, but there had never been a coward in the family.

"Mademoiselle," Helene said in a voice hoarse with distress, "I must . . . tell you . . . something. My niece, Vivica—she is perfectly normal, of course—but from her childhood she has suffered from—"

Miss Wergeland ran her big, powerful hand over her forehead, which was covered with cold sweat. That trembling hand was a curious sight, as though a block of iron had suddenly begun to fall apart.

"What did you want to say, Madame?" the Russian asked gently, throwing a surreptitious look toward the door. She could not stay here much longer without its being noticed. *Where could they be?*

In Miss Wergeland's ears there was a hollow roaring, as if great waves were beating against the rock at the foot of a fjord. As she stood here, friendless in this hostile tropical city, she imagined she heard the despairing cry of wild geese. Or was Vivie screaming in her cell? In spite of the fierce tropical heat, icy north winds seemed to be howling around her, and she had the feeling that she was tumbling from rock to rock, down into the depths below the cliff. She swayed but immediately pulled herself together; the Russian woman's frigid, strangely avaricious eyes must have hypnotized her. Good Lord, now *she* was going off her head. Briskly, she came to the point.

"My niece cannot endure a closed room. She will go completely out of her mind in prison. So you see, Mademoiselle, that we must free her at once." With that, Helene strode to the door. "Please come along, Mademoiselle!" Contrary to her habit, she had spoken softly and very politely. Until this moment she had not realized how polite people must be when they wanted something from others.

"I am inconsolable, Madame," said that voice which lulled without comforting, "but you are asking something impossible. I beg you to believe me that no secret-police force in the world would release a prisoner on account of such whimsies."

Whimsies! Helene thought.

"When political prisoners malinger, they are sent off to the insane asylum and held there until they behave reasonably. Only a few days ago a Chinese businessman—Mr. Sun, I believe—was arrested as a Chungking agent, along with his daughters. You must certainly have heard about that."

Sun, Helene thought. Was not the girl who invited Vivica to her parties named Molly Sun? Astrid had turned down the invitations. But she herself had allowed the frivolous child to walk innocently into the lion's den. She compressed her lips. Perhaps the Sun family was a starting point. She would discuss the matter with Astrid.

"Mr. Sun asked to be released," Leskaya informed her. "Didn't you read about it in the newspapers? It was very comical."

Miss Wergeland said nothing. She did not like the way Mademoiselle Leskaya found amusement in others' misfortunes.

"Mr. Sun saw tigers or bank presidents in his cell, so he said. He was therefore transferred to the madhouse at Thonburi. In a week he will return to his cell as meek as a lamb. As a lamb, Madame!"

"Would it not be possible for me to bail my niece out? We would try to raise any sum they demanded." She had property, jewelry, a share in the firm of Sun. This Sun, the Bangkok partner of the antique business which the consul had started years ago, was probably a cousin of the arrested man. Or perhaps not. All the Chinese were named Chang or Sun, all looked alike, and all dragged unsuspecting European women into trouble, Helene thought wearily and unjustly. She could not occupy herself with the Suns now. Astrid took care of that. How clever of Knut to have bought this house and land. Real estate was rising in value from month to month. By selling she could certainly buy the child's freedom.

But Mademoiselle Leskaya explained to Helene that political prisoners could not be released on bail, at least not when they were in the clutches of the Kempetai. For, if released, they might warn others to destroy evidence and cover trails. Only murderers and bank robbers enjoyed the civilized benefits of bail. However, there was the possibility of bailing out Mademoiselle Vivica after the interrogation was over. Sometimes an interrogation took very little time.

"How much time?" Miss Wergeland asked.

"Have you heard about the Japanese water cure, and the sun treatment?" Mademoiselle Leskaya asked. "Such methods often speed interrogations remarkably."

Miss Wergeland had never heard of these methods.

"All the better for your peace of mind, Madame," the Russian woman said. "It is my sorrowful lot to be compelled to mention unpleasant matters. The rest of the world, alas, has taken over Soviet Russian methods—within the secret police, I mean. Let me explain the gist of the system, Madame. The spirit of a political prisoner—"

Vera Leskaya broke off her instructive lecture and cocked her ears. From the garden sounded the excited voice of the Hindu gatekeeper, the screams of children, the furious cackling of geese, and the shrill voices of two Japanese officers barking orders in English. They were telling the Hindu to open the gate wide so that their huge American car could drive through. Vera ran to the window. "Wake up, Nina Ivanovna!" she cried, shaking the snoring colossus. "The Kempetai has come to arrest the old lady. Come, quick!"

Madame Ninette gaped drowsily at her secretary. When she grasped the sense of the words she crossed herself three times in succession and opened her full, pleasure-loving lips for a Russian scream. But before she could utter it, Vera's cold fingers sealed her lips.

"Have you gone mad?" Vera demanded without her usual humility.

"Where is a closet?" Madame Ninette whimpered through Vera's fingers. "In Russia we always hid in a big, comfortable closet: Papushka, Mamushka, Prince Nicolai, his awful wife, and me. Be calm, Leskaya. Don't scrrream, idiot!"

But by then Vera had hauled her fat employer into an adjoining room and stowed her away as well as she could in a supply closet. She herself crept modestly behind a curtain. Not a minute too soon!

Major Matsubara and Lieutenant Makoto Urata of the Kempetai were bowing politely before a petrified Miss Wergeland.

Major Matsubara looked around with the insatiable curiosity of a Japanese tourist on duty. Since he was an aesthete, Helene's Norwegian landscapes produced a faint convulsion of his stomach, and he turned his dark eyes away from the painful sight.

"Are you Miss Helene Wergeland?" he asked crossly. The name rang a faint bell in his memory, but at the moment he could connect it with nothing.

Helene nodded. She stood confronting the two visitors in the large, rather empty room. It did not occur to her to ask them to sit down.

Major Matsubara, stern and official in his uniform, considered the tall Norwegian for several seconds. Was it that she seemed rather old to him for a political conspirator, or did her face and name remind him of some other European?

"Where is your niece?" he asked abruptly.

"My niece—well—my niece—"

Miss Wergeland fell silent. This question was surely a mockery. Didn't this coldly smiling officer know far better than she where her unfortunate niece was at this moment? Was he making fun of a tormented old woman? Helene's thin lips tightened. She suddenly looked as obstinate as she had been in the good old days, when Knut was trying to wheedle something out of her. If this Japanese thought she was going to give him information, he had miscalculated! Even in her most exuberant moods, Miss Wergeland was no chatterbox.

Major Matsubara, who had been studying her fixedly and tracing her every thought in her face, smiled somewhat more amiably. It was plain to him that this angry giantess knew nothing about the Sun espionage ring. He could tell whether a person was trembling from guilty conscience, extreme fear, or righteous wrath.

"I suppose I must explain, Madame," he said in his perfect French. "Wait in the adjoining room, Lieutenant," he ordered his companion.

In the adjoining room! Helene thought. The Russian women were in there.

"You see, Madame," Major Matsubara went on, sitting down, unasked, in the chair of honor, "headquarters has decided. The business is pressing. I have already negotiated over the telephone with your niece. Two hours ago I called her"—he looked into his notebook—"but Mademoiselle Astrid Wergeland was not in her office—in the P-r-a-h-u-r-a-t." He carefully spelled out the name, meanwhile sharply eying the old foreigner from behind his notebook. Was she looking less perturbed? "And so I asked the doorman for her home address. I should like to know whether the automobiles offered us by the firm are still available. We had almost decided that they were too dear for such old models. You know we pay too much for everything in Thailand."

Helene took a deep breath. The Russian woman had almost floored her. She would bring Vivica's case to the attention of this courteous officer as soon as possible. No need to go to the Kempetai.

"My niece probably was out to lunch," she said in her normal voice. "If you drive back to her office now, she will be there."

"Do you not have a telephone here in Sathorn Road?"

"Heaven preserve me from such idiotic machinery. People would be jabbering one's ears off all day long." Miss Wergeland was by now almost her old cordial self.

Major Matsubara was vastly amused within himself at the notion of a Japanese lady's ever expressing such sentiments about her honored friends. "Thank you, Madame," he said with a stiff bow. "I shall drive right back to Pra-hu-rat. Your niece is engaged in a great deal of business at the moment, is she not? She deals in works of art, I believe. Or am I mistaken?"

"Works of art too. My brother introduced her to the trade."

"Bangkok is a meeting point of East and West," Major Matsubara remarked thoughtfully. "Hindus, Chinese—with whom is your niece connected in the art trade?"

"With Sun and Company," Helene said, and started in fright. For heaven's sake! Cousin Sun had been arrested. Or was the Russian woman misinformed?

"I admire the art of the Chinese," Major Matsubara observed quickly. His tone made it quite plain that this was all he found admirable about the Chinese. "How many nations are gathered together in this city—French, Germans, Russians. A great many White Russians, I believe."

"I assume so," Miss Wergeland said shortly. "I don't bother much with people, thank heaven. And I do not care about interesting cities. Never in my life have I seen such disorderly and extravagant people and plants as in Siam."

"You mean Thailand, Madame," Major Matsubara corrected her. "It means 'Land of the Free.'"

"Really? I consider it plain foolishness to change a country's name. When I came to Siam in nineteen-thirty everyone was quite satisfied with the old name. People are becoming crazier all the time. Oh, would you like something to drink? I quite forgot—I never have guests. In this climate one can drink gallons of lemonade, can't one?"

"It certainly is hot," Major Matsubara agreed, frowning slightly.

"But we Japanese are trained to curb our desires. In any case, thank you very much, Madame. It is very kind of you. I shall now call on your niece."

"Monsieur," Helene said hoarsely, "may I—I mean, could you tell me—" She stopped. The blood drained away from her heart.

"Aren't you well, Madame?" The major brought the second chair of honor forward for her. "What were you about to ask?"

"Nothing. It has slipped my mind."

"You do not look well, Madame. Why do you stay in a country with such a climate? You could have been repatriated with the other Norwegians in nineteen-forty-one, you know. Were you so interested in the awakening Far East?"

"Not in the least," Miss Wergeland said with almost comic candor. "I am a stupid old woman and take no interest in politics. I only keep house for my nieces."

"You have several nieces, then?"

Miss Wergeland started as if she had received a blow. He is interrogating me, she thought. He will lead me around to saying something foolish. Anger rose high in her, but she controlled herself and said quietly that Astrid had two sisters.

The Japanese officer seemed not to be listening. His attention had been caught by a scroll on the wall, "Songbird on a Dead Branch"— a masterpiece. *Where* had he seen it before? His phenomenal memory began to grind. How did Europeans come to possess such a treasure from Nippon?

"A beautiful painting, Madame," he said casually. "Do you collect Japanese painting?"

"It belonged to my deceased brother."

Brother! Wergeland. A . . . tea room in Shanghai. There, as a young man, Akiro had drunk tea with Consul Wergeland, his first and last European friend, who in 1925 had not even expressed thanks for a kimono from imperial Kyoto. And now he had this European's family in his hands. The time had come for a Japanese revenge. The longer such revenge had to wait, the sweeter it was.

"I suppose your brother always stayed in Bangkok? Or did he buy this scroll in Japan?"

"I do not know. He brought it from Shanghai to Trondheim long ago. He was very fond of it." Helene closed her eyes in exhaustion.

So it all checked. A fine family! The Mademoiselle Clermont, who in Shanghai and a few years ago in Angkor had said such cutting things about Japanese poetry, was in fact named Wergeland. He would find out why she called herself Clermont. Perhaps that was important, perhaps not.

"Madame," Major Matsubara said in a sweet voice, "permit me to give you some advice. You ought to take a vacation and go away!"

Helene stared speechlessly at him. His gentleness and politeness struck her as uncanny. Instinct had warned her a moment ago against speaking to him of Vivica. Better if Astrid went to see the officials. She was younger and understood the art of haggling.

"The bombings are surely affecting your nerves, Madame," the major remarked. "Why don't you go to the mountains of Indo-China? Dalat is an ideal resort, far from the fever and fret of Saigon. We would issue a travel permit for you at once, Madame."

"Indo-China!" Helene exclaimed, forgetting all caution. Vivica had incurred suspicion because of those trips to Saigon on orders from the Russian woman. "I would sooner visit hell."

"You do not like traveling, Madame?"

"I detest it. Talkative fools, bad and expensive food, and nothing to do all day long. No, thank you."

"Have you so much to do here, Madame?"

"I have my hands full," Helene said curtly, thinking of the pavilion filled with Chinese who looked to her for rice and protection.

"You have never been in Indo-China, Madame?" he asked casually. Helene had often heard Astrid tell of the insatiable curiosity of the Japanese, yet a tiny icy shiver ran down her spine. Suppose the man now asked whether Vivie or Astrid knew Saigon? Well, he could drag her to the gallows before he would extract a word from her about Vivie's journeys.

But Major Matsubara had no intention of leading Miss Wergeland so melodramatically to her death. As far as he was concerned, she could die in peace. In the first place, the Kempetai did not as a rule wage war against grandmothers. And then, it was obvious that Miss Wergeland was honesty personified. Major Matsubara had perceived that from the first words she spoke, and from one look into those steely blue eyes. It was ridiculous, but Miss Wergeland some-how reminded him of his own grandmother in Tokyo, although the two women were worlds apart. Old Baroness Matsubara of Itoh would sooner have thrown herself into the crater of a volcano than be caught characterizing her friends as "fools" or "chatterboxes." But she was as loyal as this Norwegian who held her lips tightly com-pressed in order not to betray her youngest niece, and she inspired the same kind of respect. Miss Wergeland's naïveté had almost prompted the major to smile. As though he did not know all there was to know about Miss Wergeland and her nieces! Mailin and the Chou families in Singapore and Shanghai were already being shad-owed, as was old Dr. Clermont, Astrid's great-uncle in Saigon. The list of visitors to the Chou and Clermont houses lay on the major's desk. The only fact that the Tiger of the Kempetai had not known was that these Wergelands were close relatives of his former Shang-hai friend. The art of old Japan had supplied him with this fact. It lent new spice to the hunt. The whole matter of the espionage ring had not yet been entirely clarified; the dragnet was out for several important Allied spies. This ring had done inordinate damage to Nip-pon in the holy war. In fact, Colonel Saito had expressed his keen displeasure with Major Matsubara for having made so little progress in the past two years. Major Matsubara had taken issue with this. He *had* made progress since Angkor Wat, but he was wary of pounc-ing prematurely on the espionage group. Hearing this, Colonel Saito had flashed his incisors and nodded, temporarily satisfied. Matsubara was, after all, his best man; and anyone who did not know how to wait had no business being in the Kempetai. Now, however, there would be an end to forbearance!

"We will send you a travel permit, Madame," Major Matsubara said gently. He actually wanted to send this woman, who reminded him of his honored grandmother, off to a place of safety and spare her the sight of things that would probably break her heart. Akiro had a cold, subtle mind, but a sensitive soul. Unwittingly Miss Wergeland had appealed directly to his soul. Old Baroness Matsu-bara would have comported herself in precisely the same way in a similar situation. If it were a question of saving Akiro, she would have allowed herself to be shot. Only she would have expressed her-self a good deal more graciously.

The major made a last ceremonial bow. He glanced into the garden, where his lieutenant was waiting stiffly beside the American police car. Fortunately Miss Wergeland did not seem struck by the remarkable fact that Lieutenant Urata had not discovered the two Russian women in the adjoining room.

At this moment there burst from Miss Wergeland a strange sound, something between a sob and a cough. The Japanese officer was on the point of going, and she still did not know whether she ought to say anything to him about Vivie. *If he helped her, Vivie could leave with her.* They could go to Laura, the former Widow from Aalesund, who lived peacefully and safely with her Danish husband in the northern part of the country. Laura would be delighted to have them visit.

"Monsieur," Helene said hoarsely to the elegant officer, "thank you for the travel permit. I—but I should like to take my youngest niece with me."

"Then I shall have it made out for you and your family, Madame," Major Matsubara said, his face immobile. He made a final ceremonial bow. "Permit me to take my leave, Madame. May the journey bring you refreshment and recuperation! I shall now try again to reach Mademoiselle Clermont-Wergeland." And then he was gone.

The big car was followed at a cautious distance by a ricksha in which sat a Chinese woman with a covered cookpot, and her youngest son beside her. Yumei had learned what had happened from Madame Ninette's ricksha coolie, who was resting in the shade of a fan palm. She had at once prepared chicken livers and rice with mango chutney, because Third Sister was fond of this dish. Yumei planned to wait with her pot and jar of chutney at the prison until some guard softened and consented to bring the food to Third Sister. Beneath Yumei's blue work smock hung a chain of heavy Norwegian silver. Miss Wergeland had sent it to her fifteen years ago at the birth of her eldest son. With this chain she planned to bribe the guards. When Missie Vivica received the chicken liver and the chutney, she would know that her old amah was still caring for her, as she had all these years since Missie Borghild fell ill and had to be taken to Dalat by Master. And in the evening Miss Wergeland would pat Yumei on the back when she heard that Third Sister was receiving her favorite dish. Of course Yumei would never mention the price. Like any Chinese, Yumei thought that a little joy in dark days was worth any ornament, no matter how precious.

Her ricksha halted in front of the Kempetai's temporary prison in Saladeng. Yumei got out, clinging tightly to her son and her cookpot.

After Major Matsubara's departure, Helene Wergeland stood frozen in the reception room, trying to collect her thoughts. Courteous though he had been, the Japanese officer had left behind an atmosphere of indefinite terror. Suddenly a glass shattered somehow in the house; the crash was followed by varied noises and a Russian curse. In her search for brandy, Madame Ninette must have broken something in the supply cupboard. Shortly afterward she reappeared in the reception room. Spots of iodine on her print dress had not made her any more attractive. "That closet is ridiculous," she growled. "Why do you keep so many bottles there if there's nothing to drink in them?"

Madame Ninette dropped heavily but nimbly into the chair for honored guests. Now that the danger was over, she saw no particular reason for rushing away. No Russian ever saw such a reason. She was enormously surprised that Miss Wergeland had not been arrested. Eyes half shut, she hummed some song of the Volga.

"Strong coffee would do me good," she announced. "I take it without sugar or cream." She went on humming in pleasurable anticipation of coffee and a good chat.

"Good-by," Miss Wergeland said hospitably. "Perhaps you will finish your song in your own house."

Madame Ninette went on singing. Twice she called out, "Leskaya, where are you? The coffee will be along in a moment!"

Miss Wergeland opened the door. "Get out!" she said. "And be quick about it!" She was trembling violently, and there flashed in her eyes that danger signal which used to warn Yvonne and Astrid that she had had enough of a quarrel or a surprise.

"Stop that noise!" Helene thundered at Madame Ninette, who was continuing to trill away. "You alone are to blame for Vivica's arrest, and I intend to see that you pay for it!"

"How do you mean that, dearest friend?"

"You sent the poor child to Saigon on your filthy business. I'll see to it that the Kempetai stops your singing once and for all."

Dead silence followed these words. Madame Ninette neither sang nor smiled; she stared at the upright, white-haired Norwegian. Then she asked her secretary, who at this moment appeared from the storage room with a bundle of letters, in a hard, sober voice, "Did you hear that, Leskaya?"

The woman in gray nodded. Her nostrils quivered like leaves in the monsoon.

"Leave this to me, my dove," Madame Ninette whispered in Russian. "Nina Ivanovna will teach this horrid hag a lesson." She assembled herself in the easy chair, preparing for a serious confrontation. She did not know, of course, how much Miss Wergeland detested scenes.

"Madame," the great mass of fat said in a voice so hard and changed that it seemed to belong to a different person, "you are mad, utterly mad. I must warn you for your own sake not to provoke me any further."

For the first time in her life Miss Wergeland did not snap back at being addressed so impudently. She stared at this new Madame Ninette. The woman was uncanny. She no longer looked comical, in spite of the incredible blond chignon. Somehow she seemed more dangerous than the ghostly secretary, though Helene could not have said why.

"I warn you not to go on spreading any such silly stories about me. *I* did not send your fine niece to Saigon. Never, not once, do you understand?"

"You did—did not send Vivica there?" Helene stammered, horrified. "But then who did? Vivica always told me that—"

"She is a liar," Madame Ninette declared, "a tramp."

Tramp! A bell rang in Helene's memory. A pale little girl stood at Helene's bedside in Trondheim. "*Maman* called the lady with the violin case *une vagabonde*. I think she stole something from *Maman*." And shortly before the catastrophe Knut had written of Borghild that she was "a creature of chaos and her art a product of the depths." Helene had never been able to forget those harsh words. Perhaps her anxious love for Vivica had sprung from Knut's harshness, which had driven Borghild to her death. Good heavens, what had the child been up to?

"Who sent my niece to Saigon?" Miss Wergeland asked tonelessly.

"How should I know that? Ask your young crrriminal!"

"You really did not?"

"I would know better than that. Your niece is a spendthrift, a reckless spender."

"Who bought your cosmetics, if not my niece?"

"*I* did the buying for Madame Ninette, of course," Vera Leskaya put in. All through this conversation her eyes had been fixed on her employer's face.

"Exactly. Vera Leskaya is my commercial agent for Saigon, milady. She has a good business head, she is not too beautiful, and she does not spend her evenings at dance halls." Madame Ninette nodded sagely. "I told your niece more than once that she was a little tramp. But she always answered that she loved to steal men's hearts. So young and already so depraved! A vixen—that is what your Vivica is!"

"Enough of that!" Miss Wergeland snapped. "You can tell your Russian fairy tales to the Kempetai. I should like to know who is responsible for my niece's arrest, if not you!"

The two visitors exchanged glances. Then Vera Leskaya stepped close to Helene. She fixed her avaricious, lifeless eyes, from which the last spark of sympathy had vanished, on Miss Wergeland. "I assure you for the last time, Madame, that my employer did not have anything to do with the arrest of your niece. We will see to it that *you* are arrested if you insult or accuse Nina Ivanovna again. Our patience has reached its limit, Madame."

"Get out!" Miss Wergeland said hoarsely.

"Don't give yourself airs because the officer did not arrest you when he was here," Vera Leskaya continued. "Perhaps it would interest you to learn that Major Kimura in person came to our salon to arrest your niece."

"No brandy, no gin, no coffee—rrridiculous!" Madame Ninette interjected. "This is a house of death." She lit Astrid's last cigarette.

Miss Wergeland did not say a word.

"The Kempetai is usually in no hurry, Madame. On the contrary, it usually watches and shadows a suspect family—or group, party, or nation. But if you insist on knowing who had your niece come to Saigon twice a month, I might be able to tell you," Vera Leskaya continued fluently.

Miss Wergeland leaned forward as if she were hard of hearing. Madame Ninette, too, was all attention.

"It is my sorrowful lot to be the bearer of ill tidings," Vera Leskaya said. "But I suppose it is better for you to know. I listened to what the two officers in our salon said to one another when they came for your niece. I know a little Japanese—"

"You marvel!" Madame Ninette said, clapping her hands. "You useful, darling bundle of secrets!"

"The officers mentioned a certain gentleman in connection with your niece's trips—a Frenchman. They said he was Mademoiselle Vivica's secret fiancé. She is so young, so dazzlingly beautiful, and knows how to handle men, doesn't she, Madame?"

"Who?" Helene asked hoarsely. "For God's sake, out with it!"

With sadistic slowness Vera took a grubby notebook from her bag and leafed through it. "I wrote down the name. Ah, here it is. The conspirator's name is Pierre de Maury, co-editor of the pro-Japanese periodical *L'Indo-Chine*. As I said, your niece Vivica's secret fiancé."

"Are you out of your head?"

Vera Leskaya shrugged away the insult. Instead of replying, she held out a bundle of letters to Miss Wergeland. "I found these letters, along with the coded material, in your niece's room. Mademoiselle Vivica must be a very disorderly person to leave such intimate missives lying around in an unlocked desk. I took the liberty of reading them while you were talking with the Japanese major, Madame. I must say, Monsieur de Maury writes letters that would turn the head of any young girl. Good day, Madame!"

The two Russians took themselves off with remarkable celerity. Helene Wergeland stood stock still in the reception room. Pierre de Maury's letters to Vivica had dropped from her hand. At last she stooped and gathered them up. Then she took them to her room to be locked away in her desk. Astrid must never be allowed to catch sight of these letters, for she would say that the tramp's daughter had stolen her fiancé. Helene did not know that Astrid already knew the contents of these letters word for word. During the long nights when Vivica danced in gardens under a green tropical moon, Astrid had almost learned by heart Pierre's letters to her half-sister. Every word remained with her, thanks to her outrageous memory. But Helene knew nothing about this, since Astrid had said not a word.

Helene was just about to leave to drive to Astrid's office when the sirens howled. The worst air raid the city had experienced since 1941 began. Countless human beings, animals, and dwellings were swept from the surface of the earth. Yumei had been waiting for over an hour in the prison yard for a chance to deliver Vivica's favorite dish to her. A bomb which scored a direct hit on the building showered deadly splinters upon Yumei. She died without a sound, the cookpot and her son held close.

When the sirens at last gave the all clear, Bangkok's two power plants lay shattered. No one knew what had happened to the prisoners. The Kempetai issued no information on the living or the dead —especially not on the dead, since surviving conspirators might then be disposed to tell the secret police lies which could not be checked against the other culprits' statements.

When Miss Wergeland came back to the house from her air-raid shelter in the garden, she did not know whether Astrid and Vivica were still alive. It was five o'clock in the afternoon—tea time. If Astrid had escaped the hail of bombs upon the center of the city, she was due to arrive at any moment.

Astrid did not return to Sathorn Road until evening. She had first helped to bring the elder Mr. Sun home. His shop was burning, and along with it much valuable Wergeland property went up in flames: scrolls, jade ornaments, china, carved chests. Since the arrest of his nephew, Mr. Sun had been in a state of nervous shock, and wanted to die with his treasures. With the aid of the staff, Astrid had saved his life.

When she returned home, exhausted and half mad with thirst, toward seven o'clock, Miss Wergeland met her on the steps, a kerosene lamp in hand.

"We have no electricity and no water! Thank heaven you're safe." In the flickering light she looked like a ghost. The whole vast stairwell was filled with quivering shadows.

"Is Vivica back yet?" Astrid asked heavily.

"No, she is not. She will not be coming."

"What has happened, Aunt Helene?" Astrid cried out in alarm. Her aunt had spoken in a voice utterly without inflection. It was as though life had passed from this strong body and energetic, eternally solicitous mind, and only a shell of the old Helene Wergeland were standing before Astrid in the flickering light of the kerosene lamp.

"Has something happened to Vivica?" A sense of unreality overcame Astrid. This was not the Aunt Helene she knew.

"I don't know, Astrid," Helene said in a flat voice. "Perhaps Vivica is still alive. I've kept some rice warm for you. Come to the dining room. Yumei's husband will serve. Yumei—" Miss Wergeland stopped. Yumei lay in the cook house. The pot still nestling in the crook of her cold arm had told Helene the whole story. The "chicken man," who knew Yumei from the market, had brought her back home, trembling and wailing lamentations. Helene had knelt beside Yumei and with her big, shaking hand had brushed the black hair back from the bloodstained forehead. Yumei, who with the passing years had become a comfortably plump Chinese mother, still had the smooth, round child's forehead she had so often leaned against Helene's knee, in touching devotion, back in Trondheim. Wen— Yumei's husband and the Wergelands' cook—stood petrified beside the bodies of his wife and his son. Why had they gone off without him? He could have accompanied them and looked out for the child.

In spite of respectful protests by Wen and the rest of the servants, Helene had washed the body with her own hands and dressed Yumei in her best clothes. Finally she had hung the silver chain around Yumei's neck. The bright Norwegian silver and the bright Chinese red of the gown looked festive and beautiful. Yumei would have taken pleasure in her appearance. The chain was a last mute tribute from Miss Wergeland of Trondheim. Let it accompany Yumei to the place where her ancestors awaited her.

In the dining room, under the flickering kerosene lamps, Astrid heard how their family's world had smashed to pieces. She sat like a statue over her cold rice. How in the world had Vivica stumbled into this pitfall? Who had pulled her down to destruction?

Astrid had removed her glasses and was looking vacantly at her aunt. Helene had reported everything except the letters of Pierre de Maury; she had not said that he was, according to the Russian woman, an enemy of Nippon disguised in the mask of a pro-Japanese collaborator.

"Eat, Astrid," Helene said wearily. But Astrid could not eat. A frightful secret had taken her appetite away. Even as a child she had always had secrets, which sooner or later she would produce for the edification of Aunt Helene. But as she studied the lifeless face in the flickering light—a face still bold, but robbed of its vitality —Astrid knew that this was one secret she must keep to herself even if it choked her.

"Why don't you eat? We will need our strength," Helene murmured. They must set out at dawn to look for Vivie, if the child were still living. Perhaps the Kempetai would be merciful. Helene had still not recovered from the shock of learning that the courteous, obliging officer had been making a fool of her. He himself had arrested Vivie! And she did not even remember his name. She could not possibly ask the Russian women, not after throwing them out of the house.

"Good night," Astrid said in a breaking voice. She was quite livid; in spite of the dim light Helene could see how all the blood had drained from her face.

She got up and brushed Astrid's hair back from her forehead. "Don't fall ill now, child; I have no one but you," she said.

Perhaps Helene should not have been affectionate, for Astrid broke down at this rare demonstration. Before Helene's eyes she seemed to go to pieces. Hands outflung, she drew back, moaning, "Don't be nice to me. I—I'm to blame for everything."

"Go to bed, Astrid," Helene said with extraordinary gentleness, for her subtle intuition and her keen mind combined to produce a fearful suspicion in her. "We'll talk more tomorrow."

She put her arm around the girl, who clung to her, sobbing uncontrollably, and took her to her own bedroom. There she undressed Astrid, drew a white blanket-sheet over the woefully thin body, and dropped a sedative powder into boiled water. Before Astrid sank at last into a feverish sleep she opened her pale nearsighted eyes once more and murmured, "I did not know . . . Aunt Helene. You must believe me!"

What had Astrid not known? It did not matter. Helene's sole purpose in life was to mend broken things and to shelter and support

Knut's daughters. "I believe you," she whispered, turning away from the bed.

She herself lay down to sleep on the couch, from which she could keep an eye on Astrid. She drew the mosquito netting close and sighed like a traveler in the desert who comes to a destination and finds no oasis but only more desert all about. The big tropical house was uncannily empty. The Chinese refugees had scurried away into hiding when the Japanese officers arrived. Yumei was dead, Vivica missing; Mailin was living in Japanese-occupied Singapore, in a similar danger zone. Over them all hung a typically Asian menace—a gentle, imperceptible, slowly creeping wave of annihilation that tossed up playful white surf before crashing down upon them all. She and Astrid were alone, and the empty house seemed to be filled to its most remote corner with Astrid's terrible secret. What had Astrid not known? Why had she said that she was to blame for everything? What strange paths had her unquiet mind taken during the long nights when she sat, wakeful, in her room, cruelly excluded from love? *What is Astrid?* Helene asked herself in the stillness of the night.

She closed her eyes in utter exhaustion and listened. She could hear a sound like a Chinese ghost-drum. Gradually she became aware that this low, insistent hammering was her own heartbeat. A strange sensation, a current hostile to life, streamed through her body. She could feel her knees becoming weak as water, her heart pounding more and more urgently, and her big, capable hands, so good at patching broken articles and picking up fallen souls, turning slowly to ice.

Why, this is fear I am feeling! Miss Wergeland thought in amazement.

3: *Variations of Fear*

Astrid rose at dawn and left the house without breakfast. Helene was still sleeping a sleep of exhaustion. Astrid had stood over her for a moment, studying her with a curious expression. Aunt Helene still did not know what she, Astrid, had done. She herself must at once take some action to save Vivie. Her mind was working clearly and logically once more. Her emotional outburst last night, solely because Aunt Helene had caressed her lovingly, had been highly inappropriate. She, who had craved love more furiously than most girls, no longer seemed able to endure it. She was no longer jealous, either, as she had been at the age of seven in Shanghai, when she killed the bird Gold Oriole; or later, at the boarding school in Lausanne, where she had plagued certain of the other children with her love as she had always plagued her father, Aunt Helene, and later Pierre de Maury. Her jealousy and her love-hatred had become like the rivers of Babylon after that outing at Angkor; the rushing waters had carried away the fragments of her virtue. If something happened to Vivica, Astrid was to blame, whether or not she had wished it. As a child she had not wanted to kill Gold Oriole either, but suddenly the bird had lain lifeless in her cold hand. At that time she had screamed, and Papa had soothed her as Aunt Helene had attempted to soothe her last night. But Gold Oriole stayed dead, and yesterday afternoon a bomb had struck the building where the Japanese were holding Vivica a prisoner.

Astrid had had no suspicion that Vivica was connected with the Sun espionage ring. Or was the whole affair a gruesome error on the part of the Kempetai, which was becoming increasingly nervous, and therefore more and more menacing, with each passing month? After all, Vivica had done nothing but dance at Molly Sun's parties under the tropical moon, while Astrid sat glumly with Aunt Helene on the dark terrace. Then she had said good night and gone into

Vivica's room. Glasses on her nose, she had read over Pierre's love letters to Vivica. He had never written *her* such letters. She had never imagined that he could be so tender and so utterly smitten by a girl's beauty. He seemed to count the hours until he could see little "Vivienne" in Saigon again. Always Saigon—he had wanted to meet her only there, because in Bangkok, Astrid would be on their scent. This was what Pierre had meant, although he had put it much more delicately: that he did not want to hurt Astrid needlessly.

These things she had read, until she knew the letters by heart, word for word. She would have liked to shed a few tears, as wall-flowers the world over do, but this gratis relief had been denied to her by her own nature. That was unfortunate, for her grief became an ulcer that consumed her virtue. Her heart was as parched as a rice field in the hot season. She burned with dry sorrow and shame over having been thrust aside by a young tramp. For Astrid was convinced that the affair had begun the day Vivica danced for Pierre.

One night, three weeks before Vivica's arrest, Astrid had sat down in her air-conditioned office and written a clear, cold letter to an agency that exercised no mercy when it received information, even if such letters were written anonymously and on a Chinese type-writer.

And now someone had been arrested whom Astrid had not dreamed of harming—her half-sister Vivica. How was that possible? The Kempetai arrested the men whom it called "foes of Nippon," interrogated them, and then did as it pleased with them; but it did not arrest the birds who sang love songs to the men, or giddy girls who danced with them in Saigon night-clubs! Had it done so, it would have had to set up women's prisons. The Japanese despised the mentality of women too greatly to go to the trouble of mass arrests. They were concerned only with the men.

Astrid had denounced Pierre de Maury to the Kempetai as a foe of Nippon.

Steeped in her tragic confusion, Astrid set out at dawn for Madame Ninette's. It was a breach of all propriety to call on a lady at half past six in the morning, but Astrid could not wait to find out as much as possible from her. They had known each other well since their first meeting in Shanghai; Madame Ninette had entertained Astrid with the biographies of total strangers, and Astrid had paid handsomely and gladly for these stories rather than for the rather wasted beauty treatments. Now, however, she would have to speak with the old Russian about someone who was not a total stranger— her own sister Vivica.

The boy, who came shuffling sleepily to the door, said that his mistress had gone away for a rest yesterday afternoon. Astrid was so upset that she forgot to tip the boy. Thereupon he slammed the door in her face. She went back to her small sports car and drove off.

Behind the curtains of the breakfast room Madame Ninette and Vera Leskaya laughed as they watched Astrid drive away. Madame Ninette rumbled with glee, and Vera Leskaya chuckled softly. Neither one of them intended to be in at any time for members of the Wergeland family.

"Wasn't that the funniest thing, Vera, my dove?"

Vera Leskaya nodded. She had spent the night at her employer's side because Madame Ninette was in such a state over Miss Wergeland's inhospitable reception. While the great mass of blubber snored, Leskaya had crept into the living room and poked around a little in the desk.

During breakfast, which Madame Ninette began with a glass of brandy, they sat in a silence oddly contrasting with their merriment over Astrid's disappointment.

"You're not eating and you're not drrinking; you're sitting around like a plaster saint with tonsilitis," Madame Ninette growled. "What's the matter with you, Leskaya?"

"I'm frightened."

"Of whom?"

"If I knew that, I would no longer be frightened," Vera Leskaya said softly.

Astrid drove in despair to her office on the Prahurat. In spite of the earliness of the hour, there was a good deal of bustle on this street of Indian silk and gold dealers. Tall Hindus with bright turbans opened their shops and placed sparkling silks and brocades on tables outside. The gold dealers wisely kept everything inside the shops; there were far too many thieves along the Prahurat. Life went on—even if the Wergelands' private world had collapsed.

Astrid's small office, from which she conducted highly profitable affairs of all sorts, was squeezed in between a gold shop and the headquarters of a dealer in foreign exchange. Directly across from it was an Indian restaurant where she often lunched. Indian food was the one thing that could still bring tears to her eyes. It was highly spiced, sweet, and burned as lingeringly as the yearning of a disdained woman.

While Astrid had been dining in this restaurant yesterday, a member of the Kempetai, disguised as a Siamese from the power company, was allegedly repairing electric wires and taking the opportunity to install a microphone in Astrid's office. The curtains had been closed to exclude the noonday sun, and the man had also found time to go through Astrid's desk. He had discovered only innocent business notes, which at once impressed him as suspicious. At any rate, he would have to find a different pretext when he wished to search offices from now on; the Allies had so thoroughly destroyed the power plants that there would evidently be little electricity for many months.

As Astrid entered the building a shrill Japanese voice sounded from her office. She could hear at once by the intonation that it was not Chinese, which she had spoken as a child in Shanghai.

They're coming for me, she thought with relief. There was nothing she wished more ardently. What else was there for her amid the ruins of her life? At this moment she suddenly felt the firm conviction that Vivica was dead. She ran to her own office, toward the voice, and pulled open the creaking door, which the boy would never oil. The boy, Yushui, was learning Japanese instead of cleaning the office. He was sitting in front of the radio, but as Astrid entered the room the Tokyo English-language broadcast began. He had already learned English from the white gods. Yushui was inspired with characteristic Chinese zeal for learning; *what* he learned was a matter of utter indifference to him.

The voice of Tokyo Radio was proclaiming: "The United States of America is a patchwork quilt; the patches are the many different peoples in the land. These patches lack the national pride and the spirit of death-defying loyalty which has inspired Nippon for thousands of years. If America does not finally abandon her feeble hope of victory, she will plunge into seething unrest and spiritual chaos."

Astrid turned off Admiral Sankichi Takahashi's speech and sat down stiffly at her desk with a feeling of hollowness only partly due to the false alarm. She pondered over the problem of why everything went awry in her life. She had loved passionately and not been requited; she had hated passionately and was not being punished. She no longer hated Pierre de Maury; wearily she asked herself how she could have committed such a crime. A girl did not bring the secret police down upon a man simply because he would not respond to her love. Astrid sighed in boundless, dull dolefulness. She had had no awareness of the depths of her jealousy. She would have readily given up her life if she could have undone the denunciation and what had followed. But evidently she lived under an unfavorable wind. It was too late. Her hatred had alienated her from God and men. She was vegetating in a wilderness equipped with radio and typewriter. She was locked within her being as in a prison cell. She could not and must not burden Aunt Helene with her terrible secret. To keep that secret was the one thing she could still do for her family, since no one seemed to want to arrest her. She longed for a tempest, and it did not descend.

She lit a cigarette because the gesture was a semblance of action. She had sent the boy to Saladeng to see if he could find out something about Vivica. She turned on the radio, and once again Nippon's hatred for the West washed over her. A strange sensation overcame her, threatening to drown out her clear intelligence. A sort of anti-life poured from that radio into her soul as she sat exposed to the torrent of words. She felt that fear of every minute passing uselessly which is one of the worst fears human beings can experience. That fear was the more dreadful in the Far East because the European who might want to do something was swallowed up in an ocean of indifference and lethargic resignation. No one helped, no one hurried, no one gave advice over so small a matter as the arrest by the Kempetai of a wrong person.

Whom could she approach for help? Suddenly she thought of Baron Matsubara. He was only an aesthete, certainly, but he could ask at the Kempetai for her. She had seen him recently at the Trocadero Hotel when she was having dinner there with a Danish customer. All the prominent Japanese, in and out of uniform, lived at the Trocadero. Baron Matsubara, to be sure, seemed to be still a

civilian. She would not mention Pierre—after all, she had not seen
him for three years—but would simply ask Matsubara to inquire
about Vivica's fate. She must still be living, she must! Perhaps she
had been taken to some other building when the air raid began. That
had been done a few weeks ago to a group of Hindus. Not one of
them had been killed. After all, the Kempetai needed its prisoners
for information. Corpses were the end-result only when there was
no more information to be got out of a prisoner—and even then, not
always. Sometimes the Kempetai set certain prisoners at liberty,
without giving any reasons. Then they secretly installed a microphone in the prisoner's home and listened to what he had to say
and what persons he inquired about. In this way it was easy to find
out things that obdurate prisoners had refused to betray.

Thinking of Baron Matsubara along these lines, Astrid suddenly
remembered the *haikku* the poetry-loving baron had recited in the
Grand Hotel at Siemréap, after the conversation on Cao Daiism. Astrid's memory functioned as efficiently as it had in the happier past.
She could see the tropical hotel lobby—the plants in expensive ce-
ramic pots, the unsteady tables and chairs, the self-effacing older
Japanese with the three protruding front teeth, and Baron Matsubara, Pierre's old friend from Shanghai and Tokyo. There had been
dust on the tabletop; three Japanese tourists in the corner of the
lobby had been staring at Astrid's Parisian hat with consuming curiosity; outside had lain the sleepy city which reeked of a glorious
past and rotting fish. A most Asian little city, charmingly neglected
and peaceable. The Grand Hotel stood like a Western provocation,
quite outside this rural and obstinately cheerful city with its young
girls in vivid sarongs, its Chinese gambling casino, its Cambodian
theater, and its mosquitoes.

The champagne cocktails had had a moldy taste. Baron Matsubara, with a smile of apology, had switched off the Tokyo Radio program. "Nasty politics, the foe of poetry, is it not?" And then he had
quoted a *haikku*:

> "Loudly, as though she sees not
> The bars of her cage,
> The nightingale sings."

How could Astrid have failed to grasp the melancholy meaning?
How could she have called this deep, subtle poetry a children's game

back in Shanghai in 1937? But at this moment, as she sat helplessly trying to think how she could save Vivica and Pierre, the power of memory brought to her an inspiration, a flash of insight wholly direct and irrational. She suddenly knew, without evidence, that Baron Matsubara had never been Pierre's friend. And she decided not to call on him at the Trocadero. Locking her office door, she began systematically searching the room. After a while she found the microphone and tucked it into her pocketbook. She would wrap it in orange peels later and throw it into the patient Menam River.

At that moment the telephone shrilled. Trembling, Astrid lifted the receiver; then she leaned back, disappointed, in her wicker chair. But habit was stronger than her confusion; unconsciously she assumed the attitude which had won her the nickname of "the duchess." Her austerely cut dress of palest lavender gave her a cool, irreproachable look. The nuance of lavender suggested that haughty resignation which Yvonne too had fallen back on after every shock. Because she had a headache, Astrid removed her glasses; there was nothing to see anyhow. This made a striking change. Her reserved, aristocratic face, now colorless and frozen with grief, contained a hidden beauty which the glasses more or less destroyed.

In a clear voice that betrayed none of her conflicts with herself, Astrid informed a French customer about the day's gold price. It had risen to dizzying heights. No, Monsieur would do better not to sell. He should hold on to his tin as well as his gold. . . . But she had bought his gold at a very favorable price only a few weeks ago, had she not? . . . Why no, it took no special talent for that. Chinese babies in the nursery were playing "gold" nowadays. . . . Yes, yes, strange times. . . . Quinine? Certainly, Astrid could obtain some for him—but only on the Chinese black market at an outrageous price. . . . *Pardon?* . . . *Naturellement* selling medicines at such prices was like selling one's own soul; Monsieur was quite right. . . . What was that? These damned Japanese troops had brought malaria to Saigon?

Astrid held her breath and asked Monsieur Duval whether he had been in Saigon recently. Was everything all right there? How was her great-uncle, Dr. Clermont. . . . No—no special reason; she was just asking out of habit. . . . What was that? . . . Someone from Saigon was with Monsieur Duval and wanted to speak with her? Who?

"Please hold the line, Mademoiselle. Monsieur de Maury is coming."

There was a crackle in the hastily mended telephone line, which had suffered from the bombing.

Astrid called desperately, "Pierre! I must speak to you!"

In the Kempetai's new office, Baron Matsubara in person replaced Monsieur Duval's handcuffs. *"Where is Monsieur de Maury?"* he demanded, hoarse with rage.

"I don't know. I have not seen him for two months. I swear I have not!"

For this, Monsieur Duval was treated to a rain of blows. He was taken back to the cellar. Major Matsubara smiled cunningly. He had given Mademoiselle Clermont-Wergeland a little shaking for this morning. The major had compared the paper in Astrid's office, and the characters of her typewriter, on which his assistant had typed a few lines while installing the microphone, with the denunciatory letter of three weeks before. His instinct alone had led him to consider the possibility that Mademoiselle Clermont, whose real name was Wergeland, might have denounced her former fiancé.

Not that he had needed Astrid's warning. As early as January, Yuriko had accumulated enough evidence to warrant de Maury's arrest. But they had hesitated because they wanted to know who the Chungking agent named Foxface was. For it was to some mysterious leader named Foxface that Pierre de Maury gave information from Bangkok and the rest of Thailand.

It was well for Mademoiselle Clermont-Wergeland to think that Monsieur de Maury was still at liberty. As a matter of fact, he was, for he had dropped out of sight in February. Ever since they had been hunting assiduously for him. But the Kempetai would surely find him.

Astrid laid down the receiver at last, got up, and looked around, wild-eyed, as though she did not see her office with its whitewashed walls and teakwood desk, but a landscape peopled by dragons. In the street below, a Chinese peddler was crying the praises of his fresh chicken soup. How strange that there still existed people who thought about chicken soup! Astrid had not breakfasted; she could not have swallowed a morsel. Vivica was different; she could eat whether or not she saw dragons. Astrid stepped away from the window, sat down at the desk again, and propped her head in her hands—blue veins and Yvonne's ruby ring against her pale blond hair. Something rolled to her feet. Mechanically she picked it up; it was the gold pencil she had taken from her handbag to write down the meeting place with Pierre. The slender, lovely pencil, a treasure of his, had been his first gift to her. She usually kept it in a particular compartment of her bag, together with one of her own treasures, Yvonne's rosary.

Astrid's eyes widened as she replaced the gold pencil in the zipper compartment. Her hands fumbled blindly for the ivory beads to which Grandmother Clermont had devoutly resorted in quiet hours. A dry sob shook her emaciated body. At eleven o'clock in the morning, in the middle of the business day, her hands clutched at the frail cord which binds the soul in the desert of life to heaven. "Holy Mary, Mother of God," Astrid Thérèse Wergeland cried, "pray for us sinners now and at the hour of our death."

There was a sharp knock at the door. Astrid jumped to her feet, hastily closed her bag, and opened the door. Her boy, Yushui, stood breathless on the threshold, his eyes glittering with sympathy and with the eternal Chinese pleasure in rumors and tale-bearing.

"They're all gone, Missie," he declaimed, tossing his smooth black hair like a colt. "Nobody knows where. Maybe jungle, maybe prison camp, maybe other town."

"Thank you, Yushui." Astrid looked for a tical to tip the fourteen-year-old office boy. But Yushui shook his head violently. "No pay till Yushui knows where Third Sister is," he said firmly. From his pocket he took a dusty, sticky cane of sugar-candy and handed it to Astrid. "For Missie Nai Hang"—Business Lady—he said, and shot out of the door. There was no grief in the world, young Yushui thought, whose bitterness could not be assuaged by a bright red and yellow sweet.

Ten days had passed. Every evening Miss Wergeland and Astrid sat in silence, by the light of a kerosene lamp, in the balcony room. They had been unable to find out anything about Vivica's fate. No one knew where the Kempetai had its headquarters at the moment. Sometimes Japanese officers went in and out of the Trocadero Hotel, which they used as they did the White Chrysanthemum in Shanghai. These hotels were unofficial headquarters and were also the stopping places of the few Europeans who were still traveling about or trying to do business in the occupied Far East.

Helene had never asked Astrid about her secret. She did not know what her eldest niece was to blame for or not to blame for. No sense discussing mistakes once they had been made, Helene thought. In truth she was afraid of Astrid's revelations. Knowledge might create a gulf that would only pain the two of them more. They must find out what had happened to Vivica; that alone was important at the moment. In spite of Astrid's pleas, Helene steadfastly refused to go to northern Siam to visit the Widow from Aalesund. She would not leave Astrid in Bangkok alone. In such a time of emergency, Helene maintained, what was left of the family must stick together.

Those evenings were a terrible nervous strain on both of them. Helene said little, and every word out of Astrid cost three pound notes. But Astrid often asked herself whether Helene knew how sick at heart she was, as she watched the erect, white-haired figure of her aunt sitting at table, her hands busy with a crochet hook. Aunt Helene was no longer rude; she treated Astrid with heartrending politeness. In the last ten days she had not once asked whether Astrid had bats in the belfry.

Miss Wergeland also never asked whether Astrid thought Vivica still alive; but at night she sat gazing, lips tightly compressed, at old photographs. By day she worked at her painting and, with the help of Yumei's husband, took care of the few bombed-out Chinese who had stolen back to big Missie's after the latest bombings and the descent of the Japanese secret police. Evenings she crocheted small jackets for Mailin's infant son and Hanna Chou's two-year-old boy. She also knitted woolen things for Hanna's boys; winters in Shanghai were harsh. Astrid read but continually removed the glasses from her tired, reddened eyes. It was not very gay at the home of the Wergelands on Sathorn Road.

One evening a ricksha rode into the garden. Both women sprang to their feet. Helene turned a shade paler, and round red spots

formed on Astrid's cheeks. Who could be visiting them at nine o'clock
at night? The Europeans, as well as the Chinese of their acquaintance, avoided the house marked by the Kempetai like the plague.
They could not be blamed; so many persons were being arrested on
the merest suspicion.

Yumei's husband, who was now cook boy and house guard in one,
brought Helene a visiting card. She saw a tall European and a Chinese boy slowly approach the house, while she stared in perplexity
at the big print, which she could read without her glasses:

ERNST AUGUST, BARON VON ZABELSDORF
GERMAN-ASIATIC BANK, SHANGHAI

Her first impulse was to refuse to see the visitor. She did not receive
the Germans, who were occupying Trondheim, where they had no
business being. She turned the card indecisively in her hand. Then
she noticed several lines of writing in English: *At the request of
Mrs. Hanna Chou, Shanghai. Bearing important news.*

"From Hanna," Helene exclaimed, her voice rising almost to its
old loudness. "Astrid, our Hanna is sending a message to us."

Astrid stood with clenched hands, unable to produce a sound. So
they still had some friends in the world! Her prayers had not gone
entirely unheard. They had been wild stammerings in deepest
spiritual distress, but apparently God was not concerned with good
style.

"Show him in," Miss Wergeland said quietly, placing her arm pro-
tectingly around her quivering niece. "Easy, easy," she whispered
to Astrid. "We want to know where we stand, don't we?"

Before Astrid could reply, the lanky, horse-faced stranger was
bowing to them and saying in his Oxford English, "Please forgive
this intrusion at such a late hour. Where can we talk without fear of
eavesdroppers, Miss Wergeland?"

Why, I know him! Astrid thought in astonishment. Her memory
began to function: We were once on a ship together—from Saigon
to Bangkok, that was it. But his right arm was not missing.

"This is Lifu, Little Tiger," Herr von Zabelsdorf said, using his left
arm to thrust a jovially grinning Chinese boy into the circle of light
cast by the lamp. "He's a rascal, and we call him 'Right Arm.'" He
repeated to Lifu in swift Chinese what he had just said. Lifu bowed

solemnly and extended both hands, offering Miss Wergeland a small tin box.

"From Missie Hanna Chou," he murmured respectfully and gave three bows for the Chou family; they had so much face in Shanghai that some reflection of their radiance fell upon Lifu. The box contained Silesian crumb cake, which Helene had liked so much at Mailin's wedding.

"Thank you, Lifu," she said, hoarse with emotion. "We had best talk in the orchid pavilion," she proposed. "If my paintings will not disturb you, Baron. To my niece Astrid's horror, I occasionally paint." She introduced Astrid.

"Haven't we met before?" Ernst von Zabelsdorf asked. Why, of course, that was *La Muette de Portici!* Good Lord, how wretched the girl looked! "Didn't we meet in 'thirty-seven on a French boat sailing from Saigon to Bangkok? Or am I mistaken?"

"I don't remember," Astrid said, avoiding the visitor's eyes.

Vivica was alive. At the moment she was in the military prison in Shanghai. Hanna Chou, who had heard of the Wergeland tragedy through the Chinese grapevine, had found out this much in a curious roundabout way. One of her husband's friends had told them that his taxi girl had been arrested and afterward released by the Kempetai. Her name was Kuei-Lan, and she worked—as Madame Chou Tso-ling had once done—in the Blue Lotus. Night after night Hanna had secretly visited the night-club until at last she caught Kuei-Lan there. The girl could not be prevailed upon to speak until Hanna had "gilded her palm," according to Chinese custom. At last she had given Hanna a note from Vivica. The note said only: *Help! Vivica.*

A lucky thing that Hanna had learned of this girl's existence, for of her own accord Kuei-Lan would never have delivered the message. It was clear now why Herr von Zabelsdorf had come to visit the Wergelands in Bangkok, wasn't it? Hanna could not possibly write, since letters to Europeans were all censored. She could not send her husband, because prominent Chinese were spied on by the Kempetai wherever they went. Hanna herself also had a Chinese passport now and did not want to endanger her three sons. But Zabelsdorf, as an old friend of the Chou family—his Annie and Hanna were as close as ever—well, in short, they had all decided that only Ernst August would be able to carry a message to Miss Wergeland and Astrid. Though the Axis was rocking like an old junk in a gale, Herr von Zabelsdorf was a German, and as such on good terms with the Japs, so to speak. He could travel wherever he pleased. So—and that was how matters stood.

Herr von Zabelsdorf fell silent because he could not endure the gratitude in Helene's and Astrid's eyes. Why, the two of them were practically *kaput*. No wonder! What in the world had that kid Vivica done? He stole a glance at Lifu, who squatted at his feet. He was thirsty, and, by God, how hungry he was! Another minute or two and he'd be out of breath.

But already Helene Wergeland was saying, "You must eat something now. Then we shall talk some more." And in an imperious voice that reminded Ernst August of his Potsdam uncle, the old general, she called out, "Wen, dinner for foreign Master!"

Ernst jumped up gratefully. Miss Wergeland was as good as gold. She knew that a man had to have something substantial in his stomach even when the world was coming to an end.

"The Wergeland ladies look as though they have been living on air for quite a while," Herr von Zabelsdorf told his wife after his return to Shanghai. "But in spite of that they didn't touch Wen's marvelous dinner."

"Then I suppose you gobbled it all up, Ernstel?" Anna asked. He had just arrived and had surprised his wife in the nursery with the children. Anna was bathing their two-year-old son, Karl Friedrich, and Luise, their five-year-old daughter, was happily helping. At the moment Luise was snooping around her father; she was searching for chocolate, and finally discovered it in his right coat pocket, where the empty sleeve hung.

Instead of his right arm Ernst had Little Tiger from Yangtzepoo, the brother of the Wu family's baby, whom Herr von Zabelsdorf had rescued from a burning house in 1937. Two months after his wedding the Wu family had appeared in their holiday dress at the Zabelsdorf home in the French Concession. Bowing and scraping, all their gold teeth grinning, they had pushed Little Tiger forward. "Master's right arm—Lifu," Father Wu had declared concisely, and refused to hear objections. Since then Lifu had been right arm, children's playmate, and Missie's helper. He sewed, darned, made charming little dresses for Luise, and served the master so tactfully and skillfully that Ernst August hardly missed his right arm any longer. Lifu was always on the spot when there was anything to lift or repair—how the rascal managed it, no one knew. (He had gained a great deal of face among the servants of the Wergeland household when he related how his master had lost his right arm. According to Lifu's tale, Master had not only rescued the baby from the burning tailor's shop in Yangtzepoo, but the entire family, one by one.)

At the moment, Lifu had vanished into the kitchen to tell the latest news about Master's trip to Bangkok. Another version of the same story was being told in the nursery.

"You'll laugh, Annie"—Herr von Zabelsdorf tweaked tenderly at Luise's long braids—"but it seemed to be turning out to be a nice pleasant evening. I'd tucked everything away. It would have been a pity to leave the Peking duck and all the rest, and the cook would have lost face, don't you think, Annie?"

"Of course. And what then? Did you explain Hanna's plan to them?"

"We drank coffee, and the cook brought in *papaofan*—a pudding of glazed rice, garnished with lotus kernels, 'dragon's eyes,' and other preserved fruits; Little Tiger wormed the recipe out of him, Annie. And I was just about to start discussing what we could do for little Vivica in Shanghai when a military car comes roaring up. Japanese flag, Rising Sun—and me right in the middle."

"For heaven's sake, Ernstel!" Anna had turned white.

"You can see I'm here," Herr von Zabelsdorf said dryly. "After all, they are our brothers of the Axis! And a man has a right to visit old friends, I should think. But I'll tell you a secret, Annie: I was really scared—knees like jelly. I gobbled up the rest of the rice pudding as fast as I could. Never know when the next meal is coming, I said to myself."

Anna caressed her husband's hair. She was very proud of him and therefore said, "You're a horrible glutton, Ernstel!"

"Then who should come walking in at the door without even knocking? Baron Matsubara! How do you like that, Annie? Astrid, the long drink of water—swank as a duchess, Annie, but not my cup of tea,

too hard around the edges—the long drink of water tells her Aunt
Helene to go to bed, *she'll* talk with the baron. He was in uniform—
and here I always took it for granted he's a civilian in cultural work,
how do you like that? Aunt Helene wouldn't stir, any more than old
Uncle Zabelsdorf, the general, who once threw three SS officers out of
the parlor with his own two hands. And our friend Baron Matsubara
—no more invitations to him, Annie, this was too much for me—he
says, sweet as sour syrup, would Miss Astrid Clermont-Wergeland
please come along to the Kempetai for a 'confrontation' with a
Frenchman?"

"How ghastly!"

"I went up to Matsubara and asked him what the idea was. And he
said—the fellow speaks French like a Parisian—that the long drink of
water—"

"Did he say 'long drink of water,' Ernstel?"

"No, that's my expression. He assured us that Miss Astrid would be
back home within the hour. And he was oh, so apologetic about the
lateness of the hour, but the Frenchman had just been—well, I suppose they had just picked him up, and now they wanted to get the
goods on him."

"How did Hanna's friend take it?"

"Like a major! That girl has guts, even if she is hard around the
edges. Walked right out with Matsubara, with her head in the air.
So help me, she looked as if she was glad they were coming for her
—and off she went like a duchess to the guillotine rather than a lamb
to the slaughter."

He wiped the drops of perspiration from his brow with his left
hand, as he always did when something affected him deeply and he
talked away brashly to drown out his emotion.

"Please, please go on, Ernstel."

"Well, I stayed with Miss Wergeland, although you know I was going to start straight back for Shanghai that night. I stuck it out there,
though she wanted to throw me out more than once—kept saying it
wasn't safe. I told her all about you and our kids and the Chous.
Time passed, and we were getting along pretty well with each
other."

"Hanna will be beside herself. After our thinking everything out so carefully! Monsignore Lavalette is due here in just two hours."

"Fine," Herr von Zabelsdorf said. "Miss Wergeland looked at the clock now and then, but that was all. I went on gabbing. Once she smiled—and I looked away. Well, then, Annie, we were just about getting ready to go to bed—Little Tiger had already taken possession of the best guest room and unpacked my shaving kit—it was getting pretty close to the witching hour, when back comes that military car. Now they're coming for me or the old lady, or both of us, I figured, and I took a long pull on Astrid's French cognac. It never does any harm to warm your bones when trouble's brewing, does it, Annie?"

"Of course not, Ernstel." Anna's eyes were filled with tears. She pressed Karl's head with the silvery-blond, downy hair against her breast.

"And just imagine, Annie—out of the car comes Astrid, free as a bird, nods graciously at the driver, and stalks into the living room, cool as a dill pickle. Then she waves a piece of paper under her aunt's nose—a permit to go to Shanghai. She might be able to clear up some matters in regard to the cases of de Maury and the Sun espionage ring, so she's told the Japanese. They're still looking for the big boss, you know. That girl has the courage of ten Japanese suicide pilots. So then we discussed everything quietly. Miss Wergeland was willing to pack her bags and go to visit a cousin who's married to a Dane in northern Siam."

"And Astrid?"

"Well—you see, now Astrid has her permit for Shanghai. She has friends here. Hanna insists she must stay with them."

"That wouldn't do at all. Tso-ling is having enough trouble as it is. The Japanese are trying to make him the scapegoat for Chinese acts of sabotage in the Shanghai spinning-mills. Hanna is always frightened that Tso-ling will not come home to dinner one of these days."

"No need to get excited, Annie. Astrid knows that; she's got a head on her shoulders. She wants to go to a hotel here in town, of course. And your Hanna wouldn't stand for that. The devil take you pigheaded Silesians."

"Oh, Ernst—" Anna von Zabelsdorf carefully placed Karl Friedrich in his bed. The baby lay quiet on his back, his keen Zabelsdorf eyes directed at the ceiling, exactly like his honorable papa, who was also in the habit of looking for a solution to the riddles of the universe on the ceiling of his room.

"What did you want to say, Annie?"

"We cannot allow Astrid Wergeland to go to a hotel, Ernst. Not in the state she's in. I met her at Hanna's three years ago, just after her engagement was broken off. She's lonely and unhappy and chews over everything inside her."

"I'm always in favor of a big bang-up when anything heartbreaking occurs. That's the only way to handle it. That's how we Berliners do it."

Anna smiled mildly and tenderly brushed her hand over his empty sleeve. She always had to hold back and not show Ernstel how fond she was of him, and how proud of him. In all the years she had never heard a word of complaint from him about his arm, only rough jokes. "Better one arm gone than two legs," was his sole comment when he returned from the hospital.

Then Anna thought of Astrid again, and her smile faded. For a moment she was back in Breslau. She and her mother waited, and her father did not come. He had been arrested by the Gestapo, and must now be in a concentration camp. No one dared to come to see them any longer—not out of indifference, but out of fear. The Gestapo had marked their house. Overnight they had become lepers, just as the Wergelands were at the moment. How long could the world go on this way, with every country shot through with fear?

"We cannot let Astrid go to a hotel," she repeated firmly. "Besides, the hotels are overcrowded with Japanese. Oh, Ernst, why didn't you use your head?"

"You may not think it possible, my dear girl," Herr von Zabelsdorf replied, "but that is exactly what I did, contrary to my habit though it is." He cleared his throat and went up to Karl's crib. "Miss Astrid, the long drink of water, is in the guest room," he declared, not looking at his wife. "Hanna is helping her unpack. Herbert, the pride of the Chou family, is there too, of course. He's also helping with the unpacking."

Anna looked at her husband with glowing eyes. Then she said mildly, "So, Herbert is here too. All that child cares about is Silesian crumb cake. I know the rascal."

When Monsignore Lavalette entered the Zabelsdorfs' living room he seemed to be stepping into a cozy family coffee hour. Even Astrid had unbent and was speaking Chinese with eight-year-old Herbert Chou and Luise, who at six spoke an amusing hodgepodge of German, French, and Chinese. Astrid loved children, although that was the last thing anyone would think of her. She had removed her glasses and looked young and terribly vulnerable. It had taken a great deal of persuasion on Hanna's part before Astrid would accept the hospitality of Hanna's best friends. Now Astrid was almost cheerful; she had children about her and knew that Aunt Helene was safely berthed with the Widow from Aalesund. Astrid and Helene did not tolerate each other very well; their relationship was one of racked nerves and lifelong loyalty.

The years had scarcely touched Monsignore Lavalette; he had only become a little more stooped and hoarse of voice. As he entered he threw a quick glance at Hanna Chou and nodded. Hanna breathed a sigh of relief. A few days ago she had called on him and made a proposal he had accepted only after long, hard reflection. Now he was here in this comfortable German living room, with its pictures of Breslau and Berlin, and a little taken aback at the sight of Astrid, with whom he had been out of touch for the past three years. Never had he imagined her quite so thin and worn. She was only twenty-six and already seemed exhausted by the business of living.

Monsignore Lavalette greeted the group in the room and then looked around. A Japanese who had come with him stood shyly in the doorway. A Japanese was the last guest Astrid had expected to see in this house and in this situation. Did Monsignore Lavalette know nothing about what had happened to them?

It developed that he had brought Dr. Yamato here because he did know. Shy Dr. Yamato, director of a small Japanese hospital in Shanghai, was their sole hope of being able to do something for Vivica. He was among the oldest members of the Catholic community in Shanghai and was a personal friend of Monsignore Lavalette. Naturally he knew all the Japanese in Shanghai, both the respectable water buffaloes and the Kempetai tigers.

There was no denying that Dr. Yamato looked quite unprepossessing at the moment, although at home, in a soft silk kimono, he commanded respect. For this visit to the foreigners he had donned his cutaway, which made his squat frame look quite absurd, for it shortened his legs grotesquely. He had neither Baron Matsubara's fine presence nor Colonel Saito's bulldog strength; he was only a ridiculous little person in a cutaway, with a saintly spirit.

Shyly he went up to Anna von Zabelsdorf and with low bows handed her a parcel wrapped in silk. It contained *habutai,* the same white taffeta-like silk which Baron Matsubara had wished to bring Borghild Lillesand at the Cathay Hotel in 1925. But although in 1945 Major Matsubara knew almost everything there was to know about the Wergeland family, he was not aware that his prisoner Vivica was the daughter of the violinist who had moved him to the depths of his soul by her playing in the consul's salon.

Anna thanked him so heartily for the precious gift that Dr. Yamato turned his wrinkled monkey face with its deep, melancholy eyes away in embarrassment. Unfortunately his glance fell upon a Japanese woodcut which Anna had hung out of politeness toward the guest. Dr. Yamato had never seen anything more frightful; it was an imitation of an imitation of Hokusai, who was, he knew, a great favorite with the foreigners. Dr. Yamato saw no nobility at all in this well-known artist; he could not be compared with Yeitoku or Kiyonaga. A rare Kiyonaga hung in the picture corner of his Shanghai home, right beneath the statue of the Blessed Virgin.

"Do you like the woodcut?" Anna asked with modest pride.

"Very lovely, very clever, Madame," Dr. Yamato replied with true Christian charity. He had banished from his voice every trace of the mild contempt he felt for the artistic taste of Europeans. "Very lovely, very clever," he repeated, for he had the annoying habit of repeating his remarks. After a polite pause he turned to more pleasant sights. Modestly he sat down beside Hanna Chou and smiled at Luise so kindly that the child trustfully started to climb on his lap, whereupon Dr. Yamato sprang to his feet with a smothered cry of horror. He certainly felt in harmony with every Christian soul in the universe, but little girls who forthrightly jumped on the laps of honored guests—this was too much!

Monsignore Lavalette noted the little crisis and drew Luise over to himself before she knew she was being spurned. He made up his mind to have a talk with his friend Yamato about the verse "Suffer the little children to come unto me."

Dr. Yamato was undoubtedly a true Christian. He led an exemplary married life, did not visit geisha houses or go to stag evenings at the White Chrysanthemum; but in spite of all requisite respect for his wife, he closed his ears when Madame Yamato expressed an opinion, which happened rarely indeed. Rome was not built in a day, and a Japanese Catholic of the first generation could not, with the best will in the world, summon up any interest in a wife's views. In his spare leisure hours he sat in a quiet corner of the house and painted a little, with the natural talent of his people for finding relaxation in artistic activity, or read with deep absorption *The Story of a Soul,* by the "Blessed Thérèse of the Child Jesus." The quiet French saint was Dr. Yamato's great love. She might have been a Japanese woman; she was the hooded *minomushi*-insect of heaven.

The kindly doctor who despised world conquest and violence, asked Astrid and Herr von Zabelsdorf about the details of Vivica's arrest. The melancholy in his eyes thickened like the fog on Seta Bridge as a plan formed in his mind—a highly Japanese, very subtle plan, with one per cent prospect of success and ninety-nine per cent risk for Dr. Yamato. But this appallingly tall and thin foreign woman prayed before the same altar as Dr. Yamato and his wife; therefore he must try to help her.

"In whose honored hands does the conduct of the case lie?" he asked after a long pause, while his plan took shape.

"As far as I know, Baron Matsubara's," Astrid replied, surveying Dr. Yamato with hunger for Vivica's rescue in her eyes. "He also calls himself Kimura, I have heard."

"Baron Matsubara comes from a great family in Japan," Dr. Yamato replied dolefully. "That is favorable," he added by way of consolation, because it could not have been more unfavorable. It *would* have to be the Tiger of the Kempetai! "Yes, it is favorable," he added politely and quite absently.

"Do you have a plan, my friend?" Monsignore Lavalette asked; he knew Dr. Yamato too well to misunderstand the true meaning of his affirmation.

Yes, Dr. Yamato had a plan. He outlined it, looking modestly at the floor while he spoke.

"You mean to do *that* for us?" Astrid asked, overwhelmed.

"Please consider it carefully, my friend," the conscientious Monsignore advised him. "After all, you know the Kempetai."

But little Dr. Yamato murmured with obstinate heroism that the situation was favorable and rose quickly, in a veritable terror of Astrid's thanks. He went to the door—an absurd, short-legged figure in striped trousers and a preposterous black cutaway, his heart filled with Christian charity. From a pocket of his cutaway he drew a small picture, wrapped in a flowered cloth, of the saintly *minomushi*-insect. With three low, solemn bows, he handed it to Astrid. "*La Sainte de Lisieux*," he murmured. "Tonight I shall lay my stupid request before her."

Then he went out, accompanied by the mistress of the house. He had often knelt in the cathedral beside Frau von Zabelsdorf at Mass. Now Anna squeezed his hand so hard that Dr. Yamato almost cried out—from pain and from shock at this breach of manners. "*Que le Bon Dieu vous bénisse*," Anna whispered.

But the homely little man scurried off, murmuring once more that the situation was favorable. Inside, Monsignore Lavalette and Astrid sat alone at the table over the rest of the crumb cake. Astrid sat with her blond head bowed. The frightful inner rigidity of the past weeks had yielded; something pure and cleansing rose up out of the mountains of guilt. "I don't deserve it," she said, sobbing. "I am so wicked, Monsignore!"

But Monsignore Lavalette thought differently. Now that Astrid had broken out of the prison of culpability, his fears for her had dropped away. For if there is anything more pleasing to Divine Love than the humility of the humble, thought Monsignore, it is the humility of the proud.

Inspired with hope, the old French cleric left this home in Shanghai where, in the critical year 1945, members of German, Japanese, French, Norwegian, and Chinese families had gathered around a coffee table and, contrary to all political rationality, had loved one another in the shadow of the cross.

"One thing is clear: America has lost the war. All that Nippon must do in the future is preserve the inconquerable Shinto spirit in the face of the enemy. The Western spirit has no chance against the gigantic power of the Orient. The West will be destroyed by its materialistic fears."

Major Matsubara turned off the Tokyo Radio broadcast with a frown, although he should have found it gratifying. For a moment he looked wildly around the Kempetai office in Shanghai, then addressed himself once more to the documents piled on his desk. It was ten o'clock; families in Shanghai were all at home and hoping for an uneventful night. Major Matsubara was reading the latest reports on the Sun espionage ring. The Chungking agent Foxface, who had been transmitting from Bangkok to Saigon information on the location of Japanese factories and the movements of Japanese troops, had not yet been found. It still appeared that this information had been carried by Vivica Wergeland—with or without her knowledge —to Pierre de Maury in Saigon. Unfortunately it had not been Monsieur de Maury whom the major had confronted with Astrid in Bangkok, but only Dr. Gaston Lafitte of the Saigon Hospital, who had been on his way to visit Astrid in Bangkok.

Now Mademoiselle Clermont was in Shanghai.

Major Matsubara had had his reasons for giving her a permit to go to Shanghai. It was a tried and true principle of the secret police not to lock up all the members of a family at the same time. On this score Vera Leskaya had correctly informed Miss Helene Wergeland only a few weeks before.

Major Matsubara looked as if he needed sleep. That was no wonder, for arrests were increasing as Nippon's sun declined. In a side pocket of his uniform was a telegram from his family in Tokyo. Matsubara Itoh, his elder brother, had died the *samurai's* death as commander of a corps of suicide pilots in the Pacific. Nippon had called these corps of heroes *kamikaze,* for that was the "divine wind" which had saved the Land of the Rising Sun from invasion by Genghis Khan in the thirteenth century. In those days the divine wind had actually scattered the attackers. Now heroic Elder Brother was dead, and Nippon's sun was still sinking. Akiro was too intelligent not to distinguish the true war news from the Shinto propaganda. Nevertheless, there were many times when he still believed in the miracle of the divine wind and of the Imperial Chrysanthemum.

The honorable death of his brother had given Akiro a fresh spur to activity. In this critical month when Germany was on her last legs and the people of Italy, the second Axis country, had hanged their leader Mussolini, when the Russians had taken Königsberg and liberated Vienna, and the United States had incredibly attacked Okinawa—in this month of disasters, the heroic death of his brother restored to the Tiger of the Kempetai that irrational pride which filled him with the *bushido* spirit, with the longing to die in battle for the Emperor. He envied Itoh; his own work suddenly seemed to him dishonorable, for all that it was so necessary. For already the secret police had to arrest Japanese who were thinking and disseminating "dangerous ideas." According to these traitors, there were better things to do than to die for the Tenno. Among such heretics was a certain lieutenant who had died ignobly of "heart attack" after questioning—just as ignobly as Mr. Sun of Bangkok, whose daughter Molly had invited yellow-haired Vivica to espionage cocktails. Mr. Sun had not been available again after his last interrogation, but he had never admitted knowing the agent Foxface. Foxface must be an extraordinarily cunning and cautious person, someone who could hear the bamboo growing—and in any case more cunning and more cautious than Mr. Sun, who had died so utterly without dignity, although he came from an honorable Shanghai family of such scholarship that they literally reeked of books. Molly Sun had been released; she had no more mentality than a noisy frog in a pond. Of course she would now be shadowed wherever she went.

Major Matsubara ordered his lieutenant to bring Prisoner Number 83 to him. When Vivica appeared, he did not look up; to try her nerves, he leafed through his documents for another ten minutes. This evening he would finish with the female. He would find out exactly how much she knew about Foxface. Vivica stood with lowered eyes; she had learned that she was not permitted to look at the mighty major-san. Abruptly, Major Matsubara clapped his hands. The agent Yuriko appeared.

"Kneel! Bow! Stand up! Kneel!" he ordered harshly.

Vivica complied, with a shadow of vexation upon her enchanting face. For several weeks she had been living in these realms of unreality and had become accustomed to them. But when everything was over here she intended to take a trip to Saigon and collect new faces. For the interrogation she was wearing the dress in which she had been arrested, a pink cotton dress, now much soiled and torn. Her hair fell in loose strands about her cheeks; she had not taken the trouble to comb it. But the untidiness, of which Astrid would never have been guilty, only brought Vivica's allure more brilliantly to the fore. She had a wild, somewhat devious charm; she was like a Nordic nymph without make-up. At the moment her greenish eyes were slightly veiled; her beautifully curved brow was faintly beaded with sweat from the exercise of bending and straightening up. Her full lips were parted like the lips of a child longing for kisses or sweets. Vivica thought the gymnastics the major in the elegant uniform insisted on both boring and silly. Not for a minute was she conscious of her deadly peril. Something within her had always longed for destruction—even in the midst of play and in the triumph of living. Now destruction had come dangerously close; she need only refuse to obey, and the abyss would open its arms to receive her.

Aunt Helene and Astrid had become for her shadowy figures, persons of another era, a different reality, belonging to another whim of existence. Vivica no longer knew precisely what Aunt Helene looked like; her memory had been slightly misted ever since the first two nights, when she had screamed so wildly behind the locked door —to the vast merriment of the guards. These foreign toads were really comical. What Japanese woman would have so much as sighed in a cell? In all situations a Japanese woman displayed stoic indifference to external difficulties, and irreproachable manners. If life became unbearable, she put an end to her miserable and unimportant existence, as had Lady Tatsue, the unwept-for wife of Major Matsubara. . . .

But after the first two nights Vivica seemed to have recovered; the guards no longer heard screams, only a faint singing and incomprehensible murmurings. Vivica had conceived for herself a small companion named Halvard, with whom she talked all the time, through this strange mist that hung over her mind.

Halvard was always with her; he was with her now, even while Major Matsubara shouted at her. The major's perfect French sounded like barking, and Vivica was tempted to laugh. She had not laughed for so long. After the interrogation she would laugh with Halvard at the major. . . .

"Back to the door. Bow!"

Vivica was so lost in thought that she did not hear the order. She had her mother's fateful talent for withdrawing from her environment by an act of the imagination. The Kempetai did not esteem such gifts. The elegant major sprang lithely to his feet, eyes half shut. He went up to Prisoner Number 83 and gave her a slap, a medium-hard box on the ear, as a gentle admonition to pay attention—not the kind that shattered a prisoner's honorable eardrum.

"Back to the door! Kneel down! Stand up! Bow!" he repeated in a significantly lower voice. This was the first time he had slapped this negligent nymph, and the act gave him pleasure. He waited for the easy tears of foreign toads, but they did not come. Vivica was so astonished that she forgot to cry. She had never in her life been struck, although a shadowy Aunt Helene had sometimes threatened to. What was she in the habit of doing, in that other existence, to escape punishments? Vivica thought hard. Ah yes, she had wooed and flattered the commanding figure on whom her well-being depended.

"I am very unhappy that I am so inattentive," Vivica whispered, raising her eyes to the commanding figure. The major looked directly into mysterious emerald depths; he saw the beads of perspiration on the childlike brow, the curved lips, the fluttering mind. If she smiled, she would look like a young vixen, he thought suddenly. *Vixen!* He started. The agent called himself Foxface—or was it "called *herself*"? The major threw a covert glance at Yuriko, who knelt whimpering in the corner, disguised as a Chinese working woman in black satin pantaloons and a torn blue jacket. The first act was about to begin.

Here was a new confrontation. This filthy Chinese woman, the major informed Prisoner Number 83, had at last confessed. At this the kneeling Yuriko produced a shrill howl, whereupon the major kicked her away so brutally that she uttered a cry of pain. "*Shikata ga nai,*" she whispered apologetically—the Japanese phrase for, "It was not possible." This was what Japanese said when the limits of endurance in an emotional crisis had been passed. With these words on their lips they also went to their deaths. "*Shikata ga nai*"—it cannot be helped. And indeed Yuriko was at the end of her endurance; of late Akiro-san, her lover, had ceased to pay attention to her. He needed only her skills nowadays. He had buried the girl Yuriko deep in the earth like a locust, and now Yuriko had uttered a cry from out of the grave of love. She could not help herself; a gnawing suspicion tormented her. Could Akiro-san have fallen in love with the foreign flour-face? He would never show it; he had too much *jicho*, too much self-respect, for that.

If the foreign woman had stolen Akiro-san's love, Yuriko would kill her, and in such a manner that no one would know. There were such convenient poisons which could be put into food. Yuriko occasionally brought the prisoners their food in order to encourage them to make confessions. She sometimes succeeded by gentle questioning and surprising little presents: a bowl of rice with chopped duck, cubed squash and sugared nuts for the Chinese, who had such a weakness for treats; a cheap little woodcut of Hiroshige's "Sudden Rain at Ohasi" for the Japanese prisoners, who were too noble or too hysterical to find consolation in good food. They quite literally could be satiated by art and nothing else. If Yuriko had to poison the foreign woman—*shikata ga nai!* But she hoped that Akiro-san would turn to her again. Therefore she kept insisting that Vivica was too stupid to have been a spy. Akiro-san's response to that was to slap Yuriko; he had seen through her. Lovestruck agents were a nuisance.

Following the established method, Major Matsubara gave the prisoner no time to reflect; he fired his questions at her at a furious tempo, so that she had no time to arrange her answers. He cleverly involved her in contradictions, and incidentally informed her that the filthy Chinese (Yuriko) had at last confessed that Vivica was the agent known as Foxface. The major had picked up the art of rapid-fire interrogation from the *Deuxième Bureau* in Paris while he was studying art in that city. The combined tiger-and-lamb method, however, was a specialty of the Kempetai. It was not, like interrogations in the West, conducted by two officials simultaneously, but by Major Matsubara alone; he displayed incredible virtuosity in shifting rapidly from the tiger attitude to the lamb attitude, throwing prisoners into paroxysms of anxiety by his abrupt kindness. They would think they were dreaming or had lost their minds; and the latter was really the worst that could happen to a prisoner of the Kempetai, for only reason restrained a prisoner from the abyss of an orgy of confession. Major-san was a spiritual inquisitor of the first rank; secretly he despised the crude methods of physical torture which he occasionally found it necessary to apply. It was not true—as was later asserted —that every Kempetai officer physically tortured prisoners. Most did so, but not Major Matsubara. He had tormented Mr. Sun so subtly with the weapons of the mind that a few burned fingertips could scarcely be said to count. The lamb method had in the end led to Mr. Sun's heart attack.

"Who is Foxface?" he asked sharply.

"That person there," Yuriko screeched, pointing at Vivica and weeping wildly.

"She is lying," Vivica said softly. The mist in her brain thickened.

"Then you tell me who Foxface is."

"I don't know."

Major Matsubara laughed so shrilly that Vivica felt a chill run down her spine. And the way this horrible Chinese woman howled! She thought that Yuriko was really Chinese—a dangerous error. Astrid would never have made such a mistake; she had known the Shanghai Chinese from childhood—their movements, their voices, their way of smiling, walking, squatting, and kneeling.

"So you don't know," Major Matsubara said after he had recovered from his fit of laughter and silenced Yuriko with a look. "So you mean to claim that this honest Chinese woman here, who lied at first only out of fear, is now lying the truth?"

"I don't understand you, Major."

"She's speaking the truth and she is lying. Is that it?"

Vivica did not answer. She wanted to sleep. Or to talk with Halvard. He was no longer in the room; he was probably afraid of this uniformed tiger with the glittering eyes.

"You will kindly answer."

"Yes, Major."

Major Matsubara then raised the subject of Saigon; how often had she crossed the border during the last few months? He had Yuriko taken out and remained alone with the prisoner.

"Why did you visit Monsieur de Maury in Saigon?"

"We would go dancing together."

"Do you like to dance?"

"When I am not tired."

"Would you like to dance now? With me?"

Vivica did not answer. She hated the tiger's jokes.

"Did de Maury call himself Foxface?"

"I don't know, Major-san."

"Are you lying the truth?"

"I don't know, Major-san."

"You don't know whether you're lying? Shall I have you taken to the madhouse? How often did you go dancing with Foxface?"

"Ten times, Major-san. I mean, with Monsieur de Maury."

"Ah, now you're telling the truth! Why didn't you say right off that Monsieur de Maury calls himself Foxface?"

Vivica stared, horrified, at the major. *What* had she said? "I didn't say that, Major-san," she said hoarsely.

"Then I am lying? Do you dare to assert that I am lying? Do you dare?" Major Matsubara bellowed, stepping up close to Vivica.

"No." Vivica held up both hands, like a child expecting a blow.

"So you don't obey? You do not want to say that I am lying?"

"You are lying, Major-san." Great beads of perspiration hung on Vivica's childlike forehead.

The major gave her a slap because she had said that he was lying. Then he went on, back and forth, up and down, tiger and lamb, lamb and tiger-san.

"Is your sister Astrid Foxface?"

"No, Major-san."

"So you know who Foxface is! Since you know so well who it is not! You know who it is! Am I lying? Are you lying? Who is lying the truth here, eh?"

"I can't go on, Major-san."

"You can't go on lying? Good, very good! You may sit down. Now let us talk like friends, Mademoiselle. So you want to confess. That is sensible. That is fine." Major Matsubara thrust a chair toward Vivica. She was so giddy that she clutched her head.

"Would you like to smoke, Mademoiselle?"

Without waiting for a reply, the major offered the prisoner a cigarette. He began to chat as though they were sitting in a salon in the Faubourg St. Germain. In between he shot out such questions as who was Foxface? and did Vivica think that all Chinese lied? What did she think of the Japanese? He informed her—likewise in a casual tone—that Pierre de Maury had been made to confess. He observed her as he said this; his X-ray eyes bored through that childlike brow. Of course this was a trial balloon; the Kempetai was desperately seeking that deceptive cultural representative. De Maury had connections with the anti-Japanese Cao Dai sect and had recently been more often in Saigon than in Hanoi. The most important group of oppositionists came from this sect, which could not be directly attacked without creating a scandal in occupied Indo-China. Scandal was the last thing Nippon desired at this juncture.

Since Vivica's arrest and Pierre's flight, the flow of information through the secret radio station in Saigon had ceased. Foxface was probably worried and crouching quietly in his den. The fury of the search for de Maury was to some extent a matter of private vengeance on the major's part. He had trusted this Frenchman for years and had been fooled and hoodwinked like a beginner. His *jicho* demanded a dramatic revenge. Once he caught Monsieur de Maury, he would start with burning cigarettes applied to the fingertips, and then expose him to the water cure: a drop of water on the traitor's head, another drop . . . another . . . , until the prisoner went three-fourths mad and confessed. Milder methods would not be appropriate for such. Painless but profound humiliations sufficed only for such innocents as Dr. Lafitte of Saigon. He had been dismissed after having knelt before the major and said thirty times, "*Kata-jikenai.*" That meant, "Thank you for the insult," for the words were ambiguous, conveying the ideas of insult and gratitude simultaneously.

The major stared into space. Vivica Wergeland had been close to Pierre de Maury. His revenge must strike her also. Her hair gleamed like the gold of the cigarette case that de Maury had sent him during their years of cultural cooperation.

Vivica had smoked greedily. The major offered her a second cigarette; these were opium cigarettes. Their purpose was to take away prisoners' fear of fear and thereby make them incautious. Major-san had found these cigarettes excellent aids with the Chinese. For every favor, the prisoners must then bow low and murmur the equivocal "*Kata-jikenai,*" which had the additional merit of signifying that the prisoner was abysmally *shamed* by kindnesses he had been the recipient of—such as blows, accusations, cigarettes, water cures, and sun treatments. Anyone who failed to express his polite gratitude was taught manners by the Kempetai. In prewar times old-fashioned shopkeepers had used this phrase to thank the honored customers for visiting their miserable shops, and the customers for their part had pronounced *"Kata-jikenai"* in that shrill whisper with which courtesies are exchanged in Japan. In this way the customers requested the honored bill, which was always "far too low" for the high excellence of the purchased object. In its benevolence the Kempetai taught manners to non-Japanese prisoners, undeserving though they might be.

Vivica rose for the bow and the ritual thanks, on which Major-san insisted. But the opium cigarette had stupefied her, since she had scarcely eaten all day. She had received burned rice and watery tea, but drunk only the tea and let the rice stand. She preferred talking to Halvard, her imaginary companion, to eating.

Therefore she staggered as she stood up. She wanted to make some excuse, but found herself unable to speak. A paralyzing weariness overcame her; it was a trancelike condition in which her body was dazed with sleepiness and her mind's keenness intensified. Suddenly she became aware of the weapon nature had given her, of her power to create dreams in others, though she had no real awareness of her innocently licentious grace, of that insouciance which rose out of the abysses of Eros. She did not need Borghild's violin in order to arouse a man's imagination. In the look from her slightly misted eyes, in her smile, which suggested delicate vexation and secret licentiousness, there was all the music in the world.

With insouciant grace, Vivica let herself fall directly into Major Matsubara's arms. Her actual physical weakness made this imitation fainting fit seem credible. She lay in his arms as if she belonged there; with closed eyes and bated breath, she let herself drop into the abyss into which the major had wanted to thrust her, and she became dangerous to him because of this very weakness.

Major Matsubara laid Vivica on the hard couch which was in the room precisely for such collapses on the part of prisoners. He fetched brandy and a cloth soaked in cold water. Now he would rouse Monsieur de Maury's mistress and extract confessions from her! Cries came from another room; his underlings were interrogating lesser insects. He was quite alone with this girl, who might be guilty and might be innocent, who might or might not know Foxface, might or might not know where Pierre de Maury was hiding.

He had power over her; she was the first European woman who had ever been completely at his mercy in a room at night. The situation pleased him, but his face remained hard and his eyes glittered dangerously as he bent over her, moistened her brow with water, and tried to force her to drink brandy. To do so, he had to touch the foreign toad who had hair that gleamed metallically. He thrust his arm under Vivica's head, wondered for a second at the silkiness of her hair, and set the mouth of the brandy flask to her lips.

Vivica swallowed a little; then she opened her eyes, but closed them again like a sleepy child, and, as in a dream, laid her head against Major Matsubara's chest, as if there she could find protection and peace. Akiro Matsubara was so aghast that he forgot to shake the woman off brutally. Vivica did not move. Major-san also did not move. This was the first time in his professional life that a political prisoner had laid her head tenderly upon his chest and looked up at him as if she were seeing something highly unusual— a man instead of a uniformed tiger.

With a single look of those veiled eyes, in which the melancholy dreaminess of the North mingled with the seductiveness of Aphrodite, Prisoner Number 83 reminded a major frozen to rigidity in the service of Nippon that he was a man of forty-one, a man who had known intimately only sterile Lady Tatsue and the lovesick spy Yuriko. Naturally he also knew Japanese flower girls, who mechanically and respectfully sold their bodies, and the magnificently garmented geishas who provided entertainment—they were carbonated lemonade with a champagne label. But romantic love was something Akiro knew only from the cinematic and novelistic lies of the West, and he had always smiled at the idea; for he had never experienced such love, or even a situation favorable to such love. The veiled and mysterious eyes of this golden-haired girl bespoke an element of wildness and chaos altogether alien to the historical amorous romances of Nippon. There lovers were well bred and killed themselves fittingly after several traditional recitations of poems and songs. There were no nymphs and Aphrodites when Japanese women loved "romantically" on the stage and in reality. It was not their part to lure a man into chaos, whether as exponents of wifely renunciation like Lady Tatsue, or as exponents of slavish amorousness like Yuriko.

Vivica looked up at Major-san in the tiger's den of the Kempetai, and the world of sadism and fading chrysanthemums vanished, became a habitation of impotent ghosts, a stupid Hall of Ten Thousand Duties. Matsubara Akiro, a degenerate *samurai*, a vicious questioner whose verbal snares sooner or later entrapped every prisoner, looked, speechless, into Vivica's eyes, instead of laughing his shrill secret policeman's laughter and giving her a few brisk slaps.

"I'm tired," Vivica whispered. She had opened her eyes wide but gave no indication of leaping to her feet and bowing. "I'm dying . . ." she murmured, and sure enough, a deathly pallor overspread her bewitching face.

Major Matsubara gave her more brandy, stooping so close to her that his eyes for a few seconds stared straight into her nymph's pupils. Vivica drank without unfastening her gaze from his. For the first time she saw the major from close up: the narrow, arrogant face that seemed to be cast out of golden bronze; the deep-set, ardent eyes; the fine nose; and the full, cruel, and yet ascetic lips. The major's eyes flashed her a look she would not soon forget—the mute sadness, the fatal, haughty boredom of the Japanese man-god who never expected anything but twittering obedience and obedient twittering on the love-mat. The major's look mingled dark, burning melancholia and haughty resignation. And there was something else in this gaze which plunged into her gleaming eyes for no more than the duration of a heartbeat—astonishment that a woman of the West was beautiful, as whitely radiant as the cherry blossoms of Kyoto, as delicate as the morning mist over Fuji, her long, straight legs and triumphant breasts as moving as the music of Beethoven-san and Mozart-san. . . . That look of his aroused fear in Vivica. Her playful mind and youthful sensuality shrank from the immeasurable loneliness that streamed from the major like a substance hostile to life. She was suddenly exposed helplessly to this confined savagery, to the flaring of the smothered craving to worship a thing that was, after all, nothing but sex, stupidity, and chaos; was helpless before the frenzied Japanese emotionality which is kindled by volcanoes and nourishes itself on the sinister gloom of love unto death.

Vivica cried out like a creature in extreme peril; she clapped her hands over her face in order to shut out the sight of this look which she had unsuspectingly provoked. And yet nothing was happening to her; Major-san was not slapping her, not undressing her, not even kissing her. He was only looking at her.

"I shall see to it that you are given something to eat," he declared at last. "One does not die so quickly. You are very hungry, that is all. You must eat tranquilly, Mademoiselle. Afterward we shall continue our talk."

Vivica was not fed in her cell. A lieutenant took her in a car with drawn curtains to the White Chrysanthemum, where her mother Borghild had dined with young Baron Matsubara twenty years before. While Vivica, clad in a guest kimono, ate reviving, sharply spiced soup and foods, Major-san entered the room reserved for the fine art of living and psychic torture. He settled gracefully beside Vivica and ordered saké. With just the faintest undertone of mockery, but with all the traditional politeness of an aristocratic Japanese, he asked her what she wished. He played the host, and was no longer in uniform, but dressed likewise in a kimono. Vivica did not dare to look up; she felt twelve years old now, so terrified was she of the major. Then the saké came—and with the hot rice wine, the traditional lyric mood.

> Loudly, as though she sees not
> The bars of her cage,
> The nightingale sings.

"Why do you not drink, Mademoiselle?" Major-san asked with dangerous gentleness, and gave her a faintly volcanic look. Vivica was slightly giddy and spilled a few drops of wine as she drank. She wanted to clean the green guest kimono with her handkerchief —Miss Wergeland had, after all, managed to teach her the rudiments of orderliness—but the major drew a silk kerchief from the neck of his kimono and dried first the precious lacquer table and then the worthless prisoner, at the same time smiling at Vivica as if there were a deep understanding between them and letting the wisp of silk flutter like a butterfly into a corner. He performed these motions with extraordinary speed and a terpsichorean grace, which was heightened by the kimono costume he wore.

"Did the Frenchman play so prettily with you, *ma petite*, that you do not want to betray him?" he asked paternally, and smilingly handed her the handleless cup of hot saké.

"What Frenchman?" Vivica asked, suddenly smiling hazily. The opium had transported her into a pleasant state poised between deathly fear and rapture. Everything was both vague and then again brilliantly distinct—the embroidered kimono the major wore, his subtle smile, the bit of white silk in the corner . . .

"What Frenchman?" Vivica asked again, smiling a little more warmly. She had never felt herself at once so powerful and so helpless, so slovenly and so beautiful. It must all be due to the major's looks.

"Aha—then you had several French friends, Mademoiselle?" the major asked, smiling radiantly. Flesh, he thought. Dust, stupidity, chaos, but so victoriously beautiful! His ascetically voluptuous mouth twisted as if in pain. He desired this beauty; his customary meditation availed him nothing against these sea-nymph eyes and gleaming golden locks. Rising from the mat, he drew the beautiful girl up to himself with a passionate, dancing movement, murmuring in the hasty, shrill whisper of Japanese ardor, *"Kino do'ku."* The words expressed gratitude; literally, they meant, "Oh, this poisonous feeling!" His French was forgotten; with growing excitement he politely thanked Prisoner Number 83 for the pleasure of beholding her beauty, and simultaneously felt a sickening shame because he had to express gratitude to so base a creature.

Matsubara Akiro, who had hitherto overcome erotic temptations with the aid of Zen discipline, stood before the foreign girl and repeated, *"Kino do'ku, kino do'ku."* He whispered more and more shrilly and hastily; the savagery of the Japanese lover was coming to the fore. He must enjoy this bundle of glory, sex, and stupidity at once, this very second, so that he would be able to toss it aside afterward. For after the embrace there came, in due order, first purifying regret at the loss of masculine force and discipline, then brutal indifference toward the giver of pleasure. The episode ended for the Japanese man by his returning home to the "pure room," where the last remnant of unstilled desire was cleared away by the chastening powers of the mind. But at the moment Akiro was totally prey to the feeling which made him kneel before Vivica and groan incessantly, *"Kino do'ku, kino do'ku."*

Vivica stared, horrified, uncomprehendingly at Major-san. What young creature from the distant West had ever seen a Japanese in the frenzy of love, had ever heard such tormented moans? What woman of the West could have witnessed, without being frightened to death, the tears which rose like smoke from Mount Asama out of Akiro's soul and gathered in his fiery black eyes?

"*Kino do'ku, kino do'ku . . .*" Thank you, thank you; oh, this poisonous feeling, this shame, this bliss. I love you, you bundle of beauty and stupidity, you goddess, you base, brainless, adorable creature; *ai . . . ai. . . .* Such was Japanese love from one in high position to a creature of the lower orders.

Major-san repeatedly struck his head against the mat. His smooth, glistening black hair hung over his forehead in wild strands; the perspiration poured down his neck. He was so frightening, so utterly strange, and in Vivica's eyes so grotesque, that for a moment she was literally numbed. But as the frenzied Japanese in his fluttering kimono uttered incomprehensible words and horrible sounds, Vivica, frightened to death and overwrought by imprisonment, opium, and saké, began to laugh. Her hysterical laughter was nothing but a tormented sobbing; out of grief, Vivica had laughed in a similar way at her father's funeral, and Miss Wergeland had had to hurry her into a car. But now she laughed out of fear, for she had unknowingly flirted with a volcano.

She did not want to laugh, of course. It was a reaction she could not control; but perhaps she also laughed in order not to lose her reason. In waves, the laughter rose up out of her agony; the tears rose into her overtired, morbidly glistening eyes. Suddenly her panting and gurgling passed over into coughing and then into painful hiccups. At last—hiccuping and laughing at once—she sank down upon the mat.

It was very bad. One might despise, lie to, betray, torture, and kill a Japanese, but in no circumstances did one dare to laugh at him. At a party given by Consul Wergeland in Shanghai some twenty years ago, a certain Mr. Bailey who was ignorant of the Japanese psyche had laughed at young Baron Matsubara. At the beginning of the war that American had, in consequence, forfeited first his business and then his life.

Still laughing, Vivica saw a tiger spring upon her. Major-san's honored pupils had shot to the farthest corners of his eyes, as in old pictures of *samurai;* the whites gleamed like an epileptic's. He seized the nineteen-year-old bundle of beauty, threw it to the floor, and began methodically beating it as he would beat a man. Then he brutally wakened Vivica from her merciful unconsciousness and dragged her by the hair around the lovely, chastely furnished room. By then the major was again wearing his uniform, which he had had concealed in a niche; his hair lay smooth and shining above an immobile face. When Vivica opened her eyes, he was standing, tall and terrible, above his victim, who lay groaning and broken on the mat, and as he kicked her repeatedly he said in his flawless French, "Death is too good for you, Mademoiselle. You will live and regret every minute of it!"

The major rang. Two officers entered, bowing low and grinning as they observed the battered girl on the floor.

"Back to the cell with her. No medical treatment! I believe I have found out during our little chat where de Maury is hiding!" Major Matsubara intended to telegraph at once to Colonel Saito, who was admiring sunsets in Laos. Pierre de Maury must be hiding in Angkor. That was not far from Laos. By the time he arrived in Shanghai for his main interrogation, Monsieur de Maury would resemble the ruins of Angkor. The thought amused the major. Smilingly he set the date for Vivica's next interrogation. The place was Room 12, the Kempetai's torture chamber. Let her wait and tremble for two weeks. How well he knew that the longnoses hated waiting. Fine, fine. Only Foxface would be missing from the party. And they would have him *sono uchi*, soon, gentlemen!

The major saluted his lieutenants ceremonially and withdrew to his private suite in the White Chrysanthemum. He would take Marionette Number 83 apart and see how many secrets and how much sawdust she still contained. And he would teach Monsieur de Maury the alphabet of fear.

In the dimly lit lobby of the White Chrysanthemum a Japanese woman stood watching as the two Kempetai men carried an unconscious Vivica into a police car. Yuriko nodded contentedly. In her stupidity she had fancied that Akiro-san was in love with the yellow-haired woman. As an old hand at secret police work she should have realized that Akiro-san was applying the lamb method before the tiger method this time. Let this be the fate of all girls who wanted to steal her Akiro-san over mulled rice wine.

Yuriko stole up to the floor on which her eternally beloved and unapproachable Akiro had his private rooms. She entered the ante-room with the *samurai* woodcuts. Soft as her footstep was—Yuriko's body was still light as a feather—Akiro-san had heard her and appeared in his night kimono. Yuriko shrank back at the sight of him.

He looked as if he were about to strangle her. The words died on her carefully rouged lips, which were dry as rice straw with longing for kisses. Sheer darkness glittered in Akiro-san's honorable eyes.

Yuriko bowed politely and backed to the door, avoiding Akiro-san's eyes. And with the hereditary fear of the Japanese woman in her disappointed soul, Yuriko murmured in polite despair, "*Kata-jikenai!*"—I thank you, I am insulted. I thank you for the insult.

In this deferential form Yuriko was attempting to express her thanks because Akiro-san had not strangled her on the spot. She drove to the hotel annex and cried herself to sleep. Woman's love was simple and simple-minded; it had not the convolutions of masculine love. Yuriko would have liked to cook for her man, sew kimonos, prepare the ceremonial tea, present him with sons, and receive his embraces with humble gratitude. Naturally she was also ready to die for Akiro-san, if opportunity offered. It would have been an unmerited honor to be permitted to serve her lover in that fashion. Such was the stupid, magnificent simplicity of Yuriko's love—the love of an average Japanese woman in a period of decline. . . .

Yuriko rose from her mat because she observed a piece of paper on the floor. It was a message from an Annamite spy in Saigon with whom she had slept on orders, in order to obtain information. She had intended to pass on this letter, which contained a curious mixture of formal vows of love and political news, to Major Matsubara earlier in the evening, but had forgotten to in her precipitate flight. It had fallen from the jacket pocket of her suit. On the streets of Shanghai, Yuriko always wore Western dress, in order not to be knocked about by Chinese. The suit was her misfortune; it emphasized all the disadvantages of her figure and none of her advantages. After having just come from Vivica, Akiro-san had felt something tantamount to physical pain at seeing his little countrywoman in a dress that was made for long, straight legs and a narrow waist.

Yuriko regretted having to turn Pierre de Maury over to the Kempetai. In this letter the Annamite agent informed her where the longnose was hiding out. Monsieur Longnose had always been amia-

ble and pleasant to Yuriko. He had given her pills from his personal
drug supply for her headaches. Yuriko made a little ceremonial bow,
privately paying tribute in her thoughts to Monsieur Longnose. But
she loved Akiro-san and Nippon. The enemy of Nippon must be ap-
prehended without delay.

Matsubara Akiro, who at this time was lord over the life and
death of several thousand foreigners in the Far East, stood motionless in his bedroom after Yuriko's retreat. It was midnight. He looked
at the *samurai* woodcuts which hung over his bed as an encouragement to right conduct. He could not make them out plainly—the savage warriors with frozen features, curved swords, and pupils high
in the corners of their eyes. Tears were swimming in his own eyes.
He dropped down on his sleeping mat and wept in despair that he
must destroy what he loved and adored. Many men mourn in secret
over a woman lost before they may embrace her. But the tears of
the fourth Baron Matsubara in war-torn Shanghai were especially
bitter because no one on all the seven continents possesses such a
talent for adoration and destruction as a Japanese.

Akiro had just dropped off to sleep when there was a knock at
his door. The two officers who had taken Vivica away brought him
an urgent message from the agent Yuriko.

Major Matsubara's eyes burned with a sinister fire as he skimmed
over the letter from the Annamite spy. At one o'clock in the morning
he held a conference with his officers. Colonel Saito was still in Laos;
the telegram to him had not yet been dispatched. He must go to
Saigon at once.

At five o'clock in the morning the major and the two officers also
flew to Saigon. In the meanwhile Akiro had signed a number of additional orders for arrests in Shanghai. Among the orders was one
for Mademoiselle Astrid Clermont-Wergeland—Shanghai address,
care of Baron von Zabelsdorf, French Concession.

The great hunt for Foxface was in full swing.

4: Flight to Laos

Three miles from Saigon lies the Chinese suburb of Cholon, a place full of factories, jolly Chinese beggars and financiers, restaurants, and nocturnal haunts for the pleasures of life. Among these were several cabarets and gambling clubs which Pierre de Maury had often visited in happier days. Mr. An T'ai, who owned the gambling club and restaurant known as the Blessed Duck, had for years been a faithful friend of the Saigon Frenchman. In his front rooms he served blessed ducks the like of which could be had nowhere else; in the rear he had an illegal gambling casino and a small dusty opium room with a wide, carved ebony couch, several inexpensive wall-paintings, and the girl Ku-ying, who served steamed crabs in the restaurant and who in the opium room warmed the little spheres of poppy over the blue flame for the customers. If anyone could banish a man's dreams, it was Ku-ying. She was deformed, had a hoarse, loud voice, and shuffled on reliable flat feet between restaurant and back room. Ku-ying, in spite of her lack of physical charms, was indispensable in the Blessed Duck. If a guest complained about the price of crabs, Ku-ying informed him that crabs naturally became more expensive when fish were scarce. If a Japanese officer came to dine and to sniff around, Ku-ying humbly informed him that they had just run out of blessed duck, the specialty of the house, and that they were inconsolable since they wanted to serve Nippon. If the Japanese asked after a particular Chinese, he had not been seen in the restaurant for months. Ku-ying had been bought at a tender age by Mr. An T'ai; he and the restaurant and its habitués were her entire world. She had never been in Saigon, although the brilliant city was only a few miles from Cholon. Like the birds, she had chosen her tree and remained there. Under this tree she served her master and his guests; she lived under it until the end of April 1945, and died in its shadow when Major Matsubara tore all the feathers out of the Blessed Duck because he had discovered in the opium room the secret radio transmitter used by Monsieur de Maury to send the Allies reports on Nippon's war materials and troop movements. They found everything all together: the cleverly camouflaged transmitter; the leftovers of roasted duck in the kitchen; Mr. An T'ai, who blubbered and trembled and maintained that he knew nothing about the whole affair; and the hunchbacked girl Ku-ying, who neither trembled nor blubbered but likewise knew nothing.

Major Matsubara therefore found everything—except for Foxface, perhaps alias Pierre de Maury. He could not find him for two reasons. In the first place, Monsieur de Maury was not the Chungking agent Foxface; he only transmitted Foxface's information from Bangkok to the Allies by means of the radio in the Blessed Duck. And then the Frenchman was not on the premises at the time of the raid.

"Where is he hiding?" Major-san asked and burned Mr. An T'ai's fingertips with his cigarette, while at the same time giving the simple-minded waitress an assortment of kicks. He stood in the main room of the restaurant, staring in a raging fury at the motto of the Blessed Duck, which hung above the counter: *No creditors on the threshold, no doctors in the house—that is happiness.*

His disappointment was as acute as his stomach cramps; he had made a hasty meal in Saigon of fish in *nuóc-mâm,* one of the national delicacies of Cochin China. The fermenting fish juices in combination with the hunt for Foxface had made him ill. But wretched as he felt, he realized that he would get nothing out of Mr. An T'ai and his misshapen waitress. He knew these Chinese scoundrels with their smiling lips, frozen faces, and humbly bowed necks; neither the silent waitress nor the babbling owner of the Blessed Duck would tell him where the French traitor was—provided that they knew. In any case, he had Mr. An T'ai shot because a secret radio had been operated in the interests of the Allies in his restaurant, with or without his complicity. The same treatment was meted out to the waitress Ku-ying so that she should not be able, afterward, to smile over Major-san's defeat. Ku-ying died without a sound, her overlarge gap-toothed mouth parted slightly in incredulous astonishment that she was going to die before her time. Ordinarily a lamp went out only when the oil was used up. To be sure, she had been riding a tiger all these last months, as she perfectly well knew. But

Pierre de Maury was the only person in Ku-ying's little world of hard work who had ever given her anything—a cheap silver armband, which Ku-ying had worn day and night. Under her work smock that band had glistened. She had often giggled to herself as she thought of her hidden adornment while she was being treated rudely by the Annamite guests, whom Chinese could not abide. It warmed her Chinese heart to conceal her fine possession from all eyes—just as the best restaurants were so often tucked away in shabby side streets. Since Ku-ying lived on work and rumors, she had learned that the Japanese were on the Frenchman's trail. Then she had acted instantly. And now she was dying, taking her secret to the grave with her. Pierre de Maury was in safety. Ku-ying had advised him where to hide. The purse of the poor may be empty, but their wisdom is a silver hoard.

Colonel Saito and Major Matsubara considered what the next step should be. The major would have to fly to Burma, where certain tribes were instigating an uprising against Nippon. Everything was conspiring against them. The major thought of Vivica's laughter and once again felt murderous rage and dark grief. The part the girl had played, knowingly or unknowingly, in transmitting information to Bangkok was unimportant at the moment. She was confined in the Kempetai prison in Shanghai and slowly going mad with fear. Or so the major assumed. He informed Colonel Saito of the arrest of the Wergeland sisters, both of whom had been closely connected with Pierre de Maury. "Yes, Colonel, Mademoiselle Clermont is the same person as Mademoiselle Wergeland."

"Is there a chance that *she* is Foxface?" Colonel Saito asked, placing his heavy peasant's finger against his nose. "I shall interrogate her personally in Shanghai," he decided. He was on the way to Shanghai, where a new anti-Japanese ring was already forming. This time massive sabotage of the Sino-Japanese spinning-mills was involved. Nippon was glorious but poor; she needed every shred of cloth from Greater East Asia.

Finally Matsubara came to his great inspiration, his inference as to the probable hiding place of the traitor de Maury. The thing was so simple that it had not at once dawned on his involuted mind. He told Colonel Saito, who stared at him open-mouthed.

"I shall go tomorrow morning, Major! You must be right. Six officers in civilian dress will accompany me. The time has come for direct measures and no consideration of the consequences!"

Major Matsubara gave a formal bow. This was his most glorious evening since the occupation of Southeast Asia. Shaken by the prospect of revenge, by unrequited passion and stomach cramps, he had envisioned combinations in a kind of clairvoyant trance, and read the solution of the riddle as if it were a motto above a restaurant counter. They might search all of Cholon and not find de Maury. But if Colonel Saito drove in a somewhat northerly direction from Saigon —not very far, the road was not bad, and the place made for an idyllic outing also—he would be sure to lay hands on that fraudulent cultural exchanger de Maury. Immediate death was too good for him. Like Vivica, Monsieur de Maury must live and regret every minute of it.

Colonel Saito awoke at half past four in the morning from a nightmare. As happened so frequently in this period of decline, which no Japanese would or could recognize as such, Joseph Kitsutaro Saito had returned in his dreams to his native town of Urakami, where his beloved wife, son, and daughter awaited the end of the glorious war. There, by the lovely Urakami River, in the vicinity of the city of Nagasaki, the Saito family worked and prayed along with thousands of good Japanese Catholics for a swift, victorious end of the war and the return of their honored dear ones. For they too rendered unto the Tenno what was the Tenno's. Had not the Son of God expressly commanded this?

In his dream Joseph Kitsutaro Saito had arranged to go with his wife and children to the river shore to picnic on tea, rice, and *manju* —bean cakes. His wife and daughter were wearing the unbecoming *mompé,* flapping cotton trousers tied together at the ankles. In peacetime only peasant women wore *mompé,* but during the war and because of the general shortage of cloth, even Madame Saito and her daughter wore the patriotic trousers which took far less material than a kimono. Colonel Saito could see it all very distinctly in this dream; this was the way his wife and daughter had received him on the occasion of his last furlough in 1943. In life as in dream, the colonel did not care what they wore; his faith had taught him to despise outward tinsel and look to a woman's heart. And awkward, ugly little Madame Saito had the heart of a saint; it was dedicated to Joseph Kitsutaro, to the children, to Our Lord Jesus Christ, and to all the poor and suffering in Urakami—in that order.

They were on the point of eating the bean cakes and the delicate tempura when a tremendous flash of lightning suddenly cast a frightful illumination over the whole region. An enormous wind—truly an "apocalyptic wind," Colonel Saito thought in his dream—rose and swept away the whole Saito family and the remains of the meal. Above the high green mountains appeared a fiery ball—or was it a tree?—which swelled, expanded horribly, filling the sky over Urakami. The brightness was so painful that Colonel Saito groaned in his dream, covered his eyes with his heavy hand, and kicked away his blanket. The fiery tree turned gray, then coal black. In his nightmare Joseph Kitsutaro saw that it was showering down greasy black beans. Suddenly everything looked greasy and black—the landscape and the remains of the food; even the *mugimeshi*, the rice boiled with wheat, of which he was especially fond, had become a greasy black mass. But then Joseph Kitsutaro saw that the black stuff was not the *mugimeshi;* it was the face and the body of his wife. His daughter and his son, who was so good a scholar and wanted to be a priest, must have run into the river—at any rate, Colonel Saito could not see them anywhere. In the dream he knelt by the black mass which had been his dear and honored wife, and cried her name, "Takeo! Takeo!"

He awoke with this hoarse cry on his lips. Tears were streaming down his rough-hewn face with its thick brows, laughing incisors, and beautiful, sad eyes, which were so unsuitable to the grimness of his trade. He knelt, his sturdy back bowed by fear and humility, and fervently prayed for the safety of his family. The crucifix which Colonel Saito always had hanging above his bed, wherever he might be pursuing the enemies of Nippon, cast a pallid gleam in Saigon's matutinal dusk. But the sight of the Crucified One poured peace and composure into the soul of this Japanese tormented by fearful dreams.

He rose from his knees, packed the crucifix into his shabby suitcase, and went to confession and early Mass in the French church. Everywhere the altar was the same; the light, the consolation, the same.

This done, Colonel Saito set about his daily work. He had to give the Tenno what was the Tenno's. Not for a moment did he question his grim duties. Only his head and his big peasant hands were occupied with these; his simple heart protested against the fatal breach between his spiritual and his worldly life. This dichotomy, which oppresses saints and sinners alike, has only one real solution: consistent rejection of a world which permits only Christian words but prevents Christian deeds. But duty, in whose faith every Japanese is reared from earliest childhood, held Colonel Saito fast in the net cast by the state.

Accompanied by six officers, he drove out to Tay-Ninh, the headquarters of the Cao Dai sect. As always throughout the past decade, Colonel Saito and his aides appeared as tourists. Supposedly they wished to visit the "pope" of the sect and be shown through the cathedral. They were all in civilian dress but had revolvers concealed in their white tropical suits. It would have been easier if Colonel Saito had been able to come as a Chinese visitor; but he looked so unmistakably Japanese that any such disguise would have seemed like a carnival joke. Therefore he came to Tay-Ninh in the role of a small businessman. Colonel Saito was in a particularly fierce mood for several reasons. In the first place, this sect of heretics was probably concealing a prominent French resistance fighter who during the past several years had been teaching the Annamites new underground methods and had been running a secret radio transmitter in Cholon, when he should have been dusting off fragments from the jungle in his museum in Hanoi! In the second place, Colonel Saito took it as a personal affront that the Cao Daiists had built their organization along the lines of the Roman Catholic Church. And it was altogether unforgivable in his eyes that these heretics had installed in their calendar of saints St. Bernard, John the Baptist, and the Maid of Orleans, alongside Victor Hugo, the Jade Emperor, and some Frenchman named de la Rochefoucauld.

His own three saints had no business in such company, thought Colonel Saito.

His first disappointment at Tay-Ninh was that the "pope" of the Cao Daiists was unable to receive Japanese tourists. In any case he never received any but high-ranking visitors, the colonel was informed; moreover, at the moment "His Holiness" was engaged in meditation which not even the highest of callers might interrupt. The still youthful Cao Dai pope had a bodyguard which protected him from all disturbances. The administrator, an Old Annamite in a Chinese mandarin coat, flashed his numerous gold teeth in a smile as he told Colonel Saito and the six tourists these things—speaking excellent Japanese, incidentally, for he was well versed in many languages, being accustomed to receiving guests from all over the world. He hated tourists and therefore smiled with supernal amiability.

Colonel Saito threw his companions a warning glance, for they showed signs of being ready to search and, if need be, occupy the administrator's palace. The fox would not be caught that way! Colonel Saito, who had also not been born yesterday, had observed a good many adherents of the sect hanging around the old mandarin's garden. Evidently the administrator also had a bodyguard. The sect's private army was not to be taken lightly. Colonel Saito bowed and murmured, "*Arigato*"—which means both "Thanks" and, in addition, "Oh, this difficulty . . ." The equivocal Japanese language left open the question of whether Colonel Saito was thanking the administrator for the information or for the fresh difficulties. It was a nuisance that the cunning old dog in the mandarin coat spoke such good Japanese, for the colonel was prevented from speaking with his officers except by signs.

The administrator invited them to sit down and had fruit juices and sweets served. He spoke with the three servants in rapid Annamite, which Colonel Saito unfortunately did not understand. It took the old fellow a little too long to give his orders, which troubled Colonel Saito. The conversation went on for fifteen minutes; every attempt on the part of the Japanese to leave the reception room and go to the cathedral was politely but unyieldingly prevented by the old man in the bright coat. He gave the Japanese guests circumstantial explanations of the nature of the sect in general and the benefits of vegetarian diet in particular; even the European guests, he said, were already beginning to recognize that "a man with few desires was a healthier man."

Colonel Saito inquired whether any Europeans were staying with the sect at the moment. Possibly, the administrator said, hesitating slightly; mass was beginning in fifteen minutes, and Frenchmen from

Saigon frequently came as guests to attend it. After mass he often served champagne to the friends of Marshal Pétain, he added benevolently; the French loved champagne almost as much as logic.

This was sheer mockery, Colonel Saito thought, and sprang brusquely to his feet. He announced his true identity, and likewise that he intended to search every nook and corner of the cathedral at once. And two of his tourists would have to search "His Holiness's" palace, naturally preserving all due respect; they would manage the business swiftly and without attracting attention.

The administrator had turned gray under his smiling mien. He requested the Japanese secret policeman not to cause any scandal, for that would surely result in a bloody uprising in Cochin China. If Colonel Saito insisted on entering the cathedral at this moment, he was welcome to attend the mass respectfully. Afterward the administrator would help him personally to search for Monsieur de Maury. He did recall a Frenchman by that name, he observed slyly, but he unfortunately did not recall just when had been the last time the man had come here to study the sect. He was an old man, he said, and his memory was not so good as it had been, and did not all the longnoses look alike?

Colonel Saito did not take the trouble to reply; he had looked carefully at Monsieur de Maury three years ago in the hotel lobby at Siemréap, and would certainly recognize him again. They accompanied the old mandarin to the cathedral.

"Where there are no quarrels, there are no uprisings, General," the administrator whispered. Colonel Saito did not condescend to answer. Since 1941 they had pulled out enough grass in Indo-China; now the roots were to be pulled. If grass is pulled out by the roots, says an old Japanese peasant proverb, nothing but dead earth remains. Without looking to the right or left, where hordes of penitents were streaming toward the cathedral to satisfy their Eastern hunger for the supernatural, Colonel Saito strode in mute rage into the resplendent and absurd church of the sect. The administrator's bodyguard followed at a respectful distance. The Cao Daiists' "mass" had begun.

Never in his life would Joseph Kitsutara Saito forget the abhorrence that overcame him at the portal and inside that cathedral. At first it was even stronger than his hunter's passion. He had placed his cheap steel spectacles on his broad peasant's nose, and looked silently around him. It was obvious to him that he could not make a fuss during the mass; if possible, he wanted to avoid one afterward as well. The sect's hall of worship was a ghastly mixture of a Chinese pagoda and an ugly baroque church—baroque in the stage of degeneracy, ornamented with hysterical exuberance. What most outraged this Japanese Christian, however, was a heretical grouping of statues: Jesus Christ was being borne on the shoulders of the Chinese sage Lao-tzu (Lao-tse), and in His turn bore Confucius and the Buddha on His shoulders. Colonel Saito inwardly crossed himself at this unspeakable sight; he asked heaven to forgive him for being compelled, in the exercise of his duties, to let his eyes linger upon such blasphemous horrors. To see his soldiers lying wounded and mutilated would not have shocked him so much as the statues above the portal of the cathedral of Tay-Ninh.

Inside, the sect's pope sat enthroned under the traditional golden parasol. He had interrupted his meditative siesta in order to conduct worship for his followers. He sat like an idol in a flowing garment, holding the marshal's staff which dispelled evil spirits. However, the staff must have possessed only limited powers, for although he distinctly waved it several times in Colonel Saito's direction, the Japanese tourist neither wavered nor retreated.

At first Colonel Saito saw only snakes writhing in hideous contortions among the groups of kneeling worshipers. Gradually he realized that the snakes were twined around tall pillars and constituted additional decoration in this overdecorated temple. The vaulted ceiling was covered with mystical signs. On the left, in a corner of the ceiling, Colonel Saito observed the sign of the cross, likewise entwined by snakes. For a moment he closed his sad, beautiful eyes in an excess of agony. In this serpentine inferno a decent Christian became aware of the whole wretchedness of the misguided passion for religion in the Far East. Colonel Saito had some respect for the Buddhists; they at least stuck to the teachings of their great founder, Buddha Gautama. But toward the Cao Dai sect and its carnival religion he felt nothing but repugnance—all the more so since they were daily gathering adherents in Indo-China. As he looked at the kneeling Annamites one after the other, vainly scanning the crowd for a European, his officers were combing the temple grounds and buildings in the manner of trained bloodhounds. Once Colonel Saito started, and the blood shot to his head; one of the kneeling men in white garment and symbol-studded hood had a lighter skin than the others. Looking more closely, he saw that the man was a Eurasian with Mongol features and Asian eyes combined with tall stature and a light skin. All the others were bronze-skinned Annamites. They gazed down at the floor; some of them wore glasses. There were many eye diseases in Cochin China.

The mass came to an end. The pope and his retinue had already returned to the papal residence when the hand grenade exploded in front of the portal. It would have torn Colonel Saito to pieces if he had not leaped back into the temple in a flash. Indescribable confusion followed. The colonel fired wildly; his officers fired; and the administrator's bodyguard, who were probably responsible for the incident, likewise fired wildly. A fantastic hunt began; during the next several hours every corner of the cathedral, the palaces of the sect and of the entire village was ransacked by Japanese soldiers. But they did not find Pierre de Maury, although he had been kneeling all the while almost at Colonel Saito's side. Asian vegetable juices had darkened his skin; the glasses had concealed his blue eyes; the flowing garment shrouded his figure; and the cape covered his close-cropped hair, which had in any case been dyed black.

Colonel Saito and his officers had looked for a European; he had knelt under their very noses and shown no sign of nervousness. For several years the sect had been cooperating with Pierre de Maury in his fight against the domination of Nippon in Southeast Asia. The little waitress's advice had been good; the Cao Dai sect's Rome had indeed been the best refuge for an arch-enemy of Nippon. The administrator had clothed the Frenchman in the Cao Dai garb, transformed his external appearance, and advised him to stay right under the noses of the police. Had Pierre de Maury hidden in the densely wooded slopes and caves of the nearby hills, Colonel Saito would have found him in the end. For weeks after the incident in Tay-Ninh the Japanese haunted these woods.

Colonel Saito, however, flew to Shanghai a few days after his defeat, in order to interrogate the women who had presumably aided Foxface. He could not imagine that he would fail to squeeze out of the stupid girls everything they knew. The evening before his departure he sat gloomily in Saigon, reading a letter from his old friend Dr. Yamato of Shanghai. Dr. Yamato wrote that he had learned of the fate of the Wergeland sisters from German friends, and he appealed to the colonel for help. He had tried four times to see a certain Major Kimura, who was holding Vivica Wergeland, but the major had refused to grant him an interview. (The last time the major had sent word to the little doctor that he was welcome to move into a cell immediately if he so craved the company of the Kempetai. Dr. Yamato did not mention this fact in his letter.) He wrote that he did not know whether his old friend Joseph Saito had any connection with the Kempetai, but it should surely be possible for so high-ranking an officer to discuss the case of Vivica Wergeland with Kimura, who was, after all, only a major. Recently, moreover, the prisoner's elder sister, Mademoiselle Clermont-Wergeland, had been taken away from the home of Dr. Yamato's honored German friends, and no one now knew where she was. He therefore begged his worthy and noble friend in the name of Christ to help the unfortunate young ladies—all the more so since Mademoiselle Clermont-Wergeland was a daughter of Holy Church. He awaited "with respectful impatience" the forthcoming arrival of his worthy friend Saito in Shanghai; Madame Yamato also wished to send her humble and most heartfelt greetings.

Colonel Saito read the letter with great care, repeatedly adjusting the position of his steel-rimmed glasses. Finally he tore the letter from his worthy Shanghai friend into a thousand pieces.

At the end of May an ambulance plane from Saigon landed in the peaceful city of Vientiane in French Laos. This city was a center of Buddhism and of silent resistance to Japan; it boasted numerous old pagodas and several good hospitals, which had been built by the French. Vientiane was situated in the quietest and most beautiful province of Laos, the "Kingdom of the Elephants and of the White Parasol." The French had always liked the wild Mekong River, the ancient heroic sagas, and the still more ancient Buddhist sanctuaries; the greater part of the aristocracy of Vientiane and Luangprabang, the former capital city, had studied in Paris, wore the cross of the Legion of Honor, and until the appearance of the Japanese in Southeast Asia had conducted the administration of the country on the

French pattern. But their pleasures, their taste for pleasant idling, their love of smiling intrigue, and the atmosphere of Buddhist legends were not imports.

For political refugees Laos was a paradise. The King of Elephants liked having them there for the sake of intrigue, and offered them the territory of the mountain peoples, which was impassable during the rainy season. Even a Japanese army of tigers and bloodhounds could do nothing in the jungles of the northern mountains. Moreover, cholera was in the air everywhere, for even in such French cities as Vientiane and Luangprabang the inhabitants had a deeply rooted dislike of injections and a deeply rooted partiality for witch doctors from the jungles, Chinese physicians, and an untroubled passing into nirvana.

It was high time for the two monks in dark red robes to return to their Laos village. The departure of the plane had been postponed repeatedly because Mr. Ninh, the Annamite pilot, had learned from the fortune-teller that the day planned for the trip was unfavorable. Mr. Ninh was a good pilot who took a childlike delight in the Western "metal birds." He was a model student of Air France, but he had his own ideas about favorable and unfavorable days for flying. How would a French army officer know the many things an Annamite pilot had to consider in order to bring his metal bird through unscathed by the spirits of the wind? In his cheerful fashion Mr. Ninh was a slave of the Annamite calendar. Lucky days were good for marrying, bringing offerings to the Buddha, praying for a large inheritance, or compounding medicines—though when thus engaged one must carefully avoid washing one's head. Unlucky days were good only for going hunting. To work on such days was inadvisable; to undertake an airplane trip, or even a ride in a buffalo cart, was sheer suicide. In the Annamite calendar there were so many unlucky days, also called "do-nothing days," that the two monks in the dark red robes of the north had already begun to doubt whether they would ever return to Laos. The rainy season was coming steadily closer. In the course of all the do-nothing days the month of May had nearly ended. Then, quite suddenly, Mr. Ninh had informed the passengers that they could start for Laos in three hours "or so." He had promised not to wash his head, and had made several other vows which had earned him a gentle smile and a sizable remuneration from the old gentleman in the mandarin coat, the administrator of the Cao Dai sect. The administrator had provided Pierre de Maury with traveling papers, for the hunted man could no more go out of doors with his own passport than with his own white skin. Pierre, eyes concealed behind sunglasses, had been the last to enter the plane. A few Chinese merchants and the pilot with the unwashed head made up the party. The ambulance plane bore the inscription: *Warning! Passengers possibly infected with cholera.* Consequently every Annamite official rejoiced when the metal bird flew on. Passports were waved away like annoying mosquitoes by the slender brown hands of the officials; paper, too, might carry cholera, and no official was going to risk his health for the sake of his duty.

In Vientiane the administrator of Tay-Ninh bade good-by to his French traveling companion. He intended to visit friends, he said, all his gold teeth flashing in his smile. When Pierre de Maury attempted to thank him, the wise and cunning protector of all foes of Japan waved his thin hand in a gesture of repudiation and observed that "big trees are a good refuge in the rain." At the gate of a remote *wat* he wished Monsieur de Maury a pleasant rainy season, and disappeared inside to exchange the dark Buddhist robe for a European suit of clothes. The administrator was flying back to Saigon as a Chinese merchant.

Pierre remained overnight in the *wat,* and set out the following morning by river boat for Luangprabang, accompanied by a Laotan monk. There his expedition into the unknown was to end for the present if the plan worked out in restless nights was successful. In Luangprabang, Pierre knew a highly influential man who had studied in Paris. He intended to appeal to him.

There was something altogether unreal about this river voyage to Luangprabang. Mornings, a cold fog veiled the mighty mountains of Laos. The searing midday sun made the eternally green woods glow like emeralds. The rowers sang; the unknown monk meditated, fasted, and smiled absently at his companion. Pierre lost track of the days. He knew only that this gliding progress through the most beautiful and tranquil lands in Southeast Asia was a temporary reprieve. Only at night did he dare remove the black sunglasses, for his blue eyes would have aroused the suspicions of the rowers.

They arrived in Luangprabang under the sheltering darkness of night and tramped on their dusty sandals toward the Xieng-Mouane monastery. Cheerful families squatted on their heels in the glow of small stoves, eating their evening rice and singing; for Laos is full of music from the old, glorious days. Above the roofs of huts and palaces rose innumerable temple towers; Luangprabang is a city of the Buddha. Rain hung heavy in air impregnated with incense. By the river knelt three old Chinese women, lighting sticks of incense set into the sand by the shore. Each old woman threw a clay pot covered with red silk-paper into the waters of the Mekong. In this way she petitioned the river-spirits for a suitable son-in-law. Pierre turned his eyes away; there was too much to see in this Franco-Oriental oasis of peace.

A great weariness overcame him; in this peaceful twilight hour, in a world bereft of terrors, he felt almost tempted to surrender to his pursuers. So many things struck him as meaningless now. Had he not sacrificed too much for France's vanishing glory? He had sacrificed his inner peace, his scholarly work in Hanoi and Pnompenh, his safety and—the safety of others. As he walked beside the taciturn Laotan monk into the garden of Xieng-Mouane Wat, he doubted whether the results had been worth the price. To Astrid and Vivica Wergeland he had brought only conflict and unrest. He did not know that both girls had been arrested. For months now he had been living in an empty world.

He spent the night as a guest of the monastery, sleeping on a straw mat under a mosquito netting, his dark red robe hung over the netting for additional protection. It was like sleeping under a curtain of coagulated blood. The cell was as empty as the political fugitive's world; it contained nothing but a few primitive boxes and crates, a picture of the home village of the monk who had given up his bed for the guest—and oppressive silence.

Pierre de Maury was grateful for his reprieve. However, he could not remain in Xieng-Mouane Wat; he brought danger and death with him wherever he appeared. If His Excellency Tran-Ky failed him, there would be no salvation for Pierre de Maury, who had come to remote tropical France as a young idealist to disseminate and eventually to receive cultural cross-stimuli. Now a warrant for his arrest was displayed all over Indo-China, Cambodia, and Laos. The Kempetai knew what it was doing. The price on his head was so high that a middling official, if he refrained from gambling, could live two years, and a rice farmer from three to five years on it. And in Laos people preferred singing and dancing to working.

His Excellency Tran-Ky had been born in Luangprabang, the son of an influential royal official. He had studied first at the College of Sisovath in Pnompenh, and then in the École Coloniale du Havre, had returned to Indo-China with a French diploma, thereafter to occupy one high administrative office after another. He was a chevalier of the French Legion of Honor and in Laos held the royal Order of the Million Elephants and the White Parasol. At the moment he was police commissioner of Luangprabang. In order to cleanse himself of the dust of office, Tran had gone to the monastery of Xieng-Mouane for meditation and prayer during the last rainy season. He was noted for three things: his friendship with the people of the École Française d'Extrême-Orient, of which Pierre de Maury had been one for many years; his three pipes of opium in the evening; and his wife, Kankharî, who represented something quite unique in Luangprabang. Madame Tran was a woman of the Miao, the almost legendary South Chinese mountain people who inhabited the remote highlands of Siam, French Laos, and Tonkin. The Miaos as a rule married only within the clan; consequently Madame Tran was noteworthy in the city not only for her austere beauty but also for her origins.

Whenever Pierre had stayed in Luangprabang he had always been a guest at His Excellency's house. He had had many a conversation in the Trans' villa, which seemed impregnated with the gentle fragrance of opium. The still youthful police chief had an unquenchable taste for the literature, the cuisine, and the conversation of the "great mother" in Europe. When Paris fell, Tran had increased his usual opium ration by a startling amount.

When this spruce gentleman with the high, curved forehead, sly but dreamy black eyes, somewhat too small nose, and vigorous, full lips saw his friend Pierre de Maury in Xieng-Mouane Wat in so precarious a situation, he mutely raised his eyebrows. They sat in the abbot's private room. Pierre had removed his glasses; his blue eyes, weakened by nervous strain and no longer accustomed to daylight, twinkled like will-o'-the-wisps in his brown-stained face.

"There is one way, my friend," His Excellency said after a long silence. "I shall speak with Madame Tran."

"But will it not be very dangerous for Madame and yourself?"

The Laotan official smiled radiantly, an indefinable expression of irony and pity in his eyes. "There are only two conditions without danger for man, *cher ami*," he said softly. "The one is in our mothers' wombs, the other in nirvana."

Serenely he turned the conversation to contemporary French letters and seemed to be in no hurry to rescue his friend. By the by he mentioned that Luangprabang was swarming with Japanese spies. Therefore it would be best if Pierre came to the Trans' after dark. A suitable disguise would be brought to the *wat* by a reliable servant. At dawn he would have to go on. He must not remain a day longer in Luangprabang, where everyone knew everyone else.

When Tran returned to his white villa by the shore of the Mekhong River, his private secretary came rushing forward. A Japanese had been waiting for His Excellency for half an hour. No one knew what he wanted. The secretary was trembling. They were all terribly frightened of all Japanese.

In the parlor, a stocky, bespectacled Japanese bowed to His Excellency. He was from the newspaper *Nichi Nichi*, he said, doing a report on Laos, Cochin China, and Cambodia. What did His Excellency think of the Japanese-Laotan Co-Prosperity Community? He fired his questions like pistol shots. Meanwhile his alert slanting eyes flew over the library of this Laotan aristocrat. It contained ancient chronicles of the country and the most up-to-date French literature. The Tourist Library—those volumes on Japanese miniatures, painting, theater, flowers, and so on, which had so delighted Pierre de Maury in Shanghai—was conspicuous by its absence. The stocky little journalist narrowed his eyes. He knew now what His Excellency Tran-Ky thought of Japanese-Laotan amity.

It was impossible for His Excellency to withhold his opinion on the Pan-Asiatic Co-Prosperity Sphere; the question hung in the air like a threat. He pointed out that great blessings usually showed their true face only after the passage of many years. One did not eat the rice sprouts but the ripened grain. Since no objection could be made to this remark, which was as objectionable as it possibly could be, the Japanese rice-eater took his leave with formal bows.

At the door he observed that certain circles among the Laotan officialdom were displaying "small affection" for Nippon. What did His Excellency Tran think to do about that?

"It is a question of influencing them," His Excellency replied quickly. The journalist from *Nichi Nichi* seemed content. Of course, influencing them! How correct, and how sly of His Excellency! He recommended to the smiling police commissioner of Luangprabang a Japanese method for influencing the populace: "A word to the wise, a blow of the lash for the stubborn steed."

The journalist laughed shrilly. His Excellency smiled gently. Truly they had had a delightful chat.

The journalist then asked the way to the famous Xieng-Mouane Wat. He wished to write a report on the monastery. People in Nippon were interested in the obscure sights of Greater East Asia.

"All is lost," Madame Tran said to her husband five minutes later. "We shall never get Monsieur out of there."

"Perhaps he really was only a reporter," the police commissioner replied. "Those journalists are buzzing about everywhere."

"What shall we do? Is there any chance to warn Monsieur de Maury now?"

"One does not point a burning candle at a concealed object. Monsieur Pierre is well disguised. If our visitor is a Kempetai agent, he will be looking for a white man."

"When is he supposed to come to us?"

"As soon as it is dark enough—four hours from now. The Abbot of Xieng-Mouane has been informed. He will do his best."

Madame Tran went out onto the veranda and stood looking silently down at the Mekhong River. A sailor in a sampan was singing. The palms and flowers of their big garden had a metallic sheen, for the sun was burning fiercely at this hour of the afternoon. A faint scent of opium hung in the air. It was beautiful and peaceful here, but Madame Tran felt suffocated. She longed for the mountains where she had spent her childhood. Where the asphalt roads of Luangprabang ended, the freedom of the mountains began.

"The Japanese bring nothing but disturbance and suffering," she said at last.

"*Bo pen nhang*"—"It is unimportant; nothing can be done about it"—Tran murmured. With this opium-eater's phrase, people in Laos expected the worst and hoped for the best.

They never found out whether the Japanese visitor had been a real journalist or one of the bloodhounds of the Kempetai. In any case, several Japanese in civilian dress were lingering in the vicinity of the monastery when Pierre de Maury, disguised as a Chinese peddler, holding a basket of fruit on a bamboo pole and wearing a pointed bamboo hat, left the *wat* by a back door. He padded slowly down to the marketplace. From there he intended to steal along the riverside to the Trans' home. In the marketplace the first person he met was a leprous beggar who extended a fingerless hand in the twilight. Pierre took this as a bad omen but immediately shook his head at his own superstition. He must be dead tired if he was beginning to believe in unlucky days as did Mr. Ninh, the pilot. As a matter of fact, he was dead tired; his head felt like a sphere of lead, and his legs were lumps of clay. He wished he could stretch out on the ground beside the leper and a boy who was selling bottle-green fruits. He did not feel any self-pity, but he pitied the world which he saw through his dark glasses. Perhaps he was already dead and only dreaming that he must go to the house of His Excellency Tran-Ky. His weariness wove floating veils about everything he looked at—the leper, the bottle-green fruit, the Asians in white tropical suits. Or were they pallbearers who had been waiting all along for him in Luangprabang? A girl with white blossoms in her hair, dressed in the long, narrow brocaded skirt of Laotan women, was humming a song—not meant for him. His mind floated in the air like a Chinese lantern, muted, weightless, playfully colorful. That must be the opium. He raised the bamboo pole from his weary shoulders and set down the baskets of pineapples. The peddlers were already packing up their wares. If he stayed here he would certainly attract attention—a Chinese on the point of going to sleep in the middle of the marketplace! But probably he was dead and it did not matter. Nothing mattered but this overwhelming tiredness. *Bo pen nhang!* He might well have told himself that three years ago, when he began working against Nippon. Someone kicked him and laughed. He jumped to his feet and picked up his baskets. How long had he been

nodding here? As he walked, he swayed like a sick man. Was the
leper walking beside him like a contagious shadow? Was he pointing
that horrible hand at him? Pierre suddenly felt overpowering terror
of the leper; he ran away in the direction of the river.

Too late. Hands reached for him. He was dragged into a curtained automobile. An Asian face bent over him. Someone pulled
the glasses from his betraying blue eyes.

A voice said, "This is he. Quick, start for Pak-Hou!"

He could have wept because it had all been in vain—his love for
France, his gamble with death, the many disguises: Cao Dai priest,
monk, Chinese peddler. But there was no sense in weeping where
tears were forbidden. Besides, he was dead anyway.

Later he realized that he was lying on a cot, eyes shut, and that
someone was watching him. Pierre de Maury had never been cow-
ardly, but now he could not summon up the resolution to open his
eyes. He did not feel capable of looking upon Major Matsubara. And
so he lay stiff with horror. He did not know where he was and how
long he had lain this way. In the car someone had pressed a cloth
dampened with narcotic to his face. Sham death was pleasant for
quarry whose running days were over.

Finally he opened his eyes after all. Madame Tran was bending
over him. Everything whirled—the room, the red tropical flowers on
the lacquered table, his own brain. It *was* Madame Tran. He had
already been at her summer residence in Pak-Hou for over a week.
She explained that she had picked him up in the marketplace because a detachment of Japanese soldiers had marched up to the villa
half an hour after the departure of the Japanese journalist. Someone
in the monastery must have been bribed by the Japanese and had
reported the visitor from Vientiane. Madame Tran was no soft, frivolous Laotan woman; she was a daughter of the mountains. The
Miaos are a South Chinese mountain folk who emigrated centuries
ago from Yunnan to the northern part of what later became French
Indo-China. Madame Tran had the Chinese gift for loyalty to friends,
and the nomad's thirst for liberty. She had followed her husband to
Luangprabang because that was where he lived and had his work,
and because a Chinese woman rests under the tree planted by her
husband's ancestors.

They spent a few more days at this lovely refuge where the Trans had built their bungalow. Two ancient hills swelled up out of the windings of a tributary of the Mekhong into a sky already pregnant with the great rains to come. A sandstone cliff opposite these hills shut off the rest of the world. Ten thousand years ago there had been only the wild Mekhong River, where now rice fields, huts, and a temple grotto with a white statue of the Buddha stood. A small bamboo bridge led from the cliffs and the rice fields off into the higher mountains. One evening Madame Tran and her French friend crossed this bridge into freedom. No one could follow them, for they traveled by jungle paths and crossed rivers the Japanese had never seen.

Madame Tran, the sandstone cliff, and the Miao mountain folk had been in Laos a good deal longer than Colonel Saito and Major Matsubara. And on the heights of Laos the laws of the hunt differ from those on the plain.

In the freedom of the mountains and the utter remoteness of a Miao village, Pierre de Maury found not only himself but something that His Excellency Tran-Ky had called "the dawn of virtue." The great political game of hide-and-seek had left him no time to reflect upon his emotions and his duties. Now he regretted that he had drawn Vivica into such dangerous paths and that he had left Astrid in a state of torment and nervous crisis.

He did not know what had befallen the two sisters, but he was aware that he had lost both. Naturally that was not his fault alone. Astrid had loved him too much, and Vivica too little. In the stillness, amid the mighty roar of the rain pelting down upon the mountains, Pierre confessed to himself with a somber melancholy that he knew far less about love than he had assumed. That was not a pleasant insight, especially for a Frenchman. But he only shrugged at the thought, for a political fugitive is first nothing but a fugitive, then a bundle of nerves, then a neuter for a while, and at last once more a man who kissed girls some centuries ago. Pierre thought of Astrid and Vivica as people think of the dead—without the sweet fever of desire, without the memory of fulfillment, without considering the possibility of seeing them again. Indeed, he thought very rarely of those remarkable sisters who had been so unlike in all things. But when he did think of them, he saw Astrid as she had been in Shang-hai—a girl in love who did not wear glasses. Undoubtedly he was to blame for the glasses, and he felt particularly sorry about that.

In one respect he was mistaken; he had *not* lost Astrid. He had inflicted so much suffering upon her that he was chained to her. The joys of love pass away and wither like the plum blossoms in rice wine. There is no denying that sorrows bind man and woman to-gether; they are the basis of that incomprehensible and continuous state known as love. On the great mountains of Laos, in one of the most ancient villages of Asia, Pierre de Maury loved lonely Astrid as she had always wanted to be loved.

The days passed and grew into months. Madame Tran and the two servants who had made the pilgrimage with them, along narrow jungle paths, in small boats, and finally on mules to the mountain village, had long since returned to the urban life of Luangprabang. Pierre was alone in a community of civilly smiling, strange figures in fantastic costume. The "black Miaos," whom he helped with the rice planting until the rainy season began in June, wore black jackets and trousers, scarlet sashes, and heavy silver jewelry. Even the small-boned but strong women wore black trousers, brilliant figured sashes, and silver chains which they wound like snakes around their slender brown necks. They wore their hair twisted into knots on top of their heads, like Burmese women or extravagant Hollywood beau-ties; but around the knot each again wove a silver snake, which she inherited from generations of mothers before her. Evenings they all ate with the foreigner around the fire in the hut and sang their tribal legends, which always dealt with their mythical wanderings.

Pierre learned their language and made notes on their customs; if the war ever ended, he would tell his fellow countrymen in Paris about these mountain people some day. In the solitude of the moun-tains the keenness of his mind slowly returned. He was not so senti-mental as to wish to live forever among these lovely primitives. Temperamentally he was no Gauguin; he was a city man. He did not think that the legends of the Miaos, their ample leisure, and their adventurous nomadic life during the dry season were a sufficient compensation for the filth amid which they lived with such serene dignity. But he was peaceful and contented as long as he remained with these nomads. They planted and sold the poppy of forgetfulness; the flavor of opium hung like the morning mist above the mountain village.

The rainy season was both salvation and trial. The paths of the village not only turned to mud; the pigs and chickens so churned up the ground that the stepping stones to the neighboring huts could be reached only by athletic leaps. Pierre sat with the chieftain, Lao Tou, and his clan, to whom Madame Tran was related, under the bamboo roof and stared into the fire on the hearth. The iron cookpot for the rice was cemented firmly into the fireplace; everything was different here from the way it was in the rest of Southeast Asia. The *ferang*—foreigner—was a highly honored guest. In the first place he had been brought by Madame Tran, who, though she had left the village as a girl, nevertheless belonged to the clan for all eternity; and in addition he had brought salt as a gift to his hosts. That was the most valuable article in this remote region. Salt was as essential to life and love as the poppy of forgetfulness, the songs, and the comfortable filth.

At the table in the chieftain's hut, Pierre took notes. A Miao girl with submissive Mongol eyes and artistic coiffure taught him by signs a number of words and phrases. Madame Tran had provided him with writing materials and medicines. Buried deep at the bottom of a rice sack Pierre had found a gift from her husband: the works of Montaigne, which His Excellency had once bought in Paris. All these years Tran had remembered his friend's fondness for Montaigne and now sent his own copies along to Pierre that "Monsieur may occasionally recuperate from nature." Tran-Ky, as has been mentioned, was enthusiastic about French cuisine, conversation, and literature. He was far less enthusiastic about French colonial policy, but this was a matter he had never discussed with Pierre.

Pierre had lost all sense of time. He had no idea where the war stood. The Miaos paid no attention to the life in the valleys; they had planted their maize and their opium and were looking forward to a good harvest. Later they would leave the exhausted soil and move to another mountain village. But in June 1945 they were still settled and gladly offered the Frenchman a hut and a woman. The girl who sat at his feet and sang legends to him was the chieftain's gift. She was young, pretty, and demanded nothing, which was all very pleasant for the guest. As proof of supreme devotion she brought him a wooden tub for his bath, and with much giggling heated the water. Neither she nor any of the other Miaos would have engaged in so perilous an activity as bathing. They oiled themselves and afterward smelled like fragrant plants. But when Pierre wanted to photograph the girl—an itinerant peddler had left a camera there during the previous dry season—she fled in wild terror. Only an ignorant foreigner would fail to realize that a camera steals a person's soul and invariably produces cholera and an early death. For this reason the girl brought many offerings to the camera, which had been placed on a wooden altar—figurines of animals, the tip of a woman's sash, and once a phallic symbol. In order to placate it fully, she strewed ashes from the fireplace in front of the door. Pierre never found out why no one threw the camera into the jungle; but evidently not even the *oa ning*, the witch doctor of the village, would have dared to incur the enmity of the demon which stole souls.

One night Pierre awoke with a piercing scream. Either the dark red rice cake had proved indigestible, or in his sleep he had wandered back into the valleys. In the valleys were Major Matsubara and Foxface. The young Miao girl rubbed his body with steaming cloths and massaged him. No wonder he cried in his sleep; that day he had held the camera in his hand, and the demon was undoubtedly angry at such disrespect. Tomorrow she would ask the witch doctor to make a sacrifice before the altar. The booming of their gongs would intimidate the camera demon.

Pierre de Maury listened in silence to her chatter. He was looking back to the world of danger and chaos he had left behind. Now he remembered that in his dream he had seen a familiar figure on her deathbed—Astrid! That was why he had cried out. He saw it now as unforgivable that he had condemned the only girl who had loved him passionately and devotedly, though sometimes vexatiously, to a slow death. This was why the mountainous world of these quiet, kindly people was no Eden to him but a purgatory. No sacrifices on strange altars could amend that.

His thoughts, moving through the valleys of the world he knew, paused in Madame Ninette's beauty parlor in Bangkok. There he had met Foxface. There Foxface had proposed to him that he have young Vivica bring information for the Allies to Saigon. No one would suspect this pretty, pleasure-loving girl of being the transmitter of vital messages. Pierre had accepted the suggestion. Foxface or his aides had hidden the information in Vivica's baggage each time. Pierre and Vivica had danced, flirted, and talked in Saigon. Of course he had briefly succumbed to Vivica's strange charm; but her Nordic complexity and conversance with chaos were alien to his clear Latin spirit. Certainly he had never loved her. It had been a charming little affair—even though it hovered on the brink of chaos, which every Frenchman instinctively avoided. Astrid with her clear intelligence, her poise, and her little hats, which for all their fantasticality were always placed precisely in the right spot on her head, was far more his dish. Vivica's manner and dress had always outraged him, despite the fact that that innocently cunning Aphrodite might sweep him off his feet for hours at a time. Through it all he had not felt bound to her, and had not hesitated to use Vivica for political ends. He understood her instinctively, as many Frenchmen did understand women. If he had fulfilled all her wishes—and Vivica had flashed him fairly frank invitations with those veiled eyes of hers— she would swiftly have tired of him, and Pierre de Maury would then no longer have received information from Foxface.

So he had used this girl—who was always in greater danger than other girls, because of her affinity to chaos—as a courier without her knowledge. The journeys had pleased Vivica no end; she had loved collecting faces and going dancing with "Uncle Pierre," but she never suspected that she was dancing on the verge of an abyss.

Now, here in this remote mountain fastness, Pierre saw everything differently. He realized that he had learned and applied the methods of the Kempetai. And he wished, helplessly and passionately, that he had never entered Madame Ninette's beauty salon. He saw it before his eyes as he lay on the bamboo couch and watched the dawn of virtue reddening in the east: Madame Ninette, forever gossiping while her sly, merry little eyes darted about in their pouches of fat; Vera Leskaya, gray, cunning, uncannily intelligent, and embittered; Vivica and the other receptionists; the clients, the womenfolk of all the nations whom the Japanese had not interned: Swedes, Danes, Swiss, and Pétain French of the Bangkok Legation. One figure in this group had been Foxface. Pierre shivered with horror. . . .

In the dream he had seen Astrid on her deathbed. And what had happened to Vivica? Astrid had once told him how Vivica's mother had ended her life. He lay on the wicker couch, and his thoughts went around in circles. It was harder to live than to die. What had happened to Astrid? What to Vivica? He could not know, here behind the great wall created by the rains.

Only Foxface knew everything and therefore could neither die nor be killed. In the Chinese view, Foxface was everywhere and nowhere and fed on the misfortunes of others. Pierre should have known that. Vivica could not possibly have known. Yet she "collected faces," as she used to say, and therefore she had also met Foxface.

Lying there, brooding on Vivica's possible fate, Pierre de Maury realized that his flight to Laos had in some respects been in vain. You could escape the Kempetai but not yourself.

5: Lessons for Backward Spies

"And then my uncle the grand duke said, 'Katharina,' he said, 'you had better take a double brrrandy!'"

The client looked dreamily up at Madame Ninette, who was rubbing her prominent Slavic cheekbones with rouge.

"Smile," Madame Ninette recommended. "Otherwise the rouge looks unnatural."

"No more unnatural than a smile on my face, Nina Ivanovna!"

"Rrridiculous," Madame Ninette said. "Anybody can smile. Are you a bar owner or an undertaker, Katharina Krylovna?"

She spoke, as always, very loudly, squinting her sharp, bright blue little eyes. "Have you heard anything?" she whispered suddenly. The client was about to reply when Madame Ninette, with a lightning movement, dropped a steaming towel over the optimistic make-up. "Wait, we'll trry it again. You look like a harrlequin."

Vera Leskaya had come in so inaudibly that Madame Ninette had perceived it only with her sixth sense for sneaks. "What should Madame Krylovna have heard?" she asked. She was wearing the dress she had worn when she informed Helene Wergeland of Vivica's arrest. Her dull, avaricious eyes seemed to be boring through the white towel that effectively shut the client's mouth.

"Where would Katharina hear anything?" Madame Ninette countered. "Her bar is a mass grave. When she says, 'Cheerio,' the guests are tempted to jump into the Menam River. Bad drrinks, bad singing, no fun, my dear Krylovna!"

"The Prahurat district has been bombed by the Allies," Katharina Krylovna announced from under the towel.

"Prahurat," Vera Leskaya said meditatively. "Isn't that where Mademoiselle Astrid Wergeland had her office?"

"What do I care about that dame and her horrible aunt?" Madame Ninette asked. "A customer, Leskaya."

A lively dispute began at the cashier's desk between Vera Leskaya and a German woman, while Madame Ninette turned back to her White Russian client. "What's that you say, Krylovna? In Shanghai? Terrible, terrible! But it serves the horrid old aunt right. She did not even offer Nina Ivanovna a drop of peppermint liqueur when Vivica, the dove, was arrested. Crazy, you say? That is verry bad, Krylovna. Crazy people talk loosely. But perhaps Vivica is crrazy like a fox; think of our *jurodivje,* our holy fools, back home in Rrrussia. Crazy like a fox, Krylovna!" At that moment Vera Leskaya returned.

"Nonsense, my dear Krylovna," Madame Ninette went on without a pause, "forty-eight is a woman's finest age. When Ninotchka was forty-eight she received three proposals a week. Not that she would accept any. She's always preferred brrrandy to any man." Madame Ninette was speaking of herself; she often included herself in her stories, speaking as if she were a perfect stranger.

"What is it, Leskaya?" she asked in the harsh, imperious tone she used toward her oldest friend and employee.

"The German client objects to the new prices for facial massage, Madame."

Madame Ninette exploded with laughter. She laughed until her face was beet-red. Every wrinkle in her complacent full moon of a face quivered with malicious pleasure.

"Did you hear that, Krylovna? Too dear! So Madame Ninette, a benefactor of aging females, is too dear! And she dares to say that two months after the Germans have lost their war! Tell Madame

Schulze that customers who lose a war have to pay the price, and
that one more or less in our beauty salon doesn't matter to us."

"I'll tell her, Madame."

"But hurry up about it. Don't stand around like Ivan the Terrible
after the bloodbath at Novgorod."

"Why are you sending me out of the room, Nina Ivanovna?"
Vera's gray face had reddened slightly.

"Now, what do you say to that, Krylovna? Would I have any reason for sending Leskaya out of the room? Not on your life, my dove.
How is the price of gold today? Did you buy any?"

Vera Leskaya had, at advantageous prices. Everyone was buying
gold. The value of paper money was declining along with the sun
of Nippon. General MacArthur had liberated the Philippines the day
before yesterday. The rainy month of July was creeping along; the
Kempetai was making arrests and shooting suspects; and the Far
Eastern revolving stage was making the jerkiest turns in the history
of the world. Only in Madame Ninette's salon nothing seemed to
have changed except the prices. Women wanted to look as beautiful
and as young as they could, whether or not the world was coming to
an end this month. Moreover, Madame Ninette's was also a great
center for buying and selling. Women brought jewelry and medicines, silver cuspidors, furniture—all the goods they had hoarded
during the war years. Leskaya bought and sold everything. *Senglee*
(selling things), as the Chinese called it, was the ruling passion during these last weeks before the downfall of Japan. The Chinese
called Vera "Miss Senglee." Soon passports and loyalties would be
for sale.

A Japanese woman entered the salon and was greeted by Madame
Ninette with all the excessive courtesy the Japanese had enjoyed
during their victorious days. Madame had always been for Nippon;
she did not mind if everyone saw that. Vera Leskaya watched the
scene in silence. She was frightfully nervous and did not dare let
her nervousness show. The sun of Nippon was sinking, and she along
with it.

A Chinese entered the beauty parlor with bowed head and looked
around for Miss Senglee. In a silk cloth he bore a stone which he
hoped would help him escape to the jungles. He had staked his future on Nippon and lost.

"Jade," he whispered in his consumptive voice. "Please buy, Miss Senglee!"

Vera took from her bag the magnifying glass with which she had examined Vivica's green letter-paper several months before.

"To Confucius jade was the symbol of virtue," the Chinese whispered.

"The stone is cloudy," Miss Senglee decided; the learned allusion had made no impression upon her. "Twenty ticals."

This was sheer mockery. Mr. Li-feng bowed politely and replaced the splendid stone in the silk cloth.

"How much?" Vera Leskaya asked curtly. A thousand ticals would not have been too much for this jade. Before the war foreigners had paid fantastic prices for jade, and they would pay them again after the war. "Three hundred ticals," she offered.

Mr. Li-feng looked pityingly at her. "I prefer to keep my miserable stone, lady," he murmured in good English. "I respect my jade, lady."

He bowed again and left the foreign devils' beauty parlor, beaten and yet relieved. He was a miserable creature, a paid spy in the service of Nippon; but he had inherited one virtue from his honorable ancestors: he respected his jade—so much so that he determined to take it with him to the hereafter. This evening he would depart from the world as one leaves a withered rice field. He would carry his jade with him between his cold lips, so that he need not appear before his ancestors stripped of all virtue. His son would arrange everything. Mr. Li-feng stepped out upon the hot, humid street, feeling tranquil and almost cheerful. "A good impulse atones for a thousand bad deeds," he had learned in his youth. He had been in Nippon's cage for a long while. Now he had found himself again.

Vera Leskaya had turned deathly pale. She guessed that the Chinese would not return, and that reminded her that years ago she had bet on the wrong horse. She must speak with Madame Ninette tonight, for the old Russian was her last hope. For weeks she had not heard from Baron Matsubara, had received no coded messages, no orders, no money. Ever since the circle around Foxface had been destroyed by the Kempetai, Vera had not heard from her employer. That was even more alarming than thoughts of her future. What did spies do when they had bet on the wrong horse? Vera closed her eyes for a moment. She knew only too well.

Finally the last client had left. Madame Krylovna, too, reluctantly prepared to go, which involved another half-hour of talk. Madame Ninette completed various biographies of unknown persons which she had begun, Madame Krylovna inquiring about details.

"Shall I write it down again, Madame?" Vera Leskaya asked, stressing the word "again."

"Devil take the person who invented high heels," Madame Krylovna replied to this hint to pay in cash. She nodded condescendingly to Vera and embraced Madame Ninette as though they would not see each other again for twenty years. Then she hastily borrowed a few ticals for the ricksha. In spite of the rouge and the facial treatment, she looked older than her years. Swaying on high heels, she left the beauty salon. Her dyed blond hair hung in a childlike bang down over her forehead; this was how Katharina Krylovna had worn it decades ago when she fled from a Russian provincial town. She was one of those women for whom a given hairdo is one of the permanent things in life. She looked like a child well provided for, who for inexplicable reasons had acquired wrinkles and experimented with dyes.

Madame Ninette dropped heavily into the wicker chair in her private office, while Vera totaled up the day's receipts. Every afternoon at five o'clock they had strong tea with candied fruit together. Afterward Madame Ninette would drive out to her villa in Bangkapi, and Mademoiselle Leskaya would go to her hotel in the Chinese quarter. This shared quarter-hour over strong, sweet tea and opium cigarettes was the mysterious communion which united these unlike companions. Vera Leskaya was counting on the atmosphere of this quarter-hour on this July day in 1945.

"How pale you are, Leskaya," Madame Ninette remarked. "It doesn't become you."

"What difference does it make?" Leskaya said, shrugging. "I have worries, Nina Ivanovna."

"Worries? Rrridiculous, Leskaya. Due to my kindness, you live a wonderful life." Madame Ninette tilted her head to one side and smiled with complacent scorn. "You have money enough for drrrinks, singing, and fun."

Money enough? Vera pricked up her ears. Was this an allusion to her subsidiary income from the Japanese? But Madame Ninette knew nothing about that. She must be referring to Leskaya's private transactions as Miss Senglee.

"What's new?" Madame Ninette asked, yawning.

"All sorts of things, Nina Ivanovna. I—I—"

"Don't entertain me in installments, Leskaya. Speak if you have anything to say."

"It is my sorrowful lot to be the bearer of ill tidings." Vera Leskaya fixed her morbid, avaricious eyes upon Madame's full-moon face. "Do you remember that some time ago we were talking about the Chungking agent Foxface? That time Mademoiselle Vivica was arrested?"

"What, what about the little Foxface? That was Vivica, the young crrriminal, if I remember rightly."

"Mademoiselle Vivica was not Foxface. She was only lured into the business. The real agent has since been discovered, Nina Ivanovna."

"Brrravo, brrravo!" Madame Ninette clapped her hands. "Is it that beanpole Astrid Werrgeland? I always suspected her." Madame reached into the desk drawer and took out a box of cigarettes. This was a sign that she was in no hurry and that Vera's talk interested her. At the bottom of the box lay a revolver. Madame Ninette sometimes stayed late at the office, long after Vera Leskaya had gone home. Thieves were as thick as the sands of the sea in this city.

"Brravo," she repeated, sweetening her tea with candied strawberries. "Sly, reprehensible little Foxface. Now she'll be groaning in the cellar. No drrinks, no singing, no fun."

"Not yet, Nina Ivanovna."

"You are speaking in riddles, Leskaya. But Nina Ivanovna has no time for your riddles." Madame's tone had hardened. And the atmosphere in the private office had changed.

Vera Leskaya was breathing heavily. "The Kempetai still does not know about the discovery, Nina Ivanovna. But *one* person now knows who Foxface is."

"And who knows, little mystifier?"

"I do, Nina Ivanovna."

"You?" Madame Ninette was overcome by a gale of laughter. "You,

you cultured goose, have found out who Foxface is? You have a fever, Leskaya! You need cold compresses and quinine, my poor dove." Madame Ninette spoke very quickly, laughing even more loudly. "May I ask when you made this discovery?"

"The night I spent in your house, Nina Ivanovna. After the arrest of Vivica Wergeland."

Madame Ninette sprang to her feet so abruptly that she knocked over a teacup and the jar of preserves. She was no longer laughing. A dangerous light sparkled in her bright blue eyes. "Watch yourself, Leskaya," she said sharply. "In my house there are no spies."

"Really not, Nina Ivanovna?"

Something crawled invisibly up to Madame Ninette—a horrible premonition, an incredible certainty, a scent of death and years of treachery. She studied Vera Leskaya as if seeing her for the first time: the clay-cold face; the thin, tightly shut lips; the death-haunted eyes. Miss Senglee . . .

"What have you to do with the business?" she demanded. "Whom were you spying on in my house? Mademoiselle Wergeland came there at dawn, remember? I didn't let her in. I was beginning to suspect something. Remember?"

Silence.

Madame Ninette went up to Vera and gripped her arm brutally. The younger woman shrank back from the look in those small eyes.

"You won't move out of this room until you've said your piece." Madame Ninette, moving with uncanny agility, locked the door. "Out with it!"

Instead of answering, Vera Leskaya opened her shabby handbag and gave Madame Ninette a typewritten document. "Please read what I have written, Nina Ivanovna. I—I have worked for the Japanese for years."

"You have worked for the Japanese for years," Madame Ninette repeated, dropping with a crash into her chair. Her fat beringed hand grasped the cigarette box with the revolver at the bottom. "So, so—so you have worked for the Japanese for years. That is amusing, Vera! Verry amusing!"

"I had to live, Nina Ivanovna."

"I see no compelling reason for that, my dove." Madame eyed her chief assistant from under half-shut lids. "No one cares whether or not you live—not even you yourself. Boris knew why he left you in Shanghai twenty years ago. No one marries a woman who is half dead."

"Stop that, Nina Ivanovna!" Vera swayed slightly. She had long ago buried Boris, but she secretly worshiped the earth she had shoveled over this grave.

"I won't stop, I'm just beginning," Madame Ninette observed, opening the document. "So she worked for the Japanese for years," she murmured. Her lower jaw trembled like that of a clown whose public has stopped laughing. She began to read, while Vera stood before her in her accustomed humble posture and was not invited to sit down. She wished she could smoke, but Madame's fat hand lay heavily on the box of cigarettes.

There was dead silence while Nina Ivanovna studied the document.

SECRET DOSSIER
To: MAJOR KIMURA (Military Secret Police)
Present location: Rangoon, Burma
From: Agent V. L.
Subject: Identification and whereabouts of Chungking agent known as
      FOXFACE
Agent V. L. wishes to set down the following observations:
The long-sought agent *Foxface*, who organized the *Sun* espionage ring (Shanghai-Bangkok-Saigon) and maintained it intact until the arrests in April 1945, is *not a Chinese*, as has been generally assumed. Nor is the still missing Frenchman named Pierre de Maury Foxface, though he was the most prominent assistant to Foxface in the Hanoi-Saigon area. Foxface *is a woman*. Agent V. L. has observed this woman's activities for years, but has hesitated to expose her because there was no conclusive evidence of her anti-Japan activities. Almost all the visitors to Madame Ninette's beauty parlor—including the Norwegian girl Mlle. Vivica Wergeland— were, with or without their knowledge, cleverly drawn into the ring. Foxface always concealed the bulletins in Mlle. Vivica Wergeland's bag when the young lady went to visit her friend Pierre de Maury in Saigon. Agent V. L. believes that Mlle. Vivica did not know what she was carrying in her luggage.
Name of Agent Foxface: Nina Ivanovna Borin
Age: 65
Special marks: Inordinately fat

Employer: Chinese followers of Generalissimo Chiang Kai-shek. Foxface succeeded for years in deceiving her associate in the Chez Ninette Beauty Parlor (first in Shanghai, later in Bangkok) about her activities. The mask of easy-going benevolence concealed her cunning, avarice, and cruelty. V. L. first obtained proofs of Foxface's activities from the agent Katharina Krylovna, whom V. L. recommended to the Kempetai for observation and shadowing of Nina Ivanovna. Since Ivanovna made a point of not inviting V. L. to her parties, V. L. bribed the said Krylovna to provide her with a list of the guests and a description of the entertainment. Thus V. L. learned that Monsieur Pierre de Maury frequently came from Indo-China to these parties, and that he flirted with Mlle. Vivica Wergeland. V. L. realized at once that this Frenchman, who was so much older than the girl, had subsidiary motives, since he frequently disappeared with Nina Ivanovna into her bedroom and carried on conversations with her there.

The scene arranged by V. L. in the home of Miss Helene Wergeland in Bangkok (April 4, 1945) strengthened the assumption that Nina Ivanovna herself was the agent Foxface and the organizer of the espionage ring. Ivanovna laughed and joked heartily while Miss Wergeland was being informed of her niece's arrest. But when V. L. lit a cigarette for her, she observed her cold hands and trembling chin—both signs of a high degree of agitation and fear in Nina Ivanovna. In the winter of 1925, when Chinese police raided the home of Nina Ivanovna in Shanghai, intending to arrest her and an old general for sale of opium, Nina Ivanovna also displayed cold hands and a trembling chin. When V. L. showed a sheet of green letter-paper, on which she herself had scribbled some signs, to Miss Helene Wergeland, maintaining that it was a secret code, Nina Ivanovna was so close to fainting that V. L. had to revive her with genuine French cognac (bill presented by V. L. at the time). Nina Ivanovna used such letter-paper to send coded messages in Vivica Wergeland's suitcase to Saigon.

During the night of April 4, 1945, while Nina Ivanovna was sleeping off the alcohol she had imbibed after all the excitement, V. L. had the opportunity to go through her desk. The locks—as is the case everywhere in Bangkok—were of Chinese manufacture, and therefore easy to open. Foxface evidently felt so secure that she did not see the necessity for a European type of secret compartment. The accompanying documents were found in this desk. Since V. L. has always been admonished to follow a trail for a long time, in order not to alarm other members of an espionage ring, she pursued the trails which the correspondence in the desk suggested might be promising. In consequence the Kempetai succeeded in netting some fifty Chungking agents in the Shanghai, Saigon, and Bangkok areas. There were only five addresses, but each arrested person betrayed others during the interrogation, as was to be expected. If Ivanovna should attempt the old trick of accusing the agent Vera Leskaya of being a double agent, Leskaya's many years of work for Nippon and his honor Major Kimura will be sufficient guarantee that this is pure slander, quite in keeping with the cruel and devious character of Foxface.

Summary: Nina Ivanovna is particularly dangerous because she plays the fool. Agent V. L. would never have suspected her if Nina Ivanovna had not made the mistake, in her agitation after the arrest of Vivica Wergeland, of taking V. L. back to her home in Bangkapi because she did not want to spend the night alone. She had always avoided, for good reason, inviting V. L. to her home, justifying this impoliteness by sadistic remarks to the effect that V. L. was too shabby, too ugly, and too dull for her parties. Foxface is at the moment unsuspecting. An arrest will cause no difficulties, since she is not contemplating flight. If she should, contrary to expectation, attempt to escape, V. L. will remain at her heels.

Postscript: It has proved impossible for V. L. to trace Mlle. Astrid Wergeland. Shortly after her sister's arrest, the Wergeland ladies disappeared from Bangkok; V. L. has not been able to locate them.

SIGNED: V. L.

Bangkok. July 1945.

Enclosures:
    Expense list for the months April to July 1945
    Ivanovna's correspondence, supplemented and partly decoded by V. L.
    Photograph of Ivanovna, supplied by Katharina Krylovna
    Photograph of her villa, supplied by V. L.
    Names of her present servants
    New list of the clients of Chez Ninette

Madame Ninette carefully laid the sheets of paper together and placed them beside the cigarette box.

"Well, well," she said with chilling calm, "so you've found all that out, you chatterbox."

Vera Leskaya did not stir.

"Do you know what Nina Ivanovna does to vipers she has nursed in her bosom?" Madame Ninette pounded herself vehemently on her ample front. "Have you lost your tongue, Leskaya?"

"There is nothing more to say."

"When did you send that dossier off?"

"I have not yet sent it off, Nina Ivanovna."

"Think of some cleverer lie five minutes before your death, you educated goose!" Madame Ninette took the revolver out of the cigarette box.

"I have unloaded it, Nina Ivanovna. I know my way about all your desks."

"You will not leave this room alive, you cursed spy!"

"That would be unfortunate for you. What you have there is only a copy that looks like an original. Only amateurs work with typewriter carbons, don't you know?"

"Quite right."

"If you kill me somehow now—I know you're terribly strong, Nina Ivanovna, and I am only a hollow husk—Mr. Cheong, my Chinese landlord, will send the original of the dossier to Major Kimura in Burma tomorrow. The major's real name is different, but that doesn't matter."

Vera Leskaya smiled wearily. But then she shrank in terror, sensitive intellectual that she was, from the murderous look in the eyes of her far more vital employer.

Madame Ninette had leaped up, hurling the rest of the tea service to the ground. For a moment she contemplated the shards. Then she sat down abruptly, smiling her foxy smile. If Leskaya were telling the truth—and she might be—there was still a chance for Nina Ivanovna.

"Sit down, Vera," she said quietly, pushing a chair toward her secretary. She took fresh teacups from a cupboard, lit the small coconut-oil cooker, and pretended not to notice that Vera Leskaya was trembling.

"Did you know Lisaveta Korsky?" Madame Ninette asked.

"No."

"She deceived and betrayed her benefactress—back home in Russia. Her benefactress took a number of small sharp shards—let us say, from broken teacups—and—hahaha . . ."

Vera Leskaya moaned. Like many intellectuals, she was terribly afraid of physical pain. She rushed up to her fat employer and clasped her knees. "The dossier has not been sent off. Please believe me, Nina Ivanovna!" She began sobbing wildly.

"Believe *you?*" Madame Ninette said sarcastically. "How idiotic do you think little Foxface is, Leskaya?"

"I wanted to send it off. And then—"

"And then you decided to ask me whether there were any details to correct. You make me laugh, Leskaya."

Vera looked at her. All was lost. It was impossible to present her offer if Nina Ivanovna did not believe her. And not to believe her was sensible and plausible—except that nothing about their relationship had ever been sensible or plausible. They had been linked by hate-love at first sight.

Nina Ivanovna did not look at the treacherous creature at her feet. If she had gambled and lost, so had Leskaya!

"You're right, Nina Ivanovna," Vera Leskaya said dully.

"The war is ending badly for Nippon anyhow, you chatterbox," Madame Ninette observed. "You have denounced me. All right!"

"Not yet, Nina Ivanovna."

"All right," Madame Ninette repeated; she had never liked being interrupted by her employee. "I shall hang, Leskaya. I won't be able to hide from that bloodhound Matsubara long—that's who your Major Kimura is, right? I'm too fat to go into hiding. But you'll hang too, chatterbox. I won't soil my hands on you. I'll leave it to the Allies to string you up. It can't be long now."

Vera looked up. In her eyes there appeared a faint glow of warmth, of embarrassment, of that demonic and indissoluble tie between Russian exiles. She brushed the hair back from her forehead, suddenly quite calm.

"Kill me or not, as you like, Nina Ivanovna. You will still find out that I have not betrayed you. The original of the dossier is lying at my landlord's. Go there and ask him!"

"Why didn't you send it off? Did you want to show me how clever you are?"

"I wanted to show you how stupid I am!" Once again she looked at her old companion, and then she bowed her head. "I—I couldn't do it," she stammered. "I—love you too much, Nina Ivanovna."

Still on her knees, she crept closer to her beloved enemy and kissed her fat beringed hands. Madame Ninette's nail polish had cracked. Some flakes of it got into Vera's mouth, and she coughed.

"Get up," Madame Ninette said hoarsely. "Get up, darling. We'll drive to my house and make some fresh tea. We'll talk everything

over, darling Leskaya. I knew you wouldn't betray your poor old
Ninotchka who picked you up out of the streets in Shanghai, would
you? You wouldn't betray her to the damned island dwarfs, would
you?"

Vera sobbed uncontrollably at her feet. All the tears she had not
been able to weep during these last thirty years, while she had been
engaged in her sinister affairs, streamed out of her overstrained eyes
at once. She wept as only Russians can—passionately, shamelessly,
with deep pleasure.

"I'll save you, Leskaya," Madame Ninette said and began sobbing
likewise. She took a huge handkerchief from her knitting bag and
wiped first her eyes and then the flowered silk of her dress, which
Vera had drenched with her tears. It was expensive silk; Vera had
better cry on cheaper material. Madame Ninette pushed the handkerchief to her.

"Let me think, Vera! The war is at its last gasp. Your poor little
Foxface will be a grrreat big shot after the war. The Allies will do
right by her. Do you want old Nina Ivanovna to save you, you bookworm, you educated gosling?"

"I'm not worth it."

"You're right, my dove. But you, you scurrilous chatterbox, you sly,
sourpussed wonder, you're my only frrriend in this icy world. Are
you or aren't you, Leskaya?" Madame Ninette suddenly screamed,
her face red, shaking the heap of misery at her feet with rough,
exuberant tenderness.

"I am, Nina Ivanovna. Please let me go. I feel dizzy!"

"Weakling, bookworm!" Madame Ninette said with good-natured
contempt. "And a creature like you wanted to cross up Foxface! Now
you repent, and Nina Ivanovna forgives you. She is generous and
sacrrrifices herself for her worthless friends."

Madame fell silent for a moment, overwhelmed by the consciousness of her own nobility. Then she swabbed away her streaming
tears and said matter-of-factly, "The war can last only a few weeks
more. The Allies will send Japan an ultimatum. There will be hear-
ings and investigations that will make the Kempetai interrogations
look like child's play, Leskaya. But I will say that my darrling
Leskaya worked as a *double agent*. I'll say she furnished the Japa-

nese with phony information supplied by the Chungking agent Foxface, that she rendered grreat secret serrvices to the Allies. She
deserrves a decoration, Nina Ivanovna will say. Well, how do you
like that, Leskaya?" Madame Ninette blinked cunningly.

"I wanted to propose something similar to you today, dearest
Ivanovna," Vera Leskaya murmured.

"Then why didn't you say so?" Madame Ninette asked. "You're
usually such a chatterbox."

They drove arm in arm to Nina Ivanovna's to drink tea, discuss the
details of Vera's change of course, and weep the rest of their senti-
mental tears. Vera needed lessons, Madame Ninette thought to herself. She had committed two unpardonable errors as a spy. In the
first place she had exposed her cards in a moment of panic, when
the rats were leaving the sinking ship. And she had believed that
old friendship was as reliable as old hatred. . . .

Madame Ninette considerately drove Vera Leskaya back to the
hotel in the Chinese quarter—in her automobile, which Chungking
had paid for. She saw to it that Mr. Cheong, the proprietor of the
hotel, beheld them go arm in arm to Vera's room, staggering, for she
had laced the tea with plenty of vodka. Together they burned the
document which Vera had addressed to Major Matsubara. Then
Madame Ninette took her leave, giving Vera a Russian kiss that took
her breath away. Vera fell happily asleep. In her dreams she smiled
and looked somewhat less weary of life than usual.

Next morning, on the way to the beauty salon, Vera was run over
by a Chinese automobile as she attempted to cross a busy intersection. She was killed instantly.

The entire White Russian colony of Bangkok came to the funeral,
although most of them had not seen Vera for years and none had
felt any affection for her. But she had been one of their own, and
her death was a loss to these Russians without a country. Madame
Ninette shed torrents of tears and told everyone that Vera Leskaya
had been her only friend in this icy world. She threw three shovel-
fuls of earth on the newly dug grave, wiped the perspiration from
her brow—it was ninety in the shade—and drove home, shattered by
emotion.

That afternoon she did not go to the beauty salon but took inventory. She thought of the many years she had spent with Vera, of the many teas after hours, of Vera's diligence, her bookworm culture, her treachery, her tears, her love, and her folly. A spy who believes in forgiveness is like a red fox that loses its cunning, she thought.

When the servant announced a caller, Madame Ninette rose heavily from her chair. It was Mr. Ling, who had run over Vera Leskaya. He had done it for China, since Vera Leskaya had been an agent of Nippon. Mr. Ling was now on his way to Shanghai.

"Tell Foxface that we have disposed of the most dangerous of Japan's agents," Madame Ninette said. "I don't think we have anything to fear now."

"Mademoiselle Leskaya rang a wooden bell, Madame," Mr. Ling whispered. He meant that Vera had made an attempt that was vain from the start. She had been a rabbit venturing to match itself against a fox.

"Vera Leskaya actually thought *I* was Foxface," the old Russian woman declared. "I made the mistake of taking her back home with me after the arrest of little Vivica."

Mr. Ling said nothing. They all made mistakes from time to time, and persons of superior character realized this.

"Now and then I indulged a little too heavily," Madame Ninette said euphemistically. Had she not drunk herself into a stupor from shock at the arrest of Vivica, Vera would never have been able to rummage through her desk.

"You were in great danger, Madame." Mr. Ling's wise, tired eyes contemplated the fat old European woman who for years had been playing such a risky game. He bowed ceremoniously. "But you won in the end, Madame," he concluded gently. "A thousand happy years to you and a free China!"

It was the usual Chungking salutation, but for Nina Ivanovna it contained a terrible irony. To be sure, she had crushed the adder she had nourished in her ample bosom. But the "thousand happy years" stretched before her mind's eye as a yawning gulf, for she had been forced to liquidate her companion of so many years. Now she was alone in a foreign land—as alone as young Vivica, the pretty, unsuspecting decoy in her Kempetai cell; as alone as Astrid in the same prison, as Helene Wergeland in northern Siam, as Pierre de

Maury behind the curtain of rain in French Laos. The war had cut
them all off, each by himself.

That night Madame Ninette awoke from a restless sleep. The monsoon rain drummed monotonously against the shutters of her Bangkok villa. Nina Ivanovna opened her eyelids, which were swollen
from the heavy sleeping draft she had taken, and looked wildly and
dazedly around her. "Vera!" she called hoarsely. "Where are you,
my dove? Come to old Ninotchka. She'll make frrresh tea." When
she at last came fully awake, fat tears ran down her complacent
clown's face. She moaned and crossed herself. Thousand-faced solitude lay upon her breast as heavily as a full sack of rice. She staggered out of bed, tearing the mosquito netting, and took a long drink
of vodka. As she did so she looked into the mirror of her dressing
table with utter incredulity. Was she really so lonesome, so old, so
sad, so pitiably victorious? Her implausible blond chignon lay on the
night table. She murmured a Russian curse, dashed it to the floor,
and trampled on it. Then she picked it up and brushed it penitently,
while the tears formed deep runnels down her fat cheeks and her
chin quivered. Inconsolable, she crept back to bed, a lonely old vixen
among other foxes.

"The hare dies and the fox mourns for him," says a Chinese peasant proverb. So it was with Nina Ivanovna in her hour of triumph
over the hare that had ventured to match itself against a fox.

Next morning Madame Ninette was as noisy and talkative as ever
with her clients in the beauty salon. She looked much the same as
usual—only somewhat more puffed-faced, as though she had drunk
too much. Shortly before the end of the day Madame Krylovna appeared. It was she who for months had supplied Vera Leskaya with
data on the parties at Madame Ninette's villa—on orders from Madame Ninette.

"You worked very well, Katharina," Madame Ninette said. "We are
pleased with you."

She walked heavily into her office, where stood the samovar, the
tea, and the opium cigarettes, and wrote out a check. Madame
Krylovna stood about in embarrassment and showed no sign of
leaving.

"Well?" Madame Ninette asked impatiently. "What else?"

"I'm dead tired from coming all this way, Nina Ivanovna. Shall we not have a cup of tea together?"

Madame Ninette stared at her. "What's that you say? *You* want to have tea with *me?*"

"Why, what has got into you, Nina Ivanovna? Are you the Emperor of Japan, that a perrrson can't drrrink tea with you?"

Madame Ninette took her heavy knitting bag and threw it at the lean, shabby agent with the idiotic frizzled bangs and the crazy high heels. "Out!" she screamed, beside herself. "How do you dare, in this verry rrroom—"

She gasped for breath and saw that she was alone. Madame Krylovna had fled at the sight of those bloodshot eyes and that powerful, reeling figure, which even in its degeneracy bristled still with the strength of a Russian peasant as it bore down on her.

Nina Ivanovna sank exhausted into her chair. Her brow was beaded with cold sweat. "Drink tea! In *our* room!" she whispered, panting. "Did you hear that, Leskaya?"

6: *Astrid and Vivica*

The day after Vera Leskaya's burial, Astrid was once again interrogated by Colonel Saito. This was the fifth interrogation since her arrest, and it was utterly fruitless. Astrid did not know where Pierre de Maury was, and Colonel Saito insisted on her telling him. This is one of the basic situations in the mournful drama of political interrogations, the questioners as a rule not having sufficient imagination to believe in that rare case, the prisoner's innocence. In response to Astrid's truthful statement that she had denounced Pierre de Maury in a fit of jealousy, Colonel Saito flashed his three front teeth in a frightful smile and pounded his fist on the table. In so doing he broke Astrid's glasses, which she always took off for these interrogations because she did not want to see the colonel too plainly. This was the one good thing the colonel did for her. Astrid had to become accustomed once more to seeing the world without the aid of glasses, and she managed. They had originally been only reading glasses anyhow, but Astrid had nothing to read in her cell; she had only her thoughts. Since no new thoughts occurred to her in her present predicament, she made do with memories. She sat upright and without stirring on the small Chinese hassock and thought about her childhood in Shanghai, about her engagement under the rain of bombs, and about the finale in Angkor.

No one could say that Astrid went downhill as the result of her arrest. She showed not the faintest trace of that dissolution and degeneration which for a single night had made Vivica irresistible to Major Matsubara in his weariness with the studied arts of geishas. Astrid sat on her hassock, cool and collected, in the posture of a duchess forgotten by the world, and received her guests from the past: her father, her amah Yumei, Aunt Helene, Mailin, the bird Gold Oriole, her hopelessly loved girl friend at the boarding school in Lausanne, slyly smiling Vivica—and Pierre, who had given her his heart in Shanghai while the bombs fell, and taken it from her among the ruins of Angkor. In the stillness of a cell, which quells the desires of the senses and allows the soul to expand, Astrid for the first time objectively pondered her tragic relationship to Pierre de Maury. And she recognized that her way of loving had been wrong. She had always considered primarily what she wanted from Pierre, and seldom thought of what he needed and of what wishes he had that she might fulfill. Happiness consisted only in giving, not in receiving, she saw. The example of her two German friends in Shanghai, Hanna Chou and Anna von Zabelsdorf, showed her that. They loved their husbands in the right way; they gave incessantly, consoled, created by their own efforts a domestic oasis where all seemed desert. Every man was a restless wanderer on the face of the earth; it was the task of every woman to provide her man with peace and consolation. For women hated the wanderings, the adventures, the dangers which in our century menaced the hearth.

Astrid began to suspect that she had misunderstood Pierre. She had been blind to his deeper nature. If any man had needed a domestic oasis, it had been Pierre in the desert of politics. What Astrid

had formerly never understood, the secret that deepened as Japan
reigned ever more victoriously in Indo-China, was his tragic attachment to his native land. That had transformed this young cultural
ambassador from Paris into a harried and imperiled sailor in the
maelstrom of Asian politics. Even in Angkor Wat, when Major
Matsubara had asked him about the Cao Dai sect, Astrid had been
blind and deaf. She had wanted to be kissed and to have a wedding date set by a lover who was wholly absorbed in political work.
The night Shanghai was bombed Pierre had given his heart to her in
trust—a skeptical Frenchman's heart, weary of emotion, which would
always belong, in a troubled way, half to France. But what he had
given to Astrid had not been enough for her. She had always wanted
everything or nothing, and so she had lost everything. Or no, she had
gained something: insight. And although understanding is the bitter weed of love, which flourishes in parched flowerbeds, it had still
the power to console and purify her soul of its selfishness. Astrid
ceased to be unhappy as she sat mutely in her cell. Her misguided
passion and her bitterness gradually melted in the sun of a new feeling of love which embraced all whom she knew—the Wergelands,
Mailin in Singapore, her German friends in Shanghai, and the
shadow of her onetime fiancé. She prayed daily for the strength to
love truly, and for Vivica's life. For Vivica's sufferings loomed terrify-
ingly large in her mind. Only divine mercy could help her here.
Astrid felt utterly empty whenever she prayed for Vivica; but it was
the emptiness of a pure heart, which had made room for God and
for charity.

So, the day after Vera Leskaya's burial, Astrid again sat calmly
facing Colonel Saito. Again she declared that she knew nothing about
Foxface. Colonel Saito drummed all his fingers upon his desk; the
sound was trying to Astrid's nerves, and was meant to be. But Colonel Saito was drumming less forcefully than usual, for in this July
before the fall of Japan a great weariness had overcome him. He
had had no news recently from his family and was worried about a
thousand matters. But even now, a month before the end, he still
could not believe in Japan's defeat.

"Where is Foxface hiding?" he asked again.

Astrid had an inspiration. "I do not think 'Foxface' exists, Colonel."

"Why do you say that, Mademoiselle?"

The Japanese interpreter pricked up his ears and held his pen ready. The longnoses had a bagful of tricks.

"I have lived among Chinese from childhood," Astrid said, knowing that Colonel Saito could not make the same claim for himself. "The Chinese love puns and concealments. My amah in Shanghai often used to tell me about Foxfaces, but when I wanted to see them she would laugh and say that she had made it all up. I think the Sun espionage ring invented the figure of an agent named Foxface in order to mislead you."

Colonel Saito had stopped drumming his fingers. He stared expressionlessly into space while the interpreter repeated the longnose's words, making a bow after each sentence, which was both time-consuming and irritating.

"Do you really think such nonsense? Or have you made up this theory in order to be released?" The colonel expressed himself far more elaborately, but the interpreter simplified what he said so that the longnose could understand. He bowed and cleared his throat humbly; one could not get around the fact that the longnoses had an extremely primitive language.

"I did not make it up," Astrid said, offended. "I never have ideas."

Colonel Saito looked at her suspiciously; she sounded as if she was speaking the truth. Perhaps it was so; but his rough, straightforward mind rebelled against such an assumption. Major Matsubara would have known immediately whether this explanation was worth anything. But the major would not be back in Shanghai for a week.

"How is my sister?" Astrid asked suddenly.

Colonel Saito stared speechlessly at her. He was the one to ask questions here. And although this prisoner was a daughter of the Church, and for that reason had been treated by him with a degree of consideration—he had applied the lamb method throughout, except for that time he had broken her glasses—he could not stand for questions on the part of his prisoners. That was going too far!

"Take her out!" he shouted, once more pounding on the desk with his fist. These women of the West talked too much; no punishment could be too harsh for that crime. For brief seconds he thought of Madame Saito, who was still as a pond in the morning mist. She guessed his thoughts and answered them with silence, or with a

favorite dish offered on her knees. Colonel Saito glanced out of the
window of the Kempetai's office. And at that moment Foxface drove
by in his old-fashioned American automobile. As the car passed,
there passed the last opportunity for the Japanese to solve the
mystery.

Colonel Saito could not catch Foxface because Foxface was not
hiding from the Kempetai. He drove about Shanghai every day, in
full view. He visited the homes of the free, ate the rice of the brave,
and "shared his opinions with the people," as Meng-Tze had recommended. With Chinese stoicism he watched his agents fight and fall,
as fate would have it, but the network he had strung three years
before, from Shanghai to Bangkok, Saigon, and radio stations in
India, held fast. A Chinese had woven it, and so it was elastic and
indestructible.

When Nina Ivanovna had proposed to him that young Vivica be
sent as an unwitting courier to Indo-China, he had shaken his head.
A female fish might too easily fall through the mesh of the great net
—and he had known the Wergelands for years. But finally he had
given his consent; the cause of freedom had meanwhile become
more important than a young foreign woman, who in any case possessed a good deal of native wit. But then something had gone
wrong; Vivica had been arrested. The Chungking net held, but a
small fish had slipped through onto the sandy shores and was gasping for air. It was sad about the pretty, glistening little fish.

Foxface's American car, which was known to every banker and
every coolie in Shanghai, stopped at the intersection of a Chapei side
street. An elegant Chinese gentleman stepped out and entered a
tailor's shop. The tailor's wife flashed into the room, bowed low, and
served green tea in handleless cups. She was the eldest sister of
Yumei, the now dead amah of the Wergeland family. Foxface sat
down in the dark back room and asked tersely, "Any news of Third
Sister?"

Yumei's sister began to cry. She had known Vivica and Astrid for
ever so long, and Miss Wergeland also. The gentleman waited patiently; women had as many tears as the Whangpoo River drops of
water; but the tears of women were cleaner and purer.

"Is she dead?" he whispered. "Then she is no longer suffering; her
spirit is already fluttering like a butterfly."

"No one knows, sir!" Yumei's eldest sister wiped away her tears with the hem of her blue jacket. "Agent Forty-one reported yesterday that Missie Vivica is no longer in the prison. Perhaps they have thrown her into the river, sir. Or crushed her with red-hot irons." Elder Sister wept self-indulgently; her Chinese imagination had taken fire and was conceiving even more horrible possibilities.

"We will seek her," Foxface said, regarding Yumei's sister with weary forbearance. One could not extract white silk from a vat of indigo! He gave her tea-money and left the shop. In front of a rice store Chinese working women were gathering, protesting in shrill, dramatic speeches against the increase in the price of rice. They seemed to have no fear of the nearby Kempetai. They were mothers of families, hence had the courage of lionesses.

Frowning, Foxface drove on to Wing On, the big department store. This was the month of the Lotus in the Chinese lunar year, and his wife had asked him to buy the traditional dragon for their eldest son. He had already explained to his eight-year-old son that the Chinese dragon was a benevolent creature who would scatter useful rain over the thousands of rice villages in China. He did not want his son to pick up from his European mother the conception of a dragon as a monster. Herbert Chou, grandson of a German and a Chinese banker, was being given a thoroughly Chinese rearing. Some day he would dwell in the free China his father Tso-ling had helped to create. Hanna and her three sons had no suspicion that Tso-ling was the celebrated weaver of espionage networks, Foxface. Nor did Tso-ling's aged mother on Great Western Road know anything about her firstborn son's double life. No one guessed that Chou Tso-ling had been indefatigably weaving his net for years, and that his life was in constant danger, for not all fish were mute. No one guessed that the house back of Bubbling Well Road, which he had inherited from old Mr. Hsin, Mailin Wergeland's grandfather, was only a stage-set representing a peaceful family life. Chou Tso-ling, master of the house, was nowadays nothing but a restive guest in the bird pavilion. He fended off the tigers from the front of his house and could never know whether they might not slip in at the back door.

It was well that the womenfolk of the house of Chou in Shanghai knew nothing of his double life, Foxface reflected as he drove through the twilight toward Bubbling Well Road, Herbert's dragon balanced carefully on his knees. Danger and death were a man's business. He should never have agreed to Vivica Wergeland's involvement. Women were too closely bound up with life; in all times, they gave life—in spring and winter, in periods of abundance and times of drought, in peacetime and wartime. They were always the archfoes of anything that endangered their sons and husbands. Even China's freedom, much as they hoped for it, was less important to them than that none of their brood should be missing from the nest. In this respect his Hanna's ideas did not differ from those of aged Madame Chou. (And did not differ from those of kindly, silent Madame Saito in Urakami, the suburb of Nagasaki.)

Hanna was sitting with Herbert and her two younger sons in the bird pavilion when Tso-ling entered. "You look tired, darling," she said. "Have you heard anything about Astrid and Vivica?"

"Unfortunately not. May I have my tea, Hanna? It is very late."

Hanna clapped her hands, and Faithful Goose waddled in with the tea things, followed by two young servant girls.

"Pack the mistress's things and the sons'," Chou Tso-ling ordered the old woman. "Your own things too; you will accompany them."

Faithful Goose bowed without a word. She was startled, but not a muscle moved in her parchment face.

"I am taking you and Mother to the country house in Soochow early tomorrow morning," Tso-ling explained to his amazed wife. "Please ask no questions, my dear. You are no longer safe in Shanghai."

"Are *you* safe here, Tso-ling?"

"I do not know, Hanna, but I think so. Above all I must know that all of you are safe."

"But we are happy here." Tears filled Hanna's lovely dark eyes.

"Don't cry, sweet!" Tso-ling kissed her tenderly. "A man who values his happiness conceals it."

"This horrible war! I am afraid for you."

"For me! Why?"

"I don't know. I scarcely see you any longer. And you are so often depressed. Won't you tell me . . ."

"No, Hanna," Tso-ling said. "Everything is all right." He wore now his firm expression, which not even love could soften.

Hanna stroked the long, slender hand that held the bowl of tea. Her delicate tact warned her against continuing this conversation. She knew that in such situations Anna von Zabelsdorf would have discussed everything for hours with her Ernst. But Hanna was the wife of a Chinese. There was an invisible boundary she must never cross. "I will pack now, Tso-ling," she said softly.

"I wish only to guard all your sleep," Tso-ling murmured, looking at her with an expression of sorrow. This was a Chinese phrase to express the ultimate degree of connubial and parental love. He watched Hanna as she went slowly into the house—a lovely, graceful, and vital woman, the mother of his three sons. She had brought the Chou family a thousand happy hours. For a while he sat still, the thoughts racing behind his high, intelligent brow. He had known that it was dangerous to ride on a tiger. But he was riding for a free China—or at least he and thousands of other Chinese followers of Chiang Kai-shek were of this opinion. They represented the core of Chinese resistance to the Japanese Empire. The generalissimo stood in the foreground of the stage. Chou Tso-ling rode the tiger in the background. And he knew, too, that the one thing more dangerous than riding the tiger through occupied Shanghai was to attempt to leap off.

Tso-ling went into the house. From Hanna's room sounded the high voices of his sons and the voice of a young Chinese whom he quickly identified as Right Arm, Herr von Zabelsdorf's servant. Evidently Right Arm had brought Hanna a message from her friend Anna. Hanna came quickly toward her husband.

"Astrid is free, Tso-ling," she cried radiantly. "She's back with Ernst and Anna. I'll drive over there at once."

"You will not. I forbid you," Chou Tso-ling said in a tone that Hanna had never before heard from her calm and courteous husband. "You will not step out of this house until we leave at dawn."

"But Tso-ling, what will Astrid think? She is my friend. If the Kempetai has released her it—"

"It has done so in order to keep watching her. Let me see the message."

With trembling hand Hanna handed him Anna von Zabelsdorf's note. Of course—there it was: *There is a restriction; Astrid is not allowed to leave Shanghai. But we are all so happy, and looking*

*forward to seeing you and Tso-ling tonight. Unfortunately we have
not been able to find out anything about Vivica. We are sending a
message through a friend to Helene Wergeland. Yours, Anna.*

Chou Tso-ling put down the note. He was already feeling repentant for having spoken so harshly to Hanna. She was much more sensitive in such matters than a Chinese wife would be. She had turned
pale and was quivering with nervousness and surprise. Never would
Bertel have adopted such a tone toward her. He would have asked
her in a kindly way and trusted to her common sense. Not so a Chinese husband, even when he knew how intelligent his wife was and
appreciated her prudence. Even study abroad and marriage to a
foreign woman did not change a Chinese husband and would not do
so in a thousand years—would not if only because Chinese women,
in spite of rapidly progressing emancipation, still found satisfaction
in service and obedience and knew how to obtain what they wished
by indirect methods.

Chou Tso-ling led Hanna to her bedroom and put her to bed like a
child. In peacetime the wife was the husband's mother; in war she
became his eldest daughter. Hanna sank back on her pillow, sobbing
quietly.

"Forgive me, darling," Tso-ling whispered. He brought a bottle of
medicine from the bathroom, which he had had outfitted in Western
style for Hanna, and gave her a glass of the "essence of long life"
which all the women of the house of Chou took when they were
expecting a child. Until late that night Chou Tso-ling sat by his wife's
bed, guarding her sleep. Outside the gates of the old-fashioned
house back of Bubbling Well Road the Japanese tiger lurked.

Politics and freedom were men's business.

A week after Hanna Chou's removal from Shanghai, Baron von
Zabelsdorf received a message from Chou Tso-ling, his old friend,
whom he had not, however, seen for the last several months—though
he had not been conscious of this until he read Tso-ling's letter. Ever
since the arrest of the Wergeland girls, Hanna had always come to
see them alone. Now Tso-ling asked him to come "for a conversation between friends" to Mr. Han's auction rooms in the Chinese
City, where Tso-ling would meet him. And would Herr von Zabelsdorf please tear up the note?

At two o'clock in the afternoon the bustle and excitement was at its height in Mr. Han's rooms, which were situated on a winding street so narrow that no automobile could enter it. This was an auction for Chinese connoisseurs of art, and consequently the long-legged foreigner attracted attention. But the fever of rivalry and the passion for jade and porcelain subdued curiosity, ordinarily so keen among Chinese. Mr. Han had just knocked down a Ming vase to an old lady who looked like a door-to-door peddler. Old Madame Yüan, who owned a large textile mill and held shares in various reputable shipping companies, was not so simple as to parade her wealth. She bid modestly but doggedly for the best pieces at this auction, at which many fine items from the households of foreigners were being offered.

A young Chinese girl plucked surreptitiously at Herr von Zabelsdorf's sleeve. He understood, but waited until the battle over a bronze mirror was going full blast before following the girl to the door. No one noticed his departure. The girl led him to a small dark room in an unprepossessing house around the corner.

He greeted his friend Chou Tso-ling with a bow that was ceremoniously returned. But what Mr. Chou had to say was anything but conventional. He proposed to have Anna and the Zabelsdorf brood taken this very day to the Chous' country home, since Shanghai would be no place for women and children for the next few weeks or months.

Zabelsdorf's keen eyes studied this generous friend of his family with almost incredulous astonishment. Tso-ling, for his part, looked full in the face of his "Ernest," who had rescued a Chinese man child from a burning house and returned it to its mother's arms.

Ernst August thanked him for the offer, tersely, hoarsely. "But it won't do, Tso-ling. We Germans have become an outcast people. Having Anna and the children might endanger all of you."

For a moment there was silence in the small dark room. Then Mr. Chou replied, "It is all arranged, my friend." His face showed no trace of expression.

"Anna will not want to leave."

"That does not count, Ernest," Mr. Chou replied mildly. A fleeting smile came and went on his grave face with its sorrowful eyes and energetic chin. "Hanna also did not want to leave, but she and our

sons departed last week. My chauffeur will call at your house at five
o'clock this afternoon. My mother is looking forward with great
pleasure to your wife's visit."

He rose and looked at the German with mute sympathy. Ernst
August heroically suppressed his impulse to shake Tso-ling's hand.
Chinese did not like that gesture.

"May your country win the peace," Mr. Chou murmured. "We remain friends, Ernest!"

Herr von Zabelsdorf observed that Germany was already a country of howls and groans. "It is funny with us, Tso-ling," he murmured.
"If there are any dishes to be broken, we lead all the rest. That runs
into money!"

Chou Tso-ling no more understood the Berliner's irony than he did
the Japanese concept of duty. Why did Ernest say such a thing, will-
fully losing face? But as he looked at his friend's tense, lined forehead and empty sleeve, as he detected the exhaustion in his voice,
an inkling of the true meaning of such humor dawned on him. Perhaps Ernest's way of joking over the bitterest facts was resigned wisdom and an expression of deep feeling he would not permit to rise
to the surface. His humor sprang from a good source, just as rough-
neck Ernest came from a good family. Tso-ling overcame his Chinese distaste for physical contact and shook hands with his friend.

"I have just thought of something else, Ernest. Hanna told me that
Miss Astrid Wergeland is staying with you again, or am I mistaken?"

No, he was not mistaken. The long drink of water was with them
again. Was she to go along to Madame Chou's or not?

Mr. Chou thought Astrid had best stay in Shanghai, since the Japanese had ordered her not to leave the city. Herr von Zabelsdorf
scratched his head and decided that he would manage all right with
Miss Astrid. To be sure, she was not exactly sweetness and light—
but still she was solid gold. She didn't bawl and she didn't brood and
she didn't grumble and she was always neat. When you got to know
her, you couldn't help liking her. The kids were crazy about her
too. No, nothing wrong with Miss Astrid. But—was it altogether
proper if a good-looking young lady of twenty-seven remained alone
in the flat with the master of the household? What would Aunt
Helene say about that? Herr von Zabelsdorf, who had conceived a
great respect for Helene Wergeland, wondered.

But Chou Tso-ling was already saying that he had arranged matters for Miss Astrid too. Ernest should go home now and encourage the ladies to pack quickly. For the present Astrid would move to Chapei, to the sister of her old amah Yumei. She had often visited there during her childhood in Shanghai. Older Sister was looking forward to young Missie's arrival. Like her dead sister, she was devoted to all the Wergelands. And fortunately Astrid still spoke Chinese fluently.

Herr von Zabelsdorf gasped for breath. Still waters certainly ran deep. Tso-ling had obviously laid his plans and arranged matters with great forethought. He seemed to be a lot smarter than any Berliner, although that was hard to conceive. "My respects!" Ernest August murmured.

Mr. Chou's smile broadened. Ernst was a man of good sense, as he had suspected. Perhaps he even comprehended that for a while now Astrid should not live with a German family, lest she be suspected by the Allies after the end of the war of having been a friend of the Axis. In fact the Berliner saw that perfectly but made no allusion to it. He knew when a man with self-respect should keep his honorable trap shut.

"Miss Astrid is terribly worried about her sister," he remarked, cautiously feeling his way. "Hasn't anything come to light, Tso-ling? Is the poor kid still in the same prison, do you think?"

"Good-by, then, Ernest," Chou Tso-ling said as if he had not heard. He knew now where Vivica was. One of his agents had found out. His agents swarmed all through the gigantic city on the Whangpoo River. "The world is like a chess game; the situation changes with every move," he murmured. "I wish you a thousand happy years, Ernest. The man with a son is an enviable person!"

Mr. Chou bowed. He had the Chinese knack of breaking off a conversation in the middle with exquisite courtesy. The world was indeed like a game of chess, and these days the situation changed radically with every move. If Vivica could hold out a little longer, she would be saved. But where she was there were no foreign newspapers to read and no foreign radio could be heard, so that there was no way for her to know how close to the end everything was. Death was the penalty for Japanese who listened to Allied broadcasts. And at the moment Vivica was in a Japanese house in Shanghai. Her mind was wandering. She did not suspect how close she was to freedom. That was too bad, but nothing could be done about it.

Vivica lay with closed eyes in a clean, bare Japanese room. There were only a few straw mats and a vase of flowers in this room—and a Western-type bed for Vivica.

She did not want to open her eyes. She was tired, like a child who out of curiosity or by chance has played ball with the terrestrial globe.

Now and then a small Japanese woman entered the clean, bare room. This was Aki-Ko, who was in charge of tending and guarding the foreign woman. She must not be permitted to run away; otherwise Major Matsubara's fury would know no bounds. She must remain in this room—quiet, shattered, dreaming and talking to herself, and beautiful as a gull gliding above dark waves, the waves of passion.

From time to time Major Matsubara appeared and stared down at Vivica. She had been screaming so terribly that she had been given a sedative by injection, and was therefore sleeping like one dead. Major Matsubara would then bend over the woman and adore her, for brief seconds, with despairing ardor. Then he would call Madame Aki-Ko or Dr. Yamato, who by gentle force had pried this victim from the Kempetai and brought her to his clinic. After all, not even Major-san could obtain information from a madwoman! Once Vivica had opened her eyes while the major stood staring fervently at her; but no recognition had appeared in her eyes, which seemed to be brooding on immense distances.

Occasionally Vivica awoke from the stupor into which she had sunk after that nocturnal dinner at the White Chrysanthemum. Gentle Dr. Yamato and his wife tended her devotedly, but they did nothing to reawaken her mind. For that would mean that the Major-san would interrogate her again. At every Holy Mass they prayed for the young foreigner, but they knew nothing more about her than that she was the sister of Mademoiselle Astrid Wergeland.

They could not tell when Vivica's mind wandered, when she was conversing with her imaginary companion Halvard, who had followed her from the prison to this lovely quiet room, and when she was conscious and sane. No one could tell that. Even in ordinary times no one had ever known precisely what was going on in Vivica's mind. At the moment she was out of danger, and yet in grave danger—a dreaming Aphrodite.

In a way Vivica felt quite happy under the care of good Dr. Yamato and his gentle wife. Her retreat from a reality she could no longer cope with had taken place as quietly and unsensationally as the flight from life of her mother, Borghild, when Consul Wergeland had been about to send her to an expensive mental hospital. But there was a difference: Borghild had had her violin until the last, and that was a tangible instrument of wonder-working. Vivica had only Halvard, her imaginary little companion, who always hid from Major-san. Halvard was one of those little trolls out of Norway's days of innocence; he was merry and irresponsible, and he could sing. Vivica often listened to him these days, as she lay on her bed with eyes closed. She no longer remembered anyone she knew—neither Aunt Helene nor Astrid, certainly not Pierre or fat, funny old Madame Ninette in her beauty salon in Bangkok.

One day Madame Yamato hung a scroll in the niche: a *haikku,* one of those pearls of poetry for which Astrid had shown no understanding when she first met Major Matsubara in Shanghai.

> When the people go home
> After the fireworks—
> What darkness!

Madame Yamato explained the words shyly in English. "This *haikku,* Miss. We love *haikku.* When poem nice sad, we cry." Sweet Madame Yamato had the confusing Japanese habit of speaking of herself in the plural, out of modesty. Only the head of a Japanese household occasionally spoke of himself in the first person singular.

Vivica turned her face to the wall and again closed her eyes. What darkness after the fireworks!

In the afternoon she suddenly screamed, as she had in the days when she was still suffering the worst after-effects of shock and Dr. Yamato had mercifully transferred her from the cell to his light, clean home. His old friend, Colonel Joseph Saito, had apparently convinced Major Matsubara that not even the secret police could wring facts out of a woman possessed by spirits. However, Major-san came frequently to see whether the prisoner was making progress.

At least Dr. Yamato and his wife imagined that was the reason, for why else should so feared and prominent an officer stand regarding Prisoner Number 83 with fiery looks?

Vivica screamed in a strange high-pitched voice, and called for someone named Halvard whom Dr. Yamato did not know. Was it her fiancé, perhaps, or her brother? Vivica groaned. A fabulous creature, half bird, half man, had suddenly appeared in the quiet, lovely room. It had a golden face with glowing eyesockets, and an iron beak, and carried eight swords on the military cap which covered its head. The huge body flaunted greenish metal feathers and advanced threateningly upon Vivica. Now it was about to fall upon her—she could feel the iron beak and the fire flashing from its eyesockets. She screamed piercingly, but the fabulous creature only said in elegant French, "Death is too good for you, Mademoiselle. You shall live and regret every minute of it."

Dr. Yamato gave Vivica an injection. He whispered, "She was showing improvement, Major-san. She must have had another nightmare."

The darkness after the fireworks was wonderful. The morphine had banished the monster, or stripped it of its metallic feathers and its fire. There were shadows in the room. The world dissolved into colors and tones. Vivica was sitting in a meadow, but all around her were nothing but ashes and bizarre ruins, and in the distance an illuminated night-club. That must be Saigon. There she had filched a man from her sister Astrid—just for fun. On the fringes of the meadow, shadows with aged faces scurried by; their clothes were coated with blood and ashes. The meadow must be in a hollow, for when she looked up she saw processions of clouds, cobalt blue and poppy red and deathly gray. Vivica gathered the nearest clouds and smiled. Gathering clouds was a delightful occupation. Now and then music poured down out of the clouds. She waited for this music; it liberated her from her dark anxieties; when she heard it no bird with metallic feathers and elegant French could frighten her.

Vivica smiled—alluringly, with innocent licentiousness and in utter vacancy of mind. Major-san stood immobile by her bed. She was wearing an old pink kimono that belonged to the mistress of the house. Madame Yamato was an aged crone of thirty-seven, after all, and dressed only in dark colors nowadays. The pink kimono and the golden hair on the pillow harmonized delicately and nostalgically. The major stared at the picture. *Asagao*, he thought—morning blossom. The smile of this damaged Aphrodite pierced him like an arrow. He looked anxiously around. Then he bent over the dreaming girl and quickly, despairingly, kissed her lips. His brow was damp with cold sweat. He rushed to the door. Outside stood Madame Yamato, holding a small kettle. He greeted her with a wintry smile as he hastened past. She looked after him in alarm and astonishment. Then she filled the kettle and returned to her rooms.

In the White Chrysanthemum, Yuriko was waiting for Major-san. He looked at her in wonderment for a moment. Then he remembered that he himself had ordered her to come to Shanghai.

"You are flying back to Tokyo in a military plane tomorrow," he said coolly. "You will go back to helping your father in his shop as though you had never been away."

Yuriko's eyes filled with tears. Why should Akiro-san be sending her home? "Have I done something wrong?" she asked tremulously. "Is my intelligence too wretched?"

"No," Akiro replied with alarming gentleness. "You have served Nippon faithfully, little sea gull. But the end is approaching, and I want to know that you are safe. Later on, you know nothing, understand? You have never seen Colonel Saito or me. Tell your father to say the same if—if it is not yet too late!"

Yuriko understood. A deadly new type of bomb had fallen upon the Island Kingdom. The sun of Nippon was sinking with furious speed. She knelt before the man she loved and whispered, "We wish to die with Akiro-san."

But Akiro-san could not grant her this wish. He could not join little Yuriko in the love-death; he had died half an hour ago beside Vivica's bed. But no one but himself knew this.

An overwhelming weariness dimmed his eyes and paralyzed his senses, already numb with sorrow and desire. "Prepare a hot bath for me," he said, again with that alarming gentleness. "I am freezing."

After Yuriko had prepared the bath, she bowed farewell to her lover and thanked him formally for the attention he had paid to her worthless person.

"*Arigato*," she whispered, smiling. In this context the word im-

plied that Yuriko felt grief because she had so much to express gratitude for and now had an *on*—a high obligation of which she was not
worthy—toward her benefactor. This Japanese *on* was like a cold
which, once caught, cannot be shaken off.

"*Arigato*," Yuriko repeated with a stiff bow, while her heart ached.
Oh, how hard it was to thank your lover and not to molest him with
importunate passion!

In her Western costume Yuriko went out of the White Chrysanthemum, where only a few Japanese officers were staying now. Young
Chinese marched by with their paper dragons, singing. Yuriko shivered in spite of the sultry heat of early August. She felt as cold as
though Akiro-san had shaken a handful of the snow of Hirayama
upon her heart.

As Yuriko entered her plane next day, American Superfortresses
were annihilating the remnants of the Japanese Navy in the Sea of
Japan. It was still several days before Nippon's unconditional surrender. During that period a great many enemies continued to be
annihilated—and in the days that followed the surrender also. For
when the political power of a nation passes to others, the process is
not usually conducted with too great circumspection.

On August 17, 1945, Vivica awoke in a strange room. She screamed
in fright. Where were Dr. Yamato and his gentle wife? Where were
the fireworks, the darkness, the meadow morphine had created for
her?

Someone bent over her. "Don't be afraid. Everything is all right.
You are free."

Vivica shrank in fear, as one always does in the presence of
unhoped-for freedom, and momentarily recognized Mr. Chou Tso-
ling, who stood by her bed beside an American in uniform, in the
old-fashioned house back of Bubbling Well Road.

"Give her time, Mr. Chou," Dr. Timothy Williams said. "She is still
suffering from the effect of the shock. Her mind is wandering, but
she's young. She'll be all right."

The young army doctor gazed at Vivica out of grave but humor-
ous eyes. He had never seen a more beautiful girl. By background
and education Dr. Williams had no taste for triumphant Aphrodites;
he gave them a wide berth. But he found suffering Aphrodites over-

whelming. What an enchanting face, with its rounded childlike forehead, the pure contours of indestructible beauty, the rose-red, softly
swelling lips, and the faint shadow of vexation and melancholy.

"What is her name?" he asked. Told it, he showed surprise and
recognition. "The Wergelands are a fine old family in Trondheim,"
he explained to Mr. Chou. "My grandmother came from Tröndelag.
Her people were foresters who emigrated to America. Doesn't Miss
Wergeland have any relations here, Mr. Chou?"

"We are expecting her sister any moment. I have had her hiding
with Chinese friends of her childhood. And there is also Miss Helene
Wergeland, her aunt. The Kempetai refused to give her a permit to
travel to Shanghai, but now we are expecting her any day. I sent
word to her at once that both her nieces are alive."

"How old is this girl, Mr. Chou?"

"Nineteen, I believe."

Vivica stirred. She was still dressed in Madame Yamato's pink
kimono. At the risk of their lives the Japanese couple had brought
her to Mr. Chou after the Emperor announced over the radio that
the holy war was over. Dr. Yamato had remembered meeting Mrs.
Hanna Chou at the Zabelsdorfs when he went there with Monsignore
de Lavalette to discuss the possibility of rescuing Vivica. Tso-ling
had looked thoughtfully after him as the ugly little man in the dreadful cutaway departed. Men *were* brothers after all, although for
decades everything had conspired to prove that they were not! He
had offered Dr. Yamato the protection of the name of Chou, but the
little doctor had smilingly refused. He wanted no protection, no ex-
ceptional position among his hated and outlawed countrymen. That
would have been a breach of propriety.

"You are with friends, Vivica," murmured Chou Tso-ling, who had
the quiet Japanese doctor to thank for the lifting of the burden on
his conscience. How could he ever have permitted a child to play
ball with the terrestrial globe?

"We are expecting your Aunt Helene," Tso-ling said insistently,
trying to catch Vivica's eye.

"Aunt Helene?" Vivica asked. "Who is that?"

7: *Variations of Power*

Vivica was once again living through an interrogation by Major-san when Miss Wergeland and Astrid entered her room in the Chous' home. Vivica walked stiffly from the door to the bed, bowed, walked from bed to door, and bowed again. When she caught sight of Helene Wergeland she fled to the bed and hid her head in the pillow.

"She doesn't know you, Aunt Helene!" Astrid had tears in her eyes. "She *wants* to dream."

Miss Wergeland, who never dreamed, said nothing. She stood stock still at the door for a moment, then slowly approached the figure cowering on the bed. The months of separation, and concern over the fate of her nieces, had engraved deep lines in her face, but her tall, commanding figure was unbent, and in her steel-blue eyes flashed the determination to put an end to this nonsense. She still did not know how she was going to bring Vivica to her senses, but she was certain she would find out. "Leave us alone, Astrid," she said quietly.

There was deep silence after Astrid had left. Miss Wergeland continued to stand in the middle of the room, unstirring and unfrightened. Vivica looked up, brushed her gleaming hair back from her forehead, and then went slowly up to her aunt. Something about this lady seemed familiar; not for nothing had Helene been the protective spirit of her childhood. Perhaps, too, something of the silent and forbearing love which emanated from Helene, in spite of the sternness in her eyes, reached the girl.

Vivica bowed stiffly from the waist, as Major-san had taught her to do, and looked at Helene. At that moment she had Borghild's look —harried, perplexed, indescribably lonely. Her lips moved, but no sound came from them. She again brushed her hand over her forehead and murmured plaintively, "I have a headache, Madame. A terrible headache!"

She had spoken French. For a moment Helene was struck dumb;

then she said in Norwegian, "You are tired, Vivie! I'll put you to bed." She spoke imploringly, but behind her words were all her matter-of-fact love and pedagogic experience. This was her old formula, what she used to say when Vivica as a child cried out over some dream.

"Yes—very tired." The words were only breathed. Vivie came hesitantly closer, staring at Helene. Into her vacant gaze came a first, tremulous look of recognition, a light that flickered and might go out again at any moment.

Vivica gave a loud scream, which shook even Helene, who ordinarily could take any noises. "Aunt Helene!" she screamed, opening her eyes wide. "Why did you go away?"

"I am with you now, Vivie," Helene Wergeland said quietly.

Vivica threw her arms around her, and Helene carried the big girl like a child over to the bed in her strong arms. She undressed her and put her, with many a headshake, into the pink kimono, since she found nothing else in the wardrobe. Vivica seemed to have fallen asleep. Helene sat upright beside her bed for one hour—two hours. . . . Now it was seven in the evening. Once Vivica put out her hand, quiveringly, uncertainly, terribly frightened of the emptiness. But the big reassuring hand immediately touched hers.

"Are you staying with me?" Vivica asked as she had asked as a child.

Helene held that trembling hand and bent silently over the sick girl. Vivica laid her silver-blond hair back on the pillow and drew the kind hand to her lips.

"Stop this nonsense, Vivie," Helene said in a choking voice. She stood up, intending to go to the door. Vivie and she must have something to eat. And Astrid must lend the child a proper nightgown. But she did not reach the door. Vivica came flying out of bed, rushed to the door, spread out both her arms, and blocked the way.

"What is the meaning of this nonsense, Vivie?" Helene said, although she knew perfectly well.

"You must not go away, Madame. Major-san takes everyone away from me. First Halvard . . ." Big tears ran down her wasted cheeks.

"Don't you have a handkerchief, child?" Helene took out her own handkerchief and dried Vivica's tears. She discovered a bell and pressed the button.

"I think—I love you, Madame!"

"Of course we love each other, Vivie. Would you like something to eat?" As she spoke, Helene guided Vivica back to the bed. Vivica shook her head. She did not want to eat, only drink something, hold that kind hand, and dream. . . .

The door opened gently. Astrid appeared, accompanied by a middle-aged Chinese woman—Yumei's elder sister, who had guarded Missie Astrid so loyally during the last critical weeks. She wanted to greet Miss Wergeland now. On a lacquer tray she brought her gifts —heavily sugared cakes, fruit and a pretty, cheap ivory necklace for Third Sister, whom the spirits were mistreating. Yumei's sister knelt down before Miss Wergeland and held out the welcoming gifts. She spoke in a hoarse, affectionate, submissive voice, like Yumei.

Vivica lay relaxed in bed. But the voices aroused her. She started up, clung, trembling, to Helene, and screamed when she caught sight of Yumei's sister. She was overcome by something that overcame thousands of Westerners in hospitals after the end of Japanese rule; an Asian face drove them frantic, even when it was as kind and friendly a face as that of Yumei's elder sister.

"Send her away," Vivica whispered. "I don't know anything. I . . . can't . . . tell her . . ." She sobbed wildly. For the first time she had spoken in Norwegian; quivering, she hid behind Helene. Yumei's sister had turned pale. Never had she been so offended, never had she lost so much face in a moment. She had not understood a word of the Norwegian, but the wild horror in Vivica's eyes and the frightened gestures were plain enough. Well, if the foreign devils did not want her and trampled on her gifts—Vivica had just thrown the ivory necklace out of the window—Black Jade knew what she must do. An unfavorable wind blew here.

Black Jade bowed first to Helene and then to Astrid. With downcast eyes she murmured that she would go now to cook the evening rice for her family. Every word cost her enormous effort, but she spoke quietly and with dignity while Vivica screamed that she would tell the spy whom Major-san had sent nothing at all. Black Jade added something else to the effect that the good understood one another silently, while the wicked bellowed like buffaloes at the good, and made her last bow.

Helene and Astrid had listened in silence, for to interrupt Black Jade, who had donned her finest dress for this visit, would have been an unforgivable breach of manners. But when Yumei's elder sister was finished and looked up expectantly at the foreign women—she had no intention of leaving the house with such a loss of face, and expected solemn apologies and a bowl of tea—Miss Wergeland said she must pay no attention to Vivie's nonsense, the girl was sick, and besides a very favorable wind blew here. Whereupon she opened the door and called in a stentorian voice for tea and sweets. Astrid meanwhile ran out into the garden to rescue the ivory necklace.

In the end reparation was made for the insult. Black Jade accepted the apology, and Vivica smiled sweetly at her. She had at last grasped that this rotund, friendly Chinese woman meant well by her. Now that her doses of morphine had been discontinued, since there was no longer any possibility of her being returned to the Kempetai, the veil over her mind was gradually clearing.

"She must stay," Vivica murmured when Black Jade began seriously considering going home. But Yumei's sister said gently that the ivory necklace—she mentioned the price of it, of course—would be staying with Little Third Sister in her place. It was settled, however, that Black Jade would share the care of Vivica with Helene and Astrid, and Helene promised her preposterously high tea-money for a daily massage.

At that moment the door opened, and Mr. Chou Tso-ling introduced to the ladies Captain Timothy Williams, who evidently was in charge in Shanghai of rehabilitation of Americans and Europeans freed from Japanese imprisonment. Dr. Williams' grandparents, he said, came from the Trondheim region and still spoke Norwegian at home in America. Captain Williams himself said that unfortunately he did not speak Norwegian, but was planning to visit the old country as soon as he had a leave.

Helene felt an instant confidence in the young army doctor. In the course of the conversation Captain Williams explained who the mysterious Halvard was—in case Miss Vivica should speak of him again.

"Will she recover?" Helene asked hoarsely.

"She ought to be taken away from the Far East as soon as possible,

Miss Wergeland. As a matter of fact, she is in much better shape than many of the men. I've seen cases of mental shock among soldiers—"

He broke off, his eyes clouding. Women, oddly enough, could endure far more than men. His eyes lingered on Vivica's face.

Miss Wergeland told him that she intended to take Vivica back to Norway as soon as possible. She was only waiting until Hanna Chou came from Soochow and Mailin from liberated Singapore.

The evening of that eventful day, Astrid sat up late with Helene, who planned to sleep in Vivica's room. A new intimacy had been created between them. Helene thought Knut's eldest daughter was altered, although she did not quite see how. At last she asked whether Astrid had heard anything from Pierre de Maury. Suddenly there was a wall between them again. Astrid, who in the solitude of her cell had vowed to exercise patience and charity toward all, even Pierre de Maury, drew herself up and said that she never wished to see or hear from Monsieur de Maury again. Whereupon Helene took a plump letter from her pocket; it had reached her in northern Siam a few days after the Japanese capitulation. "Monsieur de Maury wrote you a letter from French Laos a few days after the armistice. He is the guest there of some Excellency So-and-so."

Astrid turned fiery red, snatched the letter from her aunt, and read the envelope, full of secret terror that it might be meant for Vivica. But now— She thrust it into the pocket of her beautifully cut sports dress and prepared to continue the conversation as if nothing had happened.

But Helene took in the situation. The flush that had suddenly made Astrid look very young had not escaped her. She yawned aloud without embarrassment and said she was going to turn in; she had had enough for one day, and there was the Zabelsdorf family to call on first thing in the morning. Astrid informed her that Anna and the children were safely in Soochow, and that for the present her friend Ernst August had been placed under house-arrest by the Allies. No one was permitted to visit him.

So in her private domain Helene discovered how great a turn the stage had taken in the Far East. Japanese were no longer to be seen on the streets. Many had vanished into camps or transport ships.

Later they would be haled before war-crimes tribunals. Japanese en-
listed men and small businessmen were working for the occupation
forces; they prepared the hotels and houses of the former Japanese
rulers for the present victors; they carried water and coal, scrubbed
the decks of ships, and bowed humbly before the masters of the
hour in their spruce uniforms. The White Chrysanthemum had been
turned into an American officers' club. Captain Williams now occupied Major Matsubara's rooms, after "his boys" had trampled on the
scrolls and smashed the vases and china. A volume of poetry containing some famous *haikku* was used as toilet paper by the good
Yankees. Major Matsubara had been arrested so suddenly that he
was cheated of the chance for the ceremonial *seppuku,* the *samurai*
suicide. Later this was banned by the Emperor. Colonel Saito, of
course, did not for a moment consider suicide. That was a mortal
sin. Both officers were aboard a transport to Tokyo, while jazz blared
in the White Chrysanthemum and photographs of Hollywood stars
hung in the honored wall niches. The vicissitudes of power affected
even the art treasures of the defeated nation—in fact, wreaked havoc
among them. What the occupation troops did not destroy in the first
flush of victory was smashed by the celebrating Chinese.

Japanese to whom life was dear in spite of the defeat were at the
moment safest in Allied prisons. Their businesses were taken over
and, against the will of the Allies, plundered by the Chinese. Japanese and German firms had had their day, like the Japanese and
Germans themselves.

The night after Helene's arrival Vivica started up out of sleep.
Instantly Helene was at her bedside. Vivica looked at her quietly
and dreamily and declared that she must get dressed at once and
go to take Halvard, her little companion, out of prison.

Helene Wergeland had fought a good deal in her life, but she
had never been pitted against a creature of the imagination. However, she did not say that Vivica was dreaming or talking silly nonsense; that would only have disturbed the girl more. Instead, she
pressed Vivica gently but firmly back into her pillows, went to the
washstand, and mixed a powder which the nice American with the
Norwegian grandmother had left with her for just such occasions.

"What is this?"

"Drink it, Vivie," Helene ordered. Vivica obeyed, but she never-theless wanted to get up and rescue Halvard. He was so droll and sang so nicely. She wept bitter tears because Aunt Helene—whom she had at last really recognized—would not let her go to Halvard.

"Tomorrow, child," Helene said in a smothered voice. "We will go together for Halvard tomorrow. I promise you."

This was a magic formula. Reassured, Vivica closed her eyes and lay back. Aunt Helene had never broken a promise.

Dr. Yamato and his wife had listened in utter consternation to the Tenno's message. They did not think of themselves but of their pa-tients. Fortunately they had removed the Norwegian girl to Mr. Chou's house in good time. Now they sat on two cushions to either side of a low lacquer table, and Madame Yamato prepared the tea in formal, lovely ceremony, as she had learned to do at home. The doctor had discarded his cutaway, which he used for his visits, and was relaxing in a kimono of heavy, dark silk. It conferred a quiet dignity upon him. Rumors were sprouting everywhere through the stone pavements of the familiar city, which for the Yamatos had sud-denly become alien and hostile. But it would have been contrary to etiquette to discuss any such unpleasant topics as the variations of power during the tea hour. The tea ceremony was a creative and refreshing pause for the Yamatos, even in these evil days. In the *tokonoma* Madame Yamato had hung a scroll which accorded with the present Japanese mood of "rain in the heart": it showed sacred Mount Fuji in misty rain. The picture signified that the noble per-son preserves his bearing even in misfortune, as Mount Fuji remains beautiful in the rain.

After the tea Madame Yamato withdrew, with a little bow, to the kitchen to supervise the preparation of diet foods for the patients. Dr. Yamato remained alone in the light, almost empty room. He took from his kimono a small volume, the writings of St. Thérèse of Lisieux, that *minomushi*-insect among the saints of the Church, and with reverence and joy applied himself to the perceptions of that gentle, loving spirit. He sat with his back to the sliding door of the tea room, and his mind was shut to all noises and disturb-ances. That was how he was found by the Chinese soldiers who, intoxicated with victory, had broken into the Japanese hospital. Dr. Yamato rose slowly and walked, the book in his small, bony hand, to the door in order to get dressed and submit to arrest. Not to greet the intruders in his house dress was pure Japanese courtesy. First one dressed properly, and only then returned to greet friend or foe with a respectful bow. Perhaps it was fundamental ignorance on the part of the young Chinese officers who ought to have arrested him, perhaps the wild high spirits of victory. In any case, the manner in which Dr. Yamato attempted to pass quietly along, without a word, as though they were not in the room—they who now held the power—threw the Chinese officers into a blind rage. One of them tugged at Dr. Yamato's kimono so that he stumbled and fell; a second kicked him in the face. Covered with blood, he felt the broken glass of his spectacles in his eyes and groped, half blinded, with his right hand for the consecrated medallion which Monsignore de Lavalette had brought him from Rome years ago. His left hand held fast to the writings of the holy *minomushi*-insect. So he lay when the bullet from the Chinese victor's pistol struck him.

Dr. Yamato smiled as the merciful darkness closed above his head. It was only a short way to the light, and the saint of Lisieux was guiding him.

Ernst August von Zabelsdorf had never been so lonely in his life. Anna and the children had not yet returned from Soochow. Only Right Arm was still with him, trying to make Master "happy." Lifu cooked all his favorite foods, which Master choked down in order to please the boy. Since their memorable talk, Chou Tso-ling had not put in an appearance. And now Ernst August was under house-arrest until he was shipped home or transferred to a Shanghai prison. He made no attempt to go out, although the house in the French Concession was unguarded. This was because of Tso-ling's intervention with the Allied authorities. But in the first few weeks after the victory there had been so much for Mr. Chou to arrange and intervene in that he could do no more for his German friend. He had seen to Ernst's safety and that of his family, although at the moment the only guarantees of that safety were the name of Chou and Right Arm. Right Arm even refused to admit Miss Wergeland and Astrid because he was convinced that the "victor devils" would attempt to poison Master. It did not dawn on Lifu that he himself was one of the victors. He served Master, as he was accustomed to do, and desired nothing else. He did not think of the future at all; a sensible Chinese left that to take care of itself.

Master was lying on the couch, thinking about his girl child Luise, when three Chinese youths in uniform burst through the door of the apartment without asking the boy for permission. Right Arm promptly brandished the Chinese letter signed by Chou Tso-ling. It bore the stamp of the Allied military authorities and stated in plain Chinese and English that Ernst August, Baron von Zabelsdorf, was to remain unharmed in his home until his deportation. The first soldier spat at the sheet of paper, the second laughed heartily, and the third thrust his way onward, waving a loaded revolver. To the right of the vestibule the master of the house lay dozing in his room; to the left, at the end of the corridor, was the nursery. Ernst August awoke with a start when he heard the shrill voice of Lifu, and the laughter and stamping of the soldiers, who were apparently enjoying a private joke. Someone had told them that a German was still sitting around free in this flat.

His long legs carried Zabelsdorf in two strides to the nursery, from which the commotion was coming. He had no weapons, only his left arm and his anger. The nursery was chaos. At this moment the second soldier, who was the jester of the group, picked up Luise's doll, which had been forgotten in the haste of the flight to Soochow. Chortling, he held it up for the third soldier to shoot. It was nothing but a boyish joke, but to Ernst August von Zabelsdorf the doll Mathilde with her long braids somehow became one with his daughter Luise. He stood poised for a moment, and his long, intelligent horse-face flushed. A vein on his high forehead seemed about to burst. At this moment the shot was fired, knocking the doll's head with the braids, into which Luise had lovingly twined light blue hair ribbons, from the stiff sawdust body.

In one stride Master reached the soldier. Without thinking of the consequences, he snatched the pistol out of the young Chinese boy's hand and shouted, *"Lümmel! Rotzlöffel, verfluchter!"*

He shouted in German, for in rage and in dreams a man uses his mother tongue. Then he began slapping the "lout" with his left hand. His breath gave out. An inarticulate sound burst from him. He saw red, he saw purple, he was once again the wild young Zabelsdorf he had once been. Too much was too much! No snot-nosed brat was going to touch his girl's doll, not if they had won the war a thousand times over and were making mincemeat of the damfool Germans. When all that inarticulate sound had come out of him, fearfully low-pitched and soft, he reached his left arm clumsily out for support. For everything was whirling around in his head and vanishing behind veils. He was not fainting—that kind of thing didn't happen to a Zabelsdorf, did it?—but he was falling, tipping over, first his head and then his long legs, and then he was not there any more. . . .

He came to with a jerk and struggled to rise from Anna's chair. Why, he was still in the nursery. And there was the doll Mathilde without a head. But, after all, that happens to most dolls sooner or later. The three musketeers were standing, abashed, in the corner, and the boy, Lifu, was giving a regular Chinese theatrical performance. He was talking away at his fellow countrymen without pause for commas or periods—Chinese are laconic only in Hollywood movies. Ernst August made out "Shanghai 'thirty-seven" and the splendid, dusty legend of "Master's right arm." The number of families and man children Master had rescued from burning homes increased by the score. The soldiers bowed, smiled foolishly, and withdrew.

Lifu brought black coffee and a flask of whisky; then he fetched glue and they tried to repair little Missie's doll. The boy smiled the soul out of his body, only to sniff and snuffle as soon as Master looked away. And here the fellow had just gone and won World War Number Two; he ought to be laughing. But Lifu looked at Master like a dying swan, and then he went on with the gluing, following Master's honorable instructions precisely.

So Astrid and Chou Tso-ling found the two of them when they came tearing in two hours later. Astrid, after being turned away, had driven straight to Tso-ling at the Chinese Chamber of Commerce and had informed him that everything had worked out as agreed, but that Lifu had refused to let anyone into the apartment. He had waved an ancient revolver in front of her nose and roared out that no one would poison or kidnap Master as long as Lifu . . . and so on. And now Astrid was back with her news, and Chou Tso-ling with her. For she had had an idea, although she maintained that she never had ideas. She had gone with Mr. Chou to Allied headquarters and there professed that Herr von Zabelsdorf had for months intervened with the Kempetai in behalf of the Wergeland sisters, who were merely friends of his friend Hanna Chou—yes, of course, a Madame Chou of the famous Chous, her husband had just received a decoration—in other words, the gentleman from Potsdam had risked his own security constantly for an Allied family that had fallen into the clutches of the Kempetai. The result was that Herr von Zabelsdorf would be allowed to leave freely on a Norwegian freighter in one week. The ship's captain was Vivica's uncle, Captain Lillesand. Astrid explained all this in French to her German friend and protector, who had unexpectedly become someone she could protect. Meanwhile Tso-ling was explaining the business to Lifu in Chinese.

Then there was a pause, because all had to stop for breath. For a while Ernst August von Zabelsdorf said nothing, and still nothing. So he would see his Anna and the kids again. The Zabelsdorfs were getting out of the inferno of victory with whole skins. There stood Chou Tso-ling and Astrid, catching their breath after their joyous orations. And Ernst August, who as a Berliner usually had three answers to every remark, said not a single word, only looked dazedly from Astrid to Chou Tso-ling and back again.

At last he held out to Astrid the doll's body and the head. "Those soldier boys have made mincemeat out of Mathilde. Do you think you could glue her up, Mademoiselle Astrid?"

That was all Herr von Zabelsdorf could think to say at a moment that called for fancy speeches of gratitude. But Astrid knew the doll Mathilde; she had sewed a good many clothes for her and knew that Mathilde was part of the family. In her elegant suit and witty hat, which had a touch of the Chinese about it, Astrid sat down on the floor beside the pot of glue and began expertly putting Mathilde's component parts together. That was how Ernst August von Zabelsdorf remembered Shanghai—a good and consoling picture to carry back with him out of the witches' caldron of unconditional mess.

Vivica had improved amazingly from week to week. Helene, Astrid, and Mailin could at last begin to think of leaving for Bangkok.

There the Wergelands would have to part, hard though it was for them. Mailin would return to her family in Singapore. Astrid, after the dissolution of the household and her office, would go to Paris for good. There she intended to open a milliner's salon together with Amélie Clermont's friend—she was and would always remain more French than Norwegian. And Helene and Vivica would return to Trondheim.

Their final night in Shanghai was drawing closer. They were still staying at the Chous', in the huge house back of Bubbling Well Road, and Hanna pampered them all. Captain Williams, the young army doctor, was also a constant guest in the Chou household. With natural heartiness and naïve amazement—for the first time he was meeting Europeans and Chinese in the Far East—he entered into the strange and complicated family life of the Wergelands. Without incident he had helped move Anna von Zabelsdorf and her charming children to Shanghai, and put the whole Zabelsdorf family on the ship bound for their shattered native land. All his primer conceptions of "friend" and "foe" had gone to pieces in these last hectic weeks. In the Chou house eagle and dove, friend and foe, lived with dignity and affection their unimpaired private lives.

But the magnet that drew Captain Williams to the Chou house was Vivica, who had been transformed with astonishing rapidity from a suffering to a victorious Aphrodite. Captain Williams, it is true, was scarcely aware of this change; in the proper New England town where he had been born, women were only mothers, teachers, sisters, and sisters' girl friends. Hitherto he had not encountered Aphrodites of Vivica's fantastic and highly dangerous attractiveness; he had more or less assumed that only "bad girls" possessed such charms.

Mailin amazed him most of all; in the United States "Chinks" were not related to families like the Wergelands. Captain Williams thought Mailin "sweet," but he wondered nevertheless. Consul Wergeland, the deceased father of these young ladies, must have been a gay dog. Then again, he was surprised by Helene Wergeland; the austere old maid literally blossomed in Mailin's company and spent every free minute with her favorite niece.

Every Saturday, Tim, as they already called him, had gone dancing with Vivica. And now the last Saturday had come. Dr. Timothy

Williams was an excellent dancer, although in ordinary life he was likely to bump into things and knock down objects that stood around a room; he was adroit only with instruments in the operating room. But music released something deep and vital, something almost savage, in his tamed American soul. His intelligent, pensive eyes, which sometimes looked a little sad, shone whenever the music began. Dancing, Timothy H. Williams was a changed man, for all his rather disturbing habit of humming the idiotic tunes the band was playing. As they danced he would hold Vivica tightly, as if he did not want to let her go again. And Vivica's strange eyes smiled at him—unmoved, frivolous, tempting, and deep.

While the Chinese population of Shanghai in this "Month of the Chrysanthemum" listened to the autumnal melodies of the crickets or the rustling of leaves in the old-fashioned gardens of the city, swing bands played it hot in the former Japanese White Chrysanthemum, now the American officers' club. A few influential Chinese were always invited, but they never came. Only elegant young ladies—the Chinese variety of "bad girls"—danced in high-collared Shanghai brocades with the officers of the United States Army. The men received a shock every time they chanced to look down from the severe high-buttoned throats of the ladies and observed the generously slit skirts. Oh, boy! they thought, and tried to make something out of the deadly earnest expressions of their dancing partners. They all had the uncomfortable feeling that the womenfolk back home would not like these Chinese girls in their clever outfits. For that matter, Timothy Williams thought as he looked down on Vivica's silvery-blond hair—he was a head taller than the Norwegian Aphrodite—that the youngest Miss Wergeland would not be regarded with approval in the Women's Literary Club of his native Concord, New Hampshire. For a second his eyes became lost in the shimmering depths of hers; then he pulled himself together, blinked humorously, and hummed the tune. He was probably off his rocker if he at twenty-eight even conceived of transplanting this nineteen-year-old package of beauty, dreaminess, and temptation back to his mother and his elder sister in Concord. To be sure, Dr. Margaret Williams was a little eccentric herself, but in a wholly staid and dreamless way.

"Why are you so silent, Tim?" Vivica broke in upon his thoughts. He pressed her as closely as one could a dream from Norway without making it dissolve into mist.

"Are you going to miss me, baby?" he asked somewhat hoarsely. His dark eyes, with the crinkles of laughter in the corners and the touch of wildness the music inspired, probed her face for brief seconds. He did not want to admit to himself that the reply mattered to him.

"Of course," Vivica said. "It's been very nice with you, Tim darling!"

It was ridiculous how deeply this answer disappointed him. The lines of worry on his forehead—a heritage from his Scottish father, who had been a minister in Concord—deepened. He smiled painfully, a mere shadow of the warmhearted smile that generally won him the affection of others. Well, a fool remained a fool, back home and in Shanghai. He had nursed Vivica back to mental health patiently and competently. From the start her body had needed no repairs; it had triumphed over brutality and danger. Aphrodite is really made of iron; the delicate dreaminess conceals an invulnerable robustness that will be the ruin of generations of adorers, Timothy Williams thought in a moment of amazing clairvoyance.

Aloud, he said, "Shall we have dinner now?"

Captain Williams' rendezvous with Aphrodite probably would have been without consequences if it had not occurred to the boy to serve a Japanese dinner for "Master Captain Williams and Lady" in the only purely Japanese room left in the White Chrysanthemum. The Chinese boy had found out that the Americans were glad for a whiff of Japanese culture "just for the hell of it," now that Japan was conquered. For this reason a Japanese cook was still working in a corner of the hotel kitchen, preparing with a humble smile all the delicacies the honored victors ordered. Captain Williams had simply requested "dinner in a private room" and left everything else to the Number One Boy of the club. Since one of the higher officers of the United States Army had pronounced that Japanese scrolls and lacquer bowls had no connection with politics, Room Number Seven had been spared pin-up girls and bright lights. Naturally, neither the boy nor Captain Williams knew that Vivica had dined in this very room with Major Matsubara only a few months ago. Captain Williams, from her delirious ravings, had heard enough to conceive a deep distaste for Baron Matsubara. He had never seen the man, however; Matsubara was already one of a shipload of war criminals on the way to Tokyo when Captain Williams arrived in Shanghai.

Vivica was surprised to find an Asian room in the American officers' club, but not in the least disturbed. She had been brought to the place late at night in a curtained car, and had been carried away unconscious. Even a less abstracted girl than she might, in these circumstances, not have recognized the Oriental room at once.

"Are you looking forward to Norway?" Tim asked; he had already surveyed the menu, printed on silk, and had ordered a select dinner.

"It will be a change, anyway," Vivica replied blithely. She loved change above all else, and obviously had not had enough of it. "But I don't know how long I am going to be able to endure Aunt Helene's women's village. *Only* women and children—isn't that dreadful?"

Captain Williams learned that Villa Wergeland was a home for unmarried mothers, but that Helene, her family, and her friends would continue to occupy the west wing. He found it hard to conceive of Vivica in this "women's village."

"Then you do need a man to be happy?" he teased.

"To be amused," Vivica corrected him, smiling like a *vagabonde* with a hundred years' experience. Her blond locks had fallen forward over her forehead, giving her a faint air of irresistible negligence. She looked at Tim out of the corners of her eyes—tempting, untouched, just a bit cunning. He wanted to kiss her or to spank her. The girl aroused elemental passions in him. Did she know it?

The boy brought in more lacquer bowls. They contained the delicious *nishime*—chopped pork with carrots, bamboo sprouts, and taro roots in soy sauce—as well as Major Matsubara's favorite dish, *maki-zushi*—rice cakes with red ginger, pieces of eel, and vegetables encased in fried seaweed. Vivica ate the first bites of *maki-zushi* pensively and murmured, "I've tasted this before. It's—it's a Ja—a Japanese food."

The atmosphere of the room underwent some change.

"Don't you like it, Vivica?"

Vivica had turned deathly pale. She swayed faintly in her bamboo seat and looked around like one who had plunged head first from ordinary, pleasant reality into a dark, nightmarish cellar. Wordlessly she stared at the paper walls, the sliding doors, and the wall niche, whose scroll showed a wild and decorative warrior scene. Then she stood up slowly and walked unsteadily toward the picture, which projected the same force and diabolic quality it had possessed during that frightful dinner with Major-san. Her eyes became fixed and vacant. She quivered like bamboo in the wind. From the picture Major-san sprang at her, a tiger in *samurai* costume. His pupils had slid to the farthest corners of his eyes; the whites gleamed like those of a blind man or an epileptic. But his sensual and yet ascetic lips smiled and twisted in shame and unspeakable grief. Vivica stood with closed eyes. In a moment Major-san would kneel down before her and pay homage to her beauty by shrill whispers and a single fiery look—homage to her beauty and the violence of his volcanic and unsatiated desire.

She must have stood before the scroll for only a few seconds. Captain Williams had leaped to his feet, knocking over the saké bottle and a lacquer box filled with *daiku*—large Japanese radishes and raisins pickled in brine—and had gripped Vivica's shoulders.

"Vivica, for heaven's sake, wake up!"

Vivica opened her nymph's eyes, saw the tall, straight—outwardly and inwardly—man before her, and began to laugh. How funny Tim was—for this was certainly good Uncle Timothy from New Hampshire, U.S.A. How indescribably funny the men of the West were —naïve, good, cold-blooded as fishes! Their glances trickled off a girl like raindrops against a window pane. Such glances had no power. Such men respected woman. Oh, it was too funny!

"Wake up, Vivica," Captain Williams was saying. "Good Lord, what is it, kid?"

Yes, it was Tim, who danced so well and was so inconceivably kind and patient with her. Vivica wanted to tell him how grateful she was, and assure him that she really did not like to be on intimate terms with chaos. But unfortunately she could not say it because she had to laugh, because she was after all not like other girls. She would never marry, for she would always have to laugh at the thought that Tim and other Western men had Coca-Cola or tea in their veins.

Naturally Vivie did not want to laugh. She was awfully fond of Tim, and he had given her so much of his time. He had a wonderful calming effect on her, and he could dance too. Dancing, he seemed closer to her; but that was only fun. One did not live and marry in order to dance. That much Vivie knew, although she was neither so intelligent nor so much of a duchess as Astrid, nor so kindly and stern as Aunt Helene. Vivie had suspected all along that Tim had marriage in the back of his mind. Otherwise a man would not be constantly telling a girl about his home town and his mother and his rather terrifying elder sister, Dr. Margaret Williams, who had made a "success" out of life and was recognized as the best doctor in Concord, for all that she was a woman. Vivica hated the word "success," which Tim and other Americans seemed to be so fond of.

Suddenly Vivica felt terribly embarrassed at this compulsion to laugh when Tim was so concerned and so loving. There were so many kinds of love in this world, after all. With what infinite kindness and concern he was looking at her now, and brushing the hair back from her forehead. Any other girl would have been mad with joy if a fine fellow like Timothy Williams had given his heart to her. The girls in Concord had undoubtedly been wild about him—with the consequence that he shied away from marriage. But Vivica was not like other girls. And only Aunt Helene knew this and watched out for her and gave Vivica a helping hand whenever she started to slide toward the abyss and covertly look around for Halvard, her little friend. . . .

In successive waves, the spasms of laughter shook Vivie; she gurgled, panted, and coughed, and her eyes filled with tears from laughing so hard. Then came the painful hiccup which had driven Major-san to the point of madness in this very room a few months ago. (A hiccup was in the first place a violation of perfect beauty; then, coming from a woman, it was far too loud and presumptuous, an insult to the man-god who commanded all the power, all the laughter, and all the gifts of love.) And now here was Vivica's presumptuous hiccuping again—but Dr. Williams simply pounded her on the back, held her arms up in the air like a puppet's, and murmured with patient concern, "There, there . . . darling!" And be-

cause he was so dear and kind, Vivica had to stop panting and
moaning out of sheer astonishment. The releasing tears came like a
gentle wave at evening. Suddenly her head lay still against Tim's
broad chest, and once more everything was quiet and pleasant in
the White Chrysanthemum—which was still not entirely a genuine
American officers' club, for all that the Stars and Stripes waved
above the entrance, the light was too bright, a swing band played
in the dining room, and such typical victors' foods as ice cream and
hamburgers appeared on the menu.

Vivica lay like an utterly weary child against Tim's chest. The fit
was over, and amid her tears she looked at him so gratefully that it
cut him to the quick. "Baby . . ." he murmured. She threw her arms
around him, and her silver-blond hair, a gleaming dream-web, became misted before his eyes. "What is all this silliness?" he asked
softly. He wanted to make a joke of the whole thing, but he did
not succeed. Vivie looked up at him. No woman had ever looked
at him that way. Was Aphrodite a "bad girl" after all? But he could
not resist that look; Borghild's forlornness and Vivica's own fire were
in it. And Tim by no means had Coca-Cola in his veins, as Vivie
had imagined.

"What are you thinking of, Tim?" Vivie asked, gasping. Those
were not weak-tea kisses. Vivie was a silly young goose; she had no
experience with men. With Monsieur de Maury she had purred like
a kitten; next she had flirted with a volcano. But she still knew nothing about love, above all not about the kind of love of which poets
may not sing but by which women live, that homely and unexciting
love which radiates consolation and good-humored forbearance, and
which is the grand prize in the marital race.

Vivica felt that homely love when, after his first kisses, Tim gently
put her down on the couch in the corner, once again brushed the
unruly locks back from her forehead, and then fed her tea and rice
by the spoonful. He held her icy hand warmly and firmly in his big,
reliable doctor's paw. Something in his eyes told her that he would
unhesitatingly lay down his life if that could make her tranquil and
happy. She *was* his life, and finally he told her so. She had been that
from the first moment he saw her in the Chou house, lying helpless
and with her mind wandering. And she would always be that, even
when she was older and her hair had lost its sheen and her eyes

the compelling power of Aphrodite. In sickness and in health, for better and for worse, Tim would guard her and keep her and love her.

"We'll be married as soon as possible," he said finally, knocking over the last of the lacquer bowls. Vivica nodded. It was wonderful to be protected by Tim, even nicer than being protected by Aunt Helene—or at least more fun! What would Aunt Helene say to her engagement? And—Major-san?

But Major-san was no more than a shadow on a scroll in a niche, and shadows no longer had power over Vivica since she had felt Tim's kisses and discovered a new kind of masculine love. She snuggled close to him and smiled.

"I'll stay with you forever," she whispered. In her nymph's eyes there was an unmistakable invitation.

Captain Williams jumped up so hastily that he knocked over the vase of flowers beside the couch.

"Come, darling, I'll take you back to the Villa Chou now."

Timothy Williams of Concord, New Hampshire, had taken the considerable risk of planning a marriage with Aphrodite. He had the necessary strength and maturity, as well as that homely warmth which is needed to carry off the grand prize in the marital race. He was prepared to put up with Vivica's moods, to comb her locks out of her eyes, and to pull her back again and again from the abyss to reality; he was ready to guard and keep her and to give his life for her at any suitable or unsuitable moment. But to sleep with her before the wedding—that he would not do! That would have meant striking up a grievous intimacy with chaos!

8: *The Golden Chalice*

"I take it you are out of your mind, Captain Williams!" Helene Wergeland said amiably. "Vivica is no wife for you."

They stood facing each other in the venerable drawing room of the Chou villa like two warriors. All preparations had been made for the departure, and now this ordinarily reasonable American came at the eleventh hour and produced a surprise. Naturally he could not know how much Miss Wergeland abominated surprises.

"Have you a reason for your refusal, Miss Wergeland?"

"More than one, Captain Williams."

Helene was thinking that the Wergelands in general were not especially well suited to marriage. Her brother Olaf in Trondheim was married to the shipyard. She herself had, as the Chinese would phrase it, "become a mother to the whole village." She preferred not to think of her brother Knut's marriages. Knut as a husband had been created by God in a moment of wrath. And his youngest daughter—well, Vivie was not like other girls. If she did marry six or seven years hence, it would be in Norway and under Helene's supervision.

"Vivica is not well," she said gruffly at last.

"We have discussed this point," Captain Williams replied with a calm that gave forewarning of his obstinacy. "Vivica has been my patient. I know her, Miss Wergeland. She suffered a severe shock as the result of that Jap's cruelty, but she has almost completely overcome it by now."

"The Lillesand family suffers from hereditary melancholia. Vivica's mother threw herself out of the window of a hotel room in Dalat when my brother was about to take her to a mental institution in Europe."

Timothy Williams flinched for a moment. "There is no need for family history to repeat itself," he replied after a moment. "It will not repeat itself. I will see to that."

"Captain Williams, I am going to speak frankly with you." Evidently Miss Wergeland had the impression that she had been most reticent up to this moment. "You know as well as I that this child knows nothing whatsoever about life. All right—perhaps that isn't necessary. But I certainly will never let Vivie go to Tokyo, where you will be stationed. In such a place she would be reminded of her prison experiences day and night."

"Permit me to say otherwise, Miss Wergeland. Vivica will be coming to Tokyo as the wife of an American army officer."

"And what would that signify?"

Captain Williams flushed with anger. "As a doctor I can assure

you that the sight of defeated Japanese will be just the thing to cure
her anxieties. Haven't you seen how defeated Japanese behave?"

"I have seen only Madame Yamato, who is now in an internment
camp," Helene replied grimly. "The Chinese murdered her husband.
He took Vivica out of the clutches of the Kempetai at the risk of
his life and sheltered her in his private hospital. At the end it was
he who brought her to the Chous. Didn't you know that?"

"Chou Tso-ling never mentioned it, nor Vivica either."

"So you see, you know very little about the whole affair. Vivica
is far from having got over it."

"Can't we stick to the point, Miss Wergeland? In my country we
live for the future and shape the present accordingly. I guarantee
that Vivie in Tokyo . . ."

There was only a slight tremor in his voice, but Helene heard the
note of torment and solicitous love. Timothy Williams was really a
fine fellow, but—

"I am speaking for your good, Captain Williams," she said almost
gently. For a moment there was silence. Timothy Williams looked
in astonishment at the tall, commanding figure with the sharp eyes.
What did this strong old woman mean? His good was Vivica. In all
probability Miss Wergeland did not want to see that. She undoubtedly did not realize how robust Vivica was, in spite of her recent
breakdown. But perhaps there was another reason for her attitude.
Perhaps she had more ambitious plans for this beautiful girl who
belonged to one of the most influential families in Trondheim. The
grandson of a forester from Tröndelag might not be . . .

"I am not good enough for Vivica?" he asked roughly.

Helene had never been so surprised in her life. The boy must be
out of his mind. Not good enough for Vivica?

"The other way round," she said crossly.

A long silence followed. Captain Williams' forehead wrinkled in
those hereditary frown lines. Suddenly it occurred to Helene that
she might be seeing the matter too narrowly. She would not live forever, for all that she felt lively as a herring right now. She thought
of Hanna Chou, and of how satisfying a marriage could be if both
sides made, out of love, the inevitable concessions. Perhaps she was
really living too much in the past, like most Europeans.

"I will take care of Vivica, Miss Wergeland," said the long-legged young doctor from Concord, New Hampshire. That was a feeble expression of all he intended to do for his girl. But Helene perceived that here was no romantic and no shirker. The young man, fool that he was, had taken it into his head to have Vivie. And perhaps he, at least, was the right man for her, even though Vivica was certainly not the right woman for him. Wasn't there in all of the United States of America a nice, orderly girl for Captain Williams, a genuine life-partner who would look reality straight in the eye and not treat it as a poor substitute for a personal dream world, as did Vivica, as Knut and Borghild had done?

"Please think it over, Miss Wergeland."

Helene looked up from her brooding and straight into the intelligent, reliable eyes of the young man with the funny frown lines on his forehead.

"You may as well call me Aunt Helene," she said. "You'll marry Vivie anyway, whether I'm for or against it. . . . Hold it there, young man. That's no reason to smash the tea service."

For Astrid, Vivica's engagement meant a change of plans. She had intended going straight to Paris, but now it was decided that she would accompany the family to Trondheim and remain at Villa Wergeland until Vivica's wedding. Vivica was to make the acquaintance of her parents' native land before going back to the Far East with Tim. Captain Williams already had his furlough; he could depart for Europe when he pleased. He would go back with the Wergeland family, and intended to look up his relatives on his mother's side in Tröndelag.

Astrid had so many things to arrange in Bangkok that she scarcely had time to think about this change of plans. She too had been astounded at Vivie's engagement, for she had taken it for granted that Pierre de Maury and her youngest sister would be pairing off. She had read Pierre's letter twice with knitted brows, then torn it into fragments. That was unfortunate, for Monsieur de Maury's matter-of-fact account contained unique material on the escape and rescue of a member of the French Resistance in Japanese-occupied Southeast Asia. Pierre had expressed the hope that the Wergeland family had come safely through the terrors of the occupation period. From Bangkok, Astrid had sent him a curt note, letting him know how wrong he had been about this, and simultaneously wishing him the best of good fortune for the future. She had said nothing at all about her own plans, since she assumed that he would not be interested.

Now she was alone in the big, empty house on Sathorn Road. Aunt Helene and Vivica had already moved onto the ship which four days hence would be taking them to Europe. The furniture had been auctioned off, except for that in Astrid's room. Yumei's husband and the servants were taking care of Missie Astrid with touching solicitude on these last days. She had sold her share in the Sun antique business at a large profit. Astrid was so efficient and clearheaded that Helene had gladly left to her the winding up of all their affairs. For the first time, during these last days Helene had admitted to herself that she was tired, and that Astrid was a real support to her. Parting from Mailin had affected her deeply. The Wergelands' songbird had returned to the Chou family in Singapore, and with her a source of deep, quiet happiness had vanished from Helene's life. Mailin alone had not changed in a world that changed alarmingly year by year and hour by hour.

Astrid was sitting on Helene Wergeland's veranda, dressed in a magnificent raw-silk traveling suit and writing to her cousin Amélie Clermont, when a ricksha drove between the bougainvillaea flowers at the gate. Yumei's husband came running up. A visitor at this late hour! What did he have left to offer a guest?

Astrid stood up slowly and walked, stiffly erect, down the steps. She had turned very pale and moved like a sleepwalker toward the visitor.

"What do you want here?" she asked.

"Won't you say good evening to me first, Astride?" Pierre de Maury said, looking steadily at her.

Astrid had turned fiery red. Something in the look and that familiar alluring voice of her lost lover robbed her of her composure, but she quickly got a grip on herself.

"Good evening," she said mechanically, and turned to Yumei's husband, who had stood watching the scene with furious curiosity. "Bring cocktails and sandwiches to the orchid pavilion."

"Thank you, but I have already ordered a dinner for us at the Oriental Hotel," Monsieur de Maury said. "We ought to say good-by in style, Astride!"

For a moment Astrid succeeded in persuading herself that Pierre was a good old acquaintance with whom she could dine in perfect calm. Then she realized once more that he was the only man she had ever loved and ever would love. But during the terrible months after Vivie's arrest she had learned something; she neither regarded him with hungry looks nor let it be known by the slightest quiver of her voice that she would never be able to forget or recover from her rejection. "The tree cannot choose the bird that perches on it," Chou Tso-ling had once said. Astrid, too, had no choice. This gold oriole had flown toward her years ago; she had wanted to catch and hold it, but it had fluttered away, and she had stood there, more helpless than the tree of the proverb. That was all there was to it. There was no sense brooding over the riddles of suffering.

They had a good many things to tell each other, and they told them. Abruptly Pierre said, "I have at last found out who denounced me to the Kempetai. Isn't that curious?"

He looked at Astrid. She felt as if the world were standing still. Only the sampans on the Menam River and the misty moon above their garden table had a semblance of life. So this was why Pierre had looked her up. This time too he had come to torment her—as always. So he had learned her terrible secret.

What was the point of their sitting here, two human beings who had once loved each other and must now hate each other? For if Pierre knew what Astrid had done in her frozen despair, he could not help despising her, no matter how bitterly she had repented and atoned for her betrayal.

"Pierre," she whispered, "I—"

But Monsieur de Maury had already taken a letter from his coat pocket and was holding it out to her. "Read that, Astride!" he said equably; he had been through several hells since last seeing her, and had survived them. "Read this letter. It is quite a document."

Astrid groped for her reading glasses and discovered that she had left them at home in another bag. At first the letters swam mistily before her eyes; then she managed to read them, with growing astonishment.

Tokyo, October 1945

Monsieur,

Undersigned asks pardon for troubling Monsieur de Maury with wretched and stupid letter. Undersigned is wretched creature and deserves to have Nippon lie in dust and Monsieur punish by contempt stupid creature.

Undersigned visited Monsieur in Shanghai and Saigon and obtained honorable poppy of oblivion. Talked with Monsieur and did duty for Nippon. Monsieur was enemy of Japan; undersigned found this out, read letters, gave them to Kempetai, and Monsieur had to run away. Undersigned prays every day before great Buddha and before forbidden Shinto shrines that Monsieur is well and may forgive. Writer denounced Monsieur with bleeding heart, and weeps many worthless tears of shame and friendship. Monsieur was always friendly and did not suspect agent's poor thanks for honored kindness. But duty to country is highest duty in Nippon. Undersigned hopes that Monsieur may forgive defeated and repentant Japanese people. Letter goes to Saigon, to old address.

With expression of deep humility,
Yuriko

"She worked for Baron Matsubara for years," Pierre explained. "None of us had any idea—"

"When was the last time you saw her?"

"In—January of this year. Then she vanished."

In January. Long before Astrid herself had written to the Kempetai. Astrid breathed like one who had been given life anew by inscrutable divine goodness. The river of ice within her, which had refused to dissolve even after Vivica's rescue, was transformed all at once into a flowing warm stream. She could not help herself; big tears streamed from her pale blue eyes onto her handsome suit. She was half blind with tears and saw the face of the man she had vainly loved through the fine-spun veil of renunciation. Perhaps Pierre knew what she had done and had come to free her of her burden of guilt. She did not want to know whether that was so, did not want to know now or ever. She had lost Pierre, she sensed, chiefly because she had always wanted to know things so precisely. During her solitary confinement in the Kempetai prison she had begun to suspect that every man seeks peace in a wife, and that too many questions and too much craving to possess destroy that longed-for peace.

"Why are you crying, Astride?" Pierre asked gently. Gaston Lafitte, after his release, had told him about the letter which Major Matsubara had given him to read, stressing that Mademoiselle Clermont-Wergeland was the author of the denunciation.

"Oh, Pierre—I'm so happy." It was only the shadow of a voice.

Deeply moved, he bent over the girl who had loved him and whom he, engrossed in politics and full of fear for France, had never loved as she deserved. They had, all of them, become entangled in a great deal of guilt from the moment the sun of the West began to sink in 1941. But the greatest guilt a person can incur is always lack of love. Pierre had recognized that by now. In the solitude of the Laotan mountains he had drained to the dregs both the golden chalices of which the mystics of the West have sung; he had drunk the red wine of pain and the white wine of hope. Everyone must drink both, sooner or later, in youth or in age, in poverty or in wealth. Both together constituted the wine of life, not to be confused with cheap imitations. That is why Pierre de Maury came to Astrid before he left Indo-China forever, and brought her the golden chalice of white wine, for she had already drained to the dregs the chalice containing the red wine of pain. He could see that she had: her fine, transparent face with its haughtily arched eyebrows and thwarted mouth was marked by spiritual torment. It was a gentler face than it had been, but too resigned for a girl of twenty-seven.

Then Astrid's head with the soft hair once again lay on his breast —as once before in Shanghai when she, so young then, had listened to his heartbeat. He raised her face to his—that proud face, branded by sorrow and longing, which had always preserved the purity of the Far North—and sought her lips.

"No—oh, no, Pierre!"

"Why, yes—*chérie.*"

Only the moon and a shaded candle in the hotel garden illuminated the table where two Europeans bade good-by to Asia. This would be a surprise for Aunt Helene!

The coming together of Astrid and Pierre after a break that had seemed irreparable was a highly personal phenomenon, and yet it was typical, psychologically and socially, of the postwar era. During those months after the war the Far East swarmed with engaged couples and newlyweds. It was as though the people of the West, who had lived either free or captive for years in the Japanese "Empire," wanted in their homesickness to build nests, and with birds of their own kind. A good many of these alliances impulsively formed under the burning tropical sun fell apart in the more sober climate of the homelands; a good many lasted for life. The durability of Astrid's and Vivica's marriages was a question for the future; but the impulse of homesickness that brought the two young couples together immediately after the war was genuine and powerful. That, at any rate, was how Helene Wergeland explained to herself the surprising turn in Astrid's destiny; and the transfigured face of her eldest niece moved her in a way inexplicable to herself. Pierre de Maury, that most talkative of all Frenchmen, had never been her cup of tea; but after all, *she* was not going to marry Monsieur.

The following evening they all sat in the garden of the Oriental Hotel as Pierre's guests. Captain Williams, who came from so fundamentally different a world, and beside whom Pierre seemed rather tired and skeptical, had obviously struck up a good man-to-man friendship with Monsieur. They had one great subject in common: the war. And a second: the Wergeland sisters. A third was Tokyo, with which de Maury had become acquainted as a cultural missionary before the war, under the guidance of Baron Matsubara, and to which Captain Williams would be taking Vivica after the wedding.

Vivica had greeted "Uncle Pierre" without the slightest constraint, and with an enchanting smile. She was very proud of Tim, her "giant." After dinner they danced on the dimly lit lawn of the Oriental Hotel. After a while Pierre found Vivica in his arms. She smiled up at him like a nymph; was he too thinking of Saigon and the many little bars where they had collected faces? Monsieur de Maury's expression betrayed nothing of his thoughts. "You dance wonderfully, Uncle Pierre," Vivie whispered.

"The hem of your skirt is down, Vivienne," Pierre remarked dryly. That disorderly hem had bothered him all evening. *Une petite vagabonde* . . . Involuntarily, he glanced over at Astrid, who was dancing with Captain Williams, looking distinguished in her smart cocktail dress, with a fantastic little hat that seemed, like a bird, to have settled infallibly on the right spot on her head. He nodded gratifiedly. Astride would fit in beautifully back home. She would receive *tout Paris*—intellectual and social Paris. The de Maury family had extensive connections and took it for granted that Pierre would marry a woman of great social aplomb. *Maman* would be delighted with Astride.

Shortly before the end of the evening, Helene Wergeland found herself alone with Pierre de Maury in a quiet corner of the hotel garden. "What have you in mind for the future?" she asked bluntly.

"I have a number of plans, Madame. We will live in Paris; but first I must get in touch with my friends again."

Helene said nothing. Pierre went on hastily. "My uncle is Director-General of the Political Section in the Foreign Ministry. He has already offered me an interesting post in the press and information service for Asia and Oceania. That would involve traveling from time to time, but our headquarters would be Paris."

Helene still said nothing. Perhaps she was realizing that she would be losing Astrid too, and finding the prospect painful. Pierre took the silence for disapproval. After all, Astride had been born with a silver spoon in her mouth. She lost silver powder boxes—he remembered this well—as though they were apples or nuts. He drew himself up into a somewhat stiffer posture. Helene regarded his ascetic profile with some wonder; it was not nearly so man-of-the-world as his smile and his urbane movements.

"My family is not wealthy, Madame," he said rather arrogantly. "For many generations we have served the state or the Church. Our womenfolk live within their means by grace and intelligence. I hope you are satisfied with what I have to offer Astride."

A faint undertone of worry reached Helene's sensitive ear. It seemed to her a guarantee of the honest intentions of this man who was alien to her and would remain so.

"I shall endeavor to win for Astride the social position she has a right to demand," Pierre added stiffly.

Helene Wergeland gave the French shirker her first look of warmth since that distant day when they had first met. "Be good to her," she said hoarsely. "That's all Astrid needs. I know her pretty well."

An era had ended for Europeans in the Far East. The Wergeland family set out on their voyage home. In Europe, too, a new and different world awaited them.

While Helene, Astrid, and Vivica sailed toward the Far North—the double wedding was to be held in Trondheim next year—Baron Matsubara Akiro sat in prison in Tokyo, a war criminal. With impassive countenance he drank the red wine of pain. Sometimes he thought of the beautiful girl whom he had adored and—so he thought —destroyed. He always saw her in Dr. Yamato's hospital, wrapped in dream-clouds and fearing the fire of his eyes. When the fallen warrior of the Rising Sun thought of Vivica, he smiled obscurely to himself. In the Japanese view, something you had contemplated long and hard belonged to you.

BOOK THREE

A Moment of Glory

Perhaps it was Baron Matsubara's great good fortune that for the next five years he was absent from the revolving stage. As prisoner of the Allies he enjoyed certain benefits of which his countrymen in freedom were sometimes deprived: time for undisturbed meditation, regular meals, and the chance to recover in a Japanese way from the hurtling plunge into inconceivable depths. Above all, Matsubara Akiro enjoyed, like the other war criminals, the priceless privilege of observing only from afar the transformation of Japan into an American-type democracy. Thus, during the five years of his imprisonment, he was spared—in contrast to the Imperial Family and the nobles of Tokyo—certain humiliations that were tragic and grotesque, although—or because—they stemmed from the educational desires of the occupying power. The atom bomb had accomplished the military victory; but General MacArthur and his military moralists in Tokyo Headquarters were not content with that. This was logical enough, for the Second World War had not been an uncomplicated war such as used to be fought in the good old days, when after the victory people were satisfied with the acquisition of territory and new markets. The moralists of the United States of America tried to transplant to Tokyo and its environs the American Way of Life and the principles of democracy, precisely as they were taught in the West. Since moralists, in order to attain their ends, seldom spare money or material, the Americans poured vast sums in dollars, goods, and instructional materials into the "re-education" of the Japanese of all classes. Particularly in the early years after the defeat, the victors found their Japanese pupils passionately attentive. With the eagerness of the defeated the Japanese learned something new—namely, democracy. Baron Kenzo, a cousin of Akiro Matsubara, learned with grim determination.

Furthermore, the Americans harvested innumerable courteous bows, winsome looks from the ladies, a great deal of to-do in the newspapers, and little solid substance. The reason was that hitherto they had never met persons like the Matsubara barons and their circle. The moral intentions of the Americans were sincere; their ignorance of the Japanese psyche was, on the whole, abysmal. When the Matsubaras and the other fallen rulers of the syndicates and trusts "learned democracy," they did so solely from the rational consideration that there must be something to this system, since it had helped its adherents to win a world war. There must be some trick behind the fine moral preachings, they were convinced, and if they studied the matter hard enough they were sure to find out what the trick was. When the Japanese bowed low to the uniformed pedagogues from the United States, they did so because in the first place they were incurably polite, and then because one made oneself as small as possible during a typhoon. There was also, alas, a special quality to the beaming smile which the Japanese of all classes offered the victors. The Japanese did not smile out of pure love for democracy, as their schoolmasters sometimes imagined. In Japan every private or public disaster is treated, before other people, as a successful joke. One reason for this is a sense of tact toward the unsuspecting others; moreover, the smile of a Japanese conceals his profound pessimism and salvages his wounded pride. His smile, therefore, is by no means hypocritical; it is a moral gesture which for centuries has proved its worth in all situations of life.

Scarcely two nations under the sun are as dissimilar as the Japanese and the Americans. (And the French philosopher Rivarol maintains that similarity is the moral basis for every community.) The contrasts of political and private morality, of ways of life and social structure, could not be abolished by decree. This fact did not alter official American optimism, nor Japanese resignation (*Shikato ga nai!*). The thousand little nuances that govern Japan's art and everyday life were incomprehensible to the far cruder schoolmasters, who lived by superlatives. A traditionally feudalistic country could not grasp the healthy democratic principle that every citizen has the same opportunities provided he is committed enough to his personal success. The social hierarchy of Nippon corresponded more or less to the needs of the Japanese, who were proud that their Tenno was descended from the Sun Goddess and not from the Smith family in Chicago.

The prewar years had featured the Japanese tourist, the war years the Japanese victor and *samurai* on the Far Eastern revolving stage. The years between 1945 and 1955 brought a new figure into the limelight—the "bamboo people." These were the Japanese men and women who bent back and forth as gently and gracefully as bamboo in the high winds of the postwar era, and never broke. Baron Kenzo of the Matsubara family was such a bamboo person; so was the former spy Yuriko, now working in her father's shop on the Ginza in Tokyo; and so was every rice farmer, every official, every pompom girl, or soldier's sweetheart, on the streets and in the dance-halls of the Yoshivara. They said, "*Sah*"—"Fine, good"—to the incomprehensible ordinances, and did the opposite; they bowed at banquets and street corners until their delicate bones ached; they smiled their mute, tormented souls out of their bodies—but they did not break.

When Major Matsubara in 1950 left prison to go home, the Twelve Families who had ruled Japan were still there in the background; the yea-sayers to democracy were in the foreground; and the women were everywhere, for Japanese women are pliable, obedient, and modest. But not much had come of the idea of a democratic community. In Nippon the "group" still governed—though behind the curtain now—and their glory and advancement were still what counted. The individual, whose development is the concern of every genuine democracy, was still meaningless in postwar Japan; his joys and sorrows remained subordinate to the welfare of his social group and his family.

Now that the Americans strode the revolving stage and the bamboo people were eagerly learning democracy, millions of Japanese recollected the great hidden virtues which had in the past brought them happiness and serenity: their pleasure in nature; their ability to be content with little, so long as that little was gracefully presented; and their national discipline, which contains a mystic element of unconditional readiness to sacrifice. The power of Japanese humility, their lack of envy of American automobiles and foods, their feeling of identity with nature and their group, brought the twelve great families and the millions of little families unharmed through the terrors and temptations of that perplexing matter called democracy. Japanese gratitude for every gift or act of friendliness, no matter how slight—this is perhaps the highest virtue of the entire people —proved to be a significant experience to a great many Americans whose good hearts and warm natures made them capitulate constantly to their defeated enemy.

1: *The Darkness after the Fireworks*

═══════════════════════

In the isolation of his cell Baron Matsubara Akiro had only an inkling of Nippon's brand-new democracy. He saw only the darkness after a fireworks which had intoxicated his proud and glory-hungry soul. Very slowly he arrived at the surprising insight that Asia, since the hour Nippon had first launched its brilliant slogan in Greater East Asia, actually belonged to the Asians. At the moment, to be sure, it belonged principally to the Chinese. But Baron Akiro, like many of his fellow countrymen, took a long view in politics, and he preferred the basest Chinese to the most well-disposed American. A moral victory, even though it remained as hidden as a hooded *minomushi*-insect, did Akiro's proud and sensitive soul as much good as a hot bath and the sight of a thing of perfect beauty. But nevertheless, what darkness after the fireworks!

When on the eve of the New Year Festival of 1950 Baron Akiro made his way through a Tokyo in part destroyed and in part garishly illuminated, on his way to the Matsubara manor, he needed all his moral courage not to seek death under a passing automobile. Like shadows or *minomushi*-insects, his countrymen scurried through the occupied capital. An icy sadness filled him when he at last halted before the gate of his familial manor, which, in accordance with the best tradition, looked from the outside like a simple country house. It showed so many signs of bomb damage that no American officer had requisitioned the building. Moreover, it was so cleverly concealed among shrubbery and winding paths and bridges that at first the Americans had not even noticed it.

A strong wind was blowing this evening. Matsubara Akiro shivered in the thin coat he had borrowed from his maternal uncle. Prince Itoh was a small, delicate-boned man, and his coat was inadequate for his nephew, who was unusually big for a Japanese. Utter silence prevailed in garden and house when Baron Akiro, unnoticed, un-re-educated, and unconverted, came before the gate. In the wan moonlight the house looked like a ruin. The untended garden smelled of decay. A bat swooped over the beautifully curved roofs, from which numerous tiles were missing. The lacquer had splintered off the gate and had not been renewed. The "hermit's hut," which his great-grandfather had built and occupied in old age, stood dark and ghostly in a corner of the neglected garden. Moreover, there was no light showing in the whole house. What could have happened? Prince Itoh had informed the family in good time of Akiro's release and impending return. Where were his parents, his two daughters, his honored grandmother, who had guided and dominated the family, a politely soft-spoken tyrant, for so many years? Akiro had always been her favorite grandson.

Prince Itoh had refused to give Akiro any information on the situation at home. "See for yourself!" he had said with a gentle smile. The prince abhorred conversations on painful or sorrowful matters.

An ancient maidservant appeared at the gate with a lantern. She started back almost imperceptibly when she saw Baron Akiro in the glow of the lantern. The honorable young master looked like a ghost. In his childhood old Kikue had cradled him respectfully in her arms. She had been with the old baroness decades ago—Akiro's grandmother had been a lady of the court—and had moved with her to the Matsubara home.

Old Kikue knelt and touched her dry lips humbly to the shoes of the returned master. She did not dare cast a second look at that emaciated face with the gloomy eyes and the compressed lips. She had prepared the ceremonial bath for honored Second-Eldest Son, she murmured, and the old baroness would be pleased to receive honored Grandson after his bath.

Matsubara Akiro stooped down to the ancient, crooked little servant, and raised her to her feet with that kindly tenderness that Japanese of great houses have traditionally displayed toward their servants.

"Come into the house, Kikue," he said gently. "An ill wind is blowing."

The old woman knelt again and removed Second-Eldest Son's shoes. Then she crept along, bowed and covertly coughing, behind the fourth Baron Matsubara, who was returning not with glory but as a war criminal. She smiled beatifically as she scrubbed Young Master's honored back; one could count every knob of his spine.

Baron Akiro also smiled when old Kikue replied, in response to his question, that his honored father was unfortunately prevented by illness from greeting Second-Eldest Son. That was worse than all the other humiliations of the past five years. Thinking about it, Baron Matsubara forgot that his two daughters had also not considered it necessary to welcome him at the door. He was too proud to ask about them. Stomach cramps tormented him when he at last stepped out of the ceremonial bath for homecomers, smiling politely. He smiled also when he greeted his grandmother with low bows. The aged baroness smiled back.

Baroness Matsubara was eighty-five years old. She was as tiny, bent, and precious as a Japanese dwarf fruit tree. As a member of a *samurai* family, she had enjoyed a reflection of the Imperial Sun during her days as court lady; for her the darkness after the fireworks was not so total as it was for younger people, because in the manner of the very old she lived in the past and rejoiced her eyes in the refulgence of the three imperial jewels. On ceremonial occasions she had often visited a famous Shinto shrine where the three treasures of Nippon—a sword, a necklace, and the imperial mirror—were exhibited and Shinto priests in solemn robes made sacrifices to the gods of Nippon. Since the American occupation the state Shinto ceremonies had been banned on the grounds that they offended the newly awakened democratic feelings of the Japanese people. When Baron Jiro read out to the old baroness this article of faith from the new "religion" imported from the U.S.A., the old woman had tittered and murmured that it was odd for foreign eggs to be trying to teach the Japanese hen. The old baroness could very well have gone out into the country, accompanied by her servant Kikue, to a Shinto service. But she remained stubbornly in her bombed manor, where her sons and grandsons had been born. She, like many Japanese, had a fear of microbes and an intense dislike of foreigners; if she went to the country, she could scarcely have avoided either. Somehow the Americans reminded her of huge red-cheeked microbes, and she thought of democracy as an infectious fever which could best be escaped by remaining at home.

When her grandson Akiro entered the reception room of the house, she looked quickly down at the floor before she gave him a heartrending smile. He had always been her pride, a handsome, vigorous, and intelligent heir of the old name—her name—and of his father's power. She had pondered for a long while after Prince Itoh informed her that Akiro was being released from prison. During the interrogations Colonel Saito had taken so much guilt upon himself that he had been condemned to ten years' imprisonment. From Saito's account it would seem as though Major Matsubara had obeyed his, Colonel Saito's, diabolic instructions solely out of a penchant for obedience. Consequently Akiro's seven years of imprisonment had surprisingly been reduced to five, and now the old baroness had to inform her favorite grandson of what had taken place in his absence. In order to do so, she had hit upon an ingenious, typically Japanese solution. It would not do to wound by words this proud second-eldest son, who after Nippon's defeat had not committed suicide solely out of heroic obedience to the Emperor. Akiro was intelligent and had a penetrating eye; he would understand correctly the arrangements for his reception.

He understood! The blood seemed to stand still in his veins as, still warm and soothed by the hot bath, he paid his respects to his highly honored grandmother and saw these arrangements, which had been conceived with a tact and cleverness worthy of Akiro himself in his days of glory in Shanghai, Paris, or Indo-China. For a moment all his intestinal organs ached frightfully, and he closed his eyes, for a second not sure whether he might not be dreaming in his cell. Then he opened them wide and gave a twisted smile. What had happened? To a foreigner nothing at all; to Akiro of the house of Itoh-Matsubara the sun at this moment seemed to have set for all time to come.

A foreigner would have observed nothing but an aesthetically spare room which had been laid with clean *tatami,* the traditional straw mats, in honor of the New Year. A simple glowing *hibachi* or basin of coals spread a cozy warmth. Near the *tokonoma* was, as always, the "sacred corner," the *butsudan* or Buddhist wall shelf. It was a miniature altar, charmingly carved and painted with gold lacquer. It contained an image of the Buddha Amida, the principal figure of Shinshu Buddhism, which would assure members of the Matsubara family a good place in paradise in any case, no matter whether they learned democracy or, in the stubborn fashion of Prince Itoh and the old baroness, refused to have anything to do with Abraham Lincoln, chewing gum, or the *Reader's Digest* in Japanese translation. In front of this altar the old baroness rang a tiny brass bell every morning, and in spite of her advanced age she made as lithe a bow as any bamboo girl receiving cigarettes from an American soldier, and recited the prescribed prayer of the Shinshu sect. And on the *butsudan* Akiro at once observed the new ancestor tablet of his elder brother, who had won fame as a suicide pilot and was consequently, in spite of the lost war, the only light in the clouded sky of the Matsubara and Itoh families.

Near the altar hung a portrait of Great-Grandfather Matsubara, who had built the hermit's hut, where at the moment Baron Jiro, Akiro's honored father, had sought refuge from the representatives of the democracy. In this ascetic's den he spent his days and nights —he who had been incessantly active right up to the unconditional surrender—and only occasionally received his nephew Kenzo for whispered consultations. Baron Jiro Matsubara, one of the most capable and cunning financial despots of Japan, had been suffering since the breaking up of the *zaibatsu* from a tendency to take flight from the world in meditation, a tendency which his aged mother regarded with many a frown. She knew that Jiro was a man of action. It was not right for him to leave to his nephew Kenzo the obscure affairs and intrigues which the members of the *zaibatsu* were plotting behind the scenes. And not only the affairs . . .

Baron Jiro had adopted Kenzo as eldest son and heir of the Matsubara clan. He had stricken his son Akiro from the list because Akiro had brought shame upon the family. Obstinately wedded to old principles of conduct, Baron Jiro had refused to understand why Akiro, after the shame of arrest, had not committed honorable suicide. But that was precisely what the Tenno had forbidden, immediately after the capitulation, in a message to the entire people. It was the tragedy of thousands of death-seeking, proud Japanese that they had been compelled to subdue their own desires for death in favor of the highest virtue of the *samurai*, obedience. Matsubara Akiro, too, had obeyed, accepting the commandment to go on living; his dishonor was precisely his honor. Only his grandmother and Prince Itoh understood him and smiled their sad smiles. And now the aged baroness was compelled to wound to the quick, quietly and without words, simply by her arrangements, this humiliated patriot of a grandson.

For in the niche there was a seat of honor for guests or for the ranking member of a family, and on this seat of honor sat Cousin Kenzo, the adopted eldest son of the family. Kenzo, the son of the rice widow who in Akiro's childhood and young manhood had led a despised shadow-existence in the noble family, whose other womenfolk all came of the princely house of Itoh! Kenzo, a timid, humble, shadowy child, had served and flattered the haughty, scintillating Akiro, hoping always for a friendly word from his unattainably high cousin. He was never permitted to play with Akiro and his elder brother or participate in Western sports with them. The rice widow and Kenzo had occupied a painful middle position between the servants and the members of the powerful family. They had always been treated with less consideration than the servants. But times had changed. During the bombings of Tokyo the rice widow had saved the lives of the old baroness and Akiro's mother, dying herself as a result. Akiro's mother had soon afterward been struck down by a heart attack. Only the aged Baroness Matsubara of Itoh had survived everything—tiny, bent, precious as a Japanese dwarf tree, and as intelligent and proud as her grandson Akiro, who but for his height was the image of her. Like her he had the boldly hooked nose, the carved, arrogant lips, and the unmoving, fiery eyes of the *samurai*.

With those eyes Akiro was at the moment staring at his cousin Kenzo. He grasped in a trice the significance of the arrangement in the niche of honor, and bowed to the new head of the Matsubara family. For a moment he stood motionless, feeling the life leak out of him. Then he bowed again to his honored grandmother.

Cousin Kenzo shyly approached Akiro. He was small, inclined to stoutness, and concealed the expression in his nearsighted eyes behind huge horn-rimmed glasses.

"Welcome to the paternal household," he murmured, smiling in perplexity. If only Akiro, in spite of his humiliation, were not so tall and distinguished, and he himself so small and plump! Baron Kenzo looked a little common; his mother had not been quite the right person for a member of the Twelve Families. But Kenzo was industrious, uncommonly adroit in business, a perfect model of the bamboo man, and behind the scenes of the revolving stage he represented with infinite persistence, cleverness, and tact the economic interests of the *zaibatsu*, whom General MacArthur had smashed. There was nothing Cousin Kenzo, who had successfully taken lessons from the old baron in his hermit's hut, did not know in 1950 about the large-scale manufacturing, financial transactions, transportation, mining, and banking among the great families of Japan. But at the moment Kenzo, with his Japanese sensitivity, was utterly distracted. The looks of the one-time tiger of the Kempetai bored through him like the blade of the sacred *samurai* sword which Prince Itoh had buried and so conveniently forgotten that he could not turn it over to the American troops, although the order to do so had been issued to the old families from the very highest authority. The sword rested in the garden of a remote summer house belonging to the old baroness. She had intended this small country house in Karuizawa as a New Year gift for her grandson Akiro, and was going to present him with the deed tomorrow. Akiro could not remain in Tokyo; his savage looks too obviously gave the lie to his courteous attitude, the old baroness thought. He looked as if he would have preferred to strangle poor Kenzo with his own hands, although he went on smiling and bowing.

"We hope that tomorrow you will share in our wretched New Year meal, so that your honored presence may give joy and happiness to all." With these words Baron Kenzo took refuge in convention. He drew breath audibly through his nose, like a subordinate before a person of high rank, although *he* was now the master in the family. Becoming aware of this impropriety, he forged on. *"Ake-mashite omede toh gozai masu"*—This New Year is truly a happy occasion. Then he gasped for air like a carp, in so doing revealing the gold crowns of his teeth, which were adorned with jewels—a forgivable breach of taste in the son of a rice widow. An entire jewelry shop had found its way into Baron Kenzo's honored mouth.

"Konen mo yoro-shiku onegai itashi-masu"—I hope that the coming year will find us as close friends as ever—Cousin Akiro replied ceremonially with a murderous smile.

The old baroness clapped her hands. Promptly Kikue and her two daughters-in-law appeared. All three of them had learned so little about freedom and democracy in the past five years that they went on serving the family as in the past for their rice, their clothing, their minute wages, and the great honor. They still did not receive the legally established remuneration for domestic workers, for all their loyalty and blind submission to the matriarch of the family. As far as democratic principles were concerned, they were hopeless cases.

"How is your honored wife?" Akiro asked politely.

"Thank you for asking, Cousin Akiro. She is very well."

Why was Kenzo's face so contorted? Why was old Kikue holding her thin, workworn hand in front of her nutcracker face to suppress a giggle? Madame Kenzo had been so thoroughly abused in a courteous and oblique manner by the family and her honored husband, because she had failed to present the Matsubaras with a son and heir, that she had applied for a divorce—a concomitant of the emancipation of Japanese women. The thirty-five-year-old baroness had returned to her parental household and intended to go into politics, now that women had received the suffrage from Uncle MacArthur! All this the old baroness told her grandson after Cousin Kenzo had taken a hasty leave.

Akiro listened incredulously. Women . . . politics . . . freedom . . . right to vote! He began to laugh, and his grandmother added her refined titter to his laughter, while the serving maids listened with wooden faces and respectfully curbed delight. The gossip of the Twelve Great Families was far dearer to their hearts than all the achievements of de-mo-cra-cy.

"She said Kenzo did not understand her," Baroness Matsubara of Itoh concluded, and now she laughed outright.

Akiro too felt so relaxed that he laughed almost merrily. "Do our women want to be understood *too,* now?" he asked. "The poor creatures." Akiro had always believed that the women of the West were so frequently unhappy because their husbands "understood" them instead of teaching them the joys of obedience. "I see I have much to learn in the new Japan, honored Grandmother," he remarked gaily. "May I ask whether my two daughters have also been taking gratis lessons in freedom and democracy?"

Late that night Akiro went to bed. His daughters were still on his mind, although they had not considered it necessary to be present for his reception at the Matsubara manor. Eiko and Sadako seemed to resemble Lady Tatsue, their noble and unfortunate mother, in no respect. As children they had despised Lady Tatsue and adored their magnificent father, although he had ignored them because they were not man children. And now?

Baron Akiro stared at the walls of his bedroom.

What darkness after the fireworks!

2: *Variations of Humility*

Next morning Japan's most important holiday of the year commenced—Shogatsu, the New Year celebration. In the home of the Matsubaras too everything was being prepared for the reception of the priest who would purify the house. The traditional *mochi*—rice dumplings—stood ready in quantities for relatives and friends, in spite of the fact that rice was rationed. Baron Kenzo always found ways and means to obtain special favors and rations from his friends in the occupation forces. Nevertheless, he and the matriarch did not feel that inner joy with which the family had celebrated Shogatsu in the bad old days. For Baron Kenzo all peace and joy was gone, now that Cousin Akiro was living even temporarily under the same roof with him. Hence he smiled an especially blissful smile when he paid his New Year visit to Akiro's honored father in the hermit's hut.

Baron Jiro had heard how his mother had apprised Akiro of the new situation, and he now received his adopted eldest son Kenzo in excellent good humor, as befitted the New Year. Akiro had already paid his respects to his parent; there had been little talking and much smiling. Baron Jiro had never liked Akiro, in spite of this son's great gifts; and Akiro, like many Japanese sons, had always held the opinion that the three worst evils in life were an earthquake, a parched ricefield, and a man's highly honored father.

Akiro's father was of medium height, very thin, and looked, in spite of his ascetic exercises and meditations, like an unusually sly and good-humored fox. He possessed a high intelligence and an unostentatious refinement, and was given to pronounced likes and dislikes, which he masked by flowery speeches and amiable smiles. Miserable, diligent little Kenzo could relax a little only in his presence. But his *ko*, his duty to his parents and ancestors, oppressed him far too much for him ever to feel really at ease with the former powerful head of the family. Never would Kenzo be able to repay the old baron for the unmerited honors he had heaped upon the head of the rice widow's son. At the bottom of his grateful and humble soul Kenzo harbored the suspicion that Baron Jiro had raised him so high only in order to humiliate Akiro all the more without the need for explanations and scenes.

Kenzo shifted about on the mat so uncomfortably as to provide the old baron with ample entertainment. As with a private smile he looked upon the slightly plebeian face before him, with the disingenuous mouth to which the expensive gold teeth added neither distinction nor force, he knew exactly what was going on in Kenzo's mind.

"I am sorry, there can be no question of that, my dear son," the old baron remarked regretfully, as if he were grieved beyond words at the necessity of denying Kenzo's mute request. "I will never put Akiro in your place."

Kenzo started so violently that his glasses, which never sat properly on his stubby nose, fell off. His good-natured, shy eyes, which occasionally lit up with an economic expert's spark of cunning, fixed mournfully on the floor. This stern and powerful father-san would not even permit his wretched son the delights of humility. On New Year's Day, 1950, Kenzo was going to be condemned to run the family's affairs under Akiro's unwinking stare. For the erstwhile tiger of the Kempetai, for all that he had accepted the deed of gift to his grandmother's country house in Karuizawa with an especially low bow, had murmured that he would depart for Karuizawa as soon as he had attended to the affairs of his two daughters. This clearly meant that Cousin Akiro intended to remain in Tokyo for an indefinite time, and would be "obeying" his brand-new eldest brother.

Kenzo gulped as if he were choking over a huge New Year rice dumpling. He bowed low before the inexorable High Person who had condemned him to the frightful fate of having to give orders to Cousin Akiro. Not for a moment did it enter his head to rebel against the decision—though he was a man of forty-two!—nor even to discuss the embarrassing situation that resulted from it. The unshakable arrogance of the Matsubaras, their secret plans and involved intrigues, left no room for one of those discussions that Americans—whom Kenzo observed narrowly with fascinated envy— plunged into on the slightest pretext. Perhaps there was something to this incomprehensible de-mo-cra-cy, at least in family life. A week ago Baron Kenzo had seen two of the American longnoses slapping each other on the back and arguing heartily; finally one of these American officers, whistling piercingly, had slammed the door because his friend was jovially teasing him about a consolation girl. And all this in a realm in which, in Japan, polite language, smiles, and utmost circumspection were the rule!

After a third bow, poor Kenzo murmured his despairing thanks— "*Sumimasen!*" This expression might mean that his obligation to the family was unending, that Kenzo could never pay back all that Baron Jiro had loaded upon his humble back; it might also mean that Kenzo was altogether unhappy about the situation. Naturally, it was above all an apology for his daring to have had ideas of his own in the presence of the High Person.

With bowed head and back, Kenzo returned to the Matsubara manor. The beautiful gate, from which the lacquer had chipped off, was decorated for New Year's Day. The servants had laced pine branches and bamboo around it to symbolize long life. Above the front door hung a huge *yuzu* fruit; amid ferns and rice straw gleamed the traditional lobster. Humbly bowed, Kenzo stole like a servant torn between two harsh masters through the festively decked door, back into the honored family life.

On the second day of the New Year holiday Baron Akiro set out to visit his elder daughter, Eiko, who had run away from the family during the postwar era in order to marry a *nouveau riche* Japanese textile manufacturer. Ever since, neither Eiko nor her young husband had been received in the Matsubara manor. The old baroness had not yet recovered from the blow of having a "peddler" in the family, although Mr. Yasuda was a *narikin*—a man made of gold who, by means of paying excessively low wages to his working people and indulging in sundry black-marketing and the other usual practices of diligent bamboo men in postwar Japan, had pulled himself up into the class of "liberals" much favored by the American democrats. The longnoses knew nothing about the low wages, against which his women workers never struck, although they now belonged to a union. Nor did they know that Mr. Yasuda engaged in black-market affairs and that his wife was a Baroness Matsubara of Itoh, hence a member of a class currently forbidden to give orders, amass wealth, or engage in intrigues in the new Japan.

Eiko was so ashamed of having belonged to the Twelve Families that she tore to pieces every newspaper article in English or Japanese which dealt with these villains, so that her lord and master would not come across it. Naturally Mr. Yasuda read the articles at the geisha parties he regularly attended while his nobly born spouse waited at home for him. She had every reason to kiss the dust of his boots for having married her, daughter of a war criminal of the notorious Matsubara family. The newspaper articles restored to him

that self-assurance which sometimes left him in the presence of
Eiko. She was so completely different from the girls and women Mr.
Yasuda knew in the textile industry. She did not hold her hand vul-
garly over her mouth when she giggled—to be precise, she never
giggled at all. She prepared his tea with enchanting and distant
grace, and once she did not speak a word to him for three days
because he had given her a mild, good-natured slap as punishment
for expressing an opinion of her own. Eiko had only stared at her
husband. Her finely curved lips had set in mute disgust, and her
bold hooked nose—by all the Shinto gods, that was no rice dumpling
of a nose—had drawn in air with a sound that expressed loathing.
After three days Mr. Yasuda, who really had not meant it ill and
had only been remembering how well his sister obeyed after a slap
from her honored husband, had been in such a state of psychic col-
lapse that he made a mistake in favor of the working girls when
reckoning their wages. And on the evening of the third day Yasuda-
san had so far forgotten himself that he entered Eiko's bedroom in
the large modern house and begged her pardon. And instead of
meeting his obstinate wife's refusal to reply to him with a sound
beating, he had brought her a hideous and expensive necklace.
Whereupon Eiko had smiled pleasantly, and with *samurai* courage
thereafter wore the horrible necklace over a sweater from Mr. Yasuda's factory. Eiko had done with kimonos and stately coiffures;
these were not the thing for the wife of a Japanese democrat who
had not a stain on his record. She received guests in European clothing. Eiko was finished with Matsubara manners.

When old Kikue came stealing to the house at dawn on the first
New Year holiday to bring Eiko news of her honored father's return,
Mr. Yasuda had his way, and no mistake about it. He forbore to reproach Eiko for her idiotic aristocratic rearing, for he sincerely loved
her and would have committed suicide if she had left him. But that
his wife should return home to greet a war criminal—that was going
too far, thought Mr. Yasuda, who now belonged to the ruling class.

In short, Mr. Yasuda had strictly forbidden Eiko to accompany
the old servant, although Kikue had brought a choice kimono in
which she could make the visit. Eiko had obeyed, though with some
resentment, because she could not endure orders. She herself did

not want to see her father—in fact she wanted to see no one, not even Mr. Yasuda. At least so it seemed, for Eiko declared she was ill and did not come to the big New Year party at which so many black-market delicacies were being served. She lay on her mat and did not really know why she was crying so bitterly. All her pride flowed away along with her tears. Perhaps she longed after all to see the father she had once worshiped.

Softly the door to her room slid open. Eiko started up and suppressed a scream. On the threshold stood her handsome, powerful father. He smiled graciously at the little image of himself, although Eiko had behaved scandalously, unfilially, and altogether idiotically the day before by not coming to greet him. But she was young and uncertain of herself. And he was now well in his forties and possessed of that arrogant self-assurance which Eiko occasionally imitated. After all, he was responsible for his daughters.

Eiko leaped up and dried her tears with a silk handkerchief. She was profoundly ashamed that the High Paternal Person had seen her weeping, even though he was a war criminal and unworthy of respect. Her mind, influenced by Mr. Yasuda and the *Reader's Digest,* rebelled for a few seconds, but tradition and education in the Tokyo finishing school for aristocratic girls were stronger than her single year of marriage. Kneeling before her father, she humbly wished him a happy New Year.

Baron Matsubara raised his daughter to her feet. Eiko had burst into wild sobs. He pretended not to notice, for otherwise she would have lost too much honor and self-respect. From a briefcase that Herr von Zabelsdorf had given him in the years before the sunrise and sunset, he took out a New Year gift. After the fine old custom, it was packed in an oblong gift box and tied with a red and white paper ribbon called a *mizuhiki.* The traditional *noshi* had been added to this ribbon on the upper right side of the box—pastel-colored silk paper folded in a special fashion.

"I have brought you a scroll-painting," Baron Matsubara said, and added ironically, "If I were compelled to spend as much as an hour with the pictures hanging in this house, I would hang myself beside them! I admire your stamina, my little Eiko."

At that moment Mr. Yasuda appeared at the door, and behind him a servant girl carrying a tray laden with refreshments for Eiko.

"Go!" Mr. Yasuda ordered. At the moment it was not clear whether he meant his honored wife or the servant. In any case, the servant retreated. Eiko was still not taking orders.

"May I ask you to join us downstairs, Baron?" Mr. Yasuda said with wooden face. He had recognized Eiko's father at once from newspaper photographs. But it was New Year's. The wretched war criminal knew only too well that not even a Japanese democrat could show a guest the door on this most important holiday in the year. He must show him hospitality, wish him happiness, and more or less smile at him.

This was precisely what Mr. Yasuda did. On the question of holiday manners all Japan was united, however it might otherwise be racked by dissension.

After Baron Matsubara had partaken of ceremonial refreshments, he sat looking alternately at his little feminine image and at Mr. Yasuda the textile manufacturer. He had already heard where and how they had met. Eiko had secretly accompanied a girl friend to a party for which Mr. Yasuda had contributed the whisky and accordingly become guest of honor. Baron Matsubara had, after his sleepless night, conceived a subtle plan to extract his daughter from her present environment. This environment, he now noted, was exactly what he had imagined it to be.

Naturally he did not throw his plan at wretched Mr. Yasuda all at once. Instead, he guided the conversation from the usual holiday sentiments gently, gently around to Nippon's present economic predicament. He wanted first of all to test his son-in-law's intelligence. With exemplary patience he listened to the newly rich democrat's analyses, now and then darting in with an incisive question. It turned out that Yasuda-san not only was well informed, but harbored, behind all his democratic claptrap, highly acceptable ideas on the possibilities for economic reconstruction. Moreover, he had a number of connections which were not yet available to the *zaibatsu*, who had been excluded from economic life, in spite of Kenzo's tireless efforts. Mr. Yasuda was young, energetic, and had a good political record. He had been still a child when Baron Matsubara was working for the construction of the sacred Empire in Southeast Asia. . . . The baron's mind worked at full speed while Mr. Yasuda, en-

tirely in his element, somewhat patronizingly informed the base war
criminal about the new Japan. The country must be placed on her
own feet economically, Mr. Yasuda said emphatically—although of
course with the aid of, and not in opposition to, the United States,
he added virtuously. But the core of his disquisition was still that
Japan, in order to stand on her own honored legs, must trade with
Red China. Mr. Yasuda sincerely hoped that the United States would
have no objection. After all, the Americans did not object to Shintoism either, so long as it was not State Shinto.

Mr. Yasuda then turned to the subject of exports. That is to say,
he glided from the general principles of economic democracy to the
question of his textiles, which he was burningly eager to export to
the United States, or even to manufacture in San Francisco in such
quantities and at such shamelessly low prices that innumerable
American housewives would be able to buy blouses for a single dol-
lar, since Japanese wages were, at most, ten per cent of American
wages. Mr. Yasuda ought to know; the wages of his workers were
a considerable percentage under the average. Cheap blouses, Eiko's
young husband concluded, would undoubtedly constitute an important element in de-mo-cra-cy both in Japan and in the United States.

Since Baron Matsubara was royally amused, and on the whole
pleasantly surprised by his son-in-law's intelligence—he had been
reared to believe that in Nippon only the high nobility was capable
of thinking—he frowned rather darkly and imposed a weighty pause
on the conversation. Finally he rose with his accustomed grace and
thanked Yasuda-san for the pleasant evening and the informative
talk. He added his ceremonial New Year wishes, saying that Yasuda-
san was really a *narikin,* a man made of gold—in other words, good
as gold! But his daughter Eiko—who, like foreign women, wore instead of a kimono a shameless sweater which distinctly defined the
form of her small breasts—his daughter, Baroness Matsubara of Itoh,
nineteen years old and plainly running wild under Mr. Yasuda's influence, could not possibly remain in a house in which hung oil
paintings from America that might drive poor Eiko to suicide at any
minute. That was perfectly clear, was it not? Moreover, divorce
nowadays was just as democratic as cheap blouses and sheets. Or
did Yasuda-san think differently?

After Baron Matsubara had spoken these charming preludes to a family drama in a honeyed voice, smiling at Yasuda-san all the while, he turned to his miserable daughter and said bluntly, "You are coming home with me at once! Kikue is waiting outside in the vestibule with a kimono."

He bowed once more with utter grace and waited with undisguised impatience for Eiko to make her parting bow to her husband. Mr. Yasuda was quite capable of carrying out his plans by virtue of his intelligence and low wages; everything would go along nicely blouse by blouse and deal by deal. To all this Eiko was quite superfluous.

But Mr. Yasuda stood trembling, while Eiko seemed to have frozen into a statue. She held her head raised high, while an icy stream ran through her body. Both young people were helpless with horror and quite incapable of coping with the diabolic graciousness of the former Tiger of the Kempetai. Nor could they resist his enormous arrogance and unassailable authority. But in spite of millenniums of submission to the wills of fathers, Eiko suddenly looked up out of her numbness at her young husband. And what she saw determined her fate. Yasuda-san, who had taken her from the cloister of a dying family, which, like all its kind, was enduring hunger and scorn in proud obstinacy, and transported her to the midst of life; Yasuda-san, who was young and kind and hard-working as a bee—Yasuda-san was looking at Eiko like a man on his deathbed. His pleasure-loving lips, which had kissed her body into wakefulness, were quivering as helplessly as a boy's; but the real drama was taking place in his eyes. Those deep, shining, distressed eyes were looking at Eiko with a degree of humility and love which would have melted the snow on sacred Mount Fuji. This was something like the way Mr. Yasuda had looked at her when she refused to speak to him for three days and he had brought her that impossible necklace—just like that, really, except that there had been less of this nameless, mute sorrow and longing for death.

Eiko awoke from her numbness. She bowed low and humbly before Baron Akiro and whispered that to her infinite regret she could not follow the High Paternal Person. She would remain with Toshiyuki, and nothing and no one could change that. She would remain with him and the oil paintings if—if her honored husband still wished to have her. And Eiko flew as lightly and gracefully as a butterfly to her young husband, bowed her proud head, and in a broken voice asked him to forgive her for . . . She did not know what Toshiyuki should forgive her for, and so she knelt mutely before him, as her mother, grandmother, and great-grandmother in the bad old days had knelt before their husbands. She kept her eyes closed, ready for life or for death. As if in a dream she felt a man's arms gently lifting her, and a hand passing over her shining long hair. But it was not the hand of her husband, who was vainly groping for words. It was her father's.

"I only wanted to know whether I had a mouse or a Matsubara for a daughter," the baron said tranquilly. "I am sorry that my method alarmed you."

Later he elaborated the plan he had come with in case his daughter proved to be no mouse and his son-in-law no idiot. He knew his daughter only from the infrequent furloughs he had spent in Tokyo during Nippon's spell of glory, but on the whole he estimated her correctly. And of course he had always felt responsible for her; that was only one of his many familial duties.

"I will, of course, adopt you, Yasuda-san," Baron Akiro said suddenly. "My honored father has adopted my cousin Kenzo; our family seems to favor this method."

Adoption was nothing extraordinary; it was an old custom in important families in case there was no eldest son to beget grandsons and carry on the family name. That was the principal consideration for Matsubara Akiro; incidentally, all the Matsubaras would thereafter collaborate, and Mr. Yasuda's connections with the new authorities might well prove highly useful. Officially the reconstruction of Japan's economic life would continue under the blameless name of "Yasuda" until the Twelve Families once again came to power, which would surely be within the next five or ten years. Thereafter Mr. Yasuda would function, wherever it seemed appropriate, as Baron Matsubara of Itoh. And Eiko's prospective son would some day be, it was to be hoped, a keen and cool-headed nobleman like his grandfather Akiro and his great-grandfather in the hermit's hut.

Young Mr. Yasuda listened open-mouthed as his father-in-law expatiated on his plan for adoption and inheritance.

Feeling that he had done a good day's work, the baron rode in a shabby ricksha to Prince Itoh, who was to play the part of "intermediary" with the family. That, too, was Japanese custom. Eiko and her husband would spend the third day of the New Year holiday in the Matsubara manor. Old Kikue had placed the kimono in Eiko's wardrobe; it was as choice as that kimono from Imperial Kyoto which Baron Matsubara had presented to Consul Wergeland in 1925, without ever receiving a word of thanks from his first and last Western friend.

Akiro smiled with satisfaction. He had applied the tried and true methods of the Kempetai. First he had acted as if he wished to make Eiko purchase certain advantages by betrayal of a person close to her—the simplest way to determine a person's principles. And then he had brought Yasuda-san over to the side of the Twelve Families by a bribe on a really generous scale. Yasuda would draw other democrats after him.

The methods of the secret police were still effective, Matsubara Akiro reflected, even though their practitioners had vanished into the cellars under the new de-mo-cra-cy. Whereupon his thoughts returned once more to Colonel Saito, whose entire family had been wiped out by the atom bomb which fell upon Nagasaki and its suburb Urakami.

No one could help Colonel Saito; all the plans of his true friend and loyal associate, Matsubara Akiro, were of no avail. Akiro was genuinely grieved that this was so. He did not smile as he rode through a Tokyo ablaze with illuminated advertisements. For a few minutes he could look somber, for he was alone.

Joseph Kitsutaro Saito spent the New Year holiday of 1950, as he had so many holidays of the past, in his prison cell. He sat on the tattered mat and talked with his beloved wife and children. In a sense they were with him constantly, for no one is ultimately dead so long as someone thinks of him and prays for him.

Colonel Saito's big peasant's body had become alarmingly gaunt —not because he did not receive enough to eat, but because he could not eat. His wife had to admonish him gently before he would obediently and humbly take the chopsticks between his knobby fingers and choke down the rice. Perhaps God had prescribed a long life of penitence for His miserable son Joseph Saito, and in that case, he would need his strength.

Like those of a very old man, his thoughts often wandered back

to Urakami. He and his family would be having a picnic by the river
again, and the children swam and shouted. Or else they all knelt
together at the vesper hour in the little church and felt happy and
full of confidence. That had been before the war, long before Joseph
Kitsutara Saito had dedicated himself to the service of the rigid,
death-bringing glory of the Imperial Chrysanthemum. In the simplicity of his nature he had believed that one could hunt men by
day—men who had planned the downfall of Nippon, to be sure—
and at night pray and sleep. That had been an error, and the Lord
in His boundless grace had granted His servant, Joseph Saito of
Urakami, the privilege of partly atoning for his sins in thought, word,
and deed by ten years of strict incarceration.

Sometimes the prison chaplain, an American Catholic priest, visited him. Each time Father O'Brien left the cell shaken and almost
ashamed by such pure humility. Colonel Saito was one of the first
Japanese Christians Father O'Brien had come to know well. The
good Father had drawn up a petition for mercy, but Joseph Saito
refused to hear of it; he insisted on serving his full term. After all,
it was only ten years. And Father O'Brien had left the cell, shaking
his head. His Japanese flock was still a sealed book to him. Where
else in the world was there a human being who wished pedantically
to serve ten endless years when these might be commuted to six or
seven? But the humble request not to concern himself with so miserable and sinful a prisoner had touched the young priest to the
heart. He had asked Joseph Saito with equal humility to pray for
him at Epiphany.

Joseph Saito was not so sad as his friend Matsubara imagined.
He had returned home from the headquarters of the wolves to that
of the lambs, and done so with a swiftness and thoroughness possible
only to children and to the poor in spirit. When he knelt before his
wooden crucifix, which had accompanied him to Shanghai and Indo-
China, a premonition of mystic joy mingled with his sorrow and his
repentance. He began to see, with the vision that is vouchsafed to
saints and sometimes to sinners, that during the era of power he had
in all sincerity prayed for a false goal. For this reason his sins had
come down upon his head. And since he now recognized this, he
turned his back upon the world with absoluteness and promptness.

He refused to file a petition for mercy because he wanted to be judged sternly. In his noble simplicity he felt that God could certainly make the cherry blossoms bloom in winter, and likewise exempt the most wretched of sinners from all punishment, but that this would not be right. The cherry blossoms of grace would bloom in the heavenly Kyoto at the prescribed season. This, it seemed to him, was required by the Japanese and the divine sense of order.

Night after night Joseph Saito knelt before his inherited crucifix and prayed to Jesus with childlike trust that all should be done as was right for his country and for himself. And therefore he humbly thanked Him for the long, severe cold of the winter, and for well-regulated suffering.

3: Encounter in the Fujiya Hotel

HELENE WERGELAND TO VIVICA WILLIAMS (FUJIYA HOTEL
MYANOSHITA, JAPAN)

Trondheim, January 18, 1950

Dear Vivie,

Thank you for your good wishes for Christmas and the New Year, the which I hope will bring us no surprises. I was very happy to receive the photographs of yourself and your little Halvard. The child is big and strong for three, and reminds me of your father: the same eyes and the same smile!

I am less pleased to hear that you skipped out of Tokyo before Christmas and have taken yourself, the boy, and his Japanese nurse off to Myanoshita. Please do not tell me that you want to admire Mount Fuji, for I know perfectly well how little you care for natural beauties. Your remark about the climate is tommyrot. You are perfectly healthy and so is the child. You cannot fool me; you ought to know that by now, child!

Why have you left your husband alone for the holidays? You are only providing food for the gossip-mongers. By now you are twenty-three years old, and it is time you considered what you are doing. What is wrong? I am worried about you. Please do not make me wait another six months for a reply. I am an old woman and do not have much more time for waiting.

Not that there is anything wrong with my health. The Widow of Aalesund—whose husband, by the way, died in Copenhagen two years ago—is also enjoying good health. She has even grown quite fat. All the girls in the Mothers' Home are fond of her. She tells them and their children cloak-and-dagger stories about the Siamese jungles. The stories rarely have any point, but people like to hear about elephants and such stuff. I am happy to have Laura with me again; I know her, and she knows me.

There is only the best of news from Astrid. Her twins, Antoine and Hélène, are thriving. Astrid looks devastatingly well in her last picture, except for an insane hat. A little strange, I must admit, but I suppose that is due to Paris. Our Mailin is very sad; she has lost her Jimmy. But she will be sensible about it; I have no fears for her. It is fortunate that she has her three sons, for she is a born mother. She will spend this summer in Trondheim with the children; then we shall see about the future. Of course the Chou family of Singapore will not give up her or the children for any longer period, but I have known that since the day Mailin married. Please write to her; do not be forgetful.

No one hears anything from you. I should like to know what you have on your mind. If you find yourself bored, there is but one piece of advice I can give: work! Since Timothy has his hands full at the hospital in Tokyo—so he wrote to me—you might take care of his correspondence, or do something in the hospital. I don't want you to be doing anything foolish, Vivie!

Aunt Helene

VIVICA WILLIAMS TO HELENE WERGELAND (HELENE
WERGELAND MOTHERS' HOME, TRONDHEIM)

Myanoshita, February 1950

Dear Aunt Helene,

Thank you for your letter of January 18. I have no idea why you are angry with me. I make such an effort to please you, but you know I am not as nicely finished as Astrid or as balanced as Mailin.

I also would like to please Tim, but most of the time my efforts miss fire. I'm terribly fond of him; aside from you and Halvard, he is all I have, you know. But we do not get on too well. That has nothing to do with love. Tim is so jealous, and at the same time has so little time for me, that I prefer to be alone. He is the best person in the world, of course, and he is not to blame for his truly horrible family in Concord. I have never seen such unimaginative and such unpleasantly hard-working people as the natives of Concord. But I suppose that is because I have always lived in the tropics and am now in divine Japan. . . . There is no sense in writing long letters about that. Fortunately, Tim has so much to do with the hospital and the medical education of the Japanese that he will remain here at least another four years. Also I would never find such a child's nurse as Sumi anywhere else. Best of all I should like to live in Paris. I envy Astrid for being able to. I have been on speaking terms only with one Frenchman—Astrid's husband, of course. But how amusing he was, and how urbane, and his dancing was heavenly. Astrid sent me a copy of the photo also. Pierre is still marvelous, even though he is so awfully dapper and polished. But I prefer a person polished and amusing to easygoing and dull, and that is what Tim's friends here are, with few exceptions. He has a sweet young assistant, Bob Donnelly, but I'm not supposed to dance and laugh with him, and—oh, Aunt Helene, I'm rather tired of married life! Halvard is still too little to be a companion to me, and he screams for Sumi as soon as I want to take him. I would be happiest with you. Even though you write me such scolding letters, you know everything about me and what I have been through.

I don't know why you ask "what is wrong." *Nothing is wrong,* that's the worst of it. I went away over Christmas because we were invited to one party after the other, and I'd rather be alone with myself than alone with forty Americans. I came up here to collect a few new faces, that's all. I don't know what Tim has written to you; he is just too good for me. I'm terribly sorry for him. He is wonderfully warm and reliable, but whenever I want to warm myself the whole Tokyo "crowd" is right there with him. Americans cannot be alone, and we Norwegians cannot stand constantly having people about us. *You* cannot reproach me for that, Aunt Helene! I'm not so clever as you and the Duchess in Paris, and don't have Mailin's angelic patience. I'm terribly sorry about Jimmy. But Mailin, for all her fragility, is somehow invulnerable. And I am tall and strong, but inwardly I must be made of glass. Sometimes I hear it breaking. If Tim lets me go,

I'll pay you a visit this summer too. Or don't you want to have me? Halvard and Sumi would come also, of course. Oh, if only it were summer already! Time creeps along. Timothy is most of the time as invisible as a *minomushi*-insect; that was what a Japanese acquaintance of mine once called himself, back in Shanghai. Here in the hotel there is a chrysanthemum room also—and other flower rooms. But one scarcely sees any Japanese here; only Americans, and a few Englishmen and Swiss.

All love from your far from naughty
Vivica

DR. MARGARET WILLIAMS TO MAJOR TIMOTHY WILLIAMS (U. S. ARMY, THE COUNCIL OF MEDICAL EDUCATION, TOKYO HEADQUARTERS)

Dear Brother,

Thank you for your Christmas greetings; Mother and I send the same to you. It is very nice to have the snapshot of the three of you. The boy looks like Grandfather Williams to a T.

I was very much interested in the newspaper clippings on your new medical schools in Japan, and particularly pleased to see that a group of forward-looking Japanese doctors have taken a positive stand on your work and are actively aiding it. I have always thought that work for a common goal contributes far more to democratic development than all armchair discussions, pamphlets, and orders. And so I wish you success with all my heart, in the New Year, for the project you have helped to build. And this brings me to my main topic.

You cannot seriously mean, Tim, to spend still more years in Japan on account of the whims of your wife. You yourself write that your work has been placed in many competent hands, and that more and more Japanese doctors are attending the four-year course in laboratory work, and the clinical training, and are taking the final examinations. Under these circumstances I do not see why you should stay away from home much longer—all the more so since the boy is growing up and ought to be brought in contact with other influences besides his Japanese nurse and the American kindergartens in Tokyo.

It is hard for me to say this to you, but it must be said sometime: the manner in which you abruptly broke off your stay here two years ago, solely because your wife did not like us and Concord, is not easily forgotten or forgiven. You and I have been the best of friends from childhood, always worked for things in common, and I was deeply hurt by your action. I will say nothing at all about Mother. She swallows everything in silence and only grows weaker and paler all the time. Please do not again give me that nonsense that Vivica as a Norwegian girl cannot adjust to life in the States. The trouble is not with Concord but with Vivica. If you would for once consider the problem objectively, you would have to agree with me. To my mind, much too much is made of "national differences" in this world. It isn't half as bad as all that. In our country in particular, which has taken and continues to take in millions of immigrants who then try to make themselves into Americans—in our country especially, innumerable Norwegian families have learned to fit in perfectly well. These people, however, did not look for a dream world in the States; they adjusted to our world as it is. This is what Vivica did not even try to do. I admit that she had to pass through rather extraordinary experiences during the years in which other girls play tennis and prepare themselves for a profession. At your wedding in Trondheim, Miss Helene Wergeland had a long talk with me on this very point. I have seldom met a more admirable individual than this brave, kind, thoroughly active woman. Vivica, unfortunately, has an asocial character. As a doctor I understand her; you are quite mistaken when you think I do not. I would even say that in many aspects of this matter I see more deeply than you. And so I am not at all surprised that Vivica is unwilling to leave Japan. Her feeling for the country is a kind of hate-love such as introverted people frequently develop after experiences that were too much for them. I am speaking here as a physician, not as Vivica's "judge," to use the word you employed before your flight to Tokyo. If I spoke too harshly at that time—I could not help seeing how you were hurting Mother—I beg your pardon. I am thinking only of what is best for you; in this I am in complete accord with Helene Wergeland, who would also like to see Vivica settled in Concord as soon as possible. I wish you would consider these things soberly and not shut your mind to all that your family means to you. You have always been the pride of all of us, Tim; you know that. If so-called love can make even a person like yourself deaf and blind to realities, then I must thank God that in all my thirty-six years I have been spared the disease of love.

The immediate cause of all this is the following: dear old Dr.

Chase has had a second stroke, and in spite of his acute New England sense of responsibility is forced at last to give up his practice to a younger man. Nothing would please him and Mrs. Chase more than to see you take over for him in Concord. Of course, if you do not return in three months, someone else will have to be called in. All of us hope that you will see this as the golden opportunity it is, to be of service to the community and lead the kind of life you were intended for. It would be in every respect ideal. Mother would pick up wonderfully if you were around. I promise that we and all our friends will do our best to make Vivica like it here.

Mother is shipping you a box of Baldwin apples, to remind you of how they taste at home.

> All the best from
> Your old
> Margaret

Lips tightly compressed, Major Timothy Williams read his sister's letter on the way to the nursing school in Tokyo, which was so dear to his heart that he gave up some of his scant leisure to make these inspection trips. There was no need for him to consider; for the present he was staying in Japan—until the boy is ready for school, he thought. That would be three years hence. Then Vivie would have to listen to reason. It was rather nice that this process could be postponed a full three years. A little of the Oriental tendency to let things take their course had infected even so capable and energetic a man as Major Williams during his stay in the Far East. But the main thing was to earn a smile from Vivie; that was what Timothy Williams lived for during his scant leisure time.

The American head nurse of the hospital connected with the nursing school came to meet him, smiling with effort, eyes inflamed from weeping and hasty applications of cold water. Elizabeth Murphy was a tall, well-groomed girl from San Francisco. She had been expecting a proposal, but today she had in her pocket a good-by note from Captain Donnelly. This was the same young doctor whom Vivica considered "sweet"—a comment that Miss Wergeland in Trondheim read with a frown.

"What's the matter, Betty?" Major Williams asked, pretending not to notice her tear-stained eyes.

"Trouble," Miss Murphy replied tersely. "Do you remember Nurse

Sadako? She ran away from home three years ago. Her father was an imprisoned war criminal—the old story. Now she has left the hospital in the dead of night."

"Running away seems to be a habit of hers. What is her family name?"

"Matsu or Saru, or something like that. They're all the same."

Timothy pondered, the lines on his forehead deepening. This was embarrassing. The Japanese newspapers seized on such runaway stories almost as eagerly as on stories of suicides. And yet the new hospitals and especially the nursing schools could be counted among the real achievements of the occupation's re-education program. Before 1945 nurses in Japan had been low-paid servant girls, with a correspondingly low social position, who scrubbed floors and left most of the care of patients to the honored relatives. The family often lived in the sickrooms, prepared the meals, and entertained the sick persons with gossip, singing, and deadly delicacies.

Nurse Sadako had been hard-working and sweet-spoken. The head nurse was utterly baffled by this sudden flight. The Japanese were an incomprehensible people. You worked with them and thought you were reaching bedrock, and suddenly the ground gave way as though there had been an earthquake.

There was a shy knock at the door. Bowing repeatedly, Nurse Sumiko smilingly entered the laboratory. "Letter from Nurse Sadako," she murmured, drawing the breath audibly through her nose. "Sumiko is to say—is to give news," she added vaguely.

It turned out that Nurse Sadako had suffered a nervous breakdown and had "fled from desires for suicide" to a "small miserable country house" belonging to her maternal great-uncle. American officer loved Sadako, but Sadako had great fear of "Lady Head Nurse Murphy" and therefore "nerves all gone."

"Who is the officer?" Major Williams asked as gently as possible. "Why is Nurse Sadako afraid of Miss Murphy?"

Nurse Sumiko, a tailor's daughter, began to giggle, holding her hand over her mouth in slightly vulgar fashion. She choked over her laughter, which sprang from her sympathy for "Lady Murphy," whom she deeply admired. Finally she stammered that the "U.S. friend" of Nurse Sadako was the honored captain Bob Donnelly.

"Very well, thank you for the message, Nurse Sumiko," Major

Williams said, trying not to look at Lady Murphy. "Where is Nurse Sadako staying?"

"Don't know, Major-san. Might be Tonosawa. Might be Chiradei. Might be Myanoshita. Might—"

"Thank you." Major Williams ended the geography lesson, whose implication he fully grasped. Captain Donnelly was, of course, at the Fujiya Hotel, where he had gone for his furlough. Nurse Sadako was staying somewhere in the vicinity, in one of the villages mentioned. A charming situation! This was precisely what Tokyo and Washington expected of the members of the American Army in their role as "educators."

"Please bring me Nurse Sadako's file card, Betty," he said quietly after Nurse Sumiko had scampered out in a paroxysm of sympathetic merriment. "We must get in touch with the girl's family and report the whole thing. Otherwise they will be saying again that . . ."

He broke off, frowning. So that was why Donnelly had given Betty Murphy the go-by. Everyone had taken it for granted that they were as good as engaged. It was hard on this courageous, decent girl who had flung herself with such self-sacrificing eagerness into the work for the hospital and the nursing school. She and Bob had come to Japan from San Francisco together. Their families were close friends back home. As he skimmed through Nurse Sadako's record, while Miss Murphy stared out the window, he suddenly started. Then he said to Miss Murphy's back, "Donnelly must have a screw loose. The girl is a baroness of the Matsubara family. What a scandal that will be! Those people belong to the Twelve Families. Did you know that, Betty?"

Miss Murphy turned slowly away from the window and seemed to be studying a rack of test-tubes. Then she looked down at the floor. She felt Tim's kindly, intelligent eyes on her. He himself was not exactly living on a bed of roses with his beautiful wife, who also seemed to have a screw loose. Betty shook her head mutely, loosening the dark hair crowned by the nurse's cap.

"I'll be joining my wife at the Fujiya Hotel over the week end," Tim said. "I'll take the occasion to straighten Donnelly out. It's crazy, a fellow like Bob losing his head over a pretty little Japanese toy. He doesn't give a thought to his future."

Tim had talked himself into a rage. He pounded on the table, only in order to bring some life into the girl's numbed face. Out here all of them had to stick together against the gracious, cunning, death-loving, and secretive people who surrounded them.

"Of course it would be a pity if he ruined his career through a scandal," Miss Murphy said. "It's not a personal concern for me any more."

"You're not going to let a little Japanese pastime girl take Bob away from you?"

"They're always taking our men away, Tim. The pastime girls and the students, both. They do it with their littleness and fragility, with their kimonos and moon faces and their folderol with the tea. Ceremonial theft, my boy."

"You're exaggerating, Betty! Those helpless little creatures!"

"That helplessness is all a fake, Tim. I work with them and I know them. They're a whole lot subtler than we are. We're good pals; we give the boys their coffee and apple pie without any fuss and feathers, and call a spade a spade. Here in Japan that isn't good enough for them. Oh, Tim, next time I hear the words 'tea ceremony' I'm going to scream! I've had enough of the women here. They go all wistful and speak about suicide, and our boys fall for it like a ton of bricks."

"Not all, Betty!"

"I'm going home as soon as my contract expires." Miss Murphy pressed her forehead against the window pane. "I can't go on."

"Let's have dinner together! That's an invitation, not an order. And wear that print dress of yours, if you please. I want to have something nice to look at for a change." Tim grinned like a schoolboy. "Okay?"

"Okay. Thanks. What time, Tim?"

"Eight o'clock on the Ginza, Lady Murphy!"

Elizabeth smiled at last. Then she thought of the gossip among the American crowd in Tokyo and in the Fujiya Hotel, which the occupation authorities had taken over from a Japanese family of hoteliers rich in tradition. It was one of the finest hotels in the world, situated amid dramatically lovely volcanic landscape, flanked by blue lakes, with Mount Fuji rising in the distance. There the man with whom she had hoped to share her life was having himself a good time. Or could it possibly be that he was in love with that little Japanese girl?

"Won't your wife mind if we dine together in public here?" she asked, half jokingly, half seriously.

"Vivica?" Major Williams asked, feeling his heart suddenly begin to hammer painfully. "Don't worry about that, Betty! My wife isn't as jealous as all that." He laughed and hastily lit a cigarette.

If Miss Murphy had not been so preoccupied with her own grief, she might have noticed that Tim's laugh was a little forced, and that the humor had gone out of his eyes.

"See you later, Lady Murphy," Major Williams said, and strode out a bit precipitately.

As soon as he heard from the Tokyo nursing school, Baron Matsubara Akiro left for Myanoshita to rescue his younger daughter, Sadako, from the clutches of melancholia or the occupying power. His indispensable son-in-law, Mr. Yasuda, had business in the vicinity and could therefore obtain gasoline for the drive of several hours to Myanoshita. During the ride his father-in-law sat wrapped in gloomy silence. With the Japanese talent for resignation and pretended cheerfulness, Baron Akiro had become reconciled to a good deal within a few months. But that his miserable daughter, who resembled the noble and unfortunate Lady Tatsue in all except her limp, wished to become a plaything for an American officer—that, by all the dethroned Shinto gods, was going too far! The baron might be earnestly studying how to win a lost war with the aid of democracy; but if there was anyone who took a sterner view of "fraternization" than the authorities in Washington (whose regulations on the matter were so blithely ignored in and around Tokyo), it was this same Baron Matsubara. There was a dull, underground rumbling within him such as the craters in the Hakone region frequently produce; this rumbling stemmed partly from his fury and partly from his stomach cramps. His face, with its fiercely glowing eyes and bold hooked nose, looked terrifying as he sat in silence beside his son-in-law in the speeding car.

Mr. Yasuda hunched anxiously over the wheel to avoid the baron's looks. In Akiro's pocket was a letter which Sadako had written to

Cousin Kenzo after her flight. "Because of regrettable love-tragedy" —that was the phrase the girl had used. She was a goose, as her honored mother had been. But Lady Tatsue had had considerably superior manners.

While Mr. Yasuda took care of his business, Baron Akiro entered the familiar hotel. He must spend three hours in this now hateful place; then he would be driving back to Tokyo with his misguided daughter. In three hours the Tiger of the Kempetai could bring whole wagonloads of daughters to their knees, and even send a reminiscent shudder down the spine of an American officer. Captain Donnelly would keep his hands off the daughters of the Japanese aristocracy henceforth! Akiro did not know, of course, that Sadako had been firmly calling herself "Miss Matsu," with the result that Captain Donnelly had no suspicion of who his little Miss Nippon's amiable father was. Almost all relationships between the Japanese and the members of the occupation forces were beclouded by misunderstandings. These began with the ambiguity of the Japanese language and gestures—waving a person away, for example, is the Japanese mode of beckoning him to come closer—and ended with the clash of two different world-views. Nevertheless, as Miss Murphy had accurately noted, the Japanese girls were forever taking men away from the American women who came to teach the Miss Nippons hygiene, liberty, and enlightenment. Miss Murphy, unfortunately, was destined never to find out that "Miss Matsu's" father was at least as violently opposed to Captain Donnelly's romance as she herself.

But the misunderstanding went still further. For Sadako was no such goose as her timid mother had been. Quietly she had guided her relationship with Captain Bob to the point she had had in mind from the start. As soon as she received a special-delivery letter from her friend Sumiko in Tokyo—this was five days before her father's drive to Myanoshita—she and Captain Donnelly had hied themselves to the capital city and been married there. The necessary papers and permits had long since been obtained. Bob had only hesitated for so long because he was reluctant to hurt his old flame, Elizabeth Murphy. That was what Sadako had been referring to in her letter to the new head of the Matsubara clan when she spoke of a "regrettable love-tragedy." It was Lady Murphy's tragedy, not her own.

When Baron Akiro entered the hotel, he found awaiting him a

letter from Cousin Kenzo which as gently as possible broke the news that Youngest Daughter, without farewells or wedding celebration, had departed by plane for San Francisco with new American husband. Sadako had a gift for laying plans as subtly and ably as her honored father. But to face Miss Murphy at the side of "new American husband"—*this* Sadako could not do. She was far too shy and peace-loving to subject herself to such a scene.

Baron Akiro carefully folded Kenzo's letter and placed it in his pocket. The Japanese desk clerk, who since time immemorial had seen members of the Twelve Families enter and leave this fairy-tale hotel, looked anxiously at the Tiger of the Kempetai.

"Good news, Baron?" he asked mournfully, bowing as he might have done in the bad old days.

"That depends," Matsubara Akiro answered with a frosty smile. "My younger daughter has had an accident; she has married an American."

Since Baron Akiro still had over two hours to wait for his son-in-law, he went across the lobby of the hotel, which had been swept clean of Japanese guests, and into the small rocky landscape of the garden. He did not seem to see the foreigners who paraded about in bathrobes from their rooms to the medicinal hot springs or the steam bath—huge, red-cheeked microbes, as his honored grandmother rightly thought.

It scarcely occurred to the strangers that this dream of a hotel at the entrance to the Fuji-Hakone National Park was on intimate terms with the slumbering volcano. During the great earthquake of 1923, before young Baron Matsubara had ever been abroad, Hakone Lake had begun to boil. That was one year before the restriction of Japanese immigration into the United States, and two years before Consul Wergeland's reception in Shanghai, at which Matsubara Akiro had been unspeakably insulted by a Mr. Bailey of Clifford Motors. Baron Akiro's phenomenal memory built a curious bridge from that evening in Shanghai to his American son-in-law, whom he hoped he would never meet. As a young man Akiro had wished to abash the foreigners by wisdom and generosity; in the past twenty-five years he had graduated to other methods. Haughtily erect, he marched through the mild February air to the waterfalls, the lakes, and the fish-ponds he had loved in his youth.

By one miniature lake, stretched out in a steamer-chair and wrapped in a white woolen blanket, lay a girl in a light green jacket. Her long blond hair fell down into her beautiful face, giving her an air of faint, utterly charming abandon. Out of half-closed eyes she saw a fine-looking Japanese approaching. She wrinkled her childishly rounded forehead.

The Japanese moved toward the hidden miniature lake as though he knew it well. Then, with lithe grace, he settled down a short distance away from the girl. Something about his movements, disciplined and yet graceful, reminded the girl in the steamer-chair of something long repressed. Under half-closed eyelids Vivica saw a room devoted to the art of living and torture of the mind in Shanghai —a chrysanthemum room such as she occupied in the Fujiya Hotel, with the frozen splendor of flowers in the *tokonoma*. . . . A tall Japanese in a dark kimono asked with politeness and an undertone of mockery after the wishes of his honorable prisoner. . . . Loudly, as though she sees not the bars of her cage, the nightingale sings. . . . Why do you not drink, Mademoiselle? Death is too good for you, Mademoiselle. . . . Passionate glances probing every line of her body . . . a cruel, voluptuous, and yet ascetic mouth. . . . Oh, this poisonous feeling!

Vivica had closed her eyes. A terrible weakness overcame her. Unnoticed, a sheet of paper slipped from her hands—a delicate, fantastic sketch of the kind she often tossed off when she was afflicted by boredom. Her sketches were all curious and unusual, but incomplete. Completeness requires diligence.

A breeze picked up the sketch and deposited it at the feet of the Japanese. At once he sprang up and brought it back to its owner. "Your sketch, Mademoiselle," he said with a ceremonial bow. "May I have the honor of returning it to you?"

Vivica opened her nymph's eyes wide. She forgot to thank him. "Major Kimura?" Her voice was an insubstantial whisper.

The stranger smiled. "You must be mistaking me for someone else, Mademoiselle," he said in his Parisian accent. "I am Baron Matsubara of Tokyo."

"Have we not met before—in Shanghai?"

"Shanghai?" The baron who bore a ghostly resemblance to Major-san looked stunned. He seemed about to ask where the city of Shanghai was located. Knitting his brows over this geographical enigma, he covertly scrutinized Vivica as if he were trying to see even her thoughts, which had never interested him. Flesh, he thought; stupidity, beauty. She had become even more beautiful, although a cloud of fatal ennui darkened her brow.

"I was in Shanghai once as a young man," he replied with impassive face. "In nineteen-twenty-five. You had certainly not come into the world yet, Mademoiselle."

His calculations were correct, as always. In 1925 young Baron Matsubara had invited Borghild Lillesand to a Japanese dinner in a chrysanthemum room. Now he was forty-five. This lovely Morning Face in the steamer-chair might have been his daughter. At the thought of daughters, Akiro was overcome by an unpleasant emotion. Sadako—that little imbecile who had flouted all tradition!

Vivica had recovered from her momentary weakness. A faint flush had risen to her cheeks. Every nerve in her body was alert now. She looked directly into the stranger's face and asked casually, "Are you lying the truth, Monsieur?"

"Would you prefer me to admit a lie, Mademoiselle?" Major-san asked gently. She was no longer so stupid as she had been in Shanghai; fear must have robbed her of all her mental faculties at that time. There was a glint of admiration in Akiro's eyes. No Japanese woman could have flung into his face more graciously and cunningly the fact that she had recognized him.

"Do you live up here all the time, Madame?" he asked, for he had noticed Vivica's wedding ring.

"Unfortunately we are returning to Tokyo on Monday. But as soon as the real heat starts I'll be going up to Karuizawa for the whole summer. Do you know the place, Baron? Except for the noise in the two big hotels, it is very lovely there."

Baron Matsubara pondered the charms of Karuizawa as thoroughly as he had Shanghai's geographical position a few moments before. He threw his *asagao*—"morning face," the flower that opens only for a morning—a middling volcano look. The ennui on her child's brow, the weary and yet rebellious lines around her rich lips, told him the story of her marriage. As a Japanese he was clever at deciphering the subtlest scripts. Probably she was married to an American—why else would she be at the Fujiya Hotel?

A gust of wind in this isolated corner of the lake carried away the jacket Vivica had draped casually around her shoulders. Major-san ran after it with the terpsichorean grace of a young Japanese playing a game. He came of a stock hard as steel; his gracious and cunning father in the hermit's hut also looked ten or fifteen years younger than he was.

The baron waved the jacket like a banner and laid it gently and respectfully around Vivica's shoulders. In doing so he noted that her blanket had loosened around the steamer-chair. He stooped over Morning Face slightly, fixing his ardent eyes upon her hair for brief seconds—hair that was a magical dream-web such as only the Far North wove around the heads of nymphs. As he solicitously wrapped the blanket around Vivica, his hands touched the tips of her breasts. It must have been chance, for the next thing Baron Matsubara did was to step back a pace and look at Vivica's drawing with genuine interest. In a Japanese landscape, its contours blurred in the best Japanese manner by a soft eraser, a figure in a kimono was crossing a swaying bamboo bridge. The figure was tiny, but in its hand it held a big round fan painted with strange animals and plants. For all its smallness, the graceful, kimonoed figure was drawn realistically, whereas the fan was done with sportive fantasy. Close inspection revealed that the bamboo bridge hung free in the air above a blurred abyss. Within this abyss there was the suggestion of intertwined figures, as in a distant vision of hell by some European old master. Scribbled playfully in one corner, half obliterated by a spot of grease, were the words: *Les Rêves de Vivienne.*

"A remarkable picture," Baron Matsubara murmured. "And how true!"

Vivica had flushed a fiery red. She rudely snatched the sketch from his hand. Under the white blanket she was still trembling from his touch, and angry with herself for being so affected. Quickly she tore the sketch to pieces and scattered the scraps of paper in all directions, which highly displeased Matsubara Akiro. In a Japanese lake garden, order and beauty were one and the same.

"It is very wise of you to have torn up your sketch, Madame."

"Why?"

"It was unfortunately quite amateurish. I pray, forgive me this disrespectful criticism, Madame. But you do have talent. You even have ideas, which is not quite normal in young ladies. It would be well if you took lessons in painting. But you will not, of course."

"How do you know that, Baron?" Vivica asked. She was beginning to recover from the shock of the meeting. "After all, you do not know me!" She threw a coquettish and mysterious glance at Major-san out of half-shut eyes, a glance which would probably have earned her a slap from her Aunt Helene even at this late date.

"To my regret I must again correct an error, Madame," Thought-Policeman Matsubara said with diabolic gentleness. "As the result of our little talks in Shanghai I came to know something about you. In fact, I believe that, in spite of my abysmal stupidity, I know you better than anyone else."

"I have never heard anything more ridiculous!" Vivica abruptly burst into laughter that was very gay but a little too shrill.

"Naturally your husband must know you considerably more thoroughly," the Baron said with an increasing note of slyness in his quiet voice. "But we Japanese do have the habit of reading an entire novel in a few allusions. I should venture to assert that our modest three-line poems often say more than a three-volume Western novel."

Since Vivica never read novels or poems, and found all conversations boring which did not revolve around herself, she said abruptly, "Why do you assume that I will not take painting lessons?"

"I am inconsolable, Madame; I have forgotten the reason." Baron Matsubara looked at his watch and made a formal bow. "Is it not unfortunate that the chats we have with each other every five years are always interrupted?" he asked pensively. "But perhaps you will visit me during the summer in my small house in Karuizawa, Madame? I could consider it a high honor to serve you a ceremonial tea. That is to say, if you have not already had one in the former palace of His Highness, Prince Takamatsu?"

Akiro's eyes had narrowed; a dangerous, cold warning signal flashed in their black depths. But Vivica replied innocently that she never went to the palace because too many Americans drank ceremonial tea there.

Baron Matsubara raised his eyebrows. "Is not your honored husband also an American, Madame?"

Vivica blushed deeply; she could have slapped herself for that careless remark. "I mean that I like to be alone," she said awkwardly.

Then she sprang to her feet, flinging the white blanket thoughtlessly to the ground. Baron Matsubara at once lifted it, folded it with meticulous care, and deposited it on the steamer-chair. As he did so, he did not so much as glance at Vivica—or if he did, she did not notice.

Suddenly he approached her. "You will visit me, Madame?"

"With pleasure, Monsieur—if you promise not to ask me so many questions this time."

"Would *I* ask *you* questions?" Baron Matsubara raised both hands in mock horror. At this moment he was practicing a Japanese specialty, *naibun,* or pretended innocence. Many Americans in Japan had had more experience than they wished with *naibun.* It was a cloud around the speaker, a thing which in the end made conversation or agreement impossible.

Since Vivica did not quite know how to react to *naibun,* she asked Major-san for his address in Karuizawa. Of course she would not visit him; she really could not do such a thing to Tim and to democracy! But let Major-san think she was coming, and be angry that she did not. This way she could revenge herself for everything he had done to her. As this thought came to her, her face broke into a charming, somewhat indolent smile.

"Simply ask for the country house of old Baroness Matsubara of Itoh, Madame," Akiro replied.

"Yes, but—do people really know? The country houses out there are all so hidden."

"We have been living in the house since eighteen-eighty, Madame," Matsubara Akiro replied mildly. "Do not worry—people know us there." He added with an amiable smile, "We are better known in Karuizawa, at any rate, than in the Fujiya Hotel, which we have stopped visiting since the last earthquake."

"Do you mean the earthquake of nineteen-twenty-three, which made Hakone Lake boil over?" From sheer boredom Vivica had been studying the hotel's prospectus and wanted to show off her knowledge of Japan.

"I meant the earthquake of nineteen-forty-five," Baron Matsubara informed her. "But I can see that it bores you. I humbly beg your pardon. I had forgotten that you have no particular liking for political conversations. In Karuizawa we shall talk about pleasanter matters, Madame."

"For example?" Vivica secretly rejoiced as she imagined Major-san's disappointment over her failure to come. She remembered now that he had kissed her in Dr. Yamato's hospital. She had pretended to be sleeping and unaware of those light caresses. "I really do not know what we would have to say to each other," she added pertly, throwing a triumphant glance at the defeated tiger. The times had changed; she was on the side of the victors now.

"To tell the truth, I do not know either," Matsubara Akiro said. "But if nothing has occurred to us by then, I shall propose a subject which will entertain both of us."

"What would that be, Baron?"

"*Les Rêves de Vivienne*," Baron Matsubara whispered, and paced lightly away.

Vivica stared after him, an absent smile on her face. Never would she call upon this satan! She hated him, and yet she was glad she had seen him because now he would wait for her in vain. It really is a pity, she thought with half-shut eyes. Major-san had been so much nicer and jollier this time than in Shanghai. . . . A little flirtation on the edge of an abyss would have been just the sort of thing she enjoyed.

Baron Matsubara was glad also as he sat in Mr. Yasuda's car on the drive back to Tokyo and, to his son-in-law's astonishment, chatted pleasantly. This time he would have to wait only five months for a talk with Morning Face.

4: *Baron Matsubara's Tea Ceremony*

Vivica would not have gone to tea with Major-san if she had not been so bored by Colonel Hunter's garden party at Karuizawa, and later so irritated. She was always the youngest person at these parties, and she was the only one who enjoyed being lazy. Paid or unpaid, American women in Japan devoted themselves to the re-education of the populace. Vivica had neither talent nor inclination for such activities. The inept compliments the men paid to her striking beauty bored or annoyed her. Aphrodite always felt offended when people called her a "pretty girl." Baron Matsubara, for all his slyness, would never have dreamed of calling Vivica "pretty" or "damned pretty." He recognized beauty wherever and in whatever form he encountered it—in a Karuizawa lily, in an old temple gate, in a young nymph from Europe's Far North.

But it was not only offended vanity or her sense of emptiness that tormented Vivica at these parties. In this American society her European need for isolated joys and sorrows remained unsatisfied. Her melancholic states during and after a party sprang from hopeless rebellion against the depersonalized unerotic New World atmosphere in old Nippon. Not that these men and women had no knowledge of the abysses of Eros. Miss Murphy was currently passing through various hells, and Major Timothy Williams had not been privileged to experience the miracle of intimacy in all the four years of his marriage with Vivica. But these aspects of private life were successfully ignored by the group and by the affected persons themselves.

The Japanese too concealed their griefs under radiant smiles, but for an altogether different reason. Their pathological sensitivity, nowadays intensified by wounded pride, made them averse to troubling anyone else with their own troubles. The Americans, on the other hand, suffered from another kind of pathological anxiety: they did not wish to appear to "their crowd" as failures, whether in business or in love. Both these tendencies to disguise personal wounds were alien to Vivica; this vagabonding Aphrodite never practiced such diplomacies.

Tim had insisted that Vivica attend the garden party because the Hunters were important persons in American society in Tokyo and would take offense if Vivica stayed away. The great thing was for the whole crowd to turn up, without exception. Only then did things become really jolly, impersonal, and relaxing. Tim himself was still sweating it out in Tokyo; he intended to visit Vivica and little Halvard within the next few days, and then spend three weeks in Karuizawa, amid the stupefying scent of lilies and the electric atmosphere engendered by the nearness of a volcano.

As soon as Vivica left the party and returned to her small chalet, her self-control gave out. She threw herself down on the bed, in the lovely gown which Astrid had designed and made for her, and sobbed without restraint. Then she sat bolt upright in front of her dressing-table mirror for a while and made decisions. When Vivica sat in front of a mirror and made decisions, Helene Wergeland had always wrinkled her brow and taken care that the girl was somehow distracted.

This hot summer evening Vivica decided to have a ceremonial tea with Baron Matsubara. In the first place, she wanted to prove that she had a right to joys and sorrows of her own. In addition, she was interested in seeing the Matsubaras' summer house. But above all she was tempted by the prospect of continuing her flirtation on the edge of an abyss—far from Helene Wergeland's stern glances, far from the "crowd," and far from Timothy Williams, who had so little time for her and her dream-life.

Since she despised Baron Matsubara, nothing could happen to her, she reassured herself as she caught sight of him in his wonderfully tended garden.

"I had been expecting you sooner, Madame!" Akiro turned slowly away from his lilies.

"I am only dropping in for a moment, Baron! Isn't it odd? I've been out for a walk and stumbled on your summer house by sheer chance."

Baron Matsubara smiled sincerely at this naïve attempt to stand on dignity. "It could not be odder, Madame," he agreed earnestly, and invited her to enter the tea hut.

A pretty, sad-looking Japanese woman appeared and with a graceful bow brought the utensils for the tea ceremony. Vivica looked at her and started slightly. Where had she seen this woman before? In Shanghai . . . on the margin of the morphine meadow . . .

"M-Madame Yamato?" she stammered, paling. But the fragile Japanese with the sad smile had already scurried out. She had found a refuge for herself and her son from the hunger and the housing shortage of Tokyo here with Major-san. In this hidden summer house there were other shipwrecked Japanese from Shanghai whom the Tiger of the Kempetai had fraternally taken in. Except for Madame Yamato, who was waiting with Christian submissiveness to be reunited in Heaven with the little hero in the cutaway who had saved Vivica from the Kempetai, all the occupants of this remote summer house were waiting for the autumn. Even that lieutenant who had once accompanied "Major Kimura" to Miss Wergeland's after Vivica's arrest was now here. Akiro had picked him up on the streets of Tokyo, where he wore the white garment of the despised war invalids while he sang *samurai* ballads in front of a café and held out a beggar's bowl to the sympathetic evening breeze. They had all found in Prince Itoh's summer house "a good place in the dark" where they might wait for the autumn. In Nippon autumn is the time of chrysanthemums. . . .

Baron Matsubara's tea hut, the *sukiya,* was a plain little building surrounded by flowers and high shrubs. Ordinarily the tea hut was devoted to meditation, and no one might enter it after the master of the household was seated in it before the boiling water and the utensils. It was a hermitage dedicated to tranquillity and contemplation in this mountain resort overshadowed by Asama-Yama, the largest active volcano in the country. Sacred Asama was the favorite volcano of the suicide clubs and in its time had swallowed up many a pair of lovers and many a student or *samurai* whose honor had been impugned. Smoking or slumbering, this volcano was always in the thoughts of the Japanese. It filled the air of Karuizawa with suppressed excitement and a subterranean temptation to yield entirely to that fire which from time to time erupts through Japanese smiles, courtesy, and *naibun.*

Baron Matsubara had not spewed fire for some time. This simple room hidden among shrubbery was his oasis in the desert of de-mo-cra-cy. Here he could always have "diamond dew"—the purest tea—flowers, and the consolation of painting.

With his accustomed grace he knelt on his pillow and played the good host. He did not cast a single ardent glance at Vivica. Only now, as Major-san served her the diamond dew with modestly lowered eyes and entertained her with legends about flowers, did she realize how eagerly she had been waiting for those glances. A solitary orchid from the woods around Karuizawa lay "noiselessly" in a mossy bowl in front of the scroll in the *tokonoma.* "Noisy" flowers were banned from a tea hut—as was noisy talk.

Baron Akiro really understood Morning Face very well; he observed the cloud of vexation upon her child's brow and smiled secretly to himself. If for once a flirtation was to be carried on in the tea hut, he would direct the course of it. He had closed the paper walls; muted sunlight fell through the yellow oiled-paper windows. The painted paper doors were closed to show that the master of the house was not to be disturbed by visitors. At the moment, however, the only heated element in this room was the basin of coals for the kettle of boiling water, which Akiro spooned out with a long dipper and poured over the green powdered tea in the precious bowls, to be stirred to foam with a bamboo brush.

"I am disappointed, Madame," he observed after the second bowl of ceremonial tea, and flashed a side-glance at Morning Face. They were sitting stiffly opposite each other, as was prescribed for the tea ceremony. Akiro leaned forward slightly and asked in a whisper, "Why have you not brought me one of your drawings?"

"But I didn't know I was going to get lost and end up here with you."

"Of course. I beg your pardon a thousandfold, Madame! Incidentally, I am convinced that if you had intended to visit me you would have chosen another color."

"I don't understand."

"That you don't understand is the only point in which nothing at all has changed between us, Madame," Major-san replied with brazen gentleness. "How could you possibly understand a stupid Japanese? He lives as inconspicuously as a *minomushi*, the most invisible of insects; he raises flowers instead of democrats—pardon, Madame—and is altogether too simple-minded for a European. Is that not so, Madame?"

"I suppose you are making fun of us, Baron?"

Major-san lifted his hands in horror. "There we have it. You distrust me. I am inconsolable."

"But you look very pleased, Monsieur."

"A Japanese peculiarity, Madame. The more inconsolable we are, the more pleased we look. What I wanted to say was: You would have chosen another color for your dress. I am accustomed to seeing you in green, and I cling to my habits."

"This is a dress from Paris," Vivica said, offended. "I think it very beautiful."

"I think you very beautiful, Madame!" Baron Matsubara had risen and dropped with lithe grace beside Vivica. He put his hand to Vivica's hair, which for once she had carefully combed and arranged, and in a second he had made of it a glistening, unkempt halo. It was an act of outrageous intimacy, and so startling that Vivica held her breath.

"You know that I adore you," Matsubara Akiro murmured. "You are a picture for my wall niche."

"How dare you!"

Vivica smoothed down her hair. She was trembling all over. Major-san's eyes dropped; he placed an arm around Vivica's shoulders and said nothing. Vivica slid a little away on her cushion. A brutal arm jerked her back. "I cling to my habits," Matsubara Akiro whispered.

"Let me go! Oh . . . please . . . don't . . ."

"Are you lying the truth?" Vivica's mortal foe asked with infinite softness, looking at her. "Are you still afraid of me?"

"I—I have never been afraid of you." Vivica wanted to jump up, but she sank back feebly. The poisonous feeling that those glances transmitted to her paralyzed her will to resist.

"Poor child," her mortal foe murmured, his arm about her shoulders. "Don't you even know that fear is essential for the enjoyment of love? Or am I to begin to 'understand' you in addition to everything else?"

Major-san laughed softly. Vivica was no longer capable of replying. That golden-bronze mask with the glowing eyes was above her face when she uttered a soft cry, a birdlike cry that would have touched the heart of a more considerate lover. But Major-san began to caress her with frenzied gentleness. Morning Face!—a strange blossom that squanders its splendor in a single hour. A locket hung on a thin chain between her breasts. He saw it as he opened the tiny silver buttons of the Parisian dress. Vivica moved so violently that the chain tore and the locket sprang open. Like a tiger, Matsubara Akiro snatched at it. If the locket held the picture of another lover, he would beat this package of beauty, fear, and curiosity, and then take leave of her with a courteous bow.

"Who is it?" he asked hoarsely, his breath coming in gasps. Vivica tried to pull the trinket out of his hand, but she had not the strength. It contained a photograph, as he had suspected. Then he froze as he looked more closely at the tiny snapshot—a man child, an innocent round baby face with Vivica's forehead, wreathed in bright, silky curls. An engraved inscription informed him that this was Halvard Lillesand Williams.

Major-san's face contorted in a grief that only a Japanese woman would have understood. This package of beauty and timid sensuality had given to another man something Matsubara Akiro had hungered for all his life—a *son!* For only a son filled the cage of a thousand duties with glory; a son honored his father in life and in death, whether or not he loved him as a person; and only bearing a son could bring honor to a woman within the family.

Separated from Vivica by the greatest of gulfs, Akiro studied the photograph and the inscription and then returned it without a word to the quivering young woman. Vivica was so shaken by passion that she could scarcely breathe. Tears filled her nymph's eyes; with all her might she repressed the insane impulse to throw herself at the feet of this demon lover who unexpectedly burned and froze—to throw herself at his feet and beg for caresses that were like winds in the desert of unfulfilled desire, like poppy petals brushing over shivering skin, like flashes of lightning cutting into the slumber of the senses, like whiplashes, one moment volcanic fire and the next as gentle as the veiled moon and the fragrance of dying flowers.

But such raptures were not for a young mother, to whom every man owed only respect and admiration. From one fateful moment to the next the climate in the pure, lovely room had utterly changed. Abruptly a passionate lover had become a Japanese moralist. Matsubara Akiro had not dreamed that this flowery consolation girl, whom he had alternately adored and wished to destroy for years, was already a stroller in the golden garden of motherhood, a dreamer forgetful of her duties. Such a one was no concern of his.

"I beg your pardon," Baron Matsubara murmured, in all sincerity for the first time. "May I take you to the house now, Madame? I should like to show you some paintings by a Japanese master."

Without a word of explanation, without the slightest recognition of her state, Baron Matsubara led a numbed Vivica to the drawing room of his summer house and showed her a scroll painted at the end of the seventeenth century: "Chrysanthemums and Maple by the Brook."

Vivica suppressed a wild sob; she felt unimaginably tricked and humiliated. Her host studiously pointed out the subtleties of composition; with gentle cruelty he forced her to erase from her memory the episode in the tea hut. He was altogether indifferent to what this lonely, frivolous child whom he had pulled into the maelstrom of passion might be feeling because of his sudden, and to her utterly incomprehensible, change of mood. Madame Williams had deceived him—as always. He had thought her a spring blossom; in reality she was a son's mother, already in the summer of her life; she had borne fruit. The sweet and terrible games of love were no longer for her. A salacious comedy had been transformed into a Japanese drama of duty. Among a man's duties was respect for a woman who had brought a man child into the world. The inherited and highly cultivated sense of duty of an aristocratic Japanese was far more binding than love for women and flowers. Moreover, a Japanese lover is interested only in two seasons of the year. These two, spring and autumn, cherry-blossom raptures and moonlight romances by twilit streams, automatically inspire his passions and his sense of poetry. A woman's summer belongs to the realm of duties: obedience to mother-in-law, preparation of meals, the making of the family wardrobe, and the bearing of sons. No pampered Japanese man would arrange a tea with or without ceremony for such a utilitarian creature. But how could Vivica have known all this and been able to sense the meaning of his sudden reversal? After all, she was no *kabuki* actor on the revolving stage.

Baron Matsubara had wiped their amorous dalliance from his memory and was waiting with exemplary patience for Madame to take her leave. His keen ear had detected noises; footsteps were approaching the house. Perhaps it was his uncle, Prince Itoh. He threw a probing look at Vivica and was, in spite of his indifference, a little alarmed by her deadly pallor and the emptiness in her eyes. How, he wondered, could he tactfully ease her out of the house? She was in no state to confront other guests. But it was too late. A tall American officer came pounding up the stone steps to the house.

"What are you doing here?" Major Timothy Williams demanded in a tone Vivica had never heard from him before. He had unexpectedly found someone willing to take his place in broiling Tokyo and had lost no time coming out to Karuizawa to join Vivica and his

son. The driver who had pointed out to Madame the way to the
Matsubara house had in all innocence driven Major Williams up here.
He was by now accustomed to the fact that foreign ladies paid visits
alone and that their husbands would come for cocktails after work.
To the driver, the Williams family had gained a great deal of prestige by being invited to ceremonial tea with a member of the Matsubara of Itoh family. This was only one more of the many comic
misunderstandings between victors and vanquished in occupied
Japan.

Timothy Williams stood, stunned, at the sliding door of the drawing room. Vivica looked glazedly at him; *Les Rêves de Vivienne* were
becoming more ghastly with each passing minute. Only Baron
Matsubara was through with dreaming, whereas Tim was still hoping against hope that this was one of his usual tormenting jealous
nightmares.

Baron Matsubara welcomed the honored guest with a bow and
employed the tried and true lamb method of the Kempetai to explain the situation. Madame had lost herself in the woods around
Karuizawa; it was a stupid region, was it not? with far too few sign-
posts. Naturally he had refreshed the major's honored wife with
ceremonial tea. Naturally, quite naturally. Then he informed the un-
mannerly guest who had not even removed his shoes before entering
the drawing room that he had just been showing several works by
old Japanese masters to Madame.

Every word was true, and in a deeper sense untrue; Baron Matsubara was putting on a performance of *naibun* that would have delighted a connoisseur. As he spoke he leaned, graceful and composed, against a chest which contained more treasures of Japanese
art. Tomorrow he would change the scroll to clear the atmosphere
of these guests. He was no longer looking at Vivica. This bearer of
sons was more helpless and inexperienced in erotic matters than a
fourteen-year-old Japanese girl. How could he have expected her to
be the mother of a son? And if Morning Face wished to cast her
marital obligations to the wind, it was really not his affair to remind
her of them in his tea hut. Was he supposed to be educating the
foreigners? The Americans were re-educating him, were they not?
All this and more lay hidden within the cold and dangerous looks

Major-san directed at the heavy-shod intruder. At the moment Major Williams was helpless before him because he had lost his self-control and left his manners at home. Baron Matsubara offered tea and waited in ironic humility for Major Williams to commit further breaches of courtesy.

He did not have to wait in vain. The long-legged, mutely furious American disregarded the master of the house as if he were completely alone with his wife. Naturally he did not express thanks for the offer of refreshment, but that did not surprise Matsubara Akiro. Since 1925 he had been accustomed to having the Wergeland family and everyone attached to them omit to thank him.

"Come with me!" Major Williams snapped at his wife and strode forward, prepared, if need be, to drag Vivica by force out of the house of this notorious war criminal. The name Matsubara had aroused various associations in his mind. Hadn't a doll by that name stolen his friend Elizabeth Murphy's fiancé? And had not this fellow been in the Kempetai? Vivica could not know that, of course; but what business had she here? It was a scandal, a nightmare, a stab directly into his blindly devoted heart.

As he rushed to her he knocked something over, as usual. It was a tall, dully glazed vase that stood in front of the wall niche. The shards and the two lilies it had contained formed a shattered still life on the mats which the major's boots had stained. Baron Matsubara showed no change of expression, although the loss of the vase shook him.

"Sorry," Major Williams said curtly. "Send the bill for the thing to me, care of the Medical Council in Tokyo."

Matsubara Akiro drew himself up and replied with the indescribable arrogance of his caste. "A bill, sir? That vase was a gift of the Imperial Family to my great-grandfather. It had been in our possession for more than a hundred years. It cannot be paid for."

During the ride home to the hotel Timothy Williams said not a word to Vivica, who had sunk dazedly back into the seat of the car. Not until they drove through the garden gate did he speak. Then he said hoarsely, "Brush your hair back from your forehead. You look like a tramp. Don't you hear me?" He shook Vivica's arm roughly.

She started up out of her daze. "You're hurting me, Tim!"

"This is the last time I'll ever touch you. You can depend on that."

Vivica began to weep silently. Big tears ran down her pale, beautiful face. "Please don't be angry with me, Tim," she begged. "Nothing happened." She began to sob more loudly and received a light slap from her husband.

"Pull yourself together. The driver—"

The car stopped.

"Get out. In two hours we must go to a party."

"I can't go, Tim!"

He refused to hear the note of helpless lamentation. "You're coming to that party if I have to drag you. I'm sick and tired of your nonsense."

Vivica walked with an odd stiffness up the steps to the veranda. She threw an imploring look at this stranger who was saying such terrible things to her in a strange voice. "Do believe me, Tim, nothing happened!"

"Will you be good enough to button up your dress?" Major Williams said.

"What was the matter with our young beauty this evening?" Mrs. Hunter said to her husband when they retired to their hotel room after Major General Hopkins' party. Mrs. Hunter made a practice of referring to Vivica as "our young beauty." She employed this mildly satiric phrase to combat the effect the Nordic Aphrodite had upon the "boys," among whom she counted her gray-haired husband, a war hero who had carried away innumerable decorations from the battles in the Pacific. She took the view that men, in spite of their decorations and their competence at men's business, were never quite grown up and therefore had to be constantly watched and guided.

"I didn't notice anything the matter," Colonel Hunter said, suppressing a yawn. These parties, which the ladies could never get enough of, tired him more than any nice little jungle war had ever done.

"I don't know," Mrs. Hunter replied thoughtfully. "But there's something happening in the Williams family. Vivie sat with me most of the time, instead of dazzling the boys."

"I suppose she's learning to be sensible. Good night, my dear!"

"Edward," Mrs. Hunter said energetically, "I have the feeling that I should give a little more attention to our young beauty."

"For heaven's sake don't interfere!" Colonel Hunter had spoken somewhat more loudly than usual.

"Did you see Tim?" Mrs. Hunter asked. "He looked frightful. They must have had a terrible fight. I'll have to do something about this."

"We had our fights too when we were young, and made up again. Didn't we, honey?"

Mrs. Hunter smiled forbearingly. In spite of their gray hair and their three grown children in the States, they were still moderately in love with each other. And they were still the best of friends.

"I must tell you something," Mrs. Hunter said. Her friendly, maternal face expressed genuine concern; because of her age and social position she felt responsible for the welfare of the whole crowd. "Didn't you notice that I disappeared for a while with Vivica?"

Colonel Hunter had not noticed.

"She had a kind of fit. She began hiccuping dreadfully, and then sobbing."

"The girl is hysterical. It's just plain boredom. She ought to pitch in at the Brides' School and help you prepare these Japanese girls for life in the States."

"She doesn't know anything about life in the States herself. But listen. I wanted to go for Tim—you know how he always hovers over her, he really overdoes it sometimes, it seems to me—but Vivie clung to me and begged me not to bring him. What do you think of that?"

"Considerate of her. She didn't want to spoil his fun."

"This was the first time I've ever felt really sorry for her. She was —well, helpless. I tell you, something serious has happened. Tomorrow I'm going to have a talk with Tim."

"Please don't, Catherine!" When Colonel Hunter addressed his wife as "Catherine," he meant what he said. "You must not interfere. Williams told me over a drink this evening that he is asking for an immediate furlough and intends to return to Concord."

"Why, that leaves me speechless," Mrs. Hunter said, and proceeded to rattle on. "Tim is indispensable here. He's doing a marvelous job and—" She paused for breath. "Why should he make such a decision all of a sudden? He was planning to stay another three years in Tokyo."

"He's his own master, my dear. Besides, he has not had a furlough for years and there's the best general practice in Concord waiting for him if he goes back now. I imagine his mother and sister are pressing him hard. In the end we all do what you women want."

"And a good thing you do," Mrs. Hunter replied with dignity. She thought for a moment of Vivie's hapless little face. Vivica had no longer been the "young beauty" at that moment, but a child who has been spanked and is expecting worse. What kind of trick could the child have played on her husband to make him decide on the transfer to Concord as punishment? "The thing is, she's alone too much. That has never done anyone any good."

Colonel Hunter's thoughts had wandered. "Whom do you mean now?"

"You know perfectly well the person I'm referring to, my dear! Do you really think there is nothing we can do?" Mrs. Hunter said with the eager, warm-hearted helpfulness of so many American women.

"I have the feeling you'd better keep your hands off. Tim Williams is the kind of still water that runs deep. There's a streak tough as steel inside him somewhere. His father was a Presbyterian preacher, you know, a strong character if there ever was one. Tim told me about him once. Tim'll straighten things out by himself."

"I hope so with all my heart. It would be a pity about two such nice young people. They do make a handsome couple."

"Vivie is damned pretty—beg your pardon—but changeable as April and—a kind of hermit. Does she ever come to your teas?"

"Never. She still hasn't really made contact, but she'll learn to fit in with the crowd sooner or later. We're all trying hard."

They certainly were, and no efforts could have been more in vain.

"Well, the girl isn't my cup of tea," Colonel Hunter remarked to close the conversation.

"I certainly hope not," Mrs. Hunter said with considerable force and turned over to the side she habitually slept on.

Around midnight Major Timothy Williams sat in his bedroom with his hands covering his face. He could not stop thinking about what could have made Vivie let a Japanese . . . He groaned.

Vivica stood in pajamas at the door of his room. He started, and asked in that new, harsh voice which had so terrified her, "What do you want?"

"Tim—" A burst of sobs.

Dr. Williams stirred a strong sedative into some boiled water from a Thermos bottle. "Drink this. You must calm down now."

Vivica drank the brew. Every swallow hurt her, but she was careful not to spill a drop. Tim hated spots on the Japanese mats. He had turned his back to her; he did not want her to see his suffering.

Vivica still stood, staring at that reliable back in the silk pajama jacket. She had given the pajamas to Tim, and she remembered his warm, glad smile because she had gone to so much trouble and given such thought to pleasing him. Tim's smile, which won him hearts so easily, seemed at this moment to Vivica the most wonderful gift any girl could receive. She had treated that gift with irresponsible frivolity. Now she knew it, now that she was banished into the darkness and cold.

"Tim! Please listen to me!"

Major Williams turned around. "What else do you want?" he asked roughly.

Vivie had always suspected that her interior was made of glass. Now she could hear it crack, and it hurt. She no longer understood why she had wanted to have a ceremonial tea with Major-san. He was more alien to her than Mount Fuji towering in the distance above Myanoshita, where she had first seen Matsubara Akiro again after so many years. After all, she had hated him. Never had anyone been so brutal to her as he. The fire his caresses had kindled in her was burned to ashes now—like everything else in her life.

At last Tim relented a little. "You can sit down," he said, pushing a chair toward her. "If you're determined to talk with me, you can answer a few questions."

Vivie looked at him in alarm. Every muscle in his strong face was tense. There were dark rings under his eyes. Two deep furrows ran down from the base of his nose to his set mouth. He looked far older than his thirty-three years.

"How long have you been cheating on me with this—this man?"

"What—what's that you're asking?"

"Don't you understand English? I asked you how long you've been unfaithful to me with this fellow?"

"I've never been unfaithful to you."

In his mind he saw again the opened buttons of her blouse, her tousled hair, saw her as a quivering package of beauty and depravity. Never would he be able to banish this picture from his memory. Vivica had offended against Tim's need, so peculiarly American, to respect the person whom he simultaneously loves romantically. A Japanese is altogether different; he finds entertainment with a geisha, sensual gratification with a *joro*—a police-supervised prostitute of the red-light district—and the satisfaction of his familial feelings with a wife who bears him sons, the wife being chosen by the family for social and economic reasons. None of these things existed in the American's erotic realm; he married without consideration for money and social position, purely on the basis of romantic love, and he clung to that until the marriage relationship became familial happiness, resignation, or a thorn in the flesh.

"You can lie as well as a Jap," Major Williams responded. "But I don't care. This evening I learned by chance from a former Shanghai intelligence officer that you had a date with Matsubara in the Fujiya Hotel five months ago."

"That isn't true, Tim. I was drawing and dozing a little, and suddenly—"

"Yes?"

"Suddenly th-there he was, standing before me," Vivica stammered. It was all so horribly mixed up, and she could not explain it to Tim because this was not Tim questioning her; it was some preacher's son from Concord who was a perfect stranger to her.

"How long have you known this Baron Matsubara?"

Silence.

"'Drawing and dozing a little, and suddenly there he was, standing before me,'" Major Williams repeated. "Sounds just like Alice in Wonderland. How dumb do you think I am?"

"Don't look at me that way. It's all so different from what you think. I'm terribly tired. Tomorrow—"

"By tomorrow you'll have thought up new lies, won't you?"

Timothy Williams turned his back on Vivica again. "You've run into some hard luck, my girl," he said with icy calm. "As it happens, John Bailey was interrogated by the Kempetai in Shanghai during the war, at approximately the same time as yourself. He knows who Matsubara is."

"Stop it, Tim."

"I'm just starting. John Bailey told me he had seen Matsubara with you at the Fujiya Hotel several months ago. He thought you didn't know anything about the man's past and wanted to warn me. I let him think that."

Tim was so choked by disgust that he struggled for breath. Then he said with uncanny composure, "And with *that* man who almost drove you out of your mind in Shanghai you were willing, here, as the wife of an American officer . . ." Again his voice failed him.

"From the start you've lied and cheated on me," he finally went on. "Don't pull off a faint now. You can't make me break my heart for you that way again. You—you Jap's whore!"

Vivica clung to the wardrobe to support herself as her husband went on.

"There are some arrangements to be made. I'll keep the boy, of course. Divorce is out of the question. Halvard ought to have the illusion of a normal set-up. You can bum around Japan or Norway or wherever you like. You've money enough, God knows—too much money, in my opinion."

He wiped the sweat from his brow, where the frown lines had deepened like wheel tracks in soft mud, and looked at the clock. "We'd better go to sleep now." A pause. "What are you waiting for?"

Vivica flinched at the tone. She opened her eyes wide and murmured, "I'm—looking for—you!" This harsh stranger was not her Tim. She would find him again somewhere, when this nightmare came to an end.

Timothy Williams deliberately ignored the exclamation. He must not allow himself to be softened by this comedienne who played ball with his heart. He was utterly drained and at the moment no longer even felt hatred. Tomorrow, early in the morning, they would go back to Tokyo. He still had to write a note to Colonel Hunter saying that Vivica had fallen ill and had had to be taken back to the hospital in Tokyo. The crowd must not know.

"There is something I have to tell you, Tim!" Once more she spoke in that imploring, broken, girlish voice. "Please, Tim, please—"

"It can wait until tomorrow. I beg your pardon, Vivica, but at the moment I cannot stand the sight of you."

He opened the door, and Vivica went to her room.

At dawn Vivica, tears streaming down her face, sat writing a letter:

My dearest Tim,

I cannot go on living if you have stopped loving me. It was all intended just for a little fun—the tea ceremony and all that—I was so lonesome. I don't know how it all turned out as it did. I wanted to tell you last night that I was not unfaithful to you, as you think. But you don't want to believe me, and perhaps you cannot, poor darling!

From now on I meant to do nothing but please you all the time, even go to Mrs. Hunter's afternoon teas and listen to dreadful lectures at Mrs. Brent's and learn to cook at the YWCA in Tokyo—apple pie and griddle cakes and all that sort of thing. I even wanted to leave Japan—I never wanted to look another Japanese in the face.

I'm so confused by everything and that you cannot forgive me. I never spoke about Major-san because I wanted to forget it all. And then suddenly he stood before me—in Myanoshita, I mean. Is it absolutely impossible for you to believe me?

You've always been so good to me, Tim! And I have been so proud of you. Everyone thinks you're wonderful, the whole crowd. Excuse all the blots, I can't stop crying. You said such horrible things to me —I can't believe you mean them.

I'm cold, darling. There's a ringing in my ears. Don't be angry at my taking the car. I'll leave it by the old Buddhist temple and walk the rest of the way.

Thank you for everything. I'm going away because it is the only thing I can still do for you now. Perhaps then you will believe that I—oh, Tim, I can't express myself like Astrid or Miss Murphy—and I'm so tired and I've cried myself hollow. You must marry some nice, hard-working, well-adjusted girl who will bring up Halvard nicely. I have always been good for nothing, and Astrid used to say I was the daughter of a tramp. Only Aunt Helene liked me a little in spite of all that. Now I know that life is no picnic, of course; but it's too late. You must never tell Aunt Helene that I—

I wanted to try to stop being a tramp and—in America—

Good-by, dearest Tim. I'm sorry you had to run into me. But now everything will be all right, and perhaps you'll think better of me later on. Kiss Halvard for me. I love you—*only* you. It sounds silly to say that again and again. Good-by.

Vivica

Vivica laid the letter, smeared with tears and inkblots, on her untouched bed. She had spent the few hours of the night on the *tatami* on the floor, because she had been too weary to make it to the bed. Then, too, she would have had to wipe off her make-up; Tim hated lipstick and rouge on her pillow. She did not want to do anything more to annoy him. Perhaps he would be a little pleased when he saw the orderly room, Vivica thought hazily. She had put away all the things that usually lay in wild disarray on chairs and floor until the chambermaids cleaned up, had even set her evening dress on its hanger and hung it in the closet. For a moment she looked at herself in her light sports dress with its wide leather belt—a big, strong girl, and inwardly made entirely of glass.

She opened her jewel-case—a Japanese lacquer box with many secret drawers that fitted perfectly into one another—and put the locket with her son's picture into her pocket. The little companion whom she had imagined in the Shanghai military prison, and who had then become living flesh, would accompany her. Tim was keeping the original, after all.

She shivered and fought back sobs as she stole to the garage.

She drove cautiously through the garden gate and turned in the direction of Baron Matsubara's summer house. It was not far from the Buddhist temple where she intended to leave the car. From there a footpath led to the peak of Asama, the sacred volcano.

Timothy Williams, drugged by the heavy dose of sleeping tablets he had taken, lay in deep sleep as Vivica drove away. Halvard's nurse, Sumi, thought she heard a noise but did not get up. The foreigners were constantly doing mad things; if Master and Mistress wanted to enter honored automobile and go for a drive at dawn, they did so. *Shikato ga nai*—there was nothing to be done about it.

It was five o'clock in the morning.

5: A Moment of Glory

Half an hour later the telephone at Colonel Hunter's bedside rang. A gentle Japanese voice asked him to come down; Major Williams was waiting in the lobby. No, sir, honored visitor was speaking so quickly and so loudly that stupid Japanese, alas, not understand single word. There was a click on the telephone. Then came Tim's voice.

"Pardon, sir, something terrible has happened!"

Colonel and Mrs. Hunter did not know later how they could have dressed so quickly. Downstairs in the dusky hotel lobby stood the "finest fellow in the crowd"—or rather, his shadow. Vivica had driven off sometime during the morning toward the volcano, he stammered out, and he, Timothy Williams, had driven her to her death.

Colonel Hunter was a man of action. He thought fast and clearly and required not nearly so much supervision and advice as his wife imagined. This was bad business, and not much hope. The volcano had been behaving sensibly of late, but the girl had probably thrown herself over the brink anyhow, and there would not be much to do but recover the body. Poor kid!

"We'll drive out to Baron Matsubara's," he said, eyes averted from Timothy's face. "He knows all the footpaths around Asama. They've been living long enough in this region."

"Out of the question, sir! The dirty bastard is responsible for it all."

"Don't be childish, Williams!" The elder officer's tone had suddenly taken on a steely note. He sprinted to his car like a much younger man. "Come on, Williams! There isn't a minute to lose."

When they reached the summer house, Colonel Hunter's last faint hope vanished. No one answered all their calls and knocks. Finally a half-grown servant boy crept out from behind a tea hut hidden among pines and magnolias, but vanished after the colonel had beckoned to him. "Damn it all," the colonel growled. In his excitement he had beckoned to the Japanese in the Western manner. To a Japanese that meant that he should clear out, and the boy had promptly obeyed the order from these two imposing American soldiers.

They drove in silence to the temple, but the Williams car was not standing there. Timothy covered his eyes with his hand. The colonel patted him on the shoulder. "Take it easy, boy," he murmured.

They left their car and began the climb. Far and wide there was no track, no one in sight. It was ghostly. Even Colonel Hunter had repeatedly to assure himself that he was not dreaming. But a glance at Tim's face sufficed to convince him of the dreary reality of their mission. Again and again he kept thinking of the pretty Norwegian girl. She'd given the boys a hot time of it with those eyes of hers, but then again she would have a spell of sitting all alone by herself for days on end. That was what made for such damned nonsense as this. And then, all by herself, she had sought death in the crater of the volcano. Damn it to hell, Colonel Hunter thought, because he felt utterly wretched. But Catherine, for all her subtle intuition and warm heart, could not have mended matters. Vivica had escaped them all.

Timothy Williams was no longer thinking of anything, but looking about him in utter despair. He'd see Vivica's golden head somewhere in this desolate landscape. Somewhere she must be waiting for him to take her in his arms and carry her home. It could not be that Vivie had left him for good and all. Heaven above, God could not punish him so cruelly. Yet this seemed to be the rule: that a man was punished the rest of his life for his harshness. Tim suppressed a moan that rose up from the depths of his soul, from deep below where the darkness stopped and rage toward himself was gradually, gradually transforming a fine fellow into a good Christian.

They had long since left behind the plain, the little villages with their silvery streams and tiny houses. By now they were on the solitary heights and approaching the demon who dominated this countryside—Asama Volcano. Suddenly Colonel Hunter stopped. They were standing before a sign that bore a grinning skull as warning. From here on only the death-bound lovers, failed students, and "masterless" *samurai* proceeded. From here on the way led over cracked volcanic soil to the eternal flame of the crater.

Colonel Hunter surveyed the situation; then he placed his arm on his companion's shoulder. "We must turn back, my boy. I'm damned sorry about it."

"Thank you, sir. You turn back. I'll look for Vivica."

"No nonsense now, Williams!"

"I am going, sir!"

"It's suicide, Williams! Have you forgotten your kid?" Colonel Hunter gripped his young friend harder as Tim tried to tear away. "It's no use, man! Come back. I promise you—"

Colonel Hunter had no chance to finish his sentence. His keen soldier's eyes had discerned something. He released Timothy Williams and pointed wordlessly at a procession of people winding with infinite slowness from somewhere near the heart of the crater toward the warning sign where the two Americans stood.

"We'll wait here." Colonel Hunter's voice sounded choked. Tim Williams nodded. He did not care where he stood when God crushed him for the mortal sin of lovelessness.

It was an age—or perhaps only a quarter of an hour—before the group that crawled slowly along like a procession of black ants could at last be distinguished clearly. First the two Americans made out only some bearers carrying a shrouded bier; then they saw other figures. Might it be a suicide party of Japanese who had nothing at all to do with Tim's wife? Frequently whole groups would set out for a fiery grave and then, as the result of a sudden shift of mood, would return—all, or nearly all of them—along the path back to life.

Not until the group of Japanese came close to them did Timothy Williams recognize the leader of the group as Baron Matsubara Akiro. With the assistance of the youngest Baron Matsubara—born Yasuda—he was carrying the shrouded bier. All the members of his household, apparently, had accompanied him on this dangerous and evidently vain rescue expedition.

Matsubara Akiro bowed stiffly to the two Americans and with a silk handkerchief wiped the sweat from his high forehead. He kept his eyes fixed on the shrouded bier.

Tim had rushed to the bier to lift the sheet that draped it. A thin hand with a grip of steel restrained him. "We are taking the body to my house, sir," Matsubara said with impassive features. "We must drive to Tokyo at once to arrange the funeral."

Had Baron Matsubara gone mad? The daily newspapers frequently recounted stories of Japanese who lost their reason through grieving over loved ones.

"Don't touch the bier!" Akiro suddenly shouted. His face contorted as in the good old days when he worked for the Kempetai. Then he passed his hand over his forehead again, and murmured in the general direction of Colonel Hunter, "I beg your pardon, sir. We have just recovered the body of my honored cousin and the head of my family, Baron Kenzo Matsubara."

Once more Baron Akiro wiped his forehead with the silk handkerchief. Then, as if he were at last awakening from a trance, he turned fully toward Colonel Hunter. "Madame Williams was brought home by one of my servants, sir. At dawn Madame Yamato, my honored housekeeper, was returning from a sick-visit in the village and saw Madame set out in her automobile toward Asama."

He fell silent, evidently overexhausted. The two Americans held their breath. In spite of the unbearable tension, they had been living too long in the Orient to interrupt a Japanese.

"Fortunately we had a car at our disposal. My cousin and my son-in-law had come from Tokyo last night. We found Madame Williams in a faint in front of the Buddhist temple."

"Is she alive?" Colonel Hunter asked hoarsely.

Matsubara looked off into a private world. "We had to wake her. I am afraid that afterward we had to disregard the requirements of courtesy, sir. The young lady wanted to run away from us, determined to continue her promenade."

Baron Matsubara had disregarded the requirements of courtesy to the extent of employing the familiar methods of the Kempetai to quiet the raging Vivica and stow her into his son-in-law's car. The lamb method had been ineffectual, for in spite of her long acquaintanceship with Major-san, Madame had never formed a taste for the delights of obedience. Morning Face was and remained a mystery to him. In his experience, women sought death in the flames when they had *no* sons.

"I hope you will excuse me now, sir," Matsubara said to Colonel Hunter, bowing with exquisite politeness. "My familial duties unfortunately cannot be postponed."

He did not so much as glance at Major Williams as he rejoined his group, who were waiting by the bier.

He does not want me to thank him because he despises me, Tim thought.

But Matsubara Akiro, new head of the Matsubara family, by no means despised the lanky American. He was too indifferent to him to despise him. He had refrained from recognizing Major Williams out of Japanese tact, because he did not want to impose upon him the oppressive obligation of gratitude. Dimly he felt that no man of the West could bear this *on*, this leaden weight of gratitude, with composure and good face. Consequently he had completely ignored Major Timothy Williams. This too was but another of the many misunderstandings between victors and vanquished.

Unnoticed by the others, Baron Kenzo had stolen away from the rescue party and continued on alone up to Asama. Akiro's honored father had died suddenly in the hermit's hut, without having altered his testament in favor of his only son. Kenzo, the rice widow's son, was and remained the head of the family. Kenzo had promptly asked the newly adopted Baron Matsubara, formerly Mr. Yasuda, to drive him to Karuizawa for a conversation with Cousin Akiro. Eiko's young husband secured an extra ration of gasoline for business purposes and set off at once with Kenzo, with whom he was on the best of terms. They had arrived at the summer house two hours after Major Williams took Vivica away.

Kenzo had humbly laid his request before Cousin Akiro and had been gruffly refused. He had wished to restore Akiro's birthright; but Akiro, dutiful son that he was—whatever he might have thought in private about his honored father—had been unable to accept. His deceased father's will was sacred to him. What was more, poor Kenzo had been favored with a look of consternation from Cousin Akiro. Though Kenzo's mother might not have been quite the proper person for the family, he himself had after all grown up with Cousin Akiro and his war-hero brother within the cage of duties. Hence he ought to know how impossible his proposal was.

In abject silence Baron Kenzo had taken all this in and drawn the logical conclusion. He had not even attempted to ascend to the peak of Asama; modest as always, he cast himself down at the half-way mark and was found by his relations with a broken backbone. Now he lay at rest under a shroud in the Karuizawa summer house, a contented smile on his round face. Baron Kenzo had every reason to be content. He had honorably escaped the dreadful fate of having to give orders to Cousin Akiro.

Tim sat unmoving beside Vivica's bed. She was sleeping as peacefully as a child. Mrs. Hunter had tamed her blond curls with a blue ribbon, leaving her clear, rounded forehead free.

Tim was alone with Vivica. Mrs. Hunter and Madame Yamato, who had brought Vivica back to the chalet and put her to bed, had vanished completely after having performed their work of mercy. Little Halvard was in the garden with his nurse, crowing melodiously. He was a musical child, as his grandmother Borghild Lillesand had been. When his nurse, Sumi, hummed a song to him, Halvard sat wide-eyed, and both the wildness and the obstinacy of his inheritance dropped away from him.

Tim looked at Vivie as though he could not sate himself with looking. He was still overwhelmed by God's infinite forbearance. But in the intense stillness and thoughtfulness of these hours, Timothy Williams began clearing away the rubble of illusions and laying the cornerstone for a real marriage. In his thinking things through he could not refrain from drifting slowly back through the past, for it alone gave him the key to Vivica's nature and actions. He saw himself once more, after the end of the war, standing in the Chous' home in Shanghai, and heard Miss Wergeland tell him sharply that Vivica was no wife for him. She had spoken of Borghild Lillesand and how she died, and he had replied that such things need not be repeated. They would not be repeated. He saw his beautiful Vivica in the room in the former White Chrysanthemum, and lived through again her terror and the fit of hiccuping, the frightening laughter, and her liberating weeping in his arms. At that time Vivica had recognized in a scroll "Major-san," whom she wanted to forget. And Tim had promised her that he would guard her and keep her and love her—in sickness and in health, for better and for worse. . . .

Then their fairy-tale wedding in Trondheim, and afterward life, the failure of everyday life in Concord, and the unhealthful dream-life in Japan which Helene Wergeland and his sister Margaret had so often warned him against. Both of them had understood Vivica better than he. Both of them had suspected that Vivica had not yet resolved the experience of imprisonment. And he in his tempestuous infatuation had given her no time to resolve it. In New England she had been like a dreamer lost in the woods. After the birth of their child she had been alone so much of the time, for in occupied Japan he had been pressed by a thousand duties and had begun to leave Vivica to herself—a little more every week, a little more carelessly every month, a little more impatiently every year. Her beauty still thrilled him, but only from time to time. Theirs had gradually become a week-end marriage. He had continued to live his own life, at times longing intensely for the miracle of intimacy but doing nothing to bring about this miracle. He had been proud of his beautiful wife but had not even taken an interest in her talent for painting. At the beginning of their marriage she had shyly shown him a few of her efforts; then never again. Now it occurred to him that perhaps it had been something more than Vivica's delight in dangerous flirtations which had driven her to Baron Matsubara. Japanese loved painting. (Indeed, the baron had been the only person who had ever looked at a sketch of Vivica's with genuine interest, and who in spite of the amateurish execution had seen in it something unusual. But Tim knew nothing about this; he knew only vaguely that Vivie, at an age when other girls were playing tennis and preparing for practical life, had flirted with a volcano and played ball with the globe. And he had done nothing with this knowledge.)

As he sat studying Vivica's face, while there raged through him that purifying anger with himself which can unexpectedly lead to a higher plane of love, he abruptly grasped that this beautiful girl had been doubly imperiled from the very beginning of her life—imperiled by her beauty and by the fragile psychic constitution she had inherited from her parents. Consul Wergeland's tendency to regard reality as an inferior imitation of his dreams had been brought to a high peak of development by his youngest daughter. Finally, the melancholy and solitary disposition inherited from Borghild had been brought into collision with Tim's crowd, and the result had been almost total shattering and flight from life.

Tim stood up and went for a cigarette, for he now had to face an insight which he would have been only too happy to keep buried in the depths of his mind. The cigarette was bracing and laid down a fine mist between himself and the lovely face on the pillow.

Timothy Williams had to acknowledge the reason he had felt such murderous hatred for Vivica's host in Karuizawa, a hatred that had encompassed Vivica and almost destroyed her. At the bottom of his soul, Tim realized, he had been profoundly shocked because his wife had taken up with a Japanese. Now, with the moral courage of the New Englander, he confessed to himself that he had been moved by racial hatred, that un-Christian, irrational spiritual weed which grew so rampantly in many regions of his flourishing native land, and which was being fought so vigorously by every decent American. Yet it was Puritan tradition above all to respect one's neighbor's human dignity, no matter how he differed in color, language, or customs from his fellow citizens. Tim had been unable to understand Vivica, and understanding her was what mattered, now and in the future. He realized that his young wife had seen her northern homeland for the first time as a bride; that she had grown up among Asians and regarded them all—as she did her half-sister Mailin and the saintly Dr. Yamato—as in every respect her equals. This morally irreproachable attitude, this utterly natural and guiltless relationship with the people of the Far East, was one point in which she was far ahead of the American educators in Japan. Her flirtation on the brink of the abyss had been sinfully frivolous, but Timothy realized at this moment how great an attraction the Japanese might have for people of the West. Certainly the many marriages between American soldiers and Japanese women were ample testimony to that.

In her worst and blindest distress, Tim now realized, Vivica had grasped his nature far more than he had hers. In her farewell note she had called him "poor darling." She had tried to sympathize with him, whereas he . . .

Vivica opened her eyes and saw her husband's dark shock of hair. Tim had knelt beside her bed, his head buried in his hands. The cigarette lay half-smoked in the ash tray—a habit he had always reproved her for. Painfully Vivica sat up and seized Tim's right hand. With childlike trust she put her little face into that vessel of strength and shelter. This was her return to the warmth which is the grand prize in the lottery of marital happiness.

Tim bent over her and whispered in a choked voice, "Why do you do such things to me, baby?"

He held her tightly against his fiercely pounding heart, which had belonged to her from the first moment he saw her in the Chous' house in Shanghai. But five years ago his heart had been raw and inexperienced. Now it had suddenly matured. Vivica's joys must be his, and her mysterious sorrows his sorrows, until their days and nights were illuminated by the radiance of sharing. Before such radiance, born of the intimacy of shared sorrow, conventional American marital romanticism paled, revealed itself as nothing but the fireworks of the senses and the transient mirage of dreamers.

Tim's brow furrowed so deeply that Vivica gently tried to smooth it with her forefinger. He felt as if a butterfly's wing were brushing his forehead. Then he carefully kissed each of her fingertips in turn. She used no nail polish because he hated the stuff; his mother and Margaret had never used it either.

"What are you thinking about?" Vivie asked timidly, for the lines on his forehead were deepening still more.

"I am thinking where we should go for our honeymoon." Major Timothy Williams toyed with Vivica's bright blue hair-ribbon. "What do you think about that, Mrs. Williams? Isn't it time we got to know each other a little better?"

A delicious fragrance of fresh coffee, ham and eggs, and pancakes wafted through the chalet. In the doorway appeared Mrs. Hunter. They had not known she was still in the house.

"Breakfast, children," she called out cheerfully. "Everything is ready in the dining room. You young people seem to live on air and love!"

"Won't you eat with us?" Tim asked lamely.

"Yes—please, Mrs. Hunter," Vivie said still more lamely.

"Some other time," Mrs. Hunter replied gravely. "My old boy will want his breakfast too." She glanced at Vivica with a smile and said, "I left the recipe for pancake batter on the kitchen table, young lady."

Two months later Baron Matsubara Akiro sat waiting in his deceased father's hermit's hut. His face was almost twisted with strain, but he permitted himself not the slightest impatient movement. Over at the house, in the Matsubara manor, his daughter Eiko lay in labor. The labor had begun toward morning, and in spite of the pain that tore at her slender, girlish body, Eiko did not utter a sound. She behaved as a Japanese woman of the aristocracy was expected to behave. Baron Matsubara Toshiyuki, born Yasuda, did not display the same exemplary composure; after all he was not a *samurai* but a textile manufacturer raised to the nobility. Before Eiko's door he wept noiselessly to himself because she was undergoing such torments and refused to cry out. Old Kikue, who kept running back and forth from the aged baroness's rooms to the head of the family in the hermit's hut, thought that Baron Toshiyuki still had a good deal to learn from the Matsubaras. In this house no one had ever pitied a woman in labor because of her pain. She was pitied only if she—as had Eiko's unhappy mother—brought only girl children into the world.

Matsubara Akiro, sitting in the hut, was thinking of this very heritage and trying to prepare his mind for another blow of fate. He was the last true son in the manor. His family would die away like Nippon's Empire if Eiko followed the example of her mother Tatsue and gave birth to nothing but daughters.

Twilight had come. Matsubara Akiro still sat motionless in the hermit's hut. He had stomach cramps, of course. Kikue had prepared a hot bath for him, but it had grown as cold as Akiro's hopes. Two doctors stood at Eiko's bedside: a Japanese obstetrician and an American surgeon, who was now undertaking a Caesarean operation, in spite of all the protests from the old baroness and Kikue.

Akiro did not know how long he had waited this way. Suddenly old Kikue appeared like a ghost before him. She moved her parched lips and tried in vain to produce a sound. Akiro had leaped to his feet. He forgot his customary tender consideration for the faithful old woman and shook her thin shoulders rudely. His intestines burned like Asama Volcano before a deadly eruption, but his brain was as icy as a waterfall in wintry twilight. He saw the tears in old Kikue's eyes, her shaking hands, her jaw moving ineffectually.

"Out with it, out with it!" he screamed, beside himself. "It is a daughter!"

The old woman still stood helpless. But at last her master's numbed look reminded her of her duty of obedience and restored speech to her. She knelt humbly and whispered, "A grandson, Master! A beautiful, strong man child!"

Matsubara Akiro stood in mute triumph in the monastic room after Kikue had hurried back to the young mother. The old servant had stolen only a single glance at the bold, beloved countenance of the former young baron. It was glowing as if Nippon's mystic chrysanthemum had suddenly flowered in the Americanized wasteland of postwar Tokyo.

Later Matsubara Akiro placed in honored Grandmother's arms her great-great-grandchild. The shrunken old woman who had buried her father, her husband, her son, and her grandson—the heroic *kamikaze* of the Second World War—sat mutely regarding the man child's perfect body and clear eyes. She nodded, proud and weary unto death.

For this moment of glory she had clung tenaciously and patiently to life in a world that no longer had any meaning for her.

6: Family Reunion in Norway

The last week in May 1955 brought a stream of visitors from all over the world to Trondheim to celebrate Helene Wergeland's seventieth birthday. Astrid came with her family from Paris, Mailin with her sons from Singapore, Vivica and Timothy with Halvard and Dr. Margaret Williams from Concord, New Hampshire. And the end was not yet, for the family of Chou Tso-ling was expected from China; Herr von Zabelsdorf, with his wife and children, was due from West Berlin; and Madame Yamato, who seemed always to be present when Vivica sickened of life, was to come from Tokyo. Throughout the years Helene had remained in touch with all her friends.

Villa Wergeland was festively decorated, though Helene considered this entirely unnecessary. Some of the guests were staying in her private wing. The big dining room in the Home for Mothers had been turned into a nursery for the young guests from West and East. The children were her birthday present, she growled to the Widow from Aalesund. As usual, Laura was fluttering about like a headless chicken.

After supper on the eve of her birthday Miss Wergeland sat alone on her terrace, watching the drifting clouds as she had done in the old days. She was still unbent, still rather stern. From the huge drawing room came a babble of voices in half a dozen languages: Norwegian, English, French, German, Chinese, and Japanese. This last Vivica was speaking with Madame Yamato, who had been put on board the Trondheim steamer in Marseille by Baron Matsubara. Since the peace signed at San Francisco in 1951, Matsubara Akiro had been traveling about the world for his government, as in his younger days. He was at the moment in Paris on a trade mission, and was planning next to go to Peiping and Shanghai. Madame Yamato whispered all this news to beautiful Mrs. Williams. Madame Yamato held Baron Matsubara in the greatest respect. She considered him a wonderfully kind person. He was even paying for her son's education at a Catholic theological seminary; her son wished to be a priest.

Helene Wergeland watched the clouds. In the five years since Vivica had left Japan her anxiety about the child had almost entirely vanished. This was the first pleasant surprise in her life—that Vivie had come to her senses at last. The girl had, moreover, stayed for a year with Astrid in Paris, studying with a famous painter, while Timothy had "taken a look at Europe." Well, and now Vivie, the good-for-nothing, who had been pampered by everyone and been as lazy as an Asian princess, was having her first one-man show in Paris; all of them were going to Paris to attend the opening after the birthday. Astrid, with her customary competence, had arranged the show, and already Vivica's water-colors and sketches seemed to be creating a furor.

"They'll only succeed in turning her head," Helene had growled as she studied photographs of Vivica's paintings. There scarcely seemed to be anything on the paper.

Helene stood up and went to the children's room. With a howl of glee, young Halvard and eleven-year-old Karl Friedrich von

Zabelsdorf flung themselves upon her. Astrid's twins, Antoine and Hélène—eight years old and alarmingly well bred—were whispering in rapid French in one corner of the room. Helene somehow could not warm to Astrid's "little monsieur" and rather prissy daughter, nor to their "parlez-vous" which poured out like a waterfall, but she steadfastly refused to give way to this feeling. She went up to Mailin's eldest son, who stood with Hanna Chou's youngest boy, discussing in Chinese this assortment of odd relations. Those two were not a bit less loquacious than their French cousins. Both boys were smiling at the little Frenchman and at strapping, red-cheeked Cousin Halvard from America. Halvard and the boy from Berlin were wrestling and tussling, laughing loudly and pounding each other on the shoulders. How wildly uncouth!

Helene looked thoughtfully at the group of Oriental and Occidental children. Her steely blue eyes tried to penetrate to the hearts and minds of these children who, she hoped, would build a new and better world. But although she strictly forbade herself to declare eight-year-old Halvard her favorite, something wrung her heart when the unruly boy suddenly came over to whisper, "Great-Aunt, may I play something for you?"

His silvery-blond hair fell over his face; Borghild's veiled glance sought hers; and Halvard's hands—the slender, sensitive hands of the born violinist—shyly caressed Helene Wergeland's big, strong hands, ridged by the prominent veins of old age.

"Tomorrow, Halvard—for my birthday." Then she looked sharply down at her secret favorite and said, "But make sure your hands are clean when you play."

The big birthday banquet was over, and the guests had retired to rest. Helene had shaken hands with hundreds of visitors from Trondheim and Tröndelag, and had shaken her head time and again over the presents. How many diapers and skis might have been bought for all this artistic nonsense! But the chicks and the shirkers and the sons and grandsons of the shirkers had saved for months in order to bring some "fine" gift to Fröken Wergeland. And Helene secretly rejoiced that her protégés, old or young, had given so much thought to the matter. She expressed her thanks with unwonted politeness. She did not throw the truth like a wet dishrag into a single caller's face—there were too many guests from the Far East who would not have known what to make of that sort of thing.

At last she was left alone with her family and friends. The boys and girls had eaten the coffee table clean; even Antoine and lady-like little Hélène had taken part with amazing zest in the final battle over the cake. Now they all went to the paneled salon to hear Halvard Lillesand Williams play. In spite of her protest, Miss Wergeland had to sit on the flower-decked, richly carved armchair which stood like a Chinese seat of honor opposite the oil painting of old Olaf, who had been a forester from Tröndelag.

When Halvard tucked the violin under his chin all conversation stopped. The long-legged eight-year-old boy with the childish red cheeks and the rough shock of hair stood alone in the middle of the room and played Norwegian folk melodies which his American teacher had taught him for this occasion. Miss Wergeland sat still, her keen eyes probing Halvard's boyish face. His eyes were no longer veiled; they glowed as had Borghild's eyes whenever she played. But Helene saw also the boy's firm, energetic chin and powerful hands, which would grip reality hard when childhood was past and the struggle with art and love began.

The grown-ups sat quite still. Timothy held the hand of his beauti-ful, smiling wife, who would soon be tasting the joys of public recognition in Paris. Then came Hanna Chou, plumper than in earlier years, but still emanating that charm and poise which she owed to her education in a feudal German boarding school. Anna von Zabelsdorf still looked like a schoolgirl, for all that she was a Silesian Madonna; the years had left no mark upon her. And between them sat Astrid, her arms around these friends, as in the dark days in Shanghai when Vivica had vanished into the Kempetai's cellars and Astrid had found comfort and shelter with these two German women. Beside them Helene saw, lovely and composed, her favorite niece, Mailin, who thirty years ago had presented her with Gold Oriole at the dock in Trondheim, because Gold Oriole was tiny Mailin's dearest possession.

God had been good to her and her nieces, Helene thought. Here they were all together still. The girls had their places in life, and their children also; and her friends from the Far East modestly sur-rounded them all with quiet loyalty. It must be true after all that all men are brothers, she thought, even though all that had been happening for years in West and East seemed to belie this truth. Helene's mind conjured up the face of Yumei, who had died for Vivica during the war; she looked once more into Yumei's gleaming black eyes and recalled her simple and heroic conviction that Third Sister must have her favorite food in the Kempetai prison. Then there was Tso-ling, who had hidden Astrid in the home of Yumei's sister during the tumultuous last days of the war. And beside Vivica sat frail Madame Yamato in her dark kimono, embodying the profound Japanese principle that the inconspicuous must protect the resplendent, and the weak the strong. In the opposite corner was the Widow from Aalesund, who after the death of her Danish husband had so kindly returned to continue her mourning at Miss Wergeland's side. Laura held a small Chinese boy in each arm, for Mailin's and Hanna's sons had lost no time discovering who among this company spoke Chinese, and they clung to Laura, Helene, and Astrid. All in all, in this divided world of 1955 books and radio propaganda and conferences did not really matter so much, Miss Wergeland thought. One needed only a heart and two hands for helping. Then West and Far East understood each other very well.

She looked at Halvard and saw that, young as he was, he wielded his bow with Borghild's precision and sureness. In her heart there was a sudden ache, but it was not very painful, and not surprising. It was only that she traced her way a little further back into the past and saw Borghild, who had passed her secret magic on to this grandson. And then she saw Knut once more at the harbor of Trondheim, tall, handsome, and helpless, holding a pasty-faced little Astrid by the hand, while Yumei and Mailin followed with Gold Oriole.

"Here we are," Knut had said. It had been as simple as that for him. There they were, seeking shelter and comfort; and with her vexed smile Helene had given them that again and again. The more she had given, the richer she had become. "The unmarried woman is a mother to the whole world," the Chinese used to say. In her world, which extended from Trondheim to the Far East and the United States, she had done a little to prove the truth of that saying. And the ache which oppressed her heart as she listened to little Halvard's playing was only her lifelong mourning for Knut and the present sorrow that he could not be here now, rejoicing in his daughters and grandchildren. But at seventy Helene had grown accustomed to the pain of separation from Knut; she knew that it is possible to live with sorrows just as well as with joys, because life as it is consists of both. They had all experienced this—Helene, her three girls, and the friends who had come in her honor from all parts of the world to this clean, sober city in Europe's Far North. Not one among them had escaped suffering, but all had coped with it after their fashions.

Halvard lowered his half-size violin. He had given his first concert in Trondheim. Miss Wergeland stood up and went to a carved chest. Her hands trembled slightly as she took something out of the chest. She unwound its silk wrappings.

"This is your grandmother's violin, my boy. An Amati! If you work hard, Daddy will give it to you for your sixteenth birthday."

"What is an Amati, Great-Aunt?"

"A fairly good instrument," Miss Wergeland said dryly. It had been her family's wedding present to Borghild. She shook herself.

"Halvard," she said sternly, "there is a button missing on your jacket. Can't you sew the boy's buttons, Vivie?"

"Beg pardon," Dr. Timothy Williams said, winking. "I don't know how such a thing could have happened. *I* am the button-sewer in our family."

Amid the general laughter, only Helene observed Vivica secretly stroke her husband's sleeve. The gesture was a minor miracle of intimacy. Tim blushed like a boy at his junior prom. Then he stood up quietly to examine the Amati.

"Isn't it too precious for the boy?" he asked Helene Wergeland. The question was forgivable; he had never heard Borghild Lillesand play.

The guests sat up far into the night in the big paneled salon. They had been apart for a long time and did not know whether or when they would see one another again.

The children were in bed by now. Helene Wergeland had had one more small surprise with Astrid's little daughter. In saying good night, the child had asked her whether she loved Cousin Halvard *much* more than Antoine and herself. And once reassured on this point, Hélène had joyfully confided a "secret" to Great-Aunt Helene: that Antoine *also* played with dolls, but Papa must not know. Miss Wergeland had hugged the little creature; she was no longer an alien little lady from Paris but Astrid's daughter after all.

Shortly before the end of the birthday party there was a surprise for the guests. Mailin had established an orphanage in Singapore which bore the name of her deceased husband. Helene Wergeland was planning to go to Singapore for a year or longer to help in the James Chou Orphanage. This was work with which she had been familiar since her Bangkok days, and in addition she would have her Gold Oriole.

"You don't seriously mean this, Aunt Helene, do you?" Astrid asked.

"Have you any objection?"

The "Duchess" had all sorts of objections; foremost was that her aunt, after seeing Vivie's show—in a small, select gallery in Saint-Germain-des-Prés—was slated to stay with her in Paris for at least six months. Astrid had long been insisting on such a visit. Besides, Aunt Helene had never liked the tropics very well.

"What do you know about that!" Miss Wergeland said very loudly. Astrid seemed to be off her rocker.

"It will all be far too tiring for you, Aunt Helene!" Astrid stuck to her guns; she was a great believer in persistence, for even Pierre in the end almost always followed her advice, for all that he detested advice as strongly as did Miss Wergeland. But Astride was so perfect that this little fault made her all the more charming—Monsieur de Maury thought.

Astrid was honestly concerned about her aunt, although she was also just a little jealous of Mailin. "Please reconsider this, Aunt Helene," she gracefully concluded her arguments. "Mailin is wonderfully capable and can cope with things without you, and after all, you are not so young any more."

"Stuff and nonsense," Miss Wergeland said with her customary sweetness. "Why, *I'm not yet a day over seventy!*"

EPILOGUE

A Japanese in Paris

Baron Matsubara Akiro had enjoyed his holiday in Paris. He had revisited all the places he had made the acquaintance of, with astonishment and distrust, in 1925: the Opéra, the Faubourg Saint-Germain, the Louvre, Montparnasse, and the Parc Monceau. Thirty years ago he had come to Europe for the first time—an obedient son, a *minomushi*-insect in the City of Light, one of the many young Japanese who went to "learn about Europe" while they suffered stomach cramps from shyness and on moonlit nights longed for Nippon. Akiro had survived everything. At the moment he was a world conqueror in retirement and was working in behalf of his grandsons, who might see a new flowering of the Imperial Chrysanthemum. That was not so out of the question, if one thought in sufficiently large spans of time.

The baron had changed outwardly in the past five years. At fifty he was a person of dignity and distinction. His stern, ascetic face showed lines and the first deep grooves of age. When Matsubara Akiro smiled, he did so for specific ends. The era of romance was over for good.

For the past two years he had been kept very busy. He had placed his modest experience in political economy at the disposal of his government. In spite of defeat, Japan was still the most highly industrialized country in the East, but she needed markets more than ever. And Red China lay at her very door. The time would soon be past when leading men in Tokyo only whispered about the possibilities of such trade. The baron still considered the Japanese and the Chinese close kin, though the relative power of the two had been reversed. This change must tactfully be taken into considera-

465

tion, and the little misunderstandings of the years between 1937 and 1945 must be forgotten.

It was Akiro's last day in Paris. He intended to visit one or two more art galleries and then dine in the Bois de Boulogne. His own society sufficed him now as it had in the past. He remembered the satisfactions and forgot the darkness after the fireworks. Paris was still a center of culture, and he had always been a man for culture, after all. In Saint-Germain-des-Prés there had been a small gallery which he had visited as a student. It featured the work of unknowns; Paris had a weakness for that sort of thing. Sometimes the unknowns later became famous. Discovery is a pleasure, and people in the city on the Seine were not averse to the small effort of searching.

He was the last visitor in the small, attractive gallery. The current show was a series of water-colors collectively entitled *Les Rêves de Vivienne*. The painter was Vivica Williams, a young Norwegian woman who had spent several years in Asia, as he was informed by someone in the gallery.

With impassive face Baron Matsubara studied the pictures, which struck him as new and strange. Here Western fancy and a Japanese-oriented sense of form had produced something that astonished him. Nippon's intuition and the individualistic temperament of Europe had become reconciled on silk and paper. Baron Matsubara stood motionless before these works, which he had inspired. His assaults of terror and erotic passion had made a lasting impression upon Morning Face, so that years later visions of terse and economical beauty had emerged from her emotional shock. There were the singing nightingale in the prison, the morphine meadow, the dream-lake of Myanoshita with Mount Fuji in the clouds. And there was "The Tea Hut," a scroll which reflected, artfully sublimated, the tragedy at Karuizawa. It was Akiro's tea hut, but in it sat a Buddhist monk. The silence quivered in "Chrysanthemum and Maple by the Brook."

In these scrolls and sketches was a gravely gay spirit playing with the possibilities of painting in a manner quite unknown to the tradition-bound and formalistic Japanese masters. Here were classical arrangements which a Westerner's imagination had transformed into adventures. The last scroll was even based on the art of *bonkei*, miniature landscaping, the artistic gardens Japanese lay out in shallow bowls. But Vivica had smuggled into her composition a landscape of the Far North, which Matsubara Akiro had never seen. Wild romantic cliffs surrounded the studied Japanese garden with its little gnarled tree, its moss and stones. Here was the "noiseless" beauty of the East by the shore of a fjord. Such a synthesis of the art and nature of two worlds could be created only by a young person who had come to know Asia more deeply, more terribly, and more gloriously than other Europeans.

Confronting this picture, Matsubara Akiro experienced a profound shock. For the first time in his life, whose spring and summer he had sacrificed to the glory of Nippon, he was able to feel dynamic Western culture as an equal of the age-old, static perfection of the East. His rigid Japanese arrogance suffered a blow, for he was compelled to realize that the world outside Nippon was not only an institute of technology, not only a market for ideas and goods or a source of dollars, but also the field in which tremendous cultural and human forces vibrated. For the first time he saw the possibility of an understanding from person to person, from art to art, and from people to people. The *bonkei* by the fjord was, for all its restraint, a great symbol of hope, a gesture of ultimate reconciliation among nations.

"Do you like the pictures, Monsieur?"

Baron Matsubara came out of his meditations with a start. It was a Parisian girl who was addressing him, apparently without inhibitions on that score. She wore three-quarter-length, tight-fitting black slacks which brazenly emphasized her hips; a pink sweater; a filmy scarf; and an existentialist mane of hair—but a charming child in spite of the get-up, Baron Matsubara thought forbearingly. What had happened to the young women of Paris? Were they no longer interested in pleasing men? The girl did not look as though she could not afford to dress better. She wore genuine jewelry with that frisky sweater. And all the garments were of first-class material. In Tokyo too true elegance and modesty had disappeared; his daughter Eiko had received him in a similar pullover on New Year's Day 1950.

"I think these water-colors are enchanting," the young lady remarked; it was evident that she felt female opinions counted for something in art and in other matters too. "So much is left out of these sketches that one's own imagination is stimulated."

"You consider that to the good, Mademoiselle?"

The young art-lover did not reply. She studied Vivica's composi-
tions with every indication of interest. "I love China," she murmured.
"May I ask what city you come from, Monsieur?"

"From Tokyo," Baron Matsubara replied mildly. "Have you by
chance heard of this city, Mademoiselle? Formerly it was a center
of horticulture. Nowadays it is a favored resort for Americans on
outings."

"I beg your pardon, Monsieur. I thought you were Chinese."

"A charming compliment nowadays, Mademoiselle. We are only
the poor relations."

"You are very witty, Monsieur," the young lady said a little uncertainly. "Is this your first time in Paris?"

"Our chat has been a rare pleasure. May I express my gratitude,
Mademoiselle?" Baron Matsubara bowed with his accustomed grace.
No existentialist kittycat was going to extract information from him.

He left the room, a middle-aged, aristocratic Japanese exuding
visible courtesy and invisible *naibun*.

His thoughts drifted back to the pictures. It suddenly occurred to
him that Morning Face was the only member of the Wergeland
family who had ever expressed thanks for his modest services.

Smiling, he stepped out on the street. As he strolled down the
boulevard, Paris in May filled him with a tranquil sense of happiness,
just as it had decades ago. The twilight blurred the contours of
houses and trees. Baron Matsubara turned into the Rue Bonaparte,
feeling a deep sense of harmony with the ironic nostalgia in the air
and with the silvery dusk. This city was the tea hut of the West. The
Bois de Boulogne, where he planned to dine—that forest tamed by
the art of gardening—seemed made for Japanese guests, a rustic
haven on the edge of a metropolis. This night belonged to him and
Vivienne. His passion for her had been a moment of glory between
waking and sleeping, between birth and death. Before and afterward
there had been only the precisely determined duties laid down by
Shintoism and the Japanese family system. Like the Imperial Chrysanthemum, duties were not subject to time's mutability. Matsubara
Akiro had been born into this order, and he had no quarrel with it.

Tomorrow morning his plane would be leaving for Peiping.